Benjamin F. Greene

Finding the Error of the Marine Compass on Board Ship

Benjamin F. Greene

Finding the Error of the Marine Compass on Board Ship

ISBN/EAN: 9783337418519

Printed in Europe, USA, Canada, Australia, Japan

Cover: Foto ©Andreas Hilbeck / pixelio.de

More available books at **www.hansebooks.com**

FINDING THE ERROR

OF

THE MARINE COMPASS

ON BOARD SHIP.

BY

B. F. GREENE,
PROFESSOR OF MATHEMATICS, UNITED STATES NAVY,
SUPERINTENDENT OF COMPASSES.

BUREAU OF NAVIGATION,
NAVY DEPARTMENT.

WASHINGTON:
GOVERNMENT PRINTING OFFICE.
1875.

PREFATORY NOTE.

So much of the Text, comprising nearly all of one Chapter, together with the entire set of Tables, as here given, from the *Manual of the Marine Compass*, in course of preparation by the undersigned, it has been deemed expedient to print, in advance of its general publication, for the immediate use of the United States Navy.

Leaving any statement of particulars, as to the author's intentions, peculiarities of treatment, and acknowledgments, to a more appropriate time, he would merely remark, at present, that his aim has been, so far as "Finding the Error of the Compass" is concerned, to aid the Navigator with some additions to his appliances for an easy, expeditious, and reliable determination of this important element. And this is done, from the point of view occupied by him, *That, because there is so much unavoidable liability to error and consequent uncertainty in the use of the Compass at sea, there is the greater reason why we should neglect no available means for reducing these errors on the one hand and insuring greater certainty on the other.* If he shall succeed in commending this idea to the approval of Navigators, and in making their arduous duties enough easier in this respect to induce a more frequent determination of their Compass-Errors, he will feel somewhat compensated for the labor bestowed even upon this one Chapter of his work, not to mention that involved in the preparation of the appended Tables.

B. F. GREENE.

BUREAU OF NAVIGATION, NAVY DEPARTMENT,
Washington, March, 1875.

CONTENTS.

§ 1.—NATURE OF THE COMPASS-ERROR.

Art. — Page.

1. Different Errors of the Compass 1
2. Pointing-Errors of the Compass 1
   a) *Adjustment-Errors of the Compass.*
   b) *Adjustment-Errors of the Azimuth-Circle.*
   c) *Error from Defective Sensibility.*
   d) *Observation-Errors of the Compass.*
3. Reduction-Errors of the Compass 3
   a) *The Compass-Deviation.*
   b) *The Magnetic Variation.*
4. Total Error: called simply the Compass-Error 3
   Two Different Definitions of the Compass-Error.

§ 2.—FINDING THE COMPASS-ERROR.

5. The Basis of Procedure in all Cases 4
6. Different Methods of Finding the True Azimuth 4

I. BY OBSERVATIONS OF CELESTIAL OBJECTS.

A. Method of Horizon-Azimuths.

7. Fundamental Principles of the Horizon-Azimuth 6
8. Remark: The Amplitude 6
9. Rule: To make the Observation 7
   a) *Observation of the Sun.*
   b) *Observation of the Moon.*
   c) *Observation of a Planet or Fixed Star.*
10. Remark: Auxiliary Observations 7
11. Rule: To correct the Observed Compass-Azimuth 8
    a) *For the Sun, a Planet, or Fixed Star.*
    b) *For the Moon.*
12. Examples of Correcting Observed Azimuths 8
13. Rule: To find the True Azimuth 8
    a) *Preparation of the Data.*
    b) *Solution by Computation.*
    c) *Examples of True Azimuths by Computation.*
    d) *Solution by Inspection: Use of Tab. XXIV.*
    e) *Remark: On taking Means of Tabular Quantities.*
    f) *Examples of True Azimuths by Inspection.*
14. Examples of Finding the Compass-Error by Horizon-Azimuths 11

B. Method of Time-Azimuths.

15. Fundamental Principles of the Time-Azimuth 12
16. The Ship-Time; its Importance, etc 12

Art.		Page.
17.	**Finding the Compass-Error for a Single Heading of the Ship**	13
18.	To make a Single Time-Azimuth Observation	13
19.	Finding the True Azimuth	14
20.	Rule: Preparation of the Data	14
	a) The Object being the Sun.	
	b) The Object being the Moon, a Planet, or Fixed Star.	
	Remark on taking out the R. A.	
21.	Examples in Finding the Hour-Angle	16
22.	Rule: Solution by Logarithmic Computation	17
23.	Examples of True Azimuths by Computation	17
24.	The Tables of Time-Azimuths	18
	a) Tab. XXX, or First Part.	
	b) Tab. XXX. A, or Second Part.	
	c) Tab. XXX. B, or Third Part.	
	d) Intention, etc., with respect to these Tables.	
25.	Direct and Limiting Values of Time-Azimuths	20
26.	Rule: Solution by the Azimuth-Tables	20
27.	Examples of True Azimuths by the Azimuth-Tables	21
28.	Remark I: On the Two Cases of the Time-Azimuth	22
29.	Remark II: On the Conditions introducing the Use of the Symbols $-\infty$ and $+\infty$	23
	a) The Dec. equal to the Lat.	
	b) The Dec. nearly equal to the Lat.	
30.	Examples of Finding the Compass-Error by Time-Azimuths	24
31.	**Finding the Compass-Error for a Series of Different Headings of the Ship**	25
32.	To make the Observations of Serial Time-Azimuths	25
	Remark I: Position of the Object.	
	Remark II: Steadying the Ship.	
	Remark III: Heading-Intervals.	
	Remark IV: Care in Sighting and Reading off.	
33.	Rule: To get the Serial True Azimuths by Computation	26
34.	Rule: To get the Serial True Azimuths by the Azimuth-Tables	27
35.	Examples of Finding Serial Compass-Errors by Time-Azimuths	28

C. Method of Circumpolar Azimuths.

Art.		Page.
36.	The Circumpolar Azimuth a Modified Form of the Time-Azimuth	32
37.	Table of Circumpolar Azimuths for Polaris: Description of Tab. XL	32
38.	Two Distinct Problems in the Use of Tab. XL	33
39.	Rule: To find the True Azimuth of Polaris	33
	a) To take out the True Azimuth for any Ship-Time.	
	b) To find the Ship-Time of the greatest W. or E. E. of Polaris.	
40.	Examples of Finding the Compass Error by Circumpolar Azimuths	34

D. Method of Altitude-Azimuths.

Art.		Page.
41.	Fundamental principles of the Altitude-Azimuth	35
42.	Rule: To make the Observation	35
43.	Rule: To find the True Azimuth by Computation	35
44.	Rule: To find the True Azimuth by the Azimuth-Tables	36
	Remark I: Arguments to Odd Numbers.	
	Remark II: Direct and Limiting Values of Altitude-Azimuths.	
45.	Examples of Finding the Compass-Error by Altitude-Azimuths	37

E. Method of Time-Altitude-Azimuths.

Art. Page.

46. Fundamental Characteristics; Advantages and Defects 38
47. Rule: To find the True Azimuth by Computation 38
48. Examples of Finding the True Azimuth 39
49. Table of Time-Alt. Azimuths: Use of Tab. XLVIII 39
50. Examples of the Use of Tab. XLVIII 40

F. Method of Transition-Azimuths.

51. Fundamental Principles of the Transition-Azimuth 40
52. Remark on the Preparation of the Data 41
53. Rule: To find the True Azimuth 41
    a) *By Logarithmic Computation.*
    b) *By Tabular Inspection.*
54. Examples of Finding the Compass-Error by Transition-Azimuths 42

G. Dependence to be placed on these Methods.

55. The Data of a True Azimuth always liable to be in Error 42
56. Estimating Errors of the Azimuth-Data 42
    a) *The Latitude-Error.*
    b) *The Declination-Error.*
    c) *The Hour-Angle Error.*
    d) *The Altitude-Error.*
    e) *Recapitulation of the Limits of the Data-Errors.*
57. Tables of Azimuth-Errors: Auxiliary Tables 44
    a) *For Errors of Horizon-Azimuths.*
    b) *For Errors of Time-Azimuths.*
    c) *For Errors of Altitude-Azimuths.*
    d) *For Errors of Time-Alt. Azimuths.*
58. Finding Partial Azimuth-Errors 45
    a) *Partial Errors of Horizon-Azimuths.*
    b) *Partial Errors of Time-Azimuths.*
    c) *Partial Errors of Altitude-Azimuths.*
    d) *Partial Errors of Time-Alt. Azimuths.*
59. Probable Total Azimuth-Error 47
60. Favorable and Unfavorable Conditions 48
    a) *Conditions of Horizon-Azimuths.*
    b) *Conditions of Time-Azimuths.*
    c) *Conditions of Altitude-Azimuths.*
    d) *Conditions of Time-Alt. Azimuths.*
61. Limits of allowable Azimuth Error 49
62. Dependence on Horizon-Azimuths 51
63. Dependence on Time-Azimuths 52
    a) *Single Time-Azimuths.*
    b) *Serial Time-Azimuths.*
64. Dependence on Circumpolar Azimuths 54
65. Dependence on Altitude-Azimuths 54
    a) *Single Altitude-Azimuths.*
    b) *Serial Altitude-Azimuths.*
66. Relative Advantages of these Methods 56
    a) *Horizon-Azimuths.*
    b) *Time-Azimuths.*
    c) *Circumpolar Azimuths.*
    d) *Altitude-Azimuths.*

II. BY OBSERVATIONS OF TERRESTRIAL OBJECTS.

A. Method by Direct Bearings.

Art. Page.

67. Fundamental Conditions 58
  a) *First Condition: A Fixed Station.*
  b) *Second Condition: Means of Swinging the Ship.*
  c) *Third Condition: A Limited Parallax of Swing.*
68. Process of Finding Serial Compass-Errors 60
69. Examples of the Method by Direct Bearings 61
70. Dependence to be placed on Results 63
71. Tables of Parallactic Errors: Examples 63
72. To correct the Observations for Parallactic Errors 63
  a) *Case of Using the True Bearing of Object.*
  b) *Case of Using the Magnetic Bearing.*
  c) *Remark I: Observing two or more Objects.*
  d) *Remark II: Swinging with a Taut Cable.*
  e) *Remark III: Using the nearest whole Degree.*
73. Examples of Correcting for Parallactic Errors 65
74. Limiting Distance-Ratios 67
75. Different Methods of Finding the True Bearing of Object 67
76. Finding True Bearing by the Geographical Position 67
77. Examples of Finding T. B. by the Geographical Position 68
78. Finding True Bearing by an Astronomical Bearing 68
  a) *Rule: To make the Observation.*
  b) *Rule: To make the Computation.*
79. Examples of Finding T. B. by an Astronomical Bearing 69
80. Finding True Bearing by an Azimuth of the Vertical Circle 70
  a) *Rule: To take the Observation.*
  b) *Rule: To find the True Bearing of the Object.*
81. Examples of Fnding T. B. by an Azimuth of the Vertical Circle 71
82. Remarks relative to Finding the True Bearing of the Object 71

B. Method by Allignments.

83. Fundamental Idea 72
84. Process of Finding Serial Compass-Errors 72
85. Examples of the Method by Allignments 73
86. Dependence to be placed on Results 74

C. Method by Reciprocal Bearings.

87. Preliminary Explanations 74
88. Two Distinct Cases of Reciprocal Bearings 75
89. Essential Requisites of the Method under the First Case 75
90. Essential Requisites of the Method under the Second Case 76
  a) *The Angles measured from the True Meridian.*
  b) *The Angles measured from an Arbitrary Line.*
91. Preparations for Observations by this Method 77
92. Process of Conducting Reciprocal Observations 77
93. Reduction of Reciprocal Observations 78
  a) *Magnetic Observations on Shore.*
  b) *Angles Measured from the True Meridian on Shore.*
  c) *Angles Measured from any Arbitrary Line.*

Art.		Page.
94.	Examples of the Method by Reciprocal Bearings	79
95.	Dependence to be placed on Results	82
96.	To find the True Meridian	82
97.	Remark: To set the Instrument in a True Meridian	83
98.	Example of Finding the True Meridian	83

D. Relative Advantages of the Several Methods of Finding Serial Compass-Errors.

99.	Methods by Celestial Azimuths	84
100.	Method by Direct Bearings	85
101.	Method by Reciprocal Bearings	85

APPENDIX.

COMPASS-COMPARISONS.

102.	Definition	87

A. Compass-Comparisons on board Ship.

103.	Characteristics and Uses of Comparisons	87
104.	To make a Compass-Comparison	87
105.	Examples of Compass-Comparisons	88
106.	To convert a Given Course by Standard Compass into an Equivalent Course by a Compared Compass and Reciprocally	88
107.	Examples of Direct and Reciprocal Conversions	88
108.	Rule: To find the Error or Deviation of a Compared Compass	88
109.	Examples of Finding the Errors of Compared Compasses	89

B. Compass-Comparisons on Shore.

110.	Comparison on Shore: Detection of Local Magnetism	89

INDEX TO THE TABLES.

Table.		Page.
I.	Compass-Points and their Equivalents in Degrees	1
II.	Conversion of Arc into Time and Time into Arc	2
III.	Conversion of Mean Solar into Sidereal Time	3
IV.	Conversion of Sidereal into Mean Solar Time	3
V.	Length of a Degree in Latitude or Longitude	4
VI.	Logarithms of Numbers and Small Arcs	5
VII.	Logarithms of Numbers 1 to 1009	24
VIII.	Logarithmic Sines, Tangents, and Secants to every Eighth of a Compass-Point	26
IX.	Logarithmic Sines, Tangents, and Secants to every Minute of Arc and Fourth Minute of Time	27
X.	Logarithmic Sines to every Tenth of a Degree	72
XI.	Logarithmic Secants to every Tenth of a Degree	74
XII.	Logarithmic Tangents to every Tenth of a Degree	76
XIII.	Logarithmic Tangents to every Minute of Time	78
XIV.	Lengths of Circular Arcs to every Tenth of a Degree	79
XV.	Natural Sines and Cosines to every Tenth of a Degree	80
XVI.	Natural Tangents to every Tenth of a Degree	82
XVII.	Natural Versed Sines to every Tenth of a Degree	84
XVIII.	Decimal Parts and their Multiples of a Day	85
XIX.	Decimal Equivalents of Common Fractions	86
XX.	Proportional Parts	89
XXI.	Squares of Numbers from 0.0 to 100.9	90
XXII.	Square Roots of Numbers from 0.0 to 100.9	92
XXIII.	True Rising and Setting	94
XXIV.	Horizon-Azimuths	99
XXV.	Position-Angles for Horizon-Azimuths	104
XXVI.	Limiting-Errors of Horizon-Azimuths	104
XXVII.	Correction of the Compass-Azimuth on the Apparent Horizon	105
XXVIII.	Error of the Horizon-Azimuth for an Error of 0°.2 in the Latitude	105
XXIX.	Error of the Horizon-Azimuth for an Error of 0°.1 in the Declination	105
XXX.	Time-Azimuths: Logs A and B	106
XXX. A.	Time-Azimuths: Log C	124
XXX. B.	Time-Azimuths: Log Tangents X and Y	130
XXXI.	Time-Azimuths: Direct and Limiting Values	132
XXXII.	Position-Angles of Direct and Limiting Time-Azimuths	134
XXXIII.	Altitudes of Direct and Limiting Time-Azimuths	136
XXXIV.	Error of the Time-Azimuth for an Error of 1^m in the Hour-Angle	138
XXXV.	Error of the Time-Azimuth for an Error of 0°.2 in the Latitude	141
XXXVI.	Error of the Time-Azimuth for an Error of 0°.1 in the Declination	141
XXXVII.	Limiting-Errors of Time-Azimuths	142
XXXVIII.	Limiting-Errors of Time-Azimuths in High Latitudes	142
XXXIX.	Limiting-Errors of Serial Time-Azimuths	142
XL.	Circumpolar Azimuths: Polaris or the Pole-Star	143
XLI.	Altitude-Azimuths: Part I	144
XLI.	Altitude-Azimuths: Part II	146
XLI.	Altitude-Azimuths: Part III	146

Table.		Page.
XLII.	Altitude Azimuths: Direct and Limiting Values	148
XLIII.	Position-Angles of Direct and Limiting Altitude-Azimuths	150
XLIV.	Error of the Altitude-Azimuth for an Error of 0°.1 in the Altitude	150
XLV.	Error of the Altitude-Azimuth for an Error of 0°.2 in the Latitude	151
XLVI.	Error of the Altitude-Azimuth for an Error of 0°.1 in the Declination	152
XLVII.	Limiting-Errors of Altitude-Azimuths	152
XLVIII.	Time-Alt. Azimuths: Log A	153
XLVIII.	Time-Alt. Azimuths: Log B	154
XLIX.	Error of the Time-Alt. Azimuth for an Error of $0^m.2$ in the Hour-Angle	158
L.	Error of the Time-Alt. Azimuth for an Error of 3′ in the Altitude or Declination	158
LI.	Transition-Azimuths	159
LII.	Direct Bearings of a Fixed Object: Limiting Distance	160
LIII.	Direct Bearings of a Fixed Object: Parallactic Errors	160
LIV.	Products of Arcs Multiplied by the Sines of the Rhumbs	161
LV.	Magnetic Elements of the Earth: The Magnetic Variation in Arctic Latitudes	169
LVI.	Magnetic Elements of the Earth: The Magnetic Variation in Latitudes 70° N to 60° S	170
LVII.	Magnetic Elements of the Earth: The Magnetic Dip	174
LVIII.	Magnetic Elements of the Earth: The Horizontal Force	175
LIX.	Right Ascension of the True Sun and Equation of Time	176
LX.	Declination of the Sun	180
LXI.	Mean Places of Twenty-five Fixed Stars	182
LXII.	Meridian-Passages of Twenty-five Fixed Stars	182
LXIII.	Reductions of Meridian-Passages of the Fixed Stars	183
LXIV.	Reduction of Daily or Hourly Changes in Right Ascension	184
LXV.	Reduction of Hourly Changes in the Moon's Right Ascension	186
LXVI.	Reduction of the Mean Sun's Right Ascension	188

THE COMPASS-ERROR, AND METHODS OF FINDING IT ON BOARD SHIP.

§ 1.—NATURE OF THE COMPASS-ERROR.

1. Different Errors of the Compass.—The Errors of the Marine Compass may be considered in two different relations: First, as to the *pointing of the compass*, which, but for the influence of certain errors, would always be in precise accordance with the Directive Force, whether on board ship or on the land; and, secondly, as to the *reduction to the True Meridian* of the corrected compass-pointing, which, although in no proper sense an error of the compass, is treated like one from considerations of practical convenience. All the errors of the compass explained or referred to in the preceding Chapters[1] may therefore be regarded as forming parts of either the Pointing-Errors or Reduction-Errors of this instrument, and they will now be recapitulated under these two heads.

2. Pointing-Errors of the Compass.—The Pointing-Errors include all instrumental and observational errors which affect the accuracy of the compass-pointing. Under this head there are the following errors:

a) *Adjustment-Errors of the Compass.*—These comprise (*Chap. I*)—

1. The divergence of the zero-line from the magnetic axis of the compass-card;

2. The eccentricity of the cap with respect to the centre of the card-circle; and

3. The eccentricity of the pivot with respect to the centre of the bowl-circle.

b) *Adjustment-Errors of the Azimuth-Circle.*—These are—

1. The Direction-Error of the sight-vanes, or divergence of the vertical plane of sight from the diameter of the circle (*Chap. I*); and

2. Several possibilities of error from defective construction, which need not be mentioned in this place. (See *Chap. I.*)

c) *Error from Defective Sensibility* (*Chap. I*).

d) *Observation-Errors of the Compass.*—These comprise—

1. Equilibrium-Errors of the compass-card and bowl-circle (*Chap. V*); and

[1] The references here and elsewhere made, are to different parts of the *Manual of the Marine Compass*, not yet published, of which this is one Chapter (the *sixth*, with certain modifications), as explained in the Prefatory Note.

2. Personal Errors in sighting and reading off (*Chap. V*).

The Adjustment-Errors of both the compass and azimuth-circle should be practically unimportant, when these instruments are delivered by the makers; and the adjustments should be sufficiently stable to remain unimpaired for a long period, with careful and considerate usage. Unfortunately, even the best intentions of the most reliable maker are liable to be occasionally frustrated; and hence the only certain way to arrive at satisfactory conclusions concerning these errors is to subject the instruments to careful tests of their actual condition (*Chap. I*).

The error from Defective Sensibility of a well-made liquid compass, having a buoyant card, adjusted to a minimum pressure at the pivot, is commonly inappreciable; and, under circumstances ordinarily favorable, it may in general be relied on to continue in that condition for a long period. But other compasses, whether air or liquid, with heavy cards, and having a pivot-pressure ranging from 1,500 to 5,000 grains, are liable to an appreciable error from this source, proportional, at the least, to the greater pressure at the pivot; and not only that, but such compasses are even more than proportionally liable to the development of a very serious error as the cap and pivot become sensibly worn or otherwise altered in form (*Chap. I*).

The compasses of the United States Navy, under the inspection-tests to which they are subjected, are required to satisfy the following conditions:

The greatest error to which they may be liable must not exceed—

For Adjustment-Errors of the compass (*a*) $\pm 0^\circ.1$
For Adjustment-Errors of the az. circle (*b*) $\pm 0\ .1$
For Error from Defective Sensibility (*c*) $\pm 0\ .01$

or, in the last case, it must be inappreciable. Such a limitation of these errors is equivalent to a probable limit, in the aggregate,[1] of $\pm\ 0^\circ.14$.

These conditions, or something equivalent to them, by which the Navy compasses are required to be "practically perfect" when put on board ship, should be required by all Navigators, or at the least for one (standard) compass of their ships.

The Observation-Errors, whether depending on the circumstances of the observation or on the personal peculiarities of the observer, are alike impossible of previous estimate. Nor, indeed, can they be estimated with much pretension to accuracy—even as to their limits—after the observation has been made, unless conducted with a view to such an estimate; and this is rarely practicable or expedient with the Compass-Observations generally required for the purpose of shaping or correcting a course. Nothing can therefore be relied on but intelligence and care in making these observations as a remedy for this source of Compass-Error.

It is otherwise with observations of a serial kind, which are made for the purpose of obtaining a set of Compass-Deviations; for it is then quite practicable to get a definite estimate of the total Pointing-Error,

[1] The probable sum of these errors is $\pm\sqrt{(0^\circ.1)^2+(0^\circ.1)^2+(0^\circ.01)^2} = \pm\ 0^\circ.14$.

including the errors of observation, at least as to its limits, both in sign and amount (*Chap. IV*).

3. Reduction-Errors of the Compass.—The Reduction-Errors include such as are not, strictly speaking, errors of the compass, but those which are treated as if they were, in the reduction of the corrected compass-pointing to the Geographical or True Meridian. There are two of these, as follows:

a) *The Compass-Deviation.*—By this is meant the reduction of the corrected pointing to the Magnetic Meridian, whatever the place or heading of the ship, and whether the ship be upright or in a state of heel (*Chap. IV*).

b) *The Magnetic Variation.*—This is to be understood as the reduction of the Magnetic Meridian at the time and place to the True Meridian (*Chap. II*).

These are sometimes of the same name and sometimes of different names, and it is their resultant or combined effect which constitutes the Reduction-Error in a given case.

4. The Total Error; called simply the Compass-Error.—Each of the errors heretofore mentioned, whether belonging to the first or second class, admits of being measured on the compass-card; and each, according as it has the effect to carry the zero or N point of the card to the eastward or westward, is easterly and marked E, or westerly and marked W. Hence, as in other analogous cases, if all the individual or component errors have the same name, their sum is the total error, and takes the common name of its several components; but if a part of the components have one name, and a part the other name, then the difference of the two partial sums is the total error, and takes the name of the greater partial sum.

The total or combined effect of the several component errors of a compass will be called the *Compass-Error*, and will always be understood to represent the angular distance east or west from the True Meridian to the observed compass-pointing as read off from the compass. It may therefore be defined in two different ways, as follows:

a) The Compass-Error is the angle formed at the centre of the compass, between the N and S or zero line of the card and the True Meridian; and it is marked *E* or *W*, according as the N or zero point of the card falls to the *eastward* or *westward* of the true north; otherwise,

b) The Compass-Error is the difference between the compass-bearing and the true bearing of the same object; and it is marked *E* or *W*, according as the compass-bearing falls to the *left* or *right* of the true bearing, the observer's eye being supposed at the centre of the compass.

§ 2.—FINDING THE COMPASS-ERROR.

There are several different methods of **Finding the Compass-Error,** by which will always be meant the total or resultant error, as defined in the preceding articles. It is one of the most important problems with which the Navigator has to do; since, how important soever the problems of the Position, no accurate steering of a given course, from one position to another, can be had without a reliable determination of the Compass-Error on that course.

5. The Basis of Procedure in all Cases.—To find the Compass-Error in a given case depends on the possibility of knowing the True Azimuth of some celestial or terrestrial object, whenever the Compass-Azimuth of the same object can be had by observation. Then—

The Compass-Error is found by taking the difference between the Compass-Azimuth and the True Azimuth, and is marked *E* or *W*, according as the Compass-Azimuth falls to the *left* or *right* of the True Azimuth (4).

The problem will therefore consist of two parts: First, of finding by actual observation the Compass-Azimuth of some object; and, secondly, of finding, by computation or otherwise, the True Azimuth of the same object, if not already known by a previous determination. If the object be a celestial body, *in motion*, the True Azimuth must be found for the instant of time at which the Compass-Observation is made; but if the object be a terrestrial one, *at rest*, it is obviously not important, so far as the mere result is concerned, whether the True Azimuth be found at the time it is required, or happens to be already known, provided the observer's position remains unchanged.

6. Different Methods of Finding the True Azimuth.—There are several different methods of finding the True Azimuth of both celestial and terrestrial objects; and, accordingly, there may be at least as many different methods of finding the Compass-Error. The following methods will be considered:

I. By Observations of Celestial Objects.

Method of Horizon-Azimuths.

Method of Time-Azimuths.

Method of Circumpolar Azimuths.

Method of Altitude Azimuths.

Method of Time-Altitude Azimuths.

Method of Transition-Azimuths.

II. By Observations of Terrestrial Objects.

Method of Direct Bearings.

Method of Allignments.

Method of Reciprocal Bearings.

Other processes of getting the True Azimuth, incidental for the most part to determinations of the Time and Position, are known to Nautical Astronomers. These, if made available by corresponding Compass-Observations, would supply so many additional means of finding the Compass-Error; but the methods named above include all, probably, that can be usefully employed in a direct manner for this purpose.[1]

In practice, the Navigator may be required—

First, to find the Compass-Error on a particular heading of the ship, for immediate use, upon every change of course; or,

Secondly, to find the corresponding Compass-Errors on a series of different headings, for subsequent use, with the opportunity chosen at pleasure, either at sea or in port.

In the first case, the *Compass-Error*[2] is what is required, whether in shaping a course or in working up, in which the direct relation of the compass-course to the true course is always sought; but, in the second case, the Compass-Errors are generally required to be *reduced to Compass-Deviations*,[3] by separating the magnetic variation, and also the Pointing-Error if required (*Chap. IV*).

---

[1] The method of Time-Altitude-Azimuths, included in the foregoing list, requiring both the Altitude and Hour-Angle as data, belongs rather to the class of incidental methods, as it could hardly ever seem to be expedient to use this as a direct method in preference to the Time-Azimuth, although it is sometimes so employed.

[2] Still called the "Variation" in most of the books on navigation.

[3] The reduction of Compass-Errors to Compass-Deviations by separating the Magnetic Variation has been fully explained in a previous Chapter. It may, however, be best to repeat so much of it as may suffice to insure that this important operation shall always be performed with *certainty*.

1. Recall an application of the rule of *Art.* 4:—That, when the Var. and Dev. have the *same* name their *Sum* is the Error, which takes the name common to both; but that, if they have *unlike* names, their *Difference* is the Error, which then takes the name of the greater quantity.

2. Conceive the Error and Var. to be laid off on the compass-card, beginning at the N or zero point, and extending *East* or *West*, according as they are marked *E* or *W*, and measured on the arc of reading. Then the Dev. is always equal to the *Difference between the points of reading* of the Error and Var. (*i. e.*, equal to their *Sum* or *Difference*, according as they have *unlike* or the *same* names), and is marked *E* or *W*, according as the Var. falls to the *left* or *right* of the Error.

Always mentally test the result by the first rule.

I.—BY OBSERVATIONS OF CELESTIAL OBJECTS.

A. Method of Horizon-Azimuths.

7. Fundamental Principles of the Horizon-Azimuth.—The Method of Horizon-Azimuths consists in observing the compass-bearing of the Sun or other celestial body, while its centre is in the *True Horizon;* that is to say, either at the *True Rising or True Setting* of the body.

But since, during an observation, the object can only be referred to the Apparent or Visible Horizon, and since, moreover, it is subject to vertical displacement from refraction, parallax, and dip, it is necessary to adopt some provision by means of which the actual observation in a given case may be made to satisfy the preceding condition. There are two ways of doing this: one by observing the bearing of the object while it is elevated at a certain estimated distance above the Visible Horizon, sufficient to correct the effect of the vertical displacement above mentioned; the other, by observing the body when its centre is apparently in the Visible Horizon, and applying a suitable correction.

The former of these two provisions is that which is more commonly in use, at least by American Navigators; but, apart from the uncertainty of the estimated height, it wholly excludes the Moon as one of the objects of observation. The latter, on the other hand, not only admits of a more precise observation, but readily permits the use of the Moon as an object certainly only inferior to the Sun in importance for this purpose.

8. Remark: The Amplitude.—The method now being considered is commonly treated in the books on Navigation as an Amplitude; that is to say, by using the *complement* of the Azimuth, reckoning from the E and W points toward the N or S. But the Azimuth, besides being more natural and more convenient in the compass-reading than the Amplitude, has the advantage of being consistent with all the other forms of finding the Compass-Error.[1]

---

[1] The author may be deemed a little hardy in venturing to propose the change indicated in the text. But, so far as mere terms are concerned, why may not "Rising-Azimuth" and "Setting-Azimuth" replace the old phraseology of "Rising-Amplitude" and "Setting-Amplitude" without doing serious violence to nautical usage!

With the change proposed, every observation at sea for Compass-Error will be an Azimuth, always referred to the Meridian, and always read forward from the zero-point, rather than, as in the exceptional case of the Amplitude, referred to the prime vertical and read backward from 90°.

The *Table of Horizon-Azimuths* (XXIV) here given will at least enable the Navigator to test this question from a practical point of view; but any one, still desirous of preserving the old form, may treat his observation as an Amplitude, by simply using the difference between 90° and the quantity taken from this Table, which is the same as that taken from a Table of Amplitudes.

9. Rule: To make the Observation.—In observing objects having appreciable disks, like the Sun and Moon, no preparation is necessary beyond that of being ready at the compass a few minutes in advance, and keeping the sight-vanes pointed in the proper direction.

a) *Observation of the Sun.*—At the *rising*, when the upper limb appears in the sea-horizon, take the bearing by compass; and continue to take bearings of the centre, bisecting the disk, and reading off each bearing for an assistant to note, till the lower limb appears. Or, at the *setting*, when the lower limb touches the horizon, proceed in the same manner till the upper limb disappears. In either case take the mean of the several bearings, which will be the apparent Compass-Azimuth of the Sun's centre.

b) *Observation of the Moon.*—Proceed in the same manner as in observing the Sun, whenever the luminous portion of the disk is sufficiently large and bright for the rising to be anticipated in time to get the bearing of the upper limb as it comes upon the horizon. Otherwise, if the brightness be insufficient for a reliable observation in the horizon (as when the Moon is near her conjunction), it may be better to make the observation at a convenient altitude by one of the methods to be described.

c) *Observation of a Planet or Fixed Star.*—It is seldom practicable to obtain a reliable observation of a Planet or Fixed Star in the horizon, and especially at rising; so that it is generally better to anticipate the setting, or delay until after the rising, and take the object low in altitude by the method of Time-Azimuths. Whenever the attempt is made to obtain a Rising-Azimuth, it will be expedient to prepare for the observation as follows:

With the Lat. in, and the Dec. taken from the Naut. Almanac, or from Tab. LX, find the Time, Apparent or Mean, of rising (*Tab. XXIII* and *Introd.*) Also take out, from Tab. XXIV, the Horizon-Azimuth.

Then, a few minutes before the time of rising, having applied the latest known Compass-Error to the Horizon-Azimuth for the particular heading of the ship, and thus obtained the approximate Compass-Azimuth, place the sight-vanes upon the indicated bearing and watch for the Planet or Star to appear; and at the instant it does come distinctly into view, on or extremely near the Visible Horizon, carefully take the bearing.[1]

10. Remark: Observations auxiliary to Compass-Azimuths.—There are certain auxiliary observations which should always be made at the instant of taking any Azimuth-Observation for Compass-Error. These are—

1) The Ship's Heading by the Standard or Azimuth Compass, and by each of the other compasses on board which are suitably mounted for such observations; and

[1] In this case, of course, but a single bearing can be taken, and greater care is therefore requisite.

2) If the ship be iron-built, the Angle of Heel by clinometer, and whether to starboard or port (*Chap. IV*).

The labor of making and recording these auxiliary observations is trifling; and they are essential to a complete knowledge of the compass-situation (*Chap. IV*).

11. Rule: To correct the Observed Azimuth.—As already remarked (7), all observed Azimuths in the Apparent Horizon require certain corrections, in order to convert them into Compass-Azimuths on the True Horizon. For this correction, enter Tab. XXVII, with the Lat. and Dec., both to the nearest degree, and when taken out apply it to the observed Azimuth in the following manner:

a) *For the Sun, a Planet, or Fixed Star.*—At the rising in N Lat. and setting in S Lat., apply the whole correction to the *right;* or at the setting in N Lat. and rising in S Lat., apply it to the *left.*

b) *For the Moon.*—Apply the *half*-correction in the contrary manner

The result in either case will be the proper Compass-Azimuth, which, by comparison with the True Azimuth, will give the Compass-Error.

12. Examples of Correcting Azimuths observed in the Apparent Horizon.

Ex. 1.—With Lat. 55° N and Dec. 14° N, observed Rising-Azimuth of the Sun was N 47° E.

By Tab. XXVII:

Obs. Az.	N 47°.0 E
Corr. (R.)	1 .0
Comp. Az.	N 48 .0 E

Ex. 2.—With Lat. 47° N, Dec. 27° S, observed Setting-Azimuth of Venus was S 45°.5 W.

Obs. Az.	S 45°.5 W
Corr. (L.)	0 .9
Comp. Az.	N 135 .4 W

Ex. 3.—With Lat. 65° S and Dec. 11° S, observed Rising-Azimuth of the Sun was S 56° E.

By Tab. XXVII:

Obs. Az.	S 56°.0 E
Corr. (L.)	1 .6
Comp. Az.	S 57 .6 E

Ex. 4.—With Lat. 35°.6 S, Dec. 20°.2 N, observed Setting-Azimuth of the Moon was N 70°.2 W.

Obs. Az.	N 70°.2 W
Corr. (½ L.)	0 .3
Comp. Az.	S 129 .5 W

It will be noticed, in cases where the Lat. and Dec. have contrary names, in which it may be convenient to take the supplement of the Compass-Azimuth for comparison with the True Azimuth, as in Examples 2, 3, 4, 5, and 6 (14), that the result is the same whether the correction be applied before or after taking the supplement.

Of course, when the correction is quite small it may be neglected, as it might be in Ex. 1 of Art. 14.

13. Rule: To find the True Azimuth.—For this, proceed as follows:

a) *Preparation of Data.*—Find the Latitude in, and take out the Declination, both to the nearest tenth of a degree.[1] For the latter, observe that—

[1] It will be seen that little use is made by the author of *sexagesimal* computations, tabular or otherwise, in anything relating to the Azimuth and Compass-Error. In

1. For the Sun, it is sufficient to take it off-hand from Tab. LX.

2. For a Fixed Star, it may be taken at sight from Tab. LXI.

3. For one of the four Planets, it is sufficient to take it off-hand from the Tables of the Nautical Almanac.

4. For the Moon, it will be sufficient to find the Greenwich date to the nearest tenth of an hour, and with this take out the Declination from the Nautical Almanac.

b) *Solution by Computation: Use of Tables X and XI.*—To the secant of the Lat. add the sine of the Dec.; their sum, rejecting 10 from the index, is the cosine of an angle. This taken at sight from Tab. X to the nearest tenth of a degree, if the Lat. and Dec. have the *same* name, will be the required True Azimuth *less* than 90°; but, if they have *contrary* names, the supplement of the angle, or that found by subtracting the angle from 180°, will be the True Azimuth *greater* than 90°. In either case, mark the Azimuth N or S, according to the Lat., and *E* or *W*, according as it is found for a *rising* or *setting* of the object observed.

c) *Examples of True Azimuths by Computation:*

Ex. 1.—With Lat. 42° 25′ N and Dec. 21°.7 N, what is the True Azimuth at Rising?

Lat.	42°.4 N	sec 0.1317
Dec.	21 .7 N	sin 9.5679
T. Az.	N 60 .0 E	cos 9.6996

Ex. 2.—With Lat. 51° 30′ N and Dec. 16° 17′ S, what is the True Azimuth at Setting?

Lat.	51°.5 N	sec 0.2058
Dec.	16 .3 S	sin 9.4482
T. Az.	N 116 .8 W	cos 9.6540

Ex. 3.—With Lat. 55° 5′ S and Dec. 13°.9 S, what is the True Azimuth at Setting?

Lat.	55°.1 S	sec 0.2425
Dec.	13 .9 S	sin 9.3806
T. Az.	S 65 .2 W	cos 9.6231

Ex. 4.—With Lat. 16° 57′ S and Dec. 29° 13′ N, what is the True Azimuth at Rising?

Lat.	16°.9 S	sec 0.0194
Dec.	29 .2 N	sin 9.6883
T. Az.	S 120 .7 E	cos 9.7077

---

fact, at least in his opinion, all refinements, such as the consideration of quantities smaller than *minutes of arc* and *tenths of a minute in time*, are a waste of time and patience, being utterly useless in computations of this kind. And, moreover, so far as the finding of any single Compass-Error is concerned, it is always quite sufficient to work to the nearest *tenth of the degree in arc*, and to the nearest *minute in time*.

The practice of changing sexagesimal quantities of a lower denomination into tenths of a higher is readily done at sight, *without thinking about it*, after a little practice.

Take the series in minutes of arc—

	1′	2′	3′	4′	5′	6′	
	0°.02	0°.03	0°.05	0°.07	0°.08	0°.10	*to tenths and hundredths of degrees,*
or,	0°.0	0°.0	{ 0°.0 / 0°.1 }	0°.1	0°.1	0°.1	*to the nearest tenth.*

Again, take the series—

	24′	25′	26′	27′	28′	29′	30′	
	0°.40	0°.42	0°.43	0°.45	0°.47	0°.48	0°.50	*to tenths and hundredths,*
or,	0°.4	0°.4	0°.4	{ 0°.4 / 0°.5 }	0°.5	0°.5	0°.5	*to the nearest tenth.*

And similarly for all other cases. To annex one cipher to the minutes, divide by 6, and point off two decimal places, is to convert the sexagesimal into tenths and hundredths of degrees. Or, to divide simply by 6 and point off one decimal, is to have an equivalent in tenths. But, as remarked above, the operation becomes as involuntary as the use of the *multiplication-table*.

Ex. 5.—With Lat. 67° 17′ N and Dec. 19° 28′ S, what is the True Azimuth at Rising?

Lat.	67°.3 N	sec 0.4135
Dec.	19 .5 S	sin 9.5235
T. Az.	N 149 .9 E	cos 9.9370

Ex. 6.—With Lat. 71° 55′ N and Dec. 12° 47′ N, what is the True Azimuth at Setting?

Lat.	71°.9 N	sec 0.5077
Dec.	12 .8 N	sin 9.3455
T. Az.	N 44 .5 W	cos 9.8532

d) *Solution by Inspection: Use of Tab. XXIV.*—Enter the Table of Horizon-Azimuths with the Lat. and Dec., each to the nearest tabular argument, and take out the corresponding angle; and this, or its supplement, according as the Lat. and Dec. have the same name or contrary names, will be the True Azimuth. Mark as above (*b*).

e) *Remark.*—If either the given Lat. or Dec. be more nearly half-way between two adjacent arguments than equal to either of them, take the Mean of the two numbers corresponding to the two arguments. If both the Lat. and Dec. be more nearly half-way between adjacent arguments than equal to them, take the Mean *crosswise* of two of the four corresponding numbers.

The Mean of two numbers is most conveniently found by adding their Half-Difference to the less one.

f) *Examples of True Azimuths by Inspection* (the Data from the Examples [*c*]):

Ex. 1.—With Lat. 42°.4 N and Dec. 21°.5 N, Tab. XXIV gives—

True Az. N 60°.2 E

Ex. 2.—With Lat. 51°.5 N and Dec. 16°.3 S, we get—

True Az. N 116°.7 W

Ex. 3.—With Lat. 55°.1 S and Dec. 13°.9 S—

True Az. S 65°.1 W

Ex. 4.—With Lat. 16°.9 S and Dec. 29°.2 N—

True Az. S 120°.5 E

Ex. 5.—With Lat. 67°.3 N and Dec. 19°.5 S—

True Az. N 149°.7 E

Ex. 6.—With Lat. 71°.9 N and Dec. 12°.8 N—

True Az. N 44°.4 W

In Ex. 1, on entering Tab. XXIV, we find that the Lat. falls more nearly half-way between 42° and 43° than equal to either, and we therefore take the Mean of the corresponding Tabular Azimuths, 60°.4 and 59°.9, by subtracting their Half-Difference (0°.2) from the greater.

In Ex. 2, both the Lat. and Dec. are more nearly half-way between 51°, 52° and 16°.0, 16°.5 respectively; and, consequently, we take a crosswise Mean of the four Tabular Azimuths $\left\{ \begin{matrix} 64°.0, & 63°.2 \\ 63\ .4, & 62\ .5 \end{matrix} \right\}$, by adding the Half-Difference (0°.1) of 63°.4, 63°.2 to the less, or subtracting it from the greater.

By a similar mental process, executed at sight, the results in the other Examples are obtained, as well as those in all Examples of this kind.

It is thus seen that with no greater care than to take the Means of the Tabular Azimuths, corresponding to the arguments between which the given data fall, the results in these Examples, alike for the higher and lower Latitudes, do not differ more than 0°.2 from those obtained by computation. And they will seldom differ as much as that.

In taking Cross-Means of four numbers we may use either pair; but it will generally be found that one pair, as in this instance, has a smaller difference than the other, and we use that in preference.

14. Examples of Finding the Compass-Error by Horizon-Azimuths.

Ex. 1.—1875, June 5: At sea, in Lat. 11° 29′ N, Long. 30° W, about 6ʰ 10ᵐ A. M., the observed bearing of the Sun at rising was N 59° E: Required, the Compass-Error.

Greenwich date, June 4ᵈ 20ʰ
☉'s Dec. (Tab. LX) N 22°.5

By Tab. XXIV:

Latitude	11°.5 N	*True Az.*	N 67°.1 E
☉'s Dec.	22 .5 N		
Obs. Az.	N 59 .0 E	*Comp. Az.*	N 59 .1 E
Corr. (R.)	0 .1		
COMP. ERROR			8 .0 E

Ex. 2.—1875, May 30: At sea, in Lat. 25° 3′ S, Long. 22° W, about 6ʰ 42ᵐ A. M., the observed bearing of the Sun at rising was N 71°.5 E: Required, the Compass-Error.

Greenwich date, May 29ᵈ 20ʰ
☉'s Dec. N 21°.7

By Tab. XXIV:

Latitude	25°.0 S	*True Az.*	S 114°.1 E
☉'s Dec.	21 .7 N		
Obs. Az.	S 108 .5 E	*Comp. Az.*	S 108 .8 E
Corr. (L.)	0 .3		
COMP. ERROR			5 .3 W

Ex. 3.—1875, November 27: At sea, in Lat. 40° 27′ N, Long. 20° 7′ W, about 4ʰ 43ᵐ P. M., the observed bearing of the Sun at setting was S 73° W: Required, the Compass-Error.

Greenwich date, November 27ᵈ 6ʰ
☉'s Dec. S 21°.2

By Tab. XXIV:

Latitude	40°.5 N	*True Az.*	N 118°.5 W
☉'s Dec.	21 .2 S		
Obs. Az.	S 73 .0 W	*Comp. Az.*	N 107 .7 W
Corr. (L.)	0 .7		
COMP. ERROR			10 .8 W

Ex. 4.—1875, December 18: At sea, in Lat. 31° 35′ S, Long. 60° 13′ E, about 7ʰ 0ᵐ P. M., the observed bearing of the Sun at setting was N 83° W: Required, the Compass-Error.

Greenwich date, December 18ᵈ 3ʰ
☉'s Dec. S 23°.4

By Tab. XXIV:

Latitude	31°.6 S	*True Az.*	S 62°.1 W
☉'s Dec.	23 .4 S		
Obs. Az.	N 83 .4 W	*Comp. Az.*	S 97 .0 W
Corr. (R.)	0 .4		
COMP. ERROR			34 .9 W

Ex. 5.—1875, July 17: At sea, in Lat. 51° 13′ N, Long. 33° 47′ W, about 2ʰ 7ᵐ A. M., the observed bearing of the Moon at setting was S 62° W: Required, the Compass-Error; also the Deviation.

Ship heading W ¼ S by Standard Compass.

Greenwich date, July 16ᵈ 16ʰ.4
☾'s Dec. 28°.2 S

By Tab. XXIV:

Latitude	51°.2 N	*True Az.*	N 138°.7 W
☾'s Dec.	28 .2 S		
Obs. Az.	S 62 .0 W	*Comp. Az.*	N 117 .4 W
Corr. (½ R.)	0 .6		
COMP. ERROR			21 .3 W

Tab. LVI., Mag. Var. 37°.7 W
Comp. Dev. 16 .4 E

Ex. 6.—1871, August 16: In port, Disco Island, in Lat. 69° 14′ N, Long. 53° 18′ W, about 8ʰ 40ᵐ P. M., the observed bearing of the Sun at setting was N 6°.8 E: Required, the Compass-Error; also the Deviation.

Greenwich date, August 16ᵈ 12ʰ
☉'s Dec. N 13° 40′

Latitude	69°.2 N	*True Az.*	N 47°.8 W
☉'s Dec.	13 .7 N		
Obs. Az.	N 6 .8 E	*Comp. Az.*	N 4 .4 E
Corr. (L.)	2 .4		
COMP. ERROR			52 .2 W

By Tab. LVI, Mag. Var. 72°.5 W
Hence, also, Comp. Dev. 20 .3 E

Ex. 7.—1875, February 2: At sea, in Lat. 48° 5′ N, Long. 174° 15′ W, about 10 P. M., desired to get an observation of Jupiter at rising for Compass-Error on present course of ship, which is North.

Preparation:

Approx. Gr. date, February $2^d\ 22^h$

♃'s Dec. S 10°.7

♃'s Mer. Pass. $17^h\ 5^m$ M. T. at ship

♃'s Hour-Angle $5^h\ 12^m$ at rising (*Tab. XXIII*)

Ship M. T. $12^h\ 53^m$ of rising

Mag. Var.	15°.5 E	(*Tab. LVI*)
Comp. Dev.	10 .3 W	Dev. Table for
Comp. Er.	5 .2 E	Stand. Comp.

By Tab. XXIV:

Latitude	48°.1 N	*True Az.*	N 106°.2 E
♃'s Dec.	10 .7 S		

Approx. Comp. Er.	5°.2 E
Approx. Comp. Az.	N 101 .0 E
or,	S 79 .0 E

A few minutes before the time of rising, the compass is set upon the approximate bearing (S 79°.0 E), the appearance of the Planet in the horizon watched for, and, as soon as distinctly visible, the bearing carefully taken. In this case it is S 80°.5 E. Hence—

Obs. Az.	N 99°.5 E	*True Az.*	N 106°.2 E
Corr. (R.)	0 .8	*Comp. Az.*	N 100 .3 E
COMP. ERROR			5 .9 E

Remark.—Example 7 is given at length to illustrate the procedure in such cases, which, although in appearance somewhat complicated, is really very simple and but the work of a few moments. Still, it is quite evident that, by waiting a few minutes for the Planet to rise above the horizon, a bearing then taken and compared with a Time-Azimuth for that instant will be much simpler, and generally preferable, except when the Ship-Time is very uncertain. In such case the Horizon-Azimuth, as above, might be useful.

B. METHOD OF TIME-AZIMUTHS.

15. Fundamental Principles of the Time-Azimuth.—In a Time-Azimuth, the bearing of the Sun or other heavenly body is observed with the compass whenever practicable, the Ship or Local Time being reliably known within certain limits.

The observed bearing is itself the proper Compass-Azimuth of the body.

The True Azimuth is found by a solution of the *Triangle of Position* (*Int.*)

The Data required are—

The *Hour-Angle*, deduced from the Local Time of the observation (*Int.*);

The *Declination*, taken from the Nautical Almanac or Nautical Tables (*Int.*); and

The *Latitude* in, as brought up by the Reckoning or known from previous observation.

16. The Ship-Time.—The Ship or Local Time upon which the Hour-Angle depends, is the important element in this problem. There are two distinct means by which it is obtained, whenever required on board ship.

The first, which is the ordinary one, consists in the use of a reliable Comparing-Watch, which is always kept regulated to the Ship-Time, either Apparent or Mean, generally to the former; being set to that time, or the error noted upon it, as often as a new determination is made by any of the astronomical methods employed for that purpose. Then, whenever required at any intervening moment prior to the next determination, the Ship T. is readily deduced from the W. T., by correcting the latter for the error at the last preceding determination, for that accumulated in the rate during the subsequent interval, and for any difference of Longitude in time made good during the same interval, *subtracting* or *adding* the latter, according as it is *W* or *E* of Greenwich.

The second means is that of deducing the Ship T. from the Chronometer on board, by correcting the Chro. T. for its error on Greenwich T., and then for the place of the ship by *subtracting* or *adding* the Longitude in time, according as it is *W* or *E* of Greenwich. The Ship T., as thus found, will generally be M. T.; and if A. T. be required, it will be necessary to take out for the Greenwich date the Equation of Time and apply it to the M. T.

For the observations of the Sun, it is more convenient to have A. T.; but for observations of the Moon, Planets, or Fixed Stars, it is almost a matter of indifference whether A. T. or M. T. be used; consequently, it is generally expedient to keep one Comparing-Watch at least regulated to ship A. T.

17. Finding the Compass-Error for a Single Heading of the Ship: Objects which may be employed.—In finding the Compass-Error for a single heading of the ship, every recognizable celestial object, which is sufficiently bright to be seen through the sight-vanes of the compass, may be employed in Time-Azimuths with more or less convenience. During the day, the Sun is most commonly resorted to; next to it, the Moon may often be used with nearly equal facility, whether by daylight or during the night, except when near her conjunction; and, besides these, the planets Venus, Mars, Jupiter, and Saturn are frequently available for this purpose. The brighter Fixed Stars may be observed with advantage whenever the more conspicuous objects are in less favorable positions.

In general, it will conduce to accuracy to select an object, on a given occasion, relatively *low in altitude*, not only that, in being seen by direct vision through the sight-vanes rather than by reflection, the Compass-Azimuth is more reliable (*Chap. I*), but because the condition is more favorable for a reliable True Azimuth when the Data are considerably uncertain. Still, as will be seen in the sequel, Time-Azimuths are really available with sufficient accuracy for a single Compass-Error at sea under a wide range of circumstances.

18. To make a Single Time-Azimuth Observation.—Take a bearing of the object with the Standard Compass, or preferably a set of two or three bearings, as quickly as possible, bisecting it each time, if it have a sensible disk (Sun or Moon), and noting the times with a watch, whose error on Ship T. is known.

Note the heading of the ship with the same compass, and the corresponding headings with the other compasses; also, the Angle of Heel, if the ship be iron-built, with the clinometer (10).

The observed bearing, or the Mean if several be taken, is the required Compass-Azimuth; and the noted time, or mean if several be taken, is the corresponding W. T. of observation.

19. Finding the True Azimuth.—This method of finding the True Azimuth consists of two parts: First, the *Preparation of the Data*, and, secondly, the *Solution of the Triangle of Position.* The second part may be accomplished by Logarithmic Computation, by Azimuth Tables, or even by a Graphical Construction, and each may have certain advantages and disadvantages as compared with the others; but the first part must necessarily be the same, and can neither be simplified nor abridged, with reference to one or another of the processes employed for the second part.

20. Rule: Preparation of the Data.—In preparing the Data of a Time-Azimuth, we may proceed in the following manner, according as the object observed is the Sun, or one of the other heavenly bodies:

a) The object observed being the Sun.—This presents the simplest case. Thus—

1. *Find the Greenwich date* for the Ship-Time of observation to the nearest hour.

2. *Take out the Declination of the Sun*, with this date, from Tab. LX, at sight, to the nearest tenth of the degree; and note the *Pol. Dist.* and *Co-Lat.*, each to the nearest tenth of the degree.

3. *Find the Hour-Angle of the Sun.*—For this, convert the Watch-Time of observation into ship Ap. Time, by applying the Watch-Error on that time. Or, if the Watch-Error be known only on ship M. Time, apply this error, and in addition the Eq. of Time, taken at sight from Tab. LIX, to the nearest tenth of a minute, according to its sign, adding if +, subtracting if —. Then, if the observation be P. M., the ship A. T. so found is the Hour-Angle West; or, if the observation be A. M., the ship A. T. subtracted from 12^h gives the Hour-Angle East.

b) The object observed being the Moon, a Planet, or Fixed Star.—For these objects there is a little more to be done in getting the Hour-Angle; still, the process of finding this datum is the same for all objects except the Sun, and requires less time to execute than to describe.

1. *Find the Greenwich date*, in the usual manner:—For the Moon, to the nearest minute; and for either of the Planets or a Fixed Star, to the nearest tenth of the hour.

2. *Take out the Declination of the object*, at sight, to the nearest tenth of the degree; for the Moon and Planets from the Naut. Almanac, and for the Fixed Stars from Tab. LXI; and note the *Pol. Dist.* and *Co-Lat.*, each to the nearest tenth of the degree.

3. *Find the Hour-Angle of the object.*—For this, convert the Watch-Time of observation into ship A. T. by applying the Watch-Error on that time.

Next, to the ship A. T., expressed astronomically, *add* the *Right Ascension of the True Sun* (taken from Tab. LIX and reduced to the Greenwich date by Tab. LXIV), rejecting 24^h from the sum if greater than 24^h, and the result will be the *Right Ascension of the Meridian.* Then, the difference between this R. A. and the *R. A. of the object* (taken from the Naut. Alm. or from Tab. LXI and reduced by Tab. LXIV or LXV), will be the Hour-Angle, which will be *W* or *E* according as the latter R. A. is *less* or *greater* than the former. If the H. A. thus found be greater than 12^h, subtract it from 24^h and take the remainder as the proper H. A. with the *contrary* name.

Otherwise, if the Watch-Error be known only on ship M. T., convert the Watch-Time of observation into ship M. T. by applying the Watch-Error on that time. Next, to the ship M. T., expressed astronomically, add the *Right Ascension of the Mean Sun* (taken from Tab. LIX and reduced to the Greenwich date by Tab. LXVI), rejecting 24^h from the sum if greater than 24^h, and the result will be the *Right Ascension of the Meridian.* Then the difference between this R. A. and the *R. A. of the object* will be the Hour-Angle, as explained in the preceding paragraph.

4. *Remark.*—It is always sufficient to take out the Right Ascensions and to deduce the corresponding Hour-Angles to the nearest tenth of the minute; and Tables LXIV–LXVI afford the requisite facilities for taking out the proper corrections, at sight, to reduce the Tabular Right Ascensions[1] to the given Greenwich date.

---

[1] In order to facilitate the taking out of Right Ascensions, to the nearest tenth of the minute, without the necessity of consuming time and patience in the requisite interpolations, the several Tables referred to in the text have been constructed. The following explanations of their use may be convenient:

1. *To take out the R. A. of the True Sun.*—Enter Tab. LIX with the *day* of G. date and take out the corresponding R. A. and the *Daily Diff.* between that R. A. and the next following; or, enter the Naut. Alm. with the *day* of date and take out the R. A., noting the adjacent *Hourly Diff.;* then, in either case, enter Tab. LXIV with the Diff. and the *hour* (including tenths, if any) of the G. date, and take out the corresponding correction, which *add* to the R. A. for the day, and the result will be the required *R. A. True Sun* reduced to the date.

2. *To take out the R. A. of the Mean Sun.*—Enter Tab. LIX with the day of G. date, and take out the R. A. of the True Sun for that *day,* to which apply the corresponding Eq. of Time, according to its sign, adding if +, subtracting if —; or, take the R. A. *of the Mean Sun* directly from the Naut. Alm. for the *day* of date; then, in either case, enter Tab. LXVI with the *hour* (and tenths, if any) of the G. date, and take out the corresponding correction, which *add* to the before-mentioned sum, or R. A. of the Mean Sun for the day of G. date, and the result will be the required *R. A. Mean Sun* reduced to the date.

3. *To take out the R. A. of the Moon.*—Enter the Tables of the Naut. Alm. with the *day* and *hour* of the G. date and take out the corresponding R. A., and also note the adjacent *Diff.* for 1^m; then enter Tab. LXV with that Diff. (found at foot) and the *minutes* of the G. date and take out the corresponding correction, which *add* to the R. A. above mentioned, and the result will be the required R. A. *of the Moon* reduced to the date.

4. *To take out the R. A. of a Planet.*—Enter the Tables of the Naut. Alm. with the *day* of the G. date and take out the corresponding R. A., and note the adjacent *Diff. for* 1^h with its *sign;* then enter Tab. LXIV with that Diff. and the *hour* (and tenths, if any) of the G. date and take out the corresponding correction, which apply to the before-mentioned

21. Examples in Finding the Hour-Angle.

Ex. 1.—1875, July 17:

Required, the Moon's H. A. in Long. 33° 47′ W at $1^h\ 37^m\ 20^s$ A. M. Ship A. T.

	d.	h.	m.		h.	m.
Ship A. T. July	16	13	37	Ship A. T.	13	37.3
Long. in		+ 2	15	R. A. T.⊙[1]	7	44
Greenwich date	16	15	52	R. A. Merid.	21	21.3
				R. A. ☾	18	36.4
				H. A. ☾	2	44.6 W

Ex. 2.—1875, February 23:

Required, the H. A. of Jupiter in Long. 174° 15′ W at $1^h\ 5^m$ A. M. Ship A. T.

	d.	h.		h.	m.
Ship A. T. Feb.	22	13.1	Ship A. T.	13	5.0
Long. in		+ 11 6	R. A. T.⊙	22	25.6
Greenwich date	23	0.7	R. A. Merid.	11	30.6
			R. A. Jup.	13	59.6
			H. A. Jup.	2	29.0 E

Ex. 3.—1875, April 25:

Required, the Hour-Angle of the Moon, in Long. 155° 20′ W at $0^h\ 15^m\ 30^s$ A. M. Ship M. T.

	d.	h.	m.		h.	m.
Ship M. T. Apr.	24	12	15.5	Ship M. T.	12	15.5
Long. in		+ 10	21.3	R. A. M.⊙	2	12.1
Greenwich date	24	22	37	R. A. Merid.	14	27.6
				R. A. ☾	17	44.5
				H. A. ☾	3	16.9 E

Ex. 4.—1875, October 2:

Required, the H. A. of Venus, in Long. 42° W at $5^h\ 45^m\ 25^s$ P. M. Ship A. T.

	d.	h.		h.	m.
Ship A. T. Oct.	2	5.8	Ship A. T.	5	45.4
Long. in		+ 2.8	R. A. T.⊙	12	33.9
Greenwich date	2	8.6	R. A. Merid.	18	19.3
			R. A. Venus	12	45.1
			H. A. Venus	5	34.2 W

Ex. 5.—1875, April 4:

Required, the H. A. of Castor, in Long. 80° 39′ E at $11^h\ 9^m$ P. M. Ship A. T.

	d.	h.		h.	m.
Ship A. T. April	4	11.2	Ship A. T.	11	9
Long. in		— 5.4	R. A. T.⊙	0	53.6
Greenwich date	4	5.8	R. A. Merid.	12	2 6
			R. A. Star	7	26 6
			H. A. Star	4	36 0 W

Ex. 6.—1875, September 9:

Required, the H. A. of Fomalhaut, in Long. 33° 55′ W at $8^h\ 20^m\ 10^s$ P. M. Ship M. T.

	d.	h.		h.	m.
Ship M. T. Sept.	9	8.3	Ship M. T.	8	20.2
Long. in		+ 2.3	R. A. M.⊙	11	14.2
Greenwich date	9	10.6	R. A. Merid.	19	34.4
			R. A. Star	22	50.7
			H. A. Star	3	16.3 E

R. A. according to the sign of the Diff., and the result will be the required *R. A. of the Planet* reduced to the date.

5. *To take out the R. A. of a Fixed Star.*—Enter Tab. LXI, or the Naut. Alm., with the *year* of G. date and take out at sight the corresponding R. A. to the nearest tenth of the minute.

In taking out corrections from Tables LXIV–LXVI, it will be sufficient to enter the Tables with the nearest tabular difference, and to retain the nearest tenth's figure in the decimal part of the correction.

			h.	m.	
[1] *In Ex.* 1:—By	Tab. LIX	R. A. True Sun	7	41.4	at Greenwich noon July 16.
	Tab. LXIV	Red^n for $15^h.9$	+	2.6	Daily Diff. $4^m.0$.
		R. A. True Sun	7	44.0	for Greenwich date.

			h.	m.	
In Ex. 2:—By	Tab. LIX	{ R. A. True Sun	2	6.5	at Greenwich noon April 24.
		{ Eq. of Time	+	1.9	at Greenwich noon.
		R. A. Mean Sun	2	8.4	at Greenwich noon.
	Tab. LXV	Red^n for $22^h.6$	+	3.7	
		R. A. Mean Sun	2	12.1	for Greenwich date.

			h.	m.	
In Ex. 1:—By	N. Almanac	R. A. Moon	18	34.4	at Greenwich $15^h.0$ July 16.
	Tab. LXV	Red^n for 52^m	+	2.0	Diff. $2^s.30$ for 1^m.
		R. A. Moon	18	36.4	for Greenwich date.

			h.	m.	
In Ex. 4:—By	N. Almanac	R. A. Venus	12	43.5	at Greenwich noon Oct. 2.
	Tab. LXIV	Red^n for $8^h.6$	+	1.6	Diff. $11^s.4$ for 1^h.
		R. A. Venus	12	45.1	for Greenwich date.

22. Rule: Solution by Logarithmic Computation.—

Using Tables X, XI, XII, and XIII, we may proceed as follows:

Take the *Half-Difference* and *Half-Sum* of the Pol. Dist. and Co-Lat., also Half the Hour-Angle; then, to the sine of the ½ D. add the cosecant of the ½ S. and the cotangent of the ½ H. A.; the Sum of these three logarithms, rejecting tens from the indices, is the log tangent of the *Angle* **X.** Similarly, to the cosine of the ½ D. add the secant of the ½ S. and the same cotangent of the ½ H. A.; and the Sum of these three logarithms, rejecting tens from the indices, is the log tangent of the *Angle* **Y.**

There will now be two Cases to consider, according as the ½ S. of the Pol. Dist. and Co-Lat. is *less* or *greater* than 90°.

First Case: *½ S. of Pol. Dist. and Co-Lat.* **less** *than* 90°.—Take the *Sum* or *Difference* of the Angles **X** and **Y**, according as the Pol. Dist. is *greater* or *less* than the Co-Lat., and the result will be the *True Azimuth.*

Second Case: *½ S. of Pol. Dist.* and *Co-Lat.* **greater**[1] *than* 90°.—Always take the *Difference* of the Angles **X** and **Y**, which subtract from 180°, and the result will be the *True Azimuth.*

In either Case, mark the True Azimuth N or S according to the Lat., and E or W according to the Hour-Angle.

Remark.—It may sometimes be convenient to use the *Supplement* of the True Azimuth by subtracting from 180° and reversing the prefix N or S, in order to make it correspond to the Compass-Azimuth less than 90°.

23. Examples of True Azimuths by Computation.

Ex. 1.—With Lat. 20° 50′ N and Dec. 2°.7 S, what is the Truo Az. of the Sun at 1^h 21^m P. M. ship Ap. Time? ⊙'s Hour-Angle 1^h 21^m W.

Pol. dist.	92°.7				
Co-Lat.	69 .2				
Diff.	23 .5				
½ Diff.	11 .7	sin	9.3070	cos	9.9961
½ Sum	80 .9	cosec	0.0055	sec	0.8009
½ H. A.	0^h 40^m.5	cot	0.7488	cot	0.7488
		tan	0.0613	tan	1.5458
T. Az. N 137°.4 W:		**X**	49°.0	**Y**	88°.4

Ex. 2.—With Lat. 40° 33′ N and Dec. N 21°.8, what is the True Az. of the Sun at 5^h 24^m 43^s A. M. ship A. T.? ⊙'s Hour-Angle 6^h 35^m.3 E.

Pol. dist.	68°.2				
Co-Lat.	49 .5				
Diff.	18 .7				
½ Diff.	9 .3	sin	9.2085	cos	9.9943
½ Sum	58 .8	cosec	0.0678	sec	0.2856
½ H. A.	3^h 17^m.6	cot	9.9330	cot	9.9330
		tan	9.2093	tan	0.2129
T. Az. N 67°.7 E:		**X**	9°.2	**Y**	58°.5

Ex. 3.—With Lat. 12° 17′ S and Dec. 22°.9 S, what is the Truo Az. of the Sun at 8^h 20^m 5^s A. M. ship A. T.? ⊙'s H. A. 3^h 39^m.9 E.

Pol. dist.	67°.1				
Co-Lat.	77 .7				
Diff.	10 .6				
½ Diff.	5 .3	sin	8 9655	cos	9.9981
½ Sum	72 .4	cosec	0.0208	sec	0.5195
½ H. A.	1^h 50^m	cot	0.2835	cot	0.2835
		tan	9.2698	tan	0.8011
T. Az. S 70°.5 E:		**X**	10°.5	**Y**	81°.0

Ex. 4.—With Lat. 6° 11′ N and Dec. 23°.3 S, what is tho True Az. of the Sun at 5^h 10^m P. M. ship A. T.? ⊙'s H. A. 5^h 10^m W.

Pol. dist.	113°.3				
Co-Lat.	83 .8				
Diff.	29 .5				
½ Diff.	14 .7	sin	9.4044	cos	9.9855
½ Sum	98 .5	cosec	0.0048	sec	0.8303
½ H. A.	2^h 35^m	cot	0.0955	cot	0.0955
		tan	9.5047	tan	0.9113
T. Az. N 114°.7 W:		**X**	17°.7	**Y**	83°.0

[1] In taking out the cosecant and secant in this case, use the Supplement of ½ S. by subtracting from 180°; otherwise, and more conveniently, use the *excess* of the ½ S. over 90°, taking out the secant for cosecant and the cosecant for secant.

Ex. 5.—With Lat. 23° 24′ N and Dec. 23°.4 N, what is the True Az. of the Sun at 6^h 10^m P. M. ship A. T.? ⊙'s H. A. 6^h 10^m W.

Pol. dist.	66°.6				
Co-Lat.	66 .6				
Diff.	0 .0				
½ Diff.	0 .0	sin	—∞	cos	0.0000
½ Sum	66 .6	cosec	....	sec	0.4010
½ H. A. 3^h 5^m		cot	....	cot	9 9810
		tan	—∞	tan	0 3820
T. Az. N 67°4. W:		X	0°.0	Y	67°.4

Ex. 6.—With Lat. 21° 23′ N and Dec. 21° 23′ S, what is the True Az. of the Sun at 4^h 30^m P. M. ship A. T.? ⊙'s H. A. 4^h 30^m W.

Pol. dist.	111°.4				
Co-Lat.	68 .6				
Diff.	42 .8				
½ Diff.	21 .4	sin	9.5621	cos	....
½ Sum	90 .0	cosec	0.0000	sec	+∞
½ H. A. 2^h 15^m		cot	0.1751	cot	....
		tan	9.7372	tan	+∞
T. Az. N 118°.6 W:		X	28°.6	Y	90°.0

Ex. 7.—With Lat. 12° 17′ N and Dec. 11°.7 N, what is the True Az. of the Sun at 5^h 5^m P. M. ship A. T.? ⊙'s H. A. 5^h 5^m W.

Pol. dist.	78°.3				
Co-Lat.	77 .7				
Diff.	0 .6				
½ Diff.	0 .3	sin	7.7190	cos	0.0000
½ Sum	78 .0	cosec	0.0096	sec	0.6821
½ H. A. 2^h 32^m.5		cot	0.1053	cot	0.1053
		tan	7.8339	tan	0.7874
T. Az. N 81°.1 W:		X	0°.4	Y	80°.7

Ex. 8.—With Lat. 72° 11′ N and Dec. 29° 32′ N, required the True Az. of a Star whose Hour-Angle is 9^h 15^m W.

Pol. dist.	60°.5				
Co-Lat.	17 .8				
Diff.	42 .7				
½ Diff.	21 .3	sin	9.5602	cos	9.9693
½ Sum	39 .1	cosec	0.2002	sec	0.1101
½ H. A. 4^h 37^m.5		cot	9.5757	cot	9 5757
		tan	9.3361	tan	9.6551
T. Az. N 36°.5 W:		X	12°.2	Y	24°.3

Ex. 9.—With Lat. 30° 7′ N and Dec. 9° 17′ S, what is the True Az. of the Moon when its H. A. is 0^h 13^m.3 E?

Pol. dist.	99°.3				
Co-Lat.	59 .9				
Diff.	39 .4				
½ Diff.	19 .7	sin	9.5278	cos	9.9738
½ Sum	79 .6	cosec	0.0072	sec	0.7435
½ H. A. 0^h 6^m. 6½		cot	1.5384	cot	1.5384
		tan	1.0734	tan	2.2557
T. Az. N 174°.9 E:		X	85°.2	Y	89°.7

Ex. 10.—With Lat. 12° 17′ N and Dec. 11° 42′ S, what is the True Az. of the Sun at 6^h 30^m A. M. ship A. T.? ⊙'s H. A. 5^h 30^m E.

Pol. dist.	101°.7				
Co-Lat.	77 .7				
Diff.	24 .0				
½ Diff.	12 .0	sin	9.3179	cos	9 9904
½ Sum	89 .7	cosec	0.0000	sec	2 2810
½ H. A. 2^h 45^m		cot	0.0570	cot	0.0570
		tan	9 3749	tan	2.3284
T. Az. N 103°.1 E:		X	13°.3	Y	89°.8

Ex. 11.—With Lat. 70° 50′ N and Dec. 20°.6 N, required the True Az. of the Sun at 0^h 20^m A. M. ship A. T. ⊙'s H. A. 11^h 40^m E.

Pol. dist.	69°.4				
Co-Lat.	19 .2				
Diff.	50 .2				
½ Diff.	25 .1	sin	9 6276	cos	9.9569
½ Sum	44 .3	cosec	0.1559	sec	0.1453
½ H. A. 5^h 50^m		cot	8.6401	cot	8.6401
		tan	8.4236	tan	8.7423
T. Az. N 4°.7 E:		X	1°.5	Y	3°.2

Ex. 12.—With Lat. 1° 2′ S and Dec. 32°.1 N, required the True Az. of Castor when its H. A. is 4^h 35^m.8 W.

Pol. dist.	122°.1				
Co-Lat.	89 .0				
Diff.	33 .1				
½ Diff.	16 .5	sin	9.4533	cos	9.9817
½ Sum	105 .5	cosec	0.0161	sec	0 5731
½ H. A. 2^h 17^m.9		cot	0.1632	cot	0.1632
		tan	9.6326	tan	0.7180
T. Az. S 124°.0 W:		X	23°.2	Y	79°.2

Always, in *computing*, take secant for cosecant and cosecant for secant of the *excess* whenever the Half-Sum, as in Ex. 4, is greater than 90°.0. In the use of Table XXX, this distinction is not presented; the necessary changes being provided for in the construction of the Tables. This is one among the other advantages of tabular inspection in avoiding the mistakes of a hasty computation.

24. The Tables of Time-Azimuths.—Although, under the preceding Rule, the computation of a True Azimuth by this method is really quite simple, and may be accomplished in a few moments for any given case, still, it is possible, with the aid of special Tables, to greatly facilitate the determination of this important element. Such is the object of the Tables, in three parts (*XXX*, *XXX. A*, and *XXX. B*), of this Manual.

a) **Tab. XXX,** or the First Part, provides for taking out Logs A and B with the Lat. and Dec., or with the corresponding Co-Lat. and Pol. Dist., either being used at pleasure as arguments. These arguments comprise all Latitudes from 0° to 80° north or south of the Equator, and all Declinations from 0° to 35° of the same and contrary name. The arguments are given at intervals of *one degree ;* but the Table may be entered to the *nearest half-degree*, and the quantities taken at sight, with a sacrifice of precision that, as compared with a computation to the nearest tenth of the degree, is seldom so great as $\pm 0°.2$, or $\pm 12'$;—much within the requirements of practice in finding a single Compass-Error. The Table may, however, readily be entered with the Lat. and Dec. to the nearest tenth of the degree, by a simple interpolation, but this is rarely, if ever, required for a single Compass-Error.

b) **Tab. XXX. A,** or Second Part, provides for taking out Log C, with the Hour-Angle as argument. This argument comprises all Hour-Angles from 0^h to 12^h west or east of the Meridian, and is given throughout at intervals of *one-tenth of a minute* (every six seconds) in time.

c) **Tab. XXX. B,** or Third Part, provides for taking out the **Angles X** and **Y** among the arguments, which are given in degrees and tenths. This Table is entered to the nearest tabular quantities with the two sums obtained by adding Log C to Log A and to Log B.

d) It was intended in the construction of these Tables—

First, that they should admit of furnishing an immediate or offhand determination of the True Azimuth, with every probable combination of Data, without a moment of time or patience expended on mere interpolation, and with a degree of precision and certainty to meet every practical requirement, whether in finding single or serial Compass-Errors; and,

Secondly, that they should be as compact and portable as possible, consistently with the realization of the foregoing conditions.[1]

---

[1] Other Tables of Time-Azimuths have been given under different forms. Such are the following:

1. *Sun's True Bearing or Azimuth Tables, computed for intervals of four minutes, between the Parallels of Latitude* 30° *and* 60° *inclusive:* By JOHN BURDWOOD, Staff-Commander R. N., London, 1866.

2. *Tables des Azimuts du Soleil correspondant à l'heure vraie du bord, entre les parallèles* 55° *sud et* 55° *nord :* par F. LABROSSE, Ancien Officier de Marine, Paris, 1868. (The explanations are given in French and English.)

3. A set of Azimuth-Tables (pp. 58–107), contained in *Practical Information on the Deviation of the Compass, for the use of Masters and Mates of Iron Ships:* By JOHN THOMAS TOWSON, F.R.G.S., etc., London, 1869.

4. *Azimuth and Hour-Angle, for Latitude and Declination ; or Tables for finding Azimuth at sea by means of the Hour-Angle, in all navigable Latitudes, at every two degrees of Declina-*

25. Direct and Limiting Values of Time-Azimuths: Use of Tab. XXXI.—Tab. XXXI gives the Time-Azimuth directly, which, under very favorable conditions (60), may be taken out quite readily and with sufficient accuracy for finding the Compass-Error in numerous special instances; but the argument-intervals are too large for convenient use in the general case.

This Table is useful in showing the *limits* of the Time-Azimuth; in furnishing a *check against serious error*, through a hasty or inconsiderate procedure in getting out the True Azimuth by the ordinary methods; and it is frequently useful in giving an approximate True Azimuth, at sight, as required in estimating probable errors, etc.

26. Rule: Solution by the Azimuth-Tables.—The Data having been prepared (20), proceed as follows:

Enter Tab. XXX, either with the Lat. and Dec., or with the Co-Lat. and Pol. Dist., to the *nearest half-degree*, and take out at sight *Log A* from the *left* and *Log B* from the *right* page; next, enter **Tab. XXX. A,** with the Hour-Angle, to the *nearest tenth of the minute*, and take out *Log C*, which *add* to both *Log A* and *Log B*, calling the results *Tang X* and *Tang Y;* then, enter **Tab. XXX. B,** and take out (from the arguments) *Ang. X* with the *Tang X* and *Ang. Y* with the *Tang Y;* and, finally, complete the solution, according as it falls under the First or Second Case (*Art. 22* and *foot of Tab. XXX. B*).

b) **Remark.**—When *either* the Lat. or Dec. (in Tab. XXX) falls more nearly upon the half-degree than whole degree of the tabular argument, take the *Mean* of the *two adjacent* tabular[1] quantities; and when *both* the Lat. and Dec. fall more nearly upon the half than whole degree of the tabular arguments, take the *Cross-Mean* of the *four adjacent* quantities.[2] The same rule will be observed in using the Co-Lat. and Pol. Dist. as arguments.

---

tion between the limits of the Zodiac, etc.: By Major-General R. SHORTREDE, F.R.A.S., London.

Also, a *Time-Azimuth Diagram:* By HUGH GODFRAY, M. A., London, 1858.

This graphical method applies to all Latitudes, to all Declinations between 25° N and 25° S, and to all Hour-Angles from 2^h to 10^h, E or W of the Meridian.

[1] The Mean of two quantities is most readily found by subtracting their Half-Difference from the greater, or adding it to the smaller quantity. Most commonly, the Mean of the two adjacent quantities in this Table may be taken at sight.

[2] The Mean from *each* cross-pair of the four adjacent quantities in this Table is the same, or nearly so, and either may be used; but, in general, it will be seen that the quantities of *one* cross-pair in each case are very *nearly equal*, and, accordingly, the Mean of this pair will be taken in preference.

27. Examples of True Azimuths by the Azimuth-Tables (the data from the Examples of Art. 23).

Ex. 1.—Lat. 20°.8 N, Dec. 2°.7 S, and H. A. 1^h 21^m W: Required, the True Az.

Enter with { P. D. 92°.5
C. L. 69 .0
Diff. 23 .5
½ Sum 80 .7

Log A 9.315	Log B 0.785	*Tab. XXX*
Log C 0.748	Log C 0.748	*XXX. A*
Tan **X** 0.063	Tan **Y** 1.533	
X 49°.2	**Y** 88°.3	*XXX. B*

TRUE Az. N 137°.5 W

Ex. 2.—Lat. 40°.5 N, Dec. 21°.8 N, and H. A. 6^h $35^m.3$ E: Required, the True Az.

P. D. 68°.0
C. L. 49 .5
Diff. 18 .5
½ Sum 58 .7

9.274	0.280
9.933	9.933
9.207	0.213
X 9°.1	**Y** 58°.5

TRUE Az. N 67°.6 E

Ex. 3.—Lat. 12°.3 S, Dec. 22°.9 S, and H. A. 3^h $39^m.9$ E: Required, the True Az.

P. D. 67°.0
C. L. 77 .5
Diff. 10 .5
½ Sum 72 .2

8.982	0.514
0.284	0.284
9.266	0.798
X 10°.5	**Y** 81°.0

TRUE Az. S 70°.5 E

Ex. 4.—Lat. 6°.2 N, Dec. 23°.3 S, and H. A. 5^h 10^m W: Required, the True Az.

P. D. 113°.5
C. L. 84 .0
Diff. 29 .5
½ Sum 98 .7

9.410	0.803
0.096	0.096
9.506	0.899
X 17°.8	**Y** 82°.8

TRUE Az. N 115°.0 W

Ex. 5.—Lat. 23°.4 N, Dec. 23°.4 N, and H. A. 6^h 10^m W: Required, the True Az.

P. D. 66°.5
C. L. 66 .5
Diff. 0 .0
½ Sum 66 .5

$-\infty$	0.399
....	9.981
$-\infty$	0.380
X 0°.0	**Y** 67°.4

TRUE Az. N 67°.4 W

Ex. 6.—Lat. 21°.4 N, Dec. 21°.4 S, and H. A. 4^h 30^m W: Required, the True Az.

P. D. 111°.5
C. L. 68 .5
Diff. 43 .0
½ Sum 90 .0

9.564	$+\infty$
0.175	....
9.739	$+\infty$
X 28°.7	**Y** 90°.0

TRUE Az. N 118°.7 W

Ex. 7.—Lat. 12°.3 N, Dec. 11°.7 N, and H. A. 5^h 5^m W: Required, the True Az.

P. D. 78°.5
C. L. 77 .5
Diff. 1 .0
½ Sum 78 .0

7.950	0.682
0.105	0.105
8.055	0.787
X 0°.7	**Y** 80°.7

TRUE Az. N 81°.4 W

Ex. 8.—Lat. 72°.2 N, Dec. 29°.5 N, and H. A. 9^h 15^m W: Required, the True Az.

P. D. 60°.5
C. L. 18 .0
Diff. 42 .5
½ Sum 39 .2

9.758	0.080
9.576	9.576
9.334	9.656
X 12°.2	**Y** 24°.3

TRUE Az. N 36°.5 W

Ex. 9.—Lat. 30°.1 N, Dec. 9°.3 S, and H. A. $0^h\ 13^m.3$ E: Required, the True Az.

P. D.	99°.5
C. L.	60 .0
Diff.	39 .5
½ Sum	79 .7

	9.536	0.723
	1.537	1.537
	1.073	2.260
	X 85°.2	**Y** 89°.7

True Az. N 174°.9 E

Ex. 10.—Lat. 12°.3 N, Dec. 11°.7 S, and H. A. $5^h\ 30^m$ E: Required, the True Az.

P. D.	101°.5
C. L.	77 .5
Diff.	24 .0
½ Sum	89 .5

9.318	2.050
0.057	0.057
9.375	2.107
X 13°.3	**Y** 89°.6

True Az. N 102°.9 E

Ex. 11.—Lat. 70°.8 N, Dec. 20°.6 N, and H. A. $11^h\ 40^m$ E: Required, the True Az.

P. D.	69°.5
C. L.	19 .0
Diff.	50 .5
½ Sum	44 .2

9.786	0.100
8.640	8.640
8.426	8.740
X 1°.5	**Y** 3°.1

True Az. N 4°.6 E

Ex. 12.—Lat. 1°.0 S, Dec. 32°.1 N, and H. A. $4^h\ 35^m.8$ W: Required, the True Az.

P. D.	122°.0
C. L.	89 .0
Diff.	33 .0
½ Sum	105 .5

9.469	0.555
0.163	0.163
9.632	0.718
X 23°.2	**Y** 79°.2

True Az. S 124°.0 W

28. Remark I: On the Two Cases of the Time-Azimuth.—In obtaining the True Azimuth by this method, the first thing to be noticed, after getting the Angles **X** and **Y**, is the relation of the Half-Sum of Pol. Dist. and Co-Lat. to 90°. If the Half-Sum be *less* than 90°, the Example falls under Case I; if *greater*, under Case II. Thus, of the several preceding Examples, Nos. 1, 2, 3, 5, 7, 8, 9, 10, and 11, fall under Case I; Nos. 4 and 12 under Case II; while No. 6, having the Half-Sum *equal* to 90°, falls indifferently into either Case.

And the next thing after deciding the Case: If the Example fall under Case I, it is sufficient to observe whether the Pol. Dist. be *greater* or *less* than the Co-Lat., and to take, correspondingly, the *Sum* or the *Difference* of the Angles **X** and **Y** as the True Azimuth; or, if the Example fall under Case II, it is only necessary to take the *Difference* of the Angles **X** and **Y** and use its *Supplement* (*i. e.* subtracting the Difference from 180°.0) as the True Azimuth.

The simplicity of these precepts in the Rule of the Time-Azimuth must be evident, if it be kept in mind that they are entirely general; that is to say, are applicable to the finding of the True Azimuth of any celestial object, whatever its Declination, in any Latitude, and at any hour of the day or night.

As an aid to the memory, whenever necessary to recall these precepts (given at the foot of Tab. XXX. B, as well as in the text), the following consideration may be useful: Observing that, while "Pol. Dist." is the distance of the object from the elevated pole, Co-Lat. is also the Polar Distance of the observer, the significance of the fundamental distinction into Two Cases is found in this: that, according as the Half-Sum or Mean of the Polar Distances of the observer and object is *less* or *greater* than 90° (that is, *less* or *greater* than the Polar Distance of the Equator), the problem falls under *Case I* or *Case II*. The subordinate distinction into two varieties of Case I is obviously suggestive; while the Difference and Supplement, or Double Difference, is hardly less so, when reaching *beyond the Equator* of Case II.

29. Remark II: On the Conditions introducing the Use of the Symbols $-\infty$ and $+\infty$.—There are two conditions of the Lat. and Dec., which bring into view certain relations of the symbols $-\infty$ and $+\infty$, as found in the Azimuth-Tables, with respect to which a brief explanation may be of service to some one, possibly, who may use these Tables.

a) **The Dec. *equal* to the Lat.**—This condition is one very liable to occur, alike with the Dec. of the *same* and the *contrary* name.

First, when the Dec. has the *same* name as the Lat.: Then, whether both these Data be entered in Tab. XXX to the whole or to the half degree,[1] the Log A is always $-\infty$; and as the Log C cannot affect it,[2] the Ang. X for $-\infty$ is always 0°.0,—as in Ex. 5.

Secondly, when the Dec. has the *contrary* name: Then, whether both these Data be entered in Tab. XXX to the whole or half degree,[3] the Log B is always $+\infty$; and as the Log C cannot affect it,[4] the Ang. Y for $+\infty$ is always 90°,—as in Ex. 6.

b) **The Dec. *nearly equal* to the Lat.**—This is a condition, both when the Dec. has the *same* and when the *contrary* name, which is of course more frequently liable to occur than the first.

First, when the Dec. has the *same* name as the Lat.: Then, the smaller limit in Tab. XXX of the Log A is $-\infty$, and the adjacent or larger limit (varying from 7.941 to 8.025 in different parts of the Table) *always* differs about 0.300 from each of its own outward adjacents. Accordingly, if *both* the Lat. and Dec. be entered to the half-degree, the *Cross-Mean* is still to be taken, as in Ex. 7; but, if one be entered to the whole and the other to the half degree, the proportion is made towards the $-\infty$, by always *subtracting* 0.150 from the adjacent and larger limit;[5] as, for example, if the Lat. were 12°.0 and Dec. 11°.5, we should take 7.800 as the Log A.

Secondly, when the Dec. has the *contrary* name: Then, the *larger* limit of the Log B is $+\infty$, and the adjacent or *smaller* limit (varying from 2.059 to 1.975 in different parts of the Table) *always* differs about 0.300 from each of its outward adjacents. Accordingly, if *both* the Lat. and Dec. be entered to the half-degree, the *Cross-Mean* is to be taken, as in Ex. 10; but if one be entered to the whole and the other to the

[1] Since the ½ Diff. of the Pol. Dist. and Co-Lat. being 0°.0, the Log sine is $-\infty$.

[2] Except in the rare instance of having the Hour-Angle equal to 0h.0, when the Ang. X is *indeterminate*.

[3] Since the ½ Sum of the Pol. Dist. and Co-Lat. being 90°, the Log secant is $+\infty$.

[4] In any instance that can occur in practice.

[5] That is, by subtracting the *Half Adjacent Diff.* from the greater limit, which, although only approximate, always gives a result within about ±0°.3.

half degree, the proportion is made towards the $+\infty$, by always *adding* 0.150 to the adjacent and smaller limit;[1] as, for example, if the Lat. were 12°.0 and Dec. —11°.5, we should take 2.200 as the Log B.

Although the preceding explanation of these relations may seem at first view to imply it, there need be really no occasion whatever for embarrassment in the treatment of these symbols whenever encountered; only remembering that $-\infty$ represents an extremely *small* quantity or *nothing*, and that $+\infty$ represents an extremely *large* quantity or *infinity*.

30. Examples of Finding the Compass-Error by a Time-Azimuth.—The Examples already given (*Arts.* 21, 23, 27) fully illustrate the process of getting a True Azimuth by this method, under a considerable variety of circumstances. It will be sufficient to present a few more, merely to exhibit the entire form of procedure in finding the Compass-Error by a Time-Azimuth.

Ex. 1.—1871, August 16: At anchor, Disco Island, in Lat. 69° 14′ N, Long. 53° 18′ W, at $4^h\ 21^m\ 46^s$ P. M., Ship A. T., observed bearing of ☉'s centre was N 56° W: Required, the Compass-Error.

Greenwich date, August $16^d\ 8^h$
☉'s Dec. 13°.7 N; ☉'s H. A. $4^h\ 21^m.8$ W

Pol. Dist. 76°.3
Co-Lat. 20 .8

	9.792		0.128
	0.192		0.192
	9.984		0.320
X	44°.0	Y	64°.4

True Az.	N 108°.4 W	
Comp. Az.	N 56 .0 W	
Comp. Er.	52 .4 W	

Ex. 2.—1875, February 23: At sea, in Lat. 60° 53′ N, Long. 174° 15′ W, at $1^h\ 5^m$ A. M., Ship A. T., observed bearing of Jupiter was S 49° E: Required, the Compass-Error and Deviation.

Greenwich date, February $23^d\ 0^h.7$
♃'s Dec. 10°.7 S
♃'s H. A. $2^h\ 29^m.0$ E (*Ex.* 2, *Art.* 21)

Pol. Dist. 100°.7
Co-Lat. 29 .1

	9.811		0.280
	0.472		0.472
	0.283		0.752
X	62°.4	Y	80°.0.

True Az.	N 142°.4 E	
Comp. Az.	N 131 .0 E	
Comp. Er.	11 .4 E	
Mag. Var.	19 .3 E	(*Tab. LVI*)
Comp. Dev.	7 .9 W	

Ex. 3.—1875, April 25: At sea, in Lat. 50° 37′ N, Long 155° 20′ W, at $0^h\ 15^m\ 30^s$ A. M., Ship M. T., the observed bearing of ☾'s centre was S 66°.5 E: Required, the Compass-Error.

Greenwich date, April $24^d\ 22^h\ 37^m$
☾'s Dec. S 28°.3
☾'s H. A. $3^h\ 16^m.9$ E (*Ex.* 3, *Art.* 21)

Pol. Dist. 118°.5
Co-Lat. 39 .5

	9.812		0 607
	0.339		0.339
	0.151		0.946
X	54°.7	Y	83°.5

True Az.	N 138°.2 E
Comp. Az.	N 113 .5 E
Comp. Er.	24 .7 E

Ex. 4.—1875, July 17: At sea, in Lat. 52° 38′ N, Long. 33° 47′ W, at $1^h\ 37^m\ 20^s$ A. M., Ship A. T., observed bearing of ☾'s centre was S 66°.0 W: Required, the Compass-Error.

Greenwich date, July $16^d\ 13^h\ 37^m$
☾'s Dec. S 28°.3
☾'s H. A. $2^h\ 44^m.9$ W (*Ex.* 1, *Art.* 21)

Pol. Dist. 118°.5
Co-Lat. 52 .5

	9.738		1.029
	0.425		0.425
	0.163		1.454
X	55°.5	Y	88°.0

True Az.	N 143°.5 W
Comp. Az.	N 114 .0 W
Comp. Er.	29 .5 W

[1] That is, by adding the *Half Adjacent Diff.* to the smaller limit, which, although only approximately correct, always gives a result within about ±0°.3.

31. Finding Compass-Errors for a Series of Different Headings of the Ship.—It is occasionally desirable (*Chap. IV*) to determine the Compass-Errors for a series of different Headings of the Ship. For this, the Method of Time-Azimuths is peculiarly convenient and reliable, whether at sea or near the land.

For these observations, the Sun is the object commonly employed. Other objects, such as the Moon, the brighter Planets, and the brighter Stars, might be used, sometimes, with advantage. Generally, the opportunity may be chosen at will; and the considerations controlling the choice of an object should have reference to the slowness of its change of Declination, the ease and certainty with which it may be sighted, and the convenience with which the auxiliary observations may be made. In all cases, the object should be observed only while it is low in altitude—never, at least if it can be avoided, when the H. A. is less than 4^h; for the precision with which serial Compass-Errors should be had, in order to serve any really useful purpose, requires that those conditions be satisfied.

32. To make the Observations of Serial Time-Azimuths.—With a fine day and a smooth sea, and with the means of placing the ship upon her different Headings by steaming or sailing, and whenever necessary, near the land, by towing or warping, the requisite observations may be conducted as follows:

The ship being steady, take a bearing of the Sun's centre with the Standard Compass, noting the time with a watch, whose error on Ship T., Apparent or Mean, is known within allowable limits (G). Note the Heading of the ship with the same compass; also the corresponding Headings with the Steering-Compasses, and the Angle of Heel with the clinometer (10).

After changing the Heading to any desired extent, and again steadying, repeat the observation in all particulars; and so proceed, changing the Heading and repeating the observation, till the desired number shall have been made, completely or partially, round the Compass-Circle.

Remark I: Position of the Object.—The period should be so chosen that the Hour-Angles of the object shall not, in general, be less than 4^h, E or W of the Meridian. In no case should an H. A. be less than 3^h, E or W of the Meridian, except in cases of urgent necessity, as when threatened with thick weather.

Remark II: Steadying the Ship.—While the observations should be made with the least practicable delay, no flying bearings should be taken; but the ship should be steadied upon the recognized Heading, not only during the time of making each observation, but for a minute at the least before commencing it.[1]

[1] See *Chap. IV*.—There must be time not only for the changing induction to be accomplished, but also for the vibrations of the compass-card to cease, should there be any, if we would aim at getting really satisfactory results.

Remark III: Heading-Intervals.—It is always preferable to make the observations with the Headings upon the regular points by compass, thirty-two, sixteen, or eight, whenever practicable; but, when the circumstances make this difficult or time-consuming, the results will be equally available if obtained on any Headings distributed with approximate equality round the whole circle, or similarly through any part of it, when those on a certain part only are desired or can be had.

Remark IV: Care in Sighting and Reading off.—Strict attention should be given to Sighting and Reading off. It should be seen that the Standard Compass is in nice equilibrium. With a well-made and properly-adjusted Compass, and otherwise favorable circumstances, it should be practicable to sight and read off to the nearest quarter of a degree.

33. Rule: To get the Serial True Azimuths by Computation.—First, prepare the Data, as follows:

a) Find the Greenwich date for the *Middle* Ship T. of the set of observations, either by applying the Longitude or deducing it from the chronometer.

b) With this date take out the Sun's Declination; also, the Equation of Time, whenever necessary to convert Ship M. T. into Ship A. T.

c) Deduce the Co-Lat. and Mid. Pol. Dist. each to the nearest minute for observations in port or near the land, or when the greatest precision is desired; otherwise, to the nearest tenth of the degree, which is generally sufficient for observations at sea.

d) Prepare the Sun's Hour-Angles. For this, convert the W. Times of observation into Ap. Times; then, if the observations be P. M., the Ap. Times are the Sun's Hour-Angles W; if the observations be A. M., the Ap. Times subtracted from 12^h are the Sun's Hour-Angles E.

Next, proceed with the computations, as follows:

e) Take the Half-Difference and Half-Sum of the Mid. Pol. Dist. and Co-Lat.; then, using Tab. IX,—

To the sine of the ½ D. add the cosecant of the ½ S.; the result, rejecting 10 from the index, will be the Log A. Similarly, to the cosine of the ½ D. add the secant of the ½ S.; the result, rejecting 10 from the index, will be the Log B.

f) Now, proceed in tabular form, by ruling several vertical columns, and, dividing each Hour-Angle by 2, place the series of ½ Hour-Angles, in their order, in Col. I. Take the cotangent of each ½ H. A. and place it opposite in Col. II. *Add* Log A to each cotangent and place the resulting Tangents X in Col. III; also, do the same with Log B, and place the resulting Tangents Y in Col. IV, rejecting 10 from the index in each case.

Then, take out for each tangent in Col. III the corresponding Angles X, and place them in Col. V; also, from the tangents in Col. IV the corresponding Angles Y, which place in Col. VI.

There will now be two Cases to consider, according as the ½ S. of the P. D. and C. L. is *less* or *greater* than 90°.

g) **First Case: H. S. of P. D. and C. L. *less* than 90°.**—Take the *Sum* or *Difference* of the corresponding Angles X and Y, according as the P. D. is *greater* or *less* than the C. L., and place the resulting True Azimuths in Col. VII; or, in the—

h) **Second Case: H. S. of P. D. and C. L. *greater* than 90°.**—Always take the *Difference* of the corresponding Angles X and Y, which subtract from 180°, and place the resulting True Azimuths in Col. VII.

i) **In either Case,** mark the True Azimuth N or S according to the Latitude, and E or W according as the observations are East or West of the Meridian.

Remark.—It may sometimes be convenient to use the Supplements of the True Azimuths (22, *e*).

34. To get the Serial True Azimuths by the Azimuth-Tables.—The preceding Rule for computing the True Azimuths of a Series, for precision and facility, leaves little to be desired in an operation that is only occasionally encountered by the Navigator; nevertheless, they may be found with the requisite precision and greater facility by the Azimuth-Tables (*XXX, XXX. A, XXX. B*).

The Data having been prepared (33 *a–d*), proceed as follows:

a) Enter Tab. XXX with the Middle Dec. and Lat., or with the Mid. Pol. Dist. and Co-Lat., both to the nearest tenth of the degree, and take out Log A and Log B, proportioning for the tenths of the degree; otherwise, compute Log A and Log B (33 *c*), as may be deemed most convenient.

b) Now, proceed in tabular form, by ruling several vertical columns and placing the series of Hour-Angles, in their order, in Col. I. Then, entering Tab. XXX. A, with each H. A., in succession, take out at sight the corresponding Log C, and place it in Col. II, opposite to the H. A. to which it belongs. Next, *add* Log A to each Log C and place the Sum[1] opposite in Col. III; also, do the same with Log B, and place the corresponding Sums in Col. IV. Finally, enter Tab. XXX. B with each Sum in Col. III and take out the corresponding Ang. X, which place in Col. V; also, enter the same Table with each Sum in Col. IV and take out the corresponding Ang. Y, which place in Col. VI.

Finally, there will be the two Cases to consider, according as the Half-Sum of Pol. Dist. and Co-Lat. is *less* or *greater* than 90°.

c) **First Case:** H. S. of Pol. Dist. and Co-Lat. *less* than 90°.—Take the *Sum* or *Difference* of the corresponding Angles X and Y, according as

[1] The Sums in Col. III being *Tangents* X and those in Col. IV being *Tangents* Y.

the Pol. Dist. is *greater* or *less* than the Co-Lat., and place the resulting True Azimuths in Col. VII.

d) **Second Case:** H. S. of Pol. Dist. and Co Lat. *greater* than 90°.—Always take the *Difference* of the corresponding Angles X and Y, which subtract from 180°, and place the resulting True Azimuths in Col. VII.

e) **In either Case,** mark the True Azimuths N or S according to the Lat., and E or W according as the observations are East or West of the Meridian.

Remark.—If it be desired to take the Mid. Dec. and Lat. to the nearest minute, it will be necessary to proceed according to Par. *e* of the preceding Rule (33), instead of Par. *a* of the present Rule, to find Log A and Log B; after which, proceed according to the present Rule, observing that it will generally be sufficient to use Log A and Log B with the nearest third decimal figure, rejecting the fourth figure.

35. Examples of Finding Serial Compass-Errors by the Method of Time-Azimuths.

Ex. 1.—1875, May 13: In New York Bay, Lat. 40° 41′ N, Long. 74° 2′ W, about 5^h 45^m P. M., made the following observations of the Sun, on a careful swinging of the Ship, for Compass-Deviations.

Watch-Error on Loc. M. T. 47^s *fast;* mean from comparisons before and after the observations.

Mag. Variation 7°.9 W, from previous determinations.

a) Tabular Record of Observations.

Watch-Time.	Standard Compass.		Watch-Time.	Standard Compass.	
	Ship's Head.	☉'s Centre.		Ship's Head.	☉'s Centre.
h m s		°	h m s		°
5 18 10	North	N 72.0 W	5 37 50	South	N 70.5 W
20 30	NNE	64.5	41 0	SSW	79.5
22 0	NE	57.0	46 30	SW	80.0
25 10	ENE	51.5	48 30	WSW	89.5
27 50	East	N 49.0 W	55 0	West	88.5
30 20	ESE	48.5	57 20	WNW	85.5
32 30	SE	52.5	6 0 30	NW	80.0
34 40	SSE	60.5	3 10	NNW	73.0

b) Preparation of the Data.

Mid. date A. T. May	13^d $5^h.7$		Pol. Dist.	71° 32′					
Long. W	+ 4 .9		Co-Lat.	49 19	By Tab. IX				
Greenwich date	13 10 .6		Diff.	22 13					
			½ Diff.	11 6½	sin	9.2848	cos	9.9918	
☉'s Dec.	N 18° 21′.3	+ 0′.6	½ Sum	60 25½	cosec	0.0606	sec	0.3067	
Redⁿ for $10^h.6$	+ 6 .4	6 .0			Log A	9.3454	Log B	0.2985	
☉'s Dec. for date	18 28 N	0 .4							

Eq. of T. 3^m 51^s+ to M. T. Error of Watch on Loc. A. T. + 3^m 4^s

c) Tabular Form of Solution by Azimuth-Tables.

Sun's Hour-Angles West.	Table XXX. A.	Log A 9.345|4.	Log B 0.298|5.	Table XXX. B.		Sun's True Azimuth.	Sun's Compass-Azimuth.	Compass-Error.	Compass-Dev.
		Tan X.	Tan Y.	Ang. X.	Ang. Y.				
h m				°	°	°	°	°	°
5 21.2	0.074	9.419	0.372	14.7	67.02	N 81.7 W	N 72.0 W	9.7 W	1.8 W
23.6	069	414	367	14.55	66.77	81.3	64.5	16.8	8.9
25.1	066	411	364	14.45	66.62	81.1	57.0	24.1	16.2
28.2	060	405	358	14.3	66.32	80.6	51.5	29.1	21.2
5 30.9	0.055	400	353	14.1	66.12	80.2	49.0	31.2	23.3
33.4	051	396	349	14.0	65.92	79.9	48.5	31.4	23.5
35.6	046	391	344	13.85	65.67	79.5	52.5	27.0	19.1
37.7	042	387	340	13.7	65.47	79.2	60.5	18.7	10.8
5 40.9	0.036	381	334	13.55	65.17	78.7	70.5	8.2 W	0.3 W
44.1	030	375	328	13.35	64.87	78.2	79.5	1.3 E	9.2 E
49.6	020	365	318	13.05	64.32	77.4	86.0	8.6	16.5
51.6	016	361	314	12.95	64.12	77.1	89.5	12.4	20.3
5 58.1	0.004	349	302	12.6	63.52	76.1	88.5	12.4	20.3
6 0.4	9.999	344	297	12.45	63.22	75.7	85.5	9.8	17.7
3.6	993	338	291	12.3	62.92	75.2	80.0	4.8 E	12.7
6.2	988	333	286	12.17	62.67	74.8	73.0	1.8 W	6.1 E

In taking out the Angles X and Y it is well, in a case like this, where considerable precision is desired and can be had, to allow for the influence of the fourth figure (cut off) in Log A and Log B, and write the nearest second decimal, as here done, in the values of those Angles, retaining only the nearest tenth in the values of the Azimuths.

Ex. 2.—1866, May 5: At sea, in Lat. 50° 10′ N, Long. 13° 10′ W, about 6h P. M., made the following observations of the Sun for Compass Errors and Deviations, watch being *fast* 26m.0 on Ship A. T.:

Observations.[1]

Watch-Time.	By Standard Compass.	
	Ship's Head.	☉'s Centre.
h m	°	°
6 15	N 116 E	N 64 W
22	40	72
28	66	75
33	S 88 E	72
38	65	67
6 44	S 40 E	N 60 W
51	6	51
56	S 20 W	43
7 0	41	38
10	75	28
7 15	N 84 W	N 23 W
21	62	21
25	42	23
31	25	28
38	4	36

Ship Mid. A. T. May 5d 6h.5
Long. W + 1 .0
Greenwich date 5 7 .5

☉'s Dec. N 16° 16′ | +0′.7
Redn for 7h.5 + 5. 4.9
Red. Dec. 16 21 .3

P. D. 73°.6 { Log A 9.541 } *Tab. XXX*
C. L. 39 .8 { Log B 0.242 }

Mag. Var. 26° W

[1] The *Data* of this Example are taken from *Traité de Déviation et de Régulation des Compas:* par E. GIQUEL, Professeur d'hydrographie, Paris, 1868.

The observations are said to have been made on board the *Ville de Paris*, one of the ships of the New York and Havre Line.

Reductions and Results.

Sun's Ho. Ang. West.	Tab. XXX. A.	Log A 9.541.	Log B 0.242.	Tab. XXX. B.		Sun's True Azimuth.	Sun's Compass-Azimuth.	Comp. Error.	Comp. Dev.
		Tan X.	Tan Y.	Ang. X.	Ang. Y.				
h m				°	°		°	°	°
5 49	0.021	9.562	0.263	20.05	61.4	N 81.4 W	N 64 W	17.4 W	8.6 E
56	008	549	250	19.5	60.65	80.1	72	8.1	17.9
6 2	9.996	537	238	19.0	59.95	79.0	75	4.0	22.0
7	987	528	229	18.6	59.45	78.1	72	6.1	19.9
12	977	518	219	18.25	58.85	77.1	67	10.1	15.9
6 18	9.966	9.507	0.208	17.8	58.2	76.0	60	16.0	10.0
25	953	494	195	17.3	57.45	74.7	51	23.7	2.3 E
30	943	484	185	16.95	56.85	73.8	43	30.8	4.8 W
34	935	476	177	16.7	56.35	73.1	38	35.1	9.1
44	916	457	158	16.0	55.2	71.2	28	43.2	17.2
6 49	9.906	9.447	0.148	15.6	54.6	70.2	23	47.2	21.2
55	895	436	137	15.3	53.9	69.2	21	48.1	22.1
59	887	428	129	15.0	53.4	68.4	23	45.4	19.4
7 5	875	416	117	14.6	52.6	67.2	28	39.2	13.2
12	861	402	103	14.2	51.7	65.9	36	29.9	3.9 W

Ex. 3.—1875, Nov. 20: At sea, in Lat. 3° 58′ N, Long. 14° 3′ W, about 6^h 45^m A. M., Ship A. T., weather threatening, made the following observations, on a partial swing, to cover probable courses of the Ship, during two or three days:

Record of Observations.

Watch-Time.	Corrected A. T.	Stand. Compass.	
		Ship's Head.	Sun's Centre.
h m s	h m		°
6 38 20	6 40.5	South.	S 51.5 E
44 0	46.2	S 15° E	49.0
48 50	51.0	29	46.0
55 10	57.3	46	42.5
59 0	7 1.2	60	38.0

Watch 2^m 10^s slow on Ship A. T.

Ship Mid. A. T. Nov.	19^d	$18^h.8$
Long. in W	+	0.9
Greenwich date	19	19.7

☉'s Dec. S 19°.7

Pol. Dist. 109°.7 } Log A 9.316 } *Tab.*
Co-Lat. 86.0 } Log B 0.855 } *XXX*

Mag. Var. 19°.3 W (*Tab. LVI*)

Tabular Form by Azimuth-Tables.

Sun's H. Angles East.	Tab. XXX. A.	Log A 9.316.	Log B 0.855.	Tab. XXX. P.		☉'s True Azimuth.	Compass-Azimuth.	Compass-Error.	Compass-Dev.
		Tan X.	Tan Y.	Ang. X.	Ang. Y.				
h m				°	°	°	°	°	°
5 19.5	0.077	9.393	0.932	13.9	83.3	N 110.6 E	N 128.5 E	17.9 W	1.4 E
13.8	088	404	943	14.2	83.5	110.7	131.0	20.3	1.0 W
8.0	099	415	954	14.6	83.7	110.9	134.0	23.1	3.8 W
2.7	110	426	965	14.9	83.8	111.1	137.5	26.4	7.1
4 58.8	117	433	972	15.2	83.9	111.3	142.0	30.7	11.4

Ex. 4.—1875, July 16: At sea, in Lat. 0° 31′ S, Long. 20° 15′ W, about $11^h 30^m$ P. M., made the following observations of the Moon, on a partial swing of the Ship, for Compass-Deviations:

Observations and Deduced Data.

Watch-Time.	Standard Compass.		Ship Mean Time.	Green-wich date.	R. A. M. ☉ $7^h 37^m.8$	R. A. Moon.		
	Ship's Head.	Moon's Centre.			R. A. Mer.	At G. 12h	T. LXV Corr.	Reduced R. A. ☾
h m s		°	h m	h m	h m	h m	m	h m
11 14 20	SSW	S 16.0 W	11 20.0	12 41	18 57.8	18 27.5	+1.6	18 29.1
17 0	S by W	17.0	22.7	44	19 0.5	27.5	1.7	29.2
19 30	South	18.5	25.2	46	3.0	27.5	1.8	29.3
23 20	S by E	21.5	29.0	50	6.8	27.5	1.9	29.4
27 0	SSE	25.5	32.7	54	10.5	27.5	2.1	29.6
30 0	SE by S	29.0	35.7	57	13.5	27.5	2.2	29.7
35 40	SE	33.0	41.4	13 2	19.2	29.8	0.1	29.9

W. Time slow $5^m.7$ on Ship M. T.

Long. in $1^h 21^m$ W

Mid. M. T. July $16^d\ 11^h.5$
Long. W + 1 .3
Mid. Greenwich date 16 12 .8

☾'s Dec. S 28° 17′

Pol. Dist. 61°.7 { Log A 9.398 } *Tab.*
Co-Lat. 89 .5 { Log B 0.588 } *XXX*

R. A. Mean Sun $7^h 37^m.8$

Mag. Var. 19°.2 W (*Tab. LVI*)

Tabular Form by Azimuth-Tables.

Moon's Hour-Angles West.	Table XXX. A.	Log A 9.398.	Log B 0.588.	Table XXX. B.		☾'s True Azimuth.	Compass-Azimuth.	Compass-Error.	Compass-Dev.
		Tan X.	Tan Y.	Ang. X.	Ang. Y.				
h m				°	°	°	°	°	°
0 28.7	1.203	0.601	1.791	75.9	89.1	S 13.2 W	S 16.0 W	2.8 W	16.4 E
31.3	165	563	753	74.7	89.0	14.3	17.0	2.7	16.5
33.7	133	531	721	73.6	88.9	15.3	18.5	3.2	16.0
37.4	089	485	675	71.9	88.8	16.9	21.5	4.6	14.6
40.9	048	446	636	70.3	88.7	18.4	25.5	7.1	12.1
43.8	1.018	416	606	69.0	88.6	19.6	29.0	9.4	9.8
49.3	0.967	365	555	66.6	88.4	21.8	33.0	11.2	8.0

In this Example for a partial swing, the Moon being taken when her change of Declination was comparatively slow, the results are as reliable as they would have been if obtained from observations of the Sun under similar circumstances. The additional labor of the working-out is trifling, as it only involves the six extra columns in the first Table, which are formed easily and rapidly. The Hour-Angles are very small.

Such an operation, although performed at an unusual hour of the day, might be the means of anticipating serious embarrassment, especially if threatened with thick weather, and actually deprived of observations for two or three days.

C. Method of Circumpolar Azimuths.

36. The Circumpolar Azimuth a Modified Form of the Time-Azimuth.—Circumpolar Azimuths, as the name implies, are applicable solely to Circumpolar Stars; that is, to those which never set in the horizon of the observer, but are always found above it. The method is a modified form of the Time-Azimuth, receiving certain special simplifications, which are the more conspicuous and practically useful in proportion as the Polar Distance of the Star is *less*, or in proportion to its *nearness at all times to the Elevated Pole.* This will be evident, since, as all the Fixed Stars require sensibly the same time (nearly 24^h) in making their apparent revolutions about the Earth, or its axis, supposed indefinitely produced, it follows that the nearer they are to that axis, and the smaller the circle described by them, *the slower their apparent daily motions;* so that, when quite near the Pole, they appear almost entirely *at rest*, in comparison with those Stars which are much farther from it.

Polaris, or the "Pole-Star," is a notable example of this condition of things to observers in the Northern Hemisphere; for, its Polar Distance being at present less than 1½°, *its greatest change in Azimuth* from east to west and from west to east, to an observer so far north as in the Latitude of 60°, is less than 5°.5 during 12^h of time, while to an observer at the Equator it is even less than 3°.0 during the same time. So well is this apparent fixedness of the Pole-Star understood by Navigators, that not a few have regarded it as identical with the North Pole itself, and, in sighting it with their compasses, have deduced their Compass-Errors therefrom as if it were actually at the North Pole. But such an assumption may involve, though not necessarily so, a quarter to nearly half a Point of Error; that is to say, ± 3°.0 to ± 5°.5, according to the time and place of observation within the range of Latitudes indicated.

Now the motion, *in Azimuth*, of a Circumpolar Star, having a small Pol. Dist., is not only very slow, but really quite variable; being slowest at or near its *greatest* Elongations, east or west, and quickest when on or near the Meridian, above or below the Pole. Hence, in assuming it to be practicable to get reliable Azimuths of such a Star with the compass, it is desirable to know *when to observe*, in order to find the Star at its greatest Elongation, which is the most favorable time, or, losing that, to have its True Azimuth at any intermediate time of observation.

37. Table of Circumpolar Azimuths: Description of Tab. XL for Polaris.—Such is the object of Tab. XL, which is adapted to Polaris, and comprises the True Azimuths of this Star, at intervals of every hour in Sid. Time, and for all Latitudes from the Equator to 60° north. Thus, for any stated Lat., the True Azimuth of the Star is given—

First, at its greatest *Western* and *Eastern Elongations;* being set down in Cols. III and XV, adjacent to the corresponding Sid. Time. As, for example, in Lat. 30°, at the greatest Western Elongation, the True Az. is N 1°.6 W at $7^h\ 9^m.9$ Sid. T., while at the greatest Eastern Elongation the True Az. is N 1°.6 E at $19^h\ 16^m.1$ Sid. T.

Secondly, opposite to the Latitudes in the intermediate columns, IV–XIV, the Sid. Times of which being placed at top and bottom. The Sid. Times at *top*, commencing with the middle column at $1^h\ 13^m$, when the Star is on the Meridian *above* the Pole, increase by hourly intervals, as the Star moves westwardly *from* the Meridian to its greatest W. E., when the Sid. Times are adjacent to the Latitudes; after which, during its return eastwardly *towards* the Meridian, the Sid. Times are found at *bottom*, till at $13^h\ 13^m$ the Star is again on the Meridian *below* the Pole. Then, as the Star continues its eastwardly movement below the Pole again moving *from* the Meridian, the Sid. Times are still found at *bottom*, till it arrives at its greatest E. E., when the Sid. Times are adjacent to the Latitudes; after which, during its return *westwardly towards* the Meridian, the Sid. Times are found at top till it finally arrives at the point of departure on the Meridian above the Pole, when the Sid. T. is again $1^h\ 13^m$. This Table is computed for January 1, 1875, but will not be materially at fault for at least ten years.

38. Two Distinct Problems in the Use of Tab. XL.—Although the practical object in the use of Tab. XL, so far as the compass is concerned, is to get the True Azimuth of the Star, there are two distinct problems to be solved in connection therewith.

First, with a tolerable Lat. and Ship-Time, having observed a Compass-Azimuth of Polaris and noted the Ship T. thereof, it is required to take out the corresponding True Azimuth of the Star, and thus to obtain the Error of the Compass; or,

Secondly, with a very uncertain Lat. and Ship-Time, it is required to find the Ship T. of the Star's greatest Western or Eastern Elongation, whichever may occur during the night, to observe a Compass-Azimuth at that Time, and to take out the corresponding True Azimuth, in order to obtain a reliable Compass-Error, independently of the uncertainties of the Data.

39. Rule: To find the True Azimuth of Polaris by Tab. XL.—Thus, we shall have the following Rule:

a) To take out the True Azimuth for any Ship-Time.—Find the Greenwich date for the Ship T. to the nearest tenth of the hour, in the usual manner; then, according as the T. is *A.* or *M.*, take out the R. A. of the *True* or *Mean* Sun from Tab. LIX, correcting it for the G. date by Tab. LXIV or LXVI, and *add* it to the Ship T. (rejecting 24^h if the sum be greater than 24^h), and the result will be the Ship Sid. Time.[1] With this Time and the Lat. enter Tab. XL and take out the corresponding True Azimuth, as required.

[1] Which is the same thing as the *R. A. of the Meridian* of the preceding Articles.

b) *To find the Ship-Time of the greatest W. or E. Elongation, and to take out the corresponding True Azimuth.*—Find the Greenwich date for the supposed Time at Ship. With this date take out from Tab. LIX the R. A. of the *True* or *Mean* Sun, according as the Time is *A.* or *M.* Then, enter Tab. XL with the supposed Lat., and *subtract* the R. A. before mentioned from the corresponding Sid. T. (increased by 24^h if necessary) of that greatest Elongation, Eastern or Western, which gives a remainder as Ship-Time *appropriate to the night*, and take out the corresponding True Azimuth. Also, make the Compass-Observation at that Time.

c) Mark the Azimuth N according to the Lat. and *E* or *W* according as the Star is making its *Eastern* or *Western* Elongation.

40. Examples of Finding Compass-Error by Circumpolar Azimuths.

Ex. 1.—1875, March 15: At sea, in Lat. 50° 11′ N, Long. 45° W, about 9^h 20^m P. M., Ship A. T., the observed bearing of Polaris was N 14°.5 E: Required, the Compass-Error.

Ship A. T. Mar.	15^d	$9^h.3$
Long. W	+	3 .0
Greenwich date	15	12 .3

Ship A. T.	$9^h 20^m.0$
R. A. True ☉	23 41 .7
Ship Sid. T.	9 1 .7

True Az.	N 1°.8 W (*Tab. XL*)
Comp Az.	N 14 .5 E
Comp. Er.	16 .3 W

Ex. 2.—1875, June 25: At sea, in Lat. 42° N, Long. 155° E, at 11^h 50^m P. M., Ship M. T., the observed bearing of Polaris was N 27° W: Required, the Compass-Error and Deviation.

Ship M. T. June	25^d	$11^h.8$
Long. E	—	10 .3
Greenwich date	25	1 .5

Ship M. T.,	11^h $50^m.0$
R. A. M. ☉	6 13 .2
Ship Sid. T.	18 3 .2

True Az.	N 1°.8 E (*Tab. XL*)
Comp. Az.	N 27 .0 W
Comp. Er.	28 .8 E
Mag. Var.	17 .5 E (*Tab. LVI*)
Comp. Dev.	11 .3 E

Ex. 3.—1875, February 19: At sea, in thick weather, blowing a gale for two days, but now clearing to the northward, and Polaris visible, obtained an observation for Compass-Error of N 11° W.

Lat. 20° N, Long. 30° W } Supposed, with possible error of ± 5° each.

About 7^h P. M., Ship A. T.

Ship A. T. Feb.	19^d	7^h
Long W	+	2
Greenwich date	19	9

Ship A. T.	7^h 0^m
R. A. True ☉	22 12
Ship Sid. T.	5 12

True Az.	N 1°.3 W
Comp. Az.	N 11 .0 W
Comp. Er.	9 .7 E

And this is true within ± 0°.1, even with an error of ± 10° in Lat. and ± 5° in Long. of the Ship's place.

Ex. 4.—1875, October 17: At sea, in Lat. 52° 57′ N, Long. 26° 19′ W, about 7^h P. M., ship A. T.: Required, the Ship T. of the next greatest Elongation of Polaris.

Ship A. T. Oct.	17^d	$7^h.0$
Long. W	+	1 .8
Greenwich date	17	8 .8

Sid. T. W. E.	7^h 8^m
R. A. True ☉	13 29
Ship A. T.	17 39

Ex. 5.—1875, May 31: At sea, in Lat. 49° 15′ N, Long. 43° 50′ W, about 12^h P. M. approaching the American coast, and anticipating thick weather, desired to get a set of Azimuths for Compass-Deviations, sufficient to cover the probable courses of the ship for the next day.

Turning to Tab. LIX, the R. A. True Sun is seen to be 4^h 32^m at Greenwich noon; next, opening at Tab. XL and comparing this R. A. with the Sid. Times of the Elongations of Polaris, it is seen that the next (Eastern) Elongation will take place at $14^h\ 47^m$ Ship A. T., or at $2^h\ 47^m$ hence. Accordingly, preparations are immediately made to take the observations with the following results.

Mid. Greenwich date, May 31^d^ $15^h.6$; R. A. True Sun, $4^h\ 34^m.6$.

Ship A. T.	Ship's Head.	Compass-Azimuth.	Ship Sid. T.	True Azimuth.	Compass-Error.	Mag. Var.	Compass-Deviation.
h m		°	h m	°	°	°	°
12 30	WNW	N 26.5 E	17 35	N 1.9 E	24.6 W	36.0 W	11.4 E
35	W by N	23.0	40	1.9	21.1	36.0	14.9
39	West	20.5	44	1.9	18.6	36.0	17.4
45	W by S	18.5	50	1.9	16.6	36.0	19.4
50	WSW	17.0	55	2.0	15.0	36.0	21.0
54	SW by W	18.0	59	2.0	16.0	36.0	20.0

D. Method of Altitude-Azimuths.

41. Fundamental Principles of the Altitude-Azimuth.—In an Altitude-Azimuth the bearing of the Sun or other heavenly body is observed with the compass, at the same time that its *Altitude* is measured with a sextant, octant, or other reflecting instrument.

The True Azimuth is found by a solution of the Triangle of Position.

The Data required are—

The True Altitude, deduced by correcting the Observed Altitude;

The Declination, taken from the Nautical Almanac or Naut. Tables;

The Latitude in, as brought up by the Reckoning or known from previous observation.

42. Rule: To make the Observation of an Altitude-Azimuth.—Take a bearing of the object with the standard compass, or preferably a set of two or three bearings as quickly as possible; bisecting it each time, if it have a sensible disk (Sun or Moon), and noting the times with a watch; also, simultaneously, with each bearing, take the Altitude of the body with a sextant or octant.

Note the Heading of the ship with the same compass, and the corresponding Headings with the steering-compasses; also, if on board an iron ship, the Angle of Heel, and whether to starboard or port.

The observed bearing, or the mean if several be taken, is the required Compass-Azimuth; and the single Altitude, or the Mean if several be taken, is the observed Altitude.

43. Rule: To find the True Azimuth by Computation.—First, prepare the Data, as follows:

a) Find the Greenwich date for the Ship T. of observation, either by applying the Longitude to the Time, or deducing it from the chronometer.

b) With this date, take out the Declination of the body, and in the case of the Moon the Semi-Diameter and Horizontal Parallax.

c) Get the True Altitude of the centre by applying the proper corrections to the observed Altitude.

Next, compute the True Azimuth, as follows:

d) Add together the True Altitude, the Lat., and the Pol. Dist., and take the *Difference* between their Half-Sum and the Pol. Dist. Then, using Tab. IX or Tables X and XI, *add* together the secant of the Lat., the secant of the Alt., the cosine of the ½ Sum, and the cosine of the Difference. The Half-Sum of these four logarithms, rejecting tens from the indices, will be the cosine of *half* the True Azimuth, which take out and *double*, and the result will be the required True Azimuth. Mark it N or S according to the Lat., and *E* or *W* according as the Altitude is *increasing* or *decreasing*, or as the object is East or West of the Meridian.

44. Rule: To find the True Azimuth by Azimuth-Tables.—The preceding Rule, by Computation, is that usually given. But the process of getting out a True Azimuth may be greatly abridged, with results sufficiently exact for practical purposes, by special Azimuth-Tables.

Such is Table XLI, which has been extended and otherwise modified from that originally given by another hand.[1] It is adapted to all Latitudes from the Equator to 80° north or south; to all Declinations from 0° to 30° of the same or contrary name; and to all Altitudes from 0° to 82°.

This Table consists of three parts, to use which, after preparing the Data as before described (43), proceed as follows:

With the Lat. and Alt., both to the nearest degree, enter Tab. XLI, Part I, and take out the corresponding tabular number. With the Dec. to the nearest degree, and the Diff. of the Lat. and Alt., enter Part II, and take out the corresponding number. Then, with the *Sum* of these two tabular numbers, enter Part III, and take out the corresponding True Azimuth, which mark in the manner already described in the preceding Rule.

Remark I.—The arguments of the Table being set down for every *even* second degree, it will be necessary to take Means of the tabular numbers in Parts I and II, *adjacent* or *cross*, according as *one* or *both* of the given arguments are *odd*.

In general, the Azimuth will be obtained in this manner within a half-degree, or ±0°.5, of that found by computation. But, whenever deemed expedient to take the Data more closely, it is easy to proportion for a more precise result.

Remark II: Table of Direct and Limiting Values of the Altitude-Azimuth.—Table XLII will be found useful, in furnishing a convenient check against any serious error in getting out an Altitude-Azimuth, whether by computation or by Table XLI.

---

[1] *Azimuth Table; to facilitate the process of finding the True Bearing of the Sun, etc.*, by A. C. Johnson, R. N., London, 1867.—This is contained in a small pamphlet by that author under the title *How to find the Longitude simultaneously with the Latitude at Noon, etc.*

There is also an extensive set of Tables for finding the Altitude-Azimuth directly, consisting of 365 pages, 4to, by Thomas Lynn, London, 1829.

45. Examples of Altitude-Azimuths.

Ex. 1.—1868, August 5: At sea, in Lat. 23° 47′ N, Long. 110° 15′ W, at $4^h\ 6^m$ P. M., Ship A. T., all by account, the observed bearing of the Sun's centre was S 85° W and its True Alt. was 30° 26′.4: Required, the Compass-Error.

Ship T.	5^d	$4^h.1$
Long. in +		7 .3
Gr. date	5	11 .4

☉'s Dec.	N 16° 51′		− 0′.7
Red^n for $11^h.4$	— 8		7 .7
Red. Dec.	16 43		.3
Pol. Dist.	73 17		

By Computation:

Pol. Dist.	73° 17′		
Lat. in	23 47	sec	0.0385
True Alt.	30 26	sec	0.0644
Sum	127 30		
½ Sum	63 45	cos	9.6457
Diff.	9 32	cos	9.9940
			19.7426
½ Az.	41 58	cos	9.8713
True Az.	N 83 56 W		

By Azimuth-Tables:

Lat. 24°	Alt. 30°.0	(*Tab. XLI*)	51
Diff. 6	Dec. 17 .0		772
True Az.	N 83 .5 W		Sum 823
Comp. Az.	N 95 .0 W		
COMP. ER.	11 .5 E		

Ex. 2.—1871, April 17: At sea, in Lat. 27° 19′ S, Long. 75° 52′ E, the Sun's bearing by compass was N 75° W, at $3^h\ 51^m$ P. M., Ship A. T., and the True Alt. at the same time was 22° 29′: What was the Compass-Error?

Ship T.	17^d	$3^h.8$
Long. in	—	5 .0
Gr. date Apr.	16	22 .8
	17—	1 .2

☉'s Dec.	N 10° 25′	+ 0′.9
Red^n for $1^h.2$	— 1	1 .0
Red. Dec.	10 24	
Pol. Dist.	100 24	

By Computation:

Pol. Dist.	100° 24′		
Lat. in	27 19	sec	0.0514
True Alt.	22 29	sec	0.0343
Sum	150 12		
½ Sum	75 6	cos	9.4102
Diff.	25 18	cos	9.9562
			19.4521
½ Az.	57 21	cos	9.7260
Tr. Az.	S 115 42 W		

By Azimuth-Tables:

Lat. 27°.3	Alt. 22°.5	(*Tab. XLI*)	43
Diff. 4 .8	Dec. 10 .4		884.6
True Az.	S 115 .8 W		Sum 927.6
Comp. Az.	S 105 .0 W		
COMP. ER.	10 .8 E		

Ex. 3.—1871, August 16: At anchor, Disco Island, in Lat. 69° 14′ N, Long. 53° 18′ W. With the Data of Ex. 1 in Time-Azimuths (29), and, in addition, the True Altitude of the Sun's centre 21° 24′: Required, the Compass-Error.

By Computation:

Pol. Dist.	76° 17′		
Lat. in	69 14	sec	0.4503
True Alt.	21 24	sec	0.0310
Sum	166 55		
½ Sum	83 27½	cos	9.0566
Diff.	7 10½	cos	9.9966
			19.5345
½ Az.	54 12	cos	9.7672
True Az.	N 108 24 W		

By Azimuth-Tables:

Lat. 69°.2	Alt. 21°.4	(*Tab. XLI*)	240
Diff. 47 .8	Dec. 13 .7		668
True Az.	N 108 .3 W		Sum 908
Comp. Az.	N 36 .0 W		
COMP. ER.	52 .3 W		

Ex. 4.—1868, December 24: At sea, in Lat. 41° 57′ N, Long. 20° 19′ W, with a Time-Sight of the Moon.

Compass-Bear.	S 40° 0′ E	At $4^h\ 52^m$ P. M. Ship M. T.
True Altitude	37 22	
Dec.	7 37	

By Computation:

Pol. Dist.	82° 23′		
Lat. in	41 57	sec	0.1286
True Alt.	37 22	sec	0.0998
Sum	161 42		
½ Sum	80 51	cos	9.2015
Diff.	1 32	cos	9.9998
			19.4297
½ Az.	58 46	cos	9.7148
True Az.	N 117 32 E		

By Inspection:

Lat. 42°	Alt. 37°.0	(*Tab. XLI*)	113
Diff. 5	Dec. 7 .5		818
True Az.	N 117 .3 E		Sum 931
Comp. Az.	N 140 .0 E		
COMP. ER.	22 .7 W		

E. Method of Time-Altitude-Azimuths.

46. Fundamental Characteristics.—The Time-Altitude-Azimuth has for its Data the Hour-Angle, Altitude, and Declination; and as these comprise a part of the Data of the Time and Altitude Azimuth, which have already been fully considered when treating the last-named methods, they need no further explanation in this place.

The solution of the Triangle of Position for the Azimuth, with these Data, is at first sight more simple than for either the Time or Altitude Azimuth, inasmuch as it requires only the addition of three logarithms directly from the Data, the sum of which being the logarithm of the Azimuth. But, unfortunately, it has the very serious disadvantage of giving an ambiguous result, which, although removable in certain special cases, is not *in general* freed from the ambiguity, even with considerable complexity of cases. Moreover, as a method for finding Serial Compass-Errors, its use is attended with the further disadvantage that, as the H. A. and Alt. are both changeable from one observation to another of the series, there is really more labor required to get out a set of True Azimuths by this method than by either of the preceding.

On the whole, therefore, if to what has already been said it be added that the Data for the solution of the Time-Azimuth are generally available whenever those for the Time-Alt. Azimuth are, there would seem to be little, if any, occasion to resort to the use of the latter method in preference to the former.

Nevertheless, the following Rule for its solution is given, together with a few Examples to illustrate the application, so that it may be conveniently in hand for any use that may be made of it.

47. Rule: To find the True Azimuth by Computation.—The Data being given or prepared by the preceding Rules, proceed as follows:

a) Using Tab. IX: To the sine of the H. A. add the secant of the Alt. and the cosine of the Dec.; their Sum, rejecting 10 from the index, is the sine of the Angle Q, which take out.

There will now be two general Cases, according as the Pol. Dist. is *greater* or *less* than 90°.

b) **Case I:** The Pol. Dist. *greater* than 90°.—*Subtract* the Ang. Q from 180°, and the result will be the True Azimuth, always *greater* than 90°.

c) **Case II:** The Pol. Dist. *less* than 90°.—In this case there is generally a doubt, whether the Ang. Q or its Supplement is to be taken as the True Azimuth, with the following exception:

Whenever the Alt. is *less* than the Dec., the Ang. Q will be the True Azimuth, *less* than 90°.

Otherwise, whenever the Alt. is *greater* than the Dec. (a very common condition), the result will be in doubt, and reference must be made with the Data to Tab. XXXI, where it will generally be apparent, at sight, whether the True Azimuth is really *less* or *greater* than 90°. If *less*, the Ang. Q is the True Azimuth; if *greater*, the Supplement by subtracting from 180° is to be taken as the True Azimuth.

In many instances it will be easy to decide during the observation, whether the object is on the side of the Prime Vertical towards the Elevated Pole, or the reverse. In the former condition, the Ang. Q will be taken as the True Azimuth; in the latter, its Supplement will be taken, greater than 90°.

d) In every case, mark the True Azimuth N or S according to the Lat., and E or W according as the H. A. is E or W of the Meridian.

48. Examples of Finding the True Azimuth.

Ex. 1.—At sea, in Lat. 30° N, obtained the following Data in an observation of the Sun:

H. A. West 4h 0m
T. Alt. 13°.6
Dec. S 20 .0

Required, the True Az.

By Computation:

H. A.	4h 0m	sin 9.9375
Alt.	13°.6	sec 0.0124
Dec.	20 .0	cos 9.9730
Ang. Q	56 .9	sin 9.9229

or,

TRUE AZ. N 123°.1 W

(Since this falls into Case I.)

Ex. 2.—At sea, in Lat. 9° N, obtained the following Data in an observation of the Sun:

H. A. East 5h 42m
Alt. 7° 31′
Dec. N 22 0

Required, the True Az.

H. A.	5h 42m	sin 9.9987
Alt.	7° 31′	sec 0.0037
Dec.	22°.0	cos 9.9672
Ang. Q	68 .8	sin 9.9696

or,

TRUE AZ. N 68°.8 E

(Since this falls into the exception of Case II.)

Ex. 3.—Given the Data in Lat 40°.1 N for the Sun:

H. A. West 5h 6m.8
Alt. 22° 53′
Dec. N 20° .3

Required, the True Az.

H. A.	5h 6m.8	sin 9.9882
Alt.	22° 53′	sec 0.0356
Dec.	20° .3	cos 9.9722
Ang. Q	82 .2	sin 9.9960

This is doubtful; but a reference to Tab. XXXI shows that Ang. Q is to be taken; or,

TRUE AZ. N 82°.2 W

Ex. 4.—With the same Lat. and Dec., and—

H. A. 3h 56m.6
Alt. 36° 15′

Required, the True Az.

H. A.	3h 56m.6	sin 9.9337
Alt.	36° 15′	sec 0.0934
Dec.	20°.3	cos 9.9722
Ang. Q	86 .7	sin 9.9993

Here, again, we are in doubt, but, by Tab. XXXI, it is evident that we must use the Supplement of Q; or,

TRUE AZ. N 93°.3 W

49. Table of Time-Alt. Azimuths.—Tab. XLVIII consists of two parts, namely, of a first part, of which the arguments are the Azimuth and Declination, and of a second part, of which the arguments are *either* the Hour-Angle and Altitude, or the Position-Angle and Latitude; that is to say, *either pair of arguments at the same time.*

This Table, although having the title of *Time-Alt. Azimuths*, is not designed exclusively for that object, but to answer several purposes, as follows:

1. *To find the Time-Alt. Azimuth*, having the H. A., Alt., and Dec.;
2. *To find the Altitude*, having the Azimuth, Dec., and H. A.;

3. *To find the Hour-Angle*, having the Azimuth, Dec., and Alt.; and,

4. *To find the Position-Angle*, having the Azimuth, Dec., and Latitude.

Whenever at least two of the Data, one of which for each part of this Table, correspond exactly or very nearly to the tabular arguments, a True Azimuth, or either of the other quantities, with the requisite Data, may be taken out *at sight* with sufficient accuracy for any ordinary requirement; but, if the Data do not correspond, and interpolations are necessary, it will generally be easier to compute the Azimuth by the preceding Rule. For an off-hand, rough approximation, the Table is convenient for the several purposes for which it is designed.

50. Examples of the Use of Tab. XLVIII.

Ex. 1.—With the Data of Ex. 1 (48), what is the True Azimuth?

With H. A. $4^h\ 0^m$ and Alt. 13°.6, we find for—

Log B 0.050

And with this and Dec. 20° in first part, we find for—

True Az. 123°.0

Ex. 2.—With Az. 70°, Dec. 10°, and H. A. $2^h\ 20^m$, what is the True Alt.?

Entering first part, we find for—

Log A 0.020

With this and H. A. in second part, we find for—

True Alt. 53°.1

Ex. 3.—With Az. 151°, Dec. 20°, and Alt. 60°, what is the H. A.?

With Az. and Dec. in first part, we find for—

Log A 0.287

With this and Alt. in second part, we find for—

H. A. $1^h\ 0^m$

Ex. 4.—With T. Az. 21°, Dec. 17°, and Lat. 42°, what is the Pos. Angle?

With Az. and Dec. in first part, we find for—

Log A 0.426

With this and Lat. in second part, we find for—

Pos. Ang. 16°.2

F. Transition-Azimuths.

51. Fundamental Principles.—The method of Transition-Azimuths is based on the *relative changes* of the Hour-Angle and Altitude of a celestial object. The H. A. of an object, whatever its Position, changes uniformly; but the changes of the Alt. are variable, depending on the Position of the object with respect to the observer's Zenith. Accordingly, whenever two or more observations of an Altitude are made and the corresponding Hour-Angles noted, it will be easy to obtain a characteristic or distinguishing relation of these two elements, by deducing the *change of Alt. in a unit of the H. A. Interval;* and this definite relation, in a given case, will always correspond to a particular *Azimuth of the object;* so that whenever we have obtained the former, together with the observer's Latitude, they constitute the requisite Data, by means of which we may readily find the latter. This method is rarely, if ever, resorted to as a direct means of getting the True Azimuth; but it may be used, often with advantage, in connection with observations for the Time and Position *near the Meridian*, when the peculiar Data required for its use are sometimes obtained; it being only necessary that a Compass-Azimuth of the object be taken as near the *middle* of the Time-Interval, between the two observations of Altitude, as practicable. With the True Azimuth and Compass-Azimuth of the object known, the Compass-Error is found by the usual comparison.

52. Preliminary Remark on the Preparation of the Data.—The Data being furnished to hand by the direct observation, from which the True Azimuth is merely an incidental determination, there is no necessity to enter into details as to its preparation. It will be sufficient to remark that, the Times of the observed Altitudes being noted with a watch whose error on Ship Ap. Time is known, *the Diff. of the corrected W. Times will be the required H. A. Interval, when the Sun is the object observed.*

Moreover, as the W. Time Interval in these cases should hardly exceed a half-hour, the small Error due to the Difference between Ap. and M. Time (only seldom so much as $0^s.6$ in that Interval) may be disregarded, and the *W. T. Interval itself used as the H. A. Interval.* With this condition, this method is entirely independent, even with a large uncertainty,[1] of the Ship-Time.

For all other objects than the Sun, it will not be advisable to use the W. T. Interval for the proper H. A. Interval, as the difference between them, and the consequent Error, might be too large to be admitted; but, in such cases, the H. A. Interval should be deduced by taking the *Diff. of the Hour-Angles*[2] found for the two noted W. Times of observation in the usual manner (20, *b*).

53. Rule: To get the True Azimuth.—Having the Data prepared, the True Azimuth by this method may be found either by Logarithmic Computation or by Tabular Inspection.

a) *By Logarithmic Computation.*—Using Tab. IX: To the cosecant of the H. A. Interval (or W. Time Interval for the Sun) add the sine of the Alt. Diff. and the secant of the Lat.; their Sum, rejecting tens from their indices, will be the sine of the True Azimuth, which take out, and mark it *N* or *S* according as the object is *north* or *south* of the Prime Vertical, and *E* or *W* according as it is *east* or *west* of the Meridian.

b) *By Tabular Inspection.*—Divide the Alt. Diff. by the H. A. or W. T. Interval, as the case may be, the seconds of both being reduced to decimals of the minute, and the result will be the *Change of Alt. in* 1^m. With this, to the nearest tenth of the minute, and the Lat. enter Tab. LI, interpolating for the tenths, and the corresponding tabular number will be the True Azimuth, which mark as prescribed in the preceding Rule.

[1] It is of course necessary that the *rate* of the watch should be sensibly uniform during the Interval.

[2] These Hour-Angles would, however, generally be deduced among the Data for the direct use of the observations in question.

54. Examples of Finding the Compass-Error by a Transition-Azimuth.

Ex. 1.—At sea, in Lat. 36° N, with an observation of the Sun east of the Merid. and south of the P. V., the Alt. Diff. was 57'.5 and W. T. Interval $20^m\ 24^s$. The Compass-Az. at the middle of the Time-Interval being S 21°.5 E, what is the Compass-Error?

By Computation:

H. A. Int.	$20^m\ 24^s$	cosec	1.0511
Alt. Diff.	57'.5	sin	8.2236
Latitude	36°.0	sec	0.0920
True Az.	S 13 .4 E	sin	9.3667
Comp. Az.	S 21 .5 E		
COMP. ER.	8 .1 E		

By Inspection:

Dividing 57'.5 by $20^m.4$ we get 2'.8, as the *Change of Alt.* in 1^m. Then, entering Table LI, we find 9°.5 as the next less Azimuth, with a Tab. Diff. of 4°.8, of which 0.8 part is 3°.8 (=4°.8 × 0.8); and hence, adding to 9°.5, we get—

TRUE AZ. S 13°.3 E

Ex. 2.—At sea, in Lat. 51° 35' N, an observation of the Sun, W and S, gave the Alt. Diff. 38'.6 for a W. T. Int. of $12^m\ 43^s$. The Compass-Az. being S 3°.5 E, what is the Compass-Error?

By Computation:

H. A. Int.	$12^m\ 43^s$	cosec	1.2561
Alt. Diff.	38'.6	sin	8.0511
Latitude	51° 35'	sec	0.2066
True Az.	S 19° .0 W	sin	9.5138
Comp. Az.	S 3 .5 E		
COMP. ER.	22 .5 E		

By Inspection:

Dividing 38'.6 by $12^m.72$ we get 3'.0 to the nearest tenth of the minute. Then, entering Table LI, we find—

TRUE AZ. S 18°.7 W

G. DEPENDENCE TO BE PLACED ON THESE METHODS.

55. Possible Errors of the Azimuth-Data.—The Data employed in finding the True Azimuth are always liable to be in *Error*, more or less, according to circumstances. Consequently, the resulting Azimuth, as obtained by either of the preceding methods, will be correspondingly uncertain; and, to the end that we may be able to form an intelligent opinion of the dependence to be placed on the results, it will be necessary to consider the several relations of the Data, as well as their possible Errors, under the variable conditions of experience.

56. Estimating the Data-Errors; their Ordinary Limits.—The Data are uncertain by amounts which are different, not only among themselves but at different times. What these uncertainties are, on a given occasion, can only be a matter of special estimate under the circumstances of the case. The following considerations may serve to fix our ideas on this subject:

a) *The Latitude-Error.*—*On shore* it is not difficult for the Navigator to obtain his Latitude within 1', by suitable observations to which he is accustomed.

At sea, when the Latitude is known from a recent observation, it is commonly reliable within 2' to 5', at the most; when found through the Reckoning, after a lapse of 12^h to 18^h from a preceding observation, it is frequently uncertain by 5' to 10', and when obtained, after a lapse of 18^h to 36^h without an observation, the uncertainty may be not less than 15' to 30'. In cases of thick and stormy weather, no reliable estimate can be formed as to the Limit of the Latitude-Error.

b) *Declination-Error.*—With a chronometer, which will allow the Greenwich date to be had within 30^s or $0^m.5$, the Declination, as taken from the Nautical Almanac, may be depended on within—

1″ for the Sun, the Planets, and Fixed Stars;

7″ to 10″ for the Moon.

On the other hand, if the G. D. is obtained from the Longitude and Ship-Time, the Declination will be more uncertain. But, even then, when the G. D. is reliable within 2^m, or 30′, of Longitude, the Declination may still be depended on within—

2″ to 3″ for the Sun, the Planets, and Fixed Stars;

25″ to 35″ for the Moon.

These are Limits for the extreme cases of greatest change in the Declination; but, in proportion as the G. D. is more or less uncertain than the Limits above stated, the Declination will be more or less uncertain.

c) *The Hour-Angle Error.*—Since the Hour-Angle depends principally on the Local or Ship Time, it follows that the former cannot be expected to be more accurate than the latter. In reality, for the Sun, the Error of the Hour-Angle is identical with that of the Ship Apparent Time, to which it corresponds.

For the Moon, the Planets, and Fixed Stars, the Error of the Hour-Angle, composed mainly of the Error in the Ship-Time, is also affected by the small Errors of the Right Ascensions employed in getting the Hour-Angle (20, *b*). But, for practical purposes, the influence of the latter, even in the case of the Moon, is unimportant in comparison to that of the Ship-Time; so that it will be sufficiently exact[1] to regard the Error of the Hour-Angle, for any one of these objects, as that of the Ship-Time to which it corresponds.

Now the Local Time, *on shore*, may, without much difficulty, be found by the Navigator within 4^s. *At sea*, it may be obtained, according to circumstances, by direct Observation, within 10^s to 15^s; while, if deduced through the Reckoning, without a very recent observation, it may often be at fault by so much as 1^m or 2^m, or even more.

d) *The Altitude-Error.*—It is not difficult for the Navigator on shore to observe an Altitude within 10″, but it is entirely otherwise when he is at sea. Then he is quite fortunate if, under the most favorable circumstances, he can rely on his Altitude from a single observation within 1′ of arc. Ordinarily, it is doubtful if Altitudes can be relied on, even in the day-time, much within 2′; while, on a rough sea, or during the night, they may be in Error from 4′ to 6′.

e) *Recapitulation of the Limits of the Data-Errors.*—In recapitulation, we may take as ordinary *Limits* of the Errors of the Azimuth-Data, as follows:

---

[1] For example, with a Ship T. Error of $\pm 1^m$ and a G. D. Error of $\pm 1^m$, the greatest Error in the R. A. of the Sun would be $\pm 0^s.2$, and the greatest Error in the R. A. of the Moon $\pm 3^s$; so that the several Errors and the *probable total* would stand—

$$\sqrt{(60^s)^2 + (3^s)^2 + (0^s.2)^2} = \sqrt{3609.04} = \pm 60^s.1$$

or only $0^s.1$ different from that of the Ship T. Error alone.

On shore—

Lat. Error, within $\pm 1'$
Dec. Error, within $\pm 0'.05$ for all celestial objects
H. A. Error, within $\pm 4^s$
Alt. Error, within $\pm 0'.5$

At sea—

Lat. Error, within $\pm 3'$ to $\pm 30'$
Dec. Error, within $\pm 1'$ for all objects
H. A. Error, within $\pm 10^s$ to $\pm 2^m$
Alt. Error, within $\pm 2'$ to $\pm 6'$

in which the $\pm$ signs indicate, what must always be understood, the uncertainty as to the Error being one of excess (+) or deficiency (−).

57. Tables of Azimuth-Errors; Auxiliary Tables.— It may be expedient to estimate the effect of supposed or assumed Errors of the Data, sometimes before, but frequently after, computing or otherwise finding a True Azimuth. In either case, this may always be done accurately and quite simply, with the requisite Data, by logarithmic computation. But it may also be accomplished without any calculation, and with sufficient accuracy, by mere inspection, with the use of suitable Tables. Such is the object of the several *Tables of Azimuth-Errors.*

They are specified in the following list:

a) For Errors of Horizon-Azimuths.

Tab. XXVIII for a Lat. Error of $12'$ or $0°.2$.
Tab. XXIX for a Dec. Error of $6'$ or $0°.1$.

b) For Errors of Time-Azimuths.

Tab. XXXIV for an H. A. Error of 1^m of time or $15'$ of arc.
Tab. XXXV for a Lat. Error of $12'$ or $0°.2$.
Tab. XXXVI for a Dec. Error of $6'$ or $0°.1$.

c) For Errors of Altitude-Azimuths.

Tab. XLIV for an Alt. Error of $6'$ or $0°.1$.
Tab. XLV for a Lat. Error of $12'$ or $0°.2$.
Tab. XLVI for a Dec. Error of $6'$ or $0°.1$.

d) For Errors of Time-Alt. Azimuths.

Tab. XLIX for an H. A. Error of $0^m.2$ or 12^s.
Tab. L for an Alt. or Dec. Error of $3'$ or $0°.05$.

In these Tables the arguments are not generally the same as the Data of the Azimuth, but these are wholly or partially replaced by other quantities, such as the Azimuth itself, the Position-Angle (*Int.*), the Altitude in a Time-Azimuth, and the Hour-Angle in an Altitude-Azimuth, etc. Hence the need of auxiliary Tables to furnish these quantities for the convenient use of the Tables of Azimuth-Errors.[1] Such are the following:

Tab. XXV. Position-Angles for Horizon-Azimuths.
Tab. XXXII. Position-Angles for Time-Azimuths.
Tab. XXXIII. Altitudes for Time-Azimuths.
Tab. XLIII. Position-Angles for Altitude-Azimuths.

With these Tables, and the aid of the two Tables XXXI and XLII, of *Direct and Limiting Azimuths*, it will be easy, whenever desired, whether in advance of an observation or afterwards, to estimate the effect of a supposed or assumed Datum-Error upon the Azimuth. If the Data-Errors in a given case are the same as those for which the Tables of Azimuth-Errors are constructed, the Azimuth-Errors may be taken out at sight; if they are not the same, it will only be necessary to take *multiples* or *submultiples* of the Tabular Errors, according as the assumed Data-Errors are *larger* or *smaller* than those of the Tables. Ordinarily, the Azimuth-Errors are given to the nearest tenth of the degree, which is sufficiently exact in practice.

The result obtained in each special instance will be a *Partial Azimuth-Error* for the particular Datum-Error considered.

58. To find Partial Azimuth-Errors.—In order to illustrate the use of these Tables in finding Partial Az. Errors, for certain supposed or assumed Errors of the Data, we shall give in succession the Rules for taking out these Errors under each Azimuth-Method, following with Examples of application to the several Examples of Azimuths given under that method.

a) Partial Errors of Horizon-Azimuths.

1. *For the Lat. Error:* Enter Tab. XXVIII with the Lat. and True Az., each to the nearest whole degree, and take out the corresponding Error.

2. *For the Dec. Error:* First enter Tab. XXV with the Lat. and Dec. and take out the Pos. Ang. roughly to the nearest degree; then, with this, enter Tab. XXIX and take out the corresponding Error.

3. *Remark:* These Errors may obviously be taken out as well before as after the observation is made.

As Examples of application, we may take those of *Art.* 14, which we shall place in tabular form, including the Azimuth-Data, the Auxiliary Data, the Assumed Data-Errors, and the resulting Partial Az. Errors.

---

[1] The Tables of Errors in all cases might be constructed with the Azimuth-Data solely as arguments; but as each, with the exception of Horizon-Azimuths, would require three arguments, the Tables would need to be considerably extended, and even then be less convenient to use than these.

Examples of the Partial Errors of Horizon-Azimuths.

No. of Ex.	Az. Data.		Aux. Data.		Sup. Data-Errors.		Par. Az. Errors.		Prob. Tot. Az. Error.
	Lat.	Dec.	T. Az.	Pos. Ang.	Lat. Error.	Dec. Error.	For Lat. Error.	For Dec. Error.	
	°	°	°	°	°	°	°	°	°
1	11 N	23 N	67	79	±0.2	±0.1	0.0	±0.1	±0.1
2	25 S	22 N	114	63	0.1	0.05	0.0	0.0	0.0
3	40 N	21 S	119	46	0.4	0.2	±0.2	±0.2	±0.3
4	32 S	23 S	62	55	0.4	0.2	0.2	0.2	0.3
5	51 N	28 S	139	28	0.2	0.1	0.3	0.2	0.4
6	69 N	14 N	48	16	0.1	0.05	0.3	0.2	0.4
7	48 N	11 S	106	41	0.2	0.05	0.1	0.0	0.1

b) Partial Errors of Time-Azimuths.

1. *For the H. A. Error:* First, enter Tab. XXXII with the H. A., Lat., and Dec., and take out the Pos. Ang.; then, with the H. A., T. Az., and Pos. Ang., take out the Az. Error from Tab. XXXIV.

2. *For the Lat. Error:* First, enter Tab. XXXIII with the H. A., Dec., and T. Az., and take out the Alt.; then, with the T. Az. and Alt., take out the Az. Error from Tab. XXXV.

3. *For the Dec. Error:* First, enter Tab. XXXII with the H. A., Lat., and Dec., and take out the Pos. Ang.; also, take out the Alt. from Tab. XXXIII, if not already found (2); then, with the Pos. Ang. and Alt., take out the Az. Error from Tab. XXXVI.

4. *Remark:* If the T. Az. be unknown, as in the case of finding the Az. Error in advance of an observation, take it out approximately from Tab. XXXI, with the H. A., Lat., and Dec.

Examples of the Partial Errors of Time-Azimuths.

No. of Ex.	Azimuth-Data.			Auxiliary Data.			Partial Az. Errors.			Prob. Total Az. Error.
	H. A.	Lat.	Dec.	Az.	Pos. Ang.	Alt.	For H. A. Err. ±1ᵐ	For Lat. Err. ±12′	For Dec. Err. ±6′	
	h m	°	°	°	°	°	°	°	°	°
1	1 21	21 N	3 S	137	39	61	±0.4	±0.3	±0.1	±0.5
2	6 35	41 N	22 N	68	49	8	0.2	0.0	0.1	0.2
3	3 40	12 S	23 S	70	91	33	0.0	0.1	0.1	0.1
4	5 10	6 N	23 S	115	65	8	±0.1	0.0	0.1	0.1
5	6 10	23 N	23 N	67	67	6	0.1	0.0	0.1	0.1
6	4 30	21 N	21 S	119	61	12	0.1	0.0	0.1	0.1
7	5 5	12 N	12 N	81	80	15	0.05	0.05	0.1	0.1
8	9 15	72 N	30 N	36	12	14	0.2	0.0	0.0	0.2
9	0 13	30 N	9 S	175	4	50	0.4	0.0	0.0	0.4
10	5 30	12 N	12 S	103	76	5	0.1	0.0	0.1	0.1
11	11 40	71 N	21 N	5	2	1	0.3	0.0	0.0	0.3
12	4 36	1 S	32 N	124	56	22	0.2	0.1	0.1	0.3

c) Partial Errors of Altitude-Azimuths.

1. *For the Alt. Error:* First, enter Tab. XLIII with the Alt., Lat., and Dec., and take out the Pos. Ang.; then, with the Alt. and Pos. Ang., take out the Az. Error from Tab. XLIV.

2. *For the Lat. Error:* First, enter Tab. XLVIII with the T. Az., Dec., and Alt. and take out the H. A.; then, with the Lat. and H. A., take out the Az. Error from Tab. XLV.

3. *For the Dec. Error:* First, take out the H. A., if not already taken out (2); then, with the Lat. and H. A., take out the Az. Error from Tab. XLVI.

4. *Remark:* If the T. Az. be unknown, as in the case of finding the Az. Error in advance of an observation, take it out approximately from Tab. XLII, with the Alt., Lat., and Dec.

Examples of the Partial Errors of Altitude-Azimuths.

No of Ex.	Azimuth-Data.			Auxiliary Data.			Partial Az. Errors.			Prob. Total Az. Error.
	Alt.	Lat.	Dec.	Az.	Pos. Ang.	H. A.	For Alt. Err. ±6′	For Lat. Err. ±12′	For Dec. Err. ±6′	
	°	°	°	°	°	h	°	°	°	°
1	30	24 N	17 N	84	70	4.7	±0.05	±0.1	±0.1	±0.1
2	22	27 S	10 N	116	55	3.6	0.1	0.2	0.2	0.3
3	21	69 N	14 N	108	20	1.4	0.3	1.6	0.9	1.9
4	37	42 N	8 N	117	45	2.8	0.2	0.3	0.2	0.4

d) Partial Errors of Time-Alt. Azimuths.

The Partial Errors are taken out in a similar manner from Tables XLIX and L for Time-Alt. Azimuths, and need not be explained nor illustrated by Examples.

59. Total Azimuth-Error.—Since the signs of the Data-Errors are uncertain, it is obvious not only that the corresponding Partial Azimuth-Errors are uncertain in sign, but that the Total Azimuth-Error is uncertain in both amount and sign. Thus, the Partial Azimuth-Errors may be all + or *additive*, for which the Total Azimuth-Error will be equal to their Sum and also additive; they may be all − or *subtractive*, for which the Total Azimuth-Error will be equal to their Sum and subtractive; or they may be partly + and partly −, in which case the Total Azimuth-Error will be equal to the Difference between the Sum of the + and the Sum of the − Partial Azimuth-Errors, and will take the sign of the greater Sum; so that it is even quite possible for the + Errors to balance the − Errors and leave no effective Total Azimuth-Error.

Now, when there are several quantities of uncertain sign, whose effective total it is desired to determine, we can only resort to the most *probable* estimate. This may be done, in the present case, in assuming the Errors to have *equal weights*, by the following—

Rule: *The Probable Total of several Partial Errors is equal to the Square Root of the Sum of their Squares.*

Thus, Ex. 5 of Horizon-Azimuths gives the two Partial Azimuth-Errors $\pm 0°.3$ and $\pm 0°.2$. Then, by the rule,

Probable Total Az. Error =

$$\sqrt{(\pm 0°.3)^2 + (\pm 0°.2)^2} = \sqrt{0°.09 + 0°.04} = \sqrt{0°.13} = \pm 0°.36, \text{ or } \pm 0°.4$$

And in this manner the several Probable Totals of the last column in each of the Tables are obtained; that is to say, by squaring each Partial Azimuth-Error of an Example, taking the Sum of those squares, and extracting the Square Root of that Sum, taking the result to the nearest tenth of a degree.

Of course, the sign of the Probable Total is also uncertain. All that we determine is this: not knowing from the signs of the Partial Errors whether we should take a Sum or Difference of these quantities, we simply get *the most probable mean opinion between extreme conclusions.*

60. Favorable and Unfavorable Conditions.—A glance at the Tables of Azimuth-Errors is sufficient to show how varied are the values of the Azimuth-Error with respect to the same Datum-Error.

Thus, referring to Table XXXIV (Errors of the Time-Azimuth for an Error of 1^m in the Hour-Angle), it is seen that the Azimuth-Error is always comparatively *small* when the Azimuth itself approaches to 0° or 180°, or when the Position-Angle is nearly 90°, whether greater or less; that the Azimuth-Error is comparatively *large* when the Position-Angle approaches 0° or 180°, or when the Azimuth itself is nearly 90°, whether greater or less. Also, that, with the same Azimuth and Position-Angle, the Azimuth-Error is small so long as the Hour-Angle differs but little from 6^h; but increases, first slowly, at length quite rapidly, as the Hour-Angle recedes from 6^h, becoming very large as the Hour-Angle approaches 0^h or 12^h.

These illustrations show that there are certain relations between the several parts of the Triangle of Position (*Int.*) which are better than others for finding the Azimuth; from which it may be said that the conditions of an Azimuth are *favorable* or *unfavorable*, according as it is affected to a *less* or *greater* degree by the same Errors of the Data. These conditions of the several Azimuth-Methods may be briefly stated in the following terms:

a) **Conditions of Horizon-Azimuths.**—In these—

First, for an Error of the Latitude, the conditions are most favorable when the Latitude is lowest and the Azimuth itself nearest 90°; they are most unfavorable when the Latitude is highest and the Azimuth nearest 0° or 180°.

Secondly, for an Error of the Declination, the conditions are most favorable when the Position-Angle is nearest 90°; they are most unfavorable when the Position-Angle is nearest 0° or 180°.

Otherwise, it may be said that the conditions are most favorable when the Latitudes are lowest and the Declinations least; they are most unfavorable when the Latitudes are highest and the Declinations greatest.

b) **Conditions of Time-Azimuths.**—In these—

First, for an Error of the Hour-Angle, the conditions are most favorable when the Hour-Angle and Position-Angle are both nearest 90°, and the Azimuth itself nearest 0° or 180°; they are most unfavorable when the Hour-Angle and Position-Angle are both nearest 0° or 180°, and the Azimuth nearest 90°.

Secondly, for an Error of the Latitudes, the conditions are most favorable when the Altitude of the object is least and the Azimuth itself nearest 0° or 180°; they are most unfavorable when the Altitude is greatest and the Azimuth nearest 90°.

Thirdly, for an Error of the Declination, the conditions are most favorable when the Altitude is least and the Position-Angle nearest 0° or 180°; they are most unfavorable when the Altitude is greatest and the Position-Angle nearest 90°.

c) **Conditions of Altitude-Azimuths.**—In these—

First, for an Error of the Altitude, the conditions are most favorable when the Altitude is least and the Position-Angle nearest 90°; they are most unfavorable when the Altitude is greatest and the Position-Angle nearest 0° or 180°.

Secondly, for an Error of either the Latitude or Declination, the conditions are most favorable when the Latitude is lowest and the Hour-Angle nearest 6^h; they are most unfavorable when the Latitude is highest and the Hour-Angle nearest 0^h or 12^h.

d) **Conditions of Time-Alt. Azimuths.**—These conditions need not be particularized, as they are comprised in those stated under the two preceding heads, and may be inferred from a glance at Tables XLIX and L.

61. Limits of Allowable Azimuth-Error.—It is commonly regarded as "sufficient for the requirements of Navigation" if the Helmsman is able to steer within *a quarter of the point*, or 2°.8 of the course set for him. Let this be conceded as a limit for steering; then, it is also regarded by many Navigators as "sufficiently exact," in view of the Steersman's margin, to take out their True Azimuths, whenever it can be done by Tables, to the nearest degree; while it is also frequently admitted that little pretension is made, in the observation of their Compass-Azimuths, to get them more closely than to the nearest degree.

Now, we have here three distinct sources of Error, each of quite an appreciable amount, which are allowed to occur on every occasion of shaping and steering a ship's course, without mentioning the Error from Defective Sensibility, which, although nothing for some compasses, may be several degrees for others. There are, then, in supposing the compass to be practically perfect, as follows:

Pointing-Error ±0°.5 in observing the Comp. Az.;
Azimuth-Error ±0°.5 in taking out from Tables;
Steering-Error ±1°.4 in steering the ship's course;

giving a Probable Total Error of ±1°.6. It is true that these Errors might have *opposite* signs in some cases, when the total would be *reduced* to 0°.4; but they might with equal probability have the *same* signs, when the total would be *increased* to 2°.4.

But it must always be remembered that, as already exemplified in the preceding Articles, in consequence of the inevitable Errors of the Data, there is quite likely to be an Error of the True Azimuth, however carefully it may be computed or taken out from the Tables. This may be quite small under very favorable conditions; but it may also be quite large under different circumstances.

Hence, on the simple principle that, if "we cannot save everything, we should strive to save all we can," it would seem to be obvious that it is always advisable to avoid all *unnecessary Errors*, or to diminish them, at the least, whenever we may.

Without in this place entering further on the question of the need to allow so large a margin for Steering-Error, or so large an Error of Observation, it may be remarked, with respect to the two sources of the True Azimuth Error, that it has already been shown to be easy enough, by the methods described, to take out the True Azimuth from the Tables, within $\pm 0^\circ.2$ to $\pm 0^\circ.3$; while, of the Examples given of Az. Errors due to the Errors of the Data (58, 59), it is seldom that the Prob. Tot. Azimuth-Error from this source, with the actual conditions, need exceed $\pm 0^\circ.4$. It is evident, therefore, that we should be able, in finding any Single Compass-Error, to depend on our True Azimuth, within—

$$\sqrt{(0^\circ.3)^2+(0^\circ.4)^2} = \pm 0^\circ.5$$

for all ordinary cases of requiring it at sea.

On the other hand, in the operation of finding Serial Compass-Errors for Different Headings of the Ship, it is necessary and sufficient that for port or inshore observations our True Azimuth should be depended on within *one-tenth of a degree*, or $\pm 0^\circ.1$; while for observations at sea we must be content to get the best we can; in general, however, we may expect to get these within *three-tenths of the degree*, or $\pm 0^\circ.3$.

Accordingly, we shall take these as *Requirement-Limits* in those cases of nautical practice within which True Azimuths are to be employed in finding the Compass-Error; that is to say:

1. For the Single Compass-Error, the greatest Error of Azimuth not to exceed $\pm 0^\circ.5$;

2. For Serial Compass-Errors, the greatest Error of Azimuth not to exceed $\pm 0^\circ.1$ in port, or $\pm 0^\circ.3$ at sea.

In order to satisfy these requirements in practice, we must be assured, in the first place, that our Data-Errors (56) in any given case are certainly within the limits assumed for them, whatever those may be; and, secondly, that the conditions of the Azimuth give rise to Partial Azimuth-Errors, as found by a reference to the proper Tables (57), whose Probable Total is within the assigned Requirement-Limit.

By these means we shall be able to make a reliable estimate of the dependence to be placed on our Compass-Observations, so far at least as finding the True Azimuth is concerned, as well in advance as afterwards; so that, if the results cannot be depended on within the required limits, we may secure more favorable conditions, either by choosing a different object, or waiting for a favorable change; or so that, at the least, we may take our succeeding steps with intelligence and certainty.

We shall next proceed, in further elucidation of this important subject, with the aid of a series of Tables giving the *Limiting-Errors of Azimuths* for certain assumed limits of the Data-Errors, to show how we may safely estimate, in any given case, the dependence to be placed upon either of the several preceding methods of finding the True Azimuth.

62. Dependence on Horizon-Azimuths: Use of Tab. XXVI.—Since an Horizon-Azimuth can only be resorted to for a Single Compass-Error, it is unnecessary to consider the second Requirement-Limit. If, then, these Azimuths be restricted to the Sun, Moon, Planets, and those Stars whose Declinations never exceed about 30° north or south; and if we assume a Lat. Error within ±12′, or ±0.2, and a Dec. Error within ±6′, or ±0°.1, Tab. XXVI may be formed directly from Tables XXIV, XXV, XXVIII, and XXIX.

This Table consists of four parts, corresponding to the Declinations of 12°, 18°, 24°, and 30°; the first and second columns of each division containing the *greatest Par. Az. Errors*, to the nearest superior tenth of the degree, for the assumed Lat. and Dec. Errors, answering to the Latitudes in the left-hand column, to which they are set opposite. The third column in each division contains the *Probable Total Az. Errors;* each of which being found by taking the Square Root of the Sum of the Squares of the corresponding Par. Az. Errors.

It is thus seen that, with the Data-Errors within the limits here stated, and a Dec. not greater than 12°, the Prob. Tot. Error of an Horizon-Azimuth will not exceed ±0°.2 for all Latitudes up to 60° N or S; not exceed ±0°.6 for all Latitudes between 60° and 70°; nor exceed ±1°.0 even up to 76° of Latitude. But, as the Dec. is greater, the corresponding Az. Errors range at higher limits; so that, for example, with a Dec. of 30°, the Az. Error might be ±0°.7 for a Lat. of 55°.

The small Table at the right is a similar one for all Declinations up to 24°, in which the Lat. and Dec. Errors are each assumed to be ±0°.5, or ±30′. It shows the Prob. Tot. Error to which one is liable, when careless or indifferent about the Data, either in their preparation, or in taking out from the Azimuth-Tables.

It is not an uncommon practice with Navigators to enter the Table of Horizon-Azimuths (or Amplitudes) with the Lat. and Dec. to the nearest whole degree, on the ground of greater ease in taking out the required quantity. If these Data could be supposed *precisely correct*, then, in using them to the nearest degree, we should involve at the most an Error of ±0°.5 in each; and, accordingly, the small Table, before referred to, would give the corresponding greatest Prob. Tot. Errors to which such a practice would be liable. Thus, we might still depend on our True Azimuths within ±1°.0 for all Latitudes up to 50°, N or S.

If, on the other hand, as is most certain to be the case, the Data are both in Error, the Lat. especially being sometimes uncertain by 12′, 20′, or even 30′, we may involve the Lat. in Error, by at least a *whole degree*, in taking it to the nearest degree. Hence, the Par. Az. Errors in the second column of the small Table might be doubled, and the Prob. Tot. Error of the True Az. for a Lat. of 50° might be $\pm 1^\circ.4$.

63. Dependence on Time-Azimuths: Use of the Tables of Limiting-Errors.—Regarding Time-Azimuths as available, alike in finding Single and Serial Compass-Errors, we shall consider the True Azimuths with respect to both Requirement-Limits.

a) **Single Time-Azimuths within the First Requirement-Limit.**—In order to furnish some practical illustrations of the Errors to which a Time-Azimuth may be liable, under different possible circumstances at sea, and thus establish certain Limits of Dependence, three distinct suppositions of Data-Errors will be made, as follows:

1. Ordinary or fair-weather sailing, but with some dependence on the D. R.;

2. Cloudy, without regular or reliable observations for Time and Position, with increased dependence on the Reckoning;

3. Thick weather, but ship kept nearly to her course.

Evidently any assumptions of Data-Errors, under these supposed conditions, must be mainly arbitrary; but this will be of little consequence, with the use to be made of these Tables.

Tables XXXVII and XXXVIII are formed in accordance with these suppositions. The former answers to all Latitudes from 0° to 60° N or S, and for all Declinations from 0° to 30° of the same or contrary name; while the latter answers to all Latitudes between 60° and 80°, and for the same range of Declinations. The greatest Par. Az. Errors are given in each division of the Tables for the H. A. Limits set down in the first column.

From this Table the following conclusions may be drawn:

First. With the Data-Errors limited according to the first supposition, a Time-Azimuth of any object may be had during the day or night, without being liable to a greater Probable Error than $\pm 1^\circ.0$, whatever the Lat. up to 80°, even when the least H. A. is no more than 1^h. As the limiting H. A. is greater, the Azimuth-Error becomes less, until it comes to be less than $\pm 0^\circ.3$, for all H. Angles greater than 7^h. Moreover, for *all H. Angles* in Polar Latitudes, and for all H. Angles greater than 3^h in all other Latitudes, the True Azimuth may be depended on within $\pm 0^\circ.5$.

Secondly. With the Data-Errors limited by the second supposition, the Prob. Tot. Azimuth-Error does not exceed $\pm 0^\circ.7$, for all Latitudes, provided no H. A. smaller than 3^h is admitted. And in this case the greatest Prob. Azimuth-Error is less than $\pm 0^\circ.5$ for all H. Angles greater than 8^h.

Thirdly. Even with the Data-Errors so large as the limits of the third supposition, an uncertainty of the Data which should never exist except under severe stress of weather, the True Azimuth may still be depended on within $\pm 0^\circ.8$, provided the H. A. of the object is not allowed to be less than 5^h.

In reality, however, all the extreme conditions of Tables XXXVII and XXXVIII very seldom, if ever, concur at the same time; on the contrary, it most commonly happens that the conditions are much more favorable, even with the same Errors of Data. Consequently, the Azimuth-Errors for the same Data-Errors will generally be smaller than the maximum or limiting values of this Table.

This is seen in the Examples of Time-Azimuths (23, 25), which represent a considerable variety of actual conditions, and whose Errors are given in the Table of Art. 58, for assumed Data-Errors in accordance with the first supposition of Table XXXVII.

Table XXXVIII illustrates the convenience with which Time-Azimuths are adapted to the wants of the Navigator, even in the highest Latitudes. Thus, it is seen that the probable total effect upon the Azimuth of quite large Data-Errors is not only within the limits of $\pm 0^\circ.5$, but is nearly uniform for all Hour-Angles in the entire circle, from 0^h to 12^h, E or W of the Meridian.

b) **Serial Azimuths within the Second Requirement-Limit.**—Unlike the ordinary case, in which the Navigator may desire to find his Compass-Error with every important change of course, and where he is compelled to accept the situation and the best available result, whatever the circumstances, in the case of getting a set of Serial Compass-Errors, he may generally choose his opportunity and thus command the best obtainable conditions.

When in port, or otherwise near the land, the ship's Position and Time are always known or may be obtained with considerable precision. Thus, the Navigator may generally find his Time and Latitude, if not otherwise available, the former within $\pm 4^s$ and the latter within $\pm 1'$, by his own observations on shore.

At sea, moreover, in all Latitudes from the Equator to 60° north or south, with a proper choice of circumstances, suitable for Serial Azimuths, the Navigator should be able to get his Time within $\pm 10^s$ to $\pm 15^s$ and his Latitude within $\pm 3'$, by excluding all dependence on the Reckoning. Beyond the Latitude of 60°, the Time will be found with less precision, but the Latitude with somewhat greater certainty.

Table XXXIX is formed with reference to these supposed circumstances. The Declination is taken at a limit of 25° N or S, for the Sun and other zodiacal bodies; and the greatest Prob. Azimuth-Errors are given in each division of the Table for the H. A. Limit, set down in the first column.

From this Table, in assuming the Data-Errors to be kept within the limits here given, the following conclusions may be drawn:

First, that, while in port or near the land, in all Latitudes, Serial Time-Azimuths may be taken with any Hour-Angle, not less than $2\frac{1}{2}^h$ from the Meridian, without being liable to a greater Probable Error than $\pm 3'$, or $\pm 0^\circ.05$.

Secondly, that, anywhere at sea, within the parallels of 80° N and 80° S, Serial Time-Azimuths may be taken within the same Limit of the

Hour-Angle, under ordinary circumstances, without being liable to a greater Probable Error than ±7′, or ±0°.12.

Thirdly, that, anywhere at sea, Serial Time-Azimuths may be had within the same Limit of Hour-Angle, without being liable to a greater Probable Error than ±16′, or ±0°.3, even when the Data are considerably uncertain, as, for example, with the Data-Errors assumed in the third division.

Keeping in mind, however, that the Azimuth-Errors set down in these Tables correspond to *extreme* conditions, it will be seen that it is quite within the reach of the Navigator's appliances and of the conditions under his control to obtain a series of True Azimuths, by this method, sufficient for a complete circle of different Headings of the ship, in whatever part of the sea likely to be traversed by him, which may in general be depended on *within two to three tenths of the degree.*

Nor need the Navigator confine his observations to the Sun. For the Planets and Fixed Stars may be observed with equal accuracy, so long as the Time and Latitude are known within the above-mentioned Limits, and the observations are made under similar restrictions as to the smallness of the Hour-Angle.[1]

The Moon, with the exception of a little additional labor in preparing her Hour-Angles (20, 21), may be used with a facility hardly inferior to that in using the Sun, if taken during the period of greatest Declination. And, at other times, even when her Dec. changes most rapidly, a short or partial series of Azimuths may be had from this object, when, for a period of half an hour, the Error of the Middle Dec. need not exceed 4±′; a condition, that should still give us results which may be depended on within ±0°.3 or ±0°.4, quite sufficient for an immediate stress of circumstances which should compel a resort to this object in the absence of one more favorably conditioned.

64. Dependence on Circumpolar Azimuths.—Table XL, while giving direct values of the True Azimuth of Polaris, also furnishes at sight the requisite indications of the Errors due to uncertainties of the Data. And, with respect to these Errors, this Table illustrates, in a striking manner, how nearly complete in its independence, is this method of getting a True Azimuth, of all its Data. Not only is it sensibly free from any dependence on the Dec., but it is practically independent of the Lat.; while, as to the Hour-Angle, represented by the Sid. Time, the Azimuth varies less than 0°.1 during an hour of Time, when the Star is near one of its greatest Elongations. And, during other periods of the apparent daily revolution of this Star, its changes in Azimuth are still quite small in comparison to the changes in its H. A., or in the Time derived therefrom.

65. Dependence on Altitude-Azimuths: Use of the Tables of Limiting-Errors.—As already evident in what has

[1] The principal practical objection to the use of these objects will be found in the difficulty of sighting them with sufficient distinctness when near the Horizon, and the other attending inconveniences, especially of night-observations.

preceded, but will be further referred to in a succeeding Article, the computations, as well as the observations of Altitude-Azimuths, are less convenient than those of Time-Azimuths. Especially is this true of Serial Azimuths by this method. We shall also see, from the following considerations, that their Errors develop more rapidly under certain conditions than those of the latter.

a) **Single Azimuths within the First Requirement-Limit.**—In Table XLVII are given the greatest Azimuth-Errors relative to certain assumed Data-Errors, for a series of different Latitudes, under three different limitations of the smallest Hour-Angle, but answering also to the corresponding Supplements, or largest Hour-Angles. They are taken out for a Declination of 30°, and therefore cover all Declinations of the zodiacal bodies, like the Sun, Moon, etc.

Thus, the Data-Errors being within the limits of this Table so long as the Hour-Angle is not less than 1^h nor greater than 11^h, an Altitude-Azimuth of any object whose Declination does not exceed 30°, in whatever Latitude from the Equator to 40°, may be had with a certainty of no greater Probable Error than ±1°.2. Again, so long as the Hour-Angle is not less than 2^h nor greater than 10^h, an Altitude-Azimuth may be had in any Latitude up to 70° with no greater Probable Error than ±1°.2, and so on; as the H. A. Limit is more remote from the Meridian, upper and lower, the conditions are improved, and the maximum Probable Error diminished.

b) **Serial Azimuths within the Second Requirement-Limit.**—Altitude-Azimuths are occasionally resorted to in serial observations for Compass-Error; and it is accordingly advisable to consider the question of their liability to Error, and how far they can be depended on, when employed for this purpose.

The subjoined little Table gives the Errors of Altitude-Azimuths under the same conditions as those of Table XLVII, except that the several Data-Errors are reduced to their minimum limits for favorable circumstances at sea, and the Hour-Angle Limits of approach to the Meridian are made larger.

Limiting Errors of Serial Altitude-Azimuths.

For Limits of Hour-Angles.	For Latitudes N or S.	Par. Azimuth-Error.			Prob. Total Az. Error.
		Alt. Error ±1′	Lat. Error ±3′	Dec. Error ±1′	
h h	° °	′	′	′	′
3 to 9	0 to 30	±2	±5	±2	±6
4 8	30 60	2	4	3	6
5 7	60 70	3	3	3	6
5 7	70 30	4	4	6	10

Thus, if the Data-Errors may be safely assumed within ±1′ for the Altitude, ±3′ for the Latitude, ±1′ for the Declination, the corresponding Partial Azimuth-Errors will not exceed those set down, and the

Prob. Tot. Error of the Azimuth will not be greater than $\pm 6'$ for all Latitudes from 0° to 70°, provided the Hour-Angles are kept within the limits stated in the first column of the Table. For Latitudes beyond 70°, the Total Errors will exceed $\pm 6'$, for an Hour-Angle,[1] even if precisely 6^h.

66. Relative Advantages of these Methods.—We shall now consider very briefly the relative advantages of these methods.

a) Horizon-Azimuths.—This method, in the well-known form of *Amplitudes*, has long been used by Navigators, generally, as a means of finding the Compass-Error. The facility with which the observation is made, and the convenience with which the Table is used, have alike contributed to make this a popular method.

Whether in the form of Azimuths, as here given, or in that of Amplitudes, as heretofore used, it has been shown to admit of sufficiently precise results under a great variety of circumstances (62); and, with the provision of observing the object *in the Apparent Horizon* (7), it is equally available in observations of the Moon, and thereby its practical utilities are largely extended.

This method is subject, however, to the following disadvantages:

1. It is unavailable, except at certain moments of the day or night.[2]

2. It is entirely unavailable in high Latitudes, with respect to bodies which remain above the Horizon, or do not set.

3. Even when available for certain objects in high Latitudes, it is liable to large Errors, and must be used with caution.

b) Time-Azimuths.—Time-Azimuths have the following advantages:

1. In the simplicity and ease of the observation, which even exceeds that of the Horizon-Azimuth, or Amplitude.

2. In the facility and precision with which it may be employed in serial observations of Compass-Error, whether in port or at sea.

3. In often being available when neither of the other methods can be employed, as in the case of an obscured or ill-defined Horizon.

4. In being available whenever any celestial body is distinctly visible at a convenient Altitude for a compass-bearing, whether Sun, Moon, Planet, or Fixed Star.

5. In being available even when the Time and Latitude are uncertain to a very considerable extent, by a suitable choice of object, in order to avoid unfavorable conditions.

A prejudice against this method seems to have existed to a considerable extent, even among intelligent Navigators. Doubtless this has been due in some degree to the supposed greater labor of computation and perplexity of cases. Nevertheless, the computation, even of a

[1] The consideration of the H. A. Limit in Alt. Az. Errors has been adhered to in the text, not only because it conveniently enters into the estimate of these Errors, but for the purpose of a comparison with the conditions of Time-Azimuths.

[2] This objection may not be very serious with those Navigators who depend *solely* on morning and evening Amplitudes of the Sun for their Compass-Errors.

Time-Azimuth, is really quite as short and convenient as that of an Altitude-Azimuth of the same body, more commonly employed.

But the simplicity and certainty of this method are still further assured with the use of the Time-Azimuth Tables. By these means the operations of taking out an Azimuth may commonly be done at sight, with sufficient accuracy, in ordinary cases of finding the Compass-Error; while it is always easy to find the Azimuth to the nearest tenth of the degree, whenever required for a series of different Headings of a ship.

c) Circumpolar Azimuths.—This modification of the Time-Azimuth Method, subject only to the condition that the Star (Polaris) can be conveniently observed through the sight-vanes of the azimuth-circle, must be especially useful whenever the Hour-Angle and Latitude are very uncertain, as they not unfrequently are after long-continued thick weather, with entire absence of observations, and the Reckoning even very much at fault.

d) Altitude-Azimuths.—Altitude-Azimuths have the following disadvantages:

1. In the necessity of measuring the Altitude of the object, in addition to that of observing the Compass-Azimuth.

2. In being inconvenient for serial observations of Compass-Errors, from the much greater labor of the requisite observations and computations.

3. In being frequently unavailable, from the difficulty of observing an Altitude, in consequence of an obscured or ill-defined Horizon.

4. In being liable to rapidly-increasing Error in the higher Latitudes from the Errors of the Data.

In view of these disadvantages, without any very obvious compensation, there would seem to be little occasion for resorting to the observation of an Altitude, merely to find the Compass-Error; since, in general, whenever an Altitude-Azimuth is available, a Time-Azimuth would be both available and preferable.

If, however, the Navigator would follow the commendable practice of taking the Compass-Bearing of the object, whenever practicable, in every observation made for Time and Position, then the Altitude obtained for other purposes might be used in an Altitude-Azimuth, for finding the Compass-Error on the same occasion. Even in this case the Time-Azimuth might still be preferred, except with the somewhat rare occurrence that the Navigator has a very uncertain Ship-Time but a good Latitude, in which case the Altitude-Azimuth might give a more reliable result.

II.—OBSERVATIONS OF TERRESTRIAL OBJECTS.

A. Method by Direct Bearings.

The Method by Direct Bearings consists in observing the Compass-Bearing of some prominent and well-defined object on the land, whose True Bearing is already known, or may be found, from the station at which the observations are made.

The difference between the Compass-Bearing and True Bearing of the object is the Compass-Error (5).

67. Fundamental Conditions.—There are three requirements in the use of this method, which may be regarded as fundamental conditions.

a) **First Condition: A Fixed Station.**—The first requirement is a *fixed station*, from which, as a centre, the True Bearing of the object is determined; to which the ship may be held either directly by her anchor, or through a mooring-buoy, and about which she may be swung into every desired Heading round the compass-circle.

This requirement is usually fulfilled by selecting a point in a harbor or roadstead, round which, whatever the Heading of the ship, an unobstructed view of the distant object may be had from the compass-position on board. The selected point, as a centre or station, is sufficiently fixed for a given occasion, by casting the ship's anchor; but it is sometimes permanently marked, by leaving a mooring-buoy strongly held by a mushroom or other form of heavy anchor.

b) **Second Condition: Means of Swinging the Ship.**—The second requirement has reference to *the means of swinging the ship* upon the desired Headings. These depend somewhat on the circumstances of the location and the resources at command.

When the station is located in still or slack water, the ship may be swung by means of warps, using for this purpose kedges and hawsers; or the ship may be pulled about with great advantage, especially if large, by a steam-tug.

When the location is in a stream or tide-way, and when from other circumstances the use of warps may be inconvenient, advantage may be taken of the changing positions of the ship, as she swings at her anchor to the wind and tide, to obtain a sufficient number of different Headings; and these may sometimes be increased in number and variety with the aid of a steam-tug.

In the first case, it is generally practicable to place the ship with her Head upon the regular points by compass—32, 16, 8, or 4, as may be desired; but, in the second case, it is generally difficult, if not impossible, to do this; and the only resource is to obtain a sufficient number of different Headings round the whole compass-circle, even if they are not upon the regular points.

c) **Third Condition: A Limited Parallax of Swing.**—The third requirement is *that the distance of the object shall be sufficiently great, in comparison with the radius of swing, to cause no appreciable change in the Compass-Bearing whatever the Position or Heading of the ship round the station.*

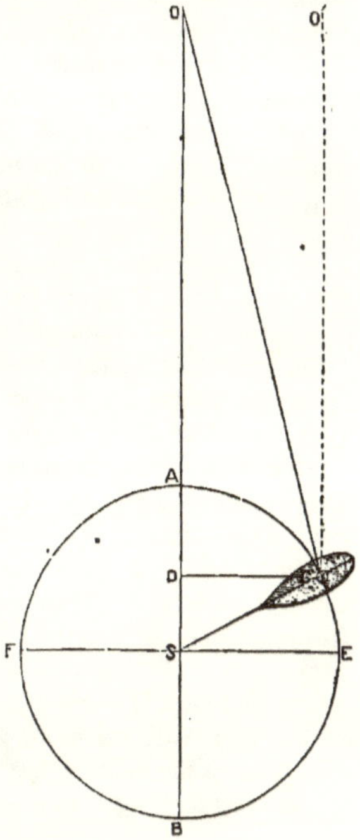

This requirement, in order to be clearly understood, may need a little detailed explanation. Referring to the figure, let O represent the place of the distant object; S the *centre of swing*, or station-centre; C the position of the Standard Compass on board.

Then, C S is the *radius of swing*, equal to the horizontal distance between the compass and the vertical at the mooring-anchor, and supposed to remain constantly the same, or, at any rate, not greater than the distance fixed by a certain length of cable; O S is the distance of the object, which is sensibly the same as O C in all positions of the ship; and A S C is the *angle of swing*, which may have any value from 0° to 180°, on each side of the *zero-line*, O A S B, through the object and centre of station.

Now, unless the distance of the object be quite considerable in comparison to the radius of swing, it will be found that the direction of the object C O, as seen from the compass at C, may be sensibly different from the true direction S O as seen from any point A or B in the zero-line. This possible change of direction, for different positions of the ship, is measured by the Angle O C O′, or its equal C O S, and is called the *Parallax of Swing.* It is evidently nothing when the ship is in the zero-line, as when headed towards O or in the opposite direction; and it increases the further the ship is swung from that line, becoming a maximum when perpendicular to it, on either side.

The Compass-Bearings of the object are accordingly liable to an Error, in consequence of this parallax, which is called the *Parallactic Error of Swing*, whose magnitude in a given case depends—

1. *On the Distance-Ratio of the Object;* that is, on the distance of the object divided by the radius of swing; and

2. *On the Angle of Swing;* being nothing when this angle is 0° or 180°, and having equal maxima when the angle is 90° and 270°.

68. Process of Finding Serial Compass-Errors.—The Method by Bearings of a Distant Object is that which is, perhaps, most commonly resorted to for obtaining a series of Compass-Errors round the compass-circle. It may be conducted in the following manner:

Everything being ready and the requisite observers at their stations, swing the ship so as to bring her head upon the nearest point by Standard Compass, gently checking her motion, and keeping her steady upon the point; then, take the Bearing of the distant object with the Standard Compass, and note the Heading of the ship with the same compass. Note, also, the Headings with the steering-compasses, and the Angle of Heel with the clinometer.

Proceed in the same careful manner to bring the ship's Head upon the next point, and, when duly stopped and steadied there, again take the Bearing of the object and note the Heading of the ship with the Standard Compass, noting also the Heading with the steering-compasses, and the Angle of Heel, as before; and so on, point after point, till the Bearings shall have been taken of the object, with the corresponding Headings of the ship and the Angles of Heel, for every point of the compass round to the point of beginning.

The operation, as thus described, may be performed upon each of the thirty-two points, sixteen points, or eight points (preferably in that case upon the octantal points), as it may be deemed expedient at the time.

Otherwise, if the circumstances of the swinging are such as to make it inexpedient to attempt obtaining the observations on the regular compass-points, proceed in all respects in the same manner, except that of trying to bring the ship's Head upon any of the regular points. It is, however, desirable in this case to distribute the observations upon Headings, approximately at an equal distance apart, round the compass-circle.

In either case, it should be the aim of the observer to get his Bearings of the object with certainty to the nearest quarter of a degree, and his Headings to the nearest *eighth of a point* or nearest whole *degree*, according as he is making his observations upon the compass-points or otherwise.

The record of the observations, which should be completely made as the work proceeds, may be kept according to the form in the subjoined Examples.

69. Examples of the Method by Direct Bearings.

Ex. 1.—1872,............ : At..............., in Lat........., Long......., Ship ...., swung for a set of Compass-Errors, by observations of a distant object,...
Distance of Object, 10 N. miles: Radius of Swing, 200 feet.
True Bearing of object, N 41°.2 W.

Ship's Head.	Direct Bearing of Object.		Error of Standard Compass.
By Standard Compass.	By Standard Compass.	True.	
North.	N 22°.7 W	N 41°.2 W	18°.5 W
N by E	26.3	"	14.9
NNE	29.8	"	11.4
NE by N	30.8	"	10.4
NE	31.0	"	10.2
NE by E	33.8	"	7.4
ENE	33.0	"	8.2
E by N	33.0	"	8.2
East.	31.8	"	9.4
E by S	30.2	"	11.0
ESE	29.2	"	12.0
SE by E	28.2	"	13.0
SE	25.5	"	15.7
SE by S	24.0	"	17.2
SSE	22.8	"	18.4
S by E	19.8	"	21.4
South.	18.0	"	23.2
S by W	15.3	"	25.9
SSW	15.0	"	26.2
SW by S	13.0	"	28.2
SW	12.8	"	28.4
SW by W	11.6	"	29.6
WSW	10.0	"	31.2
W by S	8.8	"	32.4
West.	8.4	"	32.8
W by N	9.0	"	32.2
WNW	9.8	"	31.4
NW by W	11.4	"	29.8
NW	12.4	"	28.8
NW by N	14.8	"	26.4
NNW	18.0	"	23.2
N by W	19.6	"	21.6 W

Ex. 2.—1872, February 29: At a station in New York Bay, Lat. 40°.5 N, Long. 74° W, U. S. Ship CANANDAIGUA (wood-built screw-steamer). Swung for a set of Compass-Deviations, by Direct Bearings.

Objects observed.	True Bearings.	Distances.	Rad. of Swing.
Sandy Hook L. H.	S 88°.9 E	1.2 N. M.	250 feet.
Navesink Lights.	S 27 .1 E	4.0 "	"
East Beacon.	N 60 .9 E	1.1 "	"

The Mag. Var. was 7°.6 W at the place and date.

Observations. **Reductions.**

Ship's Head. By Standard Compass.	Direct Bearing of Objects. By Standard Compass.	Direct Bearing of Objects. Magnetic.	Deviation of the Standard Compass.
North.	S 81°.5 E	S 81°.3 E	0°.2 E
N by E	S 85.0 E	81.3	3.7
NNE	S 27.7 E	S 19.5 E	8.2
NE by N	S 31.2 E	19.5	11.7
NE	S 33.2 E	19.5	13.7
NE by E	N 84.0 E	81.3	14.7
ENE	S 36.8 E	19.5	17.3
E by N	S 37.0 E	19.5	17.5
East.	S 37.2 E	S 19.5 E	17.7
E by S	N 51.5 E	N 68.5 E	17.0
ESE	N 85.2 E	S 81.3 E	13.5
SE by E	N 87.0 E	81.3	11.7
SE	N 88.8 E	81.3	9.9
SE by S	S 89.0 E	81.3	7.7
SSE	S 86.5 E	81.3	5.2
S by E	S 84.0 E	81.3	2.7 E
South.	S 81.5 E	S 81.3 E	0.2 E
S by W	S 79.0 E	81.3	2.3 W
SSW	S 75.5 E	81.3	5.8
SW by S	S 13.5 E	S 19.5 E	6.0
SW	S 11.2 E	19.5	8.3
SW by W	S 8.8 E	19.5	10.7
WSW	S 6.8 E	19.5	12.7
W by S	S 6.0 E	19.5	13.5
West.	S 5.0 E	S 19.5 E	14.5
W by N	S 67.3 E	S 81.3 E	14.0
WNW	S 4.7 E	S 19.5 E	14.8
NW by W	S 5.7 E	19.5	13.8
NW	S 8.2 E	19.5	11.3
NW by N	S 9.8 E	19.5	9.7
NNW	S 75.5 E	S 81.3 E	5.8 W
N by W	N 66.7 E	N 68.5 E	1.8 E

70. Dependence to be placed on Results.—There are two distinct sources of Error which pertain to the Method by Bearings of a Distant Object—

First, the uncertainty in the True Bearing of the object, incident to the method employed in finding it; and,

Secondly, inaccuracies in the Compass-Bearings of the object, due to the Parallactic Errors of Observation.

The first, as will be explained hereafter, should never exceed the tenth of a degree; that is, $\pm 0^\circ.1$ or $\pm 6'$. This Error, therefore, being small and constant, or affecting all the observations alike, may generally be disregarded.

The second, on the other hand, is not unfrequently a much more serious matter, since it may not only be several times as large as the former, but is attended with the complication of being unequal for the different Headings, and of having contrary signs on opposite sides of the zero-line. Nevertheless, with strict attention to the Distance-Ratio, as will presently be explained, these Errors may be kept within admissible limits; and, besides, they may always be estimated and applied as corrections of the observations, whenever it is certain that the swinging is done throughout with a taut cable.

71. Tables LII and LIII of Parallactic Errors: Examples.—Tables LII and LIII are constructed in order to afford the means of readily estimating these Errors whenever desired. They require no explanation. A few Examples will illustrate their use.

Ex. 1.—The Distance of the object is 7.4 naut. miles, the Radius of Swing 150 feet, and the Angle of Swing 90°: What is the Distance-Ratio, and what the greatest Parallactic Error?

From Tab. LII the Dist. Ratio is 300, and from Tab. LIII the greatest Parallactic Error is 12′, or 0°.2.

Ex. 2.—What is the Distance-Ratio, for which the greatest Parallactic Error shall not exceed 6′, or 0°.1?

From Tab. LIII the Dist. Ratio is between 500 and 600.

Ex. 3.—The Distance of the object is 8 naut. miles, and the greatest Parallactic Error must not exceed 6′: What is the greatest admissible Radius of Swing?

Ans. The Dist. Ratio is 500, and the Radius of Swing must not exceed 100 feet.

Ex. 4.—The Distance of the object is 2 naut. miles, and the Radius of Swing 200 feet: What is the greatest Parallactic Error?

Ans. 1°.0.

Ex. 5.—The Radius of Swing is 150 feet, and the greatest Parallactic Error is not to exceed 6′, or 0°.1: What is the least Distance of Object that will be required?

Ans. 12 N. M.

72. To correct the Observations for Parallactic Errors.—It will be the work of but a few moments, and it may sometimes be expedient, to correct the Observations of a Distant Object for Parallactic Error; or, what is the same thing, to reduce them to what they would have been if they had been made at the centre, or on the zero-line, at the station.

Thus, having deduced the Compass-Errors or Deviations, as the case may be, if it be desired to correct them for Parallax of Swing, proceed in the following manner:

a) **Rule: Case of Using the True Bearing of the Object.**—Change the Compass-Headings into True Headings, by applying the Compass-Errors to the former, to the *Right* when these Errors are *E*, to the *Left* when they are *W*.

Next, find the Angles of Swing (68), by comparing the True Headings of the ship in succession with the True Bearing of the object; setting down the Differences, or their Supplements when greater than 90°, and marking them *R.* or *L.*, according as the True Heading is *Right* or *Left* of the True Bearing of the object.[1]

Lastly, enter Tab. LIII with the Distance-Ratio and the Angles of Swing, and take out the corresponding Parallactic Errors; applying to the *Right* or *Left* of the Compass-Errors, according as the Angles of Swing are *L.* or *R.* of the zero-line (68) or True Bearing of the object from the station-centre.

b) **Rule: Case of Using the Magnetic Bearing of the Object.**—If the Magnetic Bearing of the object be used instead of the True Bearing, and the Deviations deduced instead of the Total Errors, the Rule will be the same in every particular as the preceding, except in substituting therein Magnetic for True, and Deviations for Compass-Errors.

c) **Remark I: Observing two or more Objects.**—If, instead of one object, two or more be employed with different Bearings, True or Magnetic, proceed according to the Rule, only using the proper Bearing for the Compass Error or Deviation considered.

d) **Remark II: Swinging with a Taut Cable.**—It must, of course, be understood that these corrections can only be reliably made when the entire swinging is done with a taut cable.

e) **Remark III: Using the nearest whole Degree.**—It is sufficient, in these corrections, to use the Bearings and Headings to the nearest whole degree.

---

[1] The observer's eye being supposed at the centre of the compass and looking toward the object.

73. Examples of Correcting for Parallactic Errors.

Ex. 1.—The Data and Results of *Ex.* 2 of *Art.* 69: The True Bearings being used and Compass-Errors deduced: To correct them for Parallactic Errors.

Data and Results of Ex. 2. | **Correcting for Paral. Errors.**

Ship's Head by Standard Compass.	True Bearings of Objects.	Error of Standard Compass.	Ship's Head, True.	Angles of Swing.	Parallactic Errors.	Corrected Compass-Errors.
	°	°	°	°	°	°
North.	S 89 E	7.4 W	N 7 W	82 L	1.9	5.5 W
N by E	"	3.9 W	7 E	84	1.9	2.0 W
NNE	S 27 E	0.6 E	23	50	0.3	0.9 E
NE by N	"	4.1	38	65	0.3	4.4
NE	"	6.1	51	78	0.4	6.5
NE by E	S 89 E	7.1	63	28	1.0	8.1
ENE	S 27 E	9.7	77	76	0.4	10.1
E by N	"	10.0	89	64	0.3	10.3
East.	S 27 E	10.1 E	S 80 E	53 L	0.3	10.4 E
E by S	N 61 E	9.4	69	50 R	1.5	7.9
ESE	S 89 E	5.9	62	27	0.9	5.0
SE by E	"	4.1	52	37	1.1	3.0
SE	"	2.3	43	46	1.4	0.9 E
SE by S	"	0.1 E	34	55	1.6	1.5 W
SSE	"	2.4 W	25	64	1.7	4.1
S by E	"	4.9	16	73	1.8	6.7
South.	S 89 E	7.4 W	S 7 E	81 R	1.9	9.3 W
S by W	"	9.9	1 W	90	1.9	11.8
SSW	"	13.4	9	82	1.9	15.3
SW by S	S 27 E	13.6	20	47	0.3	13.9
SW	"	15.9	29	56	0.3	16.2
SW by W	"	18.3	38	65	0.3	18.6
WSW	"	20.3	47	74	0.4	20.7
W by S	"	21.1	58	85	0.4	21.5
West.	S 27 E	22.1	S 68 W	85 R	0.4	22.5 W
W by N	S 89 E	21.6	80	11	0.4	22.0
WNW	S 27 E	22.4	N 90 W	63	0.3	22.7
NW by W	"	21.4	78	51	0.3	21.7
NW	"	18.9	64	37	0.2	19.1
NW by N	"	17.3	51	24 R	0.2	17.5
NNW	S 89 E	13.4	36	53 L	1.6	11.8
N by W	N 61 E	5.8 W	17	78	1.9	3.9

This Example supposes the Compass-Errors instead of the Deviations to have been found. It illustrates the more complicated case of several objects being observed instead of one. The procedure is entirely the same.

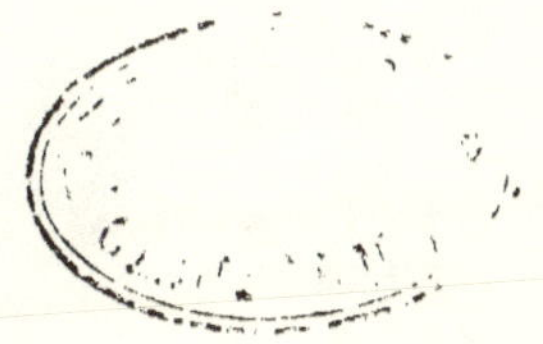

Ex. 2.—The Data and Results of *Ex.* 2 of *Art.* 69: To correct the Deviations for Parallactic Errors.

Data and Results of Ex. 2.			Correcting for Paral. Errors.			
Ship's Head by Standard Compass.	Magnetic Bearings of Objects.	Deviation of Standard Compass.	Ship's Head, Magnetic.	Angles of Swing.	Parallactic Errors.	Corrected Compass-Deviations.
North.	S 81° E	0.2° E	North.	81° L	1.9°	2.1° E
N by E	81	3.7	N 15 E	84	1.9	5.6
NNE	S 19 E	8.2	31	50	0.3	8.5
NE by N	19	11.7	45	64	0.3	12.0
NE	19	13.7	59	78	0.4	14.1
NE by E	S 81 E	14.7	71	28	1.0	15.7
ENE	19	17.3	85	76	0.4	17.7
E by N	19	17.5	S 84 E	65	0.3	17.9
East.	S 19 E	17.7	S 72 E	53 L	0.3	18.0 E
E by S	N 69 E	17.0	62	49 R	1.5	15.5
ESE	S 81 E	13.5	54	27	0.9	12.6
SE by E	81	11.7	44	37	1.1	10.6
SE	81	9.9	35	46	1.4	8.5
SE by E	81	7.7	26	55	1.6	6.1
SSE	81	5.2	17	64	1.7	3.5
S by E	81	2.7	8	73	1.8	0.9 E
South.	S 81 E	0.2 E	South.	81 R	1.9	1.7 W
S by W	81	2.3 W	S 9 W	90	1.9	4.2
SSW	81	5.8	17	82	1.9	7.7
SW by S	S 19 E	6.0	28	47	0.3	6.3
SW	19	8.3	37	56	0.3	8.6
SW by W	19	10.7	45	64	0.3	11.0
WSW	19	12.7	55	74	0.4	13.1
W by S	19	13.5	65	84	0.4	13.9
West.	S 19 E	14.5	S 76 W	85 R	0.4	14.9 W
W by N	S 81 E	14.0	87	12	0.4	14.4
WNW	S 19 E	14.8	N 82 W	63	0.3	15.1
NW by W	19	13.8	70	51	0.3	14.1
NW	19	11.3	56	37	0.2	11.5
NW by N	19	9.7	43	24 R	0.2	9.9
NNW	S 81 E	5.8 W	28	53 L	1.6	4.2 W
N by W	N 69 E	1.8 E	9	78	1.9	3.7 E

It will be seen that the Angles of Swing are the same, as they should be, in these two Cases of the same Example. The Parallactic Errors are consequently the same.

It is quite evident that *Ex.* 2, *Art.* 69, should be corrected for Parallactic Errors.

74. Limiting Distance-Ratios.—From an inspection of Tables LII, LIII, and the Examples of *Art.* 71, the need of caution in the use of this method will be evident.

Assuming that we are content to admit a maximum Parallactic Error of 0°.1, or 6′, the Distance-Ratio will have to be not less than 500; and, with this as a limit, it will be seen that, even with a Radius of Swing no greater than 100 feet, we shall require the distance of the object to be not less than 8 nautical miles.

If, however, in a given case, the Distance-Ratio be much less than 500, and we can neither find an available object farther off, nor in any practicable manner materially diminish the Radius of Swing, we shall then have to consider—

First, whether we shall still proceed and correct the observations for Parallactic Errors; or,

Secondly, whether, if this be impracticable (72, *d*), we can afford to disregard these Errors, under the circumstances of the case; or,

Thirdly, whether we should not preferably resort to one of the other methods.

75. Different Methods of Finding the True Bearing of the Object.—In using permanent stations for the observation of Compass-Errors by this method, the True Bearing of the object is commonly known from a previous determination. Whenever unknown, as when establishing a new station, temporary or otherwise, the True Bearing will be required, and it may be found by one of the methods named below:

1. By the Geographical Position.
2. By an Astronomical Bearing.
3. By an Azimuth of the Vertical Circle.

In describing these methods, we shall have to keep in mind that, among the requirements of the station (67), it must be at an anchorage, and consequently the observations for the True Bearing must be made from the deck of the ship, although it may be possible in most cases to select a smooth sea, with other favorable circumstances.

76. Finding the True Bearing by the Geographical Position.—When the Geographical Position of the object is reliably known, the True Bearing and Distance are easily determined in the following manner:

Rule:—Deduce the Co-Latitude of the object and the Co-Latitude of the station; also, the Difference of Longitudes between the object and station. Then proceed according to the method of Time-Azimuths (15); treating the Co-Latitude of the object like the Pol. Dist. and the Diff. Longitudes like the Hour-Angle of a celestial body; following the Rule (19), either by computation (22) or inspection (26), in every particular.

Having found the True Bearing, enter a Traverse-Table with this Bearing as Course and the Diff. of the two Latitudes as D. Lat. and take out the Distance of the object.

77. Examples of Finding the True Bearing by the Geographical Position.

Ex. 1.—The respective Positions of the station and object are as below stated: What is the True Bearing of the object from the station, and what is its Distance in nautical miles?

	Lat.	Long.
Station in Harbor of Yokohama	35° 26′.0 N	139° 39′.0 E
Distant object (Fusi-Yama)	35 21 .5 N	138 41 .0 E

Co-Lat.	54° 38′.5	object			
Co-Lat.	54 34 .0	station			
Diff.	4 .5				
½ Diff.	2 .2	sin	6.8159	cos	0.0000
½ Sum	54 36 .5	cosec	0.0887	sec	0.2371
½ D. Long.	28¼	cot	2.0776	cot	2.0776
		tan	8.9822	tan	2.3147

T. Bear. N 95° 12′ W: **X** 5° 29′ **Y** 89° 43′
or, S 84 48 W

With Diff. Lat. 4°.5 and True Bearing 84°.8, as Course, we take from Traverse-Table the Distance 50 N. miles.

Ex. 2.—The Positions of the station and object are as below stated: It is required to find the True Bearing and Distance of the object from the station.

	Lat.	Long.
Station at sea, in	60° 6′ N	142° 50′ W
Object, Mt. St. Elias, in	60 18 N	140 52 W

Co-Lat.	29° 42′	object			
Co-Lat.	29 54	station			
Diff.	12				
½ Diff.	6	sin	7.2419	cos	0.0000
½ Sum	29 48	cosec	0.3037	sec	0.0616
½ D. Long.	59	cot	1.7654	cot	1.7654
		tan	9.3110	tan	1.8270

T. Bear. N 77° 35′ E: **X** 11° 34′ **Y** 89° 9′

With Diff. Lat. 12′, True Bearing 77°.6, as Course, the Traverse-Table gives for Distance 57 N. miles.

78. By an Astronomical Bearing.—When the Geographical Position of the object is not reliably known, the preceding method of finding the True Bearing is no longer available. In such a case, among other means, the method by an Astronomical Bearing may be used. This consists in finding the Difference of Bearings between the object and some celestial body, whose True Azimuth is determined at the same time by one of the methods of Section (*I*).

a) **Rule: To Make the Observation.**—Measure the Angular Distance with a sextant between the defined point of the object and the Sun's limb; have a second observer measure the Altitude of the Sun at the same moment, with a sextant or octant; and note the Time with a Comparing-Watch, whose error on Local Time, Apparent or Mean, is reliably known.

Otherwise, in the absence of the second observer, first, measure the Altitude of the Sun; next, the Distance between the defined point of the object and the Sun; then, a second Altitude of the Sun; each observation being taken without unnecessary delay, and the W. Time of each being noted.

In either Case, take the Altitude of the defined point on the object above the Sea or Shore Horizon, as the circumstances may require. Note, also, whether the object is Right or Left of the observed celestial body.

b) **Rule: To Make the Computation.**—First, find the *True Az. of the celestial body*, either by the Time-Method (15) or by the Altitude-Method (41), according as the Time or Altitude is the most reliable, or as may be preferred for any other reason.

Secondly, find the *Az. Difference*, as follows: Change the Observed Altitudes of the celestial body and terrestrial object into *Apparent* Altitudes by correcting them for Index-Error of the sextant, and for Dip;[1] also, for the Semi-Diameter, if the Sun or Moon be the body observed.

Change the Observed Angular Distance into *Apparent* Ang. Distance, by correcting it for Index-Error, and for Semi-Diameter, whenever necessary.

Add together the Ap. Dist. and the two Ap. Alts.; take the Difference between their Half-Sum and the Ap. Dist. Then add together the secants of the two Ap. Alts., the cosine of the Half-Sum, and the cosine of the Difference. The Half-Sum of these four Logs, rejecting tens from their indices, will be the cosine of half the Az. Diff., which take out and double, and the result will be the required Az. Diff.

There will now be two Cases to consider, according as the Az. Diff., reckoned from the celestial body, is in the same sense as the True Az., or in the opposite sense.

First Case: The Az. Diff. in the *same* sense.—Take the Sum of the True Az. and Az. Diff., and the result will be the True Bearing of the object; which, if *less* than 180°, will have the *same* name as that of the True Az.; but, if *greater* than 180°, *subtract* from 360°, and change the meridional reference.

Second Case: The Az. Diff. in the *opposite* sense.—Take the *Difference* of the True Az. and Az. Diff., and the result will be the True Bearing of the object; which will have the *same* or *different* meridional reference, according as the True Az. is *greater* or *less* than the Az. Diff.

79. Examples of Finding the True Bearing by an Astronomical Bearing.

Ex. 1.—1870, May 20: At anchor, in Lat. 40° 30′ N, Long. 74° 0′ W, about 8¼ʰ A. M., made the following observations for finding the True Bearing of a distant light-house:

T. by Watch.	Obs. Alt. ☉̲	Ang. Dist. Lt.[2]	Obs. Alt. of Lt.[2]
8ʰ 10ᵐ 50ˢ	38° 18′ 15″		
12 50		☉| 80° 5′ 20″ R.	5° 10′ 35″
14 50	39 3 20		

Watch slow of ship A. T. 5ᵐ 10ˢ; Ht. of eye, 18 feet; Ind. Corr. — 2′ 25″.

---

[1] When, as may frequently happen in the use of this method, the Shore, instead of the proper Sea Horizon, is observed, the usual correction for a "Shore-Dip" must be used.

[2] Top of lantern.

Preparation of Data.

Mid. Ship. A. T.	19ᵈ 20ʰ 18ᵐ	⊙'s Dec.	N 19° 59'.7 + 31"	Mid. Obs. Alt.	38° 40'.8	Ind. Corr.	− 2'.4
Long. in T.	+ 4 56	Redⁿ for 1ʰ.2	+ 0.6 37.2	Alt. Corr.	+ 9.4	Dip.	− 4.0
Gr. date May	20 1 14	Red. Dec.	20 0.3	Ap. Alt. ⊙	38 50.2	Semi-D.	+15.8
or,	1.2	Pol. Dist.	70 0			Alt. Corr.	+ 9.4

Mid. Ap. T.	8ʰ 18ᵐ	Obs. Ang. Dist.	80° 5'.5	Obs. Alt. of Lt.	5° 10'.6
Mid. H. A.	3 42 E	Ind. Corr.	− 2.4	Alt. Corr.	− 6.4
		Semi-D.	+ 15.8	Ap. Alt. Lt.	5 4.2
		Ap. Ang. Dist.	80 18.9		

Computation of True Az. of Sun.

Pol. Dist.	70° 0'				
Co-Lat.	49 30				
Diff.	20 30				
½ Diff.	10 15	sin	9.2503	cos	9.9930
½ Sum	59 45	cosec	0.0636	sec	0.2978
½ H. A.	1ʰ 51ᵐ	cot	0.2789	cot	0.2789
		tan	9.5928	tan	0.5697
T. Az.	N 96° 19' E :	X	21° 23'	Y	74° 56'
Diff. Az.	81 40 R.				
T. Bear.	N 177 59 E				
or,	S 2 1 E				

Computation of Diff. Az.

Ap. dist.	80° 18'.9		
Ap. Alt. Lt.	5 4.2	sec	0.0017
Ap. Alt. ⊙	38 50.2	sec	0.1085
Sum	124 13.3		
½ Sum	62 6.6	cos	9.6700
Rem.	18 12.3	cos	9.9777
			19.7579
½ D. Az.	40 50	cos	9.8789
Diff. Az.	81 40		

Without multiplying examples in finding the True Azimuth of a celestial body, already fully exemplified, the following three Examples illustrate the Rule for deducing the True Bearing from the True Az. and Az. Diff.

Ex. 2.—Suppose the True Az. N 125° E and the Az. Diff. 87° to *right.*

Then, True Az. N 125° E
Diff. Az. 87 R. and therefore in *same* sense.
212 greater than 180.
T. Bear. N 148 W with the meridional reference changed from E to W, according to the 2d alternative of the First Case.

Ex. 3.—Suppose the True Az. N 76° W and the Az. Diff. 53° to *right.*

Then, True Az. N 76° W
53 R. in the *opposite* sense and *less* than True Az.
T. Bear. N 23 W

Ex. 4.—Suppose the True Az. N 61° E and Az. Diff. 77° to *left.*

Then, True Az. N 61° E
77 L. in the *opposite* sense and *greater* than True Az.
T. Bear. N 16 W

80. By an Azimuth of the Vertical Circle.—A convenient and simple means, which, with care in the observation, may be employed with the requisite precision, is to note the Time when the Sun or some other celestial body crosses the Vertical Circle of the object, above it, and find the True Azimuth of the body, which will be that of the terrestrial object.

a) **Rule : To take the Observation.**—Be ready with a plumb-line, so held as to cover the point of observation on the object, a few moments in advance of its expected transit by a recognized celestial body; also, with an assistant to note the time; proceeding as follows:

1. *If the Body be the Sun or the Full Moon*, note the Times, with a watch, of the first and second contact, or the instants when the inner limb

touches the plumb-line and the outer limb leaves it, and take the Mean of the two Times as the time of crossing by the centre of the body.

2. *If the Body be a Planet or Star,* note the Time at the instant the body crosses the plumb-line.

b) **Rule: To find the True Bearing of the Object.**—By the method of Time-Azimuths (19) find the True Azimuth of the celestial body for the Time at which it crosses the Vertical Circle of the object, and the result will be the required True Bearing.

81. Examples of Finding the True Bearing by an Azimuth of the Vertical Circle.

Ex. 1.—1870, July 23: At anchor, in New York Bay, in Lat. 40° 27′.6 N, Long. 74° 1′.5 W, at $6^h\ 16^m\ 56^s$ Loc. Ap. Time, P. M., the Sun's centre crossed the Vertical Circle above the Red Bank Light: Required, the True Bearing of the Light.

Loc. Ap. T.	23^d	6^h	16^m	56^s	☉'s Dec.	N 20°	5′.1	− 0′.5	H. A. W.
Long.	+	4	56	6	Redⁿ for $11^h.2$	—	5.6	5.5	$6^h\ 16^m\ 56^s$
Gr. date July	23	11	13	2	Red. Dec.	19	59.5		
		11.2			Pol. Dist.	70	0.5		

Pol. Dist.	70° 0′.5					
Co-Lat.	49 32.4					
Diff.	20 28.1					
½ Diff.	10 14	sin	9.2496	cos	9.9930	
½ Sum	59 46	cosec	0.0635	sec	0.2981	
½ H. A.	$3^h\ 8^m\ 28^s$	cot	9.9679	cot	9.9679	
		tan	9.2810	tan	0.2590	
T. BEAR. N 71° 58′ W:		**X**	10° 49′	**Y**	61° 9′	

82. Remarks relative to Finding the True Bearing of the Object.—The first method of finding the True Bearing presents the advantage of requiring no observations of Data; so that, if the Geographical Positions of the object and station are reliably known, this method is simple and convenient. Still, it should not be relied on implicitly for precision of result. The small Polar Angle (Diff. Longitudes) and correspondingly small Distance Arc are unfavorable conditions (60, *b*); but, on the other hand, the difference between the two Latitudes is always so small, that the Position-Angle of the object never differs much from 90°, which is a favorable condition (60, *b*). Consequently, Errors of the Data do not greatly influence the result. Thus, if the two Latitudes and the Difference of Longitudes may be depended on within one minute of arc, the True Bearing may generally be depended on at least within two-tenths of a degree.

The second method, though attended with greater labor of observation and computation, is rather more reliable than the first in precision of result. Thus, if each of the Data can be depended on within one minute of arc, the True Azimuth of the celestial body and the Azimuth-Difference between the body and object, may in general be depended on, each to the nearest tenth of a degree (63); so that the True Bearing of the object should be depended on within one-tenth of a degree. But even this precision, not very close, can only be assured of, in observations from the deck of a ship, with favorable circumstances and special care in the observations. The terrestrial object must have a well-defined point of observation, which may always be seized with certainty whenever referred to.[1]

The third method, so far as the True Azimuth of the Vertical Circle is concerned, should also be depended on to the nearest tenth of a degree (63). The Error of Observation, in noting the time when the centre of the celestial body crosses the plumb-line, will be different according to circumstances and the care of the observer. Its effect should not, however, exceed the proper Error of Azimuth; so that, on the whole, the True Bearing of the object should be depended on within one-tenth of a degree.

B. Method by Allignments.

83. Fundamental Idea.—From the outer approaches to almost every harbor or roadstead of importance, certain pairs of prominent objects may be sighted, such as two light-houses, two towers, etc., whose *Allignments*, or *Lines of True Bearing*, have been determined and laid down on the published charts and plans of these harbors for the convenience of Navigators.

These Allignments, among their different uses, furnish convenient means for finding the Compass-Error, whenever steaming or sailing across them. The difference between the observed Compass-Bearing of the Allignment and its True Bearing per chart is the Compass-Error.

84. Process of Finding Serial Compass-Errors.—The use of Allignments for this purpose is very simple. It is only necessary to observe the Compass-Bearing of the Allignment as the compass comes into the line, noting at the same time the Heading of the ship with the same compass.

Allignments are sometimes employed in finding Serial Compass-Errors, the operations being conducted in the following manner:

Everything being ready, and the observers at their stations, head the ship for a slow run if under sail, or bring the ship by any convenient evolution, if under steam, across the Allignment; steady the ship; and, at the precise moment when the observer at the Standard Compass gets both objects in his line of sight, note the bearing of the Allignment; note also the ship's Head by the Standard and Steering Compasses, and note the Angle of Heel by clinometer.

Proceed in the same manner, upon a second tack under sail or with a similar evolution under steam, so as to place the ship again across the Allignment, changing the Heading by the desired amount; and, again

[1] It will be noticed that this method is supposed in the text to be used only in finding the True Bearing of a terrestrial object, for observations of *Serial* Compass-Errors, at a fixed station. The "Astronomical Bearing" is commonly given in the books on Navigation as a method of finding the "Variation of the Compass," or Compass-Error; but it is difficult to conceive of a case in which the Navigator need ever resort to so cumbrous means of doing what would be better done by a small part of the process.

steadying, note the Bearing, the Heading, and Angle of Heel as before.

Continue the operation by a succession of sailing-tacks or steam-evolutions, crossing the Allignment each time under a different Heading, and making the corresponding observations, until a sufficient number shall have been obtained.

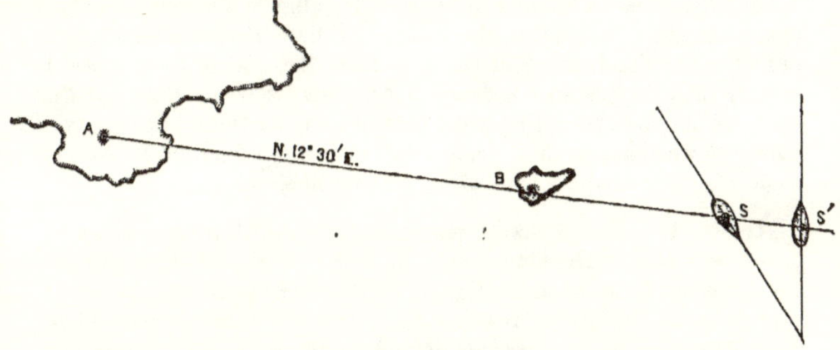

85. Examples of the Method by Allignments.

Ex. 1.—Harbor of Toulon:[1] By Compass-Bearings of an Allignment of Cape Brun and Fort Faron, made the following observations for Compass-Error:

True Bearing of Allignment N 12° 30′ W.

Distance between objects 2.2 N. miles.

Distance (average) of the ship from the outer object—not stated.

Ship's Head Stand. Comp.	Bearing of Allignment.		Compass-Error.
	Stand. Comp.	True.	
°	° ′	° ′	° ′
N 6 E	N 0 15 W	N 12 30 W	12 15 W
N 35 E	N 15 30 W	"	3 0 E
N 65 E	N 20 0 W	"	7 30 E
S 60 E	N 8 30 W	"	4 0 W
S 50 E	N 6 0 W	"	6 30 W
S 23 E	N 2 45 E	"	15 15 W
S 24 W	N 14 15 E	"	26 45 W
S 62 W	N 20 45 E	"	33 15 W
N 85 W	N 26 30 E	"	39 0 W
N 70 W	N 26 45 E	"	39 15 W
N 20 W	N 14 0 E	"	26 30 W

The order in which the observations are set down is not necessarily that in which they were made. It is obvious that the Headings are not well distributed round the compass-circle; but this is not always possible, when the observations are made by tacking across the Allignment under sail. But even in this case it will be possible to obtain a tolerable Table of Errors in the manner to be explained at a later stage.

[1] This Example is from *Traité de Déviation et de Régulation des Compas*, p. 62: par E. Giquel, Paris, 1868.

The observations are said to have been made on board the *Floride*, a sailing-ship, on a succession of tacks across the Allignment.

86. Dependence to be placed on Results.—There are two sources of Error in the Method by Allignments:

First, unless the recorded True Bearing of the Allignment has been determined by geodetical means, it is liable to be inaccurate; it may be but a few minutes, though it is quite possible to be several tenths of a degree, in Error.

Secondly, there is a liability to Errors of Parallax in observing the Compass-Bearings. In general, the liability to these Errors is increased in proportion as the distance of the ship from the first or outer object is greater than the distance between the objects. Serious Errors of this kind can only be avoided by great care in bringing the ship to a *perfect* "*steady*," when across the line, and in getting the Bearing at the moment when the compass is precisely on that line.

Remark.—Except as a convenient means of testing the compasses on a certain Heading, when running across an Allignment, this method is not likely to be much used, in preference to the other methods. And it should hardly be resorted to in preference to the method by Solar Azimuths, on any occasion of finding Serial Compass-Errors.

C. Method by Reciprocal Bearings.

87. Preliminary Explanations.—The Method by Reciprocal Bearings consists in the use of two instruments, with which *Simultaneous Bearings* are taken, each of the other; the Standard Compass on board being used for the Bearings of a station on shore, at which the second

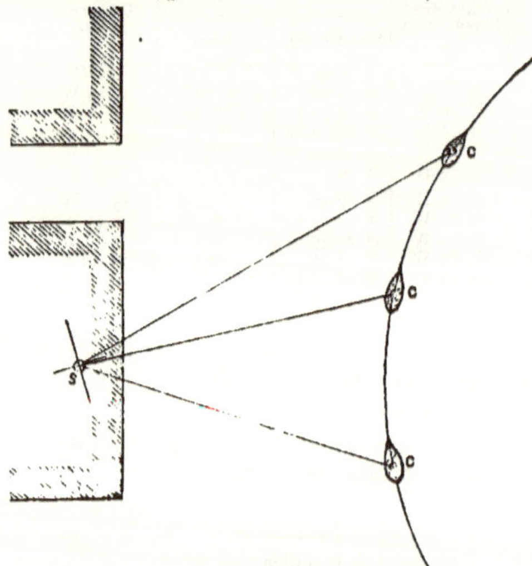

instrument is used for the corresponding Bearings of the compass-station on board.

This method differs in an important particular from the Method by Bearings of a Distant Object: There is obviously no necessity for a fixed station, round which the ship is to be swung. Each pair of Reciprocal Bearings by a direct comparison furnishes the Compass-Error for a certain Heading of the ship, *without reference to the amount by which the ship changes its position from one observation to another*, subject only to the condition, that the distance between the ship and shore does not exceed the limits of distinct vision of the signal to be sighted from each station. Thus, a steamship may steam round a circle, or by other convenient evolutions obtain the desired Headings (see figure); a sailing-ship may make a succession of tacks for the same purpose; or either, while riding at anchor, may swing to the wind and tide, and whenever expedient be pulled round either by warps or by a steam-tug.

It is not necessary to restrict the observations on shore to the use of a single station; it being entirely admissible to change the instrument from one position to another, subject to the condition above mentioned, whenever it may be expedient, in order to avoid obstructions in the line of sight, such as the masts, smoke-funnels, etc., on board.

88. Two Distinct Cases of Reciprocal Bearings.—There will be two distinct Cases, according to the nature of the instrument used in the shore-observations. This may be—

1. *An Azimuth-Compass* similar to the Standard Compass on board, or a Surveyor's Compass adapted to observations on land, with either of which *Magnetic Bearings* of the station on board may be taken, free from Deviation, but affected by Variation; or,

2. *A Theodolite* or *Dumb-Compass*, with which *True Bearings* may be taken, free from both Deviation and Variation.

In the First Case, the difference between any two Simultaneous Bearings is the Deviation of the compass on board.

In the Second Case, there are two modifications, according as the Bearings or Angles are measured from the *True Meridian*, or from *any Arbitrary Line*, passing through the station. When measured from the True Meridian, the difference between any pair of Simultaneous Bearings is the Total Error of the compass on board. When measured from any Arbitrary Line, the Differences of Simultaneous Bearings are neither Total Errors nor Deviations, but quantities which may be reduced either to Deviations or to Total Errors, as may be desired.

89. Essential Requisites of the Method under the First Case.—The ordinary procedure is to use an Azimuth-Compass for the shore-observations, which is furnished with a strong tripod fitted with a fork to receive the gimbal-ring of the compass. An air-compass is not only sufficient, but rather more portable than a liquid compass for this purpose. But, although less nautical, a good surveyor's compass is preferable to either for the shore-observations, as is readily seen in practice, and it is much less expensive as an extra instrument.

There are two requisites which must receive strict attention:

First, in selecting stations on shore which are known or ascertained to be entirely free from the influence of local magnetism, as due to masses of iron or other magnetic bodies, whether visible or concealed from view.

Secondly, in comparing the shore-compass with the standard used on board, so as to determine what differences, if any, exist between the readings of the two compasses on the same bearing.

These necessary preliminary tests and comparisons being carefully made, the shore-compass will be ready for use.

90. Essential Requisites of the Method under the Second Case.—With this method, unlike the preceding, there is no question of local disturbance. Moreover, from the nature of the instrument, whether Theodolite or Dumb-Compass, it may be relied on to the nearest tenth of a degree when in proper adjustment; so that there is no comparison required.

The stations may be selected at points on shore with reference solely to their most convenient occupation, whether upon the docks or elsewhere.

As already mentioned, the bearings of the compass-station on board may be measured from the True Meridian, or from any Arbitrary Line, passing through the station of the instrument.

a) **The Angles Measured from the True Meridian.**—In this case the graduated limb of the instrument is clamped with its zero upon the True Meridian. Hence, the True Meridian must be known in advance, and the instrument set upon it whenever required; or it must be found, for a given occasion, at the station of the instrument. Either is entirely practicable. At navy-yards, as well as in harbors and roadsteads generally, convenient Meridian-Lines may be established for this purpose, with permanent marks for reference, with suitable station-centres permanently marked upon the flagging or upon stones set in the ground; or, on any given occasion, the Meridian may be found with the requisite precision by means of a computed Solar Azimuth for a particular instant of time, and then laid down with the instrument to be used in the observations.

b) **The Angles Measured from any Arbitrary Line.**—For this it is only necessary to clamp the graduated limb, without regard to the zero,[1] and during the observations to direct the line of sight to the compass-station on board, when the readings obtained will be True Angles from the Arbitrary Line supposed to pass through the zero of the graduation. Moreover, it will be sufficient, whenever the station on shore is changed during the progress of the observations, to keep the limb clamped and continue the Angles as before. But, since

[1] It will be convenient, though not essential, to clamp so that the zero shall fall outside of the field in which the angles are to be observed.

the bearings on shore are taken without regard to any known line of reference, while the position of the ship and that of the compass-station on board are continually changing, it will be necessary to reduce the observations on board, in the manner to be explained, to what they would have been if they had been made at a fixed station and in an unchangeable direction.

91. Preparations for Observations by this Method.— All observations by this method must be directed from the ship; and, preparatory to undertaking them, proper signals should be arranged for display on board to guide the observer on shore. The following signals should, at the least, be provided for:

1. Prepare to observe!
2. Observe and register!
3. Observation is satisfactory!
4. Prepare to repeat the observation!
5. Pack the instrument and return on board!

Both observers should be prepared to note the Time of each observation, as a check against mistakes of comparison; their watches being compared before and after the set of observations. It is essential that the two observations of each pair be made simultaneously. The instrument itself at each station may be sighted as the object to be observed; but it is better to erect a more conspicuous and more nicely defined signal directly above each instrument.[1]

92. Process of Conducting Reciprocal Observations.—All things being ready, and the observers at their respective stations, bring the ship carefully upon the desired Heading, and, while being duly stopped and steadied, make the first signal; then, when ready to observe, make the second signal, upon which, at the instant, the observer at each instrument, on board and on shore, will note his Bearing of the other, and the Time by watch. Also, at the same moment, note the Ship's Head by the Standard Compass, and by each of the Steering-Compasses. Note, also, the Angle of Heel. All being completed, and the shore-observation, as posted up, apparently satisfactory, make the third signal.

Proceed, by bringing the ship upon a different Heading, making and recording the observations in a similar manner; and so on, round the compass-circle, or until the requisite observations shall have been made for a sufficient number of different Headings.

As in other cases, observations for Headings on the regular equidistant points by compass are preferable, but they are not essential.

---

[1] It is advisable, as a convenient precaution, for the observer on shore to chalk each observation upon a blackboard, so that it may be read (using a glass if necessary) by the observer on board; by which means, if there should be any apparent inconsistency, the observation may at once be repeated, and the necessity thereby avoided for again swinging the ship.

93. Reduction of Reciprocal Observations.—There are three Cases to be considered, according to the nature of the shore-observations.

a) Magnetic Observations on Shore.—In this Case the Difference between the corresponding Ship and Shore Bearings is the *Compass-Deviation*, which will be marked *E* or *W*, according as the observation on board falls to the *Left* or *Right* of that on shore.

b) Angles Measured from the True Meridian on Shore.—Here the Difference between Simultaneous Bearings is the *Compass-Error*, which is marked *E* or *W*, according as the observation on board falls to the *Left* or *Right* of that on shore.

c) Angles Measured from any Arbitrary Line on Shore.—First, note the *least*[1] among the Shore Angles, and regard it as the bearing of the *Zero-Line*, or line of reference; then, compare with this all the other Angles, setting down the corresponding Differences in a column of *Reductions for Shore-Instrument*, and marking them *R* or *L*, according as the Zero-Line falls to the *Right* or *Left* of the Angles compared with it.

Next, apply these reductions to the corresponding Bearings from the compass on board—to the *Right* or *Left*, according as they are marked *R* or *L;* which call the *Reduced Bearings by the Standard Compass.* There will now be two Cases, according as the observations are made on Equidistant Headings or at Irregular Intervals.

First: Observations on Equidistant Headings.—Take the Mean of the Reduced Bearings, whether 32, 16, or 8, and this will be the *Magnetic Bearing* of the station on shore; then, the Differences between this and the other actual Reduced Bearings will be the Deviations, to be marked *E* or *W*, according as the latter Bearings fall to the *Left* or *Right* of the Mean Bearing.

Secondly: Observations at Irregular Intervals.—Find the Reduced Bearings by the Standard Compass, as in the previous case; thence, proceed as follows:

Compare the Reduced Bearings with that of the zero-line, marking the Difference *E* or *W*, according as the former fall to the *Left* or *Right* of the zero-line.

With these Differences as Ordinates, and the Headings as Distances, construct a curve, in the manner to be explained hereafter, from which deduce the *Mean Difference* on a series of Equidistant Headings; set off this Difference according to its name, and draw a parallel to the Line of Distances; then, the Ordinates to the curve with reference to this new line of distances, for whatever Headings taken off, will be the Compass-Deviations corresponding to those Headings.

[1] Any other Shore-Angle may be chosen as that of the zero-line, as may be deemed most convenient. The least makes the Differences or Reductions take the same name; all R or all L.

94. Examples of the Method by Reciprocal Bearings.

Ex. 1.—1868, June 18: At Erie, on Lake Erie, in Lat. 42° N, Long. 80° W, U. S. Ship Michigan (iron-built paddle-wheel steamer). Swung for a set of Compass-Deviations, by Reciprocal Bearings.

Observations. **Reductions.**

Time.	Ship's Head by Standard Compass.	Simultaneous Bearings.		Deviation of the Standard Compass.
		Standard Compass on Board.	Azimuth-Compass on Shore.	
h m		°	°	°
11 13	North.	S 60.3 E	N 59.0 W	1.3 E
15	N by E	56.7	59.0	2.3 W
27	NNE	53.0	59.0	6.0
33	NE by N	48.7	59.0	10.3
12 8	NE	42.8	59.5	16.7
11	NE by E	42.0	59.5	17.5
14	ENE	41.5	60.0	18.5
17	E by N	38.0	60.0	22.0 W
12 19	East.	S 35.3 E	N 60.5	25.2 W
22	E by S	37.2	60.5	23.3
25	ESE	36.5	61.0	24.5
33	SE by E	37.2	61.0	23.8
45	SE	40.7	60.5	19.8
51	SE by S	40.5	60.0	19.5
54	SSE	49.3	60.0	10.7
58	S by E	53.7	60.0	6.3 W
1 2	South.	S 57.3 E	N 60.0 W	2.7 W
6	S by W	64.3	60.0	4.3 E
10	SSW	70.0	60.0	10.0
14	SW by S	76.0	60.0	16.0
17	SW	79.7	59.5	20.2
22	SW by W	83.0	59.0	24.0
27	WSW	85.0	58.5	26.5
36	W by S	86.7	58.0	28.7 E
1 39	West.	S 86.0 E	N 57.5 W	28.5 E
51	W by N	85.7	57.0	28.7
54	WNW	83.0	57.0	26.0
2 4	NW by W	82.7	56.5	26.2
7	NW	78.0	56.5	21.5
11	NW by N	75.3	57.0	18.3
15	NNW	70.0	57.5	12.5
19	N by W	67.8	58.0	9.8 E

Explanations.—The shore-instrument in this case being an Azimuth-Compass, the Bearings are Magnetic, and the Differences of Simultaneous Bearings are Deviations of the Standard Compass on board.

There are certain anomalies in the results, which become more obvious by a Graphical Construction, and at the same time admit of being corrected and the results reduced to more probable values.

The Standard Compass was placed on top of pilot-house on hurricane-deck, 28 feet above spar-deck.

Ex. 2.—1868, June 18: At Erie, on Lake Erie, in Lat. 42° N, Long. 80° W, U. S. Ship Michigan: The Azimuth-Compass used on shore in Ex. 1 supposed to have been replaced by a Dumb-Compass, and the Angles measured from an Arbitrary Line.

Observations.			Reductions.		
Ship's Head by Standard Compass.	Simultaneous Bearings.		Reductions to Zero-Line of Shore-Angles.	Reduced Bearings by Standard Compass.	Deviations of the Standard Compass.
	Standard Compass on Board.	Dumb-Compass on Shore.			
North.	S 60°.3 E	39°.0	2°.5 R	S 57°.8 E	0°.4 W
N by E	56.7	39.0	2.5	54.2	4.0
NNE	53.0	39.0	2.5	50.5	7.7
NE by N	48.7	39.0	2.5	46.2	12.0
NE	42.8	39.5	3.0	39.8	18.4
NE by E	42.0	39.5	3.0	39.0	19.2
ENE	41.5	40.0	3.5	38.0	20.2
E by N	38.0	40.0	3.5	34.5	23.7 W
East.	S 35.3 E	40.5	4.0 R	S 31.3 E	26.9 W
E by S	37.2	40.5	4.0	33.2	25.0
ESE	36.5	41.0	4.5	32.0	26.2
SE by E	37.2	41.0	4.5	32.7	25.5
SE	40.7	40.5	4.0	36.7	21.5
SE by S	40.5	40.0	3.5	37.0	21.2
SSE	49.3	40.0	3.5	45.8	12.4
S by E	53.7	40.0	3.5	50.2	8.0 W
South.	S 57.3 E	40.0	3.5 R	S 53.8 E	4.4 W
S by W	64.3	40.0	3.5	60.8	2.6 E
SSW	70.0	40.0	3.5	66.5	8.3
SW by S	76.0	40.0	3.5	72.5	14.3
SW	79.7	39.5	3.0	76.7	18.5
SW by W	83.0	39.0	2.5	80.5	22.3
WSW	85.0	38.5	2.0	83.0	24.8
W by S	86.7	38.0	1.5	85.2	27.0 E
West.	S 86.0 E	37.5	1.0 R	S 85.0 E	26.8 E
W by N	85.7	37.0	0.5	85.2	27.0
WNW	83.0	37.0	0.5	82.5	24.3
NW by W	82.7	36.5	0.0	82.7	24.5
NW	78.0	*36.5	0.0	78.0	19.8
NW by N	75.3	37.0	0.5	74.8	16.6
NNW	70.0	37.5	1.0	69.0	10.8
N by W	67.8	38.0	1.5	66.3	8.1 E
				Mean S 58°.2 E	

Explanations.—The Least Angle of the shore-observations is *36°.5, which is taken as that of the Zero-Line. Comparing this with all the other Shore-Angles, we get the Reductions in Col. I. These are all marked R, because the direction of the Zero-Line falls to the Right of all the other Angles.

Next, these Reductions are applied to the Right of the corresponding Bearings by the Standard Compass, and we get Col. II; the Mean of which, or S 58°.2 E, is the Magnetic Bearing of the shore-station.

Finally, comparing the Reduced Bearings of Col. II with the Mean, we get the Deviations in Col. III.

Ex. 3.—1868, June 18 : At Erie, on Lake Erie, in Lat. 42° N, Long. 80° W, U. S. Ship Michigan: The ship swung upon Irregular Headings, and the Angles on shore still measured from an Arbitrary Line with a Theodolite.

Observations. **Reductions.**

Ship's Head by Standard Compass.	Simultaneous Bearings.		Reductions to Zero-Line of Shore-Angles.	Reduced Bearings by Standard Compass.	Differences of the Standard Compass.
	Standard Compass on Board.	Theodolite on Shore.			
N 10° E	S 57°.3 E	43°.2	1°.7 R	S 55°.6 E	14°.1 E
22	53.5	44.8	3.3	50.2	8.7
40	45.7	42.8	1.3	44.4	2.9 E
53	42.4	43.9	2.4	40.0	1.5 W
71	41.2	46.0	4.5	36.7	4.8
88	36.9	45.3	3.8	33.1	8.4
S 73 E	S 36.1 E	43.9	2.4	33.7	7.8
56	37.0	44.0	2.5	34.5	7.0
40	40.3	42.6	1.1	39.2	2.3 W
27	47.2	45.1	3.6	43.6	2.1 E
10	54.7	44.8	3.3	51.4	9.9
S 5 W	S 61.0 E	42.8	1.3	59.7	18.2 E
22	69.8	42.8	1.3	68.5	27.0
36	75.3	42.5	1.0	74.3	32.8
54	82.1	43.9	2.4	79.7	38.2
65	84.5	43.1	1.6	82.9	41.4
78	86.3	42.2	0.7	85.6	44.1
89	85.9	*41.5	0.0	85.9	44.4
N 75 W	S 85.7 E	41.7	0.2	85.5	44.0 E
62	82.8	41.7	0.2	82.6	41.1
50	80.2	42.3	0.8	79.4	37.9
36	76.6	42.4	0.9	75.7	34.2
18	68.5	42.1	0.6	67.9	26.4
4	65.1	45.8	4.3 R	60.8	19.3 E

Explanations.—Having found the Reduced Bearings of Col. II, as in the preceding Example, we next compare these with the Angle of the Zero-Line (*41°.5) and get the Differences in Col. III.

95. Dependence to be placed on Results.—With the use of an Azimuth-Compass at the shore-station, there is always considerable uncertainty relative to the Magnetic Meridian, from which the Bearings are supposed to be measured, unless the requisite means are employed to have a strict comparison of the two compasses made on shore. Not only is it necessary to detect the possible influence of Local Magnetism, but to note the actual differences of the shore Compass-Readings on different parts of the compass-card, if we would be at all sure of our results. With these comparisons made, and the ascertained Errors, if any, properly applied as corrections, the shore-observations should be depended on.

With the use of a Theodolite or Dumb-Compass, on the other hand, a more satisfactory precision may be attained. It is not difficult for the Navigator, with a reliable Geographical Position and a good Local Time, to determine his True Meridian on shore to the nearest minute; and this may be established by Meridian-Marks, and worked from to a corresponding precision, with a Theodolite reading to minutes in proper adjustment. Even with a Dumb-Compass, reading only to tenths of degrees, the Bearings should be depended on to the nearest tenth of a degree.

There will not be the same degree of precision, if, instead of working from the True Meridian, the Shore-Angles are measured from an arbitrary line. In this case a certain constant Error will be introduced and merged in the Errors of Compass Adjustment and Observation, in consequence of the necessity of employing a Mean Bearing or Difference as deduced from the results of the observations. The Error from this source will be less or greater according to the greater or less care and nicety observed in conducting the operations. In general, it will rarely be so much as a degree, including the Errors of Adjustment and Observation; and, since it affects all the results alike, it may commonly be disregarded.

96. To find the True Meridian.—There are various modes of procedure for finding the True Meridian. It will, however, be quite sufficient, for the present purpose, to make use of means to which the Navigator is well accustomed, namely: That of obtaining the True Azimuth of the Sun, or other celestial object, at a particular moment of Local Time; then, of setting off the Azimuth at the designated moment, upon a Theodolite or Dumb-Compass. The whole process may be conducted as follows:

a) *Compute in advance*, for a designated Local Time, the True Azimuth of the Sun or other celestial body (19); and *add* or *subtract* the Semi-Diameter, according as the Azimuth is *greater* or *less* than 90°. The resulting Azimuth will be that of the *inner*[1] limb, if the body have a disk (Sun or Moon).

b) Having selected a convenient observing-station, set the Theodolite or Dumb-Compass at the chosen point; then turn off the ascertained

[1] That towards the Meridian.

True Azimuth from the line of zeros, and carefully clamp the alidade (telescope or sight-vanes as the case may be), and level the instrument for observation.

c) As the designated Time approaches for which the True Az. is found, point the line of sight a few minutes in advance to the inner limb of the celestial body, turning the whole instrument upon its spindle, and keeping upon the observed point of contact, by following the motion of the body, till the precise moment of time is reached; then make fast the lower or spindle clamp.

d) Unclamp the line of sight, turn to zero, and again clamp; it will now be in the True Meridian. Set up a Meridian-Mark, in the direction of the line of sight, fifty to a hundred yards in advance. Unclamp and turn[1] the line of sight 180°; unclamp, and then set up another Meridian-Mark in the opposite direction. Finally, mark the station in a permanent manner on the ground below the centre of the instrument, and it will be ready for use.

97. Remark: To set the Instrument in a True Meridian already established.—If the True Meridian be already established, proceed as follows to place the instrument: Set the instrument over the station (*d*) with a centre-plumb, and level it; then clamp the alidade to zero, and direct the line of sight to one of the permanent Meridian-Marks (*d*), turning the whole instrument upon the spindle, and, when carefully bisected, make fast the lower or spindle clamp. The instrument will be ready for use.

98. Example of Finding the True Meridian of a Shore-Station.

Ex. 1.—1872, February 20: Navy-Yard Dock, Washington, in Lat. 38° 52′.4 N, Long. 76° 59′.6 W. It is required to find the True Meridian from a True Azimuth of the Sun at $4^h.0$ P. M. Loc. A. T.: Watch *fast* on Loc. M. T. 1^m 14^s.

Loc. A. T.	4^h 0^m	☉'s Dec.	S 11° 2′.9	−54″	Eq. of T.	+ 14^m $1^s.7$	−$0^s.27$
Long.	+ 5 8	Red^n for $9^h.1$	— 8.2	486	Red^n for $9^h.1$	— 2.5	2.43
Gr. date	20 9 8	Red. Dec.	10 54.7	5	Red. Eq. T.	13 59.2	3
or,	$9^h.1$	Pol. Dist.	100 54.7			+ to A. T.	

Eq. of T.	+ 0^h 13^m 59^s				
Loc. M. T.	4 13 59	Pol. Dist.	100° 54′.7		
Er. of W. fast	+ 1 14	Co-Lat.	51 7.6		
T. by W.	4 15 13	Diff.	49 47.1		
		½ Diff.	24 53.5	sin 9.6242	cos 9.9577
		½ Sum	76 1.1	cosec 0.0131	sec 0.6168
		½ H. A.	2^h 0^m	cot 0.2386	cot 0.2386
				tan 9.8759	tan 0.8131
	True Az.	N 118° 10′ W		X 36° 55′	Y 81° 15′
	☉'s Semi-D.	+ 16			
	True Az.	N 118 26 W	Inner Limb		
	or,	S 61 34 W			

A few minutes before 4^h 15^m 13^s by *Watch*, place the theodolite firmly in position at the station chosen for the shore-observations, and level it.

[1] This is unnecessary with a theodolite whose telescope may be revolved—transit-like.

Next, turn off the Angle 61° 34′ from 0, and clamp the limb, leaving the lower or spindle clamp free.

Now, turning the whole instrument upon the spindle, pointing to the Sun, and bringing the vertical wire of the telescope into contact with its inner limb, follow its motion, carefully preserving contact, until the moment $4^h\ 15^m\ 43^s$ arrives, as shown by watch; then make fast the lower clamp.

Unclamp the limb, and turn the telescope back to 0, when it will be in the True Meridian. Set up a Meridian-Mark in the direction of the line of sight and mark the centre of the instrument, as shown by the plumb, on the ground below.[1]

The instrument is ready for the shore-observations, the lower clamp remaining all the time fixed.

Remark.—We might proceed in the direct manner, by first making the observation to a noted time by watch, subsequently computing the True Azimuth, and, finally, turning it off on the theodolite. The only objection to this mode of procedure, is the necessity of allowing the instrument to stand and the danger of its disturbance while making the computation.

D. Relative Advantages of the Several Methods of Finding Serial Compass-Errors.

We shall briefly sum up the relative advantages of the principal Methods for finding Serial Compass-Errors.

99. Methods by Celestial Azimuths.—The observations by these methods, and preferably by Time-Azimuths, are certainly the most convenient. They are all made on board ship. The ship may be at her anchorage, or standing off outside, or at sea; and the different Headings, on which the observations are made, may be had, either by swinging about her anchor, by steaming round, or by tacking under sail.

When near the land, these methods are susceptible of considerable accuracy. The True Azimuths may be depended on within ± 3′ round the entire compass-circle, the Data being reliably known and the conditions of favorable results being duly satisfied (60). The Compass-Azimuths are taken under the most favorable circumstances for precision of results.

The only drawback to this method, in comparison with the others, while superior in every particular besides, is the supposed labor of obtaining the series of True Azimuths. And yet, a set of thirty-two Azimuths may be had, with the aid of the Tables here given, in a half-hour or less.[2]

---

[1] If a dumb-compass instead of a theodolite had been used, we should have turned off instead 61°.6 and clamped the alidade, leaving the spindle free; otherwise, the description of the text is equally applicable to this instrument, only substituting "alidade" for "limb," and "sight-vanes" for "telescope."

[2] Navigators not unfrequently devote the best part of a day, sometimes two of them, at a "station" to the laborious and disagreeable duty of "swinging ship" for observations of a distant object, without always obtaining results which they can regard as

At sea, of course none but Celestial Azimuths are available for Compass-Error; and the small labor of getting a set wholly or partially round the compass by the Method of Time-Azimuths, should certainly leave no Navigator of a ship, whenever overtaken by prolonged thick weather, without *recent* determinations of the Errors on the Compass-Courses likely to be sailed at such a time.

100. Method by Direct Bearings.—The Method by Direct Bearings has also the convenience of requiring no observer on shore, but it has the disadvantage of requiring a particular station, commonly at a considerable distance from the usual anchorage, and of being attended by a large expenditure of time, labor, and patience in warping the ship about, especially if a large one. It has, moreover, the disadvantage of being liable not only to the Constant Error, whatever that may be, in getting the True Bearing of the object, but also to inaccuracies in the Compass-Bearings, from the more serious Errors of Parallax; errors which are always variable and occasionally uncertain, and which are frequently much too large to be admitted, with any regard to precision of results.[1]

101. Method by Reciprocal Bearings.—The use of this method is attended with the disadvantage of requiring observers on shore in addition to those on board. But it admits of being employed at the ordinary anchorage, either by swinging at an anchor, or by steaming about when the water-way permits. Neither Parallax nor any other consideration need interfere with entire freedom in the movements of the ship, during the operations of placing her upon different Headings, except that of keeping the distance between the ship and station on shore within the limits of distinct vision.

With the use of an instrument for measuring the Bearings, either from the True Meridian or from any Arbitrary Line at the station on shore, not only is the choice of that station independent of all regard to the influence of Local Magnetism, but the Angles admit of

"entirely satisfactory;" which in fact, are quite too frequently utterly unreliable and valueless. Whereas by merely steaming about at their anchorage (not being too near any other ship), they might get a perfect set of observations of the Sun in two or three hours after sunrise or before sunset; and another half-hour or so would enable them to reduce their observations and obtain a Table of Compass-Deviations.

[1] See the interesting and suggestive description, by the late Dr. Scoresby (pp. 168–182 of *Journal of a Voyage to Australia, etc.*, London, 1859), of his arduous labors for more than a week at Melbourne, Australia, in determining Magnetic Bearings of distant objects and in swinging the noble iron ship *Royal Charter*. With an admitted Parallax of 0°.3 to 0°.4 on some of his Headings; with an apparent uncertainty of perhaps a whole degree in the Magnetic Bearings of his objects; with probably considerable errors in the Compass-Bearings from the manner in which they were taken; and with an immense amount of labor and anxiety on his part, aided by gangs of men, boats, kedges, and warps, he obtained a series, as was to be expected, of not very satisfactory results. And yet, with steam up on one of those days, and with two or three hours devoted to a series of Solar Azimuths, what superior results, and what a saving of labor, worry, and anxiety might have been realized!

being measured with greater precision. It is quite possible to have the True Meridian laid down on shore within a minute of arc; and the Angles may be measured with equal accuracy, using a theodolite for the purpose.

When the True Meridian has not been already laid down, the Angles may be measured from Arbitrary Lines; but, in this case, the Mean of the Reduced Compass-Bearings having to be used as the Magnetic Bearing of the assumed zero-line, the results may involve a greater Constant Error.

Otherwise, in working from the Magnetic Meridian on shore, this method is not only more restricted in the choice of a station, but is liable, without great care and a troublesome comparison on shore, to considerable Errors from Local Magnetism, and differences in Compass-Readings.

In conclusion, since one or the other of the two Methods by Celestial Azimuths and Reciprocal Bearings is sufficient for all probable circumstances, and since either of these Methods may be so conducted as to insure the requisite precision of results, there would seem to be little if any occasion for resort to the less accurate Method by Bearings of a Distant Object.

APPENDIX.

COMPASS-COMPARISONS.

102. Definition.—*The Comparison* of one compass with another is the Difference of their Readings, one being taken as *Standard* for Azimuths or Bearings of the same object. It is marked *E* or *W*, according as the Bearing by the Compared Compass falls to the *Left* or *Right* of the Bearing by the Standard, the eye being supposed at the centre of the latter's compass-card.

A distinction exists between the Comparison of Compasses *on board ship* and *on shore*, which will be separately considered.

A. Compass-Comparisons on board Ship.

103. Characteristics and Uses of Comparisons.—From what has already been said, as to the nature of the Compass-Error, it may be inferred that, whenever there are several compasses set up for use in different parts of the same ship, they may generally be expected to show different Readings on the *same* Heading of the ship, and each to vary for *different* Headings. This has been fully explained in the preceding Chapters.

A Compass-Comparison on board serves several useful purposes, of which the two following may be specially mentioned:

First, in converting a Course by Standard into an equivalent Course by Compared Compass; or, *vice versâ*.

Secondly, in finding the Error of a Compared Compass, whenever we have its Comparison with the Standard and the Error of the latter.

In practice, the ship's Head is the object observed in all Compass-Comparisons on board. For this there are two reasons:

First, because the Compass-Readings, and therefore the Differences between them, depend on the direction of the ship's Head; and,

Secondly, because the *Lubber-Line*, which represents the ship's Head for each compass, is the only object which can be either conveniently or accurately observed with the Steering and other Compasses, not furnished with the sight-vanes of an Azimuth-Circle.

104. To make a Compass-Comparison.—Accordingly, the only necessary provision for Compass-Comparisons on board is, to note the Headings of the ship by the different compasses for which comparisons are desired, whenever observations for Error are made with the Standard or Azimuth Compass (10).

The Rule for the Comparison is comprised in the preceding Definition.

105. Examples of Compass-Comparisons.

Ex. 1.—Stand. Compass	N 47° E	
Steering-Compass	N 41 E	
COMPARISON	6 E	
Ex. 2.—Stand. Compass	S 67° E	
Steering-Compass	S 59 E	
COMPARISON	8 W	
Ex. 3.—Stand. Compass	N W	
Steering-Compass	N N W ¾ W	
COMPARISON	1¼ pts. W	
Ex. 4.—Stand. Compass	S 11° E	
Steering-Compass	S 2 W	
COMPARISON	13 W	
Ex. 5.—Stand. Compass	N 89° W	
Steering-Compass	S 87 W	
COMPARISON	4 E	
Ex. 6.—Stand. Compass	N E by E	
Steering-Compass	E N E ⅓ E	
COMPARISON	1⅓ pts. W	

106. To convert a Given Course by Standard Compass into an Equivalent Course by a Compared Compass, and Reciprocally.—An important application of the Comparison of Compasses is found in the conversion of a Standard-Compass Course into an equivalent Compared-Compass Course. Thus, it commonly happens, in practice, that the Sailing-Courses, while given for the Standard Compass, must be set for the Helmsman on the Steering-Compass. This conversion of the given Course is made in the following manner:

Rule: Suppose the eye at the centre of the Standard Compass, looking along the line of the given Course or Heading; then apply all *East* Comparisons to the *left* hand, and all *West* Comparisons to the *right* hand.

For Reciprocal Conversions, apply the comparison to the Course by Compared Compass in the *contrary* manner, and the result will be the equivalent Course by Standard Compass.

107. Examples of Direct and Reciprocal Conversions.

Ex. 1.—The Course or Heading by Standard is NE, and the Comparison of Steering-Compass is 6° E: Required, the Course by Steering-Compass.

Course by Standard	N 45° E
Comparison of Steering-Comp.	6 E
Course by Steering-Compass	N 41 E

Ex. 2.—The Course by Steering-Compass is NNW, and its Comparison with the Standard is 11° W: Required, the Course by Standard.

Course by Steering-Compass	N 22°.5 W
Comparison of Steering-Comp.	11 .0 W
Course by Standard	N 33 .5 W

108. Rule: To find the Error or Deviation of a Compared Compass.—Having the *Comparison* of any compass with the Standard, and the *Error* or *Deviation* of the latter, the Error or Deviation of the Compared Compass is found as follows:

Take the *Sum* or *Difference* of the Comparison and Error, or Deviation, according as they have the *same* or *different* names; and the result will be the Error or Deviation of the Compared Compass, which mark with the name of the greater number.

109. Examples of Finding the Errors of Compared Compasses.

Ex. 1.—A Comparison of Steering-Compass is ¾ pt. W with the Standard, and the Error of the latter 1¾ pts. W: Required, the Error of the Steering-Compass.

Comparison of Steer. Comp.	¾ pt.	W
Error of Standard	1¾	W
Error of Steering-Comp.	2½	W

Ex. 2.—Comparison 10° W and Dev. of Standard 20° E: Required, the Error of the Compared Compass.

Comparison	10°	W
Dev. of Standard	20	E
Dev. of Compared Comp.	10	E

Ex. 3.—Comparison 7°.5 E, and Error of Standard 16°.2 E: Required, the Error of the Compared Compass.

Comparison	7°.5 E
Error of Standard	16 .2 E
Error of Compared Comp.	23 .7 E

Ex. 4.—Comparison 15°.5 E, and Error of Standard 9°.0 W: Required, the Error of the Compared Compass.

Comparison	15°.5 W
Error of Standard	9 .0 E
Error of Compared Comp.	6 .5 W

B. Compass-Comparisons on Shore.

110. Comparison on Shore: Detection of Local Magnetism.—It is frequently desirable to carry a compass on shore for Reciprocal Observations with the Standard on board, and for other purposes. In such a case, it will be necessary to compare the compasses, if any assurance of accuracy be desired, not only to obtain their *Constant Differences* but to find the *Errors due to Local Magnetism*,[1] if, indeed, either exist. For this purpose we may proceed in the following manner:

Rule: Take both compasses on shore. Place the Shore-Compass in the selected position, and the Standard Compass at a distance of 100 to 200 feet from it.[2]

Take the Bearing of each from the other, and note their respective Readings. Again, place the Standard Compass about the same distance off, and about eight points to one side of the former position, and note the respective Readings. Finally, place the Standard about the same distance off and about sixteen points from the first position, and note their Readings as before.

Now compare these Bearings, and it will be shown—

First, if the Bearings of each pair differ exactly 16 points, or 180°, there is neither Deviation from Local Magnetism nor disagreement of Reading from any cause;

Secondly, if the difference between the Readings be more or less than 180°, but sensibly *constant*, there is probably no Deviation from Local Magnetism, but only a difference of Readings in the compasses, which must be noted as a correction to be applied; and,

[1] Arising from detached masses of iron, in sight or concealed from view, such as anchors, guns, warping-posts, chains, etc.; or from magnetic iron-ore, trap or basaltic rock, etc.

[2] It will be convenient to have a *tripod* for the Standard Compass, to be moved about. The other compass may be set up in its box on a table, block, or post; upon anything of suitable height and *stability*.

Thirdly, if the difference of Readings is not sensibly the same, there is a *Deviation* from some local cause; in which case the position selected for the Compared Compass must be changed, in order to find, by another trial, if possible, a suitable position for a station that shall be free from Local Error. Selecting a second position, make a similar series of observations; and thus proceed till a satisfactory position be found, or the particular locality abandoned as altogether impracticable.

Remark.—The necessity for comparing compasses, under the circumstances supposed in this Article, as a preparation for the observation of Serial Compass-Errors, should, we think, very seldom occur in practice. As already indicated, it is far better, in the Method by Reciprocal Bearings, to employ for the shore-observations such an angular instrument as a Theodolite or Dumb-Compass, in which *any use of the Magnetic Needle or Card is dispensed with*; not only as being intrinsically a more reliable instrument, but as relieving from all anxiety and embarrassment relative to the possible influence of Local Magnetism. Otherwise, it may often be far better to make use of Solar Azimuths.

Compass Points and their Equivalents in Degrees and parts thereof.

Name of Point.	No.	Degree Equivalents to the nearest— Second.			Hundreth.	Tenth.	No.	Name of Point.
		°	′	″	°	°		
North—East or West.	**0**	0	0	0	0.00	0.0	**0**	**South—West or East.**
	1/8	1	24	22	1.40	1.4	1/8	
	1/4	2	48	45	2.81	2.8	1/4	
	3/8	4	13	7	4.22	4.2	3/8	
	1/2	5	37	30	5.63	5.6	1/2	
	5/8	7	1	52	7.03	7.0	5/8	
	3/4	8	26	15	8.44	8.4	3/4	
	7/8	9	50	37	9.84	9.8	7/8	
N. by E. or N. by W.	**1**	11	15	0	11.25	11.3	**1**	**S. by W. or S. by E.**
	1/8	12	39	22	12.66	12.7	1/8	
	1/4	14	3	45	14.06	14.1	1/4	
	3/8	15	28	7	15.47	15.5	3/8	
	1/2	16	52	30	16.88	16.9	1/2	
	5/8	18	16	52	18.28	18.3	5/8	
	3/4	19	41	15	19.69	19.7	3/4	
	7/8	21	5	37	21.09	21.1	7/8	
N.N.E. or N.N.W.	**2**	22	30	0	22.50	22.5	**2**	**S.S.W. or S.S.E.**
	1/8	23	54	22	23.90	23.9	1/8	
	1/4	25	18	45	25.31	25.3	1/4	
	3/8	26	43	7	26.72	26.7	3/8	
	1/2	28	7	30	28.13	28.1	1/2	
	5/8	29	31	52	29.53	29.5	5/8	
	3/4	30	56	15	30.94	30.9	3/4	
	7/8	32	20	37	32.34	32.3	7/8	
N.E. by N. or N.W. by N.	**3**	33	45	0	33.75	33.8	**3**	**S.W. by S. or S.E. by S.**
	1/8	35	9	22	35.16	35.2	1/8	
	1/4	36	33	45	36.56	36.6	1/4	
	3/8	37	58	7	37.97	38.0	3/8	
	1/2	39	22	50	39.38	39.4	1/2	
	5/8	40	46	52	40.78	40.8	5/8	
	3/4	42	11	15	42.19	42.2	3/4	
	7/8	43	35	37	43.59	43.6	7/8	
N.E. or N.W.	**4**	45	0	0	45.00	45.0	**4**	**S.W. or S.E.**
	1/8	46	24	22	46.40	46.4	1/8	
	1/4	47	48	45	47.81	47.8	1/4	
	3/8	49	13	7	49.22	49.2	3/8	
	1/2	50	37	30	50.63	50.6	1/2	
	5/8	52	1	52	52.03	52.0	5/8	
	3/4	53	26	15	53.44	53.4	3/4	
	7/8	54	50	37	54.84	54.8	7/8	
N.E. by E. or N.W. by W.	**5**	56	15	0	56.25	56.3	**5**	**S.W. by W or S.E. by E.**
	1/8	57	39	22	57.66	57.7	1/8	
	1/4	59	3	45	59.06	59.1	1/4	
	3/8	60	28	7	60.47	60.5	3/8	
	1/2	61	52	30	61.88	61.9	1/2	
	5/8	63	16	52	63.28	63.3	5/8	
	3/4	64	41	15	64.69	64.7	3/4	
	7/8	66	5	37	66.09	66.1	7/8	
E.N.E. or W.N.W.	**6**	67	30	0	67.50	67.5	**6**	**W.S.W. or E.S.E.**
	1/8	68	54	22	68.90	68.9	1/8	
	1/4	70	18	45	70.31	70.3	1/4	
	3/8	71	43	7	71.72	71.7	3/8	
	1/2	73	7	30	73.13	73.1	1/2	
	5/8	74	31	52	74.53	74.5	5/8	
	3/4	75	56	15	75.94	75.9	3/4	
	7/8	77	20	37	77.34	77.3	7/8	
E. by N. or W. by N.	**7**	78	45	0	78.75	78.8	**7**	**W. by S. or E. by S.**
	1/8	80	9	22	80.16	80.2	1/8	
	1/4	81	33	45	81.56	81.6	1/4	
	3/8	82	58	7	82.97	83.0	3/8	
	1/2	84	22	30	84.38	84.4	1/2	
	5/8	85	46	52	85.78	85.8	5/8	
	3/4	87	11	15	87.19	87.2	3/4	
	7/8	88	35	37	88.59	88.6	7/8	
East or West.	**8**	90	0	0	90.00	90.0	**8**	**West or East.**

Conversion of Arc into Time, and Reciprocally.

For Degrees of Arc.												For minutes.		For sec'ds.	
°	h. m.	°	h. m.	°	h. m.	°	h. m.	°	h. m.	°	h. m.	′	m. s.	″	s.
0	0 0	**60**	4 0	**120**	8 0	**180**	12 0	**240**	16 0	**300**	20 0	**0**	0 0	**0**	0'00
1	4	61	4	121	4	181	4	241	4	301	4	1	4	1	.07
2	8	62	8	122	8	182	8	242	8	302	8	2	8	2	.13
3	12	63	12	123	12	183	12	243	12	303	12	3	12	3	.20
4	16	64	16	124	16	184	16	244	16	304	16	4	16	4	.27
5	20	65	20	125	20	185	20	245	20	305	20	5	20	5	.33
6	24	66	24	126	24	186	24	246	24	306	24	6	24	6	.40
7	28	67	28	127	28	187	28	247	28	307	28	7	28	7	.47
8	32	68	32	128	32	188	32	248	32	308	32	8	32	8	.53
9	36	69	36	129	36	189	36	249	36	309	36	9	36	9	.60
10	0 40	**70**	4 40	**130**	8 40	**190**	12 40	**250**	16 40	**310**	20 40	**10**	0 40	**10**	0.67
11	44	71	44	131	44	191	44	251	44	311	44	11	44	11	.73
12	48	72	48	132	48	192	48	252	48	312	48	12	48	12	.80
13	52	73	52	133	52	193	52	253	52	313	52	13	52	13	.87
14	56	74	56	134	56	194	56	254	56	314	56	14	56	14	.93
15	1 0	75	5 0	135	9 0	195	13 0	255	17 0	315	21 0	15	1 0	15	1.00
16	4	76	4	136	4	196	4	256	4	316	4	16	4	16	.07
17	8	77	8	137	8	197	8	257	8	317	8	17	8	17	.13
18	12	78	12	138	12	198	12	258	12	318	12	18	12	18	.20
19	16	79	16	139	16	199	16	259	16	319	16	19	16	19	.27
20	1 20	**80**	5 20	**140**	9 20	**200**	13 20	**260**	17 20	**320**	21 20	**20**	1 20	**20**	1·33
21	24	81	24	141	24	201	24	261	24	321	24	21	24	21	.40
22	28	82	28	142	28	202	28	262	28	322	28	22	28	22	.47
23	32	83	32	143	32	203	32	263	32	323	32	23	32	23	.53
24	36	84	36	144	36	204	36	264	36	324	36	24	36	24	.60
25	40	85	40	145	40	205	40	265	40	325	40	25	40	25	.67
26	44	86	44	146	44	206	44	266	44	326	44	26	44	26	.73
27	48	87	48	147	48	207	48	267	48	327	48	27	48	27	.80
28	52	88	52	148	52	208	52	268	52	328	52	28	52	28	.87
29	56	89	56	149	56	209	56	269	56	329	56	29	56	29	.93
30	2 0	**90**	6 0	**150**	10 0	**210**	14 0	**270**	18 0	**330**	22 0	**30**	2 0	**30**	2.00
31	4	91	4	151	4	211	4	271	4	331	4	31	4	31	.07
32	8	92	8	152	8	212	8	272	8	332	8	32	8	32	.13
33	12	93	12	153	12	213	12	273	12	333	12	33	12	33	.20
34	16	94	16	154	16	214	16	274	16	334	16	34	16	34	.27
35	20	95	20	155	20	215	20	275	20	335	20	35	20	35	.33
36	24	96	24	156	24	216	24	276	24	336	24	36	24	36	.40
37	28	97	28	157	28	217	28	277	28	337	28	37	28	37	.47
38	32	98	32	158	32	218	32	278	32	338	32	38	32	38	.53
39	36	99	36	159	36	219	36	279	36	339	36	39	36	39	.60
40	2 40	**100**	6 40	**160**	10 40	**220**	14 40	**280**	18 40	**340**	22 40	**40**	2 40	**40**	2.67
41	44	101	44	161	44	221	44	281	44	341	44	41	44	41	.73
42	48	102	48	162	48	222	48	282	48	342	48	42	48	42	.80
43	52	103	52	163	52	223	52	283	52	343	52	43	52	43	.87
44	56	104	56	164	56	224	56	284	56	344	56	44	56	44	.93
45	3 0	105	7 0	165	11 0	225	15 0	285	19 0	345	23 0	45	3 0	45	3.00
46	4	106	4	166	4	226	4	286	4	346	4	46	4	46	.07
47	8	107	8	167	8	227	8	287	8	347	8	47	8	47	.13
48	12	108	12	168	12	228	12	288	12	348	12	48	12	48	.20
49	16	109	16	169	16	229	16	289	16	349	16	49	16	49	.27
50	3 20	**110**	7 20	**170**	11 20	**230**	15 20	**290**	19 20	**350**	23 20	**50**	3 20	**50**	3·33
51	24	111	24	171	24	231	24	291	24	351	24	51	24	51	.40
52	28	112	28	172	28	232	28	292	28	352	28	52	28	52	.47
53	32	113	32	173	32	233	32	293	32	353	32	53	32	53	.53
54	36	114	36	174	36	234	36	294	36	354	36	54	36	54	.60
55	40	115	40	175	40	235	40	295	40	355	40	55	40	55	.67
56	44	116	44	176	44	236	44	296	44	356	44	56	44	56	.73
57	48	117	48	177	48	237	48	297	48	357	48	57	48	57	.80
58	52	118	52	178	52	238	52	298	52	358	52	58	52	58	.87
59	56	119	56	179	56	239	56	299	56	359	56	59	56	59	.93

TABLE III.

TABLE IV.

Mean Solar into Sidereal Time.						Sidereal into Mean Solar Time.					
Solar Hours.	**Add.**	**Solar Min.**	**Add.**	**Solar Sec.**	**Add.**	**Sid. Hours.**	**Subtract.**	**Sid. Min.**	**Subtract.**	**Sid. Sec.**	**Subtract.**
	m s		s		s		m s		s		s
1	0 9.86	**1**	0.16	**1**	0.00	**1**	0 9.83	**1**	0.16	**1**	0.00
2	0 19.71	**2**	0.33	**2**	0.00	**2**	0 19.66	**2**	0.33	**2**	0.00
3	0 29.57	**3**	0.49	**3**	0.01	**3**	0 29.49	**3**	0.49	**3**	0.01
4	0 39.43	**4**	0.66	**4**	0.01	**4**	0 39.32	**4**	0.66	**4**	0.01
5	0 49.28	**5**	0.82	**5**	0.01	**5**	0 49.15	**5**	0.82	**5**	0.01
6	0 59.14	**6**	0.98	**6**	0.02	**6**	0 58.98	**6**	0.98	**6**	0.02
7	1 9.00	**7**	1.15	**7**	0.02	**7**	1 8.81	**7**	1.15	**7**	0.02
8	1 18.85	**8**	1.31	**8**	0.02	**8**	1 18.64	**8**	1.31	**8**	0.02
9	1 28.71	**9**	1.48	**9**	0.02	**9**	1 28.47	**9**	1.47	**9**	0.02
10	1 38.56	**10**	1.64	**10**	0.03	**10**	1 38.30	**10**	1.64	**10**	0.03
11	1 48.42	**11**	1.81	**11**	0.03	**11**	1 48.13	**11**	1.80	**11**	0.03
12	1 58.28	**12**	1.97	**12**	0.03	**12**	1 57.95	**12**	1.97	**12**	0.03
13	2 8.13	**13**	2.13	**13**	0.04	**13**	2 7.78	**13**	2.13	**13**	0.04
14	2 17.99	**14**	2.30	**14**	0.04	**14**	2 17.61	**14**	2.29	**14**	0.04
15	2 27.85	**15**	2.46	**15**	0.04	**15**	2 27.44	**15**	2.46	**15**	0.04
16	2 37.70	**16**	2.63	**16**	0.04	**16**	2 37.27	**16**	2.62	**16**	0.04
17	2 47.56	**17**	2.79	**17**	0.05	**17**	2 47.10	**17**	2.78	**17**	0.05
18	2 57.42	**18**	2.96	**18**	0.05	**18**	2 56.93	**18**	2.95	**18**	0.05
19	3 7.27	**19**	3.12	**19**	0.05	**19**	3 6.76	**19**	3.11	**19**	0.05
20	3 17.13	**20**	3.29	**20**	0.05	**20**	3 16.59	**20**	3.28	**20**	0.05
21	3 26.99	**21**	3.45	**21**	0.06	**21**	3 26.42	**21**	3.44	**21**	0.06
22	3 36.84	**22**	3.61	**22**	0.06	**22**	3 36.25	**22**	3.60	**22**	0.06
23	3 46.70	**23**	3.78	**23**	0.06	**23**	3 46.08	**23**	3.77	**23**	0.06
24	3 56.56	**24**	3.94	**24**	0.07	**24**	3 55.91	**34**	3.93	**24**	0.07
		25	4.11	**25**	0.07			**25**	4.10	**25**	0.07
		26	4.27	**26**	0.07			**26**	4.26	**26**	0.07
		27	4.44	**27**	0.07			**27**	4.42	**27**	0.07
		28	4.60	**28**	0.08			**28**	4.59	**28**	0.08
		29	4.76	**29**	0.08			**29**	4.75	**29**	0.08
		30	4.93	**30**	0.08			**30**	4.91	**30**	0.08
		31	5.09	**31**	0.08			**31**	5.08	**31**	0.08
		32	5.26	**32**	0.09			**32**	5.24	**32**	0.09
		33	5.42	**33**	0.09			**33**	5.41	**33**	0.09
		34	5.59	**34**	0.09			**34**	5.57	**34**	0.09
		35	5.75	**35**	0.10			**35**	5.73	**35**	0.10
		36	5.91	**36**	0.10			**36**	5.90	**36**	0.10
		37	6.08	**37**	0.10			**37**	6.06	**37**	0.10
		38	6.24	**38**	0.11			**38**	6.23	**38**	0.11
		39	6.40	**39**	0.11			**39**	6.39	**39**	0.11
		40	6.57	**40**	0.11			**40**	6.55	**40**	0.11
		41	6.74	**41**	0.11			**41**	6.72	**41**	0.11
		42	6.90	**42**	0.12			**42**	6.88	**42**	0.12
		43	7.06	**43**	0.12			**43**	7.04	**43**	0.12
		44	7.23	**44**	0.12			**44**	7.21	**44**	0.12
		45	7.39	**45**	0.12			**45**	7.37	**45**	0.12
		46	7.56	**46**	0.13			**46**	7.54	**46**	0.13
		47	7.72	**47**	0.13			**47**	7.70	**47**	0.13
		48	7.89	**48**	0.13			**48**	7.86	**48**	0.13
		49	8.05	**49**	0.14			**49**	8.03	**49**	0.14
		50	8.21	**50**	0.14			**50**	8.19	**50**	0.14
		51	8.38	**51**	0.14			**51**	8.36	**51**	0.14
		52	8.54	**52**	0.14			**52**	8.52	**52**	0.14
		53	8.71	**53**	0.15			**53**	8.68	**53**	0.15
		54	8.87	**54**	0.15			**54**	8.85	**54**	0.15
		55	9.04	**55**	0.15			**55**	9.01	**55**	0.15
		56	9.20	**56**	0.15			**56**	9.17	**56**	0.15
		57	9.36	**57**	0.16			**57**	9.34	**57**	0.16
		58	9.53	**58**	0.16			**58**	9.50	**58**	0.16
		59	9.69	**59**	0.16			**59**	9.67	**59**	0.16
		60	9.86	**60**	0.16			**60**	9.83	**60**	0.16

Length of a Degree in Latitude or Longitude.

Lat.	Deg. of Long.		Deg. of Lat.		Lat.	Deg. of Long.		Deg. of Lat.	
°	*Stat. Miles.*	*Naut. Miles.*	*Stat. Miles.*	*Naut. Miles.*	°	*Stat. Miles.*	*Naut. Miles.*	*Stat. Miles.*	*Naut. Miles.*
0	69.160	60.000	68.698	59.600	**45**	48.986	42.498	69.044	59.899
1	.150	59.991	.698	.600	**46**	.126	41.752	.056	.910
2	.119	.964	.699	.601	**47**	47.251	40.993	.068	.920
3	.066	.919	.700	.602	**48**	46.362	.222	.080	.931
4	68.992	.855	.702	.603	**49**	45.459	39.439	.092	.941
5	68.898	59.773	68.704	59.605	**50**	44.542	38.643	69.104	59.951
6	.783	.673	.706	.607	**51**	43.611	37.835	.116	.962
7	.647	.555	.709	.609	**52**	42.667	.016	.128	.972
8	.491	.419	.712	.612	**53**	41.710	36.186	.140	.982
9	.314	.265	.715	.615	**54**	40.740	35.344	.151	.992
10	68.116	59.093	68.719	59.618	**55**	39.758	34.491	69.162	60.002
11	67.898	58.904	.723	.621	**56**	38.763	33.628	.173	.012
12	.659	.697	.728	.625	**57**	37.756	32.755	.184	.022
13	.400	.472	.733	.629	**58**	36.737	31.872	.195	.032
14	.120	.229	.738	.634	**59**	35.707	30.979	.206	.041
15	66.820	57.968	68.744	59.639	**60**	34.666	30.076	69.217	60.050
16	.499	.690	.750	.645	**61**	33.615	29.164	.228	.059
17	.158	.394	.757	.651	**62**	32.553	28.242	.238	.068
18	65.797	.081	.764	.657	**63**	31.481	27.311	.248	.077
19	.416	56.751	.771	.663	**64**	30.399	26.372	.258	.086
20	65.015	56.404	68.779	59.669	**65**	29.308	25.425	69.268	60.094
21	64.594	.039	.787	.676	**66**	28.208	24.471	.277	.102
22	.154	55.657	.795	.683	**67**	27.100	23.509	.286	.110
23	63.695	.258	.804	.691	**68**	25.983	22.540	.294	.117
24	.216	54.843	.813	.699	**69**	24.857	21.564	.302	.124
25	62.718	54.411	68.822	59.707	**70**	23.723	20.582	69.310	60.131
26	.201	53.962	.831	.715	**71**	22.582	19.593	.318	.137
27	61.665	.497	.840	.723	**72**	21.435	18.598	.326	.143
28	.110	.016	.850	.731	**73**	20.282	17.597	.333	.149
29	60.536	52.518	.860	.740	**74**	19.122	16.590	.339	.155
30	59.944	52.005	68.870	59.749	**75**	17.956	15.578	69.345	60.161
31	.334	51.476	.881	.758	**76**	16.784	14.561	.351	.166
32	58.706	50.931	.892	.767	**77**	15.607	13.539	.357	.171
33	.060	.370	.903	.776	**78**	14.425	12.513	.362	.175
34	57.396	49.794	.914	.786	**79**	13.238	11.484	.367	.179
35	56.715	49.203	68.925	59.796	**80**	12.047	10.452	69.371	60.183
36	.016	48.597	.936	.806	**81**	10.853	9.417	.375	.186
37	55.300	47.976	.947	.816	**82**	9.656	8.379	.378	.189
38	54.568	.340	.959	.826	**83**	8.456	7.338	.381	.192
39	53.819	46.690	.971	.836	**84**	7.253	6.294	.384	.194
40	53.053	46.026	68.983	59.846	**85**	6.048	5.248	69.387	60.196
41	52.271	45.348	.995	.856	**86**	4.841	4.200	.389	.198
42	51.473	44.656	69.007	.866	**87**	3.632	3.151	.390	.199
43	50.659	43.950	.019	.877	**88**	2.422	2.101	.391	.200
44	49.830	.231	.031	.888	**89**	1.211	1.050	.392	.201

Logarithms of Numbers and Small Arcs.

N.	Log.	N.	Log.	N.	Log.	N.	Log.	N.	Log.
0	—	**20**	3010	**40**	6021	**60**	7782	**80**	9031
1	0000	**1**	3222	**1**	6128	**1**	7853	**1**	9085
2	3010	**2**	3424	**2**	6232	**2**	7924	**2**	9138
3	4771	**3**	3617	**3**	6335	**3**	7993	**3**	9191
4	6021	**4**	3802	**4**	6435	**4**	8062	**4**	9243
5	6990	**5**	3979	**5**	6532	**5**	8129	**5**	9294
6	7782	**6**	4150	**6**	6628	**6**	8195	**6**	9345
7	8451	**7**	4314	**7**	6721	**7**	8261	**7**	9395
8	9031	**8**	4472	**8**	6812	**8**	8325	**8**	9445
9	9542	**9**	4624	**9**	6902	**9**	8388	**9**	9494
10	0000	**30**	4771	**50**	6990	**70**	8451	**90**	9542
1	0414	**1**	4914	**1**	7076	**1**	8513	**1**	9590
2	0792	**2**	5052	**2**	7160	**2**	8573	**2**	9638
3	1139	**3**	5185	**3**	7243	**3**	8633	**3**	9685
4	1461	**4**	5315	**4**	7324	**4**	8692	**4**	9731
5	1761	**5**	5441	**5**	7404	**5**	8751	**5**	9777
6	2041	**6**	5563	**6**	7482	**6**	8808	**6**	9823
7	2304	**7**	5682	**7**	7559	**7**	8865	**7**	9868
8	2553	**8**	5798	**8**	7634	**8**	8921	**8**	9912
9	2788	**9**	5911	**9**	7709	**9**	8976	**9**	9956
20	3010	**40**	6021	**60**	7782	**80**	9031	**100**	0000
N.	**Log.**	**N.**	**Log.**	**N.**	**Log.**	**N.**	**Log.**	**N.**	**Log.**

Small Arcs.

s		*h*	*m*	*s*
"		°	'	"
0	=	0	0	0
10	=	0	0	10
20	=	0	0	20
30	=	0	0	30
40	=	0	0	40
50	=	0	0	50

Small Arcs.

s		*h*	*m*	*s*
"		°	'	"
50	=	0	0	50
60	=	0	1	0
70	=	0	1	10
80	=	0	1	20
90	=	0	1	30
100	=	0	1	40

Logarithms of Numbers and Small Arcs.

No.	0	1	2	3	4	5	6	7	8	9
100	0000	0004	0009	0013	0017	0022	0026	0030	0035	0039
1	0043	0048	0052	0056	0060	0065	0069	0073	0077	0082
2	0086	0090	0095	0099	0103	0107	0111	0116	0120	0124
3	0128	0133	0137	0141	0145	0149	0154	0158	0162	0166
4	0170	0175	0179	0183	0187	0191	0195	0199	0204	0208
5	0212	0216	0220	0224	0228	0233	0237	0241	0245	0249
6	0253	0257	0261	0265	0269	0274	0278	0282	0286	0290
7	0294	0298	0302	0306	0310	0314	0318	0322	0326	0330
8	0334	0338	0342	0346	0350	0354	0358	0362	0366	0370
9	0374	0378	0382	0386	0390	0394	0398	0402	0406	0410
110	0414	0418	0422	0426	0430	0434	0438	0441	0445	0449
1	0453	0457	0461	0465	0469	0473	0477	0481	0484	0488
2	0492	0496	0500	0504	0508	0512	0515	0519	0523	0527
3	0531	0535	0538	0542	0546	0550	0554	0558	0561	0565
4	0569	0573	0577	0580	0584	0588	0592	0596	0599	0603
5	0607	0611	0615	0618	0622	0626	0630	0633	0637	0641
6	0645	0648	0652	0656	0660	0663	0667	0671	0674	0678
7	0682	0686	0689	0693	0697	0700	0704	0708	0711	0715
8	0719	0723	0726	0730	0734	0737	0741	0745	0748	0752
9	0755	0759	0763	0766	0770	0774	0777	0781	0785	0788
120	0792	0795	0799	0803	0806	0810	0813	0817	0821	0824
1	0828	0831	0835	0839	0842	0846	0849	0853	0856	0860
2	0864	0867	0871	0874	0878	0881	0885	0888	0892	0896
3	0899	0903	0906	0910	0913	0917	0920	0924	0927	0931
4	0934	0938	0941	0945	0948	0952	0955	0959	0962	0966
5	0969	0973	0976	0980	0983	0986	0990	0993	0997	1000
6	1004	1007	1011	1014	1017	1021	1024	1028	1031	1035
7	1038	1041	1045	1048	1052	1055	1059	1062	1065	1069
8	1072	1075	1079	1082	1086	1089	1092	1096	1099	1103
9	1106	1109	1113	1116	1119	1123	1126	1129	1133	1136
130	1139	1143	1146	1149	1153	1156	1159	1163	1166	1169
1	1173	1176	1179	1183	1186	1189	1193	1196	1199	1202
2	1206	1209	1212	1216	1219	1222	1225	1229	1232	1235
3	1239	1242	1245	1248	1252	1255	1258	1261	1265	1268
4	1271	1274	1278	1281	1284	1287	1290	1294	1297	1300
5	1303	1307	1310	1313	1316	1319	1323	1326	1329	1332
6	1335	1339	1342	1345	1348	1351	1355	1358	1361	1364
7	1367	1370	1374	1377	1380	1383	1386	1389	1392	1396
8	1399	1402	1405	1408	1411	1415	1418	1421	1424	1427
9	1430	1433	1436	1440	1443	1446	1449	1452	1455	1458
140	1461	1464	1467	1471	1474	1477	1480	1483	1486	1489
1	1492	1495	1498	1501	1504	1508	1511	1514	1517	1520
2	1523	1526	1529	1532	1535	1538	1541	1544	1547	1550
3	1553	1556	1559	1562	1565	1569	1572	1575	1578	1581
4	1584	1587	1590	1593	1596	1599	1602	1605	1608	1611
5	1614	1617	1620	1623	1626	1629	1632	1635	1638	1641
6	1644	1647	1649	1652	1655	1658	1661	1664	1667	1670
7	1673	1676	1679	1682	1685	1688	1691	1694	1697	1700
8	1703	1706	1708	1711	1714	1717	1720	1723	1726	1729
9	1732	1735	1738	1741	1744	1746	1749	1752	1755	1758
150	1761	1764	1767	1770	1772	1775	1778	1781	1784	1787

s ″		*h* °	*m* ′	*s* ″
100	=	0	1	40
110	=	0	1	50
120	=	0	2	0
130	=	0	2	10
140	=	0	2	20
150	=	0	2	30

s ″		*h* °	*m* ′	*s* ″
1000	=	0	16	40
1100	=	0	18	20
1200	=	0	20	0
1300	=	0	21	40
1400	=	0	23	20
1500	=	0	25	0

Logarithms of Numbers and Small Arcs.

No.	0	1	2	3	4	5	6	7	8	9
150	1761	1764	1767	1770	1772	1775	1778	1781	1784	1787
1	1790	1793	1796	1798	1801	1804	1807	1810	1813	1816
2	1818	1821	1824	1827	1830	1833	1836	1838	1841	1844
3	1847	1850	1853	1855	1858	1861	1864	1867	1870	1872
4	1875	1878	1881	1884	1886	1889	1892	1895	1898	1901
5	1903	1906	1909	1912	1915	1917	1920	1923	1926	1928
6	1931	1934	1937	1940	1942	1945	1948	1951	1953	1956
7	1959	1962	1965	1967	1970	1973	1976	1978	1981	1984
8	1987	1989	1992	1995	1998	2000	2003	2006	2009	2011
9	2014	2017	2019	2022	2025	2028	2030	2033	2036	2038
160	2041	2044	2047	2049	2052	2055	2057	2060	2063	2066
1	2068	2071	2074	2076	2079	2082	2084	2087	2090	2092
2	2095	2098	2101	2103	2106	2109	2111	2114	2117	2119
3	2122	2125	2127	2130	2133	2135	2138	2140	2143	2146
4	2148	2151	2154	2156	2159	2162	2164	2167	2170	2172
5	2175	2177	2180	2183	2185	2188	2191	2193	2196	2198
6	2201	2204	2206	2209	2212	2214	2217	2219	2222	2225
7	2227	2230	2232	2235	2238	2240	2243	2245	2248	2251
8	2253	2256	2258	2261	2263	2266	2269	2271	2274	2276
9	2279	2281	2284	2287	2289	2292	2294	2297	2299	2302
170	2305	2307	2310	2312	2315	2317	2320	2322	2325	2327
1	2330	2333	2335	2338	2340	2343	2345	2348	2350	2353
2	2355	2358	2360	2363	2365	2368	2370	2373	2375	2378
3	2380	2383	2385	2388	2390	2393	2396	2398	2401	2403
4	2405	2408	2410	2413	2415	2418	2420	2423	2425	2428
5	2430	2433	2435	2438	2440	2443	2445	2448	2450	2453
6	2455	2458	2460	2463	2465	2467	2470	2472	2475	2477
7	2480	2482	2485	2487	2490	2492	2494	2497	2499	2502
8	2504	2507	2509	2512	2514	2516	2519	2521	2524	2526
9	2529	2531	2533	2536	2538	2541	2543	2545	2548	2550
180	2553	2555	2558	2560	2562	2565	2567	2570	2572	2574
1	2577	2579	2582	2584	2586	2589	2591	2594	2596	2598
2	2601	2603	2605	2608	2610	2613	2615	2617	2620	2622
3	2625	2627	2629	2632	2634	2636	2639	2641	2643	2646
4	2648	2651	2653	2655	2658	2660	2662	2665	2667	2669
5	2672	2674	2676	2679	2681	2683	2686	2688	2690	2693
6	2695	2697	2700	2702	2704	2707	2709	2711	2714	2716
7	2718	2721	2723	2725	2728	2730	2732	2735	2737	2739
8	2742	2744	2746	2749	2751	2753	2755	2758	2760	2762
9	2765	2767	2769	2772	2774	2776	2778	2781	2783	2785
190	2788	2790	2792	2794	2797	2799	2801	2804	2806	2808
1	2810	2813	2815	2817	2819	2822	2824	2826	2828	2831
2	2833	2835	2838	2840	2842	2844	2847	2849	2851	2853
3	2856	2858	2860	2862	2865	2867	2869	2871	2874	2876
4	2878	2880	2882	2885	2887	2889	2891	2894	2896	2898
5	2900	2903	2905	2907	2909	2911	2914	2916	2918	2920
6	2923	2925	2927	2929	2931	2934	2936	2938	2940	2942
7	2945	2947	2949	2951	2953	2956	2958	2960	2962	2964
8	2967	2969	2971	2973	2975	2978	2980	2982	2984	2986
9	2989	2991	2993	2995	2997	2999	3002	3004	3006	3008
200	3010	3012	3015	3017	3019	3021	3023	3025	3028	3030

s ″		h °	m ′	s ″
150	=	0	2	30
160	=	0	2	40
170	=	0	2	50
180	=	0	3	0
190	=	0	3	10
200	=	0	3	20

s ″		h °	m ′	s ″
1500	=	0	25	0
1600	=	0	26	40
1700	=	0	28	20
1800	=	0	30	0
1900	=	0	31	40
2000	=	0	33	20

Logarithms of Numbers and Small Arcs.

No.	0	1	2	3	4	5	6	7	8	9
200	3010	3012	3015	3017	3019	3021	3023	3025	3028	3030
1	3032	3034	3036	3038	3041	3043	3045	3047	3049	3051
2	3054	3056	3058	3060	3062	3064	3066	3069	3071	3073
3	3075	3077	3079	3081	3084	3086	3088	3090	3092	3094
4	3096	3098	3101	3103	3105	3107	3109	3111	3113	3115
5	3118	3120	3122	3124	3126	3128	3130	3132	3134	3137
6	3139	3141	3143	3145	3147	3149	3151	3153	3156	3158
7	3160	3162	3164	3166	3168	3170	3172	3174	3176	3179
8	3181	3183	3185	3187	3189	3191	3193	3195	3197	3199
9	3201	3204	3206	3208	3210	3212	3214	3216	3218	3220
210	3222	3224	3226	3228	3230	3233	3235	3237	3239	3241
1	3243	3245	3247	3249	3251	3253	3255	3257	3259	3261
2	3263	3265	3267	3270	3272	3274	3276	3278	3280	3282
3	3284	3286	3288	3290	3292	3294	3296	3298	3300	3302
4	3304	3306	3308	3310	3312	3314	3316	3318	3320	3322
5	3324	3326	3328	3330	3332	3334	3336	3339	3341	3343
6	3345	3347	3349	3351	3353	3355	3357	3359	3361	3363
7	3365	3367	3369	3371	3373	3375	3377	3379	3381	3383
8	3385	3387	3389	3391	3393	3395	3397	3398	3400	3402
9	3404	3406	3408	3410	3412	3414	3416	3418	3420	3422
220	3424	3426	3428	3430	3432	3434	3436	3438	3440	3442
1	3444	3446	3448	3450	3452	3454	3456	3458	3460	3462
2	3464	3465	3467	3469	3471	3473	3475	3477	3479	3481
3	3483	3485	3487	3489	3491	3493	3495	3497	3499	3501
4	3502	3504	3506	3508	3510	3512	3514	3516	3518	3520
5	3522	3524	3526	3528	3530	3531	3533	3535	3537	3539
6	3541	3543	3545	3547	3549	3551	3553	3555	3556	3558
7	3560	3562	3564	3566	3568	3570	3572	3574	3576	3577
8	3579	3581	3583	3585	3587	3589	3591	3593	3595	3596
9	3598	3600	3602	3604	3606	3608	3610	3612	3614	3615
230	3617	3619	3621	3623	3625	3627	3629	3630	3632	3634
1	3636	3638	3640	3642	3644	3646	3647	3649	3651	3653
2	3655	3657	3659	3660	3662	3664	3666	3668	3670	3672
3	3674	3675	3677	3679	3681	3683	3685	3687	3688	3690
4	3692	3694	3696	3698	3700	3701	3703	3705	3707	3709
5	3711	3713	3714	3716	3718	3720	3722	3724	3725	3727
6	3729	3731	3733	3735	3736	3738	3740	3742	3744	3746
7	3747	3749	3751	3753	3755	3757	3758	3760	3762	3764
8	3766	3768	3769	3771	3773	3775	3777	3779	3780	3782
9	3784	3786	3788	3789	3791	3793	3795	3797	3798	3800
240	3802	3804	3806	3808	3809	3811	3813	3815	3817	3818
1	3820	3822	3824	3826	3827	3829	3831	3833	3835	3836
2	3838	3840	3842	3844	3845	3847	3849	3851	3852	3854
3	3856	3858	3860	3861	3863	3865	3867	3869	3870	3872
4	3874	3876	3877	3879	3881	3883	3885	3886	3888	3890
5	3892	3893	3895	3897	3899	3901	3902	3904	3906	3908
6	3909	3911	3913	3915	3916	3918	3920	3922	3923	3925
7	3927	3929	3930	3932	3934	3936	3938	3939	3941	3943
8	3945	3946	3948	3950	3952	3953	3955	3957	3959	3960
9	3962	3964	3965	3967	3969	3971	3972	3974	3976	3978
250	3979	3981	3983	3985	3986	3988	3990	3992	3993	3995

s	h	m	s
″	°	′	″
200 =	0	3	20
210 =	0	3	30
220 =	0	3	40
230 =	0	3	50
240 =	0	4	0
250 =	0	4	10

s	h	m	s
″	°	′	″
2000 =	0	33	20
2100 =	0	35	0
2200 =	0	36	40
2300 =	0	38	20
2400 =	0	40	0
2500 =	0	41	40

Logarithms of Numbers and Small Arcs.

No.	0	1	2	3	4	5	6	7	8	9
250	3979	3981	3983	3985	3986	3988	3990	3992	3993	3995
1	3997	3998	4000	4002	4004	4005	4007	4009	4011	4012
2	4014	4016	4017	4019	4021	4023	4024	4026	4028	4029
3	4031	4033	4035	4036	4038	4040	4041	4043	4045	4047
4	4048	4050	4052	4053	4055	4057	4059	4060	4062	4064
5	4065	4067	4069	4071	4072	4074	4076	4077	4079	4081
6	4082	4084	4086	4087	4089	4091	4093	4094	4096	4098
7	4099	4101	4103	4104	4106	4108	4109	4111	4113	4115
8	4116	4118	4120	4121	4123	4125	4126	4128	4130	4131
9	4133	4135	4136	4138	4140	4141	4143	4145	4146	4148
260	4150	4151	4153	4155	4156	4158	4160	4161	4163	4165
1	4166	4168	4170	4171	4173	4175	4176	4178	4180	4181
2	4183	4185	4186	4188	4190	4191	4193	4195	4196	4198
3	4200	4201	4203	4205	4206	4208	4209	4211	4213	4214
4	4216	4218	4219	4221	4223	4224	4226	4228	4229	4231
5	4232	4234	4236	4237	4239	4241	4242	4244	4246	4247
6	4249	4250	4252	4254	4255	4257	4259	4260	4262	4263
7	4265	4267	4268	4270	4272	4273	4275	4276	4278	4280
8	4281	4283	4285	4286	4288	4289	4291	4293	4294	4296
9	4298	4299	4301	4302	4304	4306	4307	4309	4310	4312
270	4314	4315	4317	4318	4320	4322	4323	4325	4326	4328
1	4330	4331	4333	4335	4336	4338	4339	4341	4342	4344
2	4346	4347	4349	4350	4352	4354	4355	4357	4358	4360
3	4362	4363	4365	4366	4368	4370	4371	4373	4374	4376
4	4378	4379	4381	4382	4384	4385	4387	4389	4390	4392
5	4393	4395	4396	4398	4400	4401	4403	4404	4406	4408
6	4409	4411	4412	4414	4415	4417	4419	4420	4422	4423
7	4425	4426	4428	4430	4431	4433	4434	4436	4437	4439
8	4440	4442	4444	4445	4447	4448	4450	4451	4453	4454
9	4456	4458	4459	4461	4462	4464	4465	4467	4468	4470
280	4472	4473	4475	4476	4478	4479	4481	4482	4484	4486
1	4487	4489	4490	4492	4493	4495	4496	4498	4499	4501
2	4502	4504	4506	4507	4509	4510	4512	4513	4515	4516
3	4518	4519	4521	4522	4524	4526	4527	4529	4530	4532
4	4533	4535	4536	4538	4539	4541	4542	4544	4545	4547
5	4548	4550	4552	4553	4555	4556	4558	4559	4561	4562
6	4564	4565	4567	4568	4570	4571	4573	4574	4576	4577
7	4579	4580	4582	4583	4585	4586	4588	4589	4591	4592
8	4594	4595	4597	4598	4600	4601	4603	4604	4606	4607
9	4609	4610	4612	4613	4615	4616	4618	4619	4621	4622
290	4624	4625	4627	4628	4630	4631	4633	4634	4636	4637
1	4639	4640	4642	4643	4645	4646	4648	4649	4651	4652
2	4654	4655	4657	4658	4660	4661	4663	4664	4666	4667
3	4669	4670	4672	4673	4675	4676	4678	4679	4681	4682
4	4683	4685	4686	4688	4689	4691	4692	4694	4695	4697
5	4698	4700	4701	4703	4704	4706	4707	4709	4710	4711
6	4713	4714	4716	4717	4719	4720	4722	4723	4725	4726
7	4728	4729	4730	4732	4733	4735	4736	4738	4739	4741
8	4742	4744	4745	4747	4748	4749	4751	4752	4754	4755
9	4757	4758	4760	4761	4763	4764	4765	4767	4768	4770
300	4771	4773	4774	4776	4777	4778	4780	4781	4783	4784

s		h	m	s
″		°	′	″
250	=	0	4	10
260	=	0	4	20
270	=	0	4	30
280	=	0	4	40
290	=	0	4	50
300	=	0	5	0

s		h	m	s
″		°	′	″
2500	=	0	41	40
2600	=	0	43	20
2700	=	0	45	0
2800	=	0	46	40
2900	=	0	48	20
3000	=	0	50	0

Logarithms of Numbers and Small Arcs.

No.	0	1	2	3	4	5	6	7	8	9
300	4771	4773	4774	4776	4777	4778	4780	4781	4783	4784
1	4786	4787	4789	4790	4791	4793	4794	4796	4797	4799
2	4800	4802	4803	4804	4806	4807	4809	4810	4812	4813
3	4814	4816	4817	4819	4820	4822	4823	4824	4826	4827
4	4829	4830	4832	4833	4834	4836	4837	4839	4840	4842
5	4843	4844	4846	4847	4849	4850	4852	4853	4854	4856
6	4857	4859	4860	4861	4863	4864	4866	4867	4869	4870
7	4871	4873	4874	4876	4877	4878	4880	4881	4883	4884
8	4886	4887	4888	4890	4891	4893	4894	4895	4897	4898
9	4900	4901	4902	4904	4905	4907	4908	4909	4911	4912
310	4914	4915	4916	4918	4919	4921	4922	4923	4925	4926
1	4928	4929	4930	4932	4933	4935	4936	4937	4939	4940
2	4942	4943	4944	4946	4947	4949	4950	4951	4953	4954
3	4955	4957	4958	4960	4961	4962	4964	4965	4967	4968
4	4969	4971	4972	4973	4975	4976	4978	4979	4980	4982
5	4983	4984	4986	4987	4989	4990	4991	4993	4994	4996
6	4997	4998	5000	5001	5002	5004	5005	5006	5008	5009
7	5011	5012	5013	5015	5016	5017	5019	5020	5022	5023
8	5024	5026	5027	5028	5030	5031	5032	5034	5035	5037
9	5038	5039	5041	5042	5043	5045	5046	5047	5049	5050
320	5052	5053	5054	5056	5057	5058	5060	5061	5062	5064
1	5065	5066	5068	5069	5070	5072	5073	5075	5076	5077
2	5079	5080	5081	5083	5084	5085	5087	5088	5089	5091
3	5092	5093	5095	5096	5097	5099	5100	5101	5103	5104
4	5105	5107	5108	5109	5111	5112	5113	5115	5116	5118
5	5119	5120	5122	5123	5124	5126	5127	5128	5130	5131
6	5132	5134	5135	5136	5138	5139	5140	5141	5143	5144
7	5145	5147	5148	5149	5151	5152	5153	5155	5156	5157
8	5159	5160	5161	5163	5164	5165	5167	5168	5169	5171
9	5172	5173	5175	5176	5177	5179	5180	5181	5183	5184
330	5185	5186	5188	5189	5190	5192	5193	5194	5196	5197
1	5198	5200	5201	5202	5204	5205	5206	5207	5209	5210
2	5211	5213	5214	5215	5217	5218	5219	5221	5222	5223
3	5224	5226	5227	5228	5230	5231	5232	5234	5235	5236
4	5237	5239	5240	5241	5243	5244	5245	5247	5248	5249
5	5250	5252	5253	5254	5256	5257	5258	5260	5261	5262
6	5263	5265	5266	5267	5269	5270	5271	5272	5274	5275
7	5276	5278	5279	5280	5281	5283	5284	5285	5287	5288
8	5289	5290	5292	5293	5294	5296	5297	5298	5299	5301
9	5302	5303	5305	5306	5307	5308	5310	5311	5312	5314
340	5315	5316	5317	5319	5320	5321	5322	5324	5325	5326
1	5328	5329	5330	5331	5333	5334	5335	5336	5338	5339
2	5340	5342	5343	5344	5345	5347	5348	5349	5350	5352
3	5353	5354	5355	5357	5358	5359	5361	5362	5363	5364
4	5366	5367	5368	5369	5371	5372	5373	5374	5376	5377
5	5378	5379	5381	5382	5383	5384	5386	5387	5388	5390
6	5391	5392	5393	5395	5396	5397	5398	5400	5401	5402
7	5403	5405	5406	5407	5408	5410	5411	5412	5413	5415
8	5416	5417	5418	5420	5421	5422	5423	5425	5426	5427
9	5428	5430	5431	5432	5433	5434	5436	5437	5438	5439
350	5441	5442	5443	5444	5446	5447	5448	5449	5451	5452

s ″		h °	m ′	s ″
300	=	0	5	0
310	=	0	5	10
320	=	0	5	20
330	=	0	5	30
340	=	0	5	40
350	=	0	5	50

s ″		h °	m ′	s ″
3000	=	0	50	0
3100	=	0	51	40
3200	=	0	53	20
3300	=	0	55	0
3400	=	0	56	40
3500	=	0	58	20

Logarithms of Numbers and Small Arcs.

No.	0	1	2	3	4	5	6	7	8	9
350	5441	5442	5443	5444	5446	5447	5448	5449	5451	5452
1	5453	5454	5456	5457	5458	5459	5460	5462	5463	5464
2	5465	5467	5468	5469	5470	5472	5473	5474	5475	5477
3	5478	5479	5480	5481	5483	5484	5485	5486	5488	5489
4	5490	5491	5492	5494	5495	5496	5497	5499	5500	5501
5	5502	5504	5505	5506	5507	5508	5510	5511	5512	5513
6	5515	5516	5517	5518	5519	5521	5522	5523	5524	5525
7	5527	5528	5529	5530	5532	5533	5534	5535	5536	5538
8	5539	5540	5541	5542	5544	5545	5546	5547	5549	5550
9	5551	5552	5553	5555	5556	5557	5558	5559	5561	5562
360	5563	5564	5565	5567	5568	5569	5570	5571	5573	5574
1	5575	5576	5577	5579	5580	5581	5582	5583	5585	5586
2	5587	5588	5589	5591	5592	5593	5594	5595	5597	5598
3	5599	5600	5601	5603	5604	5605	5606	5607	5609	5610
4	5611	5612	5613	5615	5616	5617	5618	5619	5621	5622
5	5623	5624	5625	5627	5628	5629	5630	5631	5632	5634
6	5635	5636	5637	5638	5640	5641	5642	5643	5644	5645
7	5647	5648	5649	5650	5651	5653	5654	5655	5656	5657
8	5658	5660	5661	5662	5663	5664	5666	5667	5668	5669
9	5670	5671	5673	5674	5675	5676	5677	5678	5680	5681
370	5682	5683	5684	5686	5687	5688	5689	5690	5691	5693
1	5694	5695	5696	5697	5698	5700	5701	5702	5703	5704
2	5705	5707	5708	5709	5710	5711	5712	5714	5715	5716
3	5717	5718	5719	5721	5722	5723	5724	5725	5726	5728
4	5729	5730	5731	5732	5733	5735	5736	5737	5738	5739
5	5740	5741	5743	5744	5745	5746	5747	5748	5750	5751
6	5752	5753	5754	5755	5757	5758	5759	5760	5761	5762
7	5763	5765	5766	5767	5768	5769	5770	5771	5773	5774
8	5775	5776	5777	5778	5780	5781	5782	5783	5784	5785
9	5786	5788	5789	5790	5791	5792	5793	5794	5796	5797
380	5798	5799	5800	5801	5802	5804	5805	5806	5807	5808
1	5809	5810	5812	5813	5814	5815	5816	5817	5818	5820
2	5821	5822	5823	5824	5825	5826	5827	5829	5830	5831
3	5832	5833	5834	5835	5837	5838	5839	5840	5841	5842
4	5843	5844	5846	5847	5848	5849	5850	5851	5852	5853
5	5855	5856	5857	5858	5859	5860	5861	5863	5864	5865
6	5866	5867	5868	5869	5870	5871	5873	5874	5875	5876
7	5877	5878	5879	5880	5882	5883	5884	5885	5886	5887
8	5888	5889	5891	5892	5893	5894	5895	5896	5897	5898
9	5900	5901	5902	5903	5904	5905	5906	5907	5908	5910
390	5911	5912	5913	5914	5915	5916	5917	5918	5920	5921
1	5922	5923	5924	5925	5926	5927	5928	5930	5931	5932
2	5933	5934	5935	5936	5937	5938	5940	5941	5942	5943
3	5944	5945	5946	5947	5948	5949	5951	5952	5953	5954
4	5955	5956	5957	5958	5959	5960	5962	5963	5964	5965
5	5966	5967	5968	5969	5970	5971	5973	5974	5975	5976
6	5977	5978	5979	5980	5981	5982	5984	5985	5986	5987
7	5988	5989	5990	5991	5992	5993	5994	5996	5997	5998
8	5999	6000	6001	6002	6003	6004	6005	6006	6008	6009
9	6010	6011	6012	6013	6014	6015	6016	6017	6018	6020
400	6021	6022	6023	6024	6025	6026	6027	6028	6029	6030

s ″		h °	m ′	s ″
350	=	0	5	50
360	=	0	6	0
370	=	0	6	10
380	=	0	6	20
390	=	0	6	30
400	=	0	6	40

s ″		h °	m ′	s ″
3500	=	0	58	20
3600	=	1	0	0
3700	=	1	1	40
3800	=	1	3	20
3900	=	1	5	0
4000	=	1	6	40

Logarithms of Numbers and Small Arcs.

No.	0	1	2	3	4	5	6	7	8	9
400	6021	6022	6023	6024	6025	6026	6027	6028	6029	6030
1	6031	6033	6034	6035	6036	6037	6038	6039	6040	6041
2	6042	6043	6044	6046	6047	6048	6049	6050	6051	6052
3	6053	6054	6055	6056	6057	6058	6060	6061	6062	6063
4	6064	6065	6066	6067	6068	6069	6070	6071	6072	6073
5	6075	6076	6077	6078	6079	6080	6081	6082	6083	6084
6	6085	6086	6087	6088	6090	6091	6092	6093	6094	6095
7	6096	6097	6098	6099	6100	6101	6102	6103	6104	6106
8	6107	6108	6109	6110	6111	6112	6113	6114	6115	6116
9	6117	6118	6119	6120	6121	6123	6124	6125	6126	6127
410	6128	6129	6130	6131	6132	6133	6134	6135	6136	6137
1	6138	6139	6141	6142	6143	6144	6145	6146	6147	6148
2	6149	6150	6151	6152	6153	6154	6155	6156	6157	6158
3	6160	6161	6162	6163	6164	6165	6166	6167	6168	6169
4	6170	6171	6172	6173	6174	6175	6176	6177	6178	6179
5	6180	6182	6183	6184	6185	6186	6187	6188	6189	6190
6	6191	6192	6193	6194	6195	6196	6197	6198	6199	6200
7	6201	6202	6203	6204	6206	6207	6208	6209	6210	6211
8	6212	6213	6214	6215	6216	6217	6218	6219	6220	6221
9	6222	6223	6224	6225	6226	6227	6228	6229	6230	6231
420	6232	6234	6235	6236	6237	6238	6239	6240	6241	6242
1	6243	6244	6245	6246	6247	6248	6249	6250	6251	6252
2	6253	6254	6255	6256	6257	6258	6259	6260	6261	6262
3	6263	6264	6265	6266	6268	6269	6270	6271	6272	6273
4	6274	6275	6276	6277	6278	6279	6280	6281	6282	6283
5	6284	6285	6286	6287	6288	6289	6290	6291	6292	6293
6	6294	6295	6296	6297	6298	6299	6300	6301	6302	6303
7	6304	6305	6306	6307	6308	6309	6310	6311	6312	6313
8	6314	6315	6316	6317	6318	6320	6321	6322	6323	6324
9	6325	6326	6327	6328	6329	6330	6331	6332	6333	6334
430	6335	6336	6337	6338	6339	6340	6341	6342	6343	6344
1	6345	6346	6347	6348	6349	6350	6351	6352	6353	6354
2	6355	6356	6357	6358	6359	6360	6361	6362	6363	6364
3	6365	6366	6367	6368	6369	6370	6371	6372	6373	6374
4	6375	6376	6377	6378	6379	6380	6381	6382	6383	6384
5	6385	6386	6387	6388	6389	6390	6391	6392	6393	6394
6	6395	6396	6397	6398	6399	6400	6401	6402	6403	6404
7	6405	6406	6407	6408	6409	6410	6411	6412	6413	6414
8	6415	6416	6417	6418	6419	6420	6421	6422	6423	6424
9	6425	6426	6427	6428	6429	6430	6431	6432	6433	6434
440	6435	6436	6437	6437	6438	6439	6440	6441	6442	6443
1	6444	6445	6446	6447	6448	6449	6450	6451	6452	6453
2	6454	6455	6456	6457	6458	6459	6460	6461	6462	6463
3	6464	6465	6466	6467	6468	6469	6470	6471	6472	6473
4	6474	6475	6476	6477	6478	6479	6480	6481	6482	6483
5	6484	6485	6486	6487	6488	6488	6489	6490	6491	6492
6	6493	6494	6495	6496	6497	6498	6499	6500	6501	6502
7	6503	6504	6505	6506	6507	6508	6509	6510	6511	6512
8	6513	6514	6515	6516	6517	6518	6519	6520	6521	6522
9	6522	6523	6524	6525	6526	6527	6528	6529	6530	6531
450	6532	6533	6534	6535	6536	6537	6538	6539	6540	6541

s		h	m	s
″		°	′	″
400	=	0	6	40
410	=	0	6	50
420	=	0	7	0
430	=	0	7	10
440	=	0	7	20
450	=	0	7	30

s		h	m	s
″		°	′	″
4000	=	1	6	40
4100	=	1	8	20
4200	=	1	10	0
4300	=	1	11	40
4400	=	1	13	20
4500	=	1	15	0

Logarithms of Numbers and Small Arcs.

No.	0	1	2	3	4	5	6	7	8	9
450	6532	6533	6534	6535	6536	6537	6538	6539	6540	6541
1	6542	6543	6544	6545	6546	6547	6548	6549	6549	6550
2	6551	6552	6553	6554	6555	6556	6557	6558	6559	6560
3	6561	6562	6563	6564	6565	6566	6567	6568	6569	6570
4	6571	6572	6572	6573	6574	6575	6576	6577	6578	6579
5	6580	6581	6582	6583	6584	6585	6586	6587	6588	6589
6	6590	6591	6592	6593	6593	6594	6595	6596	6597	6598
7	6599	6600	6601	6602	6603	6604	6605	6606	6607	6608
8	6609	6610	6611	6612	6612	6613	6614	6615	6616	6617
9	6618	6619	6620	6621	6622	6623	6624	6625	6626	6627
460	6628	6629	6629	6630	6631	6632	6633	6634	6635	6636
1	6637	6638	6639	6640	6641	6642	6643	6644	6645	6645
2	6646	6647	6648	6649	6650	6651	6652	6653	6654	6655
3	6656	6657	6658	6659	6660	6661	6661	6662	6663	6664
4	6665	6666	6667	6668	6669	6670	6671	6672	6673	6674
5	6675	6675	6676	6677	6678	6679	6680	6681	6682	6683
6	6684	6685	6686	6687	6688	6689	6689	6690	6691	6692
7	6693	6694	6695	6696	6697	6698	6699	6700	6701	6702
8	6702	6703	6704	6705	6706	6707	6708	6709	6710	6711
9	6712	6713	6714	6715	6715	6716	6717	6718	6719	6720
470	6721	6722	6723	6724	6725	6726	6727	6727	6728	6729
1	6730	6731	6732	6733	6734	6735	6736	6737	6738	6739
2	6739	6740	6741	6742	6743	6744	6745	6746	6747	6748
3	6749	6750	6750	6751	6752	6753	6754	6755	6756	6757
4	6758	6759	6760	6761	6761	6762	6763	6764	6765	6766
5	6767	6768	6769	6770	6771	6772	6772	6773	6774	6775
6	6776	6777	6778	6779	6780	6781	6782	6783	6783	6784
7	6785	6786	6787	6788	6789	6790	6791	6792	6792	6793
8	6794	6795	6796	6797	6798	6799	6800	6801	6802	6802
9	6803	6804	6805	6806	6807	6808	6809	6810	6811	6812
480	6812	6813	6814	6815	6816	6817	6818	6819	6820	6821
1	6821	6822	6823	6824	6825	6826	6827	6828	6829	6830
2	6830	6831	6832	6833	6834	6835	6836	6837	6838	6839
3	6839	6840	6841	6842	6843	6844	6845	6846	6847	6848
4	6848	6849	6850	6851	6852	6853	6854	6855	6856	6857
5	6857	6858	6859	6860	6861	6862	6863	6864	6865	6865
6	6866	6867	6868	6869	6870	6871	6872	6873	6874	6874
7	6875	6876	6877	6878	6879	6880	6881	6882	6882	6883
8	6884	6885	6886	6887	6888	6889	6890	6890	6891	6892
9	6893	6894	6895	6896	6897	6898	6898	6899	6900	6901
490	6902	6903	6904	6905	6906	6906	6907	6908	6909	6910
1	6911	6912	6913	6913	6914	6915	6916	6917	6918	6919
2	6920	6921	6921	6922	6923	6924	6925	6926	6927	6928
3	6928	6929	6930	6931	6932	6933	6934	6935	6936	6936
4	6937	6938	6939	6940	6941	6942	6943	6943	6944	6945
5	6946	6947	6948	6949	6950	6950	6951	6952	6953	6954
6	6955	6956	6957	6957	6958	6959	6960	6961	6962	6963
7	6964	6964	6965	6966	6967	6968	6969	6970	6971	6971
8	6972	6973	6974	6975	6976	6977	6978	6978	6979	6980
9	6981	6982	6983	6984	6985	6985	6986	6987	6988	6989
500	6990	6991	6991	6992	6993	6994	6995	6996	6997	6998

s ″		*h* °	*m* ′	*s* ″		*s* ″		*h* °	*m* ′	*s* ″
450	=	0	7	30		4500	=	1	15	0
460	=	0	7	40		4600	=	1	16	40
470	=	0	7	50		4700	=	1	18	20
480	=	0	8	0		4800	=	1	20	0
490	=	0	8	10		4900	=	1	21	40
500	=	0	8	20		5000	=	1	23	20

Logarithms of Numbers and Small Arcs.

No.	0	1	2	3	4	5	6	7	8	9
500	6990	6991	6991	6992	6993	6994	6995	6996	6997	6998
1	6998	6999	7000	7001	7002	7003	7004	7004	7005	7006
2	7007	7008	7009	7010	7011	7011	7012	7013	7014	7015
3	7016	7017	7017	7018	7019	7020	7021	7022	7023	7023
4	7024	7025	7026	7027	7028	7029	7029	7030	7031	7032
5	7033	7034	7035	7035	7036	7037	7038	7039	7040	7041
6	7042	7042	7043	7044	7045	7046	7047	7048	7048	7049
7	7050	7051	7052	7053	7054	7054	7055	7056	7057	7058
8	7059	7059	7060	7061	7062	7063	7064	7065	7065	7066
9	7067	7068	7069	7070	7071	7071	7072	7073	7074	7075
510	7076	7077	7077	7078	7079	7080	7081	7082	7083	7083
1	7084	7085	7086	7087	7088	7088	7089	7090	7091	7092
2	7093	7094	7094	7095	7096	7097	7098	7099	7099	7100
3	7101	7102	7103	7104	7105	7105	7106	7107	7108	7109
4	7110	7110	7111	7112	7113	7114	7115	7116	7116	7117
5	7118	7119	7120	7121	7121	7122	7123	7124	7125	7126
6	7127	7127	7128	7129	7130	7131	7132	7132	7133	7134
7	7135	7136	7137	7137	7138	7139	7140	7141	7142	7142
8	7143	7144	7145	7146	7147	7147	7148	7149	7150	7151
9	7152	7153	7153	7154	7155	7156	7157	7158	7158	7159
520	7160	7161	7162	7163	7163	7164	7165	7166	7167	7168
1	7168	7169	7170	7171	7172	7173	7173	7174	7175	7176
2	7177	7178	7178	7179	7180	7181	7182	7183	7183	7184
3	7185	7186	7187	7188	7188	7189	7190	7191	7192	7192
4	7193	7194	7195	7196	7197	7197	7198	7199	7200	7201
5	7202	7202	7203	7204	7205	7206	7207	7207	7208	7209
6	7210	7211	7212	7212	7213	7214	7215	7216	7216	7217
7	7218	7219	7220	7221	7221	7222	7223	7224	7225	7226
8	7226	7227	7228	7229	7230	7230	7231	7232	7233	7234
9	7235	7235	7236	7237	7238	7239	7239	7240	7241	7242
530	7243	7244	7244	7245	7246	7247	7248	7248	7249	7250
1	7251	7252	7253	7253	7254	7255	7256	7257	7257	7258
2	7259	7260	7261	7262	7262	7263	7264	7265	7266	7266
3	7267	7268	7269	7270	7271	7271	7272	7273	7274	7275
4	7275	7276	7277	7278	7279	7279	7280	7281	7282	7283
5	7284	7284	7285	7286	7287	7288	7288	7289	7290	7291
6	7292	7292	7293	7294	7295	7296	7297	7297	7298	7299
7	7300	7301	7301	7302	7303	7304	7305	7305	7306	7307
8	7308	7309	7309	7310	7311	7312	7313	7313	7314	7315
9	7316	7317	7318	7318	7319	7320	7321	7322	7322	7323
540	7324	7325	7326	7326	7327	7328	7329	7330	7330	7331
1	7332	7333	7334	7334	7335	7336	7337	7338	7338	7339
2	7340	7341	7342	7342	7343	7344	7345	7346	7346	7347
3	7348	7349	7350	7350	7351	7352	7353	7354	7354	7355
4	7356	7357	7358	7358	7359	7360	7361	7362	7362	7363
5	7364	7365	7366	7366	7367	7368	7369	7370	7370	7371
6	7372	7373	7374	7374	7375	7376	7377	7377	7378	7379
7	7380	7381	7381	7382	7383	7384	7385	7385	7386	7387
8	7388	7389	7389	7390	7391	7392	7393	7393	7394	7395
9	7396	7397	7397	7398	7399	7400	7400	7401	7402	7403
550	7404	7404	7405	7406	7407	7408	7408	7409	7410	7411

s		h	m	s
″		°	′	″
500	=	0	8	20
510	=	0	8	30
520	=	0	8	40
530	=	0	8	50
540	=	0	9	0
550	=	0	9	10

s		h	m	s
″		°	′	″
5000	=	1	23	20
5100	=	1	25	0
5200	=	1	26	40
5300	=	1	28	20
5400	=	1	30	0
5500	=	1	31	40

Logarithms of Numbers and Small Arcs.

No.	0	1	2	3	4	5	6	7	8	9
550	7404	7404	7405	7406	7407	7408	7408	7409	7410	7411
1	7412	7412	7413	7414	7415	7415	7416	7417	7418	7419
2	7419	7420	7421	7422	7423	7423	7424	7425	7426	7426
3	7427	7428	7429	7430	7430	7431	7432	7433	7434	7434
4	7435	7436	7437	7437	7438	7439	7440	7441	7441	7442
5	7443	7444	7444	7445	7446	7447	7448	7448	7449	7450
6	7451	7452	7452	7453	7454	7455	7455	7456	7457	7458
7	7459	7459	7460	7461	7462	7462	7463	7464	7465	7466
8	7466	7467	7468	7469	7469	7470	7471	7472	7473	7473
9	7474	7475	7476	7476	7477	7478	7479	7480	7480	7481
560	7482	7483	7483	7484	7485	7486	7487	7487	7488	7489
1	7490	7490	7491	7492	7493	7494	7494	7495	7496	7497
2	7497	7498	7499	7500	7500	7501	7502	7503	7504	7504
3	7505	7506	7507	7507	7508	7509	7510	7510	7511	7512
4	7513	7514	7514	7515	7516	7517	7517	7518	7519	7520
5	7520	7521	7522	7523	7524	7524	7525	7526	7527	7527
6	7528	7529	7530	7530	7531	7532	7533	7534	7534	7535
7	7536	7537	7537	7538	7539	7540	7540	7541	7542	7543
8	7543	7544	7545	7546	7547	7547	7548	7549	7550	7550
9	7551	7552	7553	7553	7554	7555	7556	7556	7557	7558
570	7559	7560	7560	7561	7562	7563	7563	7564	7565	7566
1	7566	7567	7568	7569	7569	7570	7571	7572	7572	7573
2	7574	7575	7575	7576	7577	7578	7579	7579	7580	7581
3	7582	7582	7583	7584	7585	7585	7586	7587	7588	7588
4	7589	7590	7591	7591	7592	7593	7594	7594	7595	7596
5	7597	7597	7598	7599	7600	7600	7601	7602	7603	7603
6	7604	7605	7606	7606	7607	7608	7609	7610	7610	7611
7	7612	7613	7613	7614	7615	7616	7616	7617	7618	7619
8	7619	7620	7621	7622	7622	7623	7624	7625	7625	7626
9	7627	7628	7628	7629	7630	7631	7631	7632	7633	7634
580	7634	7635	7636	7637	7637	7638	7639	7640	7640	7641
1	7642	7643	7643	7644	7645	7646	7646	7647	7648	7648
2	7649	7650	7651	7651	7652	7653	7654	7654	7655	7656
3	7657	7657	7658	7659	7660	7660	7661	7662	7663	7663
4	7664	7665	7666	7666	7667	7668	7669	7669	7670	7671
5	7672	7672	7673	7674	7675	7675	7676	7677	7677	7678
6	7679	7680	7680	7681	7682	7683	7683	7684	7685	7686
7	7686	7687	7688	7689	7689	7690	7691	7692	7692	7693
8	7694	7695	7695	7696	7697	7697	7698	7699	7700	7700
9	7701	7702	7703	7703	7704	7705	7706	7706	7707	7708
590	7709	7709	7710	7711	7711	7712	7713	7714	7714	7715
1	7716	7717	7717	7718	7719	7720	7720	7721	7722	7722
2	7723	7724	7725	7725	7726	7727	7728	7728	7729	7730
3	7731	7731	7732	7733	7733	7734	7735	7736	7736	7737
4	7738	7739	7739	7740	7741	7742	7742	7743	7744	7744
5	7745	7746	7747	7747	7748	7749	7750	7750	7751	7752
6	7752	7753	7754	7755	7755	7756	7757	7758	7758	7759
7	7760	7760	7761	7762	7763	7763	7764	7765	7766	7766
8	7767	7768	7768	7769	7770	7771	7771	7772	7773	7774
9	7774	7775	7776	7776	7777	7778	7779	7779	7780	7781
600	7782	7782	7783	7784	7784	7785	7786	7787	7787	7788

s ″		*h* °	*m* ′	*s* ″		*s* ″		*h* °	*m* ′	*s* ″
550	=	0	9	10		5500	=	1	31	40
560	=	0	9	20		5600	=	1	33	20
570	=	0	9	30		5700	=	1	35	0
580	=	0	9	40		5800	=	1	36	40
590	=	0	9	50		5900	=	1	38	20
600	=	0	10	0		6000	=	1	40	0

Logarithms of Numbers and Small Arcs.

No.	0	1	2	3	4	5	6	7	8	9
600	7782	7782	7783	7784	7784	7785	7786	7787	7787	7788
1	7789	7789	7790	7791	7792	7792	7793	7794	7795	7795
2	7796	7797	7797	7798	7799	7800	7800	7801	7802	7802
3	7803	7804	7805	7805	7806	7807	7807	7808	7809	7810
4	7810	7811	7812	7813	7813	7814	7815	7815	7816	7817
5	7818	7818	7819	7820	7820	7821	7822	7823	7823	7824
6	7825	7825	7826	7827	7828	7828	7829	7830	7830	7831
7	7832	7833	7833	7834	7835	7835	7836	7837	7838	7838
8	7839	7840	7840	7841	7842	7843	7843	7844	7845	7845
9	7846	7847	7848	7848	7849	7850	7850	7851	7852	7853
610	7853	7854	7855	7855	7856	7857	7858	7858	7859	7860
1	7860	7861	7862	7863	7863	7864	7865	7865	7866	7867
2	7868	7868	7869	7870	7870	7871	7872	7872	7873	7874
3	7875	7875	7876	7877	7877	7878	7879	7880	7880	7881
4	7882	7882	7883	7884	7885	7885	7886	7887	7887	7888
5	7889	7889	7890	7891	7892	7892	7893	7894	7894	7895
6	7896	7897	7897	7898	7899	7899	7900	7901	7901	7902
7	7903	7904	7904	7905	7906	7906	7907	7908	7908	7909
8	7910	7911	7911	7912	7913	7913	7914	7915	7916	7916
9	7917	7918	7918	7919	7920	7920	7921	7922	7923	7923
620	7924	7925	7925	7926	7927	7927	7928	7929	7930	7930
1	7931	7932	7932	7933	7934	7934	7935	7936	7937	7937
2	7938	7939	7939	7940	7941	7941	7942	7943	7943	7944
3	7945	7946	7946	7947	7948	7948	7949	7950	7950	7951
4	7952	7953	7953	7954	7955	7955	7956	7957	7957	7958
5	7959	7959	7960	7961	7962	7962	7963	7964	7964	7965
6	7966	7966	7967	7968	7969	7969	7970	7971	7971	7972
7	7973	7973	7974	7975	7975	7976	7977	7978	7978	7979
8	7980	7980	7981	7982	7982	7983	7984	7984	7985	7986
9	7987	7987	7988	7989	7989	7990	7991	7991	7992	7993
630	7993	7994	7995	7995	7996	7997	7998	7998	7999	8000
1	8000	8001	8002	8002	8003	8004	8004	8005	8006	8006
2	8007	8008	8009	8009	8010	8011	8011	8012	8013	8013
3	8014	8015	8015	8016	8017	8017	8018	8019	8020	8020
4	8021	8022	8022	8023	8024	8024	8025	8026	8026	8027
5	8028	8028	8029	8030	8030	8031	8032	8033	8033	8034
6	8035	8035	8036	8037	8037	8038	8039	8039	8040	8041
7	8041	8042	8043	8043	8044	8045	8045	8046	8047	8048
8	8048	8049	8050	8050	8051	8052	8052	8053	8054	8054
9	8055	8056	8056	8057	8058	8058	8059	8060	8060	8061
640	8062	8062	8063	8064	8065	8065	8066	8067	8067	8068
1	8069	8069	8070	8071	8071	8072	8073	8073	8074	8075
2	8075	8076	8077	8077	8078	8079	8079	8080	8081	8081
3	8082	8083	8083	8084	8085	8085	8086	8087	8088	8088
4	8089	8090	8090	8091	8092	8092	8093	8094	8094	8095
5	8096	8096	8097	8098	8098	8099	8100	8100	8101	8102
6	8102	8103	8104	8104	8105	8106	8106	8107	8108	8108
7	8109	8110	8110	8111	8112	8112	8113	8114	8114	8115
8	8116	8116	8117	8118	8118	8119	8120	8120	8121	8122
9	8122	8123	8124	8124	8125	8126	8126	8127	8128	8128
650	8129	8130	8130	8131	8132	8132	8133	8134	8134	8135

s ″		h °	m ′	s ″
600	=	0	10	0
610	=	0	10	10
620	=	0	10	20
630	=	0	10	30
640	=	0	10	40
650	=	0	10	50

s ″		h °	m ′	s ″
6000	=	1	40	0
6100	=	1	41	40
6200	=	1	43	20
6300	=	1	45	0
6400	=	1	46	40
6500	=	1	48	20

Logarithms of Numbers and Small Arcs.

No.	0	1	2	3	4	5	6	7	8	9
650	8129	8129	8130	8131	8132	8132	8133	8134	8134	8135
1	8136	8136	8137	8138	8138	8139	8140	8140	8141	8142
2	8142	8143	8144	8144	8145	8146	8146	8147	8148	8148
3	8149	8150	8150	8151	8152	8152	8153	8154	8154	8155
4	8156	8156	8157	8158	8158	8159	8160	8160	8161	8162
5	8162	8163	8164	8164	8165	8166	8166	8167	8168	8168
6	8169	8170	8170	8171	8172	8172	8173	8174	8174	8175
7	8176	8176	8177	8178	8178	8179	8180	8180	8181	8182
8	8182	8183	8184	8184	8185	8186	8186	8187	8188	8188
9	8189	8190	8190	8191	8191	8192	8193	8193	8194	8195
660	8195	8196	8197	8197	8198	8199	8199	8200	8201	8201
1	8202	8203	8203	8204	8205	8205	8206	8207	8207	8208
2	8209	8209	8210	8211	8211	8212	8213	8213	8214	8214
3	8215	8216	8216	8217	8218	8218	8219	8220	8220	8221
4	8222	8222	8223	8224	8224	8225	8226	8226	8227	8228
5	8228	8229	8230	8230	8231	8231	8232	8233	8233	8234
6	8235	8235	8236	8237	8237	8238	8239	8239	8240	8241
7	8241	8242	8243	8243	8244	8245	8245	8246	8246	8247
8	8248	8248	8249	8250	8250	8251	8252	8252	8253	8254
9	8254	8255	8256	8256	8257	8258	8258	8259	8259	8260
670	8261	8261	8262	8263	8263	8264	8265	8265	8266	8267
1	8267	8268	8269	8269	8270	8270	8271	8272	8272	8273
2	8274	8274	8275	8276	8276	8277	8278	8278	8279	8280
3	8280	8281	8281	8282	8283	8283	8284	8285	8285	8286
4	8287	8287	8288	8289	8289	8290	8290	8291	8292	8292
5	8293	8294	8294	8295	8296	8296	8297	8298	8298	8299
6	8299	8300	8301	8301	8302	8303	8303	8304	8305	8305
7	8306	8307	8307	8308	8308	8309	8310	8310	8311	8312
8	8312	8313	8314	8314	8315	8316	8316	8317	8317	8318
9	8319	8319	8320	8321	8321	8322	8323	8323	8324	8324
680	8325	8326	8326	8327	8328	8328	8329	8330	8330	8331
1	8332	8332	8333	8333	8334	8335	8335	8336	8337	8337
2	8338	8338	8339	8340	8340	8341	8342	8342	8343	8344
3	8344	8345	8345	8346	8347	8347	8348	8349	8349	8350
4	8351	8351	8352	8352	8353	8354	8354	8355	8356	8356
5	8357	8358	8358	8359	8359	8360	8361	8361	8362	8363
6	8363	8364	8365	8365	8366	8366	8367	8368	8368	8369
7	8370	8370	8371	8371	8372	8373	8373	8374	8375	8375
8	8376	8377	8377	8378	8378	8379	8380	8380	8381	8382
9	8382	8383	8383	8384	8385	8385	8386	8387	8387	8388
690	8388	8389	8390	8390	8391	8392	8392	8393	8394	8394
1	8395	8395	8396	8397	8397	8398	8399	8399	8400	8400
2	8401	8402	8402	8403	8404	8404	8405	8405	8406	8407
3	8407	8408	8409	8409	8410	8410	8411	8412	8412	8413
4	8414	8414	8415	8415	8416	8417	8417	8418	8419	8419
5	8420	8420	8421	8422	8422	8423	8424	8424	8425	8425
6	8426	8427	8427	8428	8429	8429	8430	8430	8431	8432
7	8432	8433	8434	8434	8435	8435	8436	8437	8437	8438
8	8439	8439	8440	8440	8441	8442	8442	8443	8444	8444
9	8445	8445	8446	8447	8447	8448	8449	8449	8450	8450
700	8451	8452	8452	8453	8453	8454	8455	8455	8456	8457

s ″		h °	m ′	s ″
650	=	0	10	50
660	=	0	11	0
670	=	0	11	10
680	=	0	11	20
690	=	0	11	30
700	=	0	11	40

s ″		h °	m ′	s ″
6500	=	1	48	20
6600	=	1	50	0
6700	=	1	51	40
6800	=	1	53	20
6900	=	1	55	0
7000	=	1	56	40

Logarithms of Numbers and Small Arcs.

No.	0	1	2	3	4	5	6	7	8	9
700	8451	8452	8452	8453	8453	8454	8455	8455	8456	8457
1	8457	8458	8458	8459	8460	8460	8461	8462	8462	8463
2	8463	8464	8465	8465	8466	8466	8467	8468	8468	8469
3	8470	8470	8471	8471	8472	8473	8473	8474	8474	8475
4	8476	8476	8477	8478	8478	8479	8479	8480	8481	8481
5	8482	8483	8483	8484	8484	8485	8486	8486	8487	8487
6	8488	8489	8489	8490	8491	8491	8492	8492	8493	8494
7	8494	8495	8495	8496	8496	8497	8498	8498	8499	8500
8	8500	8501	8502	8502	8503	8503	8504	8505	8505	8506
9	8506	8507	8508	8508	8509	8510	8510	8511	8511	8512
710	8513	8513	8514	8514	8515	8516	8516	8517	8517	8518
1	8519	8519	8520	8521	8521	8522	8522	8523	8524	8524
2	8525	8525	8526	8527	8527	8528	8528	8529	8530	8530
3	8531	8532	8532	8533	8533	8534	8535	8535	8536	8536
4	8537	8538	8538	8539	8539	8540	8541	8541	8542	8542
5	8543	8544	8544	8545	8545	8546	8547	8547	8548	8549
6	8549	8550	8550	8551	8552	8552	8553	8553	8554	8555
7	8555	8556	8556	8557	8558	8558	8559	8559	8560	8561
8	8561	8562	8562	8563	8564	8564	8565	8565	8566	8567
9	8567	8568	8569	8569	8570	8570	8571	8572	8572	8573
720	8573	8574	8575	8575	8576	8576	8577	8578	8578	8579
1	8579	8580	8581	8581	8582	8582	8583	8584	8584	8585
2	8585	8586	8587	8587	8588	8588	8589	8590	8590	8591
3	8591	8592	8593	8593	8594	8594	8595	8596	8596	8597
4	8597	8598	8599	8599	8600	8600	8601	8602	8602	8603
5	8603	8604	8605	8605	8606	8606	8607	8608	8608	8609
6	8609	8610	8611	8611	8612	8612	8613	8614	8614	8615
7	8615	8616	8617	8617	8618	8618	8619	8620	8620	8621
8	8621	8622	8623	8623	8624	8624	8625	8625	8626	8627
9	8627	8628	8628	8629	8630	8630	8631	8631	8632	8633
730	8633	8634	8634	8635	8636	8636	8637	8637	8638	8639
1	8639	8640	8640	8641	8642	8642	8643	8643	8644	8645
2	8645	8646	8646	8647	8647	8648	8649	8649	8650	8650
3	8651	8652	8652	8653	8653	8654	8655	8655	8656	8656
4	8657	8658	8658	8659	8659	8660	8661	8661	8662	8662
5	8663	8663	8664	8665	8665	8666	8666	8667	8668	8668
6	8669	8669	8670	8671	8671	8672	8672	8673	8674	8674
7	8675	8675	8676	8676	8677	8678	8678	8679	8679	8680
8	8681	8681	8682	8682	8683	8684	8684	8685	8685	8686
9	8686	8687	8688	8688	8689	8689	8690	8691	8691	8692
740	8692	8693	8693	8694	8695	8695	8696	8696	8697	8698
1	8698	8699	8699	8700	8701	8701	8702	8702	8703	8703
2	8704	8705	8705	8706	8706	8707	8708	8708	8709	8709
3	8710	8710	8711	8712	8712	8713	8713	8714	8715	8715
4	8716	8716	8717	8717	8718	8719	8719	8720	8720	8721
5	8722	8722	8723	8723	8724	8724	8725	8726	8726	8727
6	8727	8728	8729	8729	8730	8730	8731	8731	8732	8733
7	8733	8734	8734	8735	8736	8736	8737	8737	8738	8738
8	8739	8740	8740	8741	8741	8742	8743	8743	8744	8744
9	8745	8745	8746	8747	8747	8748	8748	8749	8749	8750
750	8751	8751	8752	8752	8753	8754	8754	8755	8755	8756

s (″)		h (°)	m (′)	s (″)
700	=	0	11	40
710	=	0	11	50
720	=	0	12	0
730	=	0	12	10
740	=	0	12	20
750	=	0	12	30

s (″)		h (°)	m (′)	s (″)
7000	=	1	56	40
7100	=	1	58	20
7200	=	2	0	0
7300	=	2	1	40
7400	=	2	3	20
7500	=	2	5	0

Logarithms of Numbers and Small Arcs.

No.	0	1	2	3	4	5	6	7	8	9
750	8751	8751	8752	8752	8753	8754	8754	8755	8755	8756
1	8756	8757	8758	8758	8759	8759	8760	8760	8761	8762
2	8762	8763	8763	8764	8764	8765	8766	8766	8767	8767
3	8768	8769	8769	8770	8770	8771	8771	8772	8773	8773
4	8774	8774	8775	8775	8776	8777	8777	8778	8778	8779
5	8779	8780	8781	8781	8782	8782	8783	8783	8784	8785
6	8785	8786	8786	8787	8788	8788	8789	8789	8790	8790
7	8791	8792	8792	8793	8793	8794	8794	8795	8796	8796
8	8797	8797	8798	8798	8799	8800	8800	8801	8801	8802
9	8802	8803	8804	8804	8805	8805	8806	8806	8807	8808
760	8808	8809	8809	8810	8810	8811	8812	8812	8813	8813
1	8814	8814	8815	8816	8816	8817	8817	8818	8818	8819
2	8820	8820	8821	8821	8822	8822	8823	8824	8824	8825
3	8825	8826	8826	8827	8828	8828	8829	8829	8830	8830
4	8831	8832	8832	8833	8833	8834	8834	8835	8835	8836
5	8837	8837	8838	8838	8839	8839	8840	8841	8841	8842
6	8842	8843	8843	8844	8845	8845	8846	8846	8847	8847
7	8848	8849	8849	8850	8850	8851	8851	8852	8852	8853
8	8854	8854	8855	8855	8856	8856	8857	8858	8858	8859
9	8859	8860	8860	8861	8862	8862	8863	8863	8864	8864
770	8865	8865	8866	8867	8867	8868	8868	8869	8869	8870
1	8871	8871	8872	8872	8873	8873	8874	8874	8875	8876
2	8876	8877	8877	8878	8878	8879	8880	8880	8881	8881
3	8882	8882	8883	8883	8884	8885	8885	8886	8886	8887
4	8887	8888	8889	8889	8890	8890	8891	8891	8892	8892
5	8893	8894	8894	8895	8895	8896	8896	8897	8898	8898
6	8899	8899	8900	8900	8901	8901	8902	8903	8903	8904
7	8904	8905	8905	8906	8906	8907	8908	8908	8909	8909
8	8910	8910	8911	8911	8912	8913	8913	8914	8914	8915
9	8915	8916	8916	8917	8918	8918	8919	8919	8920	8920
780	8921	8922	8922	8923	8923	8924	8924	8925	8925	8926
1	8927	8927	8928	8928	8929	8929	8930	8930	8931	8932
2	8932	8933	8933	8934	8934	8935	8935	8936	8937	8937
3	8938	8938	8939	8939	8940	8940	8941	8942	8942	8943
4	8943	8944	8944	8945	8945	8946	8946	8947	8948	8948
5	8949	8949	8950	8950	8951	8951	8952	8953	8953	8954
6	8954	8955	8955	8956	8956	8957	8958	8958	8959	8959
7	8960	8960	8961	8961	8962	8963	8963	8964	8964	8965
8	8965	8966	8966	8967	8967	8968	8969	8969	8970	8970
9	8971	8971	8972	8972	8973	8974	8974	8975	8975	8976
790	8976	8977	8977	8978	8978	8979	8980	8980	8981	8981
1	8982	8982	8983	8983	8984	8985	8985	8986	8986	8987
2	8987	8988	8988	8989	8989	8990	8991	8991	8992	8992
3	8993	8993	8994	8994	8995	8995	8996	8997	8997	8998
4	8998	8999	8999	9000	9000	9001	9002	9002	9003	9003
5	9004	9004	9005	9005	9006	9006	9007	9007	9008	9009
6	9009	9010	9010	9011	9011	9012	9012	9013	9013	9014
7	9015	9015	9016	9016	9017	9017	9018	9018	9019	9019
8	9020	9021	9021	9022	9022	9023	9023	9024	9024	9025
9	9025	9026	9027	9027	9028	9028	9029	9029	9030	9030
800	9031	9031	9032	9033	9033	9034	9034	9035	9035	9036

s		*h*	*m*	*s*
″		°	′	″
750	=	0	12	30
760	=	0	12	40
770	=	0	12	50
780	=	0	13	0
790	=	0	13	10
800	=	0	13	20

s		*h*	*m*	*s*
″		°	′	″
7500	=	2	5	0
7600	=	2	6	40
7700	=	2	8	20
7800	=	2	10	0
7900	=	2	11	40
8000	=	2	13	20

Logarithms of Numbers and Small Arcs.

No.	0	1	2	3	4	5	6	7	8	9
800	9031	9031	9032	9033	9033	9034	9034	9035	9035	9036
1	9036	9037	9037	9038	9038	9039	9040	9040	9041	9041
2	9042	9042	9043	9043	9044	9044	9045	9046	9046	9047
3	9047	9048	9048	9049	9049	9050	9050	9051	9051	9052
4	9053	9053	9054	9054	9055	9055	9056	9056	9057	9057
5	9058	9059	9059	9060	9060	9061	9061	9062	9062	9063
6	9063	9064	9064	9065	9066	9066	9067	9067	9068	9068
7	9069	9069	9070	9070	9071	9071	9072	9073	9073	9074
8	9074	9075	9075	9076	9076	9077	9077	9078	9078	9079
9	9079	9080	9081	9081	9082	9082	9083	9083	9084	9084
810	9085	9085	9086	9086	9087	9088	9088	9089	9089	9090
1	9090	9091	9091	9092	9092	9093	9093	9094	9094	9095
2	9096	9096	9097	9097	9098	9098	9099	9099	9100	9100
3	9101	9101	9102	9103	9103	9104	9104	9105	9105	9106
4	9106	9107	9107	9108	9108	9109	9109	9110	9111	9111
5	9112	9112	9113	9113	9114	9114	9115	9115	9116	9116
6	9117	9117	9118	9119	9119	9120	9120	9121	9121	9122
7	9122	9123	9123	9124	9124	9125	9125	9126	9126	9127
8	9128	9128	9129	9129	9130	9130	9131	9131	9132	9132
9	9133	9133	9134	9134	9135	9135	9136	9137	9137	9138
820	9138	9139	9139	9140	9140	9141	9141	9142	9142	9143
1	9143	9144	9144	9145	9146	9146	9147	9147	9148	9148
2	9149	9149	9150	9150	9151	9151	9152	9152	9153	9153
3	9154	9155	9155	9156	9156	9157	9157	9158	9158	9159
4	9159	9160	9160	9161	9161	9162	9162	9163	9163	9164
5	9165	9165	9166	9166	9167	9167	9168	9168	9169	9169
6	9170	9170	9171	9171	9172	9172	9173	9173	9174	9175
7	9175	9176	9176	9177	9177	9178	9178	9179	9179	9180
8	9180	9181	9181	9182	9182	9183	9183	9184	9185	9185
9	9186	9186	9187	9187	9188	9188	9189	9189	9190	9190
830	9191	9191	9192	9192	9193	9193	9194	9194	9195	9195
1	9196	9197	9197	9198	9198	9199	9199	9200	9200	9201
2	9201	9202	9202	9203	9203	9204	9204	9205	9205	9206
3	9206	9207	9207	9208	9209	9209	9210	9210	9211	9211
4	9212	9212	9213	9213	9214	9214	9215	9215	9216	9216
5	9217	9217	9218	9218	9219	9219	9220	9221	9221	9222
6	9222	9223	9223	9224	9224	9225	9225	9226	9226	9227
7	9227	9228	9228	9229	9229	9230	9230	9231	9231	9232
8	9232	9233	9233	9234	9235	9235	9236	9236	9237	9237
9	9238	9238	9239	9239	9240	9240	9241	9241	9242	9242
840	9243	9243	9244	9244	9245	9245	9246	9246	9247	9247
1	9248	9248	9249	9250	9250	9251	9251	9252	9252	9253
2	9253	9254	9254	9255	9255	9256	9256	9257	9257	9258
3	9258	9259	9259	9260	9260	9261	9261	9262	9262	9263
4	9263	9264	9264	9265	9265	9266	9267	9267	9268	9268
5	9269	9269	9270	9270	9271	9271	9272	9272	9273	9273
6	9274	9274	9275	9275	9276	9276	9277	9277	9278	9278
7	9279	9279	9280	9280	9281	9281	9282	9282	9283	9283
8	9284	9284	9285	9285	9286	9287	9287	9288	9288	9289
9	9289	9290	9290	9291	9291	9292	9292	9293	9293	9294
850	9294	9295	9295	9296	9296	9297	9297	9298	9298	9299

s ″		h °	m ′	s ″
800	=	0	13	20
810	=	0	13	30
820	=	0	13	40
830	=	0	13	50
840	=	0	14	0
850	=	0	14	10

s ″		h °	m ′	s ″
8000	=	2	13	20
8100	=	2	15	0
8200	=	2	16	40
8300	=	2	18	20
8400	=	2	20	0
8500	=	2	21	40

…garithms of Numbers and Small Arcs.

2	3	4	5	6	7	8	9
9295	9296	9296	9297	9297	9298	9298	9299
9300	9301	9301	9302	9302	9303	9303	9304
9305	9306	9306	9307	9307	9308	9308	9309
9311	9311	9312	9312	9313	9313	9314	9314
9316	9316	9317	9317	9318	9318	9319	9319
9321	9321	9322	9322	9323	9323	9324	9324
9326	9326	9327	9327	9328	9328	9329	9329
9331	9331	9332	9332	9333	9333	9334	9334
9336	9336	9337	9337	9338	9338	9339	9339
9341	9341	9342	9342	9343	9343	9344	9344
9346	9347	9347	9348	9348	9349	9349	9350
9351	9352	9352	9353	9353	9354	9354	9355
9356	9357	9357	9358	9358	9359	9359	9360
9361	9362	9362	9363	9363	9364	9364	9365
9366	9367	9367	9368	9368	9369	9369	9370
9371	9372	9372	9373	9373	9374	9374	9375
9376	9377	9377	9378	9378	9379	9379	9380
9381	9382	9382	9383	9383	9384	9384	9385
9386	9387	9387	9388	9388	9389	9389	9390
9391	9392	9392	9393	9393	9394	9394	9395
9396	9397	9397	9398	9398	9399	9399	9400
9401	9402	9402	9403	9403	9404	9404	9405
9406	9407	9407	9408	9408	9409	9409	9410
9411	9412	9412	9413	9413	9414	9414	9415
9416	9417	9417	9418	9418	9419	9419	9420
9421	9422	9422	9423	9423	9424	9424	9425
9426	9427	9427	9428	9428	9429	9429	9430
9431	9431	9432	9432	9433	9433	9434	9434
9436	9436	9437	9437	9438	9438	9439	9439
9441	9441	9442	9442	9443	9443	9444	9444
9446	9446	9447	9447	9448	9448	9449	9449
9451	9451	9452	9452	9453	9453	9454	9454
9456	9456	9457	9457	9458	9458	9459	9459
9461	9461	9462	9462	9463	9463	9464	9464
9466	9466	9466	9467	9467	9468	9468	9469
9470	9471	9471	9472	9472	9473	9473	9474
9475	9476	9476	9477	9477	9478	9478	9479
9480	9481	9481	9482	9482	9483	9483	9484
9485	9486	9486	9487	9487	9488	9488	9489
9490	9490	9491	9491	9492	9492	9493	9493
9495	9495	9496	9496	9497	9497	9498	9498
9500	9500	9501	9501	9502	9502	9503	9503
9505	9505	9506	9506	9507	9507	9508	9508
9509	9510	9510	9511	9511	9512	9512	9513
9514	9515	9515	9516	9516	9517	9517	9518
9519	9520	9520	9521	9521	9522	9522	9523
9524	9525	9525	9526	9526	9526	9527	9527
9529	9529	9530	9530	9531	9531	9532	9532
9534	9534	9535	9535	9536	9536	9537	9537
9539	9539	9540	9540	9540	9541	9541	9542
9543	9544	9544	9545	9545	9546	9546	9547

m ′	s ″
14	10
14	20
14	30
14	40
14	50
15	0

s ″		h °	m ′	s ″
8500	=	2	21	40
8600	=	2	23	20
8700	=	2	25	0
8800	=	2	26	40
8900	=	2	28	20
9000	=	2	30	0

Logarithms of Numbers and Small Arcs.

No.	0	1	2	3	4	5	6	7	8	9
900	9542	9543	9543	9544	9544	9545	9545	9546	9546	9547
1	9547	9548	9548	9549	9549	9550	9550	9551	9551	9552
2	9552	9553	9553	9554	9554	9554	9555	9555	9556	9556
3	9557	9557	9558	9558	9559	9559	9560	9560	9561	9561
4	9562	9562	9563	9563	9564	9564	9565	9565	9566	9566
5	9566	9567	9567	9568	9568	9569	9569	9570	9570	9571
6	9571	9572	9572	9573	9573	9574	9574	9575	9575	9576
7	9576	9577	9577	9578	9578	9578	9579	9579	9580	9580
8	9581	9581	9582	9582	9583	9583	9584	9584	9585	9585
9	9586	9586	9587	9587	9588	9588	9589	9589	9589	9590
910	9590	9591	9591	9592	9592	9593	9593	9594	9594	9595
1	9595	9596	9596	9597	9597	9598	9598	9599	9599	9599
2	9600	9600	9601	9601	9602	9602	9603	9603	9604	9604
3	9605	9605	9606	9606	9607	9607	9608	9608	9609	9609
4	9609	9610	9610	9611	9611	9612	9612	9613	9613	9614
5	9614	9615	9615	9616	9616	9617	9617	9618	9618	9618
6	9619	9619	9620	9620	9621	9621	9622	9622	9623	9623
7	9624	9624	9625	9625	9626	9626	9627	9627	9627	9628
8	9628	9629	9629	9630	9630	9631	9631	9632	9632	9633
9	9633	9634	9634	9635	9635	9636	9636	9636	9637	9637
920	9638	9638	9639	9639	9640	9640	9641	9641	9642	9642
1	9643	9643	9644	9644	9644	9645	9645	9646	9646	9647
2	9647	9648	9648	9649	9649	9650	9650	9651	9651	9652
3	9652	9652	9653	9653	9654	9654	9655	9655	9656	9656
4	9657	9657	9658	9658	9659	9659	9660	9660	9660	9661
5	9661	9662	9662	9663	9663	9664	9664	9665	9665	9666
6	9666	9667	9667	9668	9668	9668	9669	9669	9670	9670
7	9671	9671	9672	9672	9673	9673	9674	9674	9675	9675
8	9675	9676	9676	9677	9677	9678	9678	9679	9679	9680
9	9680	9681	9681	9682	9682	9682	9683	9683	9684	9684
930	9685	9685	9686	9686	9687	9687	9688	9688	9689	9689
1	9690	9690	9690	9691	9691	9692	9692	9693	9693	9694
2	9694	9695	9695	9696	9696	9696	9697	9697	9698	9698
3	9699	9699	9700	9700	9701	9701	9702	9702	9703	9703
4	9703	9704	9704	9705	9705	9706	9706	9707	9707	9708
5	9708	9709	9709	9710	9710	9710	9711	9711	9712	9712
6	9713	9713	9714	9714	9715	9715	9716	9716	9716	9717
7	9717	9718	9718	9719	9719	9720	9720	9721	9721	9722
8	9722	9722	9723	9723	9724	9724	9725	9725	9726	9726
9	9727	9727	9728	9728	9729	9729	9729	9730	9730	9731
940	9731	9732	9732	9733	9733	9734	9734	9735	9735	9735
1	9736	9736	9737	9737	9738	9738	9739	9739	9740	9740
2	9741	9741	9741	9742	9742	9743	9743	9744	9744	9745
3	9745	9746	9746	9747	9747	9747	9748	9748	9749	9749
4	9750	9750	9751	9751	9752	9752	9752	9753	9753	9754
5	9754	9755	9755	9756	9756	9757	9757	9758	9758	9758
6	9759	9759	9759	9760	9761	9761	9762	9762	9763	9763
7	9764	9764	9764	9765	9765	9766	9766	9767	9767	9768
8	9768	9769	9769	9769	9770	9770	9771	9771	9772	9772
9	9773	9773	9774	9774	9774	9775	9775	9776	9776	9777
950	9777	9778	9778	9779	9779	9780	9780	9780	9781	9781

s		h	m	s
″		°	′	″
900	=	0	15	0
910	=	0	15	10
920	=	0	15	20
930	=	0	15	30
940	=	0	15	40
950	=	0	15	50

s		h	m	s
″		°	′	″
9000	=	2	30	0
9100	=	2	31	40
9200	=	2	33	20
9300	=	2	35	0
9400	=	2	36	40
9500	=	2	38	20

Logarithms of Numbers and Small Arcs.

No.	0	1	2	3	4	5	6	7	8	9
950	9777	9778	9778	9779	9779	9780	9780	9780	9781	9781
1	9782	9782	9783	9783	9784	9784	9785	9785	9785	9786
2	9786	9787	9787	9788	9788	9789	9789	9790	9790	9790
3	9791	9791	9792	9792	9793	9793	9794	9794	9795	9795
4	9795	9796	9776	9797	9797	9798	9798	9799	9799	9800
5	9800	9800	9801	9801	9802	9802	9803	9803	9804	9804
6	9805	9805	9805	9806	9806	9807	9807	9808	9808	9809
7	9809	9810	9810	9810	9811	9811	9812	9812	9813	9813
8	9814	9814	9815	9815	9815	9816	9816	9817	9817	9818
9	9818	9819	9819	9820	9820	9820	9821	9821	9822	9822
960	9823	9823	9824	9824	9825	9825	9825	9826	9826	9827
1	9827	9828	9828	9829	9829	9829	9830	9830	9831	9831
2	9832	9832	9833	9833	9834	9834	9834	9835	9835	9836
3	9836	9837	9837	9838	9838	9839	9839	9839	9840	9840
4	9841	9841	9842	9842	9843	9843	9843	9844	9844	9845
5	9845	9846	9846	9847	9847	9848	9848	9848	9849	9849
6	9850	9850	9851	9851	9852	9852	9852	9853	9853	9854
7	9854	9855	9855	9856	9856	9857	9857	9857	9858	9858
8	9859	9859	9860	9860	9861	9861	9861	9862	9862	9863
9	9863	9864	9864	9865	9865	9865	9866	9866	9867	9867
970	9868	9868	9869	9869	9870	9870	9870	9871	9871	9872
1	9872	9873	9873	9874	9874	9874	9875	9875	9876	9876
2	9877	9877	9878	9878	9878	9879	9879	9880	9880	9881
3	9881	9882	9882	9882	9883	9883	9884	9884	9885	9885
4	9886	9886	9886	9887	9887	9888	9888	9889	9889	9890
5	9890	9890	9891	9891	9892	9892	9893	9893	9894	9894
6	9895	9895	9895	9896	9896	9897	9897	9898	9898	9899
7	9899	9899	9900	9900	9901	9901	9902	9902	9903	9903
8	9903	9904	9904	9905	9905	9906	9906	9907	9907	9907
9	9908	9908	9909	9909	9910	9910	9910	9911	9911	9912
980	9912	9913	9913	9914	9914	9914	9915	9915	9916	9916
1	9917	9917	9918	9918	9918	9919	9919	9920	9920	9921
2	9921	9922	9922	9922	9923	9923	9924	9924	9925	9925
3	9926	9926	9926	9927	9927	9928	9928	9929	9929	9930
4	9930	9930	9931	9931	9932	9932	9933	9933	9933	9934
5	9934	9935	9935	9936	9936	9937	9937	9937	9938	9938
6	9939	9939	9940	9940	9941	9941	9941	9942	9942	9943
7	9943	9944	9944	9944	9945	9945	9946	9946	9947	9947
8	9948	9948	9948	9949	9949	9950	9950	9951	9951	9952
9	9952	9952	9953	9953	9954	9954	9955	9955	9955	9956
990	9956	9957	9957	9958	9958	9959	9959	9959	9960	9960
1	9961	9961	9962	9962	9962	9963	9963	9964	9964	9965
2	9965	9966	9966	9966	9967	9967	9968	9968	9969	9969
3	9969	9970	9970	9971	9971	9972	9972	9973	9973	9973
4	9974	9974	9975	9975	9976	9976	9976	9977	9977	9978
5	9978	9979	9979	9980	9980	9980	9981	9981	9982	9982
6	9983	9983	9983	9984	9984	9985	9985	9986	9986	9987
7	9987	9987	9988	9988	9989	9989	9990	9990	9990	9991
8	9991	9992	9992	9993	9993	9993	9994	9994	9995	9995
9	9996	9996	9997	9997	9997	9998	9998	9999	9999	0000
1000	0000	0000	0001	0001	0002	0002	0003	0003	0003	0004

s ″		h °	m ′	s ″
950	=	0	15	50
960	=	0	16	0
970	=	0	16	10
980	=	0	16	20
990	=	0	16	30
1000	=	0	16	40

s ″		h °	m ′	s ″
9500	=	2	38	20
9600	=	2	40	0
9700	=	2	41	40
9800	=	2	43	20
9900	=	2	45	0
10000	=	2	46	40

Logarithms of Numbers: 1 to 1009.

No.	0	1	2	3	4	5	6	7	8	9	Proportional Parts. 1	2	3	4	5	6	7	8	9
0	—	0000	3010	4771	6021	6990	7782	8451	9031	9542	98	196	294	392	490	587	685	783	881
1	0000	0414	0792	1139	1461	1761	2041	2305	2553	2788	30	60	90	120	150	180	210	240	270
2	3010	3222	3424	3617	3802	3979	4150	4314	4472	4624	18	35	53	71	88	106	124	142	159
3	4771	4914	5052	5185	5315	5441	5563	5682	5798	5911	13	25	38	50	63	76	88	101	113
4	6021	6128	6232	6335	6435	6532	6628	6721	6812	6902	10	19	29	39	48	58	68	78	87
5	6990	7076	7160	7243	7324	7404	7482	7559	7634	7709	8	16	24	32	40	48	56	64	72
6	7782	7853	7924	7993	8062	8129	8195	8261	8325	8388	7	13	20	27	33	40	47	54	60
7	8451	8513	8573	8633	8692	8751	8808	8865	8921	8976	6	12	18	24	29	35	41	47	53
8	9031	9085	9138	9191	9243	9294	9345	9395	9445	9494	5	10	15	20	25	31	36	41	46
9	9542	9590	9638	9685	9731	9777	9823	9868	9912	9956	5	9	14	18	23	28	32	37	41
10	0000	0043	0086	0128	0170	0212	0253	0294	0334	0374	4	8	12	17	21	25	29	33	37
1	0414	0453	0492	0531	0569	0607	0645	0682	0719	0755	4	8	11	15	19	23	26	30	34
2	0792	0828	0864	0899	0934	0969	1004	1038	1072	1106	3	7	10	14	17	21	24	28	31
3	1139	1173	1206	1239	1271	1303	1335	1367	1399	1430	3	6	10	13	16	19	23	26	29
4	1461	1492	1523	1553	1584	1614	1644	1673	1703	1732	3	6	9	12	15	18	21	24	27
5	1761	1790	1818	1847	1875	1903	1931	1959	1987	2014	3	6	8	11	14	17	20	22	25
6	2041	2068	2095	2122	2148	2175	2201	2227	2253	2279	3	5	8	11	13	16	18	21	24
7	2304	2330	2355	2380	2405	2430	2455	2480	2504	2529	2	5	7	10	12	15	17	20	22
8	2553	2577	2601	2625	2648	2672	2695	2718	2742	2765	2	5	7	9	12	14	16	19	21
9	2788	2810	2833	2856	2878	2900	2923	2945	2967	2989	2	4	7	9	11	13	16	18	20
20	3010	3032	3054	3075	3096	3118	3139	3160	3181	3201	2	4	6	8	11	13	15	17	19
1	3222	3243	3263	3284	3304	3324	3345	3365	3385	3404	2	4	6	8	10	12	14	16	18
2	3424	3444	3464	3483	3502	3522	3541	3560	3579	3598	2	4	6	8	10	12	14	15	17
3	3617	3636	3655	3674	3692	3711	3729	3747	3766	3784	2	4	6	7	9	11	13	15	17
4	3802	3820	3838	3856	3874	3892	3909	3927	3945	3962	2	4	5	7	9	11	12	14	16
5	3979	3997	4014	4031	4048	4065	4082	4099	4116	4133	2	3	5	7	9	10	12	14	15
6	4150	4166	4183	4200	4216	4232	4249	4265	4281	4298	2	3	5	7	8	10	11	13	15
7	4314	4330	4346	4362	4378	4393	4409	4425	4440	4456	2	3	5	6	8	9	11	13	14
8	4472	4487	4502	4518	4533	4548	4564	4579	4594	4609	2	3	5	6	8	9	11	12	14
9	4624	4639	4654	4669	4683	4698	4713	4728	4742	4757	1	3	4	6	7	9	10	12	13
30	4771	4786	4800	4814	4829	4843	4857	4871	4886	4900	1	3	4	6	7	9	10	11	13
1	4914	4928	4942	4955	4969	4983	4997	5011	5024	5038	1	3	4	6	7	8	10	11	12
2	5052	5065	5079	5092	5105	5119	5132	5145	5159	5172	1	3	4	5	7	8	9	11	12
3	5185	5198	5211	5224	5237	5250	5263	5276	5289	5302	1	3	4	5	6	8	9	10	12
4	5315	5328	5340	5353	5366	5378	5391	5403	5416	5428	1	3	4	5	6	8	9	10	11
5	5441	5453	5465	5478	5490	5502	5515	5527	5539	5551	1	2	4	5	6	7	9	10	11
6	5563	5575	5587	5599	5611	5623	5635	5647	5658	5670	1	2	4	5	6	7	8	10	11
7	5682	5694	5705	5717	5729	5740	5752	5763	5775	5786	1	2	3	5	6	7	8	9	10
8	5798	5809	5821	5832	5843	5855	5866	5877	5888	5899	1	2	3	5	6	7	8	9	10
9	5911	5922	5933	5944	5955	5966	5977	5988	5999	6010	1	2	3	4	5	7	8	9	10
40	6021	6031	6042	6053	6064	6075	6085	6096	6107	6117	1	2	3	4	5	6	8	9	10
1	6128	6138	6149	6160	6170	6180	6191	6201	6212	6222	1	2	3	4	5	6	7	8	9
2	6232	6243	6253	6263	6274	6284	6294	6304	6314	6325	1	2	3	4	5	6	7	8	9
3	6335	6345	6355	6365	6375	6385	6395	6405	6415	6425	1	2	3	4	5	6	7	8	9
4	6435	6444	6454	6464	6474	6484	6493	6503	6513	6522	1	2	3	4	5	6	7	8	9
5	6532	6542	6551	6561	6571	6580	6590	6599	6609	6618	1	2	3	4	5	6	7	8	9
6	6628	6637	6646	6656	6665	6675	6684	6693	6702	6712	1	2	3	4	5	6	7	7	8
7	6721	6730	6739	6749	6758	6767	6776	6785	6794	6803	1	2	3	4	5	5	6	7	8
8	6812	6821	6830	6839	6848	6857	6866	6875	6884	6893	1	2	3	4	4	5	6	7	8
9	6902	6911	6920	6928	6937	6946	6955	6964	6972	6981	1	2	3	4	4	5	6	7	8
50	6990	6998	7007	7016	7024	7033	7042	7050	7059	7067	1	2	3	3	4	5	6	7	8

Logarithms of Numbers: 1 to 1009.

No.	0	1	2	3	4	5	6	7	8	9	PP 1	PP 2	PP 3	PP 4	PP 5	PP 6	PP 7	PP 8	PP 9
50	6990	6998	7007	7016	7024	7033	7042	7050	7059	7067	1	2	3	3	4	5	6	7	8
1	7076	7084	7093	7101	7110	7118	7126	7135	7143	7152	1	2	3	3	4	5	6	7	8
2	7160	7168	7177	7185	7193	7202	7210	7218	7226	7235	1	2	2	3	4	5	6	7	7
3	7243	7251	7259	7267	7275	7284	7292	7300	7308	7316	1	2	2	3	4	5	6	6	7
4	7324	7332	7340	7348	7356	7364	7372	7380	7388	7396	1	2	2	3	4	5	6	6	7
5	7404	7412	7419	7427	7435	7443	7451	7459	7466	7474	1	2	2	3	4	5	5	6	7
6	7482	7490	7497	7505	7513	7520	7528	7536	7543	7551	1	2	2	3	4	5	5	6	7
7	7559	7566	7574	7582	7589	7597	7604	7612	7619	7627	1	2	2	3	4	5	5	6	7
8	7634	7642	7649	7657	7664	7672	7679	7686	7694	7701	1	1	2	3	4	4	5	6	7
9	7709	7716	7723	7731	7738	7745	7752	7760	7767	7774	1	1	2	3	4	4	5	6	7
60	7782	7789	7796	7803	7810	7818	7825	7832	7839	7846	1	1	2	3	4	4	5	6	6
1	7853	7860	7868	7875	7882	7889	7896	7903	7910	7917	1	1	2	3	4	4	5	6	6
2	7924	7931	7938	7945	7952	7959	7966	7973	7980	7987	1	1	2	3	3	4	5	6	6
3	7993	8000	8007	8014	8021	8028	8035	8041	8048	8055	1	1	2	3	3	4	5	5	6
4	8062	8069	8075	8082	8089	8096	8102	8109	8116	8122	1	1	2	3	3	4	5	5	6
5	8129	8136	8142	8149	8156	8162	8169	8176	8182	8189	1	1	2	3	3	4	5	5	6
6	8195	8202	8209	8215	8222	8228	8235	8241	8248	8254	1	1	2	3	3	4	5	5	6
7	8261	8267	8274	8280	8287	8293	8299	8306	8312	8319	1	1	2	3	3	4	5	5	6
8	8325	8331	8338	8344	8351	8357	8363	8370	8376	8382	1	1	2	3	3	4	4	5	6
9	8388	8395	8401	8407	8414	8420	8426	8432	8439	8445	1	1	2	2	3	4	4	5	6
70	8451	8457	8463	8470	8476	8482	8488	8494	8500	8506	1	1	2	2	3	4	4	5	6
1	8513	8519	8525	8531	8537	8543	8549	8555	8561	8567	1	1	2	2	3	4	4	5	5
2	8573	8579	8585	8591	8597	8603	8609	8615	8621	8627	1	1	2	2	3	4	4	5	5
3	8633	8639	8645	8651	8657	8663	8669	8675	8681	8686	1	1	2	2	3	4	4	5	5
4	8692	8698	8704	8710	8716	8722	8727	8733	8739	8745	1	1	2	2	3	4	4	5	5
5	8751	8756	8762	8768	8774	8779	8785	8791	8797	8802	1	1	2	2	3	3	4	5	5
6	8808	8814	8820	8825	8831	8837	8842	8848	8854	8859	1	1	2	2	3	3	4	5	5
7	8865	8871	8876	8882	8887	8893	8899	8904	8910	8915	1	1	2	2	3	3	4	4	5
8	8921	8927	8932	8938	8943	8949	8954	8960	8965	8971	1	1	2	2	3	3	4	4	5
9	8976	8982	8987	8993	8998	9004	9009	9015	9020	9025	1	1	2	2	3	3	4	4	5
80	9031	9036	9042	9047	9053	9058	9063	9069	9074	9079	1	1	2	2	3	3	4	4	5
1	9085	9090	9096	9101	9106	9112	9117	9122	9128	9133	1	1	2	2	3	3	4	4	5
2	9138	9143	9149	9154	9159	9165	9170	9175	9180	9186	1	1	2	2	3	3	4	4	5
3	9191	9196	9201	9206	9212	9217	9222	9227	9232	9238	1	1	2	2	3	3	4	4	5
4	9243	9248	9253	9258	9263	9269	9274	9279	9284	9289	1	1	2	2	3	3	4	4	5
5	9294	9299	9304	9309	9315	9320	9325	9330	9335	9340	1	1	2	2	3	3	4	4	5
6	9345	9350	9355	9360	9365	9370	9375	9380	9385	9390	1	1	2	2	3	3	4	4	5
7	9395	9400	9405	9410	9415	9420	9425	9430	9435	9440	0	1	1	2	2	3	3	4	4
8	9445	9450	9455	9460	9465	9469	9474	9479	9484	9489	0	1	1	2	2	3	3	4	4
9	9494	9499	9504	9509	9513	9518	9523	9528	9533	9538	0	1	1	2	2	3	3	4	4
90	9542	9547	9552	9557	9562	9566	9571	9576	9581	9586	0	1	1	2	2	3	3	4	4
1	9590	9595	9600	9605	9609	9614	9619	9624	9628	9633	0	1	1	2	2	3	3	4	4
2	9638	9643	9647	9652	9657	9661	9666	9671	9675	9680	0	1	1	2	2	3	3	4	4
3	9685	9689	9694	9699	9703	9708	9713	9717	9722	9727	0	1	1	2	2	3	3	4	4
4	9731	9736	9741	9745	9750	9754	9759	9764	9768	9773	0	1	1	2	2	3	3	4	4
5	9777	9782	9786	9791	9795	9800	9805	9809	9814	9818	0	1	1	2	2	3	3	4	4
6	9823	9827	9832	9836	9841	9845	9850	9854	9859	9863	0	1	1	2	2	3	3	4	4
7	9868	9872	9877	9881	9886	9890	9894	9899	9903	9908	0	1	1	2	2	3	3	4	4
8	9912	9917	9921	9926	9930	9934	9939	9943	9948	9952	0	1	1	2	2	3	3	4	4
9	9956	9961	9965	9969	9974	9978	9983	9987	9991	9996	0	1	1	2	2	3	3	4	4
100	0000	0004	0009	0013	0017	0022	0026	0030	0035	0039	0	1	1	2	2	3	3	4	4

Column headers 1–9 under "Proportional Parts." are labelled PP 1 – PP 9.

Logarithmic Sines, Tangents, and Secants to every Eighth Point of the Compass.

Degrees.	Points.	Sine.	Cosecant.	Tangent.	Cotangent.	Secant.	Cosine.	Points.	Degrees.
0.0	0	− ∞	+ ∞	− ∞	+ ∞	10.0000	10.0000	8	90.0
1.4	⅛	8.3899	11.6101	8.3900	11.6100	10.0001	9.9999	⅞	88.6
2.8	¼	8.6908	11.3092	8.6913	11.3087	10.0005	9.9995	¾	87.2
4.2	⅜	8.8667	11.1333	8.8678	11.1322	10.0012	9.9988	⅝	85.8
5.6	½	8.9913	11.0087	8.9934	11.0066	10.0021	9.9979	½	84.4
7.0	⅝	9.0878	10.9122	9.0911	10.9089	10.0033	9.9967	⅜	83.0
8.4	¾	9.1665	10.8335	9.1713	10.8287	10.0047	9.9953	¼	81.6
9.8	⅞	9.2329	10.7671	9.2394	10.7606	10.0064	9.9936	⅛	80.2
11.3	1	9.2902	10.7098	9.2987	10.7013	10.0084	9.9916	7	78.7
12.7	⅛	9.3406	10.6594	9.3513	10.6487	10.0107	9.9893	⅞	77.3
14.1	¼	9.3856	10.6144	9.3988	10.6012	10.0132	9.9868	¾	75.9
15.5	⅜	9.4260	10.5740	9.4421	10.5579	10.0160	9.9840	⅝	74.5
16.9	½	9.4628	10.5372	9.4819	10.5181	10.0191	9.9809	½	73.1
18.3	⅝	9.4965	10.5035	9.5190	10.4810	10.0225	9.9775	⅜	71.7
19.7	¾	9.5275	10.4725	9.5537	10.4463	10.0262	9.9738	¼	70.3
21.1	⅞	9.5561	10.4439	9.5863	10.4137	10.0301	9.9699	⅛	68.9
22.5	2	9.5828	10.4172	9.6172	10.3828	10.0344	9.9656	6	67.5
23.9	⅛	9.6077	10.3923	9.6467	10.3533	10.0390	9.9610	⅞	66.1
25.3	¼	9.6310	10.3690	9.6748	10.3252	10.0438	9.9562	¾	64.7
26.7	⅜	9.6528	10.3472	9.7019	10.2981	10.0490	9.9510	⅝	63.3
28.1	½	9.6734	10.3266	9.7280	10.2720	10.0546	9.9454	½	61.9
29.5	⅝	9.6928	10.3072	9.7532	10.2468	10.0604	9.9396	⅜	60.5
30.9	¾	9.7111	10.2889	9.7777	10.2223	10.0666	9.9334	¼	59.1
32.3	⅞	9.7284	10.2716	9.8016	10.1984	10.0732	9.9268	⅛	57.7
33.7	3	9.7447	10.2553	9.8249	10.1751	10.0802	9.9198	5	56.3
35.2	⅛	9.7603	10.2397	9.8477	10.1523	10.0875	9.9125	⅞	54.8
36.6	¼	9.7750	10.2250	9.8702	10.1298	10.0952	9.9048	¾	53.4
38.0	⅜	9.7890	10.2110	9.8923	10.1077	10.1033	9.8967	⅝	52.0
39.4	½	9.8024	10.1976	9.9142	10.0858	10.1118	9.8882	½	50.6
40.8	⅝	9.8150	10.1850	9.9358	10.0642	10.1208	9.8792	⅜	49.2
42.2	¾	9.8271	10.1729	9.9573	10.0427	10.1302	9.8698	¼	47.8
43.6	⅞	9.8386	10.1614	9.9787	10.0213	10.1401	9.8599	⅛	46.4
45.0	4	9.8495	10.1505	10.0000	10.0000	10.1505	9.8495	4	45.0
Degrees.	Points.	Cosine.	Secant.	Cotangent.	Tangent.	Cosecant.	Sine.	Points.	Degrees.

The equivalents in Degrees are to the nearest Tenth.

0° = 0h 0m] **Log. Sines, Tangents, and Secants.** [11h 56m = 179°

′	m s	Sin.	Diff. 0′.1	Diff. 1s	Cosec.	Tan.	Diff. 0′.1	Diff. 1s	Cot.	Sec.	Cos.	m s	′
0	0 0	− ∞			+ ∞	− ∞			+ ∞	10.0000	10.0000	60 0	60
1	4	6.4637	301	753	13.5363	6.4637	301	753	13.5363	0000	0000	59 56	59
2	8	7648	176	440	2352	7648	176	440	2352	0000	0000	52	58
3	12	9408	125	312	0592	9408	125	312	0592	0000	0000	48	57
4	16	7.0658	97	242	12.9342	7.0658	97	242	12.9342	0000	0000	59 44	56
5	0 20	7.1627	79	198	12.8373	7.1627	79	198	12.8373	10.0000	10.0000	40	55
6	24	2419	67	167	7581	2419	67	167	7581	0000	0000	36	54
7	28	3088	58	145	6912	3088	58	145	6912	0000	0000	32	53
8	32	3668	51	128	6332	3668	51	128	6332	0000	0000	28	52
9	36	4180	40	114	5820	4180	46	114	5820	0000	0000	59 24	51
10	0 40	7.4637	41.4	103	12.5363	7.4637	41.4	103	12.5363	10.0000	10.0000	20	50
11	44	5051	37.8	94	4949	5051	37.8	94	4949	0000	0000	16	49
12	48	5429	34.8	87	4571	5429	34.8	87	4571	0000	0000	12	48
13	52	5777	32.2	80	4223	5777	32.2	80	4223	0000	0000	8	47
14	56	6099	29.9	75	3901	6099	29.9	75	3901	0000	0000	59 4	46
15	1 0	7.6398	28.0	70	12.3602	7.6398	28.0	70	12.3602	10.0000	10.0000	59 0	45
16	4	6678	26.4	66	3322	6678	26.4	66	3322	0000	0000	58 56	44
17	8	6942	24.8	62	3058	6942	24.8	62	3058	0000	0000	52	43
18	12	7190	23.5	59	2810	7190	23.5	59	2810	0000	0000	48	42
19	16	7425	22.3	56	2575	7425	22.3	56	2575	0000	0000	58 44	41
20	1 20	7.7648	21.2	53	12.2352	7.7648	21.2	53	12.2352	10.0000	10.0000	40	40
21	24	7859	20.2	50	2141	7860	20.2	50	2140	0000	0000	36	39
22	28	8061	19.3	48	1939	8062	19.3	48	1938	0000	0000	32	38
23	32	8255	18.5	46	1745	8255	18.5	46	1745	0000	0000	28	37
24	36	8439	17.7	44	1561	8439	17.7	44	1561	0000	0000	58 24	36
25	1 40	7.8617	17.0	42	12.1383	7.8617	17.0	42	12.1383	10.0000	10.0000	20	35
26	44	8787	16.4	41	1213	8787	16.4	41	1213	0000	0000	16	34
27	48	8951	15.8	39	1049	8951	15.8	39	1049	0000	0000	12	33
28	52	9109	15.2	38	0891	9109	15.2	38	0891	0000	0000	8	32
29	56	9261	14.7	37	0739	9261	14.7	37	0739	0000	0000	58 4	31
30	2 0	7.9408			12.0592	7.9409			12.0591	10.0000	10.0000	58 0	30
31	4	9551	13	31	0449	9551	13	31	0449	0000	0000	57 56	29
32	8	9689	25	62	0311	9689	25	62	0311	0000	0000	52	28
33	12	9822	38	93	0178	9823	38	93	0177	0000	0000	48	27
34	16	9952	50		0048	9952	50		0048	0000	0000	57 44	26
35	2 20	8.0078	63		11.9922	8.0078	63		11.9922	10.0000	10.0000	40	25
36	24	0200	76		9800	0200	76		9800	0000	0000	36	24
37	28	0319	88		9681	0319	88		9681	0000	0000	32	23
38	32	0435	101		9565	0435	101		9565	0000	0000	28	22
39	36	0548	113		9452	0548	113		9452	0000	0000	57 24	21
40	2 40	8.0658			11.9342	8.0658			11.9342	10.0000	10.0000	20	20
41	44	0765	10	25	9235	0765	10	25	9235	0000	0000	16	19
42	48	0870	19	49	9130	0870	19	49	9130	0000	0000	12	18
43	52	0972	29	73	9028	0972	29	73	9028	0000	0000	8	17
44	56	1072	39		8928	1072	39		8928	0000	0000	57 4	16
45	3 0	8.1169	49		11.8831	8.1170	49		11.8830	10.0000	10.0000	57 0	15
46	4	1265	58		8735	1265	58		8735	0000	0000	56 56	14
47	8	1358	68		8642	1359	68		8641	0000	0000	52	13
48	12	1450	78		8550	1450	78		8550	0000	0000	48	12
49	16	1539	87		8461	1540	87		8460	0000	0000	56 44	11
50	3 20	8.1627			11.8373	8.1627			11.8373	10.0000	10.0000	40	10
51	24	1713	8	20	8287	1713	8	20	8287	0000	0000	36	9
52	28	1797	16	39	8203	1798	16	39	8202	0000	0000	32	8
53	32	1880	24	58	8120	1880	24	58	8120	0001	9.9999	28	7
54	36	1961	32		8039	1962	32		8038	0001	9999	56 24	6
55	3 40	8.2041	40		11.7959	8.2041	40		11.7959	10.0001	9.9999	20	5
56	44	2119	47		7881	2120	47		7880	0001	9999	16	4
57	48	2196	55		7804	2196	55		7804	0001	9999	12	3
58	52	2271	63		7729	2272	63		7728	0001	9999	8	2
59	56	2346	71		7654	2346	71		7654	0001	9999	56 4	1
60	4 0	8.2419			11.7581	8.2419			11.7581	10.0001	9.9999	56 0	0
′	m s	Cos.	0′.1 Diff.	1s Diff.	Sec.	Cot.	0′.1 Diff.	1s Diff.	Tan.	Cosec.	Sin.	m s	′

90° = 6h 0m] [5h 56m = 89°

1° = 0ʰ 4ᵐ] **Log. Sines, Tangents, and Secants.** [11ʰ 52ᵐ = 178°

′	m s	Sin.	Diff. 0′.1	Diff. 1ˢ	Cosec.	Tan.	Diff. 0′.1	Diff. 1ˢ	Cot.	Sec.	Cos.	m s	′
0	4 0	8.2419			11.7581	8.2419			11.7581	10.0001	9.9999	56 0	60
1	4	2490	7	17	7510	2491	7	17	7509	0001	9999	55 56	59
2	8	2561	13	33	7439	2562	13	33	7438	0001	9999	52	58
3	12	2630	20	50	7370	2631	20	50	7369	0001	9999	48	57
4	16	2699	27		7301	2700	27		7300	0001	9999	55 44	56
5	4 20	8.2766	34		11.7234	8.2767	34		11.7233	10.0001	9.9999	40	55
6	24	2832	40		7168	2833	40		7167	0001	9999	36	54
7	28	2898	47		7102	2899	47		7101	0001	9999	32	53
8	32	2962	54		7038	2963	54		7037	0001	9999	28	52
9	36	3025	60		6975	3026	60		6974	0001	9999	55 24	51
10	4 40	8.3088			11.6912	8.3089			11.6911	10.0001	9.9999	20	50
11	44	3150	6	15	6850	3150	6	15	6850	0001	9999	16	49
12	48	3210	12	29	6790	3211	12	29	6789	0001	9999	12	48
13	52	3270	17	43	6730	3271	17	43	6729	0001	9999	8	47
14	56	3329	23		6671	3330	23		6670	0001	9999	55 4	46
15	5 0	8.3388	29		11.6612	8.3389	29		11.6611	10.0001	9.9999	55 0	45
16	4	3445	35		6555	3446	35		6554	0001	9999	54 56	44
17	8	3502	41		6498	3503	41		6497	0001	9999	52	43
18	12	3558	46		6442	3559	46		6441	0001	9999	48	42
19	16	3613	52		6387	3614	52		6386	0001	9999	54 44	41
20	5 20	8.3668			11.6332	8.3669			11.6331	10.0001	9.9999	54 40	40
21	24	3722	5	13	6278	3723	5	13	6277	0001	9999	36	39
22	28	3775	10	26	6225	3776	10	26	6224	0001	9999	32	38
23	32	3828	15	38	6172	3829	15	38	6171	0001	9999	28	37
24	36	3880	20		6120	3881	20		6119	0001	9999	54 24	36
25	5 40	8.3931	26		11.6069	8.3932	26		11.6068	10.0001	9.9999	20	35
26	44	3982	31		6018	3983	31		6017	0001	9999	16	34
27	48	4032	36		5968	4033	36		5967	0001	9999	12	33
28	52	4082	41		5918	4083	41		5917	0001	9999	8	32
29	56	4131	46		5869	4132	46		5868	0001	9999	54 4	31
30	6 0	8.4179			11.5821	8.4181			11.5819	10.0001	9.9999	54 0	30
31	4	4227	5	12	5773	4229	5	12	5771	0002	9998	53 56	29
32	8	4275	9	23	5725	4276	9	23	5724	0002	9998	52	28
33	12	4322	14	34	5678	4323	14	34	5677	0002	9998	48	27
34	16	4368	18		5632	4370	18		5630	0002	9998	53 44	26
35	6 20	8.4414	23		11.5586	8.4416	23		11.5584	10.0002	9.9998	40	25
36	24	4459	28		5541	4461	28		5539	0002	9998	36	24
37	28	4504	32		5496	4506	32		5494	0002	9998	32	23
38	32	4549	37		5451	4551	37		5449	0002	9998	28	22
39	36	4593	41		5407	4595	41		5405	0002	9998	53 24	21
40	6 40	8.4637			11.5363	8.4638			11.5362	10.0002	9.9998	20	20
41	44	4680	4	10	5320	4682	4	10	5318	0002	9998	16	19
42	48	4723	8	21	5277	4725	8	21	5275	0002	9998	12	18
43	52	4765	12	31	5235	4767	12	31	5233	0002	9998	8	17
44	56	4807	16		5193	4809	16		5191	0002	9998	53 4	16
45	7 0	8.4848	21		11.5152	8.4851	21		11.5149	10.0002	9.9998	53 0	15
46	4	4890	25		5110	4892	25		5108	0002	9998	52 56	14
47	8	4930	29		5070	4933	29		5067	0002	9998	52	13
48	12	4971	33		5029	4973	33		5027	0002	9998	48	12
49	16	5011	37		4989	5013	37		4987	0002	9998	52 44	11
50	7 20	8.5050			11.4950	8.5053			11.4947	10.0002	9.9998	40	10
51	24	5090	4	9	4910	5092	4	9	4908	0002	9998	36	9
52	28	5129	8	19	4871	5131	8	19	4869	0002	9998	32	8
53	32	5167	11	28	4833	5170	11	28	4830	0002	9998	28	7
54	36	5206	15		4794	5208	15		4792	0002	9998	52 24	6
55	7 40	8.5243	19		11.4757	8.5246	19		11.4754	10.0002	9.9998	20	5
56	44	5281	23		4719	5283	23		4717	0002	9998	16	4
57	48	5318	27		4682	5321	27		4679	0003	9997	12	3
58	52	5355	30		4645	5358	30		4642	0003	9997	8	2
59	56	5392	34		4608	5394	34		4606	0003	9997	52 4	1
60	8 0	8.5428			11.4572	8.5431			11.4569	10.0003	9.9997	52 0	0
′	m s	Cos.	0′.1 Diff.	1ˢ Diff.	Sec.	Cot.	0′.1 Diff.	1ˢ Diff.	Tan.	Cosec.	Sin.	m s	′

91° = 6ʰ 4ᵐ] [5ʰ 52ᵐ = 88°

2° = 0h 8m] **Log. Sines, Tangents, and Secants.** [11h 48m = 177°

′	m s	Sin.	Diff. 0′.1	Diff. 1s	Cosec.	Tan.	Diff. 0′.1	Diff. 1s	Cot.	Sec.	Cos.	m s	′
0	8 0	8.5428			11.4572	8.5431			11.4569	10.0003	9.9997	52 0	60
1	4	5464	4	9	4536	5467	4	9	4533	0003	9997	51 56	59
2	8	5500	7	18	4500	5503	7	18	4497	0003	9997	52	58
3	12	5535	11	27	4465	5538	11	27	4462	0003	9997	48	57
4	16	5571	14		4429	5573	14		4427	0003	9997	51 44	56
5	8 20	8.5605	17		11.4395	8.5608	17		11.4392	10.0003	9.9997	40	55
6	24	5640	21		4360	5643	21		4357	0003	9997	36	54
7	28	5674	24		4326	5677	24		4323	0003	9997	32	53
8	32	5708	28		4292	5711	28		4289	0003	9997	28	52
9	36	5742	31		4258	5745	31		4255	0003	9997	51 24	51
10	8 40	8.5776			11.4224	8.5779			11.4221	10.0003	9.9997	20	50
11	44	5809	3	8	4191	5812	3	8	4188	0003	9997	16	49
12	48	5842	6	16	4158	5845	6	16	4155	0003	9997	12	48
13	52	5875	10	24	4125	5878	10	24	4122	0003	9997	8	47
14	56	5907	13		4093	5911	13		4089	0003	9997	51 4	46
15	9 0	8.5939	16		11.4061	8.5943	16		11.4057	10.0003	9.9997	51 0	45
16	4	5972	19		4028	5975	19		4025	0003	9997	50 56	44
17	8	6003	22		3997	6007	22		3993	0003	9997	52	43
18	12	6035	26		3965	6038	26		3962	0003	9997	48	42
19	16	6066	29		3934	6070	29		3930	0004	9996	50 44	41
20	9 20	8.6097			11.3903	8.6101			11.3899	10.0004	9.9996	40	40
21	24	6128	3	8	3872	6132	3	8	3868	0004	9996	36	39
22	28	6159	6	15	3841	6163	6	15	3837	0004	9996	32	38
23	32	6189	9	22	3811	6193	9	22	3807	0004	9996	28	37
24	36	6220	12		3780	6223	12		3777	0004	9996	50 24	36
25	9 40	8.6250	15		11.3750	8.6254	15		11.3746	10.0004	9.9996	20	35
26	44	6279	18		3721	6283	18		3717	0004	9996	16	34
27	48	6309	21		3691	6313	21		3687	0004	9996	12	33
28	52	6339	24		3661	6343	24		3657	0004	9996	8	32
29	56	6368	27		3632	6372	27		3628	0004	9996	50 4	31
30	10 0	8.6397			11.3603	8.6401			11.3599	10.0004	9.9996	50 0	30
31	4	6426	3	7	3574	6430	3	7	3570	0004	9996	49 56	29
32	8	6454	6	14	3546	6459	6	14	3541	0004	9996	52	28
33	12	6483	8	21	3517	6487	8	21	3513	0004	9996	48	27
34	16	6511	11		3489	6515	11		3485	0004	9996	49 44	26
35	10 20	8.6539	14		11.3461	8.6544	14		11.3456	10.0004	9.9996	40	25
36	24	6567	17		3433	6571	17		3429	0004	9996	36	24
37	28	6595	20		3405	6599	20		3401	0005	9995	32	23
38	32	6622	22		3378	6627	22		3373	0005	9995	28	22
39	36	6650	25		3350	6654	25		3346	0005	9995	49 24	21
40	10 40	8.6677			11.3323	8.6682			11.3318	10.0005	9.9995	20	20
41	44	6704	3	7	3296	6709	3	7	3291	0005	9995	16	19
42	48	6731	5	13	3269	6736	5	13	3264	0005	9995	12	18
43	52	6758	8	19	3242	6762	8	19	3238	0005	9995	8	17
44	56	6784	10		3216	6789	10		3211	0005	9995	40 4	16
45	11 0	8.6810	13		11.3190	8.6815	13		11.3185	10.0005	9.9995	49 0	15
46	4	6837	16		3163	6842	16		3158	0005	9995	48 56	14
47	8	6863	18		3137	6868	18		3132	0005	9995	52	13
48	12	6889	21		3111	6894	21		3106	0005	9995	48	12
49	16	6914	23		3086	6920	23		3080	0005	9995	48 44	11
50	11 20	8.6940			11.3060	8.6945			11.3055	10.0005	9.9995	40	10
51	24	6965	3	6	3035	6971	3	6	3029	0005	9995	36	9
52	28	6991	5	12	3009	6996	5	12	3004	0005	9995	32	8
53	32	7016	7	19	2984	7021	7	19	2979	0005	9995	28	7
54	36	7041	10		2959	7046	10		2954	0006	9994	48 24	6
55	11 40	8.7066	12		11.2934	8.7071	12		11.2929	10.0006	9.9994	20	5
56	44	7090	15		2910	7096	15		2904	0006	9994	16	4
57	48	7115	17		2885	7121	17		2879	0006	9994	12	3
58	52	7140	20		2860	7145	20		2855	0006	9994	8	2
59	56	7164	22		2836	7170	22		2830	0006	9994	48 4	1
60	12 0	8.7188			11.2812	8.7194			11.2806	10.0006	9.9994	48 0	0
′	m s	Cos.	Diff. 0′.1	Diff. 1s	Sec.	Cot.	Diff. 0′.1	Diff. 1s	Tan.	Cosec.	Sin.	m s	′

92° = 6h 8m] [5h 48m = 87°

3° = 0h 12m] **Log. Sines, Tangents, and Secants.** [11h 44m = 176°

′	m s	Sin.	Diff. 0′.1	Diff. 1s	Cosec.	Tan.	Diff. 0′.1	Diff. 1s	Cot.	Sec.	Cos.	m s	′
0	12 0	8.7188			11.2812	8.7194			11.2806	10.0006	9.9994	48 0	60
1	4	7212	2	6	2788	7218	2	6	2782	0006	9994	47 56	59
2	8	7236	5	12	2764	7242	5	12	2758	0006	9994	52	58
3	12	7260	7	17	2740	7266	7	17	2734	0006	9994	48	57
4	16	7283	9		2717	7290	9		2710	0006	9994	47 44	56
5	12 20	8.7307	12		11.2693	8.7313	12		11.2687	10.0006	9.9994	40	55
6	24	7330	14		2670	7337	14		2663	0006	9994	36	54
7	28	7354	16		2646	7360	16		2640	0006	9994	32	53
8	32	7377	18		2623	7383	18		2617	0006	9994	28	52
9	36	7400	21		2600	7406	21		2594	0007	9993	47 24	51
10	12 40	8.7423			11.2577	8.7429			11.2571	10.0007	9.9993	20	50
11	44	7445	2	6	2555	7452	2	6	2548	0007	9993	16	49
12	48	7468	4	11	2532	7475	4	11	2525	0007	9993	12	48
13	52	7491	7	16	2509	7497	7	16	2503	0007	9993	8	47
14	56	7513	9		2487	7520	9		2480	0007	9993	47 4	46
15	13 0	8.7535	11		11.2465	8.7542	11		11.2458	10.0007	9.9993	47 0	45
16	4	7557	13		2443	7565	13		2435	0007	9993	46 56	44
17	8	7580	16		2420	7587	16		2413	0007	9993	52	43
18	12	7602	18		2398	7609	18		2391	0007	9993	48	42
19	16	7623	20		2377	7631	20		2369	0007	9993	46 44	41
20	13 20	8.7645			11.2355	8.7652			11.2348	10.0007	9.9993	40	40
21	24	7667	2	5	2333	7674	2	5	2326	0007	9993	36	39
22	28	7688	4	11	2312	7696	4	11	2304	0007	9993	32	38
23	32	7710	6	16	2290	7717	6	16	2283	0008	9992	28	37
24	36	7731	8		2269	7739	8		2261	0008	9992	46 24	36
25	13 40	8.7752	11		11.2248	8.7760	11		11.2240	10.0008	9.9992	20	35
26	44	7773	13		2227	7781	13		2219	0008	9992	16	34
27	48	7794	15		2206	7802	15		2198	0008	9992	12	33
28	52	7815	17		2185	7823	17		2177	0008	9992	8	32
29	56	7836	19		2164	7844	19		2156	0008	9992	46 4	31
30	14 0	8.7857			11.2143	8.7865			11.2135	10.0008	9.9992	46 0	30
31	4	7877	2	5	2123	7886	2	5	2114	0008	9992	45 56	29
32	8	7898	4	10	2102	7906	4	10	2094	0008	9992	52	28
33	12	7918	6	15	2082	7927	6	15	2073	0008	9992	48	27
34	16	7939	8		2061	7947	8		2053	0008	9992	45 44	26
35	14 20	8.7959	10		11.2041	8.7967	10		11.2033	10.0009	9.9991	40	25
36	24	7979	12		2021	7988	12		2012	0009	9991	36	24
37	28	7999	14		2001	8008	14		1992	0009	9991	32	23
38	32	8019	16		1981	8028	16		1972	0009	9991	28	22
39	36	8039	18		1961	8048	18		1952	0009	9991	45 24	21
40	14 40	8.8059			11.1941	8.8067			11.1933	10.0009	9.9991	20	20
41	44	8078	2	5	1922	8087	2	5	1913	0009	9991	16	19
42	48	8098	4	10	1902	8107	4	10	1893	0009	9991	12	18
43	52	8117	6	14	1883	8126	6	14	1874	0009	9991	8	17
44	56	8137	8		1863	8146	8		1854	0009	9991	45 4	16
45	15 0	8.8156	10		11.1844	8.8165	10		11.1835	10.0009	9.9991	45 0	15
46	4	8175	12		1825	8185	12		1815	0009	9991	44 56	14
47	8	8194	14		1806	8204	14		1796	0009	9991	52	13
48	12	8213	15		1787	8223	15		1777	0010	9990	48	12
49	16	8232	17		1768	8242	17		1758	0010	9990	44 44	11
50	15 20	8.8251			11.1749	8.8261			11.1739	10.0010	9.9990	40	10
51	24	8270	2	5	1730	8280	2	5	1720	0010	9990	36	9
52	28	8289	4	9	1711	8299	4	9	1701	0010	9990	32	8
53	32	8307	6	14	1693	8317	6	14	1683	0010	9990	28	7
54	36	8326	7		1674	8336	7		1664	0010	9990	44 24	6
55	15 40	8.8345	9		11.1655	8.8355	9		11.1645	10.0010	9.9990	20	5
56	44	8363	11		1637	8373	11		1627	0010	9990	16	4
57	48	8381	13		1619	8392	13		1608	0010	9990	12	3
58	52	8400	15		1600	8410	15		1590	0010	9990	8	2
59	56	8418	17		1582	8428	17		1572	0010	9990	44 4	1
60	16 0	8.8436			11.1564	8.8446			11.1554	10.0011	9.9989	44 0	0
′	m s	Cos.	0′.1 Diff.	1s Diff.	Sec.	Cot.	0′.1 Diff.	1s Diff.	Tan.	Cosec.	Sin.	m s	′

93° = 6h 12m] [5h 44m = 86°

′	m s	Sin.	Diff. 0′.1	Diff. 1s	Cosec.	Tan.	Diff. 0′.1	Diff. 1s	Cot.	Sec.	Cos.	m s	′
0	16 0	8.8436			11.1564	8.8446			11.1554	10.0011	9.9989	44 0	60
1	4	8454	2	4	1546	8465	2	4	1535	0011	9989	43 56	59
2	8	8472	4	9	1528	8483	4	9	1517	0011	9989	52	58
3	12	8490	5	13	1510	8501	5	13	1499	0011	9989	48	57
4	16	8508	7		1492	8518	7		1482	0011	9989	43 44	56
5	16 20	8.8525	9		11.1475	8.8536	9		11.1464	10.0011	9.9989	40	55
6	24	8543	11		1457	8554	11		1446	0011	9989	36	54
7	28	8560	12		1440	8572	12		1428	0011	9989	32	53
8	32	8578	14		1422	8589	14		1411	0011	9989	28	52
9	36	8595	16		1405	8607	16		1393	0011	9989	43 24	51
10	16 10	8.8613			11.1387	8.8624			11.1376	10.0011	9.9989	20	50
11	44	8630	2	4	1370	8642	2	4	1358	0012	9988	16	49
12	48	8647	3	9	1353	8659	3	9	1341	0012	9988	12	48
13	52	8665	5	13	1335	8676	5	13	1324	0012	9988	8	47
14	56	8682	7		1318	8694	7		1306	0012	9988	43 4	46
15	17 0	8.8699	9		11.1301	8.8711	9		11.1289	10.0012	9.9988	43 0	45
16	4	8716	10		1284	8728	10		1272	0012	9988	42 56	44
17	8	8733	12		1267	8745	12		1255	0012	9988	52	43
18	12	8749	14		1251	8762	14		1238	0012	9988	48	42
19	16	8766	15		1234	8778	15		1222	0012	9988	42 44	41
20	17 20	8.8783			11.1217	8.8795			11.1205	10.0012	9.9988	40	40
21	24	8799	2	4	1201	8812	2	4	1188	0013	9987	36	39
22	28	8816	3	8	1184	8829	3	8	1171	0013	9987	32	38
23	32	8833	5	12	1167	8845	5	12	1155	0013	9987	28	37
24	36	8849	7		1151	8862	7		1138	0013	9987	42 24	36
25	17 40	8.8865	8		11.1135	8.8878	8		11.1122	10.0013	9.9987	20	35
26	44	8882	10		1118	8895	10		1105	0013	9987	16	34
27	48	8898	11		1102	8911	11		1089	0013	9987	12	33
28	52	8914	13		1086	8927	13		1073	0013	9987	8	32
29	56	8930	15		1070	8944	15		1056	0013	9987	42 4	31
30	18 0	8.8946			11.1054	8.8960			11.1040	10.0013	9.9987	42 0	30
31	4	8962	2	4	1038	8976	2	4	1024	0014	9986	41 56	29
32	8	8978	3	8	1022	8992	3	8	1008	0014	9986	52	28
33	12	8994	5	12	1006	9008	5	12	0992	0014	9986	48	27
34	16	9010	6		0990	9024	6		0976	0014	9986	41 44	26
35	18 20	8.9026	8		11.0974	8.9040	8		11.0960	10.0014	9.9986	40	25
36	24	9042	9		0958	9056	9		0944	0014	9986	36	24
37	28	9057	11		0943	9071	11		0929	0014	9986	32	23
38	32	9073	13		0927	9087	13		0913	0014	9986	28	22
39	36	9089	14		0911	9103	14		0897	0014	9986	41 24	21
40	18 40	8.9104			11.0896	8.9118			11.0882	10.0014	9.9986	20	20
41	44	9119	2	4	0881	9134	2	4	0866	0015	9985	16	19
42	48	9135	3	8	0865	9150	3	8	0850	0015	9985	12	18
43	52	9150	5	11	0850	9165	5	11	0835	0015	9985	8	17
44	56	9165	6		0835	9180	6		0820	0015	9985	41 4	16
45	19 0	8.9181	8		11.0819	8.9196	8		11.0804	10.0015	9.9985	41 0	15
46	4	9196	9		0804	9211	9		0789	0015	9985	40 56	14
47	8	9211	11		0789	9226	11		0774	0015	9985	52	13
48	12	9226	12		0774	9241	12		0759	0015	9985	48	12
49	16	9241	14		0759	9256	14		0744	0015	9985	40 44	11
50	19 20	8.9256			11.0744	8.9272			11.0728	10.0015	9.9985	40	10
51	24	9271	1	4	0729	9287	1	4	0713	0016	9984	36	9
52	28	9286	3	7	0714	9302	3	7	0698	0016	9984	32	8
53	32	9301	4	11	0699	9316	4	11	0684	0016	9984	28	7
54	36	9315	6		0685	9331	6		0669	0016	9984	40 24	6
55	19 40	8.9330	7		11.0670	8.9346	7		11.0654	10.0016	9.9984	20	5
56	44	9345	9		0655	9361	9		0639	0016	9984	16	4
57	48	9359	10		0641	9376	10		0624	0016	9984	12	3
58	52	9374	12		0626	9390	12		0610	0016	9984	8	2
59	56	9388	13		0612	9405	13		0595	0016	9984	40 4	1
60	20 0	8.9403			11.0597	8.9420			11.0580	10.0017	9.9983	40 0	0
′	m s	Cos.	0′.1 Diff.	1s Diff.	Sec.	Cot.	0′.1 Diff.	1s Diff.	Tan.	Cosec.	Sin.	m s	′

$5° = 0^h\ 20^m$] **Log. Sines, Tangents, and Secants.** **[$11^h\ 36^m = 174°$**

′	m s	Sin.	Diff. 0′.1	Diff. 1ˢ	Cosec.	Tan.	Diff. 0′.1	Diff. 1ˢ	Cot.	Sec.	Cos.	m s	′
0	**20 0**	8.9403			11.0597	8.9420			11.0580	10.0017	9.9983	**40 0**	**60**
1	**4**	9417	1	4	0583	9434	1	4	0566	0017	9983	**39 56**	**59**
2	**8**	9432	3	7	0568	9449	3	7	0551	0017	9983	**52**	**58**
3	**12**	9446	4	11	0554	9463	4	11	0537	0017	9983	**48**	**57**
4	**16**	9460	6		0540	9477	6		0523	0017	9983	**39 44**	**56**
5	**20 20**	8.9475	7		11.0525	8.9492	7		11.0508	10.0017	9.9983	**40**	**55**
6	**24**	9489	8		0511	9506	8		0494	0017	9983	**36**	**54**
7	**28**	9503	10		0497	9520	10		0480	0017	9983	**32**	**53**
8	**32**	9517	11		0483	9534	11		0466	0017	9983	**28**	**52**
9	**36**	9531	13		0469	9549	13		0451	0018	9982	**39 24**	**51**
10	**20 40**	8.9545			11.0455	8.9563			11.0437	10.0018	9.9982	**20**	**50**
11	**44**	9559	1	4	0441	9577	1	4	0423	0018	9982	**16**	**49**
12	**48**	9573	3	7	0427	9591	3	7	0409	0018	9982	**12**	**48**
13	**52**	9587	4	11	0413	9605	4	11	0395	0018	9982	**8**	**47**
14	**56**	9501	6		0399	9619	6		0381	0018	9982	**39 4**	**46**
15	**21 0**	8.9614	7		11.0386	8.9633	7		11.0367	10.0018	9.9982	**39 0**	**45**
16	**4**	9628	8		0372	9646	8		0354	0018	9982	**38 56**	**44**
17	**8**	9642	10		0358	9660	10		0340	0018	9982	**52**	**43**
18	**12**	9655	11		0345	9674	11		0326	0019	9981	**48**	**42**
19	**16**	9669	13		0331	9688	13		0312	0019	9981	**38 44**	**41**
20	**21 20**	8.9682			11.0318	8.9701			11.0299	10.0019	9.9981	**40**	**40**
21	**24**	9696	1	3	0304	9715	1	3	0285	0019	9981	**36**	**39**
22	**28**	9709	3	6	0291	9729	3	6	0271	0019	9981	**32**	**38**
23	**32**	9723	4	10	0277	9742	4	10	0258	0019	9981	**28**	**37**
24	**36**	9736	5		0204	9756	5		0244	0019	9981	**38 24**	**36**
25	**21 40**	8.9750	7		11.0250	8.9769	7		11.0231	10.0019	9.9981	**20**	**35**
26	**44**	9763	8		0237	9782	8		0218	0020	9980	**16**	**34**
27	**48**	9776	9		0224	9796	9		0204	0020	9980	**12**	**33**
28	**52**	9789	10		0211	9809	10		0191	0020	9980	**8**	**32**
29	**56**	9803	12		0197	9823	12		0177	0020	9980	**38 4**	**31**
30	**22 0**	8.9816			11.0184	8.9836			11.0164	10.0020	9.9980	**38 0**	**30**
31	**4**	9829	1	3	0171	9849	1	3	0151	0020	9980	**37 56**	**29**
32	**8**	9842	3	6	0158	9862	3	6	0138	0020	9980	**52**	**28**
33	**12**	9855	4	10	0145	9875	4	10	0125	0020	9980	**48**	**27**
34	**16**	9808	5		0132	9888	5		0112	0021	9979	**37 44**	**26**
35	**22 20**	8.9881	7		11.0119	8.9901	7		11.0099	10.0021	9.9979	**40**	**25**
36	**24**	9894	8		0106	9915	8		0085	0021	9979	**36**	**24**
37	**28**	9907	9		0093	9927	9		0073	0021	9979	**32**	**23**
38	**32**	9919	10		0081	9940	10		0060	0021	9979	**28**	**22**
39	**36**	9932	12		0068	9953	12		0047	0021	9979	**37 24**	**21**
40	**22 40**	8.9945			11.0055	8.9966			11.0034	10.0021	9.9979	**20**	**20**
41	**44**	9958	1	3	0042	9979	1	3	0021	0021	9979	**16**	**19**
42	**48**	9970	3	6	0030	9992	3	6	0008	0022	9978	**12**	**18**
43	**52**	9983	4	10	0017	9.0005	4	10	10.9995	0022	9978	**8**	**17**
44	**56**	9996	5		0004	0017	5		9983	0022	9978	**37 4**	**16**
45	**23 0**	9.0008	6		10.9992	9.0030	6		10.9970	10.0022	9.9978	**37 0**	**15**
46	**4**	0021	8		9979	0043	8		9957	0022	9978	**36 56**	**14**
47	**8**	0033	9		9967	0055	9		9945	0022	9978	**52**	**13**
48	**12**	0046	10		9954	0068	10		9932	0022	9978	**48**	**12**
49	**16**	0058	12		9942	0080	12		9920	0022	9978	**36 44**	**11**
50	**23 20**	9.0070			10.9930	9.0093			10.9907	10.0023	9.9977	**40**	**10**
51	**24**	0083	1	3	9917	0105	1	3	9895	0023	9977	**36**	**9**
52	**28**	0095	2	6	9905	0118	2	6	9882	0023	9977	**32**	**8**
53	**32**	0107	4	9	9893	0130	4	9	9870	0023	9977	**28**	**7**
54	**36**	0120	5		9880	0143	5		9857	0023	9977	**36 24**	**6**
55	**23 40**	9.0132	6		10.9868	9.0155	6		10.9845	10.0023	9.9977	**20**	**5**
56	**44**	0144	7		9856	0167	7		9833	0023	9977	**16**	**4**
57	**48**	0156	8		9844	0180	8		9820	0023	9977	**12**	**3**
58	**52**	0168	10		9832	0192	10		9808	0024	9976	**8**	**2**
59	**56**	0180	11		9820	0204	11		9796	0024	9976	**36 4**	**1**
60	**24 0**	9.0192			10.9808	9.0216			10.9784	10.0024	9.9976	**36 0**	**0**
′	m s	Cos.	Diff. 0′.1	Diff. 1ˢ	Sec.	Cot.	Diff. 0′.1	Diff. 1ˢ	Tan.	Cosec.	Sin.	m s	′

$95° = 6^h\ 20^m$] **[$5^h\ 36^m = 84°$**

$6° = 0^h\ 24^m$] **Log. Sines, Tangents, and Secants.** [$11^h\ 32^m = 173°$

′	m s	Sin.	Diff. 0′.1	Diff. 1s	Cosec.	Tan.	Diff. 0′.1	Diff. 1s	Cot.	Sec.	Cos.	m s	′
0	24 0	9.0192			10.9808	9.0216			10.9784	10.0024	9.9976	36 0	60
1	4	0204	1	3	9796	0228	1	3	9772	0024	9976	35 56	59
2	8	0216	2	6	9784	0240	2	6	9760	0024	9976	52	58
3	12	0228	4	9	9772	0253	4	9	9747	0024	9976	48	57
4	16	0240	5		9760	0265	5		9735	0024	9976	35 44	56
5	24 20	9.0252	6		10.9748	9.0277	6		10.9723	10.0025	9.9975	40	55
6	24	0264	7		9736	0289	7		9711	0025	9975	36	54
7	28	0276	8		9724	0300	8		9700	0025	9975	32	53
8	32	0287	10		9713	0312	10		9688	0025	9975	28	52
9	36	0299	11		9701	0324	11		9676	0025	9975	35 24	51
10	24 40	9.0311			10.9689	9.0336			10.9664	10.0025	9.9975	20	50
11	44	0323	1	3	9677	0348	1	3	9652	0025	9975	16	49
12	48	0334	2	6	9666	0360	2	6	9640	0025	9975	12	48
13	52	0346	3	9	9654	0371	3	9	9629	0026	9974	8	47
14	56	0357	5		9643	0383	5		9617	0026	9974	35 4	46
15	25 0	9.0369	6		10.9631	9.0395	6		10.9605	10.0026	9.9974	35 0	45
16	4	0380	7		9620	0407	7		9593	0026	9974	34 56	44
17	8	0392	8		9608	0418	8		9582	0026	9974	52	43
18	12	0403	9		9597	0430	9		9570	0026	9974	48	42
19	16	0415	10		9585	0441	10		9559	0026	9974	34 44	41
20	25 20	9.0426			10.9574	9.0453			10.9547	10.0027	9.9973	40	40
21	24	0438	1	3	9562	0464	1	3	9536	0027	9973	36	39
22	28	0449	2	6	9551	0476	2	6	9524	0027	9973	32	38
23	32	0460	3	9	9540	0487	3	9	9513	0027	9973	28	37
24	36	0472	4		9528	0499	5		9501	0027	9973	34 24	36
25	25 40	9.0483	5		10.9517	9.0510	6		10.9490	10.0027	9.9973	20	35
26	44	0494	7		9506	0521	7		9479	0027	9973	16	34
27	48	0505	8		9495	0533	8		9467	0028	9972	12	33
28	52	0516	9		9484	0544	9		9456	0028	9972	8	32
29	56	0527	10		9473	0555	10		9445	0028	9972	34 4	31
30	26 0	9.0539			10.9461	9.0567			10.9433	10.0028	9.9972	34 0	30
31	4	0550	1	3	9450	0578	1	3	9422	0028	9972	33 56	29
32	8	0561	2	5	9439	0589	2	5	9411	0028	9972	52	28
33	12	0572	3	8	9428	0600	3	8	9400	0028	9972	48	27
34	16	0583	4		9417	0611	4		9389	0029	9971	33 44	26
35	26 20	9.0594	5		10.9406	9.0622	5		10.9378	10.0029	9.9971	40	25
36	24	0605	7		9395	0633	7		9367	0029	9971	36	24
37	28	0616	8		9384	0645	8		9355	0029	9971	32	23
38	32	0626	9		9374	0656	9		9344	0029	9971	28	22
39	36	0637	10		9363	0667	10		9333	0029	9971	33 24	21
40	26 40	9.0648			10.9352	9.0678			10.9322	10.0029	9.9971	20	20
41	44	0659	1	3	9341	0688	1	3	9312	0030	9970	16	19
42	48	0670	2	5	9330	0699	2	5	9301	0030	9970	12	18
43	52	0680	3	8	9320	0710	3	8	9290	0030	9970	8	17
44	56	0691	4		9309	0721	4		9279	0030	9970	33 4	16
45	27 0	9.0702	5		10.9298	9.0732	5		10.9268	10.0030	9.9970	33 0	15
46	4	0712	7		9288	0743	7		9257	0030	9970	32 56	14
47	8	0723	8		9277	0754	8		9246	0031	9969	52	13
48	12	0734	9		9266	0764	9		9236	0031	9969	48	12
49	16	0744	10		9256	0775	10		9225	0031	9969	32 44	11
50	27 20	9.0755			10.9245	9.0786			10.9214	10.0031	9.9969	40	10
51	24	0765	1	3	9235	0796	1	3	9204	0031	9969	36	9
52	28	0776	2	5	9224	0807	2	5	9193	0031	9969	32	8
53	32	0786	3	8	9214	0818	3	8	9182	0031	9969	28	7
54	36	0797	4		9203	0828	4		9172	0032	9968	32 24	6
55	27 40	9.0807	5		10.9193	9.0839	5		10.9161	10.0032	9.9968	20	5
56	44	0818	6		9182	0849	6		9151	0032	9968	16	4
57	48	0828	7		9172	0860	7		9140	0032	9968	12	3
58	52	0838	8		9162	0871	8		9129	0032	9968	8	2
59	56	0849	9		9151	0881	9		9119	0032	9968	32 4	1
60	28 0	9.0859			10.9141	9.0891			10.9109	10.0032	9.9968	32 0	0
′	m s	Cos.	0′.1 Diff.	1s	Sec.	Cot.	0′.1 Diff.	1s	Tan.	Cosec.	Sin.	m s	′

$96° = 6^h\ 24^m$] [$5^h\ 32^m = 83°$

7° = 0h 28m] **Log. Sines, Tangents, and Secants.** [11h 28m = 172°

′	m s	Sin.	Diff. 0′.1	Diff. 1s	Cosec.	Tan.	Diff. 0′.1	Diff. 1s	Cot.	Sec.	Cos.	m s	′
0	28 0	9.0859			10.9141	9.0891			10.9109	10.0032	9.9968	32 0	60
1	4	0869	1	3	9131	0902	1	3	9098	0033	9967	31 56	59
2	8	0879	2	5	9121	0912	2	5	9088	0033	9967	52	58
3	12	0890	3	8	9110	0923	3	8	9077	0033	9967	48	57
4	16	0900	4		9100	0933	4		9067	0033	9967	31 44	56
5	28 20	9.0910	5		10.9090	9.0943	5		10.9057	10.0033	9.9967	40	55
6	24	0920	6		9080	0954	6		9046	0033	9967	36	54
7	28	0930	7		9070	0964	7		9036	0034	9966	32	53
8	32	0940	8		9060	0974	8		9026	0034	9966	28	52
9	36	0951	9		9049	0984	9		9016	0034	9966	31 24	51
10	28 40	9.0961			10.9039	9.0995			10.9005	10.0034	9.9966	20	50
11	44	0971	1	3	9029	1005	1	3	8995	0034	9966	16	49
12	48	0981	2	5	9019	1015	2	5	8985	0034	9966	12	48
13	52	0991	3	7	9009	1025	3	8	8975	0035	9965	8	47
14	56	1001	4		8999	1035	4		8965	0035	9965	31 4	46
15	29 0	9.1011	5		10.8989	9.1045	5		10.8955	10.0035	9.9965	31 0	45
16	4	1020	6		8980	1055	6		8945	0035	9965	30 56	44
17	8	1030	7		8970	1066	7		8934	0035	9965	52	43
18	12	1040	8		8960	1076	8		8924	0035	9965	48	42
19	16	1050	9		8950	1086	9		8914	0036	9964	30 44	41
20	29 20	9.1060			10.8940	9.1096			10.8904	10.0036	9.9964	40	40
21	24	1070	1	2	8930	1106	1	2	8894	0036	9964	36	39
22	28	1080	2	5	8920	1116	2	5	8884	0036	9964	32	38
23	32	1089	3	7	8911	1125	3	7	8875	0036	9964	28	37
24	36	1099	4		8901	1135	4		8865	0036	9964	30 24	36
25	29 40	9.1109	5		10.8891	9.1145	5		10.8855	10.0036	9.9964	20	35
26	44	1118	6		8882	1155	6		8845	0037	9963	16	34
27	48	1128	7		8872	1165	7		8835	0037	9963	12	33
28	52	1138	8		8862	1175	8		8825	0037	9963	8	32
29	56	1147	9		8853	1185	9		8815	0037	9963	30 4	31
30	30 0	9.1157			10.8843	9.1194			10.8806	10.0037	9.9963	30 0	30
31	4	1167	1	2	8833	1204	1	2	8796	0037	9963	29 56	29
32	8	1176	2	5	8824	1214	2	5	8786	0038	9962	52	28
33	12	1186	3	7	8814	1223	3	7	8777	0038	9962	48	27
34	16	1195	4		8805	1233	4		8767	0038	9962	29 44	26
35	30 20	9.1205	5		10.8795	9.1243	5		10.8757	10.0038	9.9962	40	25
36	24	1214	6		8786	1252	6		8748	0038	9962	36	24
37	28	1224	7		8776	1262	7		8738	0038	9962	32	23
38	32	1233	8		8767	1272	8		8728	0039	9961	28	22
39	36	1242	9		8758	1281	9		8719	0039	9961	29 24	21
40	30 40	9.1252			10.8748	9.1291			10.8709	10.0039	9.9961	20	20
41	44	1261	1	2	8739	1300	1	2	8700	0039	9961	16	19
42	48	1271	2	5	8729	1310	2	5	8690	0039	9961	12	18
43	52	1280	3	7	8720	1319	3	7	8681	0040	9960	8	17
44	56	1289	4		8711	1329	4		8671	0040	9960	29 4	16
45	31 0	9.1299	5		10.8701	9.1338	5		10.8662	10.0040	9.9960	29 0	15
46	4	1308	6		8692	1348	6		8652	0040	9960	28 56	14
47	8	1317	7		8683	1357	7		8643	0040	9960	52	13
48	12	1326	7		8674	1367	7		8633	0040	9960	48	12
49	16	1336	8		8664	1376	8		8624	0041	9959	28 44	11
50	31 20	9.1345			10.8655	9.1385			10.8615	10.0041	9.9959	40	10
51	24	1354	1	2	8646	1395	1	2	8605	0041	9959	36	9
52	28	1363	2	5	8637	1404	2	5	8596	0041	9959	32	8
53	32	1372	3	7	8628	1413	3	7	8587	0041	9959	28	7
54	36	1381	4		8619	1423	4		8577	0041	9959	28 24	6
55	31 40	9.1390	5		10.8610	9.1432	5		10.8568	10.0042	9.9958	20	5
56	44	1399	5		8601	1441	5		8559	0042	9958	16	4
57	48	1409	6		8591	1450	6		8550	0042	9958	12	3
58	52	1418	7		8582	1460	7		8540	0042	9958	8	2
59	56	1427	8		8573	1469	8		8531	0042	9958	28 4	1
60	32 0	9.1436			10.8564	9.1478			10.8522	10.0042	9.9958	28 0	0
′	m s	Cos.	0′.1 Diff.	1s Diff.	Sec.	Cot.	0′.1 Diff.	1s Diff.	Tan.	Cosec.	Sin.	m s	′

97° = 6h 28m] [5h 28m = 82°

8° = 0ʰ 32ᵐ] **Log. Sines, Tangents, and Secants.** [11ʰ 24ᵐ = 171°

′	m s	Sin.	Diff. 0′.1	Diff. 1ˢ	Cosec.	Tan.	Diff. 0′.1	Diff. 1ˢ	Cot.	Sec.	Cos.	m s	′
0	32 0	9.1436			10.8564	9.1478			10.8522	10.0042	9.9958	28 0	60
1	4	1445	1	2	8555	1487	1	2	8513	0043	9957	27 56	59
2	8	1453	2	5	8547	1496	2	5	8504	0043	9957	52	58
3	12	1462	3	7	8538	1505	3	7	8495	0043	9957	48	57
4	16	1471	4		8529	1515	4		8485	0043	9957	27 44	56
5	32 20	9.1480	4		10.8520	9.1524	5		10.8476	10.0043	9.9957	40	55
6	24	1489	5		8511	1533	5		8467	0044	9956	36	54
7	28	1498	6		8502	1542	6		8458	0044	9956	32	53
8	32	1507	7		8493	1551	7		8449	0044	9956	28	52
9	36	1516	8		8484	1560	8		8440	0044	9956	27 24	51
10	32 40	9.1525			10.8475	9.1569			10.8431	10.0044	9.9956	20	50
11	44	1533	1	2	8467	1578	1	2	8422	0044	9956	16	49
12	48	1542	2	5	8458	1587	2	5	8413	0045	9955	12	48
13	52	1551	3	7	8449	1596	3	7	8404	0045	9955	8	47
14	56	1560	4		8440	1605	4		8395	0045	9955	27 4	46
15	33 0	9.1568	4		10.8432	9.1613	5		10.8387	10.0045	9.9955	27 0	45
16	4	1577	5		8423	1622	5		8378	0045	9955	26 56	44
17	8	1586	6		8414	1631	6		8369	0046	9954	52	43
18	12	1594	7		8406	1640	7		8360	0046	9954	48	42
19	16	1603	8		8397	1649	8		8351	0046	9954	26 44	41
20	33 20	9.1612			10.8388	9.1658			10.8342	10.0046	9.9954	40	40
21	24	1620	1	2	8380	1667	1	2	8333	0046	9954	36	39
22	28	1629	2	5	8371	1675	2	5	8325	0046	9954	32	38
23	32	1637	3	6	8363	1684	3	7	8316	0047	9953	28	37
24	36	1646	3		8354	1693	4		8307	0047	9953	26 24	36
25	33 40	9.1655	4		10.8345	9.1702	4		10.8298	10.0047	9.9953	20	35
26	44	1663	5		8337	1710	5		8290	0047	9953	16	34
27	48	1672	6		8328	1719	6		8281	0047	9953	12	33
28	52	1680	7		8320	1728	7		8272	0048	9952	8	32
29	56	1689	8		8311	1736	8		8264	0048	9952	26 4	31
30	34 0	9.1697			10.8303	9.1745			10.8255	10.0048	9.9952	26 0	30
31	4	1705	1	2	8295	1754	1	2	8246	0048	9952	25 56	29
32	8	1714	2	4	8286	1762	2	5	8238	0048	9952	52	28
33	12	1722	3	6	8278	1771	3	6	8229	0049	9951	48	27
34	16	1731	3		8269	1779	3		8221	0049	9951	25 44	26
35	34 20	9.1739	4		10.8261	9.1788	4		10.8212	10.0049	9.9951	40	25
36	24	1747	5		8253	1797	5		8203	0049	9951	36	24
37	28	1756	6		8244	1805	6		8195	0049	9951	32	23
38	32	1764	6		8236	1814	7		8186	0049	9951	28	22
39	36	1772	7		8228	1822	8		8178	0050	9950	25 24	21
40	34 40	9.1781			10.8219	9.1831			10.8169	10.0050	9.9950	20	20
41	44	1789	1	2	8211	1839	1	2	8161	0050	9950	16	19
42	48	1797	2	4	8203	1848	2	4	8152	0050	9950	12	18
43	52	1806	2	6	8194	1856	3	6	8144	0050	9950	8	17
44	56	1814	3		8186	1864	3		8136	0051	9949	25 4	16
45	35 0	9.1822	4		10.8178	9.1873	4		10.8127	10.0051	9.9949	25 0	15
46	4	1830	5		8170	1881	5		8119	0051	9949	24 56	14
47	8	1838	6		8162	1890	6		8110	0051	9949	52	13
48	12	1847	6		8153	1898	6		8102	0051	9949	48	12
49	16	1855	7		8145	1906	7		8094	0052	9948	24 44	11
50	35 20	9.1863			10.8137	9.1915			10.8085	10.0052	9.9948	40	10
51	24	1871	1	2	8129	1923	1	2	8077	0052	9948	36	9
52	28	1879	2	4	8121	1931	2	4	8069	0052	9948	32	8
53	32	1887	2	6	8113	1940	2	6	8060	0052	9948	28	7
54	36	1895	3		8105	1948	3		8052	0053	9947	24 24	6
55	35 40	9.1903	4		10.8097	9.1956	4		10.8044	10.0053	9.9947	20	5
56	44	1911	5		8089	1964	5		8036	0053	9947	16	4
57	48	1919	6		8081	1973	6		8027	0053	9947	12	3
58	52	1927	6		8073	1981	6		8019	0053	9947	8	2
59	56	1935	7		8065	1989	7		8011	0054	9946	24 4	1
60	36 0	9.1943			10.8057	9.1997			10.8003	10.0054	9.9946	24 0	0
′	m s	Cos.	Diff. 0′.1	Diff. 1ˢ	Sec.	Cot.	Diff. 0′.1	Diff. 1ˢ	Tan.	Cosec.	Sin.	m s	′

98° = 6ʰ 32ᵐ] [5ʰ 24ᵐ = 81°

9° = 0h 36m] **Log. Sines, Tangents, and Secants.** [11h 20m = 170°

′	m s	Sin.	Diff. 0′.1	Diff. 1s	Cosec.	Tan.	Diff. 0′.1	Diff. 1s	Cot.	Sec.	Cos.	m s	
0	36 0	9.1943			10.8057	9.1997			10.8003	10.0054	9.9946	24 0	60
1	4	1951	1	2	8049	2005	1	2	7995	0054	9946	23 56	59
2	8	1959	2	4	8041	2013	2	4	7987	0054	9946	52	58
3	12	1967	2	6	8033	2022	2	6	7978	0054	9946	48	57
4	16	1975	3		8025	2030	3		7970	0055	9945	23 44	56
5	36 20	9.1983	4		10.8017	9.2038	4		10.7962	10.0055	9.9945	40	55
6	24	1991	5		8009	2046	5		7954	0055	9945	36	54
7	28	1999	6		8001	2054	6		7946	0055	9945	32	53
8	32	2007	6		7993	2062	6		7938	0055	9945	28	52
9	36	2015	7		7985	2070	7		7930	0056	9944	23 24	51
10	36 40	9.2022			10.7978	9.2078			10.7922	10.0056	9.9944	20	50
11	44	2030	1	2	7970	2086	1	2	7914	0056	9944	16	49
12	48	2038	2	4	7962	2094	2	4	7906	0056	9944	12	48
13	52	2046	2	6	7954	2102	2	6	7898	0056	9944	8	47
14	56	2054	3		7946	2110	3		7890	0057	9943	23 4	46
15	37 0	9.2061	4		10.7939	9.2118	4		10.7882	10.0057	9.9943	23 0	45
16	4	2069	5		7931	2126	5		7874	0057	9943	22 56	44
17	8	2077	6		7923	2134	6		7866	0057	9943	52	43
18	12	2085	6		7915	2142	6		7858	0057	9943	48	42
19	16	2092	7		7908	2150	7		7850	0058	9942	22 44	41
20	37 20	9.2100			10.7900	9.2158			10.7842	10.0058	9.9942	40	40
21	24	2108	1	2	7892	2166	1	2	7834	0058	9942	36	39
22	28	2115	2	4	7885	2174	2	4	7826	0058	9942	32	38
23	32	2123	2	6	7877	2181	2	6	7819	0058	9942	28	37
24	36	2131	3		7869	2189	3		7811	0059	9941	22 24	36
25	37 40	9.2138	4		10.7862	9.2197	4		10.7803	10.0059	9.9941	20	35
26	44	2146	5		7854	2205	5		7795	0059	9941	16	34
27	48	2153	5		7847	2213	5		7787	0059	9941	12	33
28	52	2161	6		7839	2221	6		7779	0060	9940	8	32
29	56	2169	7		7831	2228	7		7772	0060	9940	22 4	31
30	38 0	9.2176			10.7824	9.2236			10.7764	10.0060	9.9940	22 0	30
31	4	2184	1	2	7816	2244	1	2	7756	0060	9940	21 56	29
32	8	2191	2	4	7809	2252	2	4	7748	0060	9940	52	28
33	12	2199	2	6	7801	2259	2	6	7741	0061	9939	48	27
34	16	2206	3		7794	2267	3		7733	0061	9939	21 44	26
35	38 20	9.2214	4		10.7786	9.2275	4		10.7725	10.0061	9.9939	40	25
36	24	2221	5		7779	2282	5		7718	0061	9939	36	24
37	28	2229	5		7771	2290	5		7710	0061	9939	32	23
38	32	2236	6		7764	2298	6		7702	0062	9938	28	22
39	36	2243	7		7757	2305	7		7695	0062	9938	21 24	21
40	38 40	9.2251			10.7749	9.2313			10.7687	10.0062	9.9938	20	20
41	44	2258	1	2	7742	2321	1	2	7679	0062	9938	16	19
42	48	2266	2	4	7734	2328	2	4	7672	0063	9937	12	18
43	52	2273	2	6	7727	2336	2	6	7664	0063	9937	8	17
44	56	2280	3		7720	2343	3		7657	0063	9937	21 4	16
45	39 0	9.2288	4		10.7712	9.2351	4		10.7649	10.0063	9.9937	21 0	15
46	4	2295	4		7705	2359	4		7641	0063	9937	20 56	14
47	8	2303	5		7697	2366	5		7634	0064	9936	52	13
48	12	2310	6		7690	2374	6		7626	0064	9936	48	12
49	16	2317	7		7683	2381	7		7619	0064	9936	20 44	11
50	39 20	9.2324			10.7676	9.2389			10.7611	10.0064	9.9936	40	10
51	24	2332	1	2	7668	2396	1	2	7604	0064	9936	36	9
52	28	2339	2	4	7661	2404	2	4	7596	0065	9935	32	8
53	32	2346	2	6	7654	2411	2	6	7589	0065	9935	28	7
54	36	2353	3		7647	2419	3		7581	0065	9935	20 24	6
55	39 40	9.2361	4		10.7639	9.2426	4		10.7574	10.0065	9.9935	20	5
56	44	2368	4		7632	2434	4		7566	0066	9934	10	4
57	48	2375	5		7625	2441	5		7559	0066	9934	12	3
58	52	2382	6		7618	2448	6		7552	0066	9934	8	2
59	56	2390	7		7610	2456	7		7544	0066	9934	20 4	1
60	40 0	9.2397			10.7603	9.2463			10.7537	10.0066	9.9934	20 0	0
′	m s	Cos.	0′.1 Diff.	1s Diff.	Sec.	Cot.	0′.1 Diff.	1s Diff.	Tan.	Cosec.	Sin.	m s	′

99° = 6h 36m] [5h 20m = 80°

10° = 0h 40m] **Log. Sines, Tangents, and Secants.** [11h 16m = 169°

′	m s	Sin.	Diff. 0′.1	Diff. 1s	Cosec.	Tan.	Diff. 0′.1	Diff. 1s	Cot.	Sec.	Cos.	m s	′
0	40 0	9.2397			10.7603	9.2463			10.7537	10.0066	9.9934	20 0	60
1	4	2404	1	2	7596	2471	1	2	7529	0067	9933	19 56	59
2	8	2411	1	4	7589	2478	2	4	7522	0067	9933	52	58
3	12	2418	2	5	7582	2485	2	6	7515	0067	9933	48	57
4	16	2425	3		7575	2493	3		7507	0067	9933	19 44	56
5	40 20	9.2432	4		10.7568	9.2500	4		10.7500	10.0068	9.9932	40	55
6	24	2439	4		7561	2507	4		7493	0068	9932	36	54
7	28	2447	5		7553	2515	5		7485	0068	9932	32	53
8	32	2454	6		7546	2522	6		7478	0068	9932	28	52
9	36	2461	6		7539	2529	7		7471	0069	9931	19 24	51
10	40 40	9.2468			10.7532	9.2536			10.7464	10.0069	9.9931	20	50
11	44	2475	1	2	7525	2544	1	2	7456	0069	9931	16	49
12	48	2482	1	4	7518	2551	2	4	7449	0069	9931	12	48
13	52	2489	2	5	7511	2558	2	6	7442	0069	9931	8	47
14	56	2496	3		7504	2565	3		7435	0070	9930	19 4	46
15	41 0	9.2503	4		10.7497	9.2573	4		10.7427	10.0070	9.9930	19 0	45
16	4	2510	4		7490	2580	4		7420	0070	9930	18 56	44
17	8	2517	5		7483	2587	5		7413	0070	9930	52	43
18	12	2524	6		7476	2594	6		7406	0071	9929	48	42
19	16	2531	6		7469	2601	7		7399	0071	9929	18 44	41
20	41 20	9.2538			10.7462	9.2609			10.7391	10.0071	9.9929	40	40
21	24	2545	1	2	7455	2616	1	2	7384	0071	9929	36	39
22	28	2551	1	4	7449	2623	2	4	7377	0071	9929	32	38
23	32	2558	2	5	7442	2630	2	5	7370	0072	9928	28	37
24	36	2565	3		7435	2637	3		7363	0072	9928	18 24	36
25	41 40	9.2572	4		10.7428	9.2644	4		10.7356	10.0072	9.9928	20	35
26	44	2579	4		7421	2651	4		7349	0072	9928	16	34
27	48	2586	5		7414	2658	5		7342	0073	9927	12	33
28	52	2593	6		7407	2666	6		7334	0073	9927	8	32
29	56	2600	6		7400	2673	6		7327	0073	9927	18 4	31
30	42 0	9.2606			10.7394	9.2680			10.7320	10.0073	9.9927	18 0	30
31	4	2613	1	2	7387	2687	1	2	7313	0074	9926	17 56	29
32	8	2620	1	4	7380	2694	1	4	7306	0074	9926	52	28
33	12	2627	2	5	7373	2701	2	5	7299	0074	9926	48	27
34	16	2634	3		7366	2708	3		7292	0074	9926	17 44	26
35	42 20	9.2640	4		10.7360	9.2715	4		10.7285	10.0075	9.9925	40	25
36	24	2647	4		7353	2722	4		7278	0075	9925	36	24
37	28	2654	5		7346	2729	5		7271	0075	9925	32	23
38	32	2661	6		7339	2736	6		7264	0075	9925	28	22
39	36	2667	6		7333	2743	6		7257	0075	9925	17 24	21
40	42 40	9.2674			10.7326	9.2750			10.7250	10.0076	9.9924	20	20
41	44	2681	1	2	7319	2757	1	2	7243	0076	9924	16	19
42	48	2687	1	3	7313	2764	1	4	7236	0076	9924	12	18
43	52	2694	2	5	7306	2770	2	5	7230	0076	9924	8	17
44	56	2701	3		7299	2777	3		7223	0077	9923	17 4	16
45	43 0	9.2707	3		10.7293	9.2784	4		10.7216	10.0077	9.9923	17 0	15
46	4	2714	4		7286	2791	4		7209	0077	9923	16 56	14
47	8	2721	5		7279	2798	5		7202	0077	9923	52	13
48	12	2727	5		7273	2805	6		7195	0078	9922	48	12
49	16	2734	6		7266	2812	6		7188	0078	9922	16 44	11
50	43 20	9.2740			10.7260	9.2819			10.7181	10.0078	9.9922	40	10
51	24	2747	1	2	7253	2825	1	2	7175	0078	9922	36	9
52	28	2754	1	3	7246	2832	1	3	7168	0079	9921	32	8
53	32	2760	2	5	7240	2839	2	5	7161	0079	9921	28	7
54	36	2767	3		7233	2846	3		7154	0079	9921	16 24	6
55	43 40	9.2773	3		10.7227	9.2853	4		10.7147	10.0079	9.9921	20	5
56	44	2780	4		7220	2859	4		7141	0080	9920	16	4
57	48	2786	5		7214	2866	5		7134	0080	9920	12	3
58	52	2793	5		7207	2873	6		7127	0080	9920	8	2
59	56	2799	6		7201	2880	6		7120	0080	9920	16 4	1
60	44 0	9.2806			10.7194	9.2887			10.7113	10.0081	9.9919	16 0	0
′	m s	Cos.	Diff. 0′.1	Diff. 1s	Sec.	Cot.	Diff. 0′.1	Diff. 1s	Tan.	Cosec.	Sin.	m s	′

100° = 6h 40m] [5h 16m = 79°

11° = 0h 44m]		Log. Sines, Tangents, and Secants.									[11h 12m = 168°		
′	m s	Sin.	Diff. 0′.1	Diff. 1s	Cosec.	Tan.	Diff. 0′.1	Diff. 1s	Cot.	Sec.	Cos.	m s	′
0	44 0	9.2806			10.7194	9.2887			10.7113	10.0081	9.9919	16 0	60
1	4	2812	1	2	7188	2893	1	2	7107	0081	9919	15 56	59
2	8	2819	1	3	7181	2900	1	3	7100	0081	9919	52	58
3	12	2825	2	5	7175	2907	2	5	7093	0081	9919	48	57
4	16	2832	3		7168	2913	3		7087	0082	9918	15 44	56
5	44 20	9.2838	3		10.7162	9.2920	3		10.7080	10.0082	9.9918	40	55
6	24	2845	4		7155	2927	4		7073	0082	9918	36	54
7	28	2851	5		7149	2933	5		7067	0082	9918	32	53
8	32	2858	5		7142	2940	5		7060	0083	9917	28	52
9	36	2864	6		7136	2947	6		7053	0083	9917	15 24	51
10	44 40	9.2870			10.7130	9.2953			10.7047	10.0083	9.9917	20	50
11	44	2877	1	2	7123	2960	1	2	7040	0083	9917	16	49
12	48	2883	1	3	7117	2967	1	3	7033	0084	9916	12	48
13	52	2890	2	5	7110	2973	2	5	7027	0084	9916	8	47
14	56	2896	3		7104	2980	3		7020	0084	9916	15 4	46
15	45 0	9.2902	3		10.7098	9.2987	3		10.7013	10.0084	9.9916	15 0	45
16	4	2909	4		7091	2993	4		7007	0085	9915	14 56	44
17	8	2915	5		7085	3000	5		7000	0085	9915	52	43
18	12	2921	5		7079	3006	5		6994	0085	9915	48	42
19	16	2928	6		7072	3013	6		6987	0085	9915	14 44	41
20	45 20	9.2934			10.7066	9.3020			10.6980	10.0086	9.9914	40	40
21	24	2940	1	2	7060	3026	1	2	6974	0086	9914	36	39
22	28	2947	1	3	7053	3033	1	3	6967	0086	9914	32	38
23	32	2953	2	5	7047	3039	2	5	6961	0086	9914	28	37
24	36	2959	3		7041	3046	3		6954	0087	9913	14 24	36
25	45 40	9.2965	3		10.7035	9.3052	3		10.6948	10.0087	9.9913	20	35
26	44	2972	4		7028	3059	4		6941	0087	9913	16	34
27	48	2978	4		7022	3065	5		6935	0087	9913	12	33
28	52	2984	5		7016	3072	5		6928	0088	9912	8	32
29	56	2990	6		7010	3078	6		6922	0088	9912	14 4	31
30	46 0	9.2997			10.7003	9.3085			10.6915	10.0088	9.9912	14 0	30
31	4	3003	1	2	6997	3091	1	2	6909	0088	9912	13 56	29
32	8	3009	1	3	6991	3098	1	3	6902	0089	9911	52	28
33	12	3015	2	5	6985	3104	2	5	6896	0089	9911	48	27
34	16	3021	2		6979	3110	3		6890	0089	9911	13 44	26
35	46 20	9.3027	3		10.6973	9.3117	3		10.6883	10.0089	9.9911	40	25
36	24	3034	4		6966	3123	4		6877	0090	9910	36	24
37	28	3040	4		6960	3130	4		6870	0090	9910	32	23
38	32	3046	5		6954	3136	5		6864	0090	9910	28	22
39	36	3052	5		6948	3142	6		6858	0090	9910	13 24	21
40	46 40	9.3058			10.6942	9.3149			10.6851	10.0091	9.9909	20	20
41	44	3064	1	2	6936	3155	1	2	6845	0091	9909	16	19
42	48	3070	1	3	6930	3162	1	3	6838	0091	9909	12	18
43	52	3077	2	5	6923	3168	2	5	6832	0091	9909	8	17
44	56	3083	2		6917	3174	3		6826	0092	9908	13 4	16
45	47 0	9.3089	3		10.6911	9.3181	3		10.6819	10.0092	9.9908	13 0	15
46	4	3095	4		6905	3187	4		6813	0092	9908	12 56.	14
47	8	3101	4		6899	3193	4		6807	0092	9908	52	13
48	12	3107	5		6893	3200	5		6800	0093	9907	48	12
49	16	3113	5		6887	3206	6		6794	0093	9907	12 44	11
50	47 20	9.3119			10.6881	9.3212			10.6788	10.0093	9.9907	40	10
51	24	3125	1	2	6875	3219	1	2	6781	0094	9906	36	9
52	28	3131	1	3	6869	3225	1	3	6775	0094	9906	32	8
53	32	3137	2	5	6863	3231	2	5	6769	0094	9906	28	7
54	36	3143	2		6857	3237	3		6763	0094	9906	12 24	6
55	47 40	9.3149	3		10.6851	9.3244	3		10.6756	10.0095	9.9905	20	5
56	44	3155	4		6845	3250	4		6750	0095	9905	16	4
57	48	3161	4		6839	3256	4		6744	0095	9905	12	3
58	52	3167	5		6833	3262	5		6738	0095	9905	8	2
59	56	3173	5		6827	3269	6		6731	0096	9904	12 4	1
60	48 0	9.3179			10.6821	9.3275			10.6725	10.0096	9.9904	12 0	0
′	m s	Cos.	Diff. 0′.1	Diff. 1s	Sec.	Cot.	Diff. 0′.1	Diff. 1s	Tan.	Cosec.	Sin.	m s	′
101° = 6h 44m]											[5h 12m = 78°		

12° = 0ʰ 48ᵐ] **Log. Sines, Tangents, and Secants.** **[11ʰ 8ᵐ = 167°**

′	m s	Sin.	Diff. 0′.1	Diff. 1ˢ	Cosec.	Tan.	Diff. 0′.1	Diff. 1ˢ	Cot.	Sec.	Cos.	m s	′
0	48 0	9.3179			10.6821	9.3275			10.6725	10.0096	9.9904	12 0	60
1	4	3185	1	2	6815	3281	1	2	6719	0096	9904	11 56	59
2	8	3191	1	3	6809	3287	1	3	6713	0096	9904	52	58
3	12	3197	2	5	6803	3293	2	5	6707	0097	9903	48	57
4	16	3202	2		6798	3300	2		6700	0097	9903	11 44	56
5	48 20	9.3208	3		10.6792	9.3306	3		10.6694	10.0097	9.9903	40	55
6	24	3214	4		6786	3312	4		6688	0098	9902	36	54
7	28	3220	4		6780	3318	4		6682	0098	9902	32	53
8	32	3226	5		6774	3324	5		6676	0098	9902	28	52
9	36	3232	5		6768	3330	5		6670	0098	9902	11 24	51
10	48 40	9.3238			10.6762	9.3336			10.6664	10.0099	9.9901	20	50
11	44	3244	1	2	6756	3343	1	2	6657	0099	9901	16	49
12	48	3250	1	3	6750	3349	1	3	6651	0099	9901	12	48
13	52	3255	2	5	6745	3355	2	5	6645	0099	9901	8	47
14	56	3261	2		6739	3361	2		6639	0100	9900	11 4	46
15	49 0	9.3267	3		10.6733	9.3367	3		10.6633	10.0100	9.9900	11 0	45
16	4	3273	4		6727	3373	4		6627	0100	9900	10 56	44
17	8	3279	4		6721	3379	4		6621	0101	9899	52	43
18	12	3284	5		6716	3385	5		6615	0101	9899	48	42
19	16	3290	5		6710	3391	5		6609	0101	9899	10 44	41
20	49 20	9.3296			10.6704	9.3397			10.6603	10.0101	9.9899	40	40
21	24	3302	1	2	6698	3403	1	2	6597	0102	9898	36	39
22	28	3308	1	3	6692	3409	1	3	6591	0102	9898	32	38
23	32	3313	2	5	6687	3416	2	5	6584	0102	9898	28	37
24	36	3319	2		6681	3422	2		6578	0103	9897	10 24	36
25	49 40	9.3325	3		10.6675	9.3428	3		10.6572	10.0103	9.9897	20	35
26	44	3331	4		6669	3434	4		6566	0103	9897	16	34
27	48	3336	4		6664	3440	4		6560	0103	9897	12	33
28	52	3342	5		6658	3446	5		6554	0104	9896	8	32
29	56	3348	5		6652	3452	5		6548	0104	9896	10 4	31
30	50 0	9.3353			10.6647	9.3458			10.6542	10.0104	9.9896	10 0	30
31	4	3359	1	1	6641	3464	1	2	6536	0104	9896	9 56	29
32	8	3365	1	3	6635	3469	1	3	6531	0105	9895	52	28
33	12	3370	2	5	6630	3475	2	5	6525	0105	9895	48	27
34	16	3376	2		6624	3481	2		6519	0105	9895	9 44	26
35	50 20	9.3382	3		10.6618	9.3487	3		10.6513	10.0106	9.9894	40	25
36	24	3387	3		6613	3493	4		6507	0106	9894	36	24
37	28	3393	4		6607	3499	4		6501	0106	9894	32	23
38	32	3399	5		6601	3505	5		6495	0106	9894	28	22
39	36	3404	5		6596	3511	5		6489	0107	9893	9 24	21
40	50 40	9.3410			10.6590	9.3517			10.6483	10.0107	9.9893	20	20
41	44	3416	1	1	6584	3523	1	2	6477	0107	9893	16	19
42	48	3421	1	3	6579	3529	1	3	6471	0108	9892	12	18
43	52	3427	2	5	6573	3535	2	5	6465	0108	9892	8	17
44	56	3432	2		6568	3541	2		6459	0108	9892	9 4	16
45	51 0	9.3438	3		10.6562	9.3546	3		10.6454	10.0108	9.9892	9 0	15
46	4	3444	3		6556	3552	4		6448	0109	9891	8 56	14
47	8	3449	4		6551	3558	4		6442	0109	9891	52	13
48	12	3455	5		6545	3564	5		6436	0109	9891	48	12
49	16	3460	5		6540	3570	5		6430	0110	9890	8 44	11
50	51 20	9.3466			10.6534	9.3576			10.6424	10.0110	9.9890	40	10
51	24	3471	1	1	6529	3581	1	1	6419	0110	9890	36	9
52	28	3477	1	3	6523	3587	1	3	6413	0110	9890	32	8
53	32	3482	2	4	6518	3593	2	5	6407	0111	9889	28	7
54	36	3488	2		6512	3599	2		6401	0111	9889	8 24	6
55	51 40	9.3493	3		10.6507	9.3605	3		10.6395	10.0111	9.9889	20	5
56	44	3499	3		6501	3611	3		6389	0112	9888	16	4
57	48	3504	4		6496	3616	4		6384	0112	9888	12	3
58	52	3510	4		6490	3622	5		6378	0112	9888	8	2
59	56	3515	5		6485	3628	5		6372	0112	9888	8 4	1
60	52 0	9.3521			10.6479	9.3634			10.6366	10.0113	9.9887	8 0	0
′	m s	Cos.	0′.1 Diff.	1ˢ Diff.	Sec.	Cot.	0′.1 Diff.	1ˢ Diff.	Tan.	Cosec.	Sin.	m s	′

102° = 6ʰ 48ᵐ] **[5ʰ 8ᵐ = 77°**

13° = 0h 52m]		Log. Sines, Tangents, and Secants.										[11h 4m = 166°	
′	m s	Sin.	Diff. 0′.1	Diff. 1s	Cosec.	Tan.	Diff. 0′.1	Diff. 1s	Cot.	Sec.	Cos.	m s	′
0	52 0	9.3521			10.6479	9.3634			10.6366	10.0113	9.9887	8 0	60
1	4	3526	1	1	6474	3639	1	1	6361	0113	9887	7 56	59
2	8	3532	1	3	6468	3645	1	3	6355	0113	9887	52	58
3	12	3537	2	4	6463	3651	2	5	6349	0114	9886	48	57
4	16	3543	2		6457	3657	2		6343	0114	9886	7 44	56
5	52 20	9.3548	3		10.6452	9.3662	3		10.6338	10.0114	9.9886	40	55
6	24	3554	3		6446	3668	3		6332	0115	9885	36	54
7	28	3559	4		6441	3674	4		6326	0115	9885	32	53
8	32	3504	4		6436	3680	5		6320	0115	9885	28	52
9	36	3570	5		6430	3685	5		6315	0115	9885	7 24	51
10	52 40	9.3575			10.6425	9.3691			10.6309	10.0116	9.9884	20	50
11	44	3581	1	1	6419	3697	1	1	6303	0116	9884	16	49
12	48	3586	1	3	6414	3702	1	3	6298	0116	9884	12	48
13	52	3591	2	4	6409	3708	2	5	6292	0117	9883	8	47
14	56	3597	2		6403	3714	2		6286	0117	9883	7 4	46
15	53 0	9.3602	3		10.6398	9.3719	3		10.6281	10.0117	9.9883	7 0	45
16	4	3608	3		6392	3725	3		6275	0117	9883	6 56	44
17	8	3613	4		6387	3731	4		6269	0118	9882	52	43
18	12	3618	4		6382	3736	5		6264	0118	9882	48	42
19	16	3624	5		6376	3742	5		6258	0118	9882	6 44	41
20	53 20	9.3629			10.6371	9.3748			10.6252	10.0119	9.9881	40	40
21	24	3634	1	1	6366	3753	1	1	6247	0119	9881	36	39
22	28	3640	1	3	6360	3759	1	3	6241	0119	9881	32	38
23	32	3645	2	4	6355	3764	2	4	6236	0120	9880	28	37
24	36	3650	2		6350	3770	2		6230	0120	9880	6 24	36
25	53 40	9.3655	3		10.6345	9.3776	3		10.6224	10.0120	9.9880	20	35
26	44	3661	3		6339	3781	3		6219	0120	9880	16	34
27	48	3666	4		6334	3787	4		6213	0121	9879	12	33
28	52	3671	4		6329	3792	4		6208	0121	9879	8	32
29	56	3677	5		6323	3798	5		6202	0121	9879	6 4	31
30	54 0	9.3682			10.6318	9.3804			10.6196	10.0122	9.9878	6 0	30
31	4	3687	1	1	6313	3809	1	1	6191	0122	9878	5 56	29
32	8	3692	1	3	6308	3815	1	3	6185	0122	9878	52	28
33	12	3698	2	4	6302	3820	2	4	6180	0123	9877	48	27
34	16	3703	2		6297	3826	2		6174	0123	9877	5 44	26
35	54 20	9.3709	3		10.6291	9.3831	3		10.6169	10.0123	9.9877	40	25
36	24	3713	3		6287	3837	3		6163	0124	9876	36	24
37	28	3719	4		6281	3842	4		6158	0124	9876	32	23
38	32	3724	4		6276	3848	4		6152	0124	9876	28	22
39	36	3729	5		6271	3853	5		6147	0124	9876	5 24	21
40	54 40	9.3734			10.6266	9.3859			10.6141	10.0125	9.9875	20	20
41	44	3739	1	1	6261	3864	1	1	6136	0125	9875	16	19
42	48	3745	1	3	6255	3870	1	3	6130	0125	9875	12	18
43	52	3750	2	4	6250	3875	2	4	6125	0126	9874	8	17
44	56	3755	2		6245	3881	2		6119	0126	9874	5 4	16
45	55 0	9.3760	3		10.6240	9.3886	3		10.6114	10.0126	9.9874	5 0	15
46	4	3765	3		6235	3892	3		6108	0127	9873	4 56	14
47	8	3770	4		6230	3897	4		6103	0127	9873	52	13
48	12	3775	4		6225	3903	4		6097	0127	9873	48	12
49	16	3780	5		6220	3908	5		6092	0128	9872	4 44	11
50	55 20	9.3786			10.6214	9.3914			10.6086	10.0128	9.9872	40	10
51	24	3791	1	1	6209	3919	1	1	6081	0128	9872	36	9
52	28	3796	1	3	6204	3924	1	3	6076	0128	9872	32	8
53	32	3801	2	4	6199	3930	2	4	6070	0129	9871	28	7
54	36	3806	2		6194	3935	2		6065	0129	9871	4 24	6
55	55 40	9.3811	3		10.6189	9.3941	3		10.6059	10.0129	9.9871	20	5
56	44	3816	3		6184	3946	3		6054	0130	9870	16	4
57	48	3822	4		6178	3952	4		6048	0130	9870	12	3
58	52	3827	4		6173	3957	4		6043	0130	9870	8	2
59	56	3832	5		6168	3962	5		6038	0131	9869	4	1
60	56 0	9.3837			10.6163	9.3968			10.6032	10.0131	9.9869	4 0	0
′	m s	Cos.	Diff. 0′.1	Diff. 1s	Sec.	Cot.	Diff. 0′.1	Diff. 1s	Tan.	Cosec.	Sin.	m s	′
103° = 6h 52m]												[5h 4m = 76°	

14° = 0h 56m] **Log. Sines, Tangents, and Secants.** [11h 0m = 165°

′	m s	Sin.	Diff. 0′.1	Diff. 1s	Cosec.	Tan.	Diff. 0′.1	Diff. 1s	Cot.	Sec.	Cos.	m s	′
0	56 0	9.3837			10.6163	9.3968			10.6032	10.0131	9.9869	4 0	60
1	4	3842	1	1	6158	3973	1	1	6027	0131	9869	3 56	59
2	8	3847	1	3	6153	3978	1	3	6022	0132	9868	52	58
3	12	3852	2	4	6148	3984	2	4	6016	0132	9868	48	57
4	16	3857	2		6143	3989	2		6011	0132	9868	3 44	56
5	56 20	9.3862	3		10.6138	9.3995	3		10.6005	10.0133	9.9867	40	55
6	24	3867	3		6133	4000	3		6000	0133	9867	36	54
7	28	3872	4		6128	4005	4		5995	0133	9867	32	53
8	32	3877	4		6123	4011	4		5989	0133	9867	28	52
9	36	3882	5		6118	4016	5		5984	0134	9866	3 24	51
10	56 40	9.3887			10.6113	9.4021			10.5979	10.0134	9.9866	20	50
11	44	3892	1	1	6108	4027	1	1	5973	0134	9866	16	49
12	48	3897	1	3	6103	4032	1	3	5968	0135	9865	12	48
13	52	3902	2	4	6098	4037	2	4	5963	0135	9865	8	47
14	56	3907	2		6093	4042	2		5958	0135	9865	3 4	46
15	57 0	9.3912	3		10.6088	9.4048	3		10.5952	10.0136	9.9864	3 0	45
16	4	3917	3		6083	4053	3		5947	0136	9864	2 56	44
17	8	3922	4		6078	4058	4		5942	0136	9864	52	43
18	12	3927	4		6073	4064	4		5936	0137	9863	48	42
19	16	3932	5		6068	4069	5		5931	0137	9863	2 44	41
20	57 20	9.3937			10.6063	9.4074			10.5926	10.0137	9.9863	40	40
21	24	3942	1	1	6058	4079	1	1	5921	0138	9862	36	39
22	28	3947	1	3	6053	4085	1	3	5915	0138	9862	32	38
23	32	3952	2	4	6048	4090	2	4	5910	0138	9862	28	37
24	36	3957	2		6043	4095	2		5905	0139	9861	2 24	36
25	57 40	9.3961	3		10.6039	9.4100	3		10.5900	10.0139	9.9861	20	35
26	44	3966	3		6034	4106	3		5894	0139	9861	16	34
27	48	3971	4		6029	4111	4		5889	0140	9860	12	33
28	52	3976	4		6024	4116	4		5884	0140	9860	8	32
29	56	3981	5		6019	4121	5		5879	0140	9860	2 4	31
30	58 0	9.3986			10.6014	9.4127			10.5873	10.0141	9.9859	2 0	30
31	4	3991	1	1	6009	4132	1	1	5868	0141	9859	1 56	29
32	8	3996	1	3	6004	4137	1	3	5863	0141	9859	52	28
33	12	4001	2	4	5999	4142	2	4	5858	0142	9858	48	27
34	16	4005	2		5995	4147	2		5853	0142	9858	1 44	26
35	58 20	9.4010	3		10.5990	9.4153	3		10.5847	10.0142	9.9858	40	25
36	24	4015	3		5985	4158	3		5842	0143	9857	36	24
37	28	4020	4		5980	4163	4		5837	0143	9857	32	23
38	32	4025	4		5975	4168	4		5832	0143	9857	28	22
39	36	4030	5		5970	4173	5		5827	0144	9856	1 24	21
40	58 40	9.4035			10.5965	9.4178			10.5822	10.0144	9.9856	20	20
41	44	4039	1	1	5961	4184	1	1	5816	0144	9856	16	19
42	48	4044	1	2	5956	4189	1	3	5811	0145	9855	12	18
43	52	4049	1	4	5951	4194	2	4	5806	0145	9855	8	17
44	56	4054	2		5946	4199	2		5801	0145	9855	1 4	16
45	59 0	9.4059	2		10.5941	9.4204	3		10.5796	10.0146	9.9854	1 0	15
46	4	4063	3		5937	4209	3		5791	0146	9854	0 56	14
47	8	4068	3		5932	4214	4		5786	0146	9854	52	13
48	12	4073	4		5927	4220	4		5780	0147	9853	48	12
49	16	4078	4		5922	4225	5		5775	0147	9853	0 44	11
50	59 20	9.4083			10.5917	9.4230			10.5770	10.0147	9.9853	40	10
51	24	4087	1	1	5913	4235	1	1	5765	0148	9852	36	9
52	28	4092	1	2	5908	4240	1	3	5760	0148	9852	32	8
53	32	4097	1	4	5903	4245	2	4	5755	0148	9852	28	7
54	36	4102	2		5898	4250	2		5750	0149	9851	0 24	6
55	59 40	9.4106	2		10.5894	9.4255	3		10.5745	10.0149	9.9851	20	5
56	44	4111	3		5889	4260	3		5740	0149	9851	16	4
57	48	4116	3		5884	4265	4		5735	0150	9850	12	3
58	52	4121	4		5879	4270	4		5730	0150	9850	8	2
59	56	4125	4		5875	4275	5		5725	0150	9850	0 4	1
60	60 0	9.4130			10.5870	9.4281			10.5719	10.0151	9.9849	0 0	0
′	m s	Cos.	0′.1 Diff.	1s	Sec.	Cot.	0′.1 Diff.	1s	Tan.	Cosec.	Sin.	m s	′

104° = 6h 56m] [5h 0m = 75°

15° = 1h 0m]			Log. Sines, Tangents, and Secants.								[10h 56m = 164°		
′	m s	Sin.	Diff. 0′.1	Diff. 1s	Cosec.	Tan.	Diff. 0′.1	Diff. 1s	Cot.	Sec.	Cos.	m s	′
0	0 0	9.4130			10.5870	9.4281			10.5719	10.0151	9.9849	60 0	60
1	4	4135	1	1	5865	4286	1	1	5714	0151	9849	59 56	59
2	8	4139	1	2	5861	4291	1	3	5709	0151	9849	52	58
3	12	4144	1	4	5856	4296	2	4	5704	0152	9848	48	57
4	16	4149	2		5851	4301	2		5699	0152	9848	59 44	56
5	0 20	9.4153	2		10.5847	9.4306	3		10.5694	10.0152	9.9848	40	55
6	24	4158	3		5842	4311	3		5689	0153	9847	36	54
7	28	4163	3		5837	4316	4		5684	0153	9847	32	53
8	32	4168	4		5832	4321	4		5679	0153	9847	28	52
9	36	4172	4		5828	4326	5		5674	0154	9846	59 24	51
10	0 40	9.4177			10.5823	9.4331			10.5669	10.0154	9.9846	20	50
11	44	4181	1	1	5819	4336	1	1	5664	0154	9846	16	49
12	48	4186	1	2	5814	4341	1	3	5659	0155	9845	12	48
13	52	4191	1	4	5809	4346	2	4	5654	0155	9845	8	47
14	56	4195	2		5805	4351	2		5649	0155	9845	59 4	46
15	1 0	9.4200	2		10.5800	9.4356	3		10.5644	10.0156	9.9844	59 0	45
16	4	4205	3		5795	4361	3		5639	0156	9844	58 56	44
17	8	4209	3		5791	4366	4		5634	0156	9844	52	43
18	12	4214	4		5786	4371	4		5629	0157	9843	48	42
19	16	4219	4		5781	4376	5		5624	0157	9843	58 44	41
20	1 20	9.4223			10.5777	9.4381			10.5619	10.0157	9.9843	40	40
21	24	4228	1	1	5772	4386	1	1	5614	0158	9842	36	39
22	28	4232	1	2	5768	4390	1	3	5610	0158	9842	32	38
23	32	4237	1	4	5763	4395	2	4	5605	0158	9842	28	37
24	36	4242	2		5758	4400	2		5600	0159	9841	58 24	36
25	1 40	9.4246	2		10.5754	9.4405	3		10.5595	10.0159	9.9841	20	35
26	44	4251	3		5749	4410	3		5590	0159	9841	16	34
27	48	4255	3		5745	4415	4		5585	0160	9840	12	33
28	52	4260	4		5740	4420	4		5580	0160	9840	8	32
29	56	4264	4		5736	4425	5		5575	0161	9839	58 4	31
30	2 0	9.4269			10.5731	9.4430			10.5570	10.0161	9.9839	58 0	30
31	4	4274	0	1	5726	4435	1	1	5565	0161	9839	57 56	29
32	8	4278	1	2	5722	4440	1	3	5560	0162	9838	52	28
33	12	4283	1	3	5717	4445	2	4	5555	0162	9838	48	27
34	16	4287	2		5713	4449	2		5551	0162	9838	57 44	26
35	2 20	9.4292	2		10.5708	9.4454	3		10.5546	10.0163	9.9837	40	25
36	24	4296	3		5704	4459	3		5541	0163	9837	36	24
37	28	4301	3		5699	4464	4		5536	0163	9837	32	23
38	32	4305	4		5695	4469	4		5531	0164	9836	28	22
39	36	4310	4		5690	4474	5		5526	0164	9836	57 24	21
40	2 40	9.4314			10.5686	9.4479			10.5521	10.0164	9.9836	20	20
41	44	4319	0	1	5681	4484	1	1	5516	0165	9835	16	19
42	48	4323	1	2	5677	4488	1	2	5512	0165	9835	12	18
43	52	4328	1	3	5672	4493	1	4	5507	0165	9835	8	17
44	56	4332	2		5668	4498	2		5502	0166	9834	57 4	16
45	3 0	9.4337	2		10.5633	9.4503	2		10.5497	10.0166	9.9834	57 0	15
46	4	4341	3		5659	4508	3		5492	0167	9833	56 56	14
47	8	4346	3		5654	4513	3		5487	0167	9833	52	13
48	12	4350	4		5650	4517	4		5483	0167	9833	48	12
49	16	4355	4		5645	4522	4		5478	0168	9832	56 44	11
50	3 20	9.4359			10.5641	9.4527			10.5473	10.0168	9.9832	40	10
51	24	4364	0	1	5636	4532	1	1	5468	0168	9832	36	9
52	28	4368	1	2	5632	4537	1	2	5463	0169	9831	32	8
53	32	4372	1	3	5628	4541	1	4	5459	0169	9831	28	7
54	36	4377	2		5623	4546	2		5454	0169	9831	56 24	6
55	3 40	9.4381	2		10.5619	9.4551	2		10.5449	10.0170	9.9830	20	5
56	44	4386	3		5614	4556	3		5444	0170	9830	16	4
57	48	4390	3		5610	4561	3		5439	0170	9830	12	3
58	52	4395	4		5605	4565	4		5435	0171	9829	8	2
59	56	4399	4		5601	4570	4		5430	0171	9829	56 4	1
60	4 0	9.4403			10.5597	9.4575			10.5425	10.0172	9.9828	56 0	0
′	m s	Cos.	Diff. 0′.1	Diff. 1s	Sec.	Cot.	Diff. 0′.1	Diff. 1s	Tan.	Cosec.	Sin.	m s	′
105° = 7h 0m]											[4h 56m = 74°		

16° = 1h 4m]		Log. Sines, Tangents, and Secants.										[10h 52m = 163°	
′	m s	Sin.	Diff. 0′.1	Diff. 1s	Cosec.	Tan.	Diff. 0′.1	Diff. 1s	Cot.	Sec.	Cos.	m s	′
0	4 0	9.4403			10.5597	9.4575			10.5425	10.0172	9.9828	56 0	60
1	4	4408	0	1	5592	4580	1	1	5420	0172	9828	55 56	59
2	8	4412	1	2	5588	4584	1	2	5416	0172	9828	52	58
3	12	4417	1	3	5583	4589	1	4	5411	0173	9827	48	57
4	16	4421	2		5579	4594	2		5406	0173	9827	55 44	56
5	4 20	9.4425	2		10.5575	9.4599	2		10.5401	10.0173	9.9827	40	55
6	24	4430	3		5570	4603	3		5397	0174	9826	36	54
7	28	4434	3		5565	4608	3		5392	0174	9826	32	53
8	32	4438	4		5562	4613	4		5387	0174	9826	28	52
9	36	4443	4		5557	4618	4		5382	0175	9825	55 24	51
10	4 40	9.4447			10.5553	9.4622			10.5378	10.0175	9.9825	20	50
11	44	4452	0	1	5548	4627	1	1	5373	0176	9824	16	49
12	48	4456	1	2	5544	4632	1	2	5368	0176	9824	12	48
13	52	4460	1	3	5540	4637	1	4	5363	0176	9824	8	47
14	56	4465	2		5535	4641	2		5359	0177	9823	55 4	46
15	5 0	9.4469	2		10.5531	9.4646	2		10.5354	10.0177	9.9823	55 0	45
16	4	4473	3		5527	4651	3		5349	0177	9823	54 56	44
17	8	4478	3		5522	4655	3		5345	0178	9822	52	43
18	12	4482	4		5518	4660	4		5340	0178	9822	48	42
19	16	4486	4		5514	4665	4		5335	0179	9821	54 44	41
20	5 20	9.4491			10.5509	9.4669			10.5331	10.0179	9.9821	40	40
21	24	4495	0	1	5505	4674	1	1	5326	0179	9821	36	39
22	28	4499	1	2	5501	4679	1	2	5321	0180	9820	32	38
23	32	4503	1	3	5497	4683	1	4	5317	0180	9820	28	37
24	36	4508	2		5492	4688	2		5312	0180	9820	54 24	36
25	5 40	9.4512	2		10.5488	9.4693	2		10.5307	10.0181	9.9819	20	35
26	44	4516	3		5484	4697	3		5303	0181	9819	16	34
27	48	4521	3		5479	4702	3		5298	0182	9818	12	33
28	52	4525	3		5475	4707	4		5293	0182	9818	8	32
29	56	4529	4		5471	4711	4		5289	0182	9818	54 4	31
30	6 0	9.4533			10.5467	9.4716			10.5284	10.0183	9.9817	54 0	30
31	4	4538	0	1	5462	4721	1	1	5279	0183	9817	53 56	29
32	8	4542	1	2	5458	4725	1	2	5275	0183	9817	52	28
33	12	4546	1	3	5454	4730	1	4	5270	0184	9816	48	27
34	16	4550	2		5450	4735	2		5265	0184	9816	53 44	26
35	6 20	9.4555	2		10.5445	9.4739	2		10.5261	10.0185	9.9815	40	25
36	24	4559	3		5441	4744	3		5256	0185	9815	36	24
37	28	4563	3		5437	4748	3		5252	0185	9815	32	23
38	32	4567	3		5433	4753	4		5247	0186	9814	28	22
39	36	4572	4		5428	4758	4		5242	0186	9814	53 24	21
40	6 40	9.4576			10.5424	9.4762			10.5238	10.0186	9.9814	20	20
41	44	4580	0	1	5420	4767	0	1	5233	0187	9813	16	19
42	48	4584	1	2	5416	4771	1	2	5229	0187	9813	12	18
43	52	4588	1	3	5412	4776	1	3	5224	0188	9812	8	17
44	56	4593	2		5407	4781	2		5219	0188	9812	53 4	16
45	7 0	9.4597	2		10.5403	9.4785	2		10.5215	10.0188	9.9812	53 0	15
46	4	4601	3		5399	4790	3		5210	0189	9811	52 56	14
47	8	4605	3		5395	4794	3		5206	0189	9811	52	13
48	12	4609	3		5391	4799	4		5201	0189	9811	48	12
49	16	4614	4		5386	4803	4		5197	0190	9810	52 44	11
50	7 20	9.4618			10.5382	9.4808			10.5192	10.0190	9.9810	40	10
51	24	4622	0	1	5378	4813	0	1	5187	0191	9809	36	9
52	28	4626	1	2	5374	4817	1	2	5183	0191	9809	32	8
53	32	4630	1	3	5370	4822	1	3	5178	0191	9809	28	7
54	36	4634	2		5366	4826	2		5174	0192	9808	52 24	6
55	7 40	9.4639	2		10.5361	9.4831	2		10.5169	10.0192	9.9808	20	5
56	44	4643	3		5357	4835	3		5165	0192	9808	16	4
57	48	4647	3		5353	4840	3		5160	0193	9807	12	3
58	52	4651	3		5349	4844	4		5156	0193	9807	8	2
59	56	4655	4		5345	4849	4		5151	0194	9806	52 4	1
60	8 0	9.4659			10.5341	9.4853			10.5147	10.0194	9.9806	52 0	0
′	m s	Cos.	0′.1 Diff.	1s Diff.	Sec.	Cot.	0′.1 Diff.	1s Diff.	Tan.	Cosec.	Sin.	m s	′
106° = 7h 4m]												[4h 52m = 73°	

17° = 1h 8m]		Log. Sines, Tangents, and Secants.										[10h 48m = 162°	
′	m s	Sin.	Diff. 0′.1	Diff. 1s	Cosec.	Tan.	Diff. 0′.1	Diff. 1s	Cot.	Sec.	Cos.	m s	′
0	8 0	9.4659			10.5341	9.4853			10.5147	10.0194	9.9806	52 0	60
1	4	4663	0	1	5337	4858	0	1	5142	0194	9806	51 56	59
2	8	4668	1	2	5332	4862	1	2	5138	0195	9805	52	58
3	12	4672	1	3	5328	4867	1	3	5133	0195	9805	48	57
4	16	4676	2		5324	4871	2		5129	0196	9804	51 44	56
5	8 20	9.4680	2		10.5320	9.4876	2		10.5124	10.0196	9.9804	40	55
6	24	4684	2		5316	4880	3		5120	0196	9804	36	54
7	28	4688	3		5312	4885	3		5115	0197	9803	32	53
8	32	4692	3		5308	4889	4		5111	0197	9803	28	52
9	36	4696	4		5304	4894	4		5106	0198	9802	51 24	51
10	8 40	9.4700			10.5300	9.4898			10.5102	10.0198	9.9802	20	50
11	44	4705	0	1	5295	4903	0	1	5097	0198	9802	16	49
12	48	4709	1	2	5291	4907	1	2	5093	0199	9801	12	48
13	52	4713	1	3	5287	4912	1	3	5088	0199	9801	8	47
14	56	4717	2		5283	4916	2		5084	0199	9801	51 4	46
15	9 0	9.4721	2		10.5279	9.4921	2		10.5079	10.0200	9.9800	51 0	45
16	4	4725	2		5275	4925	3		5075	0200	9800	50 56	44
17	8	4729	3		5271	4930	3		5070	0201	9799	52	43
18	12	4733	3		5267	4934	4		5066	0201	9799	48	42
19	16	4737	4		5263	4939	4		5061	0201	9799	50 44	41
20	9 20	9.4741			10.5259	9.4943			10.5057	10.0202	9.9798	40	40
21	24	4745	0	1	5255	4947	0	1	5053	0202	9798	36	39
22	28	4749	1	2	5251	4952	1	2	5048	0203	9797	32	38
23	32	4753	1	3	5247	4956	1	3	5044	0203	9797	28	37
24	36	4757	2		5243	4961	2		5039	0203	9797	50 24	36
25	9 40	9.4761	2		10.5239	9.4965	2		10.5035	10.0204	9.9796	20	35
26	44	4765	2		5235	4970	3		5030	0204	9796	16	34
27	48	4769	3		5231	4974	3		5026	0205	9795	12	33
28	52	4773	3		5227	4978	4		5022	0205	9795	8	32
29	56	4777	4		5223	4983	4		5017	0205	9795	50 4	31
30	10 0	9.4781			10.5219	9.4987			10.5013	10.0206	9.9794	50 0	30
31	4	4785	0	1	5215	4992	0	1	5008	0206	9794	49 56	29
32	8	4789	1	2	5211	4996	1	2	5004	0207	9793	52	28
33	12	4793	1	3	5207	5000	1	3	5000	0207	9793	48	27
34	16	4797	2		5203	5005	2		4995	0207	9793	49 44	26
35	10 20	9.4801	2		10.5199	9.5009	2		10.4991	10.0208	9.9792	40	25
36	24	4805	2		5195	5014	3		4986	0208	9792	36	24
37	28	4809	3		5191	5018	3		4982	0209	9791	32	23
38	32	4813	3		5187	5022	4		4978	0209	9791	28	22
39	36	4817	4		5183	5027	4		4973	0209	9791	49 24	21
40	10 40	9.4821			10.5179	9.5031			10.4969	10.0210	9.9790	20	20
41	44	4825	0	1	5175	5035	0	1	4965	0210	9790	16	19
42	48	4829	1	2	5171	5040	1	2	4960	0211	9789	12	18
43	52	4833	1	3	5167	5044	1	3	4956	0211	9789	8	17
44	56	4837	2		5163	5049	2		4951	0211	9789	49 4	16
45	11 0	9.4841	2		10.5159	9.5053	2		10.4947	10.0212	9.9788	49 0	15
46	4	4845	2		5155	5057	3		4943	0212	9788	48 56	14
47	8	4849	3		5151	5062	3		4938	0213	9787	52	13
48	12	4853	3		5147	5066	4		4934	0213	9787	48	12
49	16	4857	4		5143	5070	4		4930	0213	9787	48 44	11
50	11 20	9.4861			10.5139	9.5075			10.4925	10.0214	9.9786	40	10
51	24	4865	0	1	5135	5079	0	1	4921	0214	9786	36	9
52	28	4869	1	2	5131	5083	1	2	4917	0215	9785	32	8
53	32	4873	1	3	5127	5088	1	3	4912	0215	9785	28	7
54	36	4876	2		5124	5092	2		4908	0215	9785	48 24	6
55	11 40	9.4880	2		10.5120	9.5096	2		10.4904	10.0216	9.9784	20	5
56	44	4884	2		5116	5101	3		4899	0216	9784	16	4
57	48	4888	3		5112	5105	3		4895	0217	9783	12	3
58	52	4892	3		5108	5109	4		4891	0217	9783	8	2
59	56	4896	4		5104	5113	4		4887	0218	9782	48 4	1
60	12 0	9.4900			10.5100	9.5118			10.4882	10.0218	9.9782	48 0	0
′	m s	Cos.	Diff. 0′.1	Diff. 1s	Sec.	Cot.	Diff. 0′.1	Diff. 1s	Tan.	Cosec.	Sin.	m s	′
107° = 7h 8m]												[4h 48m = 72°	

$18^{\circ} = 1^{h}\ 12^{m}$] **Log. Sines, Tangents, and Secants.** [$10^{h}\ 44^{m} = 161^{\circ}$

′	m s	Sin.	Diff. 0′.1	Diff. 1s	Cosec.	Tan.	Diff. 0′.1	Diff. 1s	Cot.	Sec.	Cos.	m s	′
0	12 0	9.4900			10.5100	9.5118			10.4882	10.0218	9.9782	48 0	60
1	4	4904	0	1	5096	5122	0	1	4878	0218	9782	47 56	59
2	8	4908	1	2	5092	5126	1	2	4874	0219	9781	52	58
3	12	4911	1	3	5089	5131	1	3	4869	0219	9781	48	57
4	16	4915	2		5085	5135	2		4865	0220	9780	47 44	56
5	12 20	9.4919	2		10.5081	9.5139	2		10.4861	10.0220	9.9780	40	55
6	24	4923	2		5077	5143	3		4857	0220	9780	36	54
7	28	4927	3		5073	5148	3		4852	0221	9779	32	53
8	32	4931	3		5069	5152	4		4848	0221	9779	28	52
9	36	4935	4		5065	5156	4		4844	0222	9778	47 24	51
10	12 40	9.4939			10.5061	9.5161			10.4839	10.0222	9.9778	20	50
11	44	4942	0	1	5058	5165	0	1	4835	0222	9778	16	49
12	48	4946	1	2	5054	5169	1	2	4831	0223	9777	12	48
13	52	4950	1	3	5050	5173	1	3	4827	0223	9777	8	47
14	56	4954	2		5046	5178	2		4822	0224	9776	47 4	46
15	13 0	9.4958	2		10.5042	9.5182	2		10.4818	10.0224	9.9776	47 0	45
16	4	4962	2		5038	5186	3		4814	0225	9775	46 56	44
17	8	4965	3		5035	5190	3		4810	0225	9775	52	43
18	12	4969	3		5031	5195	4		4805	0225	9775	48	42
19	16	4973	4		5027	5199	4		4801	0226	9774	46 44	41
20	13 20	9.4977			10.5023	9.5203			10.4797	10.0226	9.9774	40	40
21	24	4981	0	1	5019	5207	0	1	4793	0227	9773	36	39
22	28	4984	1	2	5016	5212	1	2	4788	0227	9773	32	38
23	32	4988	1	3	5012	5216	1	3	4784	0227	9773	28	37
24	36	4992	2		5008	5220	2		4780	0228	9772	46 24	36
25	13 40	9.4996	2		10.5004	9.5224	2		10.4776	10.0228	9.9772	20	35
26	44	5000	2		5000	5228	3		4772	0229	9771	16	34
27	48	5003	3		4997	5233	3		4767	0229	9771	12	33
28	52	5007	3		4993	5237	4		4763	0230	9770	8	32
29	56	5011	4		4989	5241	4		4759	0230	9770	46 4	31
30	14 0	9.5015			10.4985	9.5245			10.4755	10.0230	9.9770	46 0	30
31	4	5019	0	1	4981	5249	0	1	4751	0231	9769	45 56	29
32	8	5022	1	2	4978	5254	1	2	4746	0231	9769	52	28
33	12	5026	1	3	4974	5258	1	3	4742	0232	9768	48	27
34	16	5030	2		4970	5262	2		4738	0232	9768	45 44	26
35	14 20	9.5034	2		10.4966	9.5266	2		10.4734	10.0233	9.9767	40	25
36	24	5037	2		4963	5270	3		4730	0233	9767	36	24
37	28	5041	3		4959	5275	3		4725	0233	9767	32	23
38	32	5045	3		4955	5279	4		4721	0234	9766	28	22
39	36	5049	4		4951	5283	4		4717	0234	9766	45 24	21
40	14 40	9.5052			10.4948	9.5287			10.4713	10.0235	9.9765	20	20
41	44	5056	0	1	4944	5291	0	1	4709	0235	9765	16	19
42	48	5060	1	2	4940	5295	1	2	4705	0236	9764	12	18
43	52	5064	1	3	4936	5300	1	3	4700	0236	9764	8	17
44	56	5067	2		4933	5304	2		4696	0236	9764	45 4	16
45	15 0	9.5071	2		10.4929	9.5308	2		10.4692	10.0237	9.9763	45 0	15
46	4	5075	2		4925	5312	2		4688	0237	9763	44 56	14
47	8	5078	3		4922	5316	3		4684	0238	9762	52	13
48	12	5082	3		4918	5320	3		4680	0238	9762	48	12
49	16	5086	4		4914	5324	4		4676	0239	9761	44 44	11
50	15 20	9.5090			10.4910	9.5329			10.4671	10.0239	9.9761	40	10
51	24	5093	0	1	4907	5333	0	1	4667	0239	9761	36	9
52	28	5097	1	2	4903	5337	1	2	4663	0240	9760	32	8
53	32	5101	1	3	4899	5341	1	3	4659	0240	9760	28	7
54	36	5104	1		4896	5345	2		4655	0241	9759	44 24	6
55	15 40	9.5108	2		10.4892	9.5349	2		10.4651	10.0241	9.9759	20	5
56	44	5112	2		4888	5353	2		4647	0242	9758	16	4
57	48	5115	3		4885	5357	3		4643	0242	9758	12	3
58	52	5119	3		4881	5362	3		4638	0242	9758	8	2
59	56	5123	3		4877	5366	4		4634	0243	9757	44 4	1
60	16 0	9.5126			10.4874	9.5370			10.4630	10.0243	9.9757	44 0	0
′	m s	Cos.	0′.1 Diff.	1s Diff.	Sec.	Cot.	0′.1 Diff.	1s Diff.	Tan.	Cosec.	Sin.	m s	′

$108^{\circ} = 7^{h}\ 12^{m}$] [$4^{h}\ 44^{m} = 71^{\circ}$

19° = 1h 16m]		Log. Sines, Tangents, and Secants.										[10h 40m = 160°	
′	m s	Sin.	Diff. 0′.1	Diff. 1s	Cosec.	Tan.	Diff. 0′.1	Diff. 1s	Cot.	Sec.	Cos.	m s	′
0	16 0	9.5126			10.4874	9.5370			10.4630	10.0243	9.9757	44 0	60
1	4	5130	0	1	4870	5374	0	1	4626	0244	9756	43 56	59
2	8	5134	1	2	4866	5378	1	2	4622	0244	9756	52	58
3	12	5137	1	3	4863	5382	1	3	4618	0245	9755	48	57
4	16	5141	1		4859	5386	2		4614	0245	9755	43 44	56
5	16 20	9.5145	2		10.4855	9.5390	2		10.4610	10.0245	9.9755	40	55
6	24	5148	2		4852	5394	2		4606	0246	9754	36	54
7	28	5152	3		4848	5398	3		4602	0246	9754	32	53
8	32	5156	3		4844	5402	3		4598	0247	9753	28	52
9	36	5159	3		4841	5407	4		4593	0247	9753	43 24	51
10	16 40	9.5163			10.4837	9.5411			10.4589	10.0248	9.9752	20	50
11	44	5167	0	1	4833	5415	0	1	4585	0248	9752	16	49
12	48	5170	1	2	4830	5419	1	2	4581	0249	9751	12	48
13	52	5174	1	3	4826	5423	1	3	4577	0249	9751	8	47
14	56	5177	1		4823	5427	2		4573	0249	9751	43 4	46
15	17 0	9.5181	2		10.4819	9.5431	2		10.4569	10.0250	9.9750	43 0	45
16	4	5185	2		4815	5435	2		4565	0250	9750	42 56	44
17	8	5188	3		4812	5439	3		4561	0251	9749	52	43
18	12	5192	3		4808	5443	3		4557	0251	9749	48	42
19	16	5196	3		4804	5447	4		4553	0252	9748	42 44	41
20	17 20	9.5199			10.4801	9.5451			10.4549	10.0252	9.9748	40	40
21	24	5203	0	1	4797	5455	0	1	4545	0253	9747	36	39
22	28	5206	1	2	4794	5459	1	2	4541	0253	9747	32	38
23	32	5210	1	3	4790	5463	1	3	4537	0253	9747	28	37
24	36	5213	1		4787	5467	2		4533	0254	9746	42 24	36
25	17 40	9.5217	2		10.4783	9.5471	2		10.4529	10.0254	9.9746	20	35
26	44	5221	2		4779	5475	2		4525	0255	9745	16	34
27	48	5224	3		4776	5479	3		4521	0255	9745	12	33
28	52	5228	3		4772	5483	3		4517	0256	9744	8	32
29	56	5231	3		4769	5487	4		4513	0256	9744	42 4	31
30	18 0	9.5235			10.4765	9.5491			10.4509	10.0257	9.9743	42 0	30
31	4	5239	0	1	4761	5495	0	1	4505	0257	9743	41 56	29
32	8	5242	1	2	4758	5500	1	2	4500	0257	9743	52	28
33	12	5246	1	3	4754	5504	1	3	4496	0258	9742	48	27
34	16	5249	1		4751	5508	2		4492	0258	9742	41 44	26
35	18 20	9.5253	2		10.4747	9.5512	2		10.4488	10.0259	9.9741	40	25
36	24	5256	2		4744	5516	2		4484	0259	9741	36	24
37	28	5260	3		4740	5520	3		4480	0260	9740	32	23
38	32	5263	3		4737	5524	3		4476	0260	9740	28	22
39	36	5267	3		4733	5528	4		4472	0261	9739	41 24	21
40	18 40	9.5270			10.4730	9.5531			10.4469	10.0261	9.9739	20	20
41	44	5274	0	1	4726	5535	0	1	4465	0261	9739	16	19
42	48	5278	1	2	4722	5539	1	2	4461	0262	9738	12	18
43	52	5281	1	3	4719	5543	1	3	4457	0262	9738	8	17
44	56	5285	1		4715	5547	2		4453	0263	9737	41 4	16
45	19 0	9.5288	2		10.4712	9.5551	2		10.4449	10.0263	9.9737	41 0	15
46	4	5292	2		4708	5555	2		4445	0264	9736	40 56	14
47	8	5295	3		4705	5559	3		4441	0264	9736	52	13
48	12	5299	3		4701	5563	3		4437	0265	9735	48	12
49	16	5302	3		4698	5567	4		4433	0265	9735	40 44	11
50	19 20	9.5306			10.4694	9.5571			10.4429	10.0266	9.9734	40	10
51	24	5309	0	1	4691	5575	0	1	4425	0266	9734	36	9
52	28	5313	1	2	4687	5579	1	2	4421	0266	9734	32	8
53	32	5316	1	3	4684	5583	1	3	4417	0267	9733	28	7
54	36	5320	1		4680	5587	2		4413	0267	9733	40 24	6
55	19 40	9.5323	2		10.4677	9.5591	2		10.4409	10.0268	9.9732	20	5
56	44	5327	2		4673	5595	2		4405	0268	9732	16	4
57	48	5330	3		4670	5599	3		4401	0269	9731	12	3
58	52	5334	3		4666	5603	3		4397	0269	9731	8	2
59	56	5337	3		4663	5607	4		4393	0270	9730	40 4	1
60	20 0	9.5341			10.4659	9.5611			10.4389	10.0270	9.9730	40 0	0
′	m s	Cos.	Diff. 0′.1	Diff. 1s	Sec.	Cot.	Diff. 0′.1	Diff. 1s	Tan.	Cosec.	Sin.	m s	′
109° = 7h 16m]												[4h 40m = 70°	

20° = 1h 20m] **Log. Sines, Tangents, and Secants.** **[10h 36m = 159°**

′	m s	Sin.	Diff. 0′.1	Diff. 1s	Cosec.	Tan.	Diff. 0′.1	Diff. 1s	Cot.	Sec.	Cos.	m s	′
0	20 0	9.5341			10.4659	9.5611			10.4389	10.0270	9.9730	40 0	60
1	4	5344	0	1	4656	5615	0	1	4385	0271	9729	39 56	59
2	8	5347	1	2	4653	5619	1	2	4381	0271	9729	52	58
3	12	5351	1	3	4649	5622	1	3	4378	0272	9728	48	57
4	16	5354	1		4646	5626	2		4374	0272	9728	39 44	56
5	20 20	9.5358	2		10.4642	9.5630	2		10.4370	10.0272	9.9728	40	55
6	24	5361	2		4639	5634	2		4366	0273	9727	36	54
7	28	5365	3		4635	5638	3		4362	0273	9727	32	53
8	32	5368	3		4632	5642	3		4358	0274	9726	28	52
9	36	5372	3		4628	5646	4		4354	0274	9726	39 24	51
10	20 40	9.5375			10.4625	9.5650			10.4350	10.0275	9.9725	20	50
11	44	5379	0	1	4621	5654	0	1	4346	0275	9725	16	49
12	48	5382	1	2	4618	5658	1	2	4342	0276	9724	12	48
13	52	5385	1	3	4615	5662	1	3	4338	0276	9724	8	47
14	56	5389	1		4611	5665	2		4335	0277	9723	39 4	46
15	21 0	9.5392	2		10.4608	9.5669	2		10.4331	10.0277	9.9723	39 0	45
16	4	5396	2		4604	5673	2		4327	0278	9722	38 56	44
17	8	5399	3		4601	5677	3		4323	0278	9722	52	43
18	12	5402	3		4598	5681	3		4319	0278	9722	48	42
19	16	5406	3		4594	5685	4		4315	0279	9721	38 44	41
20	21 20	9.5409			10.4591	9.5689			10.4311	10.0279	9.9721	40	40
21	24	5413	0	1	4587	5693	0	1	4307	0280	9720	36	39
22	28	5416	1	2	4584	5696	1	2	4304	0280	9720	32	38
23	32	5420	1	3	4580	5700	1	3	4300	0281	9719	28	37
24	36	5423	1		4577	5704	2		4296	0281	9719	38 24	36
25	21 40	9.5426	2		10.4574	9.5708	2		10.4292	10.0282	9.9718	20	35
26	44	5430	2		4570	5712	2		4288	0282	9718	16	34
27	48	5433	3		4567	5716	3		4284	0283	9717	12	33
28	52	5436	3		4564	5720	3		4280	0283	9717	8	32
29	56	5440	3		4560	5724	4		4276	0284	9716	38 4	31
30	22 0	9.5443			10.4557	9.5727			10.4273	10.0284	9.9716	38 0	30
31	4	5447	0	1	4553	5731	0	1	4269	0285	9715	37 56	29
32	8	5450	1	2	4550	5735	1	2	4265	0285	9715	52	28
33	12	5453	1	3	4547	5739	1	3	4261	0286	9714	48	27
34	16	5457	1		4543	5743	2		4257	0286	9714	37 44	26
35	22 20	9.5460	2		10.4540	9.5747	2		10.4253	10.0286	9.9714	40	25
36	24	5463	2		4537	5750	2		4250	0287	9713	36	24
37	28	5467	3		4533	5754	3		4246	0287	9713	32	23
38	32	5470	3		4530	5758	3		4242	0288	9712	28	22
39	36	5474	3		4526	5762	4		4238	0288	9712	37 24	21
40	22 40	9.5477			10.4523	9.5766			10.4234	10.0289	9.9711	20	20
41	44	5480	0	1	4520	5770	0	1	4230	0289	9711	16	19
42	48	5484	1	2	4516	5773	1	2	4227	0290	9710	12	18
43	52	5487	1	3	4513	5777	1	3	4223	0290	9710	8	17
44	56	5490	1		4510	5781	2		4219	0291	9709	37 4	16
45	23 0	9.5494	2		10.4506	9.5785	2		10.4215	10.0291	9.9709	37 0	15
46	4	5497	2		4503	5789	2		4211	0292	9708	36 56	14
47	8	5500	2		4500	5792	3		4208	0292	9708	52	13
48	12	5504	3		4496	5796	3		4204	0293	9707	48	12
49	16	5507	3		4493	5800	4		4200	0293	9707	36 44	11
50	23 20	9.5510			10.4490	9.5804			10.4196	10.0294	9.9706	40	10
51	24	5514	0	1	4486	5808	0	1	4192	0294	9706	36	9
52	28	5517	1	2	4483	5811	1	2	4189	0295	9705	32	8
53	32	5520	1	3	4480	5815	1	3	4185	0295	9705	28	7
54	36	5523	1		4477	5819	2		4181	0296	9704	36 24	6
55	23 40	9.5527	2		10.4473	9.5823	2		10.4177	10.0296	9.9704	20	5
56	44	5530	2		4470	5827	2		4173	0297	9703	16	4
57	48	5533	2		4467	5830	3		4170	0297	9703	12	3
58	52	5537	3		4463	5834	3		4166	0298	9702	8	2
59	56	5540	3		4460	5838	4		4162	0298	9702	36 4	1
60	21 0	9.5543			10.4457	9.5842			10.4158	10.0298	9.9702	36 0	0
′	m s	Cos.	Diff. 0′.1	Diff. 1s	Sec.	Cot.	Diff. 0′.1	Diff. 1s	Tan.	Cosec.	Sin.	m s	′

110° = 7h 20m] **[4h 36m = 69°**

21° = 1h 24m]		Log. Sines, Tangents, and Secants.									[10h 32m = 158°		
′	m s	Sin.	Diff. 0′.1	Diff. 1″	Cosec.	Tan.	Diff. 0′.1	Diff. 1″	Cot.	Sec.	Cos.	m s	′
0	24 0	9.5543			10.4457	9.5842			10.4158	10.0298	9.9702	36 0	60
1	4	5547	0	1	4453	5846	0	1	4154	0299	9701	35 56	59
2	8	5550	1	2	4450	5849	1	2	4151	0299	9701	52	58
3	12	5553	1	3	4447	5853	1	3	4147	0300	9700	48	57
4	16	5556	1		4444	5857	2		4143	0300	9700	35 44	56
5	24 20	9.5560	2		10.4440	9.5861	2		10.4139	10.0301	9.9699	40	55
6	24	5563	2		4437	5864	3		4136	0301	9699	36	54
7	28	5566	2		4434	5868	3		4132	0302	9698	32	53
8	32	5570	3		4430	5872	3		4128	0302	9698	28	52
9	36	5573	3		4427	5876	4		4124	0303	9697	35 24	51
10	24 40	9.5576			10.4424	9.5879			10.4121	10.0303	9.9697	20	50
11	44	5579	0	1	4421	5883	0	1	4117	0304	9696	16	49
12	48	5583	1	2	4417	5887	1	2	4113	0304	9696	12	48
13	52	5586	1	3	4414	5891	1	3	4109	0305	9695	8	47
14	56	5589	1		4411	5894	2		4106	0305	9695	35 4	46
15	25 0	9.5592	2		10.4408	9.5898	2		10.4102	10.0306	9.9694	35 0	45
16	4	5596	2		4404	5902	3		4098	0306	9694	34 56	44
17	8	5599	2		4401	5906	3		4094	0307	9693	52	43
18	12	5602	3		4398	5909	3		4091	0307	9693	48	42
19	16	5605	3		4395	5913	4		4087	0308	9692	34 44	41
20	25 20	9.5609			10.4391	9.5917			10.4083	10.0308	9.9692	40	40
21	24	5612	0	1	4388	5921	0	1	4079	0309	9691	36	39
22	28	5615	1	2	4385	5924	1	2	4076	0309	9691	32	38
23	32	5618	1	2	4382	5928	1	3	4072	0310	9690	28	37
24	36	5621	1		4379	5932	2		4068	0310	9690	34 24	36
25	25 40	9.5625	2		10.4375	9.5935	2		10.4065	10.0311	9.9689	20	35
26	44	5628	2		4372	5939	3		4061	0311	9689	16	34
27	48	5631	2		4369	5943	3		4057	0312	9688	12	33
28	52	5634	3		4366	5947	3		4053	0312	9688	8	32
29	56	5638	3		4362	5950	4		4050	0313	9687	34 4	31
30	26 0	9.5641			10.4359	9.5954			10.4046	10.0313	9.9687	34 0	30
31	4	5644	0	1	4356	5958	0	1	4042	0314	9686	33 56	29
32	8	5647	1	2	4353	5961	1	2	4039	0314	9686	52	28
33	12	5650	1	2	4350	5965	1	3	4035	0315	9685	48	27
34	16	5654	1		4346	5969	2		4031	0315	9685	33 44	26
35	26 20	9.5657	2		10.4343	9.5972	2		10.4028	10.0316	9.9684	40	25
36	24	5660	2		4340	5976	3		4024	0316	9684	36	24
37	28	5663	2		4337	5980	3		4020	0317	9683	32	23
38	32	5666	3		4334	5984	3		4016	0317	9683	28	22
39	36	5670	3		4330	5987	4		4013	0318	9682	33 24	21
40	26 40	9.5673			10.4327	9.5991			10.4009	10.0318	9.9682	20	20
41	44	5676	0	1	4324	5995	0	1	4005	0319	9681	16	19
42	48	5679	1	2	4321	5998	1	2	4002	0319	9681	12	18
43	52	5682	1	2	4318	6002	1	3	3998	0320	9680	8	17
44	56	5685	1		4315	6006	2		3994	0320	9680	33 4	16
45	27 0	9.5689	2		10.4311	9.6009	2		10.3991	10.0321	9.9679	33 0	15
46	4	5692	2		4308	6013	3		3987	0321	9679	32 56	14
47	8	5695	2		4305	6017	3		3983	0322	9678	52	13
48	12	5698	3		4302	6020	3		3980	0322	9678	48	12
49	16	5701	3		4299	6024	4		3976	0323	9677	32 44	11
50	27 20	9.5704			10.4296	9.6028			10.3972	10.0323	9.9677	40	10
51	24	5708	0	1	4292	6031	0	1	3969	0324	9676	36	9
52	28	5711	1	2	4289	6035	1	2	3965	0324	9676	32	8
53	32	5714	1	2	4286	6039	1	3	3961	0325	9675	28	7
54	36	5717	1		4283	6042	2		3958	0325	9675	32 24	6
55	27 40	9.5720	2		10.4280	9.6046	2		10.3954	10.0326	9.9674	20	5
56	44	5723	2		4277	6050	3		3950	0326	9674	16	4
57	48	5726	2		4274	6053	3		3947	0327	9673	12	3
58	52	5729	3		4271	6057	3		3943	0327	9673	8	2
59	56	5733	3		4267	6060	4		3940	0328	9672	32 4	1
60	28 0	9.5736			10.4264	9.6064			10.3936	10.0328	9.9672	32 0	0
′	m s	Cos.	0′.1 Diff.	1″ Diff.	Sec.	Cot.	0′.1 Diff.	1″ Diff.	Tan.	Cosec.	Sin.	m s	′
111° = 7h 24m]											[4h 32m = 68°		

22° = 1h 28m] **Log. Sines, Tangents, and Secants.** [10h 28m = 157°

′	m s	Sin.	Diff. 0′.1	Diff. 1s	Cosec.	Tan.	Diff. 0′.1	Diff. 1s	Cot.	Sec.	Cos.	m s	′
0	28 0	9.5736			10.4264	9.6064			10.3936	10.0328	9.9672	32 0	60
1	4	5739	0	1	4261	6068	0	1	3932	0329	9671	31 56	59
2	8	5742	1	2	4258	6071	1	2	3929	0329	9671	52	58
3	12	5745	1	2	4255	6075	1	3	3925	0330	9670	48	57
4	16	5748	1		4252	6079	2		3921	0330	9670	31 44	56
5	28 20	9.5751	2		10.4249	9.6082	2		10.3918	10.0331	9.9669	40	55
6	24	5754	2		4246	6086	3		3914	0331	9669	36	54
7	28	5758	2		4242	6090	3		3910	0332	9668	32	53
8	32	5761	3		4239	6093	3		3907	0332	9668	28	52
9	36	5764	3		4236	6097	4		3903	0333	9667	31 24	51
10	28 40	9.5767			10.4233	9.6100			10.3900	10.0333	9.9667	20	50
11	44	5770	0	1	4230	6104	0	1	3896	0334	9666	16	49
12	48	5773	1	2	4227	6108	1	2	3892	0334	9666	12	48
13	52	5776	1	2	4224	6111	1	3	3889	0335	9665	8	47
14	56	5779	1		4221	6115	2		3885	0336	9664	31 4	46
15	29 0	9.5782	2		10.4218	9.6118	2		10.3882	10.0336	9.9664	31 0	45
16	4	5785	2		4215	6122	3		3878	0337	9663	30 56	44
17	8	5789	2		4211	6126	3		3874	0337	9663	52	43
18	12	5792	3		4208	6129	3		3871	0338	9662	48	42
19	16	5795	3		4205	6133	4		3867	0338	9662	30 44	41
20	29 20	9.5798			10.4202	9.6136			10.3864	10.0339	9.9661	40	40
21	24	5801	0	1	4199	6140	0	1	3860	0339	9661	36	39
22	28	5804	1	2	4196	6144	1	2	3856	0340	9660	32	38
23	32	5807	1	2	4193	6147	1	3	3853	0340	9660	28	37
24	36	5810	1		4190	6151	2		3849	0341	9659	30 24	36
25	29 40	9.5813	2		10.4187	9.6154	2		10.3846	10.0341	9.9659	20	35
26	44	5816	2		4184	6158	3		3842	0342	9658	16	34
27	48	5819	2		4181	6162	3		3838	0342	9658	12	33
28	52	5822	3		4178	6165	3		3835	0343	9657	8	32
29	56	5825	3		4175	6169	4		3831	0343	9657	30 4	31
30	30 0	9.5828			10.4172	9.6172			10.3828	10.0344	9.9656	30 0	30
31	4	5831	0	1	4169	6176	0	1	3824	0344	9656	29 56	29
32	8	5834	1	2	4166	6179	1	2	3821	0345	9655	52	28
33	12	5838	1	2	4162	6183	1	3	3817	0345	9655	48	27
34	16	5841	1		4159	6187	2		3813	0346	9654	29 44	26
35	30 20	9.5844	2		10.4156	9.6190	2		10.3810	10.0346	9.9654	40	25
36	24	5847	2		4153	6194	3		3806	0347	9653	36	24
37	28	5850	2		4150	6197	3		3803	0348	9652	32	23
38	32	5853	3		4147	6201	3		3799	0348	9652	28	22
39	36	5856	3		4144	6204	4		3796	0349	9651	29 24	21
40	30 40	9.5859			10.4141	9.6208			10.3792	10.0349	9.9651	20	20
41	44	5862	0	1	4138	6211	0	1	3789	0350	9650	16	19
42	48	5865	1	2	4135	6215	1	2	3785	0350	9650	12	18
43	52	5868	1	2	4132	6219	1	3	3781	0351	9649	8	17
44	56	5871	1		4129	6222	2		3778	0351	9649	29 4	16
45	31 0	9.5874	2		10.4126	9.6226	2		10.3774	10.0352	9.9648	29 0	15
46	4	5877	2		4123	6229	3		3771	0352	9648	28 56	14
47	8	5880	2		4120	6233	3		3767	0353	9647	52	13
48	12	5883	3		4117	6236	3		3764	0353	9647	48	12
49	16	5886	3		4114	6240	4		3760	0354	9646	28 44	11
50	31 20	9.5889			10.4111	9.6243			10.3757	10.0354	9.9646	40	10
51	24	5892	0	1	4108	6247	0	1	3753	0355	9645	36	9
52	28	5895	1	2	4105	6250	1	2	3750	0355	9645	32	8
53	32	5898	1	2	4102	6254	1	3	3746	0356	9644	28	7
54	36	5901	1		4099	6257	2		3743	0357	9643	28 24	6
55	31 40	9.5904	2		10.4096	9.6261	2		10.3739	10.0357	9.9643	20	5
56	44	5907	2		4093	6264	3		3736	0358	9642	16	4
57	48	5910	2		4090	6268	3		3732	0358	9642	12	3
58	52	5913	3		4087	6271	3		3729	0359	9641	8	2
59	56	5916	3		4084	6275	4		3725	0359	9641	28 4	1
60	32 0	9.5919			10.4081	9.6279			10.3721	10.0360	9.9640	28 0	0
′	m s	Cos.	0′.1 Diff.	1s Diff.	Sec.	Cot.	0′.1 Diff.	1s Diff.	Tan.	Cosec.	Sin.	m s	′

112° = 7h 28m] [4h 28m = 67°

23° = 1ʰ 32ᵐ] **Log. Sines, Tangents, and Secants.** **[10ʰ 21ᵐ = 156°**

′	m s	Sin.	Diff. 0′.1	Diff. 1ˢ	Cosec.	Tan.	Diff. 0′.1	Diff. 1ˢ	Cot.	Sec.	Cos.	m s	′
0	32 0	9.5919			10.4081	9.6279			10.3721	10.0360	9.9640	28 0	60
1	4	5922	0	1	4078	6282	0	1	3718	0360	9640	27 56	59
2	8	5925	1	2	4075	6286	1	2	3714	0361	9639	52	58
3	12	5928	1	2	4072	6289	1	3	3711	0361	9639	48	57
4	16	5931	1		4069	6293	2		3707	0362	9638	27 44	56
5	32 20	9.5934	2		10.4066	9.6296	2		10.3704	10.0362	9.9638	40	55
6	24	5937	2		4063	6300	3		3700	0363	9637	36	54
7	28	5940	2		4060	6303	3		3697	0364	9636	32	53
8	32	5943	3		4057	6307	3		3693	0364	9636	28	52
9	36	5945	3		4055	6310	4		3690	0365	9635	27 24	51
10	32 40	9.5948			10.4052	9.6314			10.3686	10.0365	9.9635	20	50
11	44	5951	0	1	4049	6317	0	1	3683	0366	9634	16	49
12	48	5954	1	2	4046	6321	1	2	3679	0366	9634	12	48
13	52	5957	1	2	4043	6324	1	3	3676	0367	9633	8	47
14	56	5960	1		4040	6328	2		3672	0367	9633	27 4	46
15	33 0	9.5963	2		10.4037	9.6331	2		10.3669	10.0368	9.9632	27 0	45
16	4	5966	2		4034	6334	3		3666	0368	9632	26 56	44
17	8	5969	2		4031	6338	3		3662	0369	9631	52	43
18	12	5972	3		4028	6341	3		3659	0369	9631	48	42
19	16	5975	3		4025	6345	4		3655	0370	9630	26 44	41
20	33 20	9.5978			10.4022	9.6348			10.3652	10.0371	9.9629	40	40
21	24	5981	0	1	4019	6352	0	1	3648	0371	9629	36	39
22	28	5984	1	2	4016	6355	1	2	3645	0372	9628	32	38
23	32	5987	1	2	4013	6359	1	3	3641	0372	9628	28	37
24	36	5990	1		4010	6362	2		3638	0373	9627	26 24	36
25	33 40	9.5992	2		10.4008	9.6366	2		10.3634	10.0373	9.9627	20	35
26	44	5995	2		4005	6369	3		3631	0374	9626	16	34
27	48	5998	2		4002	6373	3		3627	0374	9626	12	33
28	52	6001	3		3999	6376	3		3624	0375	9625	8	32
29	56	6004	3		3996	6380	4		3620	0375	9625	26 4	31
30	34 0	9.6007			10.3993	9.6383			10.3617	10.0376	9.9624	26 0	30
31	4	6010	0	1	3990	6386	0	1	3614	0377	9623	25 56	29
32	8	6013	1	2	3987	6390	1	2	3610	0377	9623	52	28
33	12	6016	1	2	3984	6393	1	3	3607	0378	9622	48	27
34	16	6019	1		3981	6397	2		3603	0378	9622	25 44	26
35	34 20	9.6021	2		10.3979	9.6400	2		10.3600	10.0379	9.9621	40	25
36	24	6024	2		3976	6404	3		3596	0379	9621	36	24
37	28	6027	2		3973	6407	3		3593	0380	9620	32	23
38	32	6030	3		3970	6411	3		3589	0380	9620	28	22
39	36	6033	3		3967	6414	4		3586	0381	9619	25 24	21
40	34 40	9.6036			10.3964	9.6417			10.3583	10.0382	9.9618	20	20
41	44	6039	0	1	3961	6421	0	1	3579	0382	9618	16	19
42	48	6042	1	2	3958	6424	1	2	3576	0383	9617	12	18
43	52	6045	1	2	3955	6428	1	3	3572	0383	9617	8	17
44	56	6047	1		3953	6431	2		3569	0384	9616	25 4	16
45	35 0	9.6050	2		10.3950	9.6435	2		10.3565	10.0384	9.9616	25 0	15
46	4	6053	2		3947	6438	3		3562	0385	9615	24 56	14
47	8	6056	2		3944	6441	3		3559	0385	9615	52	13
48	12	6059	3		3941	6445	3		3555	0386	9614	48	12
49	16	6062	3		3938	6448	4		3552	0387	9613	24 44	11
50	35 20	9.6065			10.3935	9.6452			10.3548	10.0387	9.9613	40	10
51	24	6068	0	1	3932	6455	0	1	3545	0388	9612	36	9
52	28	6070	1	2	3930	6459	1	2	3541	0388	9612	32	8
53	32	6073	1	2	3927	6462	1	3	3538	0389	9611	28	7
54	36	6076	1		3924	6465	2		3535	0389	9611	24 24	6
55	35 40	0.6079	2		10.3921	9.6469	2		10.3531	10.0390	9.9610	20	5
56	44	6082	2		3918	6472	3		3528	0390	9610	16	4
57	48	6085	2		3915	6476	3		3524	0391	9609	12	3
58	52	6087	3		3913	6479	3		3521	0392	9608	8	2
59	56	6090	3		3910	6482	4		3518	0392	9608	24 4	1
60	36 0	9.6093			10.3907	9.6486			10.3514	10.0393	9.9607	24 0	0
′	m s	Cos.	0′.1 Diff.	1ˢ	Sec.	Cot.	0′.1 Diff.	1ˢ	Tan.	Cosec.	Sin.	m s	′

113° = 7ʰ 32ᵐ] **[4ʰ 24ᵐ = 66°**

24° = 1h 36m] **Log. Sines, Tangents, and Secants.** **[10h 20m = 155°**

′	m s	Sin.	Diff. 0′.1	Diff. 1s	Cosec.	Tan.	Diff. 0′.1	Diff. 1s	Cot.	Sec.	Cos.	m s	′
0	36 0	9.6093			10.3907	9.6486			10.3514	10.0393	9.9607	24 0	60
1	4	6096	0	1	3904	6489	0	1	3511	0393	9607	23 56	59
2	8	6099	1	2	3901	6493	1	2	3507	0394	9606	52	58
3	12	6102	1	2	3898	6496	1	3	3504	0394	9606	48	57
4	16	6104	1		3896	6499	2		3501	0395	9605	23 44	56
5	36 20	9.6107	1		10.3893	9.6503	2		10.3497	10.0396	9.9604	40	55
6	24	6110	2		3890	6506	3		3494	0396	9604	36	54
7	28	6113	2		3887	6510	3		3490	0397	9603	32	53
8	32	6116	2		3884	6513	3		3487	0397	9603	28	52
9	36	6119	2		3881	6516	4		3484	0398	9602	23 24	51
10	36 40	9.6121			10.3879	9.6520			10.3480	10.0398	9.9602	20	50
11	44	6124	0	1	3876	6523	0	1	3477	0399	9601	16	49
12	48	6127	1	2	3873	6527	1	2	3473	0399	9601	12	48
13	52	6130	1	2	3870	6530	1	3	3470	0400	9600	8	47
14	56	6133	1		3867	6533	2		3467	0401	9599	23 4	46
15	37 0	9.6135	1		10.3865	9.6537	2		10.3463	10.0401	9.9599	23 0	45
16	4	6138	2		3862	6540	3		3460	0402	9598	22 56	44
17	8	6141	2		3859	6543	3		3457	0402	9598	52	43
18	12	6144	2		3856	6547	3		3453	0403	9597	48	42
19	16	6147	2		3853	6550	4		3450	0403	9597	22 44	41
20	37 20	9.6149			10.3851	9.6553			10.3447	10.0404	9.9596	40	40
21	24	6152	0	1	3848	6557	0	1	3443	0405	9595	36	39
22	28	6155	1	2	3845	6560	1	2	3440	0405	9595	32	38
23	32	6158	1	2	3842	6564	1	3	3436	0406	9594	28	37
24	36	6161	1		3839	6567	2		3433	0406	9594	22 24	36
25	37 40	9.6163	1		10.3837	9.6570	2		10.3430	10.0407	9.9593	20	35
26	44	6166	2		3834	6574	3		3426	0407	9593	16	34
27	48	6169	2		3831	6577	3		3423	0408	9592	12	33
28	52	6172	2		3828	6580	3		3420	0409	9591	8	32
29	56	6174	2		3826	6584	4		3416	0409	9591	22 4	31
30	38 0	9.6177			10.3823	9.6587			10.3413	10.0410	9.9590	22 0	30
31	4	6180	0	1	3820	6590	0	1	3410	0410	9590	21 56	29
32	8	6183	1	2	3817	6594	1	2	3406	0411	9589	52	28
33	12	6186	1	2	3814	6597	1	3	3403	0411	9589	48	27
34	16	6188	1		3812	6600	2		3400	0412	9588	21 44	26
35	38 20	9.6191	1		10.3809	9.6604	2		10.3396	10.0413	9.9587	40	25
36	24	6194	2		3806	6607	3		3393	0413	9587	36	24
37	28	6197	2		3803	6610	3		3390	0414	9586	32	23
38	32	6199	2		3801	6614	3		3386	0414	9586	28	22
39	36	6202	2		3798	6617	4		3383	0415	9585	21 24	21
40	38 40	9.6205			10.3795	9.6620			10.3380	10.0416	9.9584	20	20
41	44	6208	0	1	3792	6624	0	1	3376	0416	9584	16	19
42	48	6210	1	2	3790	6627	1	2	3373	0417	9583	12	18
43	52	6213	1	2	3787	6630	1	3	3370	0417	9583	8	17
44	56	6216	1		3784	6634	2		3366	0418	9582	21 4	16
45	39 0	9.6219	1		10.3781	9.6637	2		10.3363	10.0418	9.9582	21 0	15
46	4	6221	2		3779	6640	3		3360	0419	9581	20 56	14
47	8	6224	2		3776	6644	3		3356	0420	9580	52	13
48	12	6227	2		3773	6647	3		3353	0420	9580	48	12
49	16	6230	2		3770	6650	4		3350	0421	9579	20 44	11
50	39 20	9.6232			10.3768	9.6654			10.3346	10.0421	9.9579	40	10
51	24	6235	0	1	3765	6657	0	1	3343	0422	9578	36	9
52	28	6238	1	2	3762	6660	1	2	3340	0423	9577	32	8
53	32	6240	1	2	3760	6664	1	3	3336	0423	9577	28	7
54	36	6243	1		3757	6667	2		3333	0424	9576	20 24	6
55	39 40	9.6246	1		10.3754	9.6670	2		10.3330	10.0424	9.9576	20	5
56	44	6249	2		3751	6674	3		3326	0425	9575	16	4
57	48	6251	2		3749	6677	3		3323	0425	9575	12	3
58	52	6254	2		3746	6680	3		3320	0426	9574	8	2
59	56	6257	2		3743	6683	4		3317	0427	9573	20 4	1
60	40 0	9.6259			10.3741	9.6687			10.3313	10.0427	9.9573	20 0	0
′	m s	Cos.	0′.1 Diff.	1s	Sec.	Cot.	0′.1 Diff.	1s	Tan.	Cosec.	Sin.	m s	′

114° = 7h 36m] **[4h 20m = 65°**

25° = 1h 40m] Log. Sines, Tangents, and Secants. [10h 16m = 154°

′	m s	Sin.	Diff. 0′.1	Diff. 1s	Cosec.	Tan.	Diff. 0′.1	Diff. 1s	Cot.	Sec.	Cos.	m s	′
0	40 0	9.6259			10.3741	9.6687			10.3313	10.0427	9.9573	20 0	60
1	4	6262	0	1	3738	6690	0	1	3310	0428	9572	19 56	59
2	8	6265	1	2	3735	6693	1	2	3307	0428	9572	52	58
3	12	6268	1	2	3732	6697	1	2	3303	0429	9571	48	57
4	16	6270	1		3730	6700	1		3300	0430	9570	19 44	56
5	40 20	9.6273	1		10.3727	9.6703	2		10.3297	10.0430	9.9570	40	55
6	24	6276	2		3724	6706	2		3294	0431	9569	36	54
7	28	6278	2		3722	6710	3		3290	0431	9569	32	53
8	32	6281	2		3719	6713	3		3287	0432	9568	28	52
9	36	6284	2		3716	6716	3		3284	0433	9567	19 24	51
10	40 40	9.6286			10.3714	9.6720			10.3280	10.0433	9.9567	20	50
11	44	6289	0	1	3711	6723	0	1	3277	0434	9566	16	49
12	48	6292	1	2	3708	6726	1	2	3274	0434	9566	12	48
13	52	6295	1	2	3705	6729	1	2	3271	0435	9565	8	47
14	56	6297	1		3703	6733	1		3267	0436	9564	19 4	46
15	41 0	9.6300	1		10.3700	9.6736	2		10.3264	10.0436	9.9564	19 0	45
16	4	6303	2		3697	6739	2		3261	0437	9563	18 56	44
17	8	6305	2		3695	6743	3		3257	0437	9563	52	43
18	12	6308	2		3692	6746	3		3254	0438	9562	48	42
19	16	6311	2		3689	6749	3		3251	0439	9561	18 44	41
20	41 20	9.6313			10.3687	9.6752			10.3248	10.0439	9.6561	40	40
21	24	6316	0	1	3684	6756	0	1	3244	0440	9560	36	39
22	28	6319	1	2	3681	6759	1	2	3241	0440	9560	32	38
23	32	6321	1	2	3679	6762	1	2	3238	0441	9559	28	37
24	36	6324	1		3676	6765	1		3235	0442	9558	18 24	36
25	41 40	9.6327	1		10.3673	9.6769	2		10.3231	10.0442	9.9558	20	35
26	44	6329	2		3671	6772	2		3228	0443	9557	16	34
27	48	6332	2		3668	6775	3		3225	0443	9557	12	33
28	52	6335	2		3665	6778	3		3222	0444	9556	8	32
29	56	6337	2		3663	6782	3		3218	0445	9555	18 4	31
30	42 0	9.6340			10.3660	9.6785			10.3215	10.0445	9.9555	18 0	30
31	4	6342	0	1	3658	6788	0	1	3212	0446	9554	17 56	29
32	8	6345	1	2	3655	6791	1	2	3209	0446	9554	52	28
33	12	6348	1	2	3652	6795	1	2	3205	0447	9553	48	27
34	16	6350	1		3650	6798	1		3202	0448	9552	17 44	26
35	42 20	9.6353	1		10.3647	9.6801	2		10.3199	10.0448	9.9552	40	25
36	24	6356	2		3644	6804	2		3196	0449	9551	36	24
37	28	6358	2		3642	6808	3		3192	0449	9551	32	23
38	32	6361	2		3639	6811	3		3189	0450	9550	28	22
39	36	6364	2		3636	6814	3		3186	0451	9549	17 24	21
40	42 40	9.6366			10.3634	9.6817			10.3183	10.0451	9.9549	20	20
41	44	6369	0	1	3631	6821	0	1	3179	0452	9548	16	19
42	48	6371	1	2	3629	6824	1	2	3176	0452	9548	12	18
43	52	6374	1	2	3626	6827	1	2	3173	0453	9547	8	17
44	56	6377	1		3623	6830	1		3170	0454	9546	17 4	16
45	43 0	9.6379	1		10.3621	9.6834	2		10.3166	10.0454	9.9546	17 0	15
46	4	6382	2		3618	6837	2		3163	0455	9545	16 56	14
47	8	6385	2		3615	6840	3		3160	0455	9545	52	13
48	12	6387	2		3613	6843	3		3157	0456	9544	48	12
49	16	6390	2		3610	6846	3		3154	0457	9543	16 44	11
50	43 20	9.6392			10.3608	9.6850			10.3150	10.0457	9.9543	40	10
51	24	6395	0	1	3605	6853	0	1	3147	0458	9542	36	9
52	28	6398	1	2	3602	6856	1	2	3144	0458	9542	32	8
53	32	6400	1	2	3600	6859	1	2	3141	0459	9541	28	7
54	36	6403	1		3597	6863	1		3137	0460	9540	16 24	6
55	43 40	9.6405	1		10.3595	9.6866	2		10.3134	10.0460	9.9540	20	5
56	44	6408	2		3592	6869	2		3131	0461	9539	16	4
57	48	6411	2		3589	6872	3		3128	0462	9538	12	3
58	52	6413	2		3587	6875	3		3125	0462	9538	8	2
59	56	6416	2		3584	6879	3		3121	0463	9537	16 4	1
60	44 0	9.6418			10.3582	9.6882			10.3118	10.0463	9.9537	16 0	0

′	m s	Cos.	0′.1 Diff.	1s Diff.	Sec.	Cot.	0′.1 Diff.	1s Diff.	Tan.	Cosec.	Sin.	m s	′

115° = 7h 40m] [4h 16m = 64°

26° = 1h 44m] **Log. Sines, Tangents, and Secants.** [10h 12m = 153°

′	m s	Sin.	Diff. 0′.1	Diff. 1″	Cosec.	Tan.	Diff. 0′.1	Diff. 1″	Cot.	Sec.	Cos.	m s	′
0	44 0	9.6418			10.3582	9.6882			10.3118	10.0463	9.9537	16 0	60
1	4	6421	0	1	3579	6885	0	1	3115	0464	9536	15 56	59
2	8	6424	1	2	3576	6888	1	2	3112	0465	9535	52	58
3	12	6426	1	2	3574	6891	1	2	3109	0465	9535	48	57
4	16	6429	1		3571	6895	1		3105	0466	9534	15 44	56
5	44 20	9.6431	1		10.3569	9.6898	2		10.3102	10.0466	9.9534	40	55
6	24	6434	2		3566	6901	2		3099	0467	9533	36	54
7	28	6437	2		3563	6904	3		3096	0468	9532	32	53
8	32	6439	2		3561	6907	3		3093	0468	9532	28	52
9	36	6442	2		3558	6911	3		3089	0469	9531	15 24	51
10	44 40	9.6444			10.3556	9.6914			10.3086	10.0470	9.9530	20	50
11	44	6447	0	1	3553	6917	0	1	3083	0470	9530	16	49
12	48	6449	1	2	3551	6920	1	2	3080	0471	9529	12	48
13	52	6452	1	2	3548	6923	1	2	3077	0471	9529	8	47
14	56	6454	1		3546	6927	1		3073	0472	9528	15 4	46
15	45 0	9.6457	1		10.3543	9.6930	2		10.3070	10.0473	9.9527	15 0	45
16	4	6460	2		3540	6933	2		3067	0473	9527	14 56	44
17	8	6462	2		3538	6936	3		3064	0474	9526	52	43
18	12	6465	2		3535	6939	3		3061	0475	9525	48	42
19	16	6467	2		3533	6942	3		3058	0475	9525	14 44	41
20	45 20	9.6470			10.3530	9.6946			10.3054	10.0476	9.9524	40	40
21	24	6472	0	1	3528	6949	0	1	3051	0476	9524	36	39
22	28	6475	1	2	3525	6952	1	2	3048	0477	9523	32	38
23	32	6477	1	2	3523	6955	1	2	3045	0478	9522	28	37
24	36	6480	1		3520	6958	1		3042	0478	9522	14 24	36
25	45 40	9.6483	1		10.3517	9.6962	2		10.3038	10.0479	9.9521	20	35
26	44	6485	2		3515	6965	2		3035	0480	9520	16	34
27	48	6488	2		3512	6968	3		3032	0480	9520	12	33
28	52	6490	2		3510	6971	3		3029	0481	9519	8	32
29	56	6493	2		3507	6974	3		3026	0481	9519	14 4	31
30	46 0	9.6495			10.3505	9.6977			10.3023	10.0482	9.9518	14 0	30
31	4	6498	0	1	3502	6981	0	1	3019	0483	9517	13 56	29
32	8	6500	1	2	3500	6984	1	2	3016	0483	9517	52	28
33	12	6503	1	2	3497	6987	1	2	3013	0484	9516	48	27
34	16	6505	1		3495	6990	1		3010	0485	9515	13 44	26
35	46 20	9.6508	1		10.3492	9.6993	2		10.3007	10.0485	9.9515	40	25
36	24	6510	2		3490	6996	2		3004	0486	9514	36	24
37	28	6513	2		3487	6999	3		3001	0487	9513	32	23
38	32	6515	2		3485	7003	3		2997	0487	9513	28	22
39	36	6518	2		3482	7006	3		2994	0488	9512	13 24	21
40	46 40	9.6521			10.3479	9.7009			10.2991	10.0488	9.9512	20	20
41	44	6523	0	1	3477	7012	0	1	2988	0489	9511	16	19
42	48	6526	1	2	3474	7015	1	2	2985	0490	9510	12	18
43	52	6528	1	2	3472	7018	1	2	2982	0490	9510	8	17
44	56	6531	1		3469	7022	1		2978	0491	9509	13 4	16
45	47 0	9.6533	1		10.3467	9.7025	2		10.2975	10.0492	9.9508	13 0	15
46	4	6536	2		3464	7028	2		2972	0492	9508	12 56	14
47	8	6538	2		3462	7031	3		2969	0493	9507	52	13
48	12	6541	2		3459	7034	3		2966	0494	9506	48	12
49	16	6543	2		3457	7037	3		2963	0494	9506	12 44	11
50	47 20	9.6546			10.3454	9.7040			10.2960	10.0495	9.9505	40	10
51	24	6548	0	1	3452	7043	0	1	2957	0495	9505	36	9
52	28	6551	1	2	3449	7047	1	2	2953	0496	9504	32	8
53	32	6553	1	2	3447	7050	1	2	2950	0497	9503	28	7
54	36	6556	1		3444	7053	1		2947	0497	9503	12 24	6
55	47 40	9.6558	1		10.3442	9.7056	2		10.2944	10.0498	9.9502	20	5
56	44	6561	2		3439	7059	2		2941	0499	9501	16	4
57	48	6563	2		3437	7062	3		2938	0499	9501	12	3
58	52	6566	2		3434	7065	3		2935	0500	9500	8	2
59	56	6568	2		3432	7069	3		2931	0501	9499	12 4	1
60	48 0	9.6570			10.3430	9.7072			10.2928	10.0501	9.9499	12 0	0
′	m s	Cos.	0′.1 Diff.	1″ Diff.	Sec.	Cot.	0′.1 Diff.	1″ Diff.	Tan.	Cosec.	Sin.	m s	′

116° = 7h 44m] [4h 12m = 63°

27° = 1h 48m]			Log. Sines, Tangents, and Secants.									[10h 8m = 152°	
′	m s	Sin.	Diff. 0′.1	Diff. 1s	Cosec.	Tan.	Diff. 0′.1	Diff. 1s	Cot.	Sec.	Cos.	m s	′
0	48 0	9.6570			10.3430	9.7072			10.2928	10.0501	9.9499	12 0	60
1	4	6573	0	1	3427	7075	0	1	2925	0502	9498	11 56	59
2	8	6575	1	1	3425	7078	1	2	2922	0502	9498	52	58
3	12	6578	1	2	3422	7081	1	2	2919	0503	9497	48	57
4	16	6580	1		3420	7084	1		2916	0504	9496	11 44	56
5	48 20	9.6583	1		10.3417	9.7087	2		10.2913	10.0504	9.9496	40	55
6	24	6585	2		3415	7090	2		2910	0505	9495	36	54
7	28	6588	2		3412	7093	3		2907	0506	9494	32	53
8	32	6590	2		3410	7097	3		2903	0506	9494	28	52
9	36	6593	2		3407	7100	3		2900	0507	9493	11 24	51
10	48 40	9.6595			10.3405	9.7103			10.2897	10.0508	9.9492	20	50
11	44	6598	0	1	3402	7106	0	1	2894	0508	9492	16	49
12	48	6600	1	1	3400	7109	1	2	2891	0509	9491	12	48
13	52	6603	1	2	3397	7112	1	2	2888	0510	9490	8	47
14	56	6605	1		3395	7115	1		2885	0510	9490	11 4	46
15	49 0	9.6607	1		10.3393	9.7118	2		10.2882	10.0511	9.9489	11 0	45
16	4	6610	2		3390	7121	2		2879	0512	9488	10 56	44
17	8	6612	2		3388	7125	3		2875	0512	9488	52	43
18	12	6615	2		3385	7128	3		2872	0513	9487	48	42
19	16	6617	2		3383	7131	3		2869	0514	9486	10 44	41
20	49 20	9.6620			10.3380	9.7134			10.2866	10.0514	9.9486	40	40
21	24	6622	0	1	3378	7137	0	1	2863	0515	9485	36	39
22	28	6625	1	1	3375	7140	1	2	2860	0515	9485	32	38
23	32	6627	1	2	3373	7143	1	2	2857	0516	9484	28	37
24	36	6629	1		3371	7146	1		2854	0517	9483	10 24	36
25	49 40	9.6632	1		10.3368	9.7149	2		10.2851	10.0517	9.9483	20	35
26	44	6634	2		3366	7152	2		2848	0518	9482	16	34
27	48	6637	2		3363	7156	3		2844	0519	9481	12	33
28	52	6639	2		3361	7159	3		2841	0519	9481	8	32
20	56	6642	2		3358	7162	3		2838	0520	9480	10 4	31
30	50 0	9.6644			10.3356	9.7165			10.2835	10.0521	9.9479	10 0	30
31	4	6646	0	1	3354	7168	0	1	2832	0521	9479	9 56	20
32	8	6649	1	1	3351	7171	1	2	2829	0522	9478	52	28
33	12	6651	1	2	3349	7174	1	2	2826	0523	9477	48	27
34	16	6654	1		3346	7177	1		2823	0523	9477	9 44	26
35	50 20	9.6656	1		10.3344	9.7180	2		10.2820	10.0524	9.9476	40	25
36	24	6659	2		3341	7183	2		2817	0525	9475	36	24
37	28	6661	2		3339	7186	3		2814	0525	9475	22	23
38	32	6663	2		3337	7189	3		2811	0526	9474	28	22
39	36	6666	2		3334	7192	3		2808	0527	9473	9 24	21
40	50 40	9.6668			10.3332	9.7196			10.2804	10.0527	9.9473	20	20
41	44	6671	0	1	3329	7199	0	1	2801	0528	9472	16	19
42	48	6673	1	1	3327	7202	1	2	2798	0529	9471	12	18
43	52	6675	1	2	3325	7205	1	2	2795	0529	9471	8	17
44	56	6678	1		3322	7208	1		2792	0530	9470	9 4	16
45	51 0	9.6680	1		10.3320	9.7211	2		10.2789	10.0531	9.9469	9 0	15
46	4	6683	2		3317	7214	2		2786	0531	9469	8 56	14
47	8	6685	2		3315	7217	3		2783	0532	9468	52	13
48	12	6687	2		3313	7220	3		2780	0533	9467	48	12
49	16	6690	2		3310	7223	3		2777	0533	9467	8 44	11
50	51 20	9.6692			10.3308	9.7226			10.2774	10.0534	9.9466	40	10
51	24	6695	0	1	3305	7229	0	1	2771	0535	9465	36	9
52	28	6697	1	1	3303	7232	1	2	2768	0535	9465	32	8
53	32	6699	1	2	3301	7235	1	2	2765	0536	9464	28	7
54	36	6702	1		3298	7238	1		2762	0537	9463	8 24	6
55	51 40	9.6704	1		10.3296	9.7241	2		10.2759	10.0537	9.9463	20	5
56	44	6707	2		3293	7245	2		2755	0538	9462	16	4
57	48	6709	2		3291	7248	3		2752	0539	9461	12	3
58	52	6711	2		3289	7251	3		2749	0539	9461	8	2
59	56	6714	2		3286	7254	3		2746	0540	9460	8 4	1
60	52 0	9.6716			10.3284	9.7257			10.2743	10.0541	9.9459	8 0	0
′	m s	Cos.	0′.1 Diff.	1s Diff.	Sec.	Cot.	0′.1 Diff.	1s Diff.	Tan.	Cosec.	Sin.	m s	′
117° = 7h 48m]												[4h 8m = 62°	

28° = 1h 52m] **Log. Sines, Tangents, and Secants.** **[10h 4m = 151°**

′	m s	Sin.	Diff. 0′.1	Diff. 1s	Cosec.	Tan.	Diff. 0′.1	Diff. 1s	Cot.	Sec.	Cos.	m s	′
0	52 0	9.6716			10.3284	9.7257			10.2743	10.0541	9.9459	8 0	60
1	4	6718	0	1	3282	7260	0	1	2740	0541	9459	7 56	59
2	8	6721	1	1	3279	7263	1	2	2737	0542	9458	52	58
3	12	6723	1	2	3277	7266	1	2	2734	0543	9457	48	57
4	16	6726	1		3274	7269	1		2731	0543	9457	7 44	56
5	52 20	9.6728	1		10.3272	9.7272	2		10.2728	10.0544	9.9456	40	55
6	24	6730	2		3270	7275	2		2725	0545	9455	36	54
7	28	6733	2		3267	7278	3		2722	0545	9455	32	53
8	32	6735	2		3265	7281	3		2719	0546	9454	28	52
9	36	6737	2		3263	7284	3		2716	0547	9453	7 24	51
10	52 40	9.6740			10.3260	9.7287			10.2713	10.0547	9.9453	20	50
11	44	6742	0	1	3258	7290	0	1	2710	0548	9452	16	49
12	48	6744	1	1	3256	7293	1	2	2707	0549	9451	12	48
13	52	6747	1	2	3253	7296	1	2	2704	0549	9451	8	47
14	56	6749	1		3251	7299	1		2701	0550	9450	7 4	46
15	53 0	9.6752	1		10.3248	9.7302	2		10.2698	10.0551	9.9449	7 0	45
16	4	6754	2		3246	7305	2		2695	0551	9449	6 56	44
17	8	6756	2		3244	7308	3		2692	0552	9448	52	43
18	12	6759	2		3241	7311	3		2689	0553	9447	48	42
19	16	6761	2		3239	7314	3		2686	0553	9447	6 44	41
20	53 20	9.6763			10.3237	9.7317			10.2683	10.0554	9.9446	40	40
21	24	6766	0	1	3234	7320	0	1	2680	0555	9445	36	39
22	28	6768	1	1	3232	7324	1	2	2676	0556	9444	32	38
23	32	6770	1	2	3230	7327	1	2	2673	0556	9444	28	37
24	36	6773	1		3227	7330	1		2670	0557	9443	6 24	36
25	53 40	9.6775	1		10.3225	9.7333	2		10.2667	10.0558	9.9442	20	35
26	44	6777	2		3223	7336	2		2664	0558	9442	16	34
27	48	6780	2		3220	7339	3		2661	0559	9441	12	33
28	52	6782	2		3218	7342	3		2658	0560	9440	8	32
29	56	6784	2		3216	7345	3		2655	0560	9440	6 4	31
30	54 0	9.6787			10.3213	9.7348			10.2652	10.0561	9.9439	6 0	30
31	4	6789	0	1	3211	7351	0	1	2649	0562	9438	5 56	29
32	8	6791	1	1	3209	7354	1	2	2646	0562	9438	52	28
33	12	6794	1	2	3206	7357	1	2	2643	0563	9437	48	27
34	16	6796	1		3204	7360	1		2640	0564	9436	5 44	26
35	54 20	9.6798	1		10.3202	9.7363	2		10.2637	10.0564	9.9436	40	25
36	24	6801	2		3199	7366	2		2634	0565	9435	36	24
37	28	6803	2		3197	7369	3		2631	0566	9434	32	23
38	32	6805	2		3195	7372	3		2628	0567	9433	28	22
39	36	6808	2		3192	7375	3		2625	0567	9433	5 24	21
40	54 40	9.6810			10.3190	9.7378			10.2622	10.0568	9.9432	20	20
41	44	6812	0	1	3188	7381	0	1	2619	0569	9431	16	19
42	48	6814	1	1	3186	7384	1	2	2616	0569	9431	12	18
43	52	6817	1	2	3183	7387	1	2	2613	0570	9430	8	17
44	56	6819	1		3181	7390	1		2610	0571	9429	5 4	16
45	55 0	9.6821	1		10.3179	9.7393	2		10.2607	10.0571	9.9429	5 0	15
46	4	6824	2		3176	7396	2		2604	0572	9428	4 56	14
47	8	6826	2		3174	7399	3		2601	0573	9427	52	13
48	12	6828	2		3172	7402	3		2598	0573	9427	48	12
49	16	6831	2		3169	7405	3		2595	0574	9426	4 44	11
50	55 20	9.6833			10.3167	9.7408			10.2592	10.0575	9.9425	40	10
51	24	6835	0	1	3165	7411	0	1	2589	0576	9424	36	9
52	28	6837	1	1	3163	7414	1	2	2586	0576	9424	32	8
53	32	6840	1	2	3160	7417	1	2	2583	0577	9423	28	7
54	36	6842	1		3158	7420	1		2580	0578	9422	4 24	6
55	55 40	9.6844	1		10.3156	9.7423	2		10.2577	10.0578	9.9422	20	5
56	44	6847	2		3153	7426	2		2574	0579	9421	16	4
57	48	6849	2		3151	7429	3		2571	0580	9420	12	3
58	52	6851	2		3149	7432	3		2568	0580	9420	8	2
59	56	6853	2		3147	7435	3		2565	0581	9419	4 4	1
60	56 0	9.6856			10.3144	9.7438			10.2562	10.0582	9.9418	4 0	0
′	m s	Cos.	0′.1 Diff.	1s Diff.	Sec.	Cot.	0′.1 Diff.	1s Diff.	Tan.	Cosec.	Sin.	m s	′

118° = 7h 52m] **[4h 4m = 61°**

29° = 1h 56m]		Log. Sines, Tangents, and Secants.										[10h 0m = 150°	
′	m s	Sin.	Diff. 0′.1	Diff. 1s	Cosec.	Tan.	Diff. 0′.1	Diff. 1s	Cot.	Sec.	Cos.	m s	′
0	56 0	9.6856			10.3144	9.7438			10.2562	10.0582	9.9418	4 0	60
1	4	6858	0	1	3142	7440	0	1	2560	0583	9417	3 56	59
2	8	6860	1	1	3140	7443	1	2	2557	0583	9417	52	58
3	12	6863	1	2	3137	7446	1	2	2554	0584	9416	48	57
4	16	6865	1		3135	7449	1		2551	0585	9415	3 44	56
5	56 20	9.6867	1		10.3133	9.7452	1		10.2548	10.0585	9.9415	40	55
6	24	6869	1		3131	7455	2		2545	0586	9414	36	54
7	28	6872	2		3128	7458	2		2542	0587	9413	32	53
8	32	6874	2		3126	7461	2		2539	0587	9413	28	52
9	36	6876	2		3124	7464	3		2536	0588	9412	3 24	51
10	56 40	9.6878			10.3122	9.7467			10.2533	10.0589	9.9411	20	50
11	44	6881	0	1	3119	7470	0	1	2530	0590	9410	16	49
12	48	6883	1	1	3117	7473	1	2	2527	0590	9410	12	48
13	52	6885	1	2	3115	7476	1	2	2524	0591	9409	8	47
14	56	6887	1		3113	7479	1		2521	0592	9408	3 4	46
15	57 0	9.6890	1		10.3110	9.7482	1		10.2518	10.0592	9.9408	3 0	45
16	4	6892	1		3108	7485	2		2515	0593	9407	2 56	44
17	8	6894	2		3106	7488	2		2512	0594	9406	52	43
18	12	6896	2		3104	7491	2		2509	0594	9406	48	42
19	16	6899	2		3101	7494	3		2506	0595	9405	2 44	41
20	57 20	9.6901			10.3099	9.7497			10.2503	10.0596	9.9404	40	40
21	24	6903	0	1	3097	7500	0	1	2500	0597	9403	36	39
22	28	6905	1	1	3095	7503	1	2	2497	0597	9403	32	38
23	32	6908	1	2	3092	7506	1	2	2494	0598	9402	28	37
24	36	6910	1		3090	7509	1		2491	0599	9401	2 24	36
25	57 40	9.6912	1		10.3088	9.7512	1		10.2488	10.0599	9.9401	20	35
26	44	6914	1		3086	7515	2		2485	0600	9400	16	34
27	48	6917	2		3083	7518	2		2482	0601	9399	12	33
28	52	6919	2		3081	7521	2		2479	0602	9398	8	32
29	56	6921	2		3079	7523	3		2477	0602	9398	2 4	31
30	58 0	9.6923			10.3077	9.7526			10.2474	10.0603	9.9397	2 0	30
31	4	6926	0	1	3074	7529	0	1	2471	0604	9396	1 56	29
32	8	6928	1	1	3072	7532	1	2	2468	0604	9396	52	28
33	12	6930	1	2	3070	7535	1	2	2465	0605	9395	48	27
34	16	6932	1		3068	7538	1		2462	0606	9394	1 44	26
35	58 20	9.6935	1		10.3065	9.7541	1		10.2459	10.0607	9.9393	40	25
36	24	6937	1		3063	7544	2		2456	0607	9393	36	24
37	28	6939	2		3061	7547	2		2453	0608	9392	32	23
38	32	6941	2		3059	7550	2		2450	0609	9391	28	22
39	36	6943	2		3057	7553	3		2447	0609	9391	1 24	21
40	58 40	9.6946			10.3054	9.7556			10.2444	10.0610	9.9390	20	20
41	44	6948	0	1	3052	7559	0	1	2441	0611	9389	16	19
42	48	6950	1	1	3050	7562	1	2	2438	0612	9388	12	18
43	52	6952	1	2	3048	7565	1	2	2435	0612	9388	8	17
44	56	6955	1		3045	7568	1		2432	0613	9387	1 4	16
45	59 0	9.6957	1		10.3043	9.7571	1		10.2429	10.0614	9.9386	1 0	15
46	4	6959	1		3041	7573	2		2427	0615	9385	0 56	14
47	8	6961	2		3039	7576	2		2424	0615	9385	52	13
48	12	6963	2		3037	7579	2		2421	0616	9384	48	12
49	16	6966	2		3034	7582	3		2418	0617	9383	0 44	11
50	59 20	9.6968			10.3032	9.7585			10.2415	10.0617	9.9383	40	10
51	24	6970	0	1	3030	7588	0	1	2412	0618	9382	36	9
52	28	6972	1	1	3028	7591	1	2	2409	0619	9381	32	8
53	32	6974	1	2	3026	7594	1	2	2406	0620	9380	28	7
54	36	6977	1		3023	7597	1		2403	0620	9380	0 24	6
55	59 40	9.6979	1		10.3021	9.7600	1		10.2400	10.0621	9.9379	20	5
56	44	6981	1		3019	7603	2		2397	0622	9378	16	4
57	48	6983	2		3017	7606	2		2394	0623	9377	12	3
58	52	6985	2		3015	7609	2		2391	0623	9377	8	2
59	56	6988	2		3012	7611	3		2389	0624	9376	0 4	1
60	60 0	9.6990			10.3010	9.7614			10.2386	10.0625	9.9375	0 0	0
′	m s	Cos.	0′.1 Diff.	1s Diff.	Sec.	Cot.	0′.1 Diff.	1s Diff.	Tan.	Cosec.	Sin.	m s	′
119° = 7h 56m]												[4h 0m = 60°	

30° = 2h 0m]		Log. Sines, Tangents, and Secants.										[9h 56m = 149°	
′	m s	Sin.	Diff. 0′.1	Diff. 1s	Cosec.	Tan.	Diff. 0′.1	Diff. 1s	Cot.	Sec.	Cos.	m s	′
0	0 0	9.6990			10.3010	9.7614			10.2386	10.0625	9.9375	60 0	60
1	4	6992	0	1	3008	7617	0	1	2383	0625	9375	59 56	59
2	8	6994	0	1	3006	7620	1	2	2380	0626	9374	52	58
3	12	6996	1	2	3004	7623	1	2	2377	0627	9373	48	57
4	16	6998	1		3002	7626	1		2374	0628	9372	59 44	56
5	0 20	9.7001	1		10.2999	9.7629	1		10.2371	10.0628	9.9372	40	55
6	24	7003	1		2997	7632	2		2368	0629	9371	36	54
7	28	7005	1		2995	7635	2		2365	0630	9370	32	53
8	32	7007	2		2993	7638	2		2362	0631	9369	28	52
9	36	7009	2		2991	7641	3		2359	0631	9369	59 24	51
10	0 40	9.7012			10.2988	9.7644			10.2356	10.0632	9.9368	20	50
11	44	7014	0	1	2986	7646	0	1	2354	0633	9367	16	49
12	48	7016	0	1	2984	7649	1	2	2351	0633	9367	12	48
13	52	7018	1	2	2982	7652	1	2	2348	0634	9366	8	47
14	56	7020	1		2980	7655	1		2345	0635	9365	59 4	46
15	1 0	9.7022	1		10.2978	9.7658	1		10.2342	10.0636	9.9364	59 0	45
16	4	7025	1		2975	7661	2		2339	0636	9364	58 56	44
17	8	7027	1		2973	7664	2		2336	0637	9363	52	43
18	12	7029	2		2971	7667	2		2333	0638	9362	48	42
19	16	7031	2		2969	7670	3		2330	0639	9361	58 44	41
20	1 20	9.7033			10.2967	9.7673			10.2327	10.0639	9.9361	40	40
21	24	7035	0	1	2965	7675	0	1	2325	0640	9360	36	39
22	28	7037	0	1	2963	7678	1	2	2322	0641	9359	32	38
23	32	7040	1	2	2960	7681	1	2	2319	0642	9358	28	37
24	36	7042	1		2958	7684	1		2316	0642	9358	58 24	36
25	1 40	9.7044	1		10.2956	9.7687	1		10.2313	10.0643	9.9357	20	35
26	44	7046	1		2954	7690	2		2310	0644	9356	16	34
27	48	7048	1		2952	7693	2		2307	0645	9355	12	33
28	52	7050	2		2950	7696	2		2304	0645	9355	8	32
29	56	7053	2		2947	7699	3		2301	0646	9354	58 4	31
30	2 0	9.7055			10.2945	9.7701			10.2299	10.0647	9.9353	58 0	30
31	4	7057	0	1	2943	7704	0	1	2296	0648	9352	57 56	29
32	8	7059	0	1	2941	7707	1	2	2293	0648	9352	52	28
33	12	7061	1	2	2939	7710	1	2	2290	0649	9351	48	27
34	16	7063	1		2937	7713	1		2287	0650	9350	57 44	26
35	2 20	9.7065	1		10.2935	9.7716	1		10.2284	10.0651	9.9349	40	25
36	24	7068	1		2932	7719	2		2281	0651	9349	36	24
37	28	7070	1		2930	7722	2		2278	0652	9348	32	23
38	32	7072	2		2928	7725	2		2275	0653	9347	28	22
39	36	7074	2		2926	7727	3		2273	0654	9346	57 24	21
40	2 40	9.7076			10.2924	9.7730			10.2270	10.0654	9.9346	20	20
41	44	7078	0	1	2922	7733	0	1	2267	0655	9345	16	19
42	48	7080	0	1	2920	7736	1	2	2264	0656	9344	12	18
43	52	7082	1	2	2918	7739	1	2	2261	0657	9343	8	17
44	56	7085	1		2915	7742	1		2258	0657	9343	57 4	16
45	3 0	9.7087	1		10.2913	9.7745	1		10.2255	10.0658	9.9342	57 0	15
46	4	7089	1		2911	7748	2		2252	0659	9341	56 56	14
47	8	7091	1		2909	7750	2		2250	0660	9340	52	13
48	12	7093	2		2907	7753	2		2247	0660	9340	48	12
49	16	7095	2		2905	7756	3		2244	0661	9339	56 44	11
50	3 20	9.7097			10.2903	9.7759			10.2241	10.0662	9.9338	40	10
51	24	7099	0	1	2901	7762	0	1	2238	0663	9337	36	9
52	28	7102	0	1	2898	7765	1	2	2235	0663	9337	32	8
53	32	7104	1	2	2896	7768	1	2	2232	0664	9336	28	7
54	36	7106	1		2894	7771	1		2229	0665	9335	56 24	6
55	3 40	9.7108	1		10.2892	9.7773	1		10.2227	10.0666	9.9334	20	5
56	44	7110	1		2890	7776	2		2224	0666	9334	16	4
57	48	7112	1		2888	7779	2		2221	0667	9333	12	3
58	52	7114	2		2886	7782	2		2218	0668	9332	8	2
59	56	7116	2		2884	7785	3		2215	0669	9331	56 4	1
60	4 0	9.7118			10.2882	9.7788			10.2212	10.0669	9.9331	56 0	0
′	m s	Cos.	0′.1 Diff.	1s Diff.	Sec.	Cot.	0′.1 Diff.	1s Diff.	Tan.	Cosec.	Sin.	m s	′
120° = 8h 0m]												[3h 56m = 59°	

31° = 2h 4m] **Log. Sines, Tangents, and Secants.** [9h 52m = 148°

′	m s	Sin.	Diff. 0′.1	Diff. 1s	Cosec.	Tan.	Diff. 0′.1	Diff. 1s	Cot.	Sec.	Cos.	m s	′
0	4 0	9.7118			10.2882	9.7788			10.2212	10.0669	9.9331	56 0	60
1	4	7120	0	1	2880	7791	0	1	2209	0670	9330	55 56	59
2	8	7123	0	1	2877	7793	1	2	2207	0671	9329	52	58
3	12	7125	1	2	2875	7796	1	2	2204	0672	9328	48	57
4	16	7127	1		2873	7799	1		2201	0672	9328	55 44	56
5	4 20	9.7129	1		10.2871	9.7802	1		10.2198	10.0673	9.9327	40	55
6	24	7131	1		2869	7805	2		2195	0674	9326	36	54
7	28	7133	1		2867	7808	2		2192	0675	9325	32	53
8	32	7135	2		2865	7811	2		2189	0675	9325	28	52
9	36	7137	2		2863	7813	3		2187	0676	9324	55 24	51
10	4 40	9.7139			10.2861	9.7816			10.2184	10.0677	9.9323	20	50
11	44	7141	0	1	2859	7819	0	1	2181	0678	9322	16	49
12	48	7144	0	1	2856	7822	1	2	2178	0678	9522	12	48
13	52	7146	1	2	2854	7825	1	2	2175	0679	9321	8	47
14	56	7148	1		2852	7828	1		2172	0680	9320	55 4	46
15	5 0	9.7150	1		10.2850	9.7831	1		10.2169	10.0681	9.9319	55 0	45
16	4	7152	1		2848	7833	2		2167	0682	9318	51 56	44
17	8	7154	1		2846	7836	2		2164	0682	9318	52	43
18	12	7156	2		2844	7839	2		2161	0683	9317	48	42
19	16	7158	2		2842	7842	3		2158	0684	9316	54 44	41
20	5 20	9.7160			10.2840	9.7845			10.2155	10.0685	9.9315	40	40
21	24	7162	0	1	2838	7848	0	1	2152	0685	9315	36	39
22	28	7164	0	1	2836	7850	1	2	2150	0686	9314	32	38
23	32	7166	1	2	2834	7853	1	2	2147	0687	9313	28	37
24	36	7168	1		2832	7856	1		2144	0688	9312	51 24	36
25	5 40	9.7171	1		10.2829	9.7859	1		10.2141	10.0688	9.9312	20	35
26	44	7173	1		2827	7862	2		2138	0689	9311	16	34
27	48	7175	1		2825	7865	2		2135	0690	9310	12	33
28	52	7177	2		2823	7868	2		2132	0691	9309	8	32
29	56	7179	2		2821	7870	3		2130	0692	9308	51 4	31
30	6 0	9.7181			10.2819	9.7873			10.2127	10.0692	9.9308	54 0	30
31	4	7183	0	1	2817	7876	0	1	2124	0693	9307	53 56	29
32	8	7185	0	1	2815	7879	1	2	2121	0694	9306	52	28
33	12	7187	1	2	2813	7882	1	2	2118	0695	9305	48	27
34	16	7189	1		2811	7885	1		2115	0695	9305	53 44	26
35	6 20	9.7191	1		10.2809	9.7887	1		10.2113	10.0696	9.9304	40	25
36	24	7193	1		2807	7890	2		2110	0697	9303	36	24
37	28	7195	1		2805	7893	2		2107	0698	9302	32	23
38	32	7197	2		2803	7896	2		2104	0699	9301	28	22
39	36	7199	2		2801	7899	3		2101	0699	9301	53 24	21
40	6 40	9.7201			10.2799	9.7902			10.2098	10.0700	9.9300	20	20
41	44	7203	0	1	2797	7904	0	1	2096	0701	9299	16	19
42	48	7205	0	1	2795	7907	1	2	2093	0702	9298	12	18
43	52	7208	1	2	2792	7910	1	2	2090	0702	9298	8	17
44	56	7210	1		2790	7913	1		2087	0703	9297	53 4	16
45	7 0	9.7212	1		10.2788	9.7916	1		10.2084	10.0704	9.9296	53 0	15
46	4	7214	1		2786	7918	2		2082	0705	9295	52 56	14
47	8	7216	1		2784	7921	2		2079	0706	9294	52	13
48	12	7218	2		2782	7924	2		2076	0706	9294	48	12
49	16	7220	2		2780	7927	3		2073	0707	9293	52 44	11
50	7 20	9.7222			10.2778	9.7930			10.2070	10.0708	9.9292	40	10
51	24	7224	0	1	2776	7933	0	1	2067	0709	9291	36	9
52	28	7226	0	1	2774	7935	1	2	2065	0709	9291	32	8
53	32	7228	1	2	2772	7938	1	2	2062	0710	9290	28	7
54	36	7230	1		2770	7941	1		2059	0711	9289	52 24	6
55	7 40	9.7232	1		10.2768	9.7944	1		10.2056	10.0712	9.9288	20	5
56	44	7234	1		2766	7947	2		2053	0713	9287	16	4
57	48	7236	1		2764	7949	2		2051	0713	9287	12	3
58	52	7238	2		2762	7952	2		2048	0714	9286	8	2
59	56	7240	2		2760	7955	3		2045	0715	9285	52 4	1
60	8 0	9.7242			10.2758	9.7958			10.2042	10.0716	9.9284	52 0	0
′	m s	Cos.	Diff. 0′.1	Diff. 1s	Sec.	Cot.	Diff. 0′.1	Diff. 1s	Tan.	Cosec.	Sin.	m s	′

121° = 8h 4m] [3h 52m = 58°

32° = 2h 8m] **Log. Sines, Tangents, and Secants.** [9h 48m = 147°

′	m s	Sin.	Diff. 0′.1	Diff. 1s	Cosec.	Tan.	Diff. 0′.1	Diff. 1s	Cot.	Sec.	Cos.	m s	′
0	8 0	9.7242			10.2758	9.7958			10.2042	10.0716	9.9284	52 0	60
1	4	7244	0	1	2756	7961	0	1	2039	0717	9283	51 56	59
2	8	7246	0	1	2754	7964	1	2	2036	0717	9283	52	58
3	12	7248	1	2	2752	7966	1	2	2034	0718	9282	48	57
4	16	7250	1		2750	7969	1		2031	0719	9281	51 44	56
5	8 20	9.7252	1		10.2748	9.7972	1		10.2028	10.0720	9.9280	40	55
6	24	7254	1		2746	7975	2		2025	0721	9279	36	54
7	28	7256	1		2744	7978	2		2022	0721	9279	32	53
8	32	7258	2		2742	7980	2		2020	0722	9278	28	52
9	36	7260	2		2740	7983	3		2017	0723	9277	51 24	51
10	8 40	9.7262			10.2738	9.7986			10.2014	10.0724	9.9276	20	50
11	44	7264	0	1	2736	7989	0	1	2011	0725	9275	16	49
12	48	7266	0	1	2734	7992	1	2	2008	0725	9275	12	48
13	52	7268	1	2	2732	7994	1	2	2006	0726	9274	8	47
14	56	7270	1		2730	7997	1		2003	0727	9273	51 4	46
15	9 0	9.7272	1		10.2728	9.8000	1		10.2000	10.0728	9.9272	51 0	45
16	4	7274	1		2726	8003	2		1997	0728	9272	50 56	44
17	8	7276	1		2724	8006	2		1994	0729	9271	52	43
18	12	7278	2		2722	8008	2		1992	0730	9270	48	42
19	16	7280	2		2720	8011	3		1989	0731	9269	50 44	41
20	9 20	9.7282			10.2718	9.8014			10.1986	10.0732	9.9268	40	40
21	24	7284	0	1	2716	8017	0	1	1983	0732	9268	36	39
22	28	7286	0	1	2714	8020	1	2	1980	0733	9267	32	38
23	32	7288	1	2	2712	8022	1	2	1978	0734	9266	28	37
24	36	7290	1		2710	8025	1		1975	0735	9265	50 24	36
25	9 40	9.7292	1		10.2708	9.8028	1		10.1972	10.0736	9.9264	20	35
26	44	7294	1		2706	8031	2		1969	0736	9264	16	34
27	48	7296	1		2704	8034	2		1966	0737	9263	12	33
28	52	7298	2		2702	8036	2		1964	0738	9262	8	32
29	56	7300	2		2700	8039	3		1961	0739	9261	50 4	31
30	10 0	9.7302			10.2698	9.8042			10.1958	10.0740	9.9260	50 0	30
31	4	7304	0	1	2696	8045	0	1	1955	0741	9259	49 56	29
32	8	7306	0	1	2694	8047	1	2	1953	0741	9259	52	28
33	12	7308	1	2	2692	8050	1	2	1950	0742	9258	48	27
34	16	7310	1		2690	8053	1		1947	0743	9257	49 44	26
35	10 20	9.7312	1		10.2688	9.8056	1		10.1944	10.0744	9.9256	40	25
36	24	7314	1		2686	8059	2		1941	0745	9255	36	24
37	28	7316	1		2684	8061	2		1939	0745	9255	32	23
38	32	7318	2		2682	8064	2		1936	0746	9254	28	22
39	36	7320	2		2680	8067	3		1933	0747	9253	49 24	21
40	10 40	9.7322			10.2678	9.8070			10.1930	10.0748	9.9252	20	20
41	44	7324	0	1	2676	8072	0	1	1928	0749	9251	16	19
42	48	7326	0	1	2674	8075	1	2	1925	0749	9251	12	18
43	52	7328	1	2	2672	8078	1	2	1922	0750	9250	8	17
44	56	7330	1		2670	8081	1		1919	0751	9249	49 4	16
45	11 0	9.7332	1		10.2668	9.8084	1		10.1916	10.0752	9.9248	49 0	15
46	4	7334	1		2666	8086	2		1914	0753	9247	48 56	14
47	8	7336	1		2664	8089	2		1911	0753	9247	52	13
48	12	7338	2		2662	8092	2		1908	0754	9246	48	12
49	16	7340	2		2660	8095	3		1905	0755	9245	48 44	11
50	11 20	9.7342			10.2658	9.8097			10.1903	10.0756	9.9244	40	10
51	24	7344	0	1	2656	8100	0	1	1900	0757	9243	36	9
52	28	7345	0	1	2655	8103	1	2	1897	0758	9242	32	8
53	32	7347	1	2	2653	8106	1	2	1894	0758	9242	28	7
54	36	7349	1		2651	8109	1		1891	0759	9241	48 24	6
55	11 40	9.7351	1		10.2649	9.8111	1		10.1889	10.0760	9.9240	20	5
56	44	7353	1		2647	8114	2		1886	0761	9239	16	4
57	48	7355	1		2645	8117	2		1883	0762	9238	12	3
58	52	7357	2		2643	8120	2		1880	0762	9238	8	2
59	56	7359	2		2641	8122	3		1878	0763	9237	48 4	1
60	12 0	9.7361			10.2639	9.8125			10.1875	10.0764	9.6236	48 0	0
′	m s	Cos.	0′.1 Diff.	1s	Sec.	Cot.	0′.1 Diff.	1s	Tan.	Cosec.	Sin.	m s	′

122° = 8h 8m] [3h 48m = 57°

33° = 2h 12m] Log. Sines, Tangents, and Secants. [9h 44m = 146°

′	m s	Sin.	Diff. 0′.1	Diff. 1s	Cosec.	Tan.	Diff. 0′.1	Diff. 1s	Cot.	Sec.	Cos.	m s	′
0	12 0	9.7361			10.2639	9.8125			10.1875	10.0764	9.9236	48 0	60
1	4	7363	0	1	2637	8128	0	1	1872	0765	9235	47 56	59
2	8	7365	0	1	2635	8131	1	2	1869	0766	9234	52	58
3	12	7367	1	2	2633	8133	1	2	1867	0767	9233	48	57
4	16	7369	1		2631	8136	1		1864	0767	9233	47 44	56
5	12 20	9.7371	1		10.2629	9.8139	1		10.1861	10.0768	9.9232	40	55
6	24	7373	1		2627	8142	2		1858	0769	9231	36	54
7	28	7375	1		2625	8145	2		1855	0770	9230	32	53
8	32	7377	2		2623	8147	2		1853	0771	9229	28	52
9	36	7379	2		2621	8150	3		1850	0771	9229	47 24	51
10	12 40	9.7380			10.2620	9.8153			10.1847	10.0772	9.9228	20	50
11	44	7382	0	1	2618	8156	0	1	1844	0773	9227	16	49
12	48	7384	0	1	2616	8158	1	2	1842	0774	9226	12	48
13	52	7386	1	2	2614	8161	1	2	1839	0775	9225	8	47
14	56	7388	1		2612	8164	1		1836	0776	9224	47 4	46
15	13 0	9.7390	1		10.2610	9.8167	1		10.1833	10.0776	9.9224	47 0	45
16	4	7392	1		2608	8169	2		1831	0777	9223	46 56	44
17	8	7394	1		2606	8172	2		1828	0778	9222	52	43
18	12	7396	2		2604	8175	2		1825	0779	9221	48	42
19	16	7398	2		2602	8178	3		1822	0780	9220	46 44	41
20	13 20	9.7400			10.2600	9.8180			10.1820	10.0781	9.9219	40	40
21	24	7402	0	1	2598	8183	0	1	1817	0781	9219	36	39
22	28	7404	0	1	2596	8186	1	2	1814	0782	9218	32	38
23	32	7406	1	2	2594	8189	1	2	1811	0783	9217	28	37
24	36	7407	1		2593	8191	1		1809	0784	9216	46 24	36
25	13 40	9.7409	1		10.2591	9.8194	1		10.1806	10.0785	9.9215	20	35
26	44	7411	1		2589	8197	2		1803	0786	9214	16	34
27	48	7413	1		2587	8200	2		1800	0786	9214	12	33
28	52	7415	2		2585	8202	2		1798	0787	9213	8	32
29	56	7417	2		2583	8205	3		1795	0788	9212	46 4	31
30	14 0	9.7419			10.2581	9.8208			10.1792	10.0789	9.9211	46 0	30
31	4	7421	0	1	2579	8211	0	1	1789	0790	9210	45 56	29
32	8	7423	0	1	2577	8213	1	2	1787	0791	9209	52	28
33	12	7425	1	2	2575	8216	1	2	1784	0791	9209	48	27
34	16	7427	1		2573	8219	1		1781	0792	9208	45 44	26
35	14 20	9.7428	1		10.2572	9.8222	1		10.1778	10.0793	9.9207	40	25
36	24	7430	1		2570	8224	2		1776	0794	9206	36	24
37	28	7432	1		2568	8227	2		1773	0795	9205	32	23
38	32	7434	2		2566	8230	2		1770	0796	9204	28	22
39	36	7436	2		2564	8233	3		1767	0796	9204	45 24	21
40	14 40	9.7438			10.2562	9.8235			10.1765	10.0797	9.9203	20	20
41	44	7440	0	1	2560	8238	0	1	1762	0798	9202	16	19
42	48	7442	0	1	2558	8241	1	2	1759	0799	9201	12	18
43	52	7444	1	2	2556	8243	1	2	1757	0800	9200	8	17
44	56	7445	1		2555	8246	1		1754	0801	9199	45 4	16
45	15 0	9.7447	1		10.2553	9.8249	1		10.1751	10.0802	9.9198	45 0	15
46	4	7449	1		2551	8252	2		1748	0802	9198	44 56	14
47	8	7451	1		2549	8254	2		1746	0803	9197	52	13
48	12	7453	2		2547	8257	2		1743	0804	9196	48	12
49	16	7455	2		2545	8260	3		1740	0805	9195	44 44	11
50	15 20	9.7457			10.2543	9.8263			10.1737	10.0806	9.9194	40	10
51	24	7459	0	1	2541	8265	0	1	1735	0807	9193	36	9
52	28	7461	0	1	2539	8268	1	2	1732	0807	9193	32	8
53	32	7462	1	2	2538	8271	1	2	1729	0808	9192	28	7
54	36	7464	1		2536	8274	1		1726	0809	9191	44 24	6
55	15 40	9.7466	1		10.2534	9.8276	1		10.1724	10.0810	9.9190	20	5
56	44	7468	1		2532	8279	2		1721	0811	9189	16	4
57	48	7470	1		2530	8282	2		1718	0812	9188	12	3
58	52	7472	2		2528	8284	2		1716	0813	9187	8	2
59	56	7474	2		2526	8287	3		1713	0813	9187	44 4	1
60	16 0	9.7476			10.2524	9.8290			10.1710	10.0814	9.9186	44 0	0
′	m s	Cos.	Diff. 0′.1	Diff. 1s	Sec.	Cot.	Diff. 0′.1	Diff. 1s	Tan.	Cosec.	Sin.	m s	′

123° = 8h 12m] [3h 44m = 56°

34° = 2h 16m] **Log. Sines, Tangents, and Secants.** [9h 40m = 145°

′	m s	Sin.	Diff. 0′.1	Diff. 1s	Cosec.	Tan.	Diff. 0′.1	Diff. 1s	Cot.	Sec.	Cos.	m s	′
0	16 0	9.7476			10.2524	9.8290			10.1710	10.0814	9.9186	44 0	60
1	4	7477	0	1	2523	8293	0	1	1707	0815	9185	43 56	59
2	8	7479	0	1	2521	8295	1	2	1705	0816	9184	52	58
3	12	7481	1	2	2519	8298	1	2	1702	0817	9183	48	57
4	16	7483	1		2517	8301	1		1699	0818	9182	43 44	56
5	16 20	9.7485	1		10.2515	9.8303	1		10.1697	10.0819	9.9181	40	55
6	24	7487	1		2513	8306	2		1694	0819	9181	36	54
7	28	7489	1		2511	8309	2		1691	0820	9180	32	53
8	32	7491	2		2509	8312	2		1688	0821	9179	28	52
9	36	7492	2		2508	8314	2		1686	0822	9178	43 24	51
10	16 40	9.7494			10.2506	9.8317			10.1683	10.0823	9.9177	20	50
11	44	7496	0	1	2504	8320	0	1	1680	0824	9176	16	49
12	48	7498	0	1	2502	8323	1	2	1677	0825	9175	12	48
13	52	7500	1	2	2500	8325	1	2	1675	0825	9175	8	47
14	56	7502	1		2498	8328	1		1672	0826	9174	43 4	46
15	17 0	9.7504	1		10.2496	9.8331	1		10.1669	10.0827	9.9173	43 0	45
16	4	7505	1		2495	8333	2		1667	0828	9172	42 56	44
17	8	7507	1		2493	8336	2		1664	0829	9171	52	43
18	12	7509	2		2491	8339	2		1661	0830	9170	48	42
19	16	7511	2		2489	8342	2		1658	0831	9169	42 44	41
20	17 20	9.7513			10.2487	9.8344			10.1656	10.0831	9.9169	40	40
21	24	7515	0	1	2485	8347	0	1	1653	0832	9168	36	39
22	28	7517	0	1	2483	8350	1	2	1650	0833	9167	32	38
23	32	7518	1	2	2482	8352	1	2	1648	0834	9166	28	37
24	36	7520	1		2480	8355	1		1645	0835	9165	42 24	36
25	17 40	9.7522	1		10.2478	9.8358	1		10.1642	10.0836	9.9164	20	35
26	44	7524	1		2476	8361	2		1639	0837	9163	16	34
27	48	7526	1		2474	8363	2		1637	0837	9163	12	33
28	52	7528	2		2472	8366	2		1634	0838	9162	8	32
29	56	7529	2		2471	8369	2		1631	0839	9161	42 4	31
30	18 0	9.7531			10.2469	9.8371			10.1629	10.0840	9.9160	42 0	30
31	4	7533	0	1	2467	8374	0	1	1626	0841	9159	41 56	29
32	8	7535	0	1	2465	8377	1	2	1623	0842	9158	52	28
33	12	7537	1	2	2463	8379	1	2	1621	0843	9157	48	27
34	16	7539	1		2461	8382	1		1618	0844	9156	41 44	26
35	18 20	9.7540	1		10.2460	9.8385	1		10.1615	10.0844	9.9156	40	25
36	24	7542	1		2458	8388	2		1612	0845	9155	36	24
37	28	7544	1		2456	8390	2		1610	0846	9154	32	23
38	32	7546	2		2454	8393	2		1607	0847	9153	28	22
39	36	7548	2		2452	8396	2		1604	0848	9152	41 24	21
40	18 40	9.7550			10.2450	9.8398			10.1602	10.0849	9.9151	20	20
41	44	7551	0	1	2449	8401	0	1	1599	0850	9150	16	19
42	48	7553	0	1	2447	8404	1	2	1596	0851	9149	12	18
43	52	7555	1	2	2445	8406	1	2	1594	0851	9149	8	17
44	56	7557	1		2443	8409	1		1591	0852	9148	41 4	16
45	19 0	9.7559	1		10.2441	9.8412	1		10.1588	10.0853	9.9147	41 0	15
46	4	7561	1		2439	8415	2		1585	0854	9146	40 56	14
47	8	7562	1		2438	8417	2		1583	0855	9145	52	13
48	12	7564	2		2436	8420	2		1580	0856	9144	48	12
49	16	7566	2		2434	8423	2		1577	0857	9143	40 44	11
50	19 20	9.7568			10.2432	9.8425			10.1575	10.0858	9.9142	40	10
51	24	7570	0	1	2430	8428	0	1	1572	0858	9142	36	9
52	28	7571	0	1	2429	8431	1	2	1569	0859	9141	32	8
53	32	7573	1	2	2427	8433	1	2	1567	0860	9140	28	7
54	36	7575	1		2425	8436	1		1564	0861	9139	40 24	6
55	19 40	9.7577	1		10.2423	9.8439	1		10.1561	10.0862	0.9138	20	5
56	44	7579	1		2421	8442	2		1558	0863	9137	16	4
57	48	7580	1		2420	8444	2		1556	0864	9136	12	3
58	52	7582	2		2428	8447	2		1553	0865	9135	8	2
59	56	7584	2		2426	8450	2		1550	0865	9135	40 4	1
60	20 0	9.7586			10.2424	9.8452			10.1548	10.0866	9.9134	40 0	0
′	m s	Cos.	Diff. 0′.1	Diff. 1s	Sec.	Cot.	Diff. 0′.1	Diff. 1s	Tan.	Cosec.	Sin.	m s	′

124° = 8h 16m] [3h 40m = 55°

35° = 2^h 20^m] **Log. Sines, Tangents, and Secants.** [9^h 36^m = 144°

′	m s	Sin.	Diff. 0′.1	Diff. 1^s	Cosec.	Tan.	Diff. 0′.1	Diff. 1^s	Cot.	Sec.	Cos.	m s	′
0	20 0	9.7586			10.2414	9.8452			10.1548	10.0866	9.9134	40 0	60
1	4	7588	0	0	2412	8455	0	1	1545	0867	9133	39 56	59
2	8	7590	0	1	2410	8458	1	2	1542	0868	9132	52	58
3	12	7591	1	1	2409	8460	1	2	1540	0869	9131	48	57
4	16	7593	1		2407	8463	1		1537	0870	9130	39 44	56
5	20 20	9.7595	1		10.2405	9.8466	1		10.1534	10.0871	9.9129	40	55
6	24	7597	1		2403	8468	2		1532	0872	9128	36	54
7	28	7599	1		2401	8471	2		1529	0873	9127	32	53
8	32	7600	2		2400	8474	2		1526	0873	9127	28	52
9	36	7602	2		2398	8476	2		1524	0874	9126	39 24	51
10	20 40	9.7604			10.2396	9.8479			10.1521	10.0875	9.9125	20	50
11	44	7606	0	0	2394	8482	0	1	1518	0876	9124	16	49
12	48	7607	0	1	2393	8484	1	2	1516	0877	9123	12	48
13	52	7609	1	1	2391	8487	1	2	1513	0878	9122	8	47
14	56	7611	1		2389	8490	1		1510	0879	9121	39 4	46
15	21 0	9.7613	1		10.2387	9.8493	1		10.1507	10.0880	9.9120	39 0	45
16	4	7615	1		2385	8495	2		1505	0881	9119	38 56	44
17	8	7616	1		2384	8498	2		1502	0881	9119	52	43
18	12	7618	2		2382	8501	2		1499	0882	9118	48	42
19	16	7620	2		2380	8503	2		1497	0883	9117	38 44	41
20	21 20	9.7622			10.2378	9.8506			10.1494	10.0884	9.9116	40	40
21	24	7624	0	0	2376	8509	0	1	1491	0885	9115	36	39
22	28	7625	0	1	2375	8511	1	2	1489	0886	9114	32	38
23	32	7627	1	1	2373	8514	1	2	1486	0887	9113	28	37
24	36	7629	1		2371	8517	1		1483	0888	9112	38 24	36
25	21 40	9.7631	1		10.2369	9.8519	1		10.1481	10.0889	9.9111	20	35
26	44	7632	1		2368	8522	2		1478	0890	9110	16	34
27	48	7634	1		2366	8525	2		1475	0890	9110	12	33
28	52	7636	2		2364	8527	2		1473	0891	9109	8	32
29	56	7638	2		2362	8530	2		1470	0892	9108	38 4	31
30	22 0	9.7640			10.2360	9.8533			10.1467	10.0893	9.9107	38 0	30
31	4	7641	0	0	2359	8535	0	1	1465	0894	9106	37 56	29
32	8	7643	0	1	2357	8538	1	2	1462	0895	9105	52	28
33	12	7645	1	1	2355	8541	1	2	1459	0896	9104	48	27
34	16	7647	1		2353	8543	1		1457	0897	9103	37 44	26
35	22 20	9.7648	1		10.2352	9.8546	1		10.1454	10.0898	9.9102	40	25
36	24	7650	1		2350	8549	2		1451	0899	9101	36	24
37	28	7652	1		2348	8551	2		1449	0899	9101	32	23
38	32	7654	1		2346	8554	2		1446	0900	9100	28	22
39	36	7655	2		2345	8557	2		1443	0901	9099	37 24	21
40	22 40	9.7657			10.2343	9.8559			10.1441	10.0902	9.9098	20	20
41	44	7659	0	0	2341	8562	0	1	1438	0903	9097	16	19
42	48	7661	0	1	2339	8565	1	2	1435	0904	9096	12	18
43	52	7662	1	1	2338	8567	1	2	1433	0905	9095	8	17
44	56	7664	1		2336	8570	1		1430	0906	9094	37 4	16
45	23 0	9.7666	1		10.2334	9.8573	1		10.1427	10.0907	9.9093	37 0	15
46	4	7668	1		2332	8575	2		1425	0908	9092	36 56	14
47	8	7669	1		2331	8578	2		1422	0909	9091	52	13
48	12	7671	1		2329	8581	2		1419	0909	9091	48	12
49	16	7673	2		2327	8583	2		1417	0910	9090	36 44	11
50	23 20	9.7675			10.2325	9.8586			10.1414	10.0911	9.9089	40	10
51	24	7676	0	0	2324	8589	0	1	1411	0912	9088	36	9
52	28	7678	0	1	2322	8591	1	2	1409	0913	9087	32	8
53	32	7680	1	1	2320	8594	1	2	1406	0914	9086	28	7
54	36	7682	1		2318	8597	1		1403	0915	9085	36 24	6
55	23 40	9.7683	1		10.2317	9.8599	1		10.1401	10.0916	9.9084	20	5
56	44	7685	1		2315	8602	2		1398	0917	9083	16	4
57	48	7687	1		2313	8605	2		1395	0918	9082	12	3
58	52	7689	1		2311	8607	2		1393	0919	9081	8	2
59	56	7690	2		2310	8610	2		1390	0920	9080	36 4	1
60	24 0	9.7692			10.2308	9.8613			10.1387	10.0920	9.9080	36 0	0
′	m s	Cos.	Diff. 0′.1	Diff. 1^s	Sec.	Cot.	Diff. 0′.1	Diff. 1^s	Tan.	Cosec.	Sin.	m s	′

125° = 8^h 20^m] [3^h 36^m = 54°

36° = 2h 24m] **Log. Sines, Tangents, and Secants.** [9h 32m = 143°

′	m s	Sin.	Diff. 0′.1	Diff. 1s	Cosec.	Tan.	Diff. 0′.1	Diff. 1s	Cot.	Sec.	Cos.	m s	′
0	24 0	9.7692			10.2308	9.8613			10.1387	10.0920	9.9080	36 0	60
1	4	7694	0	0	2306	8615	0	1	1385	0921	9079	35 56	59
2	8	7696	0	1	2304	8618	1	1	1382	0922	9078	52	58
3	12	7697	1	1	2303	8621	1	2	1379	0923	9077	48	57
4	16	7699	1		2301	8623	1		1377	0924	9076	35 44	56
5	24 20	9.7701	1		10.2299	9.8626	1		10.1374	10.0925	9.9075	40	55
6	24	7703	1		2297	8629	1		1371	0926	9074	36	54
7	28	7704	1		2296	8631	2		1369	0927	9073	32	53
8	32	7706	1		2294	8634	2		1366	0928	9072	28	52
9	36	7708	2		2292	8637	2		1364	0929	9071	35 24	51
10	24 40	9.7710			10.2290	9.8639			10.1361	10.0930	9.9070	20	50
11	44	7711	0	0	2289	8642	0	1	1358	0931	9069	16	49
12	48	7713	0	1	2287	8644	1	1	1356	0931	9069	12	48
13	52	7715	1	1	2285	8647	1	2	1353	0932	9068	8	47
14	56	7716	1		2284	8650	1		1350	0933	9067	35 4	46
15	25 0	9.7718	1		10.2282	9.8652	1		10.1348	10.0934	9.9066	35 0	45
16	4	7720	1		2280	8655	1		1345	0935	9065	34 56	44
17	8	7722	1		2278	8658	2		1342	0936	9064	52	43
18	12	7723	1		2277	8660	2		1340	0937	9063	48	42
19	16	7725	2		2275	8663	2		1337	0938	9062	34 44	41
20	25 20	9.7727			10.2273	9.8666			10.1334	10.0939	9.9061	40	40
21	24	7728	0	0	2272	8668	0	1	1332	0940	9060	36	39
22	28	7730	0	1	2270	8671	1	1	1329	0941	9059	32	38
23	32	7732	1	1	2268	8674	1	2	1326	0942	9058	28	37
24	36	7734	1		2266	8676	1		1324	0943	9057	34 24	36
25	25 40	9.7735	1		10.2265	9.8679	1		10.1321	10.0944	9.9056	20	35
26	44	7737	1		2263	8682	1		1318	0944	9056	16	34
27	48	7739	1		2261	8684	2		1316	0945	9055	12	33
28	52	7740	1		2260	8687	2		1313	0946	9054	8	32
29	56	7742	2		2258	8689	2		1311	0947	9053	34 4	31
30	26 0	9.7744			10.2256	9.8692			10.1308	10.0948	9.9052	34 0	30
31	4	7745	0	0	2254	8695	0	1	1305	0949	9051	33 56	29
32	8	7747	0	1	2253	8697	1	1	1303	0950	9050	52	28
33	12	7749	1	1	2251	8700	1	2	1300	0951	9049	48	27
34	16	7751	1		2249	8703	1		1297	0952	9048	33 44	26
35	26 20	9.7752	1		10.2248	9.8705	1		10.1295	10.0953	9.9047	40	25
36	24	7754	1		2246	8708	1		1292	0954	9046	36	24
37	28	7756	1		2244	8711	2		1289	0955	9045	32	23
38	32	7758	1		2242	8713	2		1287	0956	9044	28	22
39	36	7759	2		2241	8716	2		1284	0957	9043	33 24	21
40	26 40	9.7761			10.2239	9.8718			10.1282	10.0958	9.9042	20	20
41	44	7763	0	0	2237	8721	0	1	1279	0959	9041	16	19
42	48	7764	0	1	2236	8724	1	1	1276	0959	9041	12	18
43	52	7766	1	1	2234	8726	1	2	1274	0960	9040	8	17
44	56	7768	1		2232	8729	1		1271	0961	9039	33 4	16
45	27 0	9.7769	1		10.2231	9.8732	1		10.1268	10.0962	9.9038	33 0	15
46	4	7771	1		2229	8734	1		1266	0963	9037	32 56	14
47	8	7773	1		2227	8737	2		1263	0964	9036	52	13
48	12	7774	1		2226	8740	2		1260	0965	9035	48	12
49	16	7776	2		2224	8742	2		1258	0966	9034	32 44	11
50	27 20	9.7778			10.2222	9.8745			10.1255	10.0967	9.9033	40	10
51	24	7780	0	0	2220	8747	0	1	1253	0968	9032	36	9
52	28	7781	0	1	2219	8750	1	1	1250	0969	9031	32	8
53	32	7783	1	1	2217	8753	1	2	1247	0970	9030	28	7
54	36	7785	1		2215	8755	1		1245	0971	9029	32 24	6
55	27 40	9.7786	1		10.2214	9.8758	1		10.1242	10.0972	9.9028	20	5
56	44	7788	1		2212	8761	1		1239	0973	9027	16	4
57	48	7790	1		2210	8763	2		1237	0974	9026	12	3
58	52	7791	1		2209	8766	2		1234	0975	9025	8	2
59	56	7793	2		2207	8769	2		1231	0976	9024	32 4	1
60	28 0	9.7795			10.2205	9.8771			10.1229	10.0977	9.9023	32 0	0
′	m s	Cos.	Diff. 0′.1	Diff. 1s	Sec.	Cot.	Diff. 0′.1	Diff. 1s	Tan.	Cosec.	Sin.	m s	′

126° = 8h 24m] [3h 32m = 53°

37° = 2h 28m] **Log. Sines, Tangents, and Secants.** **[9h 28m = 142°**

′	m s	Sin.	Diff. 0′.1	Diff. 1s	Cosec.	Tan.	Diff. 0′.1	Diff. 1s	Cot.	Sec.	Cos.	m s	′
0	**28 0**	9.7795			10.2205	9.8771			10.1229	10.0977	9.9023	**32 0**	**60**
1	**4**	7796	0	0	2204	8774	0	1	1226	0977	9023	**31 56**	**59**
2	**8**	7798	0	1	2202	8776	1	1	1224	0978	9022	**52**	**58**
3	**12**	7800	1	1	2200	8779	1	2	1221	0979	9021	**48**	**57**
4	**16**	7801	1		2199	8782	1		1218	0980	9020	**31 44**	**56**
5	**28 20**	9.7803	1		10.2197	9.8784	1		10.1216	10.0981	9.9019	**40**	**55**
6	**24**	7805	1		2195	8787	1		1213	0982	9018	**36**	**54**
7	**28**	7806	1		2194	8790	2		1210	0983	9017	**32**	**53**
8	**32**	7808	1		2192	8792	2		1208	0984	9016	**28**	**52**
9	**36**	7810	2		2190	8795	2		1205	0985	9015	**31 24**	**51**
10	**28 40**	9.7811			10.2189	9.8797			10.1203	10.0986	9.9014	**20**	**50**
11	**44**	7813	0	0	2187	8800	0	1	1200	0987	9013	**16**	**49**
12	**48**	7815	0	1	2185	8803	1	1	1197	0988	9012	**12**	**48**
13	**52**	7816	1	1	2184	8805	1	2	1195	0989	9011	**8**	**47**
14	**56**	7818	1		2182	8808	1		1192	0990	9010	**31 4**	**46**
15	**29 0**	9.7820	1		10.2180	9.8811	1		10.1189	10.0991	9.9009	**31 0**	**45**
16	**4**	7821	1		2179	8813	1		1187	0992	9008	**30 56**	**44**
17	**8**	7823	1		2177	8816	2		1184	0993	9007	**52**	**43**
18	**12**	7825	1		2175	8818	2		1182	0994	9006	**48**	**42**
19	**16**	7826	2		2174	8821	2		1179	0995	9005	**30 44**	**41**
20	**29 20**	9.7828			10.2172	9.8824			10.1176	10.0996	9.9004	**40**	**40**
21	**24**	7830	0	0	2170	8826	0	1	1174	0997	9003	**36**	**39**
22	**28**	7831	0	1	2169	8829	1	1	1171	0998	9002	**32**	**38**
23	**32**	7833	1	1	2167	8831	1	2	1169	0999	9001	**28**	**37**
24	**36**	7835	1		2165	8834	1		1166	1000	9000	**30 24**	**36**
25	**29 40**	9.7836	1		10.2164	9.8837	1		10.1163	10.1000	9.9000	**20**	**35**
26	**44**	7838	1		2162	8839	1		1161	1001	8999	**16**	**34**
27	**48**	7840	1		2160	8842	2		1158	1002	8998	**12**	**33**
28	**52**	7841	1		2159	8845	2		1155	1003	8997	**8**	**32**
29	**56**	7843	2		2157	8847	2		1153	1004	8996	**30 4**	**31**
30	**30 0**	9.7844			10.2156	9.8850			10.1150	10.1005	9.8995	**30 0**	**30**
31	**4**	7846	0	0	2154	8852	0	1	1148	1006	8994	**29 56**	**29**
32	**8**	7848	0	1	2152	8855	1	1	1145	1007	8993	**52**	**28**
33	**12**	7849	1	1	2151	8858	1	2	1142	1008	8992	**48**	**27**
34	**16**	7851	1		2149	8860	1		1140	1009	8991	**29 44**	**26**
35	**30 20**	9.7853	1		10.2147	9.8863	1		10.1137	10.1010	9.8990	**40**	**25**
36	**24**	7854	1		2146	8865	1		1135	1011	8989	**36**	**24**
37	**28**	7856	1		2144	8868	2		1132	1012	8988	**32**	**23**
38	**32**	7858	1		2142	8871	2		1129	1013	8987	**28**	**22**
39	**36**	7859	2		2141	8873	2		1127	1014	8986	**29 24**	**21**
40	**30 40**	9.7861			10.2139	9.8876			10.1124	10.1015	9.8985	**20**	**20**
41	**44**	7863	0	0	2137	8879	0	1	1121	1016	8984	**16**	**19**
42	**48**	7864	0	1	2136	8881	1	1	1119	1017	8983	**12**	**18**
43	**52**	7866	1	1	2134	8884	1	2	1116	1018	8982	**8**	**17**
44	**56**	7867	1		2133	8886	1		1114	1019	8981	**29 4**	**16**
45	**31 0**	9.7869	1		10.2131	9.8889	1		10.1111	10.1020	9.8980	**29 0**	**15**
46	**4**	7871	1		2129	8892	1		1108	1021	8979	**28 56**	**14**
47	**8**	7872	1		2128	8894	2		1106	1022	8978	**52**	**13**
48	**12**	7874	1		2126	8897	2		1103	1023	8977	**48**	**12**
49	**16**	7876	2		2124	8899	2		1101	1024	8976	**28 44**	**11**
50	**31 20**	9.7877			10.2123	9.8902			10.1098	10.1025	9.8975	**40**	**10**
51	**24**	7879	0	0	2121	8905	0	1	1095	1026	8974	**36**	**9**
52	**28**	7880	0	1	2120	8907	1	1	1093	1027	8973	**32**	**8**
53	**32**	7882	1	1	2118	8910	1	2	1090	1028	8972	**28**	**7**
54	**36**	7884	1		2116	8912	1		1088	1029	8971	**28 24**	**6**
55	**31 40**	9.7885	1		10.2115	9.8915	1		10.1085	10.1030	9.8970	**20**	**5**
56	**44**	7887	1		2113	8918	1		1082	1031	8969	**16**	**4**
57	**48**	7889	1		2111	8920	2		1080	1032	8968	**12**	**3**
58	**52**	7890	1		2110	8923	2		1077	1033	8967	**8**	**2**
59	**56**	7892	2		2108	8925	2		1075	1034	8966	**28 4**	**1**
60	**32 0**	9.7893			10.2107	9.8928			10.1072	10.1035	9.8965	**28 0**	**0**
′	m s	Cos.	0′.1 Diff.	1s Diff.	Sec.	Cot.	0′.1 Diff.	1s Diff.	Tan.	Cosec.	Sin.	m s	′

127° = 8h 28m] **[3h 28m = 52°**

38° = 2h 32m]		Log. Sines, Tangents, and Secants.										[9h 24m = 141°	
′	m s	Sin.	Diff. 0′.1	Diff. 1s	Cosec.	Tan.	Diff. 0′.1	Diff. 1s	Cot.	Sec.	Cos.	m s	′
0	32 0	9.7893			10.2107	9.8928			10.1072	10.1035	9.8965	28 0	60
1	4	7895	0	0	2105	8931	0	1	1069	1036	8964	27 56	59
2	8	7897	0	1	2103	8933	1	1	1067	1037	8963	52	58
3	12	7898	1	1	2102	8936	1	2	1064	1038	8962	48	57
4	16	7900	1		2100	8939	1		1061	1039	8961	27 44	56
5	32 20	9.7901	1		10.2099	9.8941	1		10.1059	10.1040	9.8960	40	55
6	24	7903	1		2097	8944	1		1056	1041	8959	36	54
7	28	7905	1		2095	8946	2		1054	1042	8958	32	53
8	32	7906	1		2094	8949	2		1051	1043	8957	28	52
9	36	7908	2		2092	8952	2		1048	1044	8956	27 24	51
10	32 40	9.7910			10.2090	9.8954			10.1046	10.1045	9.8955	20	50
11	44	7911	0	0	2089	8957	0	1	1043	1046	8954	16	49
12	48	7913	0	1	2087	8959	1	1	1041	1047	8953	12	48
13	52	7914	1	1	2086	8962	1	2	1038	1048	8952	8	47
14	56	7916	1		2084	8965	1		1035	1049	8951	27 4	46
15	33 0	9.7918	1		10.2082	9.8967	1		10.1033	10.1050	9.8950	27 0	45
16	4	7919	1		2081	8970	1		1030	1051	8949	26 56	44
17	8	7921	1		2079	8972	2		1028	1052	8948	52	43
18	12	7922	1		2078	8975	2		1025	1053	8947	48	42
19	16	7924	2		2076	8978	2		1022	1054	8946	26 44	41
20	33 20	9.7926			10.2074	9.8980			10.1020	10.1055	9.8945	40	40
21	24	7927	0	0	2073	8983	0	1	1017	1056	8944	36	39
22	28	7929	0	1	2071	8985	1	1	1015	1057	8943	32	38
23	32	7930	1	1	2070	8988	1	2	1012	1058	8942	28	37
24	36	7932	1		2068	8990	1		1010	1059	8941	26 24	36
25	33 40	9.7934	1		10.2066	9.8993	1		10.1007	10.1060	9.8940	20	35
26	44	7935	1		2065	8996	1		1004	1061	8939	16	34
27	48	7937	1		2063	8998	2		1002	1062	8938	12	33
28	52	7938	1		2062	9001	2		0999	1063	8937	8	32
29	56	7940	2		2060	9003	2		0997	1064	8936	26 4	31
30	31 0	9.7941			10.2059	9.9006			10.0994	10.1065	9.8935	26 0	30
31	4	7943	0	0	2057	9009	0	1	0991	1066	8934	25 56	29
32	8	7945	0	1	2055	9011	1	1	0989	1067	8933	52	28
33	12	7946	1	1	2054	9014	1	2	0986	1068	8932	48	27
34	16	7948	1		2052	9016	1		0984	1069	8931	25 44	26
35	34 20	9.7949	1		10.2051	9.9019	1		10.0981	10.1070	9.8930	40	25
36	24	7951	1		2049	9022	1		0978	1071	8929	36	24
37	28	7953	1		2047	9024	2		0976	1072	8928	32	23
38	32	7954	1		2046	9027	2		0973	1073	8927	28	22
39	36	7956	2		2044	9029	2		0971	1074	8926	25 24	21
40	34 40	9.7957			10.2043	9.9032			10.0968	10.1075	9.8925	20	20
41	44	7959	0	0	2041	9035	0	1	0965	1076	8924	16	19
42	48	7960	0	1	2040	9037	1	1	0963	1077	8923	12	18
43	52	7962	1	1	2038	9040	1	2	0960	1078	8922	8	17
44	56	7964	1		2036	9042	1		0958	1079	8921	25 4	16
45	35 0	0.7965	1		10.2035	9.9045	1		10.0955	10.1080	9.8920	25 0	15
46	4	7967	1		2033	9047	1		0953	1081	8919	24 56	14
47	8	7968	1		2032	9050	2		0950	1082	8918	52	13
48	12	7970	1		2030	9053	2		0947	1083	8917	48	12
49	16	7972	2		2028	9055	2		0945	1084	8916	24 44	11
50	35 20	9.7973			10.2027	9.9058			10.0942	10.1085	9.8915	40	10
51	24	7975	0	0	2025	9060	0	1	0940	1086	8914	36	9
52	28	7976	0	1	2024	9063	1	1	0937	1087	8913	32	8
53	32	7978	1	1	2022	9066	1	2	0934	1088	8912	28	7
54	36	7979	1		2021	9068	1		0932	1089	8911	24 24	6
55	35 40	9.7981	1		10.2019	9.9071	1		10.0929	10.1090	9.8910	20	5
56	44	7982	1		2018	9073	1		0927	1091	8909	16	4
57	48	7984	1		2016	9076	2		0924	1092	8908	12	3
58	52	7986	1		2014	9079	2		0921	1093	8907	8	2
59	56	7987	2		2013	9081	2		0919	1094	8906	24 4	1
60	36 0	9.7989			10.2011	9.9084			10.0916	10.1095	9.8905	24 0	0
′	m s	Cos.	0′.1 Diff.	1s Diff.	Sec.	Cot.	0′.1 Diff.	1s Diff.	Tan.	Cosec.	Sin.	m s	′
128° = 8h 32m]												[3h 24m = 51°	

39° = 2h 36m]			Log. Sines, Tangents, and Secants.									[9h 20m = 140°	
°	m s	Sin.	Diff. 0′.1	Diff. 1s	Cosec.	Tan.	Diff. 0′.1	Diff. 1s	Cot.	Sec.	Cos.	m s	′
0	36 0	9.7989			10.2011	9.9084			10.0916	10.1095	9.8905	24 0	60
1	4	7990	0	0	2010	9086	0	1	0914	1096	8904	23 56	59
2	8	7992	0	1	2008	9089	0	1	0911	1097	8903	52	58
3	12	7993	0	1	2007	9091	1	2	0909	1098	8902	48	57
4	16	7995	1		2005	9094	1		0906	1099	8901	23 44	56
5	36 20	9.7997	1		10.2003	9.9097	1		10.0903	10.1100	9.8900	40	55
6	24	7998	1		2002	9099	1		0901	1101	8899	36	54
7	28	8000	1		2000	9102	2		0898	1102	8898	32	53
8	32	8001	1		1999	9104	2		0896	1103	8897	28	52
9	36	8003	1		1997	9107	2		0893	1104	8896	23 24	51
10	36 40	9.8004			10.1996	9.9110			10.0890	10.1105	9.8895	20	50
11	44	8006	0	0	1994	9112	0	1	0888	1106	8894	16	49
12	48	8007	0	1	1993	9115	0	1	0885	1107	8893	12	48
13	52	8009	0	1	1991	9117	1	2	0883	1108	8892	8	47
14	56	8010	1		1990	9120	1		0880	1109	8891	23 4	46
15	37 0	9.8012	1		10.1988	9.9122	1		10.0878	10.1110	9.8890	23 0	45
16	4	8014	1		1986	9125	1		0875	1111	8889	22 56	44
17	8	8015	1		1985	9128	2		0872	1112	8888	52	43
18	12	8017	1		1983	9130	2		0870	1113	8887	48	42
19	16	8018	1		1982	9133	2		0867	1115	8885	22 44	41
20	37 20	9.8020			10.1980	9.9135			10.0865	10.1116	9.8884	40	40
21	24	8021	0	0	1979	9138	0	1	0862	1117	8883	36	39
22	28	8023	0	1	1977	9140	0	1	0860	1118	8882	32	38
23	32	8024	0	1	1976	9143	1	2	0857	1119	8881	28	37
24	36	8026	1		1974	9146	1		0854	1120	8880	22 24	36
25	37 40	9.8027	1		10.1973	9.9148	1		10.0852	10.1121	9.8879	20	35
26	44	8029	1		1971	9151	1		0849	1122	8878	16	34
27	48	8031	1		1969	9153	2		0847	1123	8877	12	33
28	52	8032	1		1968	9156	2		0844	1124	8876	8	32
29	56	8034	1		1966	9158	2		0842	1125	8875	22 4	31
30	38 0	9.8035			10.1965	9.9161			10.0839	10.1126	9.8874	22 0	30
31	4	8037	0	0	1963	9164	0	1	0836	1127	8873	21 56	29
32	8	8038	0	1	1962	9166	0	1	0834	1128	8872	52	28
33	12	8040	0	1	1960	9169	1	2	0831	1129	8871	48	27
34	16	8041	1		1959	9171	1		0829	1130	8870	21 44	26
35	38 20	9.8043	1		10.1957	9.9174	1		10.0826	10.1131	9.8869	40	25
36	24	8044	1		1956	9176	1		0824	1132	8868	36	24
37	28	8046	1		1954	9179	2		0821	1133	8867	32	23
38	32	8047	1		1953	9182	2		0818	1134	8866	28	22
39	36	8049	1		1951	9184	2		0816	1135	8865	21 24	21
40	38 40	9.8050			10.1950	9.9187			10.0813	10.1136	9.8864	20	20
41	44	8052	0	0	1948	9189	0	1	0811	1137	8863	16	19
42	48	8053	0	1	1947	9192	0	1	0808	1138	8862	12	18
43	52	8055	0	1	1945	9194	1	2	0806	1140	8860	8	17
44	56	8056	1		1944	9197	1		0803	1141	8859	21 4	16
45	39 0	9.8058	1		10.1942	9.9200	1		10.0800	10.1142	9.8858	21 0	15
46	4	8060	1		1940	9202	1		0798	1143	8857	20 56	14
47	8	8061	1		1939	9205	2		0795	1144	8856	52	13
48	12	8063	1		1937	9207	2		0793	1145	8855	48	12
49	16	8064	1		1936	9210	2		0790	1146	8854	20 44	11
50	39 20	9.8066			10.1934	9.9212			10.0788	10.1147	9.8853	40	10
51	24	8067	0	0	1933	9215	0	1	0785	1148	8852	36	9
52	28	8069	0	1	1931	9218	0	1	0782	1149	8851	32	8
53	32	8070	0	1	1930	9220	1	2	0780	1150	8850	28	7
54	36	8072	1		1928	9223	1		0777	1151	8849	20 24	6
55	39 40	9.8073	1		10.1927	9.9225	1		10.0775	10.1152	9.8848	20	5
56	44	8075	1		1925	9228	1		0772	1153	8847	16	4
57	48	8076	1		1924	9230	2		0770	1154	8846	12	3
58	52	8078	1		1922	9233	2		0767	1155	8845	8	2
59	56	8079	1		1921	9236	2		0764	1156	8844	20 4	1
60	40 0	9.8081			10.1919	9.9238			10.0762	10.1157	9.8843	20 0	0
′	m s	Cos.	Diff. 0′.1	Diff. 1s	Sec.	Cot.	Diff. 0′.1	Diff. 1s	Tan.	Cosec.	Sin.	m s	′
129° = 8h 36m]												[3h 20m = 50°	

40° = 2h 40m] **Log. Sines, Tangents, and Secants.** [9h 16m = 139°

′	m s	Sin.	Diff. 0′.1	Diff. 1s	Cosec.	Tan.	Diff. 0′.1	Diff. 1s	Cot.	Sec.	Cos.	m s	′
0	40 0	9.8081			10.1919	9.9238			10.0762	10.1157	9.8843	20 0	60
1	4	8082	0	0	1918	9241	0	1	0759	1159	8841	19 56	59
2	8	8084	0	1	1916	9243	0	1	0757	1160	8840	52	58
3	12	8085	0	1	1915	9246	1	2	0754	1161	8839	48	57
4	16	8087	1		1913	9248	1		0752	1162	8838	19 44	56
5	40 20	9.8088	1		10.1912	9.9251	1		10.0749	10.1163	9.8837	40	55
6	24	8090	1		1910	9254	1		0746	1164	8836	36	54
7	28	8091	1		1909	9256	2		0744	1165	8835	32	53
8	32	8093	1		1907	9259	2		0741	1166	8834	28	52
9	36	8094	1		1906	9261	2		0739	1167	8833	19 24	51
10	40 40	9.8096			10.1904	9.9264			10.0736	10.1168	9.8832	20	50
11	44	8097	0	0	1903	9266	0	1	0734	1169	8831	16	49
12	48	8099	0	1	1901	9269	0	1	0731	1170	8830	12	48
13	52	8100	0	1	1900	9271	1	2	0729	1171	8829	8	47
14	56	8102	1		1898	9274	1		0726	1172	8828	19 4	46
15	41 0	9.8103	1		10.1897	9.9277	1		10.0723	10.1173	9.8827	19 0	45
16	4	8105	1		1895	9279	1		0721	1175	8825	18 56	44
17	8	8106	1		1894	9282	2		0718	1176	8824	52	43
18	12	8108	1		1892	9284	2		0716	1177	8823	48	42
19	16	8109	1		1891	9287	2		0713	1178	8822	18 44	41
20	41 20	9.8111			10.1889	9.9289			10.0711	10.1179	9.8821	40	40
21	24	8112	0	0	1888	9292	0	1	0708	1180	8820	36	39
22	28	8114	0	1	1886	9295	0	1	0705	1181	8819	32	38
23	32	8115	0	1	1885	9297	1	2	0703	1182	8818	28	37
24	36	8117	1		1883	9300	1		0700	1183	8817	18 24	36
25	41 40	9.8118	1		10.1882	9.9302	1		10.0698	10.1184	9.8816	20	35
26	44	8120	1		1880	9305	1		0695	1185	8815	16	34
27	48	8121	1		1879	9307	2		0693	1186	8814	12	33
28	52	8122	1		1878	9310	2		0690	1187	8813	8	32
29	56	8124	1		1876	9312	2		0688	1188	8812	18 4	31
30	42 0	9.8125			10.1875	9.9315			10.0685	10.1190	9.8810	18 0	30
31	4	8127	0	0	1873	9318	0	1	0682	1191	8809	17 56	29
32	8	8128	0	1	1872	9320	0	1	0680	1192	8808	52	28
33	12	8130	0	1	1870	9323	1	2	0677	1193	8807	48	27
34	16	8131	1		1869	9325	1		0675	1194	8806	17 44	26
35	42 20	9.8133	1		10.1867	9.9328	1		10.0672	10.1195	9.8805	40	25
36	24	8134	1		1866	9330	1		0670	1196	8804	36	24
37	28	8136	1		1864	9333	2		0667	1197	8803	32	23
38	32	8137	1		1863	9335	2		0665	1198	8802	28	22
39	36	8139	1		1861	9338	2		0662	1199	8801	17 24	21
40	42 40	9.8140			10.1860	9.9341			10.0659	10.1200	9.8800	20	20
41	44	8142	0	0	1858	9343	0	1	0657	1201	8799	16	19
42	48	8143	0	1	1857	9346	0	1	0654	1203	8797	12	18
43	52	8145	0	1	1855	9348	1	2	0652	1204	8796	8	17
44	56	8146	1		1854	9351	1		0649	1205	8795	17 4	16
45	43 0	9.8148	1		10.1852	9.9353	1		10.0647	10.1206	9.8794	17 0	15
46	4	8149	1		1851	9356	1		0644	1207	8793	16 56	14
47	8	8150	1		1850	9358	2		0642	1208	8792	52	13
48	12	8152	1		1848	9361	2		0639	1209	8791	48	12
49	16	8153	1		1847	9364	2		0636	1210	8790	16 44	11
50	43 20	9.8155			10.1845	9.9366			10.0634	10.1211	9.8789	40	10
51	24	8156	0	0	1844	9369	0	1	0631	1212	8788	36	9
52	28	8158	0	1	1842	9371	0	1	0629	1213	8787	32	8
53	32	8159	0	1	1841	9374	1	2	0626	1215	8785	28	7
54	36	8161	1		1839	9376	1		0624	1216	8784	16 24	6
55	43 40	9.8162	1		10.1838	9.9379	1		10.0621	10.1217	9.8783	20	5
56	44	8164	1		1836	9381	1		0619	1218	8782	16	4
57	48	8165	1		1835	9384	2		0616	1219	8781	12	3
58	52	8167	1		1833	9387	2		0613	1220	8780	8	2
59	56	8168	1		1832	9389	2		0611	1221	8779	16 4	1
60	44 0	9.8169			10.1831	9.9392			10.0608	10.1222	9.8778	16 0	0
′	m s	Cos.	0′.1 Diff.	1s Diff.	Sec.	Cot.	0′.1 Diff.	1s Diff.	Tan.	Cosec.	Sin.	m s	′

130° = 8h 40m] [3h 16m = 49°

41° = 2h 44m] **Log. Sines, Tangents, and Secants.** **[9h 12m = 138°**

′	m s	Sin.	Diff. 0′.1	Diff. 1s	Cosec.	Tan.	Diff. 0′.1	Diff. 1s	Cot.	Sec.	Cos.	m s	
0	44 0	9.8169			10.1831	9.9392			10.0608	10.1222	9.8778	16 0	60
1	4	8171	0	0	1829	9394	0	1	0606	1223	8777	15 56	59
2	8	8172	0	1	1828	9397	0	1	0603	1224	8776	52	58
3	12	8174	0	1	1826	9399	1	2	0601	1225	8775	48	57
4	16	8175	1		1825	9402	1		0598	1227	8773	15 44	56
5	44 20	9.8177	1		10.1823	9.9404	1		10.0596	10.1228	9.3772	40	55
6	24	8178	1		1822	9407	1		0593	1229	8771	36	54
7	28	8180	1		1820	9409	2		0591	1230	8770	32	53
8	32	8181	1		1819	9412	2		0588	1231	8769	28	52
9	36	8182	1		1818	9415	2		0585	1232	8768	15 24	51
10	44 40	9.8184			10.1816	9.9417			10.0583	10.1233	9.8767	20	50
11	44	8185	0	0	1815	9420	0	1	0580	1234	8766	16	49
12	48	8187	0	1	1813	9422	0	1	0578	1235	8765	12	48
13	52	8188	0	1	1812	9425	1	2	0575	1237	8763	8	47
14	56	8190	1		1810	9427	1		0573	1238	8762	15 4	46
15	45 0	9.8191	1		10.1809	9.9430	1		10.0570	10.1239	9.8761	15 0	45
16	4	8193	1		1807	9432	1		0568	1240	8760	14 56	44
17	8	8194	1		1806	9435	2		0565	1241	8759	52	43
18	12	8195	1		1805	9438	2		0562	1242	8758	48	42
19	16	8197	1		1803	9440	2		0560	1243	8757	14 44	41
20	45 20	9.8198			10.1802	9.9443			10.0557	10.1244	9.8756	40	40
21	24	8200	0	0	1800	9445	0	1	0555	1245	8755	36	39
22	28	8201	0	1	1799	9448	0	1	0552	1247	8753	32	38
23	32	8203	0	1	1797	9450	1	2	0550	1248	8752	28	37
24	36	8204	1		1796	9453	1		0547	1249	8751	14 24	36
25	45 40	9.8205	1		10.1795	9.9455	1		10.0545	10.1250	9.8750	20	35
26	44	8207	1		1793	9458	1		0542	1251	8749	16	34
27	48	8208	1		1792	9460	2		0540	1252	8748	12	33
28	52	8210	1		1790	9463	2		0537	1253	8747	8	32
29	56	8211	1		1789	9466	2		0534	1254	8746	4	31
30	46 0	9.8213			10.1787	9.9468			10.0532	10.1255	9.8745	14 0	30
31	4	8214	0	0	1786	9471	0	1	0529	1257	8743	13 56	29
32	8	8216	0	1	1784	9473	0	1	0527	1258	8742	52	28
33	12	8217	0	1	1783	9476	1	2	0524	1259	8741	48	27
34	16	8218	1		1782	9478	1		0522	1260	8740	13 44	26
35	46 20	9.8220	1		10.1780	9.9481	1		10.0519	10.1261	9.8739	40	25
36	24	8221	1		1779	9483	1		0517	1262	8738	36	24
37	28	·8223	1		1777	9486	2		0514	1263	8737	32	23
38	32	8224	1		1776	9488	2		0512	1264	8736	28	22
39	36	8225	1		1775	9491	2		0509	1266	8734	13 24	21
40	46 40	9.8227			10.1773	9.9494			10.0506	10.1267	9.8733	20	20
41	44	8228	0	0	1772	9496	0	1	0504	1268	8732	16	19
42	48	8230	0	1	1770	9499	0	1	0501	1269	8731	12	18
43	52	8231	0	1	1769	9501	1	2	0499	1270	8730	8	17
44	56	8233	1		1767	9504	1		0496	1271	8729	13 4	16
45	47 0	9.8234	1		10.1766	9.9506	1		10.0494	10.1272	9.8728	13 0	15
46	4	8235	1		1765	9509	1		0491	1273	8727	12 56	14
47	8	8237	1		1763	9511	2		0489	1275	8725	52	13
48	12	8238	1		1762	9514	2		0486	1276	8724	48	12
49	16	8240	1		1760	9516	2		0484	1277	8723	12 44	11
50	47 20	9.8241			10.1759	9.9519			10.0481	10.1278	9.8722	40	10
51	24	8242	0	0	1758	9522	0	1	0478	1279	8721	36	9
52	28	8244	0	1	1756	9524	0	1	0476	1280	8720	32	8
53	32	8245	0	1	1755	9527	1	2	0473	1281	8719	28	7
54	36	8247	1		1753	9529	1		0471	1282	8718	12 24	6
55	47 40	9.8248	1		10.1752	9.9532	1		10.0468	10.1284	9.8716	20	5
56	44	8249	1		1751	9534	1		0466	1285	8715	16	4
57	48	8251	1		1749	9537	2		0463	1286	8714	12	3
58	52	8252	1		1748	9539	2		0461	1287	8713	8	2
59	56	8254	1		1746	9542	2		0458	1288	8712	12 4	1
60	48 0	9.8255			10.1745	9.9544			10.0456	10.1289	9.8711	12 0	0
′	m s	Cos.	Diff. 0′.1	Diff. 1s	Sec.	Cot.	Diff. 0′.1	Diff. 1s	Tan.	Cosec.	Sin.	m s	′

131° = 8h 44m] **[3h 12m = 48°**

42° = 2h 48m] **Log. Sines, Tangents, and Secants.** [9h 8m = 137°

′	m s	Sin.	Diff. 0′.1	Diff. 1s	Cosec.	Tan.	Diff. 0′.1	Diff. 1s	Cot.	Sec.	Cos.	m s	′
0	48 0	9.8255			10.1745	9.9544			10.0456	10.1289	9.8711	12 0	60
1	4	8257	0	0	1743	9547	0	1	0453	1290	8710	11 56	59
2	8	8258	0	1	1742	9549	0	1	0451	1292	8708	52	58
3	12	8259	0	1	1741	9552	1	2	0448	1293	8707	48	57
4	16	8261	1		1739	9555	1		0445	1294	8706	11 44	56
5	48 20	9.8262	1		10.1738	9.9557	1		10.0443	10.1295	9.8705	40	55
6	24	8264	1		1736	9560	1		0440	1296	8704	36	54
7	28	8265	1		1735	9562	2		0438	1297	8703	32	53
8	32	8266	1		1734	9565	2		0435	1298	8702	28	52
9	36	8268	1		1732	9567	2		0433	1300	8700	11 24	51
10	48 40	9.8269			10.1731	9.9570			10.0430	10.1301	9.8699	20	50
11	44	8270	0	0	1730	9572	0	1	0428	1302	8698	16	49
12	48	8272	0	1	1728	9575	0	1	0425	1303	8697	12	48
13	52	8273	0	1	1727	9577	1	2	0423	1304	8696	8	47
14	56	8275	1		1725	9580	1		0420	1305	8695	11 4	46
15	49 0	9.8276	1		10.1724	9.9582	1		10.0418	10.1306	9.8694	11 0	45
16	4	8277	1		1723	9585	1		0415	1308	8692	10 56	44
17	8	8279	1		1721	9588	2		0412	1309	8691	52	43
18	12	8280	1		1720	9590	2		0410	1310	8690	48	42
19	16	8282	1		1718	9593	2		0407	1311	8689	10 44	41
20	49 20	9.8283			10.1717	9.9595			10.0405	10.1312	9.8688	40	40
21	24	8284	0	0	1716	9598	0	1	0402	1313	8687	36	39
22	28	8286	0	1	1714	9600	0	1	0400	1314	8686	32	38
23	32	8287	0	1	1713	9603	1	2	0397	1316	8684	28	37
24	36	8289	1		1711	9605	1		0395	1317	8683	10 24	36
25	49 40	9.8290	1		10.1710	9.9608	1		10.0392	10.1318	9.8682	20	35
26	44	8291	1		1709	9610	1		0390	1319	8681	16	34
27	48	8293	1		1707	9613	2		0387	1320	8680	12	33
28	52	8294	1		1706	9615	2		0385	1321	8679	8	32
29	56	8295	1		1705	9618	2		0382	1323	8677	10 4	31
30	50 0	9.8297			10.1703	9.9621			10.0379	10.1324	9.8676	10 0	30
31	4	8298	0	0	1702	9623	0	1	0377	1325	8675	9 56	29
32	8	8300	0	1	1700	9626	0	1	0374	1326	8674	52	28
33	12	8301	0	1	1699	9628	1	2	0372	1327	8673	48	27
34	16	8302	1		1698	9631	1		0369	1328	8672	9 44	26
35	50 20	9.8304	1		10.1696	9.9633	1		10.0367	10.1329	9.8671	40	25
36	24	8305	1		1695	9636	1		0364	1331	8669	36	24
37	28	8306	1		1694	9638	2		0362	1332	8668	32	23
38	32	8308	1		1692	9641	2		0359	1333	8667	28	22
39	36	8309	1		1691	9643	2		0357	1334	8666	9 24	21
40	50 40	9.8311			10.1689	9.9646			10.0354	10.1335	9.8665	20	20
41	44	8312	0	0	1688	9648	0	1	0352	1336	8664	16	19
42	48	8313	0	1	1687	9651	0	1	0349	1338	8662	12	18
43	52	8315	0	1	1685	9653	1	2	0347	1339	8661	8	17
44	56	8316	1		1684	9656	1		0344	1340	8660	9 4	16
45	51 0	9.8317	1		10.1683	9.9659	1		10.0341	10.1341	9.8659	9 0	15
46	4	8319	1		1681	9661	1		0339	1342	8658	8 56	14
47	8	8320	1		1680	9664	2		0336	1343	8657	52	13
48	12	8322	1		1678	9666	2		0334	1345	8655	48	12
49	16	8323	1		1677	9669	2		0331	1346	8654	8 44	11
50	51 20	9.8324			10.1676	9.9671			10.0329	10.1347	9.8653	40	10
51	24	8326	0	0	1674	9674	0	1	0326	1348	8652	36	9
52	28	8327	0	1	1673	9676	0	1	0324	1349	8651	32	8
53	32	8328	0	1	1672	9679	1	2	0321	1350	8650	28	7
54	36	8330	1		1670	9681	1		0319	1352	8648	8 24	6
55	51 40	9.8331	1		10.1669	9.9684	1		10.0316	10.1353	9.8647	20	5
56	44	8332	1		1668	9686	1		0314	1354	8646	16	4
57	48	8334	1		1666	9689	2		0311	1355	8645	12	3
58	52	8335	1		1665	9691	2		0309	1356	8644	8	2
59	56	8336	1		1664	9694	2		0306	1358	8642	8 4	1
60	52 0	9.8338			10.1662	9.9697			10.0303	10.1359	9.8641	8 0	0
′	m s	Cos.	0′.1 Diff.	1s Diff.	Sec.	Cot.	0′.1 Diff.	1s Diff.	Tan.	Cosec.	Sin.	m s	′

132° = 8h 48m] [3h 8m = 47°

43° = 2h 52m]			Log. Sines, Tangents, and Secants.									[9h 4m = 136°	
′	m s	Sin.	Diff. 0′.1	Diff. 1s	Cosec.	Tan.	Diff. 0′.1	Diff. 1s	Cot.	Sec.	Cos.	m s	′
0	52 0	9.8338			10.1662	9.9697			10.0303	10.1359	9.8641	8 0	60
1	4	8339	0	0	1661	9699	0	1	0301	1360	8640	7 56	59
2	8	8341	0	1	1659	9702	0	1	0298	1361	8639	52	58
3	12	8342	0	1	1658	9704	1	2	0296	1362	8638	48	57
4	16	8343	0		1657	9707	1		0293	1363	8637	7 44	56
5	52 20	9.8345	1		10.1655	9.9709	1		10.0291	10.1365	9.8635	40	55
6	24	8346	1		1654	9712	1		0288	1366	8634	36	54
7	28	8347	1		1653	9714	2		0286	1367	8633	32	53
8	32	8349	1		1651	9717	2		0283	1368	8632	28	52
9	36	8350	1		1650	9719	2		0281	1369	8631	7 24	51
10	52 40	9.8351			10.1649	9.9722			10.0278	10.1371	9.8629	20	50
11	44	8353	0	0	1647	9724	0	1	0276	1372	8628	16	49
12	48	8354	0	1	1646	9727	0	1	0273	1373	8627	12	48
13	52	8355	0	1	1645	9729	1	2	0271	1374	8626	8	47
14	56	8357	0		1643	9732	1		0268	1375	8625	7 4	46
15	53 0	9.8358	1		10.1642	9.9735	1		10.0265	10.1376	9.8624	7 0	45
16	4	8359	1		1641	9737	1		0263	1378	8622	6 56	44
17	8	8361	1		1639	9740	2		0260	1379	8621	52	43
18	12	8362	1		1638	9742	2		0258	1380	8620	48	42
19	16	8363	1		1637	9745	2		0255	1381	8619	6 44	41
20	53 20	9.8365			10.1635	9.9747			10.0253	10.1382	9.8618	40	40
21	24	8366	0	0	1634	9750	0	1	0250	1384	8616	36	39
22	28	8367	0	1	1633	9752	0	1	0248	1385	8615	32	38
23	32	8369	0	1	1631	9755	1	2	0245	1386	8614	28	37
24	36	8370	0		1630	9757	1		0243	1387	8613	6 24	36
25	53 40	9.8371	1		10.1629	9.9760	1		10.0240	10.1388	9.8612	20	35
26	44	8373	1		1627	9762	1		0238	1390	8610	16	34
27	48	8374	1		1626	9765	2		0235	1391	8609	12	33
28	52	8375	1		1625	9767	2		0233	1392	8608	8	32
29	56	8377	1		1623	9770	2		0230	1393	8607	6 4	31
30	54 0	9.8378			10.1622	9.9773			10.0227	10.1394	9.8606	6 0	30
31	4	8379	0	0	1621	9775	0	1	0225	1396	8604	5 56	29
32	8	8381	0	1	1619	9778	0	1	0222	1397	8603	52	28
33	12	8382	0	1	1618	9780	1	2	0220	1398	8602	48	27
34	16	8383	0		1617	9783	1		0217	1399	8601	5 21	26
35	54 20	9.8385	1		10.1615	9.9785	1		10.0215	10.1400	9.8600	40	25
36	24	8386	1		1614	9788	1		0212	1402	8598	36	24
37	28	8387	1		1613	9790	2		0210	1403	8597	32	23
38	32	8389	1		1611	9793	2		0207	1404	8596	28	22
39	36	8390	1		1610	9795	2		0205	1405	8595	5 24	21
40	54 40	9.8391			10.1609	9.9798			10.0202	10.1406	9.8594	20	20
41	44	8393	0	0	1607	9800	0	1	0200	1408	8592	16	19
42	48	8394	0	1	1606	9803	0	1	0197	1409	8591	12	18
43	52	8395	0	1	1605	9805	1	2	0195	1410	8590	8	17
44	56	8397	0		1603	9808	1		0192	1411	8589	5 4	16
45	55 0	9.8398	1		10.1602	9.9810	1		10.0190	10.1412	9.8588	5 0	15
46	4	8399	1		1601	9813	1		0187	1414	8586	4 56	14
47	8	8401	1		1599	9816	2		0184	1415	8585	52	13
48	12	8402	1		1598	9818	2		0182	1416	8584	48	12
49	16	8403	1		1597	9821	2		0179	1417	8583	4 44	11
50	55 20	9.8405			10.1595	9.9823			10.0177	10.1418	9.8582	40	10
51	24	8406	0	0	1594	9826	0	1	0174	1420	8580	36	9
52	28	8407	0	1	1593	9828	0	1	0172	1421	8579	32	8
53	32	8409	0	1	1591	9831	1	2	0169	1422	8578	28	7
54	36	8410	0		1590	9833	1		0167	1423	8577	4 24	6
55	55 40	9.8411	1		10.1589	9.9836	1		10.0164	10.1425	9.8575	20	5
56	44	8412	1		1588	9838	1		0162	1426	8574	16	4
57	48	8414	1		1586	9841	2		0159	1427	8573	12	3
58	52	8415	1		1585	9843	2		0157	1428	8572	8	2
59	56	8416	1		1584	9846	2		0154	1429	8571	4 4	1
60	56 0	9.8418			10.1582	9.9848			10.0152	10.1431	9.8569	4 0	0
′	m s	Cos.	Diff. 0′.1	Diff. 1s	Sec.	Cot.	Diff. 0′.1	Diff. 1s	Tan.	Cosec.	Sin.	m s	′
133° = 8h 52m]												[3h 4m = 46°	

44° = 2h 56m]		Log. Sines, Tangents, and Secants.										[9h 0m = 135°	
′	m s	Sin.	Diff. 0′.1	Diff. 1s	Cosec.	Tan.	Diff. 0′.1	Diff. 1s	Cot.	Sec.	Cos.	m s	′
0	56 0	9.8418			10.1582	9.9848			10.0152	10.1431	9.8569	4 0	60
1	4	8419	0	0	1581	9851	0	1	0149	1432	8568	3 56	59
2	8	8420	0	0	1580	9853	0	1	0147	1433	8567	52	58
3	12	8422	0	1	1578	9856	1	2	0144	1434	8566	48	57
4	16	8423	0		1577	9858	1		0142	1436	8564	3 44	56
5	56 20	9.8424	0		10.1576	9.9861	1		10.0139	10.1437	9.8563	40	55
6	24	8426	1		1574	9864	1		0136	1438	8562	36	54
7	28	8427	1		1573	9866	2		0134	1439	8561	32	53
8	32	8428	1		1572	9869	2		0131	1440	8560	28	52
9	36	8429	1		1571	9871	2		0129	1442	8558	3 24	51
10	56 40	9.8431			10.1569	9.9874			10.0126	10.1443	9.8557	20	50
11	44	8432	0	0	1568	9876	0	1	0124	1444	8556	16	49
12	48	8433	0	0	1567	9879	0	1	0121	1445	8555	12	48
13	52	8435	0	1	1565	9881	1	2	0119	1447	8553	8	47
14	56	8436	0		1564	9884	1		0116	1448	8552	3 4	46
15	57 0	9.8437	0		10.1563	9.9886	1		10.0114	10.1449	9.8551	3 0	45
16	4	8439	1		1561	9889	1		0111	1450	8550	2 56	44
17	8	8440	1		1560	9891	2		0109	1452	8548	52	43
18	12	8441	1		1559	9894	2		0106	1453	8547	48	42
19	16	8442	1		1558	9896	2		0104	1454	8546	2 44	41
20	57 20	9.8444			10.1556	9.9899			10.0101	10.1455	9.8545	40	40
21	24	8445	0	0	1555	9901	0	1	0099	1456	8544	36	39
22	28	8446	0	0	1554	9904	0	1	0096	1458	8542	32	38
23	32	8448	0	1	1552	9907	1	2	0093	1459	8541	28	37
24	36	8449	0		1551	9909	1		0091	1460	8540	2 24	36
25	57 40	9.8450	0		10.1550	9.9912	1		10.0088	10.1461	9.8539	20	35
26	44	8451	1		1549	9914	1		0086	1463	8537	16	34
27	48	8453	1		1547	9917	2		0083	1464	8536	12	33
28	52	8454	1		1546	9919	2		0081	1465	8535	8	32
29	56	8455	1		1545	9922	2		0078	1466	8534	2 4	31
30	58 0	9.8457			10.1543	9.9924			10.0076	10.1468	9.8532	2 0	30
31	4	8458	0	0	1542	9927	0	1	0073	1469	8531	1 56	29
32	8	8459	0	0	1541	9929	0	1	0071	1470	8530	52	28
33	12	8460	0	1	1540	9932	1	2	0068	1471	8529	48	27
34	16	8462	0		1538	9934	1		0066	1473	8527	1 44	26
35	58 20	9.8463	0		10.1537	9.9937	1		10.0063	10.1474	9.8526	40	25
36	24	8464	1		1536	9939	1		0061	1475	8525	36	24
37	28	8466	1		1534	9942	2		0058	1476	8524	32	23
38	32	8467	1		1533	9944	2		0056	1478	8522	28	22
39	36	8468	1		1532	9947	2		0053	1479	8521	1 24	21
40	58 40	9.8469			10.1531	9.9949			10.0051	10.1480	9.8520	20	20
41	44	8471	0	0	1529	9952	0	1	0048	1481	8519	16	19
42	48	8472	0	0	1528	9955	0	1	0045	1483	8517	12	18
43	52	8473	0	1	1527	9957	1	2	0043	1484	8516	8	17
44	56	8475	0		1525	9960	1		0040	1485	8515	1 4	16
45	59 0	9.8476	0		10.1524	9.9962	1		10.0038	10.1486	9.8514	1 0	15
46	4	8477	1		1523	9965	1		0035	1488	8512	0 56	14
47	8	8478	1		1522	9967	2		0033	1489	8511	52	13
48	12	8480	1		1520	9970	2		0030	1490	8510	48	12
49	16	8481	1		1519	9972	2		0028	1491	8509	0 44	11
50	59 20	9.8482			10.1518	9.9975			10.0025	10.1493	9.8507	40	10
51	24	8483	0	0	1517	9977	0	1	0023	1494	8506	36	9
52	28	8485	0	0	1515	9980	0	1	0020	1495	8505	32	8
53	32	8486	0	1	1514	9982	1	2	0018	1496	8504	28	7
54	36	8487	0		1513	9985	1		0015	1498	8502	0 24	6
55	59 40	9.8489	0		10.1511	9.9987	1		10.0013	10.1499	9.8501	20	5
56	44	8490	1		1510	9990	1		0010	1500	8500	16	4
57	48	8491	1		1509	9992	2		0008	1501	8499	12	3
58	52	8492	1		1508	9995	2		0005	1503	8497	8	2
59	56	8494	1		1506	9997	2		0003	1504	8496	0 4	1
60	60 0	9.8495			10.1505	10.0000			10.0000	10.1505	9.8495	0 0	0
′	m s	Cos.	0′.1 Diff.	1s Diff.	Sec.	Cot.	0′.1 Diff.	1s Diff.	Tan.	Cosec.	Sin.	m s	′
134° = 8h 56m]												[3h 0m = 45°	

Log. Sines to every Tenth of a Degree.

Degrees.	0°.0	0°.1	0°.2	0°.3	0°.4	0°.5	0°.6	0°.7	0°.8	0°.9	1°.0	Degrees.
	0′	6′	12′	18′	24′	30′	36′	42′	48′	54′	60′	
0	−∞	7.2419	7.5429	7.7190	7.8439	7.9408	8.0200	8.0870	8.1450	8.1961	8.2419	89
1	8.2419	8.2832	8.3210	8.3558	8.3880	8.4179	4459	4723	4971	5206	5428	88
2	5428	5640	5842	6035	6220	6397	6567	6731	6889	7041	7188	87
3	7188	7330	7468	7602	7731	7857	7979	8098	8213	• 8326	8436	86
4	8436	8543	8647	8749	8849	8946	9042	9135	9226	9315	9403	85
5	8.9403	8.9489	8.9573	8.9655	8.9736	8.9816	8.9894	8.9970	9.0046	9.0120	9.0192	84
6	9.0192	9.0264	9.0334	9.0403	9.0472	9.0539	9.0605	9.0670	0734	0797	0859	83
7	0859	0920	0981	1040	1099	1157	1214	1271	1326	1381	1436	82
8	1436	1489	1542	1594	1646	1697	1747	1797	1847	1895	1943	81
9	1943	1991	2038	2085	2131	2176	2221	2266	2310	2353	2397	80
10	9.2397	9.2439	9.2482	9.2524	9.2565	9.2606	9.2647	9.2687	9.2727	9.2767	9.2806	79
11	2806	2845	2883	2921	2959	2997	3034	3070	3107	3143	3179	78
12	3179	3214	3249	3284	3319	3353	3387	3421	3455	3488	3521	77
13	3521	3554	3586	3618	3650	3682	3713	3745	3775	3806	3837	76
14	3837	3867	3897	3927	3957	3986	4015	4044	4073	4102	4130	75
15	9.4130	9.4158	9.4186	9.4214	9.4242	9.4269	9.4296	9.4323	9.4350	9.4377	9.4403	74
16	4403	4430	4456	4482	4508	4533	4559	4584	4609	4634	4659	73
17	4659	4684	4709	4733	4757	4781	4805	4829	4853	4876	4900	72
18	4900	4923	4946	4969	4992	5015	5037	5060	5082	5104	5126	71
19	5126	5148	5170	5192	5213	5235	5256	5278	5299	5320	5341	70
20	9.5341	9.5361	9.5382	9.5402	9.5423	9.5443	9.5463	9.5484	9.5504	9.5523	9.5543	69
21	5543	5563	5583	5602	5621	5641	5660	5679	5698	5717	5736	68
22	5736	5754	5773	5792	5810	5828	5847	5865	5883	5901	5919	67
23	5919	5937	5954	5972	5990	6007	6024	6042	6059	6076	6093	66
24	6093	6110	6127	6144	6161	6177	6194	6210	6227	6243	6259	65
25	9.6259	9.6276	9.6292	9.6308	9.6324	9.6340	9.6356	9.6371	9.6387	9.6403	9.6418	64
26	6418	6434	6449	6465	6480	6495	6510	6526	6541	6556	6570	63
27	6570	6585	6600	6615	6629	6644	6659	6673	6687	6702	6716	62
28	6716	6730	6744	6759	6773	6787	6801	6814	6828	6842	6856	61
29	6856	6869	6883	6896	6910	6923	6937	6950	6963	6977	6990	60
30	9.6990	9.7003	9.7016	9.7029	9.7042	9.7055	9.7068	9.7080	9.7093	9.7106	9.7118	59
31	7118	7131	7144	7156	7168	7181	7193	7205	7218	7230	7242	58
32	7242	7254	7266	7278	7290	7302	7314	7326	7338	7349	7361	57
33	7361	7373	7384	7396	7407	7419	7430	7442	7453	7464	7476	56
34	7476	7487	7498	7509	7520	7531	7542	7553	7564	7575	7586	55
35	9.7586	9.7597	9.7607	9.7618	9.7629	9.7640	9.7650	9.7661	9.7671	9.7682	9.7692	54
36	7692	7703	7713	7723	7734	7744	7754	7764	7774	7785	7795	53
37	7795	7805	7815	7825	7835	7844	7854	7864	7874	7884	7893	52
38	7893	7903	7913	7922	7932	7941	7951	7960	7970	7979	7989	51
39	7989	7998	8007	8017	8026	8035	8044	8053	8063	8072	8081	50
40	9.8081	9.8090	9.8099	9.8108	9.8117	9.8125	9.8134	9.8143	9.8152	9.8161	9.8169	49
41	8169	8178	8187	8195	8204	8213	8221	8230	8238	8247	8255	48
42	8255	8264	8272	8280	8289	8297	8305	8313	8322	8330	8338	47
43	8338	8346	8354	8362	8370	8378	8386	8394	8402	8410	8418	46
44	8418	8426	8433	8441	8449	8457	8464	8472	8480	8487	8495	45
Degrees.	60′	54′	48′	42′	36′	30′	24′	18′	12′	6′	0′	Degrees.
	1°.0	0°.9	0°.8	0°.7	0°.6	0°.5	0°.4	0°.3	0°.2	0°.1	0°.0	

Logarithmic Cosines.

Log. Sines to every Tenth of a Degree.

Degrees.	0°.0 0′	0°.1 6′	0°.2 12′	0°.3 18′	0°.4 24′	0°.5 30′	0°.6 36′	0°.7 42′	0°.8 48′	0°.9 54′	1°.0 60′	Degrees.
45	9.8495	9.8502	9.8510	9.8517	9.8525	9.8532	9.8540	9.8547	9.8555	9.8562	9.8569	44
46	8569	8577	8584	8591	8598	8606	8613	8620	8627	8634	8641	43
47	8641	8648	8655	8662	8669	8676	8683	8690	8697	8704	8711	42
48	8711	8718	8724	8731	8738	8745	8751	8758	8765	8771	8778	41
49	8778	8784	8791	8797	8804	8810	8817	8823	8830	8836	8843	40
50	9.8843	9.8849	9.8855	9.8862	9.8868	9.8874	9.8880	9.8887	9.8893	9.8899	9.8905	39
51	8905	8911	8917	8923	8929	8935	8941	8947	8953	8959	8965	38
52	8965	8971	8977	8983	8989	8995	9000	9006	9012	9018	9023	37
53	9023	9029	9035	9041	9046	9052	9057	9063	9069	9074	9080	36
54	9080	9085	9091	9096	9101	9107	9112	9118	9123	9128	9134	35
55	9.9134	9.9139	9.9144	9.9149	9.9155	9.9160	9.9165	9.9170	9.9175	9.9181	9.9186	34
56	9186	9191	9196	9201	9206	9211	9216	9221	9226	9231	9236	33
57	9236	9241	9246	9251	9255	9260	9265	9270	9275	9279	9284	32
58	9284	9289	9294	9298	9303	9308	9312	9317	9322	9326	9331	31
59	9331	9335	9340	9344	9349	9353	9358	9362	9367	9371	9375	30
60	9.9375	9.9380	9.9384	9.9388	9.9393	9.9397	9.9401	9.9406	9.9410	9.9414	9.9418	29
61	9418	9422	9427	9431	9435	9439	9443	9447	9451	9455	9459	28
62	9459	9463	9467	9471	9475	9479	9483	9487	9491	9495	9499	27
63	9499	9503	9506	9510	9514	9518	9522	9525	9529	9533	9537	26
64	9537	9540	9544	9548	9551	9555	9558	9562	9566	9569	9573	25
65	9.9573	9.9576	9.9580	9.9583	9.9587	9.9590	9.9594	9.9597	9.9601	9.9604	9.9607	24
66	9607	9611	9614	9617	9621	9624	9627	9631	9634	9637	9640	23
67	9640	9643	9647	9650	9653	9656	9659	9662	9665	9669	9672	22
68	9672	9675	9678	9681	9684	9687	9690	9693	9696	9699	9702	21
69	9702	9704	9707	9710	9713	9716	9719	9722	9724	9727	9730	20
70	9.9730	9.9733	9.9735	9.9738	9.9741	9.9743	9.9746	9.9749	9.9751	9.9754	9.9757	19
71	9757	9759	9762	9764	9767	9770	9772	9775	9777	9780	9782	18
72	9782	9785	9787	9789	9792	9794	9797	9799	9801	9804	9806	17
73	9806	9808	9811	9813	9815	9817	9820	9822	9824	9826	9828	16
74	9828	9831	9833	9835	9837	9839	9841	9843	9845	9847	9849	15
75	9.9849	9.9851	9.9853	9.9855	9.9857	9.9859	9.9861	9.9863	9.9865	9.9867	9.9869	14
76	9869	9871	9873	9875	9876	9878	9880	9882	9884	9885	9887	13
77	9887	9889	9891	9892	9894	9896	9897	9899	9901	9902	9904	12
78	9904	9906	9907	9909	9910	9912	9913	9915	9916	9918	9919	11
79	9919	9921	9922	9924	9925	9927	9928	9929	9931	9932	9934	10
80	9.9934	9.9935	9.9936	9.9937	9.9939	9.9940	9.9941	9.9943	9.9944	9.9945	9.9946	9
81	9946	9947	9949	9950	9951	9952	9953	9954	9955	9956	9958	8
82	9958	9959	9960	9961	9962	9963	9964	9965	9966	9967	9968	7
83	9968	9968	9969	9970	9971	9972	9973	9974	9975	9975	9976	6
84	9976	9977	9978	9978	9979	9980	9981	9981	9982	9983	9983	5
85	9.9983	9.9984	9.9985	9.9985	9.9986	9.9987	9.9987	9.9988	9.9988	9.9989	9.9989	4
86	9989	9990	9990	9991	9991	9992	9992	9993	9993	9994	9994	3
87	9994	9994	9995	9995	9996	9996	9996	9996	9997	9997	9997	2
88	9997	9998	9998	9998	9998	9999	9999	9999	9999	9999	9999	1
89	9999	9999	10.0000	10.0000	10.0000	10.0000	10.0000	10.0000	10.0000	10.0000	10.0000	0
Degrees.	60′ 1°.0	54′ 0°.9	48′ 0°.8	42′ 0°.7	36′ 0°.6	30′ 0°.5	24′ 0°.4	18′ 0°.3	12′ 0°.2	6′ 0°.1	0′ 0°.0	Degrees.

Logarithmic Cosines.

Log. Secants to every Tenth of a Degree.

Degrees.	0°.0 0′	0°.1 6′	0°.2 12′	0°.3 18′	0°.4 24′	0°.5 30′	0°.6 36′	0°.7 42′	0°.8 48′	0°.9 54′	1°.0 60′	Degrees.
0	10.0000	10.0000	10.0000	10.0000	10.0000	10.0000	10.0000	10.0000	10.0000	10.0001	10.0001	89
1	0001	0001	0001	0001	0001	0001	0002	0002	0002	0002	0003	88
2	0003	0003	0003	0003	0004	0004	0004	0005	0005	0006	0006	87
3	0006	0006	0007	0007	0008	0008	0009	0009	0010	0010	0011	86
4	0011	0011	0012	0012	0013	0013	0014	0015	0015	0016	0017	85
5	10.0017	10.0017	10.0018	10.0019	10.0019	10.0020	10.0021	10.0022	10.0022	10.0023	10.0024	84
6	0024	0025	0025	0026	0027	0028	0029	0030	0031	0032	0032	83
7	0032	0033	0034	0035	0036	0037	0038	0039	0040	0041	0042	82
8	0042	0044	0045	0046	0047	0048	0049	0050	0051	0053	0054	81
9	0054	0055	0056	0057	0059	0060	0061	0063	0064	0065	0066	80
10	10.0066	10.0068	10.0069	10.0071	10.0072	10.0073	10.0075	10.0076	10.0078	10.0079	10.0081	79
11	0081	0082	0084	0085	0087	0088	0090	0091	0093	0094	0096	78
12	0096	0098	0099	0101	0103	0104	0106	0108	0109	0111	0113	77
13	0113	0115	0116	0118	0120	0122	0124	0125	0127	0129	0131	76
14	0131	0133	0135	0137	0139	0141	0143	0145	0147	0149	0151	75
15	10.0151	10.0153	10.0155	10.0157	10.0159	10.0161	10.0163	10.0165	10.0167	10.0169	10.0172	74
16	0172	0174	0176	0178	0180	0183	0185	0187	0189	0192	0194	73
17	0194	0196	0199	0201	0203	0206	0208	0211	0213	0215	0218	72
18	0218	0220	0223	0225	0228	0230	0233	0236	0238	0241	0243	71
19	0243	0246	0249	0251	0254	0257	0259	0262	0265	0267	0270	70
20	10.0270	10.0273	10.0276	10.0278	10.0281	10.0284	10.0287	10.0290	10.0293	10.0296	10.0298	69
21	0298	0301	0304	0307	0310	0313	0316	0319	0322	0325	0328	68
22	0328	0331	0334	0338	0341	0344	0347	0350	0353	0357	0360	67
23	0360	0363	0366	0369	0373	0376	0379	0383	0386	0389	0393	66
24	0393	0396	0399	0403	0406	0410	0413	0417	0420	0424	0427	65
25	10.0427	10.0431	10.0434	10.0438	10.0442	10.0445	10.0449	10.0452	10.0456	10.0460	10.0463	64
26	0463	0467	0471	0475	0478	0482	0486	0490	0494	0497	0501	63
27	0501	0505	0509	0513	0517	0521	0525	0529	0533	0537	0541	62
28	0541	0545	0549	0553	0557	0561	0565	0569	0573	0578	0582	61
29	0582	0586	0590	0594	0599	0603	0607	0612	0616	0620	0625	60
30	10.0625	10.0629	10.0633	10.0638	10.0642	10.0647	10.0651	10.0656	10.0660	10.0665	10.0669	59
31	0669	0674	0678	0683	0688	0692	0697	0702	0706	0711	0716	58
32	0716	0721	0725	0730	0735	0740	0745	0749	0754	0759	0764	57
33	0764	0769	0774	0779	0784	0789	0794	0799	0804	0809	0814	56
34	0814	0819	0825	0830	0835	0840	0845	0851	0856	0861	0866	55
35	10.0866	10.0872	10.0877	10.0882	10.0888	10.0893	10.0899	10.0904	10.0909	10.0915	10.0920	54
36	0920	0926	0931	0937	0943	0948	0954	0959	0965	0971	0977	53
37	0977	0982	0988	0994	1000	1005	1011	1017	1023	1029	1035	52
38	1035	1041	1047	1053	1059	1065	1071	1077	1083	1089	1095	51
39	1095	1101	1107	1113	1120	1126	1132	1138	1145	1151	1157	50
40	10.1157	10.1164	10.1170	10.1177	10.1183	10.1190	10.1196	10.1203	10.1209	10.1216	10.1222	49
41	1222	1229	1235	1242	1249	1255	1262	1269	1276	1282	1289	48
42	1289	1296	1303	1310	1317	1324	1331	1338	1345	1352	1359	47
43	1359	1366	1373	1380	1387	1394	1402	1409	1416	1423	1431	46
44	1431	1438	1445	1453	1460	1468	1475	1483	1490	1498	1505	45
Degrees.	60′ 1°.0	54′ 0°.9	48′ 0°.8	42′ 0°.7	36′ 0°.6	30′ 0°.5	24′ 0°.4	18′ 0°.3	12′ 0°.2	6′ 0°.1	0′ 0°.0	Degrees.

Logarithmic Cosecants.

Log. Secants to every Tenth of a Degree.

Degrees.	0°.0 0′	0°.1 6′	0°.2 12′	0°.3 18′	0°.4 24′	0°.5 30′	0°.6 36′	0°.7 42′	0°.8 48′	0°.9 54′	1°.0 60′	Degrees.
45	10.1505	10.1513	10.1520	10.1528	10.1536	10.1543	10.1551	10.1559	10.1567	10.1574	10.1582	44
46	1582	1590	1598	1606	1614	1622	1630	1638	1646	1654	1662	43
47	1662	1670	1678	1687	1695	1703	1711	1720	1728	1736	1745	42
48	1745	1753	1762	1770	1779	1787	1796	1805	1813	1822	1831	41
49	1831	1839	1848	1857	1866	1875	1883	1892	1901	1910	1919	40
50	10.1919	10.1928	10.1937	10.1947	10.1956	10.1965	10.1974	10.1983	10.1993	10.2002	10.2011	39
51	2011	2021	2030	2040	2049	2058	2068	2078	2087	2097	2107	38
52	2107	2116	2126	2136	2146	2156	2165	2175	2185	2195	2205	37
53	2205	2215	2226	2236	2246	2256	2266	2277	2287	2297	2308	36
54	2308	2318	2329	2339	2350	2360	2371	2382	2393	2403	2414	35
55	10.2414	10.2425	10.2436	10.2447	10.2458	10.2469	10.2480	10.2491	10.2502	10.2513	10.2524	34
56	2524	2536	2547	2558	2570	2581	2593	2604	2616	2627	2639	33
57	2639	2651	2662	2674	2686	2698	2710	2722	2734	2746	2758	32
58	2758	2770	2782	2795	2807	2819	2832	2844	2856	2869	2882	31
59	2882	2894	2907	2920	2932	2945	2958	2971	2984	2997	3010	30
60	10.3010	10.3023	10.3037	10.3050	10.3063	10.3077	10.3090	10.3104	10.3117	10.3131	10.3144	29
61	3144	3158	3172	3186	3199	3213	3227	3241	3256	3270	3284	28
62	3284	3298	3313	3327	3341	3356	3371	3385	3400	3415	3430	27
63	3430	3444	3460	3474	3490	3505	3520	3535	3551	3566	3582	26
64	3582	3597	3613	3629	3644	3660	3676	3692	3708	3724	3741	25
65	10.3741	10.3757	10.3773	10.3790	10.3806	10.3823	10.3839	10.3856	10.3873	10.3890	10.3907	24
66	3907	3924	3941	3958	3976	3993	4010	4028	4046	4063	4081	23
67	4081	4099	4117	4135	4153	4172	4190	4208	4227	4246	4264	22
68	4264	4283	4302	4321	4340	4359	4379	4398	4417	4437	4457	21
69	4457	4477	4496	4516	4537	4557	4577	4598	4618	4639	4659	20
70	10.4659	10.4680	10.4701	10.4722	10.4744	10.4765	10.4787	10.4808	10.4830	10.4852	10.4874	19
71	4874	4896	4918	4940	4963	4985	5008	5031	5054	5077	5100	18
72	5100	5124	5147	5171	5195	5219	5243	5267	5291	5316	5341	17
73	5341	5366	5391	5416	5441	5467	5492	5518	5544	5570	5597	16
74	5597	5623	5650	5677	5704	5731	5758	5786	5814	5842	5870	15
75	10.5870	10.5898	10.5927	10.5956	10.5985	10.6014	10.6043	10.6073	10.6103	10.6133	10.6163	14
76	6163	6194	6225	6255	6287	6318	6350	6382	6414	6446	6479	13
77	6479	6512	6545	6579	6613	6647	6681	6716	6750	6786	6821	12
78	6821	6857	6893	6930	6966	7003	7041	7079	7117	7155	7194	11
79	7194	7233	7273	7313	7353	7394	7435	7476	7518	7561	7603	10
80	10.7603	10.7647	10.7690	10.7734	10.7779	10.7824	10.7869	10.7915	10.7962	10.8009	10.8057	9
81	8057	8105	8153	8203	8253	8303	8354	8406	8458	8511	8564	8
82	8564	8619	8674	8729	8786	8843	8901	8960	9019	9080	9141	7
83	9141	9203	9266	9330	9395	9461	9528	9597	9666	9736	9808	6
84	9808	9880	9954	11.0030	11.0106	11.0184	11.0264	11.0345	11.0427	11.0511	11.0597	5
85	11.0597	11.0685	11.0774	11.0865	11.0958	11.1054	11.1151	11.1251	11.1353	11.1457	11.1564	4
86	1564	1674	1787	1902	2021	2143	2269	2398	2532	2670	2812	3
87	2812	2959	3111	3269	3433	3603	3780	3965	4158	4360	4572	2
88	4572	4794	5029	5277	5541	5821	6120	6442	6790	7168	7581	1
89	7581	8039	8550	9130	9800	12.0592	12.1561	12.2810	12.4571	12.7581	+ ∞	0
Degrees.	60′ 1°.0	54′ 0°.9	48′ 0°.8	42′ 0°.7	36′ 0°.6	30′ 0°.5	24′ 0°.4	18′ 0°.3	12′ 0°.2	6′ 0°.1	0′ 0°.0	Degrees.

Logarithmic Cosecants.

Logarithmic Tangents to every Tenth of a Degree.

Degrees.	0°.0 0′	0°.1 6′	0°.2 12′	0°.3 18′	0°.4 24′	0°.5 30′	0°.6 36′	0°.7 42′	0°.8 48′	0°.9 54′	1°.0 60′	Degrees.
0	—∞	7.2419	7.5429	7.7190	7.8439	7.9409	8.0200	8.0870	8.1450	8.1962	8.2419	89
1	8.2419	8.2833	8.3211	8.3559	8.3881	8.4181	4461	4725	4973	5208	5431	88
2	5431	5643	5845	6038	6223	6401	6571	6736	6894	7046	7194	87
3	7194	7337	7475	7609	7739	7865	7988	8107	8223	8336	8446	86
4	8446	8554	8659	8762	8862	8960	9056	9150	9241	9331	9420	85
5	8.9420	8.9506	8.9591	8.9674	8.9756	8.9836	8.9915	8.9992	9.0068	9.0143	9.0216	84
6	9.0216	9.0289	9.0360	9.0430	9.0499	9.0567	9.0633	9.0699	0764	0828	0891	83
7	0891	0954	1015	1076	1135	1194	1252	1310	1367	1423	1478	82
8	1478	1533	1587	1640	1693	1745	1797	1848	1898	1948	1997	81
9	1997	2046	2094	2142	2189	2236	2282	2328	2374	2419	2463	80
10	9.2463	9.2507	9.2551	9.2594	9.2637	9.2680	9.2722	9.2764	9.2805	9.2846	9.2887	79
11	2887	2927	2967	3006	3046	3085	3123	3162	3200	3237	3275	78
12	3275	3312	3349	3385	3422	3458	3493	3529	3564	3599	3634	77
13	3634	3668	3702	3736	3770	3804	3837	3870	3903	3935	3968	76
14	3968	4000	4032	4064	4095	4127	4158	4189	4220	4250	4281	75
15	9.4281	9.4311	9.4341	9.4371	9.4400	9.4430	9.4459	9.4488	9.4517	9.4546	9.4575	74
16	4575	4603	4632	4660	4688	4716	4744	4771	4799	4826	4853	73
17	4853	4880	4907	4934	4961	4987	5014	5040	5066	5092	5118	72
18	5118	5143	5169	5195	5220	5245	5270	5295	5320	5345	5370	71
19	5370	5394	5419	5443	5467	5491	5516	5539	5563	5587	5611	70
20	9.5611	9.5634	9.5658	9.5681	9.5704	9.5727	9.5750	9.5773	9.5796	9.5819	9.5842	69
21	5842	5864	5887	5909	5932	5954	5976	5998	6020	6042	6064	68
22	6064	6086	6108	6129	6151	6172	6194	6215	6236	6257	6279	67
23	6279	6300	6321	6341	6362	6383	6404	6424	6445	6465	6486	66
24	6485	6506	6527	6547	6567	6587	6607	6627	6647	6667	6687	65
25	9.6687	9.6706	9.6726	9.6746	9.6765	9.6785	9.6804	9.6824	9.6843	9.6863	9.6882	64
26	6882	6901	6920	6939	6958	6977	6996	7015	7034	7053	7072	63
27	7072	7090	7109	7128	7146	7165	7183	7202	7220	7238	7257	62
28	7257	7275	7293	7311	7330	7348	7366	7384	7402	7420	7438	61
29	7438	7455	7473	7491	7509	7526	7544	7562	7579	7597	7614	60
30	9.7614	9.7632	9.7649	9.7667	9.7684	9.7701	9.7719	9.7736	9.7753	9.7771	9.7788	59
31	7788	7805	7822	7839	7856	7873	7890	7907	7924	7941	7958	58
32	7958	7975	7992	8008	8025	8042	8059	8075	8092	8109	8125	57
33	8125	8142	8158	8175	8191	8208	8224	8241	8257	8274	8290	56
34	8290	8306	8323	8339	8355	8371	8388	8404	8420	8436	8452	55
35	9.8452	9.8468	9.8484	9.8501	9.8517	9.8533	9.8549	9.8565	9.8581	9.8597	9.8613	54
36	8613	8629	8644	8660	8676	8692	8708	8724	8740	8755	8771	53
37	8771	8787	8803	8818	8834	8850	8865	8881	8897	8912	8928	52
38	8928	8944	8959	8975	8990	9006	9022	9037	9053	9068	9084	51
39	9084	9099	9115	9130	9146	9161	9176	9192	9207	9223	9238	50
40	9.9238	9.9254	9.9269	9.9284	9.9300	9.9315	9.9330	9.9346	9.9361	9.9376	9.9392	49
41	9392	9407	9422	9438	9453	9468	9483	9499	9514	9529	9544	48
42	9544	9560	9575	9590	9605	9621	9636	9651	9666	9681	9697	47
43	9697	9712	9727	9742	9757	9772	9788	9803	9818	9833	9848	46
44	9848	9864	9879	9894	9909	9924	9939	9955	9970	9985	10.0000	45
Degrees.	60′ 1°.0	54′ 0°.9	48′ 0°.8	42′ 0°.7	36′ 0°.6	30′ 0°.5	24′ 0°.4	18′ 0°.3	12′ 0°.2	6′ 0°.1	0′ 0°.0	Degrees.

Logarithmic Cotangents.

Logarithmic Tangents to every Tenth of a Degree.

Degrees.	0°.0 0′	0°.1 6′	0°.2 12′	0°.3 18′	0°.4 24′	0°.5 30′	0°.6 36′	0°.7 42′	0°.8 48′	0°.9 54′	1°.0 60′	Degrees.
45	10.0000	10.0015	10.0030	10.0045	10.0061	10.0076	10.0091	10.0106	10.0121	10.0136	10.0152	44
46	0152	0167	0182	0197	0212	0227	0243	0258	0273	0288	0303	43
47	0303	0319	0334	0349	0364	0379	0395	0410	0425	0440	0456	42
48	0456	0471	0486	0501	0517	0532	0547	0562	0578	0593	0608	41
49	0608	0624	0639	0654	0670	0685	0700	0716	0731	0746	0762	40
50	10.0762	10.0777	10.0793	10.0808	10.0824	10.0839	10.0854	10.0870	10.0885	10.0901	10.0916	39
51	0916	0932	0947	0963	0978	0994	1010	1025	1041	1056	1072	38
52	1072	1088	1103	1119	1135	1150	1166	1182	1197	1213	1229	37
53	1229	1245	1260	1276	1292	1308	1324	1340	1356	1371	1387	36
54	1387	1403	1419	1435	1451	1467	1483	1499	1516	1532	1548	35
55	10.1548	10.1564	10.1580	10.1596	10.1612	10.1629	10.1645	10.1661	10.1677	10.1694	10.1710	34
56	1710	1726	1743	1759	1776	1792	1809	1825	1842	1858	1875	33
57	1875	1891	1908	1925	1941	1958	1975	1992	2008	2025	2042	32
58	2042	2059	2076	2093	2110	2127	2144	2161	2178	2195	2212	31
59	2212	2229	2247	2264	2281	2299	2316	2333	2351	2368	2386	30
60	10.2386	10.2403	10.2421	10.2438	10.2456	10.2474	10.2491	10.2509	10.2527	10.2545	10.2562	29
61	2562	2580	2598	2616	2634	2652	2670	2689	2707	2725	2743	28
62	2743	2762	2780	2798	2817	2835	2854	2872	2891	2910	2928	27
63	2928	2947	2966	2985	3004	3023	3042	3061	3080	3099	3118	26
64	3118	3137	3157	3176	3196	3215	3235	3254	3274	3294	3313	25
65	10.3313	10.3333	10.3353	10.3373	10.3393	10.3413	10.3433	10.3453	10.3473	10.3494	10.3514	24
66	3514	3535	3555	3576	3596	3617	3638	3659	3679	3700	3721	23
67	3721	3743	3764	3785	3806	3828	3849	3871	3892	3914	3936	22
68	3936	3958	3980	4002	4024	4046	4068	4091	4113	4136	4158	21
69	4158	4181	4204	4227	4250	4273	4296	4319	4342	4366	4389	20
70	10.4389	10.4413	10.4437	10.4461	10.4484	10.4509	10.4533	10.4557	10.4581	10.4606	10.4630	19
71	4630	4655	4680	4705	4730	4755	4780	4805	4831	4857	4882	18
72	4882	4908	4934	4960	4986	5013	5039	5066	5093	5120	5147	17
73	5147	5174	5201	5229	5256	5284	5312	5340	5368	5397	5425	16
74	5425	5454	5483	5512	5541	5570	5600	5629	5659	5689	5719	15
75	10.5719	10.5750	10.5780	10.5811	10.5842	10.5873	10.5905	10.5936	10.5968	10.6000	10.6032	14
76	6032	6065	6097	6130	6163	6196	6230	6264	6298	6332	6366	13
77	6366	6401	6436	6471	6507	6542	6578	6615	6651	6688	6725	12
78	6725	6763	6800	6838	6877	6915	6954	6994	7033	7073	7113	11
79	7113	7154	7195	7236	7278	7320	7363	7406	7449	7493	7537	10
80	10.7537	10.7581	10.7626	10.7672	10.7718	10.7764	10.7811	10.7858	10.7906	10.7954	10.8003	9
81	8003	8052	8102	8152	8203	8255	8307	8360	8413	8467	8522	8
82	8522	8577	8633	8690	8748	8806	8865	8924	8985	9046	9109	7
83	9109	9172	9236	9301	9367	9433	9501	9570	9640	9711	9784	6
84	9784	9857	9932	11.0008	11.0085	11.0164	11.0244	11.0326	11.0409	11.0494	11.0580	5
85	11.0580	11.0669	11.0759	11.0850	11.0944	11.1040	11.1138	11.1238	11.1341	11.1446	11.1554	4
86	1554	1664	1777	1893	2012	2135	2261	2391	2525	2663	2806	3
87	2806	2954	3106	3264	3429	3599	3777	3962	4155	4357	4569	2
88	4569	4792	5027	5275	5539	5819	6119	6441	6789	11.7167	7581	1
89	7581	8038	8550	9130	9800	12.0591	12.1561	12.2810	12.4571	12.7581	+∞	0
Degrees.	60′ 1°.0	54′ 0°.9	48′ 0°.8	42′ 0°.7	36′ 0°.6	30′ 0°.5	24′ 0°.4	18′ 0°.3	12′ 0°.2	6′ 0°.1	0′ 0°.0	Degrees.

Logarithmic Cotangents.

Log. Tangents and Cotangents in Time.

m	0h	Diff. 0m.1	1h	Diff. 0m.1	2h	Diff. 0m.1	3h	Diff. 0m.1	4h	Diff. 0m.1	5h	Diff. 0m.1	m
	6h		7h		8h		9h		10h		11h		
0	− ∞		9.4281		9.7614		10.0000		10.2386		10.5719		60
1	7.6398	301	4356	7	7658	4	0038	4	2429	4	5796	8	59
2	7.9409	176	4430	14	7701	9	0076	8	2474	9	5873	16	58
3	8.1170	125	4503	21	7745	13	0114	11	2518	13	5952	25	57
4	8.2419	97	4575	28	7788	17	0152	15	2562	18	6032	33	56
5	8.3389	79	9.4646	35	9.7831	21	10.0190	19	10.2607	22	10.6114	41	55
6	4181	67	4716	42	7873	26	0228	23	2652	27	6196	49	54
7	4851	58	4785	49	7916	30	0265	27	2698	31	6281	57	53
8	5431	51	4853	56	7958	34	0303	30	2743	36	6366	66	52
9	5943	46	4921	63	8000	39	0341	34	2789	40	6454	74	51
10	8.6401	41	9.4987		9.8042		10.0379		10.2835		10.6542		50
11	6815	38	5053	6	8084	4	0418	4	2882	5	6633	10	49
12	7194	35	5118	13	8125	8	0456	8	2928	9	6725	20	48
13	7542	32	5182	19	8167	12	0494	11	2975	13	6819	29	47
14	7865	30	5245	25	8208	16	0532	15	3023	19	6915	39	46
15	8.8165	28	9.5308	31	9.8249	20	10.0570	19	10.3070	24	10.7013	49	45
16	8446	26	5370	38	8290	25	0608	23	3118	28	7113	59	44
17	8711	25	5431	44	8331	29	0647	27	3166	33	7216	69	43
18	8960	24	5491	50	8371	33	0685	30	3215	38	7320	78	42
19	9196	22	5551	56	8412	37	0723	34	3264	43	7427	88	41
20	8.9420	21	9.5611		9.8452		10.0762		10.3313		10.7537		40
21	9633	20	5669	6	8493	4	0800	4	3363	5	7649	13	39
22	9836	19	5727	11	8533	8	0839	8	3413	10	7764	26	38
23	9.0030	19	5785	17	8573	12	0878	12	3463	15	7882	39	37
24	0216	18	5842	22	8613	16	0916	16	3514	20	8003	52	36
25	9.0395	17	9.5898	28	9.8652	20	10.0955	19	10.3565	25	10.8127	65	35
26	0567	16	5954	34	8692	24	0994	23	3617	31	8255	78	34
27	0732	16	6009	39	8732	28	1033	27	3669	36	8387	91	33
28	0891	15	6064	45	8771	32	1072	31	3721	41	8522	104	32
29	1045	15	6118	50	8811	36	1111	35	3774	46	8662	117	31
30	9.1194		9.6172		9.8850		10.1150		10.3828		10.8806	14	30
31	1338	13	6226	5	8889	4	1189	4	3882	6	8955	15	29
32	1478	26	6279	10	8928	8	1229	8	3936	11	9109	15	28
33	1613	39	6331	16	8967	12	1268	12	3991	17	9268	16	27
34	1745	52	6383	21	9006	16	1308	16	4046	22	9433	16	26
35	9.1873	65	9.6435	26	9.9045	19	10.1348	20	10.4102	28	10.9605	17	25
36	1997	78	6486	31	9084	23	1387	24	4158	34	9784	18	24
37	2118	91	6537	36	9122	27	1427	28	4215	39	9970	19	23
38	2236	104	6587	42	9161	31	1467	32	4273	45	11.0164	19	22
39	2351	117	6637	47	9200	35	1507	36	4331	50	0367	20	21
40	9.2463		9.6687		9.9238		10.1548		10.4389		11.0580	21	20
41	2573	10	6736	5	9277	4	1588	4	4449	6	0804	22	19
42	2680	20	6785	10	9315	8	1629	8	4509	12	1040	24	18
43	2784	29	6834	14	9353	11	1669	12	4569	19	1289	25	17
44	2887	39	6882	19	9392	15	1710	16	4630	25	1554	26	16
45	9.2987	49	9.6930	24	9.9430	19	10.1751	20	10.4692	31	11.1835	28	15
46	3085	59	6977	29	9468	23	1792	25	4755	37	2135	30	14
47	3181	69	7025	34	9506	27	1833	29	4818	43	2458	32	13
48	3275	78	7072	38	9544	30	1875	33	4882	50	2806	35	12
49	3367	88	7118	43	9582	34	1916	37	4947	56	3185	38	11
50	9.3458		9.7165		9.9621		10.1958		10.5013		11.3599	41	10
51	3546	8	7211	5	9659	4	2000	4	5079	7	4057	46	9
52	3634	16	7257	9	9697	8	2042	8	5147	14	4569	51	8
53	3719	25	7302	13	9735	11	2084	13	5215	21	5150	58	7
54	3804	33	7348	18	9773	15	2127	17	5284	28	5819	67	6
55	9.3886	41	9.7393	22	9.9810	19	10.2169	21	10.5354	35	11.6611	79	5
56	3968	49	7438	27	9848	23	2212	25	5425	43	7581	97	4
57	4048	57	7482	31	9886	27	2255	30	5497	50	8830	125	3
58	4127	66	7526	36	9924	30	2299	34	5570	57	12.0591	176	2
59	4204	74	7571	40	9962	34	2342	38	5644	64	3602	301	1
60	9.4281		9.7614		10.0000		10.2386		10.5719		+ ∞		0
m	11h	Diff. 0m.1	10h	Diff. 0m.1	9h	Diff. 0m.1	8h	Diff. 0m.1	7h	Diff. 0m.1	6h	Diff. 0m.1	m
	5h		4h		3h		2h		1h		0h		

☞ Read "Tangents" in upper line and "Cotangents" in lower line of Hour Arguments alike at top and bottom, taking the minutes in left or right column according as the hours are taken at top or bottom.

Lengths of Circular Arcs.

Degrees.	0°.0 0′	0°.1 6′	0°.2 12′	0°.3 18′	0°.4 24′	0°.5 30′	0°.6 36′	0°.7 42′	0°.8 48′	0°.9 54′
0	0.0000	0.0017	0.0035	0.0052	0.0070	0.0087	0.0105	0.0122	0.0140	0.0157
1	0175	0192	0209	0227	0244	0262	0280	0297	0317	0332
2	0349	0367	0384	0401	0419	0436	0454	0471	0489	0506
3	0524	0541	0559	0576	0594	0611	0628	0646	0664	0681
4	0698	0716	0733	0750	0768	0785	0803	0820	0838	0855
5	0.0873	0.0890	0.0908	0.0925	0.0943	0.0960	0.0978	0.0995	0.1012	0.1030
6	1047	1065	1082	1099	1117	1134	1152	1169	1187	1204
7	1222	1239	1257	1274	1292	1309	1327	1344	1361	1379
8	1396	1414	1431	1449	1466	1484	1501	1518	1536	1553
9	1571	1588	1606	1623	1641	1658	1676	1693	1710	1728
10	0.1745	0.1763	0.1780	0.1798	0.1815	0.1833	0.1850	0.1867	0.1885	0.1902
11	1920	1937	1955	1972	1990	2007	2025	2042	2059	2077
12	2094	2112	2129	2147	2164	2182	2199	2216	2234	2251
13	2269	2286	2304	2321	2339	2356	2374	2391	2409	2426
14	2443	2461	2478	2496	2513	2531	2548	2566	2583	2601
15	0.2618	0.2635	0.2653	0.2670	0.2688	0.2705	0.2723	0.2740	0.2758	0.2775
16	2793	2810	2827	2845	2862	2880	2897	2915	2932	2950
17	2967	2985	3002	3019	3037	3054	3072	3089	3107	3124
18	3142	3159	3177	3194	3212	3229	3246	3264	3281	3299
19	3316	3334	3351	3368	3386	3403	3421	3438	3456	3473
20	0.3491	0.3508	0.3526	0.3543	0.3561	0.3578	0.3596	0.3613	0.3630	0.3648
21	3665	3683	3700	3718	3735	3752	3770	3787	3805	3822
22	3840	3857	3875	3892	3910	3927	3945	3962	3979	3997
23	4014	4032	4049	4067	4084	4102	4119	4136	4154	4171
24	4189	4206	4224	4241	4259	4276	4294	4311	4328	4346
25	0.4363	0.4381	0.4398	0.4416	0.4433	0.4451	0.4468	0.4486	0.4503	0.4520
26	4538	4555	4573	4590	4608	4625	4643	4660	4678	4695
27	4712	4730	4747	4765	4782	4800	4817	4835	4852	4869
28	4887	4904	4922	4939	4957	4974	4992	5009	5027	5044
29	5061	5079	5096	5114	5131	5149	5166	5184	5201	5219
30	0.5236	0.5253	0.5271	0.5288	0.5306	0.5323	0.5341	0.5358	0.5376	0.5393
31	5411	5428	5445	5463	5480	5498	5515	5533	5550	5568
32	5585	5603	5620	5638	5655	5673	5690	5707	5725	5743
33	5760	5777	5795	5812	5830	5847	5865	5882	5899	5917
34	5934	5952	5969	5986	6004	6021	6039	6056	6074	6091
35	0.6109	0.6126	0.6144	0.6161	0.6179	0.6196	0.6213	0.6231	0.6248	0.6266
36	6283	6301	6318	6336	6353	6370	6388	6405	6423	6440
37	6458	6475	6493	6510	6528	6545	6563	6580	6597	6615
38	6632	6650	6667	6685	6702	6720	6737	6754	6772	6789
39	6807	6824	6842	6859	6877	6894	6912	6929	6946	6964
40	0.6981	0.6999	0.7016	0.7034	0.7051	0.7069	0.7086	0.7103	0.7121	0.7138
41	7156	7173	7191	7208	7226	7243	7261	7278	7296	7313
42	7330	7348	7365	7383	7400	7418	7435	7453	7470	7487
43	7505	7522	7540	7557	7575	7592	7610	7627	7645	7662
44	7679	7697	7714	7732	7749	7767	7784	7802	7819	7836
45	0.7854	0.7871	0.7889	0.7906	0.7924	0.7941	0.7959	0.7976	0.7994	0.8011
46	8029	8046	8063	8081	8098	8116	8133	8151	8168	8186
47	8203	8220	8238	8255	8273	8290	8308	8325	8343	8360
48	8378	8395	8413	8430	8448	8465	8482	8500	8517	8535
49	8552	8570	8587	8604	8622	8639	8657	8674	8692	8709
50	0.8727	0.8744	0.8762	0.8779	0.8797	0.8814	0.8831	0.8849	0.8866	0.8884
51	8901	8919	8936	8953	8971	8988	9006	9023	9041	9058
52	9076	9093	9111	9128	9146	9163	9181	9198	9215	9233
53	9250	9268	9285	9303	9320	9338	9355	9372	9390	9407
54	9425	9442	9460	9477	9495	9512	9530	9547	9564	9582
55	0.9599	0.9617	0.9634	0.9652	0.9669	0.9687	0.9704	0.9721	0.9739	0.9756
56	9774	9791	9809	9826	9844	9861	9879	9896	9914	9931
57	9948	9966	9983	1.0001	1.0018	1.0036	1.0053	1.0071	1.0088	1.0105
58	1.0123	1.0140	1.0158	0175	0193	0210	0228	0245	0263	0280
59	0297	0315	0332	0350	0367	0385	0402	0420	0437	0455

Natural Sines.

Degrees.	0°.0 0′	0°.1 6′	0°.2 12′	0°.3 18′	0°.4 24′	0°.5 30′	0°.6 36′	0°.7 42′	0°.8 48′	0°.9 54′	1°.0 60′	Degrees.
0	0.0000	0.0017	0.0035	0.0052	0.0070	0.0087	0.0105	0.0122	0.0140	0.0157	0.0175	**89**
1	0175	0192	0209	0227	0244	0262	0279	0297	0314	0332	0349	**88**
2	0349	0366	0384	0401	0419	0436	0454	0471	0488	0506	0523	**87**
3	0523	0541	0558	0576	0593	0610	0628	0645	0663	0680	0698	**86**
4	0698	0715	0732	0750	0767	0785	0802	0819	0837	0854	0872	**85**
5	0.0872	0.0889	0.0906	0.0924	0.0941	0.0958	0.0976	0.0993	0.1011	0.1028	0.1045	**84**
6	1045	1063	1080	1097	1115	1132	1149	1167	1184	1201	1219	**83**
7	1219	1236	1253	1271	1288	1305	1323	1340	1357	1374	1392	**82**
8	1392	1409	1426	1444	1461	1478	1495	1513	1530	1547	1564	**81**
9	1564	1582	1599	1616	1633	1650	1668	1685	1702	1719	1736	**80**
10	0.1736	0.1754	0.1771	0.1788	0.1805	0.1822	0.1840	0.1857	0.1874	0.1891	0.1908	**79**
11	1908	1925	1942	1959	1977	1994	2011	2028	2045	2062	2079	**78**
12	2079	2096	2113	2130	2147	2164	2181	2198	2215	2233	2250	**77**
13	2250	2267	2284	2300	2317	2334	2351	2368	2385	2402	2419	**76**
14	2419	2436	2453	2470	2487	2504	2521	2538	2554	2571	2588	**75**
15	0.2588	0.2605	0.2622	0.2639	0.2656	0.2672	0.2689	0.2706	0.2723	0.2740	0.2756	**74**
16	2756	2773	2790	2807	2823	2840	2857	2874	2890	2907	2924	**73**
17	2924	2940	2957	2974	2990	3007	3024	3040	3057	3074	3090	**72**
18	3090	3107	3123	3140	3156	3173	3190	3206	3223	3239	3256	**71**
19	3256	3272	3289	3305	3322	3338	3355	3371	3387	3404	3420	**70**
20	0.3420	0.3437	0.3453	0.3469	0.3486	0.3502	0.3518	0.3535	0.3551	0.3567	0.3584	**69**
21	3584	3600	3616	3633	3649	3665	3681	3697	3714	3730	3746	**68**
22	3746	3762	3778	3795	3811	3827	3843	3859	3875	3891	3907	**67**
23	3907	3923	3939	3955	3971	3987	4003	4019	4035	4051	4067	**66**
24	4067	4083	4099	4115	4131	4147	4163	4179	4195	4210	4226	**65**
25	0.4226	0.4242	0.4258	0.4274	0.4289	0.4305	0.4321	0.4337	0.4352	0.4368	0.4384	**64**
26	4384	4399	4415	4431	4446	4462	4478	4493	4509	4524	4540	**63**
27	4540	4555	4571	4586	4602	4617	4633	4648	4664	4679	4695	**62**
28	4695	4710	4726	4741	4756	4772	4787	4802	4818	4833	4848	**61**
29	4848	4863	4879	4894	4909	4924	4939	4955	4970	4985	5000	**60**
30	0.5000	0.5015	0.5030	0.5045	0.5060	0.5075	0.5090	0.5105	0.5120	0.5135	0.5150	**59**
31	5150	5165	5180	5195	5210	5225	5240	5255	5270	5284	5299	**58**
32	5299	5314	5329	5344	5358	5373	5388	5402	5417	5432	5446	**57**
33	5446	5461	5476	5490	5505	5519	5534	5548	5563	5577	5592	**56**
34	5592	5606	5621	5635	5650	5664	5678	5693	5707	5721	5736	**55**
35	0.5736	0.5750	0.5764	0.5779	0.5793	0.5807	0.5821	0.5835	0.5850	0.5864	0.5878	**54**
36	5878	5892	5906	5920	5934	5948	5962	5976	5990	6004	6018	**53**
37	6018	6032	6046	6060	6074	6088	6101	6115	6129	6143	6157	**52**
38	6157	6170	6184	6198	6211	6225	6239	6252	6266	6280	6293	**51**
39	6293	6307	6320	6334	6347	6361	6374	6388	6401	6414	6428	**50**
40	0.6428	0.6441	0.6455	0.6468	0.6481	0.6494	0.6508	0.6521	0.6534	0.6547	0.6561	**49**
41	6561	6574	6587	6600	6613	6626	6639	6652	6665	6678	6691	**48**
42	6691	6704	6717	6730	6743	6756	6769	6782	6794	6807	6820	**47**
43	6820	6833	6845	6858	6871	6884	6896	6909	6921	6934	6947	**46**
44	6947	6959	6972	6984	6997	7009	7022	7034	7046	7059	7071	**45**
Degrees.	60′ 1°.0	54′ 0°.9	48′ 0°.8	42′ 0°.7	36′ 0°.6	30′ 0°.5	24′ 0°.4	18′ 0°.3	12′ 0°.2	6′ 0°.1	0′ 0°.0	Degrees.

Natural Cosines.

Natural Sines.

Degrees.	0°.0 0′	0°.1 6′	0°.2 12′	0°.3 18′	0°.4 24′	0°.5 30′	0°.6 36′	0°.7 42	0°.8 48′	0°.9 54′	1°.0 60′	Degrees.
45	0.7071	0.7083	0.7096	0.7108	0.7120	0.7133	0.7145	0.7157	0.7169	0.7181	0.7193	44
46	7193	7206	7218	7230	7242	7254	7266	7278	7290	7302	7314	43
47	7314	7325	7337	7349	7361	7373	7385	7396	7408	7420	7431	42
48	7431	7443	7455	7466	7478	7490	7501	7513	7524	7536	7547	41
49	7547	7559	7570	7581	7593	7604	7615	7627	7638	7649	7660	40
50	0.7660	0.7672	0.7683	0.7694	0.7705	0.7716	0.7727	0.7738	0.7749	0.7760	0.7771	39
51	7771	7782	7793	7804	7815	7826	7837	7848	7859	7869	7880	38
52	7880	7891	7902	7912	7923	7934	7944	7955	7965	7976	7986	37
53	7986	7997	8007	8018	8028	8039	8049	8059	8070	8080	8090	36
54	8090	8100	8111	8121	8131	8141	8151	8161	8171	8181	8192	35
55	0.8192	0.8202	0.8211	0.8221	0.8231	0.8241	0.8251	0.8261	0.8271	0.8281	0.8290	34
56	8290	8300	8310	8320	8329	8339	8348	8358	8368	8377	8387	33
57	8387	8396	8406	8415	8425	8434	8443	8453	8462	8471	8480	32
58	8480	8490	8499	8508	8517	8526	8536	8545	8554	8563	8572	31
59	8572	8581	8590	8599	8607	8616	8625	8634	8643	8652	8660	30
60	0.8660	0.8669	0.8678	0.8686	0.8695	0.8704	0.8712	0.8721	0.8729	0.8738	0.8746	29
61	8746	8755	8763	8771	8780	8788	8796	8805	8813	8821	8829	28
62	8829	8838	8846	8854	8862	8870	8878	8886	8894	8902	8910	27
63	8910	8918	8926	8934	8942	8949	8957	8965	8973	8980	8988	26
64	8988	8996	9003	9011	9018	9026	9033	9041	9048	9056	9063	25
65	0.9063	0.9070	0.9078	0.9085	0.9092	0.9100	0.9107	0.9114	0.9121	0.9128	0.9135	24
66	9135	9143	9150	9157	9164	9171	9178	9184	9191	9198	9205	23
67	9205	9212	9219	9225	9232	9239	9245	9252	9259	9265	9272	22
68	9272	9278	9285	9291	9298	9304	9311	9317	9323	9330	9336	21
69	9336	9342	9348	9354	9361	9367	9373	9379	9385	9391	9397	20
70	0.9397	0.9403	0.9409	0.9415	0.9421	0.9426	0.9432	0.9438	0.9444	0.9449	0.9455	19
71	9455	9461	9466	9472	9478	9483	9489	9494	9500	9505	9511	18
72	9511	9516	9521	9527	9532	9537	9542	9548	9553	9558	9563	17
73	9563	9568	9573	9578	9583	9588	9593	9598	9603	9608	9613	16
74	9613	9617	9622	9627	9632	9636	9641	9646	9650	9655	9659	15
75	0.9659	0.9664	0.9668	0.9673	0.9677	0.9681	0.9686	0.9690	0.9694	0.9699	0.9703	14
76	9703	9707	9711	9715	9720	9724	9728	9732	9736	9740	9744	13
77	9744	9748	9751	9755	9759	9763	9767	9770	9774	9778	9781	12
78	9781	9785	9789	9792	9796	9799	9803	9806	9810	9813	9816	11
79	9816	9820	9823	9826	9829	9833	9836	9839	9842	9845	9848	10
80	0.9848	0.9851	0.9854	0.9857	0.9860	0.9863	0.9866	0.9869	0.9871	0.9874	0.9877	9
81	9877	9880	9882	9885	9888	9890	9893	9895	9898	9900	9903	8
82	9903	9905	9907	9910	9912	9914	9917	9919	9921	9923	9925	7
83	9925	9928	9930	9932	9934	9936	9938	9940	9942	9943	9945	6
84	9945	9947	9949	9951	9952	9954	9956	9957	9959	9960	9962	5
85	0.9962	0.9963	0.9965	0.9966	0.9968	0.9969	0.9971	0.9972	0.9973	0.9974	0.9976	4
86	9976	9977	9978	9979	9980	9981	9982	9983	9984	9985	9986	3
87	9986	9987	9988	9989	9990	9990	9991	9992	9993	9993	9994	2
88	9994	9995	9995	9996	9996	9997	9997	9997	9998	9998	9998	1
89	9998	9999	9999	9999	9999	1.0000	1.0000	1.0000	1.0000	1.0000	1.0000	0
Degrees.	60′ 1°.0	54′ 0°.9	48′ 0°.8	42′ 0°.7	36′ 0°.6	30′ 0°.5	24′ 0°.4	18′ 0°.3	12′ 0°.2	6′ 0°.1	0′ 0°.0	Degrees.

Natural Cosines.

6

Natural Tangents.

Degrees.	0°.0 0′	0°.1 6′	0°.2 12′	0°.3 18′	0°.4 24′	0°.5 30′	0°.6 36′	0°.7 42′	0°.8 48′	0°.9 54′	1°.0 60′	Degrees.
0	0.0000	0.0017	0.0035	0.0052	0.0070	0.0087	0.0105	0.0122	0.0140	0.0157	0.0175	**89**
1	0175	0192	0209	0227	0244	0262	0279	0297	0314	0332	0349	**88**
2	0349	0367	0384	0402	0419	0437	0454	0472	0489	0507	0524	**87**
3	0524	0542	0559	0577	0594	0612	0629	0647	0664	0682	0699	**86**
4	0699	0717	0734	0752	0769	0787	0805	0822	0840	0857	0875	**85**
5	0.0875	0.0892	0.0910	0.0928	0.0945	0.0963	0.0981	0.0998	0.1016	0.1033	0.1051	**84**
6	1051	1069	1086	1104	1122	1139	1157	1175	1192	1210	1228	**83**
7	1228	1246	1263	1281	1299	1317	1334	1352	1370	1388	1405	**82**
8	1405	1423	1441	1459	1477	1495	1512	1530	1548	1566	1584	**81**
9	1584	1602	1620	1638	1655	1673	1691	1709	1727	1745	1763	**80**
10	0.1763	0.1781	0.1799	0.1817	0.1835	0.1853	0.1871	0.1890	0.1908	0.1926	0.1944	**79**
11	1944	1962	1980	1998	2016	2035	2053	2071	2089	2107	2126	**78**
12	2126	2144	2162	2180	2199	2217	2235	2254	2272	2290	2309	**77**
13	2309	2327	2345	2364	2382	2401	2419	2438	2456	2475	2493	**76**
14	2493	2512	2530	2549	2568	2586	2605	2623	2642	2661	2679	**75**
15	0.2679	0.2698	0.2717	0.2736	0.2754	0.2773	0.2792	0.2811	0.2830	0.2849	0.2867	**74**
16	2867	2886	2905	2924	2943	2962	2981	3000	3019	3038	3057	**73**
17	3057	3076	3096	3115	3134	3153	3172	3191	3211	3230	3249	**72**
18	3249	3269	3288	3307	3327	3346	3365	3385	3404	3424	3443	**71**
19	3443	3463	3482	3502	3522	3541	3561	3581	3600	3620	3640	**70**
20	0.3640	0.3659	0.3679	0.3699	0.3719	0.3739	0.3759	0.3779	0.3799	0.3819	0.3839	**69**
21	3839	3859	3879	3899	3919	3939	3959	3979	4000	4020	4040	**68**
22	4040	4061	4081	4101	4122	4142	4163	4183	4204	4224	4245	**67**
23	4245	4265	4286	4307	4327	4348	4369	4390	4411	4431	4452	**66**
24	4452	4473	4494	4515	4536	4557	4578	4599	4621	4642	4663	**65**
25	0.4663	0.4684	0.4706	0.4727	0.4748	0.4770	0.4791	0.4813	0.4834	0.4856	0.4877	**64**
26	4877	4899	4921	4942	4964	4986	5008	5029	5051	5073	5095	**63**
27	5095	5117	5139	5161	5184	5206	5228	5250	5272	5295	5317	**62**
28	5317	5340	5362	5384	5407	5430	5452	5475	5498	5520	5543	**61**
29	5543	5566	5589	5612	5635	5658	5681	5704	5727	5750	5774	**60**
30	0.5774	0.5797	0.5820	0.5844	0.5867	0.5890	0.5914	0.5938	0.5961	0.5985	0.6009	**59**
31	6009	6032	6056	6080	6104	6128	6152	6176	6200	6224	6249	**58**
32	6249	6273	6297	6322	6346	6371	6395	6420	6445	6469	6494	**57**
33	6494	6519	6544	6569	6594	6619	6644	6669	6694	6720	6745	**56**
34	6745	6771	6796	6822	6847	6873	6899	6924	6950	6976	7002	**55**
35	0.7002	0.7028	0.7054	0.7080	0.7107	0.7133	0.7159	0.7186	0.7212	0.7239	0.7265	**54**
36	7265	7292	7319	7346	7373	7400	7427	7454	7481	7508	7536	**53**
37	7536	7563	7590	7618	7646	7673	7701	7729	7757	7785	7813	**52**
38	7813	7841	7869	7898	7926	7954	7983	8012	8040	8069	8098	**51**
39	8098	8127	8156	8185	8214	8243	8273	8302	8332	8361	8391	**50**
40	0.8391	0.8421	0.8451	0.8481	0.8511	0.8541	0.8571	0.8601	0.8632	0.8662	0.8693	**49**
41	8693	8724	8754	8785	8816	8847	8878	8910	8941	8972	9004	**48**
42	9004	9036	9067	9099	9131	9163	9195	9228	9260	9293	9325	**47**
43	9325	9358	9391	9424	9457	9490	9523	9556	9590	9623	9657	**46**
44	9657	9691	9725	9759	9793	9827	9861	9896	9930	9965	1.0000	**45**
Degrees.	60′ 1°.0	54′ 0°.9	48′ 0°.8	42′ 0°.7	36′ 0°.6	30′ 0°.5	24′ 0°.4	18′ 0°.3	12′ 0°.2	6′ 0°.1	0′ 0°.0	Degrees.

Natural Cotangents.

Natural Tangents.

Degrees.	0°.0 0′	0°.1 6′	0°.2 12′	0°.3 18′	0°.4 24′	0°.5 30′	0°.6 36′	0°.7 42′	0°.8 48′	0°.9 54′	1°.0 60′	Degrees.
45	1.0000	1.0035	1.0070	1.0105	1.0141	1.0176	1.0212	1.0247	1.0283	1.0319	1.0355	44
46	0355	0392	0428	0464	0501	0538	0575	0612	0649	0686	0724	43
47	0724	0761	0799	0837	0875	0913	0951	0990	1028	1067	1106	42
48	1106	1145	1184	1224	1263	1303	1343	1383	1423	1463	1504	41
49	1504	1544	1585	1626	1667	1708	1750	1792	1833	1875	1918	40
50	1.1918	1.1960	1.2002	1.2045	1.2088	1.2131	1.2174	1.2218	1.2261	1.2305	1.2349	39
51	2349	2393	2437	2482	2527	2572	2617	2662	2708	2753	2799	38
52	2799	2846	2892	2938	2985	3032	3079	3127	3175	3222	3270	37
53	3270	3319	3367	3416	3465	3514	3564	3613	3663	3713	3764	36
54	3764	3814	3865	3916	3968	4019	4071	4124	4176	4229	4281	35
55	1.4281	1.4335	1.4388	1.4442	1.4496	1.4550	1.4605	1.4660	1.4715	1.4770	1.4826	34
56	4826	4882	4938	4994	5051	5108	5166	5224	5282	5340	5399	33
57	5399	5458	5517	5577	5637	5697	5757	5818	5880	5941	6003	32
58	6003	6066	6128	6191	6255	6319	6383	6447	6512	6577	6643	31
59	6643	6709	6775	6842	6909	6977	7045	7113	7182	7251	7321	30
60	1.7321	1.7391	1.7461	1.7532	1.7603	1.7675	1.7747	1.7820	1.7893	1.7966	1.8040	29
61	8040	8115	8190	8265	8341	8418	8495	8572	8650	8728	8807	28
62	8807	8887	8967	9047	9128	9210	9292	9375	9458	9542	9626	27
63	9626	9711	9797	9883	9970	2.0057	2.0145	2.0233	2.0323	2.0413	2.0503	26
64	2.0503	2.0594	2.0686	2.0778	2.0872	0965	1060	1155	1251	1348	1445	25
65	2.1445	2.1543	2.1642	2.1742	2.1842	2.1943	2.2045	2.2148	2.2251	2.2355	2.2460	24
66	2460	2566	2673	2781	2889	2998	3109	3220	3332	3445	3559	23
67	3559	3673	3789	3906	4023	4142	4262	4383	4504	4627	4751	22
68	4751	4876	5002	5129	5257	5386	5517	5649	5782	5916	6051	21
69	6051	6187	6325	6464	6605	6746	6889	7034	7179	7326	7475	20
70	2.7475	2.7625	2.7776	2.7929	2.8083	2.8239	2.8397	2.8556	2.8716	2.8878	2.9042	19
71	9042	9208	9375	9544	9714	9887	3.0061	3.0237	3.0415	3.0595	3.0777	18
72	3.0777	3.0961	3.1146	3.1334	3.1524	3.1716	1910	2106	2305	2506	2709	17
73	2709	2914	3122	3332	3544	3759	3977	4197	4420	4646	4874	16
74	4874	5105	5339	5576	5816	6059	6305	6554	6806	7062	7321	15
75	3.7321	3.7583	3.7848	3.8118	3.8391	3.8667	3.8947	3.9232	3.9520	3.9812	4.0108	14
76	4.0108	4.0408	4.0713	4.1022	4.1335	4.1653	4.1976	4.2303	4.2635	4.2972	3315	13
77	3315	3662	4015	4373	4737	5107	5483	5864	6252	6646	7046	12
78	7046	7453	7867	8288	8716	9152	9594	5.0045	5.0504	5.0970	5.1446	11
79	5.1446	5.1929	5.2422	5.2924	5.3435	5.3955	5.4486	5026	5578	6140	6713	10
80	5.6713	5.7297	5.7894	5.8502	5.9124	5.9758	6.0405	6.1066	6.1742	6.2432	6.3138	9
81	6.3138	6.3859	6.4596	6.5350	6.6122	6.6912	6.7720	6.8548	6.9395	7.0264	7.1154	8
82	7.1154	7.2066	7.3002	7.3962	7.4947	7.5958	7.6996	7.8062	7.9158	8.0285	8.1443	7
83	8.1443	8.2636	8.3863	8.5126	8.6427	8.7769	8.9152	9.0579	9.2052	9.3572	9.5144	6
84	9.5144	9.6768	9.8448	10.0187	10.1988	10.3854	10.5789	10.7797	10.9882	11.2048	11.4301	5
85	11.4301	11.6645	11.9087	12.1632	12.4289	12.7062	12.9962	13.2996	13.6174	13.9507	14.3007	4
86	14.3007	14.6685	15.0557	15.4638	15.8945	16.3499	16.8319	17.3432	17.8863	18.4645	19.0811	3
87	19.0811	19.7403	20.4465	21.2049	22.0217	22.9038	23.8593	24.8978	26.0307	27.2715	28.6363	2
88	28.6363	30.1446	31.8205	33.6935	35.8006	38.1885	40.9174	44.0661	47.7395	52.0807	57.2900	1
89	57.2900	63.6567	71.6151	81.8470	95.4895	114.5886	143.2371	190.9842	286.4777	572.9572	∞	0
Degrees.	60′ 1°.0	54′ 0°.9	48′ 0°.8	42′ 0°.7	36′ 0°.6	30′ 0°.5	24′ 0°.4	18′ 0°.3	12′ 0°.2	6′ 0°.1	0′ 0°.0	Degrees.

Natural Cotangents.

Natural Versed Sines.

Degrees.	0°.0 0′	0°.1 6′	0°.2 12′	0°.3 18′	0°.4 24′	0°.5 30′	0°.6 36′	0°.7 42′	0°.8 48′	0°.9 54′
0	0.0000	0.0000	0.0000	0.0000	0.0000	0.0000	0.0001	0.0001	0.0001	0.0001
1	0002	0002	0002	0003	0003	0003	0004	0004	0005	0015
2	0006	0007	0007	0008	0009	0010	0010	0011	0012	0003
3	0014	0015	0016	0017	0018	0019	0020	0021	0022	0013
4	0024	0026	0027	0028	0029	0031	0032	0034	0035	0037
5	0.0038	0.0040	0.0041	0.0043	0.0044	0.0046	0.0048	0.0049	0.0051	0.0053
6	0055	0057	0058	0060	0062	0064	0066	0068	0070	0072
7	0075	0077	0079	0081	0083	0086	0088	0090	0093	0095
8	0097	0100	0102	0105	0107	0110	0112	0115	0118	0120
9	0123	0126	0129	0131	0134	0137	0140	0143	0146	0149
10	0.0152	0.0155	0.0158	0.0161	0.0164	0.0167	0.0171	0.0174	0.0177	0.0180
11	0184	0187	0190	0194	0197	0201	0204	0208	0211	0215
12	0219	0222	0226	0230	0233	0237	0241	0245	0249	0252
13	0256	0260	0264	0268	0272	0276	0280	0285	0289	0293
14	0297	0301	0306	0310	0314	0319	0323	0327	0332	0336
15	0.0341	0.0345	0.0350	0.0354	0.0359	0.0364	0.0368	0.0373	0.0378	0.0383
16	0387	0392	0397	0402	0407	0412	0417	0422	0427	0432
17	0437	0442	0447	0452	0458	0463	0468	0473	0479	0484
18	0489	0495	0500	0506	0511	0517	0522	0528	0534	0539
19	0545	0551	0556	0562	0568	0574	0579	0585	0591	0597
20	0.0603	0.0609	0.0615	0.0621	0.0627	0.0633	0.0639	0.0646	0.0652	0.0658
21	0664	0670	0677	0683	0689	0696	0702	0709	0715	0722
22	0728	0735	0741	0748	0755	0761	0768	0775	0781	0788
23	0795	0802	0809	0816	0822	0829	0836	0843	0850	0857
24	0865	0872	0879	0886	0893	0900	0908	0915	0922	0930
25	0.0937	0.0944	0.0952	0.0959	0.0967	0.0974	0.0982	0.0989	0.0997	0.1004
26	1012	1020	1027	1035	1043	1051	1058	1066	1074	1082
27	1090	1098	1106	1114	1122	1130	1138	1146	1154	1162
28	1171	1179	1187	1195	1204	1212	1220	1229	1237	1245
29	1254	1262	1271	1279	1288	1296	1305	1314	1322	1331
30	0.1340	0.1348	0.1357	0.1366	0.1375	0.1384	0.1393	0.1401	0.1410	0.1419
31	1428	1437	1446	1455	1464	1474	1483	1492	1501	1510
32	1520	1529	1538	1547	1557	1566	1575	1585	1594	1604
33	1613	1623	1632	1642	1652	1661	1671	1680	1690	1700
34	1710	1719	1729	1739	1749	1759	1769	1779	1789	1798
35	0.1808	0.1819	0.1829	0.1839	0.1849	0.1859	0.1869	0.1879	0.1889	0.1900
36	1910	1920	1930	1941	1951	1961	1972	1982	1993	2003
37	2014	2024	2035	2045	2056	2066	2077	2088	2098	2109
38	2120	2131	2141	2152	2163	2174	2185	2196	2207	2218
39	2229	2240	2251	2262	2273	2284	2295	2306	2317	2328
40	0.2340	0.2351	0.2362	0.2373	0.2385	0.2396	0.2407	0.2419	0.2430	0.2441
41	2453	2464	2476	2487	2499	2510	2522	2534	2545	2557
42	2569	2580	2592	2604	2615	2627	2639	2651	2663	2675
43	2686	2698	2710	2722	2734	2746	2758	2770	2782	2794
44	2807	2819	2831	2843	2855	2867	2880	2892	2904	2917
45	0.2929	0.2941	0.2954	0.2966	0.2978	0.2991	0.3003	0.3016	0.3028	0.3041
46	3053	3066	3079	3091	3104	3116	3129	3142	3155	3167
47	3180	3193	3206	3218	3231	3244	3257	3270	3283	3296
48	3309	3322	3335	3348	3361	3374	3387	3400	3413	3426
49	3439	3453	3466	3479	3492	3506	3519	3532	3545	3559
50	0.3572	0.3586	0.3599	0.3612	0.3626	0.3639	0.3653	0.3666	0.3680	0.3693
51	3707	3720	3734	3748	3761	3775	3789	3802	3816	3830
52	3843	3857	3871	3885	3899	3912	3926	3940	3954	3968
53	3982	3996	4010	4024	4038	4052	4066	4080	4094	4108
54	4122	4136	4150	4165	4179	4193	4207	4221	4236	4250
55	0.4264	0.4279	0.4293	0.4307	0.4322	0.4336	0.4350	0.4365	0.4379	0.4394
56	4408	4423	4437	4452	4466	4481	4495	4510	4524	4539
57	4554	4568	4583	4598	4612	4627	4642	4656	4671	4686
58	4701	4716	4730	4745	4760	4775	4790	4805	4820	4835
59	4850	4865	4880	4895	4910	4925	4940	4955	4970	4985

Decimal Parts and their Multiples of a Day.

Hrs.	Dec'l Parts of Day.	Multipliers.								Hrs.	Dec'l Parts of Day.	Multipliers.							
		2	3	4	5	6	7	8	9			2	3	4	5	6	7	8	9
0.0	0.000	0.00	0.00	0.00	0.00	0.00	0.00	0.00	0.00	**12.0**	0.500	1.00	1.50	2.00	2.50	3.00	3.50	4.00	4.50
2	008	02	03	03	04	05	06	07	08	**2**	508	02	53	03	54	05	56	07	58
4	017	03	05	07	08	10	12	13	15	**4**	517	03	55	07	58	10	62	13	65
6	025	05	08	10	13	15	18	20	23	**6**	525	05	58	10	63	15	68	20	73
8	033	07	10	13	17	20	23	27	30	**8**	533	07	60	13	67	20	73	27	80
1.0	0.042	0.08	0.13	0.17	0.21	0.25	0.29	0.33	0.38	**13.0**	0.542	1.08	1.63	2.17	2.71	3.25	3.79	4.33	4.88
2	050	10	15	20	25	30	35	40	45	**2**	550	10	65	20	75	30	85	40	95
4	058	12	18	23	29	35	41	47	53	**4**	558	12	68	23	79	35	91	47	5.03
6	067	13	20	27	33	40	47	53	60	**6**	567	13	70	27	83	40	97	53	10
8	075	15	23	30	37	45	53	60	68	**8**	575	15	73	30	87	45	4.03	60	18
2.0	0.083	0.17	0.25	0.33	0.42	0.50	0.58	0.67	0.75	**14.0**	0.583	1.17	1.75	2.33	2.92	3.50	4.08	4.67	5.25
2	092	18	28	37	46	55	64	73	83	**2**	592	18	78	37	96	55	14	73	33
4	100	20	30	40	50	60	70	80	90	**4**	600	20	80	40	3.00	60	20	80	40
6	108	22	33	43	54	65	76	87	98	**6**	608	22	83	43	04	65	26	87	48
8	117	23	35	47	58	70	82	93	1.05	**8**	617	23	85	47	08	70	32	93	55
3.0	0.125	0.25	0.38	0.50	0.63	0.75	0.88	1.00	1.13	**15.0**	0.625	1.25	1.88	2.50	3.13	3.75	4.38	5.00	5.63
2	133	27	40	53	67	80	93	07	20	**2**	633	27	90	53	17	80	43	07	70
4	142	28	43	57	71	85	99	13	28	**4**	642	28	93	57	21	85	49	13	78
6	150	30	45	60	75	90	1.05	20	35	**6**	650	30	95	60	25	90	55	20	85
8	158	32	48	63	79	95	11	27	43	**8**	658	32	98	63	29	95	61	27	93
4.0	0.167	0.33	0.50	0.67	0.83	1.00	1.17	1.33	1.50	**16.0**	0.667	1.33	2.00	2.67	3.33	4.00	4.67	5.33	6.00
2	175	35	53	70	87	05	23	40	58	**2**	675	35	03	70	37	05	73	40	08
4	183	37	55	73	91	10	28	47	65	**4**	683	37	05	73	41	10	78	47	15
6	192	38	58	77	95	15	34	53	73	**6**	692	38	08	77	45	15	84	53	23
8	200	40	60	80	1.00	20	40	60	80	**8**	700	40	10	80	50	20	90	60	30
5.0	0.208	0.42	0.63	0.83	1.04	1.25	1.46	1.67	1.88	**17.0**	0.708	1.42	2.13	2.83	3.54	4.25	4.96	5.67	6.38
2	217	43	65	87	08	30	52	73	95	**2**	717	43	15	87	58	30	5.02	73	45
4	225	45	68	90	12	35	58	80	2.03	**4**	725	45	18	90	62	35	08	80	53
6	233	47	70	93	17	40	63	87	10	**6**	733	47	20	93	67	40	13	87	60
8	242	48	73	97	21	45	69	93	18	**8**	742	48	23	97	71	45	19	93	68
6.0	0.250	0.50	0.75	1.00	1.25	1.50	1.75	2.00	2.25	**18.0**	0.750	1.50	2.25	3.00	3.75	4.50	5.25	6.00	6.75
2	258	52	78	03	29	55	81	07	33	**2**	758	52	28	03	79	55	31	07	83
4	267	53	80	07	33	60	87	13	40	**4**	767	53	30	07	83	60	37	13	90
6	275	55	83	10	37	65	93	20	48	**6**	775	55	33	10	87	65	43	20	98
8	283	57	85	13	42	70	98	27	55	**8**	783	57	35	13	92	70	48	27	7.05
7.0	0.292	0.58	0.88	1.17	1.46	1.75	2.04	2.33	2.63	**19.0**	0.792	1.58	2.38	3.17	3.96	4.75	5.54	6.33	7.13
2	300	60	90	20	50	80	10	40	70	**2**	800	60	40	20	4.00	80	60	40	20
4	308	62	93	23	54	85	16	47	78	**4**	808	62	43	23	04	85	66	47	28
6	317	63	95	27	58	90	22	53	85	**6**	817	63	45	27	08	90	72	53	35
8	325	65	98	30	62	95	28	60	93	**8**	825	65	48	30	12	95	78	60	43
8.0	0.333	0.67	1.00	1.33	1.67	2.00	2.33	2.67	3.00	**20.0**	0.833	1.67	2.50	3.33	4.17	5.00	5.83	6.67	7.50
2	342	68	03	37	71	05	39	73	08	**2**	842	68	53	37	21	05	89	73	58
4	350	70	05	40	75	10	45	80	15	**4**	850	70	55	40	25	10	95	80	65
6	358	72	08	43	79	15	51	87	23	**6**	858	72	58	43	29	15	6.01	87	73
8	367	73	10	47	83	20	57	93	30	**8**	867	73	60	47	33	20	07	93	80
9.0	0.375	0.75	1.13	1.50	1.87	2.25	2.63	3.00	3.38	**21.0**	0.875	1.75	2.63	3.50	4.37	5.25	6.13	7.00	7.88
2	383	77	15	53	92	30	68	07	45	**2**	883	77	65	53	42	30	18	07	95
4	392	78	18	57	96	35	74	13	53	**4**	892	78	68	57	46	35	24	13	8.03
6	400	80	20	60	2.00	40	80	20	60	**6**	900	80	70	60	50	40	30	20	10
8	408	82	23	63	04	45	86	27	68	**8**	908	82	73	63	54	45	36	27	18
10.0	0.417	0.83	1.25	1.67	2.08	2.50	2.92	3.33	3.75	**22.0**	0.917	1.83	2.75	3.67	4.58	5.50	6.42	7.33	8.25
2	425	85	28	70	12	55	98	40	83	**2**	925	85	78	70	62	55	48	40	33
4	433	87	30	73	17	60	3.03	47	90	**4**	933	87	80	73	67	60	53	47	40
6	442	88	33	77	21	65	09	53	98	**6**	942	88	83	77	71	65	59	53	48
8	450	90	35	80	25	70	15	60	4.05	**8**	950	90	85	80	75	70	65	60	55
11.0	0.458	0.92	1.38	1.83	2.29	2.75	3.21	3.67	4.13	**23.0**	0.958	1.92	2.88	3.83	4.79	5.75	6.71	7.67	8.63
2	467	93	40	87	33	80	27	73	20	**2**	967	93	90	87	83	80	77	73	70
4	475	95	43	90	37	85	33	80	28	**4**	975	95	93	90	87	85	83	80	78
6	483	97	45	93	42	90	38	87	35	**6**	983	97	95	93	92	90	88	87	85
8	492	98	47	97	46	95	44	93	43	**8**	992	98	97	97	96	95	94	93	93
12.0	0.500	1.00	1.50	2.00	2.50	3.00	3.50	4.00	4.50	**24.0**	1.000	2.00	3.00	4.00	5.00	6.00	7.00	8.00	9.00

Decimal Equivalents to two places of Common Fractions.

D.	Numerator of Fraction.																					D.
	0	**1**	**2**	**3**	**4**	**5**	**6**	**7**	**8**	**9**	**10**	**11**	**12**	**13**	**14**	**15**	**16**	**17**	**18**	**19**	**20**	
10	00	10	20	30	40	50	60	70	80	90												**10**
11	00	09	18	27	36	45	54	64	73	82	91											**11**
12	00	08	17	25	33	42	50	58	67	75	83	91										**12**
13	00	08	15	23	31	38	46	54	61	69	77	85	92									**13**
14	00	07	14	21	29	36	43	50	57	64	71	78	86	93								**14**
15	00	07	13	20	27	33	40	47	53	60	67	73	80	87	93							**15**
16	00	06	12	19	25	31	37	44	50	56	62	69	75	81	87	94						**16**
17	00	06	12	18	23	29	35	41	47	53	59	65	71	76	82	88	94					**17**
18	00	06	11	17	22	28	33	39	44	50	56	61	67	72	78	83	89	94				**18**
19	00	05	10	16	21	26	32	37	42	47	53	58	63	68	74	79	84	89	95			**19**
20	00	05	10	15	20	25	30	35	40	45	50	55	60	65	70	75	80	85	90	95		**20**
21	00	05	09	14	19	24	29	33	38	43	48	52	57	62	67	71	76	81	86	90	95	**21**
22	00	04	09	14	18	23	27	32	36	41	45	50	54	59	64	68	73	77	82	86	91	**22**
23	00	04	09	13	17	22	26	30	35	39	43	48	52	56	61	65	70	74	78	83	87	**23**
24	00	04	08	12	17	21	25	29	33	37	42	46	50	54	58	62	67	71	75	79	83	**24**
25	00	04	08	12	16	20	24	28	32	36	40	44	48	52	56	60	64	68	72	76	80	**25**
26	00	04	08	11	15	19	23	27	31	35	38	43	46	50	54	58	61	65	69	73	77	**26**
27	00	04	07	11	15	18	22	26	30	33	37	41	44	48	52	56	59	63	67	70	74	**27**
28	00	04	07	11	14	18	21	25	29	32	36	39	43	46	50	54	57	61	64	68	71	**28**
29	00	03	07	10	14	17	21	24	28	31	34	38	41	45	48	52	55	59	62	65	69	**29**
30	00	03	07	10	13	17	20	23	27	30	33	37	40	43	47	50	53	57	60	63	67	**30**
31	00	03	06	10	13	16	19	23	26	29	32	35	39	42	45	48	52	55	58	61	64	**31**
32	00	03	06	09	12	16	19	22	25	28	31	34	37	41	44	47	50	53	56	59	62	**32**
33	00	03	06	09	12	15	18	21	24	27	30	33	36	39	42	45	48	51	54	58	61	**33**
34	00	03	06	09	12	15	18	21	23	26	29	32	35	38	41	44	47	50	53	56	59	**34**
35	00	03	06	09	11	14	17	20	23	26	29	31	34	37	40	43	46	49	51	54	57	**35**
36	00	03	06	08	11	14	17	19	22	25	28	31	33	36	39	42	44	47	50	53	56	**36**
37	00	03	05	08	11	13	16	19	22	24	27	30	32	35	38	40	43	46	49	51	54	**37**
38	00	03	05	08	10	13	16	18	21	24	26	29	32	34	37	39	42	45	47	50	53	**38**
39	00	03	05	08	10	13	15	18	20	23	26	28	31	33	36	38	41	43	46	49	51	**39**
40	00	02	05	07	10	12	15	17	20	22	25	27	30	32	35	37	40	42	45	47	50	**40**
42	00	02	05	07	09	12	14	17	19	21	24	26	29	31	33	36	38	40	43	45	48	**42**
44	00	02	04	06	09	11	14	16	18	20	23	25	27	29	32	34	36	39	41	43	45	**44**
46	00	02	04	06	09	11	13	15	17	20	22	24	26	28	30	33	35	37	39	41	43	**46**
48	00	02	04	06	08	10	12	15	17	19	21	23	25	27	29	31	33	35	37	39	42	**48**
50	00	02	04	06	08	10	12	14	16	18	20	22	24	26	28	30	32	34	36	38	40	**50**
52	00	02	04	06	08	10	11	13	15	17	19	21	23	25	27	29	31	33	35	36	38	**52**
54	00	02	04	06	07	09	11	13	15	17	18	20	22	24	26	28	30	31	33	35	37	**54**
56	00	02	04	05	07	09	11	12	14	16	18	20	21	23	25	27	29	30	32	34	36	**56**
58	00	02	03	05	07	09	10	12	14	15	17	19	21	22	24	26	27	29	31	33	34	**58**
60	00	02	03	05	07	08	10	12	13	15	17	18	20	22	23	25	27	28	30	32	33	**60**
62	00	02	03	05	06	08	10	11	13	14	16	18	19	21	23	24	26	27	29	31	32	**62**
64	00	02	03	05	06	08	09	11	12	14	16	17	18	20	22	23	25	26	28	30	31	**64**
66	00	01	03	05	06	08	09	11	12	14	15	17	18	20	21	23	24	26	27	29	30	**66**
68	00	01	03	04	06	07	09	10	12	13	15	16	18	19	21	22	23	25	26	28	29	**68**
70	00	01	03	04	06	07	09	10	11	13	14	16	17	19	20	21	23	24	26	27	29	**70**
72	00	01	03	04	06	07	08	10	11	12	14	15	17	18	19	21	22	24	25	26	28	**72**
74	00	01	03	04	05	07	08	09	11	12	13	15	16	18	19	20	22	23	24	26	27	**74**
76	00	01	03	04	05	07	08	09	10	12	13	14	16	17	18	20	21	22	24	25	26	**76**
78	00	01	03	04	05	06	08	09	10	11	13	14	15	17	18	19	20	22	23	24	26	**78**
80	00	01	02	04	05	06	07	09	10	11	12	14	15	16	17	19	20	21	22	24	25	**80**
82	00	01	02	04	05	06	07	08	10	11	12	13	15	16	17	18	19	21	22	23	24	**82**
84	00	01	02	04	05	06	07	08	09	11	12	13	14	15	17	18	19	20	21	23	24	**84**
86	00	01	02	03	05	06	07	08	09	10	12	13	14	15	16	17	19	20	21	22	23	**86**
88	00	01	02	03	04	06	07	08	09	10	11	12	14	15	16	17	18	19	20	22	23	**88**
90	00	01	02	03	04	06	07	08	09	10	11	12	13	14	15	17	18	19	20	21	22	**90**
92	00	01	02	03	04	05	06	08	09	10	11	12	13	14	15	16	17	18	20	21	22	**92**
94	00	01	02	03	04	05	06	07	08	09	11	12	13	14	15	16	17	18	19	20	21	**94**
96	00	01	02	03	04	05	06	07	08	09	10	11	12	13	15	16	17	18	19	20	21	**96**
98	00	01	02	03	04	05	06	07	08	09	10	11	12	13	14	15	16	17	18	19	20	**98**
100	00	01	02	03	04	05	06	07	08	09	10	11	12	13	14	15	16	17	18	19	20	**100**

Decimal Equivalents to two places of Common Fractions.

D.	Numerator of Fraction.																					D.
	20	21	22	23	24	25	26	27	28	29	30	31	32	33	34	35	36	37	38	39	40	
20																						20
21	95																					21
22	91	95																				22
23	87	91	96																			23
24	83	87	92	96																		24
25	80	84	88	92	96																	25
26	77	81	85	88	92	96																26
27	74	78	81	85	89	93	96															27
28	71	75	79	82	86	89	93	96														28
29	69	72	76	79	83	86	90	93	97													29
30	67	70	73	77	80	83	87	90	93	97												30
31	64	68	71	74	77	81	84	87	90	94	97											31
32	62	66	69	72	75	78	81	84	87	91	94	97										32
33	61	64	67	70	73	76	79	82	85	88	91	94	97									33
34	59	62	65	68	71	73	76	79	82	85	88	91	94	97								34
35	57	60	63	66	69	71	74	77	80	83	86	89	91	94	97							35
36	56	58	61	64	67	69	72	75	78	81	83	86	89	92	94	97						36
37	54	57	59	62	65	68	70	73	76	78	81	84	86	89	92	95	97					37
38	53	55	58	60	63	66	68	71	74	76	79	81	84	87	89	92	95	97				38
39	51	54	56	59	61	64	67	69	72	74	77	79	82	85	87	90	92	95	97			39
40	50	52	55	57	60	62	65	67	70	72	75	77	80	82	85	87	90	92	95	97		40
42	48	50	52	55	57	59	62	64	67	69	71	74	76	78	81	83	86	88	90	93	95	42
44	45	48	50	52	55	57	59	61	64	66	68	70	73	75	77	80	82	84	86	89	91	44
46	43	46	48	50	52	54	56	59	61	63	65	67	69	72	74	76	78.	80	83	85	87	46
48	42	44	46	48	50	52	54	56	58	60	62	65	67	69	71	73	75	77	79	81	83	48
50	40	42	44	46	48	50	52	54	56	58	60	62	64	66	68	70	72	74	76	78	80	50
52	38	40	42	44	46	48	50	52	54	56	58	60	61	63	65	67	69	71	73	75	77	52
54	37	39	41	43	44	46	48	50	52	54	56	57	59	61	63	65	67	69	70	72	74	54
56	36	37	39	41	43	45	46	48	50	52	54	55	57	59	61	62	64	66	68	70	71	56
58	34	36	38	40	41	43	45	47	48	50	52	53	55	57	59	60	62	64	65	67	69	58
60	33	35	37	38	40	42	43	45	47	48	50	52	53	55	57	58	60	62	63	65	67	60
62	32	34	35	37	39	40	42	44	45	47	48	50	52	53	55	56	58	60	61	63	64	62
64	31	33	34	36	37	39	41	42	44	45	47	48	50	52	53	55	56	58	59	61	62	64
66	30	32	33	35	36	38	39	41	42	44	45	47	48	50	52	53	55	56	58	59	61	66
68	29	30	32	34	35	37	38	40	41	43	44	46	47	48	50	51	53	54	56	57	59	68
70	29	30	31	33	34	36	37	39	40	41	43	44	46	47	48	50	51	53	54	56	57	70
72	28	29	31	32	33	35	36	37	39	40	42	43	44	46	47	49	50	51	53	54	56	72
74	27	28	30	31	32	34	35	36	38	39	40	42	43	45	46	47	49	50	51	53	54	74
76	26	28	29	30	32	33	34	35	37	38	39	41	42	43	45	46	47	49	50	51	53	76
78	26	27	28	29	31	32	33	35	36	37	38	40	41	42	44	45	46	47	49	50	51	78
80	25	26	27	29	30	31	32	34	35	36	37	39	40	41	42	44	45	46	47	49	50	80
82	24	26	27	28	29	30	32	33	34	35	37	38	39	40	41	43	44	45	46	48	49	82
84	24	25	26	27	29	30	31	32	33	34	36	37	38	39	40	42	43	44	45	46	48	84
86	23	24	25	27	28	29	30	31	32	34	35	36	37	38	39	41	42	43	44	45	46	86
88	23	24	25	26	27	28	29	31	32	33	34	35	36	37	39	40	41	42	43	44	45	88
90	22	23	24	25	27	28	29	30	31	32	33	34	36	37	38	39	40	41	42	43	44	90
92	22	23	24	25	26	27	28	29	30	31	33	34	35	36	37	38	39	40	41	42	43	92
94	21	22	23	24	25	27	28	29	30	31	32	33	34	35	36	37	38	39	40	41	42	94
96	21	22	23	24	25	26	27	28	29	30	31	32	33	34	35	36	37	38	39	41	42	96
98	20	21	22	23	24	25	26	27	29	30	31	32	33	34	35	36	37	38	39	40	41	98
100	20	21	22	23	24	25	26	27	28	29	30	31	32	33	34	35	36	37	38	39	40	100
D.	**1**	**5**	**10**	**15**	**20**	**25**	**30**	**35**	**40**	**45**	**50**	**55**	**60**	**65**	**70**	**75**	**80**	**85**	**90**	**95**	**100**	**D.**
125	01	04	08	12	16	20	24	28	32	36	40	44	48	52	56	60	64	68	72	76	80	125
176	01	03	06	08	11	14	17	20	23	25	28	31	34	37	40	43	46	48	51	54	57	176
301	00	02	03	05	07	08	10	12	13	15	17	18	20	22	23	25	26	28	30	32	33	301
D.	**100**	**105**	**110**	**115**	**120**	**125**	**130**	**135**	**140**	**145**	**150**	**155**	**160**	**165**	**170**	**175**	**200**	**225**	**250**	**275**	**300**	**D.**
125	80	84	88	92	96																	125
176	57	60	63	65	68	71	74	77	80	82	85	88	91	94	97							176
301	33	35	36	38	40	41	43	45	46	48	50	52	53	55	56	58	66	74	83	91		301

TABLE XIX.

Decimal Equivalents to two places of Common Fractions.

D.	Numerator of Fraction.																					D.
	40	41	42	43	44	45	46	47	48	49	50	51	52	53	54	55	56	57	58	59	60	
42	95	97																				42
44	91	93	95	98																		44
46	87	90	91	93	96	98																46
48	83	85	87	89	92	94	96	98														48
50	80	82	84	86	88	90	92	94	96	98												50
52	77	79	81	83	85	86	88	90	92	94	96	98										52
54	74	76	78	80	81	83	85	87	89	91	93	94	96	98								54
56	71	73	75	77	78	80	82	84	86	87	89	91	93	95	96	98						56
58	69	71	72	74	76	78	79	81	83	84	86	88	90	91	93	95	97	98				58
60	67	68	70	72	73	75	77	78	80	82	83	85	87	88	90	92	93	95	97	98		60
62	64	66	68	69	71	73	74	76	77	79	81	82	84	85	87	89	90	92	94	95	97	62
64	62	64	66	67	69	70	72	73	75	77	78	80	81	83	84	86	87	89	91	92	94	64
66	61	62	64	65	67	68	70	71	73	74	76	77	79	80	82	83	85	86	88	89	91	66
68	59	60	62	63	65	66	68	69	71	72	73	75	76	78	79	81	82	84	85	87	88	68
70	57	58	60	61	63	64	66	67	69	70	71	73	74	76	77	78	80	81	83	84	86	70
72	56	57	58	60	61	62	64	65	67	68	69	71	72	74	75	76	78	79	81	82	83	72
74	54	55	57	58	59	61	62	63	65	66	68	69	70	72	73	74	76	77	78	80	81	74
76	53	54	55	56	58	59	60	62	63	64	66	67	68	70	71	72	74	75	76	78	79	76
78	51	53	54	55	56	58	59	60	61	63	64	65	67	68	69	70	72	73	74	76	77	78
80	50	51	52	54	55	56	57	59	60	61	62	64	65	66	67	69	70	71	72	74	75	80
82	49	50	51	52	54	55	56	57	59	60	61	62	63	65	66	67	68	69	70	72	73	82
84	48	49	50	51	52	53	55	56	57	58	59	61	62	63	64	65	67	68	69	70	71	84
86	46	48	49	50	51	52	53	55	56	57	58	59	60	61	63	64	65	66	67	68	70	86
88	45	46	48	49	50	51	52	53	55	56	57	58	59	60	61	62	64	65	66	67	68	88
90	44	45	47	48	49	50	51	52	53	54	56	57	58	59	60	61	62	63	64	66	67	90
92	43	44	46	47	48	49	50	51	52	53	54	55	56	58	59	60	61	62	63	64	65	92
94	42	44	45	46	47	48	49	50	51	52	53	54	55	56	57	58	60	61	62	63	64	94
96	42	43	44	45	46	47	48	49	50	51	52	53	54	55	56	57	58	59	60	61	62	96
98	41	42	43	44	45	46	47	48	49	50	51	52	53	54	55	56	57	58	59	60	61	98
100	40	41	42	43	44	45	46	47	48	49	50	51	52	53	54	55	56	57	58	59	60	100
D.	60	61	62	63	64	65	66	67	68	69	70	71	72	73	74	75	76	77	78	79	80	D.
62	97	98																				62
64	94	95	97	98																		64
66	91	92	94	95	97	98																66
68	88	90	91	93	94	96	97	98														68
70	86	87	89	90	91	93	94	96	97	99												70
72	83	85	86	88	89	90	92	93	94	96	97	99										72
74	81	82	84	85	86	88	89	91	92	93	95	96	97	99								74
76	79	80	81	83	84	85	87	88	89	91	92	93	95	96	97	99						76
78	77	78	79	81	82	83	85	86	87	88	90	91	92	93	95	96	97	99				78
80	75	76	77	79	80	81	82	84	85	86	87	89	90	91	92	94	95	96	97	99		80
82	73	74	75	77	78	79	80	82	83	84	85	87	88	89	90	91	93	94	95	96	98	82
84	71	72	74	75	76	77	78	80	81	82	83	84	86	87	88	89	90	92	93	94	95	84
86	70	71	72	73	74	75	77	78	79	80	81	83	84	85	86	87	88	89	91	92	93	86
88	68	69	70	72	73	74	75	76	77	78	80	81	82	83	84	85	86	87	89	90	91	88
90	67	68	69	70	71	72	73	74	76	77	78	79	80	81	82	83	84	86	87	88	89	90
92	65	66	67	68	69	71	72	73	74	75	76	77	78	79	80	81	83	84	85	86	87	92
94	64	65	66	67	68	69	70	71	72	73	74	76	77	78	79	80	81	82	83	84	85	94
96	62	63	65	66	67	68	69	70	71	72	73	74	75	76	77	78	79	80	81	82	83	96
98	61	62	63	64	65	66	67	68	69	70	71	73	73	74	75	76	77	78	80	81	82	98
100	60	61	62	63	64	65	66	67	68	69	70	71	72	73	74	75	76	77	78	79	80	100
D	80	81	82	83	84	85	86	87	88	89	90	91	92	93	94	95	96	97	98	99	100	D.
82	98	99																				82
84	95	96	98	99																		84
86	93	94	95	96	98	99																86
88	91	92	93	94	95	97	98	99														88
90	89	90	91	92	93	94	96	97	98	99												90
92	87	88	89	90	91	92	93	95	96	97	98	99										92
94	85	86	87	88	89	90	91	92	94	95	96	97	98	99								94
96	83	84	85	86	87	88	89	91	92	93	94	95	96	97	98	99						96
98	82	83	84	85	86	87	88	89	90	91	92	93	94	95	96	97	98	99				98
100	80	81	82	83	84	85	86	87	88	89	90	91	92	93	94	95	96	97	98	99		100

Proportional Parts.

Numbers.	Tenths and their Multiples.									Numbers.	Tenths and their Multiples.								
	0.1	0.2	0.3	0.4	0.5	0.6	0.7	0.8	0.9		0.1	0.2	0.3	0.4	0.5	0.6	0.7	0.8	0.9
1	0.1	0.2	0.3	0.4	0.5	0.6	0.7	0.8	0.9	**56**	5.6	11.2	16.8	22.4	28.0	33.6	39.2	44.8	50.4
2	0.2	0.4	0.6	0.8	1.0	1.2	1.4	1.6	1.8	**57**	5.7	11.4	17.1	22.8	28.5	34.2	39.9	45.6	51.3
3	0.3	0.6	0.9	1.2	1.5	1.8	2.1	2.4	2.7	**58**	5.8	11.6	17.4	23.2	29.0	34.8	40.6	46.4	52.2
4	0.4	0.8	1.2	1.6	2.0	2.4	2.8	3.2	3.6	**59**	5.9	11.8	17.7	23.6	29.5	35.4	41.3	47.2	53.1
5	0.5	1.0	1.5	2.0	2.5	3.0	3.5	4.0	4.5	**60**	6.0	12.0	18.0	24.0	30.0	36.0	42.0	48.0	54.0
6	0.6	1.2	1.8	2.4	3.0	3.6	4.2	4.8	5.4	**61**	6.1	12.2	18.3	24.4	30.5	36.6	42.7	48.8	54.9
7	0.7	1.4	2.1	2.8	3.5	4.2	4.9	5.6	6.3	**62**	6.2	12.4	18.6	24.8	31.0	37.2	43.4	49.6	55.8
8	0.8	1.6	2.4	3.2	4.0	4.8	5.6	6.4	7.2	**63**	6.3	12.6	18.9	25.2	31.5	37.8	44.1	50.4	56.7
9	0.9	1.8	2.7	3.6	4.5	5.4	6.3	7.2	8.1	**64**	6.4	12.8	19.2	25.6	32.0	38.4	44.8	51.2	57.6
10	1.0	2.0	3.0	4.0	5.0	6.0	7.0	8.0	9.0	**65**	6.5	13.0	19.5	26.0	32.5	39.0	45.5	52.0	58.5
11	1.1	2.2	3.3	4.4	5.5	6.6	7.7	8.8	9.9	**66**	6.6	13.2	19.8	26.4	33.0	39.6	46.2	52.8	59.4
12	1.2	2.4	3.6	4.8	6.0	7.2	8.4	9.6	10.8	**67**	6.7	13.4	20.1	26.8	33.5	40.2	46.9	53.6	60.3
13	1.3	2.6	3.9	5.2	6.5	7.8	9.1	10.4	11.7	**68**	6.8	13.6	20.4	27.2	34.0	40.8	47.6	54.4	61.2
14	1.4	2.8	4.2	5.6	7.0	8.4	9.8	11.2	12.6	**69**	6.9	13.8	20.7	27.6	34.5	41.4	48.3	55.2	62.1
15	1.5	3.0	4.5	6.0	7.5	9.0	10.5	12.0	13.5	**70**	7.0	14.0	21.0	28.0	35.0	42.0	49.0	56.0	63.0
16	1.6	3.2	4.8	6.4	8.0	9.6	11.2	12.8	14.4	**71**	7.1	14.2	21.3	28.4	35.5	42.6	49.7	56.8	63.9
17	1.7	3.4	5.1	6.8	8.5	10.2	11.9	13.6	15.3	**72**	7.2	14.4	21.6	28.8	36.0	43.2	50.4	57.6	64.8
18	1.8	3.6	5.4	7.2	9.0	10.8	12.6	14.4	16.2	**73**	7.3	14.6	21.9	29.2	36.5	43.8	51.1	58.4	65.7
19	1.9	3.8	5.7	7.6	9.5	11.4	13.3	15.2	17.1	**74**	7.4	14.8	22.2	29.6	37.0	44.4	51.8	59.2	66.6
20	2.0	4.0	6.0	8.0	10.0	12.0	14.0	16.0	18.0	**75**	7.5	15.0	22.5	30.0	37.5	45.0	52.5	60.0	67.5
21	2.1	4.2	6.3	8.4	10.5	12.6	14.7	16.8	18.9	**76**	7.6	15.2	22.8	30.4	38.0	45.6	53.2	60.8	68.4
22	2.2	4.4	6.6	8.8	11.0	13.2	15.4	17.6	19.8	**77**	7.7	15.4	23.1	30.8	38.5	46.2	53.9	61.6	69.3
23	2.3	4.6	6.9	9.2	11.5	13.8	16.1	18.4	20.7	**78**	7.8	15.6	23.4	31.2	39.0	46.8	54.6	62.4	70.2
24	2.4	4.8	7.2	9.6	12.0	14.4	16.8	19.2	21.6	**79**	7.9	15.8	23.7	31.6	39.5	47.4	55.3	63.2	71.1
25	2.5	5.0	7.5	10.0	12.5	15.0	17.5	20.0	22.5	**80**	8.0	16.0	24.0	32.0	40.0	48.0	56.0	64.0	72.0
26	2.6	5.2	7.8	10.4	13.0	15.6	18.2	20.8	23.4	**81**	8.1	16.2	24.3	32.4	40.5	48.6	56.7	64.8	72.9
27	2.7	5.4	8.1	10.8	13.5	16.2	18.9	21.6	24.3	**82**	8.2	16.4	24.6	32.8	41.0	49.2	57.4	65.6	73.8
28	2.8	5.6	8.4	11.2	14.0	16.8	19.6	22.4	25.2	**83**	8.3	16.6	24.9	33.2	41.5	49.8	58.1	66.4	74.7
29	2.9	5.8	8.7	11.6	14.5	17.4	20.3	23.2	26.1	**84**	8.4	16.8	25.2	33.6	42.0	50.4	58.8	67.2	75.6
30	3.0	6.0	9.0	12.0	15.0	18.0	21.0	24.0	27.0	**85**	8.5	17.0	25.5	34.0	42.5	51.0	59.5	68.0	76.5
31	3.1	6.2	9.3	12.4	15.5	18.6	21.7	24.8	27.9	**86**	8.6	17.2	25.8	34.4	43.0	51.6	60.2	68.8	77.4
32	3.2	6.4	9.6	12.8	16.0	19.2	22.4	25.6	28.8	**87**	8.7	17.4	26.1	34.8	43.5	52.2	60.9	69.6	78.3
33	3.3	6.6	9.9	13.2	16.5	19.8	23.1	26.4	29.7	**88**	8.8	17.6	26.4	35.2	44.0	52.8	61.6	70.4	79.2
34	3.4	6.8	10.2	13.6	17.0	20.4	23.8	27.2	30.6	**89**	8.9	17.8	26.7	35.6	44.5	53.4	62.3	71.2	80.1
35	3.5	7.0	10.5	14.0	17.5	21.0	24.5	28.0	31.5	**90**	9.0	18.0	27.0	36.0	45.0	54.0	63.0	72.0	81.0
36	3.6	7.2	10.8	14.4	18.0	21.6	25.2	28.8	32.4	**91**	9.1	18.2	27.3	36.4	45.5	54.6	63.7	72.8	81.9
37	3.7	7.4	11.1	14.8	18.5	22.2	25.9	29.6	33.3	**92**	9.2	18.4	27.6	36.8	46.0	55.2	64.4	73.6	82.8
38	3.8	7.6	11.4	15.2	19.0	22.8	26.6	30.4	34.2	**93**	9.3	18.6	27.9	37.2	46.5	55.8	65.1	74.4	83.7
39	3.9	7.8	11.7	15.6	19.5	23.4	27.3	31.2	35.1	**94**	9.4	18.8	28.2	37.6	47.0	56.4	65.8	75.2	84.6
40	4.0	8.0	12.0	16.0	20.0	24.0	28.0	32.0	36.0	**95**	9.5	19.0	28.5	38.0	47.5	57.0	66.5	76.0	85.5
41	4.1	8.2	12.3	16.4	20.5	24.6	28.7	32.8	36.9	**96**	9.6	19.2	28.8	38.4	48.0	57.6	67.2	76.8	86.4
42	4.2	8.4	12.6	16.8	21.0	25.2	29.4	33.6	37.8	**97**	9.7	19.4	29.1	38.8	48.5	58.2	67.9	77.6	87.3
43	4.3	8.6	12.9	17.2	21.5	25.8	30.1	34.4	38.7	**98**	9.8	19.6	29.4	39.2	49.0	58.8	68.6	78.4	88.2
44	4.4	8.8	13.2	17.6	22.0	26.4	30.8	35.2	39.6	**99**	9.9	19.8	29.7	39.6	49.5	59.4	69.3	79.2	89.1
45	4.5	9.0	13.5	18.0	22.5	27.0	31.5	36.0	40.5	**100**	10.0	20.0	30.0	40.0	50.0	60.0	70.0	80.0	90.0
46	4.6	9.2	13.8	18.4	23.0	27.6	32.2	36.8	41.4	**101**	10.1	20.2	30.3	40.4	50.5	60.6	70.7	80.8	90.9
47	4.7	9.4	14.1	18.8	23.5	28.2	32.9	37.6	42.3	**102**	10.2	20.4	30.6	40.8	51.0	61.2	71.4	81.6	91.8
48	4.8	9.6	14.4	19.2	24.0	28.8	33.6	38.4	43.2	**103**	10.3	20.6	30.9	41.2	51.5	61.8	72.1	82.4	92.7
49	4.9	9.8	14.7	19.6	24.5	29.4	34.3	39.2	44.1	**104**	10.4	20.8	31.2	41.6	52.0	62.4	72.8	83.2	93.6
50	5.0	10.0	15.0	20.0	25.0	30.0	35.0	40.0	45.0	**105**	10.5	21.0	31.5	42.0	52.5	63.0	73.5	84.0	94.5
51	5.1	10.2	15.3	20.4	25.5	30.6	35.7	40.8	45.9	**106**	10.6	21.2	31.8	42.4	53.0	63.6	74.2	84.8	95.4
52	5.2	10.4	15.6	20.8	26.0	31.2	36.4	41.6	46.8	**107**	10.7	21.4	32.1	42.8	53.5	64.2	74.9	85.6	96.3
53	5.3	10.6	15.9	21.2	26.5	31.8	37.1	42.4	47.7	**108**	10.8	21.6	32.4	43.2	54.0	64.8	75.6	86.4	97.2
54	5.4	10.8	16.2	21.6	27.0	32.4	37.8	43.2	48.6	**109**	10.9	21.8	32.7	43.6	54.5	65.4	76.3	87.2	98.1
55	5.5	11.0	16.5	22.0	27.5	33.0	38.5	44.0	49.5	**110**	11.0	22.0	33.0	44.0	55.0	66.0	77.0	88.0	99.0

Squares of Numbers increasing by Tenths from 0.0 to 100.9.

No.	0.0	0.1	0.2	0.3	0.4	0.5	0.6	0.7	0.8	0.9	Diff. 0.01
0	0.0	0.0	0.0	0.1	0.2	0.3	0.4	0.5	0.6	0.8	0.01
1	1.0	1.2	1.4	1.7	2.0	2.3	2.6	2.9	3.2	3.6	03
2	4.0	4.4	4.8	5.3	5.8	6.3	6.8	7.3	7.8	8.4	05
3	9.0	9.6	10.2	10.9	11.6	12.3	13.0	13.7	14.4	15.2	07
4	16.0	16.8	17.6	18.5	19.4	20.3	21.2	22.1	23.0	24.0	09
5	25.0	26.0	27.0	28.1	29.2	30.3	31.4	32.5	33.6	34.8	0.11
6	36.0	37.2	38.4	39.7	41.0	42.3	43.6	44.9	46.2	47.6	13
7	49.0	50.4	51.8	53.3	54.8	56.3	57.8	59.3	60.8	62.4	15
8	64.0	65.6	67.2	68.9	70.6	72.3	74.0	75.7	77.4	79.2	17
9	81.0	82.8	84.6	86.5	88.4	90.3	92.2	94.1	96.0	98.0	19
10	100.0	102.0	104.0	106.1	108.2	110.3	112.4	114.5	116.6	118.8	0.21
11	121.0	123.2	125.4	127.7	130.0	132.3	134.6	136.9	139.2	141.6	23
12	144.0	146.4	148.8	151.3	153.8	156.3	158.8	161.3	163.8	166.4	25
13	169.0	171.6	174.2	176.9	179.6	182.3	185.0	187.7	190.4	193.2	27
14	196.0	198.8	201.6	204.5	207.4	210.3	213.2	216.1	219.0	222.0	29
15	225.0	228.0	231.0	234.1	237.2	240.3	243.4	246.5	249.6	252.8	0.31
16	256.0	259.2	262.4	265.7	269.0	272.3	275.6	278.9	282.2	285.6	33
17	289.0	292.4	295.8	299.3	302.8	306.3	309.8	313.3	316.8	320.4	35
18	324.0	327.6	331.2	334.9	338.6	342.3	346.0	349.7	353.4	357.2	37
19	361.0	364.8	368.6	372.5	376.4	380.3	384.2	388.1	392.0	396.0	39
20	400.0	404.0	408.0	412.1	416.2	420.3	424.4	428.5	432.6	436.8	0.41
21	441.0	445.2	449.4	453.7	458.0	462.3	466.6	470.9	475.2	479.6	43
22	484.0	488.4	492.8	497.3	501.8	506.3	510.8	515.3	519.8	524.4	45
23	529.0	533.6	538.2	542.9	547.6	552.3	557.0	561.7	566.4	571.2	47
24	576.0	580.8	585.6	590.5	595.4	600.3	605.2	610.1	615.0	620.0	49
25	625.0	630.0	635.0	640.1	645.2	650.3	655.4	660.5	665.6	670.8	0.51
26	676.0	681.2	686.4	691.7	697.0	702.3	707.6	712.9	718.2	723.6	53
27	729.0	734.4	739.8	745.3	750.8	756.3	761.8	767.3	772.8	778.4	55
28	784.0	789.6	795.2	800.9	806.6	812.3	818.0	823.7	829.4	835.2	57
29	841.0	846.8	852.6	858.5	864.4	870.3	876.2	882.1	888.0	894.0	59
30	900.0	906.0	912.0	918.1	924.2	930.3	936.4	942.5	948.6	954.8	0.61
31	961.0	967.2	973.4	979.7	986.0	992.3	998.6	1004.9	1011.2	1017.6	63
32	1024.0	1030.4	1036.8	1043.3	1049.8	1056.3	1062.8	1069.3	1075.8	1082.4	65
33	1089.0	1095.6	1102.2	1108.9	1115.6	1122.3	1129.0	1135.7	1142.4	1149.2	67
34	1156.0	1162.8	1169.6	1176.5	1183.4	1190.3	1197.2	1204.1	1211.0	1218.0	69
35	1225.0	1232.0	1239.0	1246.1	1253.2	1260.3	1267.4	1274.5	1281.6	1288.8	0.71
36	1296.0	1303.2	1310.4	1317.7	1325.0	1332.3	1339.6	1346.9	1354.2	1361.6	73
37	1369.0	1376.4	1383.8	1391.3	1398.8	1406.3	1413.8	1421.3	1428.8	1436.4	75
38	1444.0	1451.6	1459.2	1466.9	1474.6	1482.3	1490.0	1497.7	1505.4	1513.2	77
39	1521.0	1528.8	1536.6	1544.5	1552.4	1560.3	1568.2	1576.1	1584.0	1592.0	79
40	1600.0	1608.0	1616.0	1624.1	1632.2	1640.3	1648.4	1656.5	1664.6	1672.8	0.81
41	1681.0	1689.2	1697.4	1705.7	1714.0	1722.3	1730.6	1738.9	1747.2	1755.6	83
42	1764.0	1772.4	1780.8	1789.3	1797.8	1806.3	1814.8	1823.3	1831.8	1840.4	85
43	1849.0	1857.6	1866.2	1874.9	1883.6	1892.3	1901.0	1909.7	1918.4	1927.2	87
44	1936.0	1944.8	1953.6	1962.5	1971.4	1980.3	1989.2	1998.1	2007.0	2016.0	89
45	2025.0	2034.0	2043.0	2052.1	2061.2	2070.3	2079.4	2088.5	2097.6	2106.8	0.91
46	2116.0	2125.2	2134.4	2143.7	2153.0	2162.3	2171.6	2180.9	2190.2	2199.6	93
47	2209.0	2218.4	2227.8	2237.3	2246.8	2256.3	2265.8	2275.3	2284.8	2294.4	95
48	2304.0	2313.6	2323.2	2332.9	2342.6	2352.3	2362.0	2371.7	2381.4	2391.2	97
49	2401.0	2410.8	2420.6	2430.5	2440.4	2450.3	2460.2	2470.1	2480.0	2490.0	99
50	2500.0	2510.0	2520.0	2530.1	2540.2	2550.3	2560.4	2570.5	2580.6	2590.8	1.01

Squares of Numbers increasing by Tenths from 0.0 to 100.9.

No.	0.0	0.1	0.2	0.3	0.4	0.5	0.6	0.7	0.8	0.9	Diff. 0.01
50	2500.0	2510.0	2520.0	2530.1	2540.2	2550.3	2560.4	2570.5	2580.6	2590.8	1.01
51	2601.0	2611.2	2621.4	2631.7	2642.0	2652.3	2662.6	2672.9	2683.2	2693.6	03
52	2704.0	2714.4	2724.8	2735.3	2745.8	2756.3	2766.8	2777.3	2787.8	2798.4	05
53	2809.0	2819.6	2830.2	2840.9	2851.6	2862.3	2873.0	2883.7	2894.4	2905.2	07
54	2916.0	2926.8	2937.6	2948.5	2959.4	2970.3	2981.2	2992.1	3003.0	3014.0	09
55	3025.0	3036.0	3047.0	3058.1	3069.2	3080.3	3091.4	3002.5	3013.6	3124.8	1.11
56	3136.0	3147.2	3158.4	3169.7	3181.0	3192.3	3203.6	3214.9	3226.2	3237.6	13
57	3249.0	3260.4	3271.8	3283.3	3294.8	3306.3	3317.8	3329.3	3340.8	3352.4	15
58	3364.0	3375.6	3387.2	3398.9	3410.6	3422.3	3434.0	3445.7	3457.4	3469.2	17
59	3481.0	3492.8	3504.6	3516.5	3528.4	3540.3	3552.2	3564.1	3576.0	3588.0	19
60	3600.0	3612.0	3624.0	3636.1	3648.2	3660.3	3672.4	3684.5	3696.6	3708.8	1.21
61	3721.0	3733.2	3745.4	3757.7	3770.0	3782.3	3794.6	3806.9	3819.2	3831.6	23
62	3844.0	3856.4	3868.8	3881.3	3893.8	3906.3	3918.8	3931.3	3943.8	3956.4	25
63	3969.0	3981.6	3994.2	4006.9	4019.6	4032.3	4045.0	4057.7	4070.4	4083.2	27
64	4096.0	4108.8	4121.6	4134.5	4147.4	4160.3	4173.2	4186.1	4199.0	4212.0	29
65	4225.0	4238.0	4251.0	4264.1	4277.2	4290.3	4303.4	4316.5	4329.6	4342.8	1.31
66	4356.0	4369.2	4382.4	4395.7	4409.0	4422.3	4435.6	4448.9	4462.2	4475.6	33
67	4489.0	4502.4	4515.8	4529.3	4542.8	4556.3	4569.8	4583.3	4596.8	4610.4	35
68	4624.0	4637.6	4651.2	4664.9	4678.6	4692.3	4706.0	4719.7	4733.4	4747.2	37
69	4761.0	4774.8	4788.6	4802.5	4816.4	4830.3	4844.2	4858.1	4872.0	4886.0	39
70	4900.0	4914.0	4928.0	4942.1	4956.2	4970.3	4984.4	4998.5	5012.6	5026.8	1.41
71	5041.0	5055.2	5069.4	5083.7	5098.0	5112.3	5126.6	5140.9	5155.2	5169.6	43
72	5184.0	5198.4	5212.8	5227.3	5241.8	5256.3	5270.8	5285.3	5299.8	5314.4	45
73	5329.0	5343.6	5358.2	5372.9	5387.6	5402.3	5417.0	5431.7	5446.4	5461.2	47
74	5476.0	5490.8	5505.6	5520.5	5535.4	5550.3	5565.2	5580.1	5595.0	5610.0	49
75	5625.0	5640.0	5655.0	5670.1	5685.2	5700.3	5715.4	5730.5	5745.6	5760.8	1.51
76	5776.0	5791.2	5806.4	5821.7	5837.0	5852.3	5867.6	5882.9	5898.2	5913.6	53
77	5929.0	5944.4	5959.8	5975.3	5990.8	6006.3	6021.8	6037.3	6052.8	6068.4	55
78	6084.0	6099.6	6115.2	6130.9	6146.6	6162.3	6178.0	6193.7	6209.4	6225.2	57
79	6241.0	6256.8	6272.6	6288.5	6304.4	6320.3	6336.2	6352.1	6368.0	6384.0	59
80	6400.0	6416.0	6432.0	6448.1	6464.2	6480.3	6496.4	6512.5	6528.6	6544.8	1.61
81	6561.0	6577.2	6593.4	6609.7	6626.0	6642.3	6658.6	6674.9	6691.2	6707.6	63
82	6724.0	6740.4	6756.8	6773.3	6789.8	6806.3	6822.8	6839.3	6855.8	6872.4	65
83	6889.0	6905.6	6922.2	6938.9	6955.6	6972.3	6989.0	7005.7	7022.4	7039.2	67
84	7056.0	7072.8	7089.6	7106.5	7123.4	7140.3	7157.2	7174.1	7191.0	7208.0	69
85	7225.0	7242.0	7259.0	7276.1	7293.2	7310.3	7327.4	7344.5	7361.6	7378.8	1.71
86	7396.0	7413.2	7430.4	7447.7	7465.0	7482.3	7499.6	7516.9	7534.2	7551.6	73
87	7569.0	7586.4	7603.8	7621.3	7638.8	7656.3	7673.8	7691.3	7708.8	7726.4	75
88	7744.0	7761.6	7779.2	7796.9	7814.6	7832.3	7850.0	7867.7	7885.4	7903.2	77
89	7921.0	7938.8	7956.6	7974.5	7992.4	8010.3	8028.2	8046.1	8064.0	8082.0	79
90	8100.0	8118.0	8136.0	8154.1	8172.2	8190.3	8208.4	8226.5	8244.6	8262.8	1.81
91	8281.0	8299.2	8317.4	8335.7	8354.0	8372.3	8390.6	8408.9	8427.2	8445.6	83
92	8464.0	8482.4	8500.8	8519.3	8537.8	8556.3	8574.8	8593.3	8611.8	8630.4	85
93	8649.0	8667.6	8686.2	8704.9	8723.6	8742.3	8761.0	8779.7	8798.4	8817.2	87
94	8836.0	8854.8	8873.6	8892.5	8911.4	8930.3	8949.2	8963.1	8987.0	9006.0	89
95	9025.0	9044.0	9063.0	9082.1	9101.2	9120.3	9139.4	9158.5	9177.6	9196.8	1.91
96	9216.0	9235.2	9254.4	9273.7	9293.0	9312.3	9331.6	9350.9	9370.2	9389.6	93
97	9409.0	9428.4	9447.8	9467.3	9486.8	9506.3	9525.8	9545.3	9564.8	9584.4	95
98	9604.0	9623.6	9643.2	9662.9	9682.6	9702.3	9722.0	9741.7	9761.4	9781.2	97
99	9801.0	9820.8	9840.6	9860.5	9880.4	9900.3	9920.2	9940.1	9960.0	9980.0	1.99
100	10000.0	10020.0	10040.0	10060.1	10080.2	10100.3	10120.4	10140.5	10160.6	10180.8	2.01

Square Roots of Numbers increasing by Tenths from 0.0 to 100.9.

No.	0.0	0.1	0.2	0.3	0.4	0.5	0.6	0.7	0.8	0.9	Diff. 0.01
0	0.000	0.316	0.447	0.548	0.632	0.707	0.775	0.837	0.894	0.949	
1	1.000	4.049	1.095	1.140	1.183	1.225	1.265	1.304	1.342	1.378	4.15
2	414	449	483	517	549	581	612	643	673	703	3.19
3	732	761	789	817	844	871	897	924	950	975	2.69
4	2.000	2.025	2.049	2.074	2.098	2.121	2.145	2.168	2.191	2.214	2.37
5	2.236	2.258	2.280	2.302	2.324	2.345	2.366	2.387	2.408	2.429	2.14
6	449	470	490	510	530	550	569	588	608	627	1.97
7	646	665	683	702	720	739	757	775	793	811	1.83
8	828	846	864	881	898	915	933	950	966	983	1.72
9	3.000	3.017	3.033	3.050	3.066	3.082	3.098	3.114	3.130	3.146	1.63
10	3.162	3.178	3.194	3.210	3.225	3.240	3.256	3.271	3.286	3.302	1.55
11	317	332	347	362	376	391	406	421	435	450	48
12	464	479	493	507	521	536	550	564	578	592	42
13	606	619	633	647	661	674	688	701	715	728	36
14	742	755	768	782	795	808	821	834	847	860	32
15	3.873	3.886	3.899	3.912	3.924	3.937	3.950	3.962	3.975	3.987	1.27
16	4.000	4.612	4.025	4.037	4.050	4.062	4.074	4.087	4.099	4.111	23
17	123	135	147	159	171	183	195	207	219	231	20
18	243	254	266	278	290	301	313	324	336	348	16
19	359	370	382	393	405	416	427	438	450	461	13
20	4.472	4.483	4.494	4.506	4.517	4.528	4.539	4.550	4.561	4.572	1.10
21	583	593	604	615	626	637	648	658	669	680	08
22	690	701	712	722	733	743	754	764	775	785	06
23	796	806	817	827	837	848	858	868	879	889	03
24	899	909	919	930	940	950	960	970	980	990	01
25	5.000	5.010	5.020	5.030	5.040	5.050	5.060	5.070	5.079	5.089	0.99
26	099	109	119	128	138	148	158	167	177	187	97
27	196	206	215	225	235	244	254	263	273	282	95
28	292	301	310	320	329	339	348	357	367	376	94
29	385	394	404	413	422	431	441	450	459	468	92
30	5.477	5.486	5.495	5.505	5.514	5.523	5.532	5.541	5.550	5.559	0.91
31	568	577	586	595	604	612	621	630	639	648	89
32	657	666	675	683	692	701	710	718	727	736	88
33	745	753	762	771	779	788	797	805	814	822	87
34	831	840	848	857	865	874	882	891	899	908	85
35	5.916	5.925	5.933	5.941	5.950	5.958	5.967	5.975	5.983	5.992	0.85
36	6.000	6.008	6.017	6.025	6.033	6.042	6.050	6.058	6.066	6.075	83
37	083	091	099	107	116	124	132	140	148	156	82
38	164	173	181	189	197	205	213	221	229	237	81
39	245	253	261	269	277	285	293	301	309	317	80
40	6.325	6.332	6.340	6.348	6.356	6.364	6.372	6.380	6.387	6.395	0.79
41	403	411	419	427	434	442	450	458	465	473	78
42	481	488	496	504	512	519	527	535	542	550	77
43	557	565	573	580	588	595	603	611	618	626	76
44	633	641	648	656	663	671	678	686	693	701	75
45	6.708	6.716	6.723	6.731	6.738	6.745	6.753	6.760	6.768	6.775	0.74
46	782	790	797	804	812	819	826	834	841	848	73
47	856	863	870	877	885	892	899	907	914	921	73
48	928	935	943	950	957	964	971	979	986	993	72
49	7.000	7.007	7.014	7.021	7.029	7.036	7.043	7.050	7.057	7.064	71
50	7.071	7.078	7.085	7.092	7.099	7.106	7.113	7.120	7.127	7.134	0.70

Square Roots of Numbers increasing by Tenths from 0.0 to 100.9.

No.	0.0	0.1	0.2	0.3	0.4	0.5	0.6	0.7	0.8	0.9	Diff. 0.01
50	7.071	7.078	7.085	7.092	7.099	7.106	7.113	7.120	7.127	7.134	0.70
51	141	148	155	162	169	176	183	190	197	204	70
52	211	218	225	232	239	246	253	259	266	273	69
53	280	287	294	301	308	314	321	328	335	342	68
54	348	355	362	369	376	382	389	396	403	409	68
55	7.416	7.423	7.430	7.436	7.443	7.450	7.457	7.463	7.470	7.477	0.67
56	483	490	497	503	510	517	523	530	537	543	67
57	550	556	563	570	576	583	589	596	603	609	66
58	616	622	629	635	642	649	655	662	668	675	65
59	681	688	694	701	707	714	720	727	733	740	65
60	7.746	7.752	7.759	7.765	7.772	7.778	7.785	7.791	7.797	7.804	0.64
61	810	817	823	829	836	842	849	855	861	868	64
62	874	880	887	893	899	906	912	918	925	931	63
63	937	944	950	956	962	969	975	981	987	994	63
64	8.000	8.006	8.012	8.019	8.025	8.031	8.037	8.044	8.050	8.056	62
65	8.062	8.068	8.075	8.081	8.087	8.093	8.099	8.106	8.112	8.118	0.62
66	124	130	136	142	149	155	161	167	173	179	61
67	185	191	198	204	210	216	222	228	234	240	61
68	246	252	258	264	270	276	283	289	295	301	60
69	307	313	319	325	331	337	343	349	355	361	60
70	8.367	8.373	8.379	8.385	8.390	8.396	8.402	8.408	8.414	8.420	0.60
71	426	432	438	444	450	456	462	468	473	479	59
72	485	491	497	503	509	515	521	526	532	538	59
73	544	550	556	562	567	573	579	585	591	597	58
74	602	608	614	620	626	631	637	643	649	654	58
75	8.660	8.666	8.672	8.678	8.683	8.689	8.695	8.701	8.706	8.712	0.58
76	718	724	729	735	741	746	752	758	764	769	57
77	775	781	786	792	798	803	809	815	820	826	57
78	832	837	843	849	854	860	866	871	877	883	56
79	888	894	899	905	911	916	922	927	933	939	56
80	8.944	8.950	8.955	8.961	8.967	8.972	8.978	8.983	8.989	8.994	0.56
81	9.000	9.006	9.011	9.017	9.022	9.028	9.033	9.039	9.044	9.050	56
82	055	061	066	072	077	083	088	094	099	105	55
83	110	116	121	127	132	138	143	149	154	160	55
84	165	171	176	182	187	192	198	203	209	214	54
85	9.220	9.225	9.230	9.236	9.241	9.247	9.252	9.257	9.263	9.268	0.54
86	274	279	284	290	295	301	306	311	317	322	54
87	327	333	338	343	349	354	359	365	370	375	53
88	381	386	391	397	402	407	413	418	423	429	53
89	434	439	445	450	455	460	466	471	476	482	53
90	9.487	9.492	9.497	9.503	9.508	9.513	9.518	9.524	9.529	9.534	0.53
91	539	545	550	555	560	566	571	576	581	586	52
92	592	597	602	607	612	618	623	628	633	638	52
93	644	649	654	659	664	670	675	680	685	690	52
94	695	701	706	711	716	721	726	731	737	742	51
95	9.747	9.752	9.757	9.762	9.767	9.772	9.778	9.783	9.788	9.793	0.51
96	798	803	808	813	818	823	829	834	839	844	51
97	849	854	859	864	869	874	879	884	889	894	51
98	899	905	910	915	920	925	930	935	940	945	50
99	950	955	960	965	970	975	980	985	990	995	50
100	10.000	10.005	10.010	10.015	10.020	10.025	10.030	10.035	10.040	10.045	0.50

True Rising and Setting.

Declination of same name as the Latitude.

Latitude.	0° Ris.	0° Set.	1° Ris.	1° Set.	2° Ris.	2° Set.	3° Ris.	3° Set.	4° Ris.	4° Set.	5° Ris.	5° Set.	6° Ris.	6° Set.	Latitude.
°	h m	h m	h m	h m	h m	h m	h m	h m	h m	h m	h m	h m	h m	h m	°
0	6 0	6 0	6 0	6 0	6 0	6 0	6 0	6 0	6 0	6 0	6 0	6 0	6 0	6 0	0
4	0	0	0	0	5 59	1	5 59	1	5 59	1	5 59	1	5 58	2	4
8	0	0	5 59	1	59	1	58	2	58	2	57	3	57	3	8
12	0	0	59	1	58	2	57	3	57	3	56	4	55	5	12
16	0	0	59	1	58	2	57	3	55	5	54	6	53	7	16
20	6 0	6 0	5 59	6 1	5 57	6 3	5 56	6 4	5 54	6 6	5 53	6 7	5 51	6 9	20
22	0	0	58	2	57	3	55	5	54	6	52	8	50	10	22
24	0	0	58	2	56	4	55	5	53	7	51	9	49	11	24
26	0	0	58	2	56	4	54	6	52	8	50	10	48	12	26
28	0	0	58	2	56	4	54	6	51	9	49	11	47	13	28
30	6 0	6 0	5 58	6 2	5 55	6 5	5 53	6 7	5 51	6 9	5 48	6 12	5 46	6 14	30
32	0	0	58	2	55	5	53	7	50	10	47	13	45	15	32
34	0	0	57	3	55	5	52	8	49	11	46	14	44	16	34
36	0	0	57	3	54	6	51	9	48	12	45	15	42	18	36
38	0	0	57	3	54	6	51	9	47	13	44	16	41	19	38
40	6 0	6 0	5 57	6 3	5 53	6 7	5 50	6 10	5 47	6 13	5 43	6 17	5 40	6 20	40
41	0	0	57	3	53	7	50	10	46	14	43	17	39	21	41
42	0	0	56	4	53	7	49	11	46	14	42	18	38	22	42
43	0	0	56	4	53	7	49	11	45	15	41	19	38	22	43
44	0	0	56	4	52	8	48	12	45	15	41	19	37	23	44
45	6 0	6 0	5 56	6 4	5 52	6 8	5 48	6 12	5 44	6 16	5 40	6 20	5 36	6 24	45
46	0	0	56	4	52	8	48	12	43	17	39	21	35	25	46
47	0	0	56	4	51	9	47	13	43	17	38	22	34	26	47
48	0	0	56	4	51	9	47	13	42	18	38	22	33	27	48
49	0	0	55	5	51	9	46	14	42	18	37	23	32	28	49
50	6 0	6 0	5 55	6 5	5 50	6 10	5 46	6 14	5 41	6 19	5 36	6 24	5 31	6 29	50
51	0	0	55	5	50	10	45	15	40	20	35	25	30	30	51
52	0	0	55	5	50	10	45	15	39	21	34	26	29	31	52
53	0	0	55	5	49	11	44	16	39	21	33	27	28	32	53
54	0	0	55	5	49	11	44	16	38	22	32	28	27	33	54
55	6 0	6 0	5 54	6 6	5 49	6 11	5 43	6 17	5 37	6 23	5 31	6 29	5 25	6 35	55
56	0	0	54	6	48	12	42	18	36	24	30	30	24	36	56
57	0	0	54	6	48	12	41	19	35	25	29	31	23	37	57
58	0	0	54	6	47	13	41	19	34	26	28	32	21	39	58
59	0	0	53	7	47	13	40	20	33	27	27	33	20	40	59
60	6 0	6 0	5 53	6 7	5 46	6 14	5 39	6 21	5 32	6 28	5 25	6 35	5 18	6 42	60
61	0	0	53	7	46	14	38	22	31	29	24	36	16	44	61
62	0	0	52	8	45	15	37	23	30	30	22	38	14	46	62
63	0	0	52	8	44	16	36	24	28	32	20	40	12	48	63
64	0	0	52	8	44	16	35	25	27	33	19	41	10	50	64
65	6 0	6 0	5 51	6 9	5 43	6 17	5 34	6 26	5 26	6 34	5 18	6 42	5 8	6 52	65
66	0	0	51	9	42	18	33	27	24	36	15	45	5	55	66
67	0	0	51	9	41	19	32	28	22	38	12	48	3	57	67
68	0	0	50	10	40	20	30	30	20	40	10	50	0	7 0	68
69	0	0	50	10	39	21	29	31	18	42	7	53	4 56	4	69
70	6 0	6 0	5 49	6 11	5 38	6 22	5 27	6 33	5 16	6 44	5 4	6 56	4 53	7 7	70
71	0	0	48	12	37	23	25	35	13	47	1	59	49	11	71
72	0	0	48	12	35	25	23	37	10	50	4 58	7 2	45	15	72
73	0	0	47	13	34	26	21	39	7	53	53	7	40	20	73
74	0	0	46	14	32	28	18	42	4	56	49	11	34	26	74
75	6 0	6 0	5 45	6 15	5 30	6 30	5 15	6 45	5 0	7 0	4 44	7 16	4 28	7 32	75
76	0	0	44	16	28	32	11	49	4 55	5	38	22	20	40	76
77	0	0	43	17	25	35	7	53	49	11	31	29	11	49	77
78	0	0	41	19	22	38	3	57	43	17	23	37	1	59	78
79	0	0	39	21	19	41	4 57	7 3	36	24	13	47	3 49	8 11	79
Latitude.	Set.	Ris.	Set.	Ris.	Set.	Ris.	Set.	Ris.	Set.	Ris.	Set.	Ris.	Set.	Ris.	Latitude.
	0°		1°		2°		3°		4°		5°		6°		

Declination of contrary name.

True Rising and Setting.

Latitude.	Declination of same name as the Latitude.														Latitude.
	6°		7°		8°		9°		10°		11°		12°		
	Ris.	Set.	Ris.	Set.	Ris.	Set.	Ris.	Set.	Ris.	Set.	Ris.	Set.	Ris.	Set.	
°	h m	h m	h m	h m	h m	h m	h m	h m	h m	h m	h m	h m	h m	h m	°
0	6 0	6 0	6 0	6 0	6 0	6 0	6 0	6 0	6 0	6 0	6 0	6 0	6 0	6 0	0
4	5 58	2	5 58	2	5 58	2	5 57	3	5 57	3	5 57	3	5 57	3	4
8	57	3	56	4	55	5	55	5	54	6	54	6	53	7	8
12	55	5	54	6	53	7	52	8	51	9	51	9	50	10	12
16	53	7	52	8	51	9	50	10	48	12	47	13	46	14	16
20	5 51	6 9	5 50	6 10	5 48	6 12	5 47	6 13	5 45	6 15	5 44	6 16	5 42	6 18	20
22	50	10	49	11	47	13	45	15	44	16	42	18	40	20	22
24	49	11	47	13	46	14	44	16	42	18	40	20	38	22	24
26	48	12	46	14	44	16	42	18	40	20	38	22	36	24	26
28	47	13	45	15	43	17	41	19	38	22	36	24	34	26	28
30	5 46	6 14	5 44	6 16	5 41	6 19	5 39	6 21	5 37	6 23	5 34	6 26	5 32	6 28	30
32	45	15	42	18	40	20	37	23	35	25	32	28	29	31	32
34	44	16	41	19	38	22	35	25	33	27	30	30	27	33	34
36	42	18	40	20	37	23	34	26	31	29	28	32	24	36	36
38	41	19	38	22	35	25	32	28	28	32	25	35	22	38	38
40	5 40	6 20	5 36	6 24	5 33	6 27	5 29	6 31	5 26	6 34	5 22	6 38	5 19	6 41	40
41	39	21	35	25	32	28	28	32	25	35	21	39	17	43	41
42	38	22	35	25	31	29	27	33	23	37	20	40	16	44	42
43	38	22	34	26	30	30	26	34	22	38	18	42	14	45	43
44	37	23	33	27	29	31	25	35	21	39	17	43	13	47	44
45	5 36	6 24	5 32	6 28	5 28	6 32	5 24	6 36	5 19	6 41	5 15	6 45	5 11	6 49	45
46	35	25	31	29	27	33	22	38	18	42	14	46	9	51	46
47	34	26	30	30	25	35	21	39	16	44	12	48	7	53	47
48	33	27	29	31	24	36	19	41	15	45	10	50	5	55	48
49	32	28	28	32	23	37	18	42	13	47	8	52	3	57	49
50	5 31	6 29	5 26	6 34	5 21	6 39	5 16	6 44	5 11	6 49	5 6	6 54	5 1	6 59	50
51	30	30	25	35	20	40	15	45	10	50	4	56	4 59	7 1	51
52	29	31	24	36	19	41	13	47	8	52	2	58	57	3	52
53	28	32	22	38	17	43	11	49	6	54	0	7 0	54	6	53
54	27	33	21	39	15	45	10	50	4	56	4 58	2	52	8	54
55	5 25	6 35	5 20	6 40	5 14	6 46	5 8	6 52	5 2	6 58	4 56	7 4	4 49	7 11	55
56	24	36	18	42	12	48	6	54	4 59	7 1	53	7	47	13	56
57	23	37	16	44	10	50	4	56	57	3	50	10	44	16	57
58	21	39	15	45	8	52	1	59	54	6	48	12	41	19	58
59	20	40	13	47	6	54	4 59	7 1	52	8	44	16	37	23	59
60	5 18	6 42	5 11	6 49	5 4	6 56	4 56	7 4	4 49	7 11	4 41	7 19	4 34	7 26	60
61	16	44	9	51	1	59	54	6	45	14	38	22	30	30	61
62	14	46	7	53	4 59	7 1	51	9	43	17	34	26	26	34	62
63	12	48	4	56	56	4	48	12	39	21	30	30	21	39	63
64	10	50	2	58	53	7	44	16	35	25	26	34	17	43	64
65	5 8	6 52	5 0	7 0	4 50	7 10	4 41	7 19	4 31	7 29	4 21	7 39	4 12	7 48	65
66	5	55	4 56	4	46	14	37	23	27	33	16	44	6	54	66
67	3	57	53	7	43	17	33	27	22	38	11	49	0	8 0	67
68	0	7 0	49	11	39	21	28	32	16	44	5	55	3 53	7	68
69	4 56	4	45	15	34	26	23	37	11	49	3 58	8 2	46	14	69
70	4 53	7 7	4 41	7 19	4 29	7 31	4 17	7 43	4 4	7 56	3 51	8 9	3 37	8 23	70
71	49	11	36	24	23	37	10	50	3 57	8 3	43	17	28	32	71
72	45	15	31	29	17	43	3	57	49	11	33	27	17	43	72
73	40	20	25	35	10	50	3 55	8 5	39	21	22	38	4	56	73
74	34	26	19	41	3	57	46	14	28	32	9	51	2 49	9 11	74
75	4 28	7 32	4 11	7 49	3 54	8 6	3 35	8 25	3 15	8 45	2 54	9 6	2 30	9 30	75
76	20	40	2	58	43	17	22	38	0	9 0	35	25	6	54	76
77	11	49	3 51	8 9	30	30	7	53	2 41	19	11	49	1 32	10 28	77
78	1	59	39	21	14	46	2 47	9 13	16	44	1 35	10 25	0 0	12 0	78
79	3 49	8 11	23	37	2 55	9 5	22	38	1 40	10 20	0 0	12 0			79
	Set.	Ris.	Set.	Ris.	Set.	Ris.	Set.	Ris.	Set.	Ris.	Set.	Ris.	Set.	Ris.	
Latitude.	6°		7°		8°		9°		10°		11°		12°		Latitude.
	Declination of contrary name.														

True Rising and Setting.

Declination of same name as the Latitude.

Latitude.	12°		13°		14°		15°		16°		17°		18°		Latitude.
	Ris.	Set.	Ris	Set.	Ris.	Set.	Ris.	Set.	Ris.	Set.	Ris.	Set.	Ris.	Set.	
°	h m	h m	h m	h m	h m	h m	h m	h m	h m	h m	h m	h m	h m	h m	
0	6 0	6 0	6 0	6 0	6 0	6 0	6 0	6 0	6 0	6 0	6 0	6 0	6 0	6 0	0
2	5 58	2	5 58	2	5 58	2	5 58	2	5 58	2	5 58	2	5 57	3	2
4	57	3	56	4	56	4	56	4	55	5	55	5	55	5	4
6	55	5	54	6	54	6	54	6	53	7	53	7	52	8	6
8	53	7	53	7	52	8	51	9	51	9	50	10	50	10	8
10	5 51	6 9	5 51	6 9	5 50	6 10	5 49	6 11	5 48	6 12	5 48	6 12	5 47	6 13	10
12	50	10	49	11	48	12	47	13	46	14	45	15	44	16	12
14	48	12	47	13	46	14	45	15	44	16	43	17	41	19	14
16	46	14	45	15	44	16	42	18	41	19	40	20	39	21	16
18	44	16	43	17	41	19	40	20	39	21	37	23	36	24	18
20	5 42	6 18	5 41	6 19	5 39	6 21	5 38	6 22	5 36	6 24	5 34	6 26	5 33	6 27	20
22	40	20	39	21	37	23	35	25	33	27	32	28	30	30	22
24	38	22	36	24	34	26	33	27	31	29	29	31	27	33	24
26	36	24	34	26	32	28	30	30	28	32	26	34	24	36	26
28	34	26	32	28	30	30	27	33	25	35	23	37	20	40	28
30	5 32	6 28	5 29	6 31	5 27	6 33	5 24	6 36	5 22	6 38	5 19	6 41	5 17	6 43	30
32	29	31	27	33	24	36	21	39	19	41	16	44	13	47	32
34	27	33	24	36	21	39	18	42	15	45	12	48	9	51	34
36	24	36	21	39	18	42	15	45	12	48	9	51	5	55	36
38	22	38	18	42	15	45	12	48	8	52	5	55	1	59	38
40	5 19	6 41	5 15	6 45	5 12	6 48	5 8	6 52	5 4	6 56	5 1	6 59	4 57	7 3	40
41	17	43	14	46	10	50	6	54	2	58	4 58	7 2	54	6	41
42	16	44	12	48	8	52	4	56	0	7 0	56	4	52	8	42
43	14	46	10	50	6	54	2	58	4 58	2	54	6	49	11	43
44	13	47	8	52	4	56	0	7 0	56	4	51	9	47	13	44
45	5 11	6 49	5 7	6 53	5 2	6 58	4 58	7 2	4 53	7 7	4 49	7 11	4 44	7 16	45
46	9	51	5	55	0	7 0	56	4	51	9	46	14	41	19	46
47	7	53	3	57	4 58	2	53	7	48	12	43	17	38	22	47
48	5	55	1	59	56	4	51	9	46	14	41	19	35	25	48
49	3	57	4 58	7 2	53	7	48	12	43	17	38	22	32	28	49
50	5 1	6 59	4 56	7 4	4 51	7 9	4 46	7 14	4 40	7 20	4 35	7 25	4 29	7 31	50
51	4 59	7 1	54	6	48	12	43	17	37	23	31	29	25	35	51
52	57	3	51	9	46	14	40	20	34	26	28	32	22	38	52
53	54	6	49	11	43	17	37	23	31	29	24	36	18	42	53
54	52	8	46	14	40	20	33	27	27	33	20	40	14	46	54
55	4 49	7 11	4 43	7 17	4 37	7 23	4 30	7 30	4 23	7 37	4 16	7 44	4 9	7 51	55
56	47	13	40	20	33	27	26	34	19	41	12	48	5	55	56
57	44	16	37	23	30	30	22	38	15	45	8	52	0	8 0	57
58	41	19	33	27	26	34	18	42	11	49	3	57	3 55	5	58
59	37	23	30	30	22	38	14	46	6	54	3 58	8 2	49	11	59
60	4 34	7 26	4 26	7 34	4 18	7 42	4 9	7 51	4 1	7 59	3 52	8 8	3 43	8 17	60
61	30	30	22	38	13	47	4	56	3 55	8 5	46	14	36	24	61
62	26	34	17	43	8	52	3 59	8 1	49	11	40	20	29	31	62
63	21	39	12	48	3	57	53	7	43	17	33	27	22	38	63
64	17	43	7	53	3 57	8 3	47	13	36	24	25	35	13	47	64
65	4 12	7 48	4 1	7 59	3 51	8 9	3 40	8 20	3 28	8 32	3 16	8 44	3 3	8 57	65
66	6	54	3 54	8 6	44	16	32	28	20	40	7	53	2 53	9 7	66
67	0	8 0	48	12	36	24	23	37	10	50	2 56	9 4	40	20	67
68	3 53	7	41	19	28	32	14	46	2 59	9 1	43	17	26	34	68
69	46	14	32	28	18	42	3	57	46	14	29	31	9	51	69
70	3 37	8 23	3 23	8 37	3 7	8 53	2 50	9 10	2 32	9 28	2 12	9 48	1 47	10 13	70
71	28	32	12	48	2 54	9 6	36	24	15	45	1 50	10 10	17	43	71
72	17	43	2 59	9 1	40	20	18	42	1 52	10 8	19	41	0 0	12 0	72
73	4	56	44	16	21	39	1 55	10 5	21	39	0 0	12 0			73
74	2 49	9 11	25	35	1 58	10 2	23	37	0 0	12 0					74
Latitude.	Set.	Ris.	Set.	Ris.	Set.	Ris.	Set.	Ris.	Set.	Ris.	Set.	Ris.	Set.	Ris.	Latitude.
	12°		13°		14°		15°		16°		17°		18°		

Declination of contrary name.

True Rising and Setting.

Latitude.	Declination of same name as the Latitude.														Latitude.
	18°		19°		20°		21°		22°		23°		24°		
	Ris.	Set.	Ris.	Set.	Ris.	Set.	Ris.	Set.	Ris.	Set.	Ris.	Set.	Ris.	Set.	
°	h m	h m	h m	h m	h m	h m	h m	h m	h m	h m	h m	h m	h m	h m	°
0	6 0	6 0	6 0	6 0	6 0	6 0	6 0	6 0	6 0	6 0	6 0	6 0	6 0	6 0	0
2	5 57	3	5 57	3	5 57	3	5 57	3	5 57	3	5 57	3	5 56	4	2
4	55	5	54	6	54	6	54	6	54	6	53	7	53	7	4
6	52	8	52	8	51	9	51	9	50	10	50	10	49	11	6
8	50	10	49	11	48	12	48	12	47	13	46	14	46	14	8
10	5 47	6 13	5 46	6 14	5 45	6 15	5 44	6 16	5 44	6 16	5 43	6 17	5 42	6 18	10
12	44	16	43	17	42	18	41	19	40	20	39	21	38	22	12
14	41	19	40	20	39	21	38	22	37	23	36	24	35	25	14
16	39	21	37	23	36	24	35	25	33	27	32	28	31	29	16
18	36	24	34	26	33	27	31	29	30	30	28	32	27	33	18
20	5 33	6 27	5 31	6 29	5 30	6 30	5 28	6 32	5 26	6 34	5 24	6 36	5 23	6 37	20
22	30	30	28	32	26	34	24	36	22	38	20	40	19	41	22
24	27	33	25	35	23	37	21	39	19	41	16	44	14	46	24
26	24	36	21	39	19	41	17	43	15	45	12	48	10	50	26
28	20	40	18	42	15	45	13	47	10	50	8	52	5	55	28
30	5 17	6 43	5 14	6 46	5 11	6 49	5 9	6 51	5 6	6 54	5 3	6 57	5 0	7 0	30
31	15	45	12	48	9	51	7	53	4	56	1	59	4 58	2	31
32	13	47	10	50	7	53	4	56	2	58	4 59	7 1	55	5	32
33	11	49	8	52	5	55	2	58	4 59	7 1	56	4	53	7	33
34	9	51	6	54	3	57	0	7 0	57	3	53	7	50	10	34
35	5 7	6 53	5 4	6 56	5 1	6 59	4 58	7 2	4 54	7 6	4 51	7 9	4 47	7 13	35
36	5	55	2	58	4 59	7 1	55	5	52	8	48	12	44	16	36
37	3	57	0	7 0	56	4	53	7	49	11	45	15	42	18	37
38	1	59	4 58	2	54	6	50	10	46	14	43	17	39	21	38
39	4 59	7 1	55	5	51	9	48	12	44	16	40	20	35	25	39
40	4 57	7 3	4 53	7 7	4 49	7 11	4 45	7 15	4 41	7 19	4 37	7 23	4 32	7 28	40
41	54	6	50	10	46	14	42	18	38	22	33	27	29	31	41
42	52	8	48	12	43	17	39	21	35	25	30	30	25	35	42
43	49	11	45	15	41	19	36	24	31	29	27	33	22	38	43
44	47	13	42	18	38	22	33	27	28	32	23	37	18	42	44
45	4 44	7 16	4 39	7 21	4 35	7 25	4 30	7 30	4 25	7 35	4 20	7 40	4 14	7 46	45
46	41	19	36	24	31	29	26	34	21	39	16	44	10	50	46
47	38	22	33	27	28	32	23	37	17	43	12	48	6	54	47
48	35	25	30	30	25	35	19	41	13	47	7	53	1	59	48
49	32	28	27	33	21	39	15	45	9	51	3	57	3 57	8 3	49
50	4 29	7 31	4 23	7 37	4 17	7 43	4 11	7 49	4 5	7 55	3 58	8 2	3 52	8 8	50
51	25	35	19	41	13	47	7	53	0	8 0	53	7	47	13	51
52	22	38	15	45	9	51	2	58	3 55	5	48	12	41	19	52
53	18	42	11	49	4	56	3 57	8 3	50	10	43	17	35	25	53
54	14	46	7	53	0	8 0	52	8	45	15	37	23	29	31	54
55	4 9	7 51	4 2	7 58	3 55	8 5	3 47	8 13	3 39	8 21	3 31	8 29	3 22	8 38	55
56	5	55	3 57	8 3	49	11	41	19	33	27	24	36	15	45	56
57	0	8 0	52	8	44	16	35	25	26	34	17	43	7	53	57
58	3 55	5	46	14	38	22	28	32	19	41	9	51	2 58	9 2	58
59	49	11	40	20	31	29	21	39	11	49	0	9 0	49	11	59
60	3 43	8 17	3 34	8 26	3 24	8 36	3 13	8 47	3 2	8 58	2 51	9 9	2 38	9 22	60
61	36	24	26	34	16	44	5	55	2 53	9 7	40	20	26	34	61
62	29	31	18	42	7	53	2 55	9 5	42	18	28	32	13	47	62
63	22	38	10	50	2 58	9 2	44	16	30	30	14	46	1 56	10 4	63
64	13	47	1	59	47	13	32	28	16	44	1 58	10 2	36	24	64
65	3 3	8 57	2 50	9 10	2 35	9 25	2 18	9 42	2 0	10 0	1 38	10 22	1 9	10 51	65
66	2 53	9 7	37	23	21	39	2	58	1 39	21	10	50	0 0	12 0	66
67	40	20	23	37	4	56	1 41	10 19	11	49	0 0	12 0			67
68	26	34	6	54	1 43	10 17	13	47	0 0	12 0					68
69	9	51	1 45	10 15	14	46	0 0	12 0							69
Latitude.	Set.	Ris.	Set.	Ris.	Set.	Ris.	Set.	Ris.	Set.	Ris.	Set.	Ris.	Set.	Ris.	Latitude.
	18°		19°		20°		21°		22°		23°		24°		
	Declination of contrary name.														

True Rising and Setting.

Latitude.	Declination of same name as the Latitude.														Latitude.
	24°		25°		26°		27°		28°		29°		30°		
	Ris.	Set.	Ris.	Set.	Ris.	Set.	Ris.	Set.	Ris.	Set.	Ris.	Set.	Ris.	Set.	
°	h m	h m	h m	h m	h m	h m	h m	h m	h m	h m	h m	h m	h m	h m	°
0	6 0	6 0	6 0	6 0	6 0	6 0	6 0	6 0	6 0	6 0	6 0	6 0	6 0	6 0	0
2	5 56	4	5 56	4	5 56	4	5 56	4	5 56	4	5 56	4	5 55	5	2
4	53	7	53	7	52	8	52	8	51	9	51	9	51	9	4
6	49	11	49	11	48	12	48	12	47	13	47	13	46	14	6
8	46	14	45	15	44	16	44	16	43	17	42	18	41	19	8
10	5 42	6 18	5 41	6 19	5 40	6 20	5 39	6 21	5 38	6 22	5 38	6 22	5 37	6 23	10
12	38	22	37	23	36	24	35	25	34	26	33	27	32	28	12
14	35	25	33	27	32	28	31	29	30	30	28	32	27	33	14
16	31	29	29	31	28	32	26	34	25	35	23	37	22	38	16
18	27	33	25	35	24	36	22	38	20	40	18	42	17	43	18
20	5 23	6 37	5 21	6 39	5 19	6 41	5 17	6 43	5 15	6 45	5 13	6 47	5 11	6 49	20
22	19	41	17	43	15	45	12	48	10	50	8	52	6	54	22
24	14	46	12	48	10	50	8	52	5	55	3	57	0	7 0	24
26	10	50	7	53	5	55	2	58	0	7 0	4 57	7 3	4 55	5	26
28	5	55	3	57	0	7 0	4 57	7 3	4 54	6	51	9	49	11	28
30	5 0	7 0	4 58	7 2	4 55	7 5	4 52	7 8	4 48	7 12	4 45	7 15	4 42	7 18	30
31	4 58	2	55	5	52	8	49	11	46	14	42	18	39	21	31
32	55	5	52	8	49	11	46	14	42	18	39	21	35	25	32
33	53	7	49	11	46	14	43	17	39	21	36	24	32	28	33
34	50	10	47	13	43	17	40	20	36	24	32	28	28	32	34
35	4 47	7 13	4 44	7 16	4 40	7 20	4 36	7 24	4 33	7 27	4 29	7 31	4 25	7 35	35
36	44	16	41	19	37	23	33	27	29	31	25	35	21	39	36
37	42	18	38	22	34	26	30	30	26	34	21	39	17	43	37
38	39	21	35	25	30	30	26	34	22	38	17	43	13	47	38
39	35	25	31	29	27	33	23	37	18	42	13	47	9	51	39
40	4 32	7 28	4 28	7 32	4 23	7 37	4 19	7 41	4 14	7 46	4 9	7 51	4 4	7 56	40
41	29	31	24	36	20	40	15	45	10	50	5	55	0	8 0	41
42	25	35	21	39	16	44	11	49	5	55	0	8 0	3 55	5	42
43	22	38	17	43	12	48	7	53	1	59	3 56	4	50	10	43
44	18	42	13	47	8	52	2	58	3 56	8 4	51	9	44	16	44
45	4 14	7 46	4 9	7 51	4 3	7 57	3 57	8 3	3 52	8 8	3 45	8 15	3 39	8 21	45
46	10	50	5	55	3 59	8 1	53	7	46	14	40	20	33	27	46
47	6	54	0	8 0	54	6	48	12	41	19	34	26	27	33	47
48	1	59	3 55	5	49	11	42	18	35	25	28	32	20	40	48
49	3 57	8 3	50	10	43	17	36	24	29	31	22	38	13	47	49
50	3 52	8 8	3 45	8 15	3 38	8 22	3 30	8 30	3 23	8 37	3 15	8 45	3 6	8 54	50
51	47	13	39	21	32	28	24	36	16	44	7	53	2 58	9 2	51
52	41	19	33	27	25	35	17	43	8	52	2 59	9 1	49	11	52
53	35	25	27	33	19	41	10	50	0	9 0	51	9	40	20	53
54	29	31	20	40	11	49	2	58	2 52	8	41	19	30	30	54
55	3 22	8 38	3 13	8 47	3 3	8 57	2 53	9 7	2 42	9 18	2 31	9 29	2 18	9 42	55
56	15	45	5	55	2 55	9 5	44	16	32	28	19	41	5	55	56
57	7	53	2 56	9 4	45	15	33	27	20	40	6	54	1 49	10 11	57
58	2 58	9 2	47	13	35	25	22	38	7	53	1 50	10 10	30	30	58
59	49	11	36	24	23	37	8	52	1 51	10 9	31	29	4	56	59
60	2 38	9 22	2 25	9 35	2 9	9 51	1 52	10 8	1 32	10 28	1 5	10 55	0 0	12 0	60
61	26	34	11	49	1 53	10 7	33	27	1 6	54	0 0	12 0			61
62	13	47	1 55	10 5	34	26	6	54	0 0	12 0					62
63	1 56	10 4	35	25	7	53	0 0	12 0							63
64	36	24	8	52	0 0	12 0									64
65	1 9	10 51	0 0	12 0											65
66	0 0	12 0													66
67															67
68															68
69															69
Latitude.	Set.	Ris.	Set.	Ris.	Set.	Ris.	Set.	Ris.	Set.	Ris.	Set.	Ris.	Set.	Ris.	Latitude.
	24°		25°		26°		27°		28°		29°		30°		
	Declination of contrary name.														

Horizon-Azimuths.

Latitude.	Declination of same name as the Latitude.													Latitude.
	0°.0	0°.5	1°.0	1°.5	2°.0	2°.5	3°.0	3°.5	4°.0	4°.5	5°.0	5°.5	6°.0	
°	°	°	°	°	°	°	°	°	°	°	°	°	°	°
0	90.0	89.5	89.0	88.5	88.0	87.5	87.0	86.5	86.0	85.5	85.0	84.5	84.0	0
10	0.0	9.5	9.0	8.5	8.0	7.5	7.0	6.5	5.9	5.4	4.9	4.4	3.9	10
15	0.0	9.5	9.0	8.5	7.9	7.4	6.9	6.4	5.8	5.3	4.8	4.3	3.8	15
20	0.0	9.5	8.9	8.4	7.9	7.3	6.8	6.3	5.7	5.2	4.7	4.2	3.6	20
25	0.0	9.5	8.9	8.4	7.8	7.2	6.7	6.2	5.6	5.0	4.5	4.0	3.4	25
30	90.0	89.4	88.8	88.3	87.7	87.1	86.6	86.0	85.4	84.8	84.2	83.7	83.1	30
32	0.0	9.4	8.8	8.2	7.6	7.1	6.5	5.9	5.3	4.7	4.1	3.5	3.0	32
34	0.0	9.4	8.8	8.2	7.6	7.0	6.4	5.8	5.2	4.6	4.0	3.4	2.8	34
36	0.0	9.4	8.8	8.2	7.5	6.9	6.3	5.7	5.1	4.4	3.9	3.2	2.6	36
38	0.0	9.4	8.7	8.1	7.5	6.8	6.2	5.6	4.9	4.3	3.7	3.0	2.4	38
40	90.0	89.3	88.7	88.0	87.4	86.7	86.1	85.4	84.8	84.1	83.5	82.8	82.2	40
42	0.0	9.3	8.7	8.0	7.3	6.6	6.0	5.3	4.6	3.9	3.3	2.6	2.0	42
44	0.0	9.3	8.6	7.9	7.2	6.5	5.8	5.1	4.4	3.7	3.1	2.4	1.7	44
46	0.0	9.3	8.6	7.8	7.1	6.4	5.7	5.0	4.2	3.5	2.8	2.1	1.4	46
48	0.0	9.3	8.5	7.8	7.0	6.3	5.5	4.8	4.0	3.3	2.5	1.8	1.0	48
50	90.0	89.2	88.5	87.7	86.9	86.1	85.3	84.6	83.8	83.0	82.2	81.4	80.7	50
51	0.0	9.2	8.4	7.6	6.8	6.0	5.2	4.4	3.6	2.8	2.0	1.2	0.5	51
52	0.0	9.2	8.4	7.6	6.7	5.9	5.1	4.3	3.5	2.7	1.9	1.0	0.3	52
53	0.0	9.2	8.4	7.5	6.7	5.8	5.0	4.2	3.3	2.5	1.7	0.8	0.0	53
54	0.0	9.1	8.3	7.5	6.6	5.7	4.9	4.0	3.2	2.3	1.5	0.6	79.8	54
55	90.0	89.1	88.3	87.4	86.5	85.6	84.8	83.9	83.0	82.1	81.3	80.4	79.5	55
56	0.0	9.1	8.2	7.3	6.4	5.5	4.6	3.7	2.8	1.9	1.0	0.1	9.2	56
57	0.0	9.1	8.2	7.3	6.3	5.4	4.5	3.6	2.6	1.7	0.8	79.9	8.9	57
58	0.0	9.1	8.1	7.2	6.2	5.3	4.3	3.4	2.4	1.5	0.5	9.6	8.6	58
59	0.0	9.0	8.1	7.1	6.1	5.1	4.2	3.2	2.2	1.2	0.3	9.3	8.3	59
60	90.0	89.0	88.0	87.0	86.0	85.0	84.0	83.0	82.0	81.0	80.0	79.0	77.9	60
61	0.0	9.0	7.9	6.9	5.9	4.8	3.8	2.8	1.7	0.7	79.7	8.6	7.5	61
62	0.0	8.9	7.9	6.8	5.7	4.7	3.6	2.5	1.5	0.4	9.3	8.2	7.1	62
63	0.0	8.9	7.8	6.7	5.5	4.5	3.4	2.3	1.2	0.1	8.9	7.8	6.6	63
64	0.0	8.9	7.7	6.6	5.4	4.3	3.1	2.0	0.8	79.7	8.5	7.4	6.1	64
65.0	90.0	88.8	87.6	86.5	85.2	84.1	82.9	81.7	80.5	79.3	78.1	76.9	75.6	65.0
5.5	0.0	8.8	7.6	6.4	5.2	4.0	2.8	1.5	0.3	9.1	7.9	6.6	5.4	5.5
6.0	0.0	8.8	7.5	6.3	5.1	3.9	2.6	1.4	0.1	8.9	7.6	6.4	5.1	6.0
6.5	0.0	8.8	7.5	6.2	5.0	3.7	2.5	1.2	79.9	8.7	7.4	6.1	4.8	6.5
7.0	0.0	8.7	7.4	6.2	4.9	3.6	2.3	1.0	9.7	8.4	7.1	5.8	4.5	7.0
67.5	90.0	88.7	87.4	86.1	84.8	83.5	82.1	80.8	79.5	78.2	76.8	75.5	74.1	67.5
8.0	0.0	8.7	7.3	6.0	4.7	3.3	2.0	0.6	9.3	7.9	6.5	5.2	3.8	8.0
8.5	0.0	8.6	7.3	5.9	4.6	3.2	1.8	0.4	9.0	7.6	6.2	4.8	3.4	8.5
9.0	0.0	8.6	7.2	5.8	4.5	3.0	1.6	0.2	8.8	7.4	5.9	4.5	3.0	9.0
9.5	0.0	8.6	7.1	5.7	4.3	2.8	1.4	0.0	8.5	7.1	5.6	4.1	2.6	9.5
70.0	90.0	88.5	87.1	85.6	84.2	82.7	81.2	79.7	78.2	76.7	75.2	73.7	72.2	70.0
0.5	0.0	8.5	7.0	5.5	4.0	2.5	1.0	9.5	7.9	6.4	4.9	3.3	1.8	0.5
1.0	0.0	8.5	6.9	5.4	3.8	2.3	0.7	9.2	7.6	6.1	4.5	2.9	1.3	1.0
1.5	0.0	8.4	6.8	5.3	3.7	2.1	0.5	8.9	7.3	5.7	4.1	2.4	0.8	1.5
2.0	0.0	8.4	6.8	5.1	3.5	1.9	0.2	8.6	7.0	5.3	3.6	1.9	0.2	2.0
72.5	90.0	88.3	86.7	85.0	83.3	81.7	80.0	78.3	76.6	74.9	73.1	71.4	69.7	72.5
3.0	0.0	8.3	6.6	4.9	3.1	1.4	79.7	8.0	6.2	4.5	2.6	0.9	9.1	3.0
3.5	0.0	8.2	6.5	4.8	2.9	1.2	9.4	7.6	5.8	4.0	2.1	0.3	8.4	3.5
4.0	0.0	8.2	6.4	4.6	2.7	0.9	9.1	7.2	5.4	3.5	1.6	69.7	7.7	4.0
4.5	0.0	8.1	6.3	4.4	2.5	0.6	8.7	6.8	4.9	2.9	1.0	9.0	7.0	4.5
75.0	90.0	88.1	86.2	84.2	82.3	80.3	78.3	76.4	74.4	72.3	70.3	68.3	66.2	75.0
5.5	0.0	8.0	6.1	4.0	2.0	0.0	7.9	5.9	3.8	1.7	69.6	7.5	5.3	5.5
6.0	0.0	7.9	6.0	3.8	1.7	79.6	7.5	5.4	3.2	1.1	8.9	6.7	4.4	6.0
6.5	0.0	7.9	5.8	3.6	1.4	9.2	7.0	4.8	2.6	0.4	8.1	5.8	3.4	6.5
7.0	0.0	7.8	5.6	3.4	1.1	8.8	6.5	4.2	1.9	69.6	7.2	4.8	2.3	7.0

With Declination of contrary name enter the Table as above, but subtract the tabular azimuth from 180°.0.

Horizon-Azimuths.

Declination of same name as the Latitude.

Latitude.	6.0	6.5	7.0	7.5	8.0	8.5	9.0	9.5	10.0	10.5	11.0	11.5	12.0	Latitude.
°	°	°	°	°	°	°	°	°	°	°	°	°	°	°
0	84.0	83.5	83.0	82.5	82.0	81.5	81.0	80.5	80.0	79.5	79.0	78.5	78.0	0
10	3.9	3.4	2.9	2.4	1.9	1.4	0.9	0.3	79.9	9.3	8.8	8.3	7.8	10
15	3.8	3.3	2.8	2.2	1.7	1.2	0.7	0.2	9.6	9.1	8.6	8.1	7.5	15
20	3.6	3.1	2.6	2.0	1.5	0.9	0.4	79.9	9.3	8.8	8.3	7.7	7.2	20
25	3.4	2.9	2.3	1.7	1.2	0.6	0.1	9.5	8.9	8.4	7.8	7.2	6.7	25
30	83.1	82.5	81.9	81.3	80.7	80.2	79.6	79.0	78.5	77.9	77.3	76.7	76.1	30
32	3.0	2.3	1.7	1.2	0.5	0.0	9.4	8.8	8.2	7.6	7.0	6.4	5.8	32
34	2.8	2.2	1.5	1.0	0.3	79.7	9.2	8.5	7.9	7.3	6.7	6.1	5.5	34
36	2.6	2.0	1.3	0.7	0.1	9.5	8.9	8.2	7.6	7.0	6.4	5.7	5.1	36
38	2.4	1.8	1.1	0.5	79.8	9.2	8.6	7.9	7.3	6.6	6.0	5.3	4.7	38
40	82.2	81.5	80.9	80.2	79.5	78.9	78.3	77.6	76.9	76.2	75.6	74.9	74.3	40
42	2.0	1.2	0.6	79.9	9.2	8.5	7.9	7.2	6.5	5.8	5.2	4.4	3.8	42
44	1.7	0.9	0.3	9.5	8.9	8.1	7.5	6.7	6.0	5.3	4.7	3.9	3.2	44
46	1.4	0.6	79.9	9.2	8.5	7.7	7.0	6.2	5.5	4.8	4.1	3.3	2.6	46
48	1.0	0.3	9.5	8.8	8.0	7.2	6.5	5.7	5.0	4.2	3.4	2.7	1.9	48
50	80.7	79.9	79.1	78.3	77.5	76.7	75.9	75.1	74.3	73.5	72.7	71.9	71.1	50
51	0.5	9.6	8.8	8.0	7.2	6.4	5.6	4.8	4.0	3.2	2.3	1.5	0.7	51
52	0.3	9.4	8.6	7.8	6.9	6.1	5.3	4.4	3.6	2.8	1.9	1.1	0.3	52
53	0.0	9.2	8.3	7.5	6.6	5.8	4.9	4.1	3.2	2.4	1.5	0.6	69.8	53
54	79.8	8.9	8.0	7.2	6.3	5.4	4.6	3.7	2.8	1.9	1.1	0.2	9.3	54
55	79.5	78.6	77.7	76.9	76.0	75.1	74.2	73.3	72.4	71.5	70.6	69.7	68.8	55
56	9.2	8.3	7.4	6.5	5.6	4.7	3.8	2.8	1.9	1.0	0.1	9.1	8.2	56
57	8.9	8.0	7.1	6.1	5.2	4.2	3.3	2.3	1.4	0.4	69.5	8.5	7.6	57
58	8.6	7.7	6.7	5.7	4.8	3.8	2.8	1.8	0.9	69.9	8.9	7.9	6.9	58
59	8.3	7.3	6.3	5.3	4.3	3.3	2.3	1.3	0.3	9.3	8.3	7.2	6.2	59
60	77.9	76.9	75.9	74.9	73.8	72.8	71.8	70.7	69.7	68.6	67.6	66.5	65.4	60
61	7.5	6.5	5.4	4.4	3.3	2.2	1.2	0.1	9.0	7.9	6.9	5.7	4.6	61
62	7.1	6.1	4.9	3.9	2.7	1.6	0.6	69.4	8.3	7.1	6.1	4.8	3.7	62
63	6.6	5.6	4.4	3.3	2.1	1.0	69.9	8.7	7.5	6.3	5.2	3.9	2.8	63
64	6.1	5.0	3.8	2.7	1.5	0.3	9.1	7.9	6.7	5.4	4.3	2.9	1.7	64
65.0	75.6	74.5	73.2	72.0	70.7	69.5	68.3	67.0	65.8	64.4	63.2	61.8	60.5	65.0
5.5	5.4	4.2	2.9	1.7	0.4	9.1	7.8	6.5	5.3	3.9	2.6	1.3	59.9	5.5
6.0	5.1	3.8	2.6	1.3	0.0	8.7	7.4	6.1	4.7	3.4	2.0	0.7	9.3	6.0
6.5	4.8	3.5	2.2	0.9	69.6	8.2	6.9	5.6	4.2	2.8	1.4	0.0	8.6	6.5
7.0	4.5	3.2	1.8	0.5	9.1	7.8	6.4	5.0	3.6	2.2	0.8	59.3	7.9	7.0
67.5	74.1	72.8	71.4	70.1	68.7	67.3	65.9	64.5	63.0	61.6	60.1	58.6	57.1	67.5
8.0	3.8	2.4	1.0	69.6	8.2	6.8	5.3	3.9	2.4	0.9	59.4	7.8	6.3	8.0
8.5	3.4	2.0	0.6	9.1	7.7	6.2	4.7	3.2	1.7	0.2	8.6	7.0	5.4	8.5
9.0	3.0	1.6	0.1	8.6	7.2	5.6	4.1	2.6	1.0	59.4	7.8	6.2	4.5	9.0
9.5	2.6	1.1	69.6	8.1	6.6	5.0	3.5	1.9	0.3	8.6	7.0	5.3	3.6	9.5
70.0	72.2	70.7	69.1	67.6	66.0	64.4	62.8	61.2	59.5	57.8	56.1	54.3	52.6	70.0
0.5	1.8	0.2	8.6	7.0	5.4	3.7	2.1	0.4	8.7	6.9	5.1	3.3	1.5	0.5
1.0	1.3	69.7	8.0	6.4	4.7	3.0	1.3	59.5	7.8	6.0	4.1	2.2	0.3	1.0
1.5	0.8	9.1	7.4	5.7	4.0	2.2	0.5	8.6	6.8	5.0	3.0	1.1	49.1	1.5
2.0	0.2	8.5	6.8	5.0	3.2	1.4	59.6	7.7	5.8	3.9	1.9	49.8	7.7	2.0
72.5	69.7	67.9	66.1	64.3	62.4	60.5	58.6	56.7	54.7	52.7	50.6	48.5	46.3	72.5
3.0	9.1	7.2	5.4	3.5	1.6	59.6	7.6	5.6	3.5	1.4	49.2	7.0	4.7	3.0
3.5	8.4	6.5	4.6	2.6	0.7	8.6	6.6	4.5	2.3	0.1	7.8	5.4	3.0	3.5
4.0	7.7	5.7	3.8	1.7	59.7	7.5	5.4	3.2	0.9	48.6	6.2	3.7	1.1	4.0
4.5	7.0	4.9	2.9	0.7	8.6	6.4	4.2	1.8	49.5	7.0	4.4	1.8	38.9	4.5
75.0	66.2	64.0	61.9	59.7	57.5	55.2	52.8	50.4	47.9	45.2	42.5	39.6	36.5	75.0
5.5	5.3	3.1	0.9	8.6	6.2	3.8	1.3	48.8	6.1	3.3	0.3	7.2	3.8	5.5
6.0	4.4	2.1	59.8	7.4	4.9	2.3	49.7	7.0	4.1	1.1	37.9	4.5	0.7	6.0
6.5	3.4	1.0	8.6	6.0	3.4	0.7	7.9	5.0	1.9	38.7	5.2	1.3	27.0	6.5
7.0	2.3	59.8	7.2	4.5	1.8	48.9	5.9	2.8	39.5	5.9	2.0	27.6	22.4	7.0

With Declination of contrary name enter the Table as above, but subtract the tabular azimuth from 180°.0.

Horizon-Azimuths.

Latitude.	Declination of same name as the Latitude.													Latitude.
	12°.0	12°.5	13°.0	13°.5	14°.0	14°.5	15°.0	15°.5	16°.0	16°.5	17°.0	17°.5	18°.0	
°	°	°	°	°	°	°	°	°	°	°	°	°	°	°
0	78.0	77.5	77.0	76.5	76.0	75.5	75.0	74.5	74.0	73.5	73.0	72.5	72.0	0
10	77.8	7.3	6.8	6.3	5.8	5.3	4.7	4.2	3.7	3.2	2.7	2.2	1.7	10
15	7.5	7.1	6.5	6.0	5.5	5.0	4.4	3.9	3.4	2.9	2.3	1.8	1.3	15
20	7.2	6.7	6.2	5.6	5.1	4.5	4.0	3.5	2.9	2.4	1.9	1.3	0.8	20
25	6.7	6.2	5.6	5.1	4.5	3.9	3.4	2.9	2.3	1.7	1.2	0.6	0.1	25
30	76.1	75.5	75.0	74.4	73.8	73.2	72.6	72.0	71.4	70.8	70.3	69.7	69.1	30
32	5.8	5.2	4.7	4.0	3.4	2.8	2.2	1.6	1.0	0.4	69.8	9.2	8.6	32
34	5.5	4.9	4.3	3.6	3.0	2.4	1.8	1.2	0.5	0.0	9.3	8.7	8.1	34
36	5.1	4.5	3.9	3.2	2.6	2.0	1.3	0.7	0.0	69.5	8.8	8.2	7.5	36
38	4.7	4.0	3.4	2.8	2.1	1.5	0.8	0.2	69.5	8.9	8.2	7.6	6.9	38
40	74.3	73.6	72.9	72.2	71.6	70.9	70.3	69.6	68.9	68.2	67.6	66.9	66.2	40
41	4.0	3.3	2.7	2.0	1.3	0.6	0.0	9.2	8.6	7.9	7.2	6.5	5.8	41
42	3.8	3.1	2.4	1.7	1.0	0.3	69.6	8.9	8.2	7.5	6.8	6.1	5.4	42
43	3.5	2.8	2.1	1.4	0.7	0.0	9.3	8.6	7.8	7.1	6.4	5.7	5.0	43
44	3.2	2.5	1.8	1.1	0.4	69.6	8.9	8.2	7.4	6.7	6.0	5.3	4.6	44
45	72.9	72.2	71.5	70.7	70.0	69.3	68.5	67.8	67.0	66.3	65.6	64.8	64.1	45
46	2.6	1.8	1.1	0.4	69.6	8.9	8.1	7.4	6.6	5.9	5.1	4.3	3.6	46
47	2.3	1.5	0.7	0.0	9.2	8.5	7.7	6.9	6.2	5.4	4.6	3.8	3.1	47
48	1.9	1.1	0.3	69.6	8.8	8.0	7.2	6.4	5.7	4.9	4.1	3.3	2.5	48
49	1.5	0.7	69.9	9.2	8.4	7.6	6.8	5.9	5.1	4.3	3.5	2.7	1.9	49
50	71.1	70.3	69.5	68.7	67.9	67.1	66.3	65.4	64.6	63.8	63.0	62.1	61.3	50
51	0.7	69.9	9.1	8.2	7.4	6.5	5.7	4.9	4.0	3.2	2.4	1.5	0.6	51
52	0.3	9.4	8.6	7.7	6.9	6.0	5.1	4.3	3.4	2.5	1.7	0.8	59.9	52
53	69.8	8.9	8.1	7.2	6.3	5.4	4.5	3.6	2.7	1.8	1.0	0.0	9.1	53
54	9.3	8.4	7.5	6.6	5.7	4.8	3.9	2.9	2.0	1.1	0.2	59.2	8.3	54
55	68.8	67.8	66.9	66.0	65.1	64.1	63.2	62.2	61.3	60.3	59.4	58.4	57.4	55
56	8.2	7.2	6.3	5.3	4.4	3.4	2.4	1.4	0.5	59.5	8.5	7.5	6.4	56
57	7.6	6.6	5.6	4.6	3.6	2.6	1.6	0.6	59.6	8.6	7.5	6.5	5.4	57
58	6.9	5.9	4.9	3.9	2.8	1.8	0.8	59.7	8.7	7.6	6.5	5.4	4.3	58
59	6.2	5.2	4.1	3.1	2.0	0.9	59.8	8.7	7.7	6.5	5.4	4.3	3.1	59
60	65.4	64.4	63.3	62.2	61.1	59.9	58.8	57.7	56.6	55.4	54.2	53.1	51.8	60
61	4.6	3.5	2.4	1.2	0.1	8.9	7.8	6.5	5.4	4.2	2.9	1.7	0.4	61
62	3.7	2.5	1.4	0.2	59.0	7.8	6.6	5.3	4.1	2.8	1.5	0.2	48.8	62
63	2.8	1.5	0.3	59.0	7.8	6.5	5.3	3.9	2.6	1.3	49.9	48.5	7.1	63
64	1.7	0.4	59.1	7.8	6.5	5.2	3.8	2.4	1.0	49.6	8.2	6.7	5.2	64
65.0	60.5	59.2	57.8	56.5	55.1	53.7	52.2	50.8	49.3	47.8	46.2	44.6	43.0	65.0
5.5	59.9	8.5	7.1	5.7	4.3	2.9	1.4	49.9	8.4	6.8	5.2	3.5	1.8	5.5
6.0	9.3	7.8	6.4	5.0	3.5	2.0	0.5	8.9	7.3	5.7	4.1	2.3	0.6	6.0
6.5	8.6	7.1	5.7	4.2	2.7	1.1	49.5	7.9	6.2	4.6	2.9	1.1	39.2	6.5
7.0	7.9	6.4	4.9	3.3	1.8	0.2	8.5	6.8	5.1	3.4	1.6	39.7	7.7	7.0
67.5	57.1	55.6	54.0	52.4	50.8	49.2	47.4	45.7	43.9	42.1	40.2	38.2	36.1	67.5
8.0	6.3	4.7	3.1	1.4	49.8	8.1	6.3	4.5	2.6	0.7	38.7	6.6	4.4	8.0
8.5	5.4	3.8	2.1	0.4	8.7	6.9	5.1	3.2	1.2	39.2	7.1	4.9	2.5	8.5
9.0	4.5	2.8	1.1	49.3	7.5	5.7	3.8	1.8	39.7	7.6	5.4	3.0	0.4	9.0
9.5	3.6	1.8	0.0	8.2	6.3	4.4	2.4	0.3	8.1	5.8	3.5	0.9	28.1	9.5
70.0	52.6	50.7	48.9	47.0	45.0	43.0	40.8	38.6	36.3	33.9	31.3	28.5	25.4	70.0
0.5	1.5	49.6	7.6	5.6	3.6	1.4	39.2	6.8	4.3	1.7	28.9	5.7	2.2	0.5
1.0	0.3	8.3	6.3	4.2	2.0	39.7	7.4	4.8	2.1	29.3	6.1	2.5	18.3	1.0
1.5	49.1	7.0	4.9	2.6	0.3	7.9	5.4	2.6	29.7	6.5	2.9	18.6	13.1	1.5
2.0	7.7	5.6	3.3	0.9	38.5	5.9	3.1	0.1	6.9	3.2	18.9	13.3	0.0	2.0
72.5	46.3	44.0	41.6	39.1	36.4	33.6	30.6	27.3	23.6	19.1	13.5	0.0		72.5
3.0	4.7	2.3	39.7	7.0	4.1	1.1	27.8	3.9	19.4	13.7	0.0			3.0
3.5	3.0	0.4	7.7	4.7	1.6	28.2	4.4	19.7	13.9	0.0				3.5
4.0	1.1	38.3	5.3	2.1	28.6	4.7	0.2	14.1	0.0					4.0
4.5	38.9	5.9	2.7	29.1	5.1	0.5	14.5	0.0						4.5

With Declination of contrary name enter the Table as above, but subtract the tabular azimuth from 180°.0.

Horizon-Azimuths.

Latitude.	Declination of same name as the Latitude.													Latitude.
	18°.0	18°.5	19°.0	19°.5	20°.0	20°.5	21°.0	21°.5	22°.0	22°.5	23°.0	23°.5	24°.0	
°	°	°	°	°	°	°	°	°	°	°	°	°	°	°
0	72.0	71.5	71.0	70.5	70.0	69.5	69.0	68.5	68.0	67.5	67.0	66.5	66.0	0
10	1.7	1.2	0.7	0.2	69.7	9.2	8.7	8.2	7.7	7.1	6.6	6.1	5.6	10
15	1.3	0.8	0.3	69.8	9.3	8.7	8.2	7.7	7.2	6.7	6.1	5.6	5.1	15
20	0.8	0.3	69.7	9.2	8.6	8.1	7.6	7.0	6.5	6.0	5.4	4.9	4.3	20
25	0.1	69.5	8.9	8.4	7.8	7.3	6.7	6.1	5.6	5.0	4.5	3.9	3.3	25
30	69.1	68.5	67.9	67.3	66.7	66.2	65.6	65.0	64.4	64.8	63.2	62.6	62.0	30
32	8.6	8.0	7.4	6.8	6.2	5.6	5.0	4.4	3.8	3.2	2.6	2.0	1.3	32
34	8.1	7.5	6.9	6.2	5.6	5.0	4.4	3.8	3.1	2.5	1.9	1.3	0.6	34
36	7.5	6.9	6.3	5.6	5.0	4.3	3.7	3.1	2.4	1.8	1.1	0.5	59.8	36
38	6.9	6.2	5.6	4.9	4.3	3.6	3.0	2.3	1.6	0.9	0.3	59.6	8.9	38
40	66.2	65.6	64.9	64.2	63.5	62.8	62.1	61.4	60.7	60.0	59.3	58.7	57.9	40
41	5.8	5.2	4.5	3.8	3.1	2.3	1.7	0.9	0.2	59.5	8.8	8.2	7.4	41
42	5.4	4.7	4.0	3.3	2.6	1.9	1.2	0.4	59.7	9.0	8.3	7.6	6.8	42
43	5.0	4.3	3.6	2.8	2.1	1.4	0.7	59.9	9.2	8.4	7.7	7.0	6.2	43
44	4.6	3.8	3.1	2.3	1.6	0.9	0.2	9.4	8.6	7.8	7.1	6.4	5.6	44
45	64.1	63.3	62.6	61.8	61.1	60.3	59.6	58.8	58.0	57.2	56.5	55.7	54.9	45
46	3.6	2.8	2.1	1.3	0.5	59.7	9.0	8.2	7.4	6.6	5.8	5.0	4.2	46
47	3.1	2.3	1.5	0.7	59.9	9.1	8.3	7.5	6.7	5.9	5.1	4.3	3.4	47
48	2.5	1.7	0.9	0.1	9.3	8.4	7.6	6.8	6.0	5.1	4.3	3.5	2.6	48
49	1.9	1.1	0.3	59.4	8.6	7.7	6.9	6.0	5.2	4.3	3.5	2.6	1.7	49
50	61.3	60.4	59.6	58.7	57.9	57.0	56.1	55.2	54.4	53.5	52.6	51.7	50.8	50
51	0.6	59.7	8.9	8.0	7.1	6.2	5.3	4.4	3.5	2.6	1.6	0.7	49.8	51
52	59.9	9.0	8.1	7.2	6.3	5.3	4.4	3.5	2.5	1.6	0.6	49.7	8.7	52
53	9.1	8.2	7.3	6.3	5.4	4.4	3.4	2.5	1.5	0.5	49.5	8.6	7.5	53
54	8.3	7.3	6.4	5.4	4.4	3.4	2.4	1.4	0.4	49.4	8.3	7.4	6.2	54
55	57.4	56.4	55.4	54.4	53.4	52.4	51.3	50.3	49.2	48.1	47.1	46.0	44.8	55
56	6.4	5.4	4.4	3.3	2.3	1.2	0.2	49.0	7.9	6.8	5.7	4.6	3.3	56
57	5.4	4.4	3.3	2.2	1.1	0.0	48.9	7.7	6.5	5.4	4.2	3.0	1.7	57
58	4.3	3.2	2.1	0.9	49.8	48.6	7.5	6.2	5.0	3.8	2.5	1.2	39.9	58
59	3.1	2.0	0.8	49.6	8.4	7.2	5.9	4.6	3.3	2.0	0.7	39.3	7.8	59
60.0	51.8	50.6	49.4	48.1	46.8	45.5	44.2	42.8	41.4	40.1	38.6	37.1	35.6	60.0
0.5	1.1	49.9	8.6	7.3	6.0	4.6	3.3	1.9	0.4	39.0	7.5	5.9	4.3	0 5
1.0	0.4	9.1	7.8	6.5	5.1	3.7	2.3	0.9	39.4	7.9	6.3	4.7	3.0	1.0
1.5	49.6	8.3	7.0	5.6	4.2	2.7	1.3	39.8	8.3	6.7	5.0	3.3	1.5	1.5
2.0	8.8	7.5	6.1	4.7	3.2	1.7	0.2	8.7	7.1	5.4	3.7	1.9	0.0	2.0
62.5	48.0	46.6	45.1	43.7	42.2	40.6	39.0	37.4	35.8	34.0	32.2	30.3	28.3	62.5
3.0	7.1	5.7	4.1	2.6	1.1	39.5	7.8	6.1	4.4	2.5	0.6	28.6	6.4	3.0
3.5	6.2	4.7	3.1	1.5	39.9	8.3	6.5	4.7	2.9	0.9	28.9	6.6	4.3	3.5
4.0	5.2	3.6	2.0	0.3	8.7	7.0	5.1	3.3	1.3	29.2	7.0	4.5	1.9	4.0
4.5	4.1	2.5	0.8	39.1	7.4	5.5	3.6	1.6	29.5	7.2	4.8	2.2	19.1	4.5
65.0	43.0	41.3	39.6	37.8	36.0	34.0	32.0	29.8	27.5	25.1	22.4	19.4	15.6	65.0
5.5	1.8	0.0	8.2	6.4	4.4	2.4	0.2	7.8	5.3	2.7	19.6	15.9	11.1	5.5
6.0	0.6	38.7	6.8	4.9	2.7	0.6	28.2	5.6	2.9	19.8	16.2	11.4	0.0	6.0
6.5	39.2	7.3	5.3	3.2	0.9	28.6	6.0	3.2	0.0	16.3	11.6	0.0		6.5
7.0	7.7	5.7	3.6	1.3	28.9	6.3	3.5	0.2	16.5	11.7	0.0			7.0
67.5	36.1	34.0	31.7	29.3	26.6	23.8	20.5	16.7	11.8	0.0				67.5
8.0	4.4	2.1	29.7	7.0	4.1	0.8	17.0	11.9	0.0					8.0
8.5	2.5	0.0	7.4	4.4	1.1	17.2	12.1	0.0						8.5
9.0	0.4	27.7	4.7	1.3	17.3	12.3	0.0							9.0
9.5	28.1	5.0	1.6	17.6	12.4	0.0								9.5
70.0	25.4	21.9	17.8	12.6	0.0									70.0
0.5	2.2	18.1	12.8	0.0										0.5
1.0	18.3	12.9	0.0											1 0
1.5	13.1	0.0												1.5
2.0	0.0													2.0

With Declination of contrary name enter the Table as above, but subtract the tabular azimuth from 180°.0.

Horizon-Azimuths.

Latitude.	Declination of same name as the Latitude.													Latitude.
	24°.0	24° 5	25°.0	25°.5	26°.0	26°.5	27°.0	27°.5	28°.0	28°.5	29°.0	29°.5	30°.0	
°	°	°	°	°	°	°	°	°	°	°	°	°	°	°
0	66.0	65.5	65.0	64.5	64.0	63.5	63.0	62.5	62.0	61.5	61.0	60.5	60.0	0
4	5.9	5.4	4.9	4.4	3.9	3.4	2.9	2.4	1.9	1.4	0.9	0.4	59.9	4
8	5.7	5.2	4.7	4.2	3.7	3.2	2.7	2.2	1.7	1.2	0.7	0.2	9.7	8
12	5.4	4.9	4.4	3.9	3.4	2.9	2.4	1.9	1.3	0.8	0.3	59.8	9.3	12
16	5.0	4.4	3.9	3.4	2.9	2.4	1.8	1.3	0.8	0.2	59.7	9.2	8.7	16
20	64.3	63.8	63.3	62.7	62.2	61.7	61.1	60.6	60.0	59.5	58.9	58.4	57.9	20
22	4.0	3.4	2.9	2.3	1.8	1.2	0.7	0.1	59.6	9.0	8.5	7.9	7.4	22
24	3.6	3.0	2.4	1.9	1.3	0.8	0.2	59.6	9.1	8.5	8.0	7.4	6.8	24
26	3.1	2.5	1.9	1.4	0.8	0.3	59.7	9.1	8.5	7.9	7.4	6.8	6.2	26
28	2.6	2.0	1.4	0.8	0.2	59.7	9.1	8.5	7.9	7.3	6.7	6.1	5.5	28
30	62.0	61.4	60.8	60.2	59.6	59.0	58.4	57.8	57.2	56.6	56.0	55.3	54.7	30
31	1.7	1.1	0.5	59.9	9.2	8.6	8.0	7.4	6.8	6.2	5.5	4.9	4.3	31
32	1.3	0.7	0.1	9.5	8.9	8.3	7.6	7.0	6.4	5.8	5.1	4.5	3.9	32
33	1.0	0.4	59.8	9.1	8.5	7.9	7.2	6.6	6.0	5.3	4.7	4.0	3.4	33
34	0.6	0.0	9.4	8.7	8.1	7.4	6.8	6.2	5.5	4.9	4.2	3.6	2.9	34
35	60.2	59.6	58.9	58.3	57.7	57.0	56.4	55.7	55.0	54.4	53.7	53.1	52.4	35
36	59.8	9.2	8.5	7.9	7.2	6.5	5.9	5.2	4.5	3.9	3.2	2.5	1.8	36
37	9.4	8.7	8.1	7.4	6.7	6.0	5.4	4.7	4.0	3.3	2.6	1.9	1.2	37
38	8.9	8.3	7.6	6.9	6.2	5.5	4.8	4.1	3.4	2.7	2.0	1.3	0.6	38
39	8.4	7.8	7.1	6.4	5.7	5.0	4.3	3.5	2.8	2.1	1.4	0.7	0.0	39
40	57.9	57.2	56.5	55.8	55.1	54.4	53.7	52.9	52.2	51.5	50.7	50.0	49.3	40
41	7.4	6.7	5.9	5.2	4.5	3.8	3.0	2.3	1.5	0.8	0.0	49.3	8.5	41
42	6.8	6.1	5.3	4.6	3.9	3.1	2.3	1.6	0.8	0.1	49.3	8.5	7.7	42
43	6.2	5.5	4.7	3.9	3.2	2.4	1.6	0.8	0.1	49.3	8.5	7.7	6.9	43
44	5.6	4.8	4.0	3.2	2.5	1.7	0.9	0.0	49.3	8.4	7.6	6.8	6.0	44
45	54.9	54.1	53.3	52.5	51.7	50.9	50.1	49.2	48.4	47.5	46.7	45.9	45.0	45
46	4.2	3.4	2.5	1.7	0.9	0.0	49.2	8.3	7.5	6.6	5.7	4.9	4.0	46
47	3.4	2.6	1.7	0.9	0.0	49.1	8.3	7.4	6.5	5.6	4.7	3.8	2.9	47
48	2.6	1.7	0.8	0.0	49.1	8.2	7.3	6.4	5.4	4.5	3.6	2.6	1.7	48
49	1.7	0.8	49.9	49.0	8.1	7.2	6.2	5.3	4.3	3.3	2.4	1.4	0.4	49
50	50.8	49.8	48.9	48.0	47.0	46.1	45.1	44.1	43.1	42.1	41.1	40.0	38.9	50
51	49.8	8.8	7.8	6.8	5.9	4.9	3.8	2.8	1.8	0.7	39.6	38.5	7.4	51
52	8.7	7.7	6.7	5.6	4.6	3.6	2.5	1.4	0.3	39.2	8.0	6.9	5.7	52
53	7.5	6.5	5.4	4.3	3.3	2.2	1.0	39.9	38.7	7.5	6.3	5.1	3.8	53
54	6.2	5.1	4.0	2.9	1.8	0.6	39.4	8.2	7.0	5.7	4.4	3.1	1.7	54
55.0	44.8	43.7	42.5	41.4	40.2	38.9	37.7	36.4	35.1	33.7	32.3	30.9	29.3	55.0
5.5	4.1	2.9	1.7	0.5	39.3	8.0	6.7	5.4	4.0	2.6	1.1	29.6	8.0	5.5
6.0	3.3	2.1	0.9	39.6	8.4	7.1	5.7	4.3	2.9	1.4	29.9	8.3	6.6	6.0
6.5	2.5	1.2	0.0	8.7	7.4	6.1	4.6	3.2	1.7	0.1	8.5	6.8	5.0	6.5
7.0	1.7	0.4	39.1	7.8	6.4	5.0	3.5	2.0	0.5	28.8	7.1	5.3	3.4	7.0
57.5	40.8	39.5	38.1	36.8	35.3	33.8	32.3	30.7	29.1	27.4	25.5	23.6	21.5	57.5
8.0	39.9	8.5	7.1	5.7	4.2	2.6	1.1	29.4	7.6	5.8	3.8	1.7	19.3	8.0
8 5	8.9	7.5	6.0	4.5	3.0	1.4	29.7	7.9	6.1	4.0	1.9	19.6	16.9	8.5
9.0	7.8	6.4	4.9	3.3	1.7	0.0	8.2	6.3	4.3	2.1	19.7	17.0	13.8	9.0
9.5	6.7	5.2	3.6	2.0	0.3	28.5	6.6	4.5	2.3	19.9	17.2	14.1	9.9	9.5
60.0	35.6	34.0	32.3	30.6	28.8	26.8	24.8	2.6	20.1	17.4	14.2	10.0	0.0	60.0
0.5	4.3	2.6	0.9	29.0	7.1	5 0	2.8	0.4	17.6	14.2	10.1	0.0		0.5
1.0	3.0	1.2	29.3	7.4	5.3	3.0	0.5	17.7	14.5	10.2	0.0			1.0
1.5	1.5	29.7	7.7	5.6	3.3	0.8	18.0	14.6	10.3	0.0				1.5
2.0	0.0	8.0	5.8	3.5	1.0	18.1	14.8	10.4	0.0					2.0
62.5	28.3	26.1	23.8	21.2	18.3	14.9	10.5	0.0						62.5
3.0	6.4	4.0	1.4	18.5	15.1	10.6	0.0							3.0
3.5	4.3	1.7	18.7	15.2	10.7	0.0								3.5
4.0	1.9	18.9	15.4	10.8	0.0									4.0
4.5	19.1	15.6	11.0	0.0										4.5

With Declination of contrary name enter the Table as above, but subtract the tabular azimuth from 180°.0.

Position-Angles for Horizon-Azimuths.

Lat.	Declination of same or contrary name.													Lat.
	0°	5°	10°	12°	14°	16°	18°	20°	22°	24°	26°	28°	30°	
°	°	°	°	°	°	°	°	°	°	°	°	°	°	°
0	90.0	90.0	90.0	90.0	90.0	90.0	90.0	90.0	90.0	90.0	90.0	90.0	90.0	0
2	88.0	88.0	88.0	88.0	87.9	87.9	87.9	87.9	87.8	87.8	87.8	87.7	87.7	2
4	6.0	6.0	6.0	5.9	5.9	5.8	5.8	5.8	5.7	5.6	5.6	5.5	5.4	4
6	4.0	4.0	3.9	3.9	3.8	3.8	3.7	3.6	3.5	3.4	3.3	3.2	3.1	6
8	2.0	2.0	1.9	1.8	1.8	1.7	1.6	1.5	1.4	1.2	1.1	0.9	0.8	8
10	80.0	80.0	79.9	79.8	79.7	79.6	79.5	79.4	79.2	79.0	78.9	78.6	78.4	10
12	78.0	77.9	7.8	7.7	7.6	7.5	7.4	7.2	7.0	6.8	6.6	6.4	6.1	12
14	6.0	5.9	5.8	5.7	5.6	5.4	5.3	5.1	4.9	4.6	4.4	4.1	3.8	14
16	4.0	3.9	3.8	3.6	3.5	3.3	3.1	3.0	2.7	2.4	2.1	1.8	1.4	16
18	2.0	1.9	1.7	1.6	1.4	1.2	1.0	0.8	0.5	0.2	69.9	69.5	69.1	18
20	70.0	69.9	69.7	69.5	69.4	69.2	68.9	68.7	68.4	68.0	67.6	67.2	66.7	20
22	68.0	7.9	7.7	7.5	7.3	7.1	6.8	6.5	6.2	5.8	5.4	4.9	4.4	22
24	6.0	5.9	5.6	5.4	5.2	5.0	4.7	4.4	4.0	3.6	3.1	2.6	2.0	24
26	4.0	3.9	3.6	3.4	3.1	2.9	2.5	2.2	1.8	1.3	0.8	0.2	59.6	26
28	2.0	1.9	1.5	1.3	1.1	0.8	0.4	0.0	59.6	59.1	58.5	57.9	7.2	28
30	60.0	59.9	59.5	59.2	59.0	58.6	58.3	57.8	57.4	56.8	56.2	55.5	54.7	30
32	58.0	7.9	7.5	7.2	6.9	6.5	6.1	5.7	5.1	4.5	3.9	3.1	2.2	32
34	6.0	5.9	5.4	5.1	4.8	4.4	4.0	3.5	2.9	2.2	1.5	0.7	49.7	34
36	4.0	3.8	3.4	3.1	2.7	2.3	1.8	1.3	0.7	49.9	49.2	48.3	7.2	36
38	2.0	1.8	1.3	1.0	0.6	0.2	49.7	49.1	48.4	7.6	6.8	5.8	4.7	38
40	50.0	49.8	49.3	48.9	48.5	48.0	47.5	46.8	46.1	45.3	44.3	43.3	42.1	40
42	48.0	7.8	7.2	6.8	6.4	5.9	5.3	4.6	3.8	2.9	1.9	0.7	39.4	42
44	6.0	5.8	5.1	4.7	4.3	3.7	3.1	2.3	1.5	0.5	39.4	38.1	6.7	44
46	4.0	3.8	3.1	2.7	2.1	1.5	0.9	0.0	39.1	38.0	6.8	5.4	3.8	46
48	2.0	1.7	1.0	0.6	0.0	39.3	38.6	37.7	6.7	5.5	4.2	2.7	0.9	48
50	40.0	39.7	38.9	38.5	37.9	37.1	36.3	35.4	34.3	33.0	31.5	29.8	27.8	50
52	38.0	7.7	6.9	6.3	5.7	4.9	4.0	3.0	1.8	0.4	28.8	6.8	4.5	52
54	6.0	5.7	4.8	4.2	3.5	2.7	1.7	0.6	29.2	27.7	5.8	3.6	0.9	54
56	4.0	3.7	2.7	2.0	1.3	0.4	29.3	28.1	6.6	4.8	2.7	0.1	17.0	56
58	2.0	1.6	0.6	29.9	29.1	28.1	6.9	5.5	3.8	1.8	19.4	16.1	11.7	58
60	30.0	29.6	28.4	27.7	26.8	25.7	24.4	22.9	20.9	18.6	15.5	11.2	0.0	60
62	28.0	7.6	6.3	5.5	4.5	3.3	1.8	20.0	17.8	14.9	10.8	0.0		62
64	6.0	5.6	4.1	3.2	2.1	0.7	19.1	17.0	14.2	10.2	0.0			64
66	4.0	3.5	1.9	0.9	19.7	18.1	16.1	13.6	9.9	0.0				66
68	2.0	1.5	19.7	18.6	17.1	15.3	12.8	9.4	0.0					68
70	20.0	19.4	17.4	16.1	14.4	12.1	8.8	0.0						70
72	18.0	17.3	15.0	13.5	11.4	8.3	0.0							72
74	16.0	15.2	12.6	10.7	7.9	0.0								74
76	14.0	13.1	9.8	7.3	0.0									76
78	12.0	10.9	6.7	0.0										78
80	10.0	8.7	0.0											80

TABLE XXVI.

Limiting Errors of Horizon-Azimuths.

Latitude.	Dec. 12°.			Dec. 18°.			Dec. 24°.			Dec. 30°.		
	Partial Az. Error.		Prob. Total Az. Error.	Partial Az. Error.		Prob. Total Az. Error.	Partial Az. Error.		Prob. Total Az. Error.	Partial Az. Error.		Prob. Total Az. Error
	Lat. Error ± 12′.	Dec. Error ± 6′.		Lat. Error ± 12′.	Dec. Error ± 6′.		Lat. Error ± 12′.	Dec. Error ± 6′.		Lat. Error ± 12′.	Dec. Error ± 6′.	
°	°	°	°	°	°	°	°	°	°	°	°	°
0	0.0	±0.1	±0.1	0.0	±0.1	±0.1	0.0	±0.1	±0.1	0.0	±0.1	±0.1
30	0.0	0.1	0.1	±0.1	0.1	0.2	±0.1	0.1	0.2	±0.1	0.1	0.2
40	±0.1	0.2	0.2	0.1	0.2	0.2	0.2	0.2	0.3	0.2	0.1	0.2
50	0.1	0.2	0.2	0.2	0.2	0.3	0.2	0.2	0.3	0.3	0.2	0.4
60	0.1	0.2	0.2	0.3	0.3	0.4	0.5	0.4	0.7	*0.6	*0.3	0.7
62	0.2	0.3	0.4	0.4	0.3	0.5	0.7	0.4	0.8	†1.0	†0.6	1.2
64	0.2	0.3	0.4	0.5	0.4	0.7	1.1	0.7	1.3			
66	0.3	0.3	0.4	0.7	0.5	0.9						
68	0.3	0.3	0.5	1.1	0.6	1.3						
70	0.4	0.4	0.6									
72	0.5	0.4	0.7									
74	0.6	0.5	0.8									
76	0.8	0.6	1.0									

* For Lat. 53°.
† For Lat. 58°.

Latitude.	Dec. 24°.		
	Partial Az. Error.		Prob Total Az. Error.
	Lat. Error ±0°.5.	Dec. Error ±0°.5.	
°	°	°	°
0	0.0	±0.5	±0.5
10	±0.1	0.5	0.5
20	0.2	0.5	0.6
30	0.2	0.6	0.7
40	0.3	0.8	0.9
50	0.5	0.9	1.0
60	1.3	1.7	2.1

Correction of the observed Compass-Azimuth as taken on the Apparent Horizon.

Lat.	Declination of same or contrary name.													Lat.
	0°	5°	10°	12°	14°	16°	18°	20°	22°	24°	26°	28°	30°	
°	°	°	°	°	°	°	°	°	°	°	°	°	°	°
0	0.0	0.0	0.0	0.0	0.0	0.0	0.0	0.0	0.0	0.0	0.0	0.0	0.0	0
5	1	1	1	1	1	1	1	1	1	1	1	1	1	5
10	1	1	1	1	1	1	1	1	1	1	1	1	1	10
15	2	2	2	2	2	2	2	2	2	2	2	2	2	15
20	2	2	2	2	2	2	3	3	3	3	3	3	3	20
24	0.3	0.3	0.3	0.3	0.3	0.3	0.3	0.3	0.3	0.3	0.3	0.4	0.4	24
28	3	4	4	4	4	4	4	4	4	4	4	4	4	28
32	4	4	4	4	4	4	4	5	5	5	5	5	5	32
36	5	5	5	5	5	5	5	5	6	6	6	6	6	36
38	5	5	5	5	6	6	6	6	6	6	6	7	7	38
40	0.6	0.6	0.6	0.6	0.6	0.6	0.6	0.6	0.6	0.7	0.7	0.7	0.7	40
42	6	6	6	6	6	7	7	7	7	7	8	8	8	42
44	6	6	7	7	7	7	7	7	8	8	8	9	9	44
46	7	7	7	7	7	8	8	8	8	9	9	9	1.0	46
48	7	8	8	8	8	8	8	9	9	1.0	1.0	1.0	1	48
50	0.8	0.8	0.8	0.8	0.9	0.9	0.9	0.9	1.0	1.1	1.1	1.1	1.3	50
52	8	9	9	9	9	1.0	1.0	1.0	1	2	2	3	5	52
54	9	9	1.0	1.0	1.0	1	1	1	2	3	4	5	8	54
56	1.0	1.0	1	1	1	2	2	2	3	5	6	8	2.2	56
58	1	1	2	2	2	3	3	4	5	7	9	2.3	3.2	58
60	1.2	1.2	1.3	1.3	1.3	1.4	1.5	1.6	1.7	2.0	2.4	3.4	∞	60
62	3	3	4	4	4	6	7	8	2.1	5	3.5	∞		62
64	4	4	5	5	6	8	9	2.2	6	3.7	∞			64
66	5	5	7	7	9	2.0	2.3	8	3.8	∞				66
68	6	7	9	2.0	2.2	4	9	4.0	∞					68
70	1.8	1.9	2.1	2.3	2.6	3.1	4.3	∞						70
72	2.0	2.1	5	8	3.3	4.6	∞							72
74	2	5	3.0	3.5	4.8	∞								74
76	6	3.0	8	5.2	∞									76
78	3.1	6	5.7	∞										78
80	3.8	4.4	∞											80

TABLE XXVIII.

Error of the Horizon-Azimuth for an Error of 12′, or 0°.2, in the Latitude.

Lat.	Azimuth.												Lat.
	90°	80°	70°	60°	50°	40°	30°	20°	15°	10°	5°	0°	
°	°	°	°	°	°	°	°	°	°	°	°	°	°
0	0.0	0.0	0.0	0.0	0.0	0.0	0.0	0.0	0.0	0.0	0.0	0.0	0
10	0	0	0	0	0	0	1	1	1	2	4	∞	10
20	0	0	0	0	1	1	1	2	3	4	8	∞	15
30	0	0	0	1	1	1	2	3	4	6	1.3	∞	20
35	0	0	1	1	1	2	2	4	5	8	6	∞	25
40	0.0	0.0	0.1	0.1	0.1	0.2	0.3	0.5	0.6	1.0	1.9	∞	40
45	0	0	1	1	2	2	3	6	8	1	2.3	∞	45
50	0	0	1	1	2	3	4	7	9	3	8	∞	50
55	0	1	1	2	2	3	5	8	1.1	6	3.3	∞	55
60	0	1	1	2	3	4	6	9	3	2.0	4.0	∞	60
62	0.0	0.1	0.1	0.2	0.3	0.5	0.6	1.0	1.4	2.1	4.3	∞	62
64	0	1	1	2	3	5	7	1	5	3	7	∞	64
66	0	1	2	3	4	5	8	2	7	5	5.1	∞	66
68	0	1	2	3	4	6	9	4	8	8	7	∞	68
70	0	1	2	3	5	7	1.0	5	2.0	3.1	6.3	∞	70
72	0.0	0.1	0.2	0.3	0.5	0.8	1.1	1.7	2.3	3.5	7.0	∞	72
74	0	1	2	4	6	9	2	9	6	9	8.0	∞	74
76	0	1	3	5	7	1.0	4	2.2	3.0	4.5	9.2	∞	76
78	0	2	3	5	8	1	6	6	5	5.3	10.7	∞	78
80	0	2	4	6	9	3	2.0	3.1	4.2	6.4	13.0	∞	80
Lat.	90°	100°	110°	120°	130°	140°	150°	160°	165°	170°	175°	180°	Lat.
	Azimuth.												

TABLE XXIX.

Error of the Horizon-Azimuth for an Error of 6′, or 0°.1, in the Declination.

Position-Angle.	Azimuth-Error.
°	°
90	0.1
80	1
70	1
60	1
50	1
40	0.1
35	2
30	2
25	2
20	3
18	0.3
16	4
14	4
12	5
10	6
8	0.7
6	1.0
4	4
2	2.9
0	∞

Time-Azimuths: Log A.

Dec.	Latitude.											Polar Dist.
	0°	1°	2°	3°	4°	5°	6°	7°	8°	9°	10°	
35°	9.499	9.488	9.476	9.465	9.453	9.440	9.427	9.413	9.399	9.385	9.370	55°
34	485	474	462	450	437	424	411	397	382	367	351	56
33	472	460	447	435	422	408	394	379	364	348	331	57
32	458	445	432	419	406	391	376	361	345	328	310	58
31	443	430	417	403	389	374	358	342	325	308	289	59
30	9.428	9.415	9.401	9.386	9.371	9.356	9.340	9.323	9.305	9.286	9.267	60
29	413	399	384	369	354	337	320	302	284	264	243	61
28	397	382	367	351	335	318	300	281	262	241	219	62
27	380	365	349	333	316	298	279	259	238	216	193	63
26	363	347	331	314	296	277	257	236	214	190	165	64
25	9.346	9.329	9.312	9.294	9.275	9.255	9.234	9.211	9.188	9.163	9.136	65
24	328	310	292	273	253	232	209	186	161	134	105	66
23	309	290	271	251	230	207	184	159	132	103	072	67
22	289	269	249	228	206	182	157	130	101	070	036	68
21	268	248	226	204	180	155	128	099	068	034	8.998	69
20	9.246	9.225	9.202	9.179	9.153	9.126	9.097	9.066	9.032	8.996	8.955	70
19	224	201	177	152	125	096	064	030	8.994	953	909	71
18	200	176	150	123	094	063	029	8.992	952	907	857	72
17	175	149	122	093	061	027	8.990	950	905	855	798	73
16	148	121	091	060	026	8.989	948	903	853	796	730	74
15	9.119	9.090	9.059	9.025	8.988	8.947	8.902	8.852	8.795	8.728	8.650	75
14	089	058	023	8.986	946	901	850	793	727	649	552	76
13	057	022	8.985	944	899	849	792	725	647	551	427	77
12	022	8.984	943	898	848	791	724	646	549	425	250	78
11	8.984	943	897	847	789	723	645	548	424	249	7.948	79
10	8.942	8.897	8.846	8.789	8.722	8.643	8.547	8.423	8.247	7.947	— ∞	80
9	896	845	788	721	643	546	422	246	7.946	— ∞	7.947	81
8	845	787	721	642	545	421	245	7.945	— ∞	7.946	8.247	82
7	787	720	641	545	420	244	7.944	— ∞	7.945	8.246	423	83
6	719	641	544	419	244	7.943	— ∞	7.944	8.245	422	547	84
5	8.640	8.543	8.419	8.243	7.942	— ∞	7.943	8.244	8.421	8.546	8.643	85
4	543	418	243	7.941	— ∞	7.942	8.244	420	545	643	722	86
3	418	242	7.941	— ∞	7.941	8.243	419	545	642	721	789	87
2	242	7.941	— ∞	7.941	8.242	419	544	641	721	788	846	88
1	7.941	— ∞	7.941	8.242	418	543	641	720	787	845	897	89
0	— ∞	7.941	8.242	8.418	8.543	8.640	8.719	8.787	8.845	8.896	8.942	90
— 1	7.941	8.242	418	543	640	719	786	844	895	941	983	91
— 2	8.242	418	543	640	719	786	844	895	941	982	9.020	92
— 3	418	543	640	719	786	844	895	941	982	9.020	055	93
— 4	543	640	719	786	844	895	940	982	9.019	054	087	94
— 5	8.640	8.719	8.786	8.844	8.895	8.940	8.982	9.019	9.054	9.086	9.116	95
— 6	719	786	844	895	940	982	9.019	054	086	116	144	96
— 7	787	844	895	941	982	9.019	054	086	116	144	170	97
— 8	845	895	941	982	9.019	054	086	116	144	170	194	98
— 9	896	941	982	9.020	054	086	116	144	170	194	218	99
—10	8.942	8.983	9.020	9.055	9.087	9.116	9.144	9.170	9.194	9.218	9.240	100
—11	984	9.021	055	087	117	144	170	194	218	240	261	101
—12	9.022	056	088	117	145	170	195	218	240	261	281	102
—13	057	088	118	145	171	195	218	240	261	281	300	103
—14	089	119	146	172	196	219	241	261	281	300	318	104
—15	9.119	9.147	9.173	9.197	9.220	9.241	9.262	9.282	9.301	9.318	9.336	105
—16	148	173	197	220	242	263	282	301	319	336	353	106
—17	175	198	221	243	263	283	302	320	337	353	369	107
—18	200	222	244	264	284	303	320	337	354	369	385	108
—19	224	245	265	285	303	321	338	354	370	385	400	109
—20	9.246	9.267	9.286	9.305	9.322	9.339	9.355	9.371	9.386	9.401	9.415	110
—21	268	287	306	323	340	356	372	387	401	416	429	111
—22	289	307	325	341	357	373	388	402	416	430	443	112
—23	309	326	343	359	374	389	403	417	431	444	456	113
—24	328	344	360	375	390	405	418	432	444	457	469	114
Dec.	90°	89°	88°	87°	86°	85°	84°	83°	82°	81°	80°	Polar Dist.
	Co-Latitude.											

Time-Azimuths: Log B.

Dec.	Latitude.											Polar Dist.
	0°	1°	2°	3°	4°	5°	6°	7°	8°	9°	10°	
35°	0.501	0.491	0.480	0.470	0.460	0.451	0.442	0.433	0.424	0.415	0.407	55°
34	514	504	493	482	472	462	453	444	434	425	417	56
33	528	517	506	495	484	474	464	455	445	436	427	57
32	542	531	519	508	497	486	476	466	456	447	437	58
31	557	545	533	521	510	499	488	478	467	458	448	59
30	0.572	0.559	0.547	0.534	0.523	0.512	0.500	0.490	0.479	0.469	0.459	60
29	587	574	561	548	536	524	513	502	491	481	470	61
28	603	589	576	563	550	538	526	515	503	493	482	62
27	620	605	591	578	564	552	539	528	516	505	494	63
26	637	621	607	593	579	566	553	541	529	517	506	64
25	0.654	0.638	0.623	0.608	0.594	0.580	0.567	0.554	0.542	0.530	0.518	65
24	672	656	640	624	610	595	582	568	556	543	531	66
23	691	674	657	641	626	611	597	583	570	556	544	67
22	711	693	675	659	643	627	612	598	584	570	557	68
21	732	713	694	677	660	644	628	613	599	585	571	69
20	0.754	0.733	0.714	0.695	0.678	0.661	0.645	0.629	0.614	0.600	0.585	70
19	776	755	735	715	697	679	662	646	630	615	600	71
18	800	778	756	736	716	697	680	663	646	631	615	72
17	825	802	779	757	737	717	698	680	663	647	631	73
16	852	827	803	780	758	737	718	699	681	664	647	74
15	0.881	0.853	0.827	0.803	0.780	0.759	0.738	0.718	0.699	0.681	0.664	75
14	911	881	854	828	804	781	759	739	719	700	682	76
13	943	912	882	855	829	805	782	760	739	719	700	77
12	978	944	912	883	855	829	805	782	760	739	719	78
11	1.016	979	945	913	883	856	830	805	782	760	739	79
10	1.058	1.117	0.979	0.945	0.913	0.884	0.856	0.830	0.806	0.782	0.760	80
9	104	059	1.018	980	946	914	884	856	830	806	782	81
8	155	105	059	1.018	981	946	914	884	856	830	806	82
7	213	156	105	059	1.018	981	946	914	884	856	830	83
6	281	214	156	105	060	1.018	981	946	914	884	856	84
5	1.360	1.281	1.214	1.156	1.105	1.060	1.018	0.981	0.946	0.914	0.884	85
4	457	360	281	214	156	105	060	1.018	981	946	913	86
3	582	457	360	281	214	156	105	059	1.018	980	945	87
2	758	582	457	360	281	214	156	105	059	1.018	980	88
1	2.059	758	582	457	360	281	214	156	105	059	1.017	89
0	+ ∞	2.059	1.758	1.582	1.457	1.360	1.281	1.213	1.155	1.104	1.058	90
− 1	2.059	+ ∞	2.059	758	582	457	359	280	213	155	103	91
− 2	1.758	2.059	+ ∞	2.059	757	581	456	359	279	212	154	92
− 3	582	1.758	2.059	+ ∞	2.058	757	581	455	358	279	211	93
− 4	457	582	1.757	2.058	+ ∞	2.058	756	580	455	357	278	94
− 5	1.360	1.457	1.581	1.757	2.058	+ ∞	2.057	1.756	1.579	1.454	1.357	95
− 6	281	359	456	581	1.756	2.057	+ ∞	2.056	755	578	453	96
− 7	213	280	359	455	580	1.756	2.056	+ ∞	2.055	754	577	97
− 8	155	213	279	358	455	579	1.755	2.055	+ ∞	2.054	753	98
− 9	104	155	212	279	357	454	578	1.754	2.054	+ ∞	2.053	99
−10	1.058	1.103	1.154	1.211	1.278	1.357	1.453	1.577	1.753	2.053	+ ∞	100
−11	016	057	103	153	211	277	355	452	576	1.751	2.052	101
−12	0.978	016	057	102	152	209	276	354	451	575	1.750	102
−13	943	0.978	015	056	101	151	208	275	353	449	573	103
−14	911	942	0.977	014	054	099	150	207	273	351	448	104
−15	0.881	0.910	0.941	0.975	1.012	1.053	1.098	1.148	1.205	1.272	1.350	105
−16	852	879	909	940	0.974	011	052	097	147	204	270	106
−17	825	851	878	907	939	0.973	010	050	095	145	202	107
−18	800	824	850	877	906	937	0.971	008	048	093	143	108
−19	776	799	823	848	875	904	936	0.970	006	047	091	109
−20	0.754	0.775	0.798	0.821	0.847	0.874	0.903	0.934	0.968	1.004	1.045	110
−21	732	752	774	796	820	845	872	901	932	0.966	002	111
−22	711	731	751	772	794	818	843	870	899	930	0.964	112
−23	691	710	729	749	770	793	816	841	868	897	928	113
−24	672	690	708	727	747	768	791	814	839	866	895	114
Dec.	90°	89°	88°	87°	86°	85°	84°	83°	82°	81°	80°	Polar Dist.
	Co-Latitude.											

Time-Azimuths: Log A.

Dec.	Latitude. 10°	11°	12°	13°	14°	15°	16°	17°	18°	19°	20°	Polar Dist.
35°	9.370	9.354	9.337	9.320	9.302	9.282	9.262	9.241	9.218	9.194	9.168	55°
34	351	334	317	298	279	259	237	214	190	164	136	56
33	331	313	295	276	255	234	211	186	160	132	102	57
32	310	292	273	252	230	207	183	157	129	098	065	58
31	289	270	249	227	204	180	153	125	095	062	026	59
30	9.267	9.246	9.224	9.201	9.176	9.150	9.122	9.092	9.058	9.023	8.983	60
29	243	221	198	173	147	119	088	055	019	8.980	936	61
28	219	195	171	144	116	085	052	016	8.976	932	883	62
27	193	168	141	113	082	049	013	8.973	929	880	823	63
26	165	139	110	080	046	010	8.970	926	876	820	755	64
25	9.136	9.108	9.077	9.043	9.007	8.967	8.923	8.873	8.817	8.752	8.674	65
24	105	075	041	005	8.965	920	871	814	749	671	576	66
23	072	039	002	8.962	918	868	811	746	668	573	449	67
22	036	000	8.960	915	865	809	743	665	570	446	8.272	68
21	8.998	8.957	913	863	806	741	663	567	444	269	7.969	69
20	8.955	8.911	8.861	8.804	8.738	8.660	8.565	8.441	8.266	7.967	— ∞	70
19	909	859	802	736	658	562	439	264	7.964	— ∞	7.966	71
18	857	800	734	656	560	436	261	7.961	— ∞	7.964	8.266	72
17	798	732	654	558	434	259	7.959	— ∞	7.961	8.264	441	73
16	730	652	556	432	257	7.957	— ∞	7.959	8.261	439	565	74
15	8.650	8.554	8.430	8.255	7.955	— ∞	7.957	8.259	8.436	8.562	8.660	75
14	552	428	253	7.953	— ∞	7.955	8.257	434	560	658	738	76
13	427	252	7.951	— ∞	7.953	8.255	432	558	656	736	804	77
12	250	7.950	— ∞	7.951	8.253	430	556	654	734	802	861	78
11	7.948	— ∞	7.950	8.252	428	554	652	732	800	859	911	79
10	— ∞	7.948	8.250	8.427	8.552	8.650	8.730	8.798	8.857	8.909	8.955	80
9	7.947	8.249	425	551	649	728	796	855	907	953	996	81
8	8.247	424	549	647	727	795	853	905	952	994	9.032	82
7	423	548	646	725	793	852	903	950	992	9.030	066	83
6	547	645	724	792	850	902	948	990	9.029	064	097	84
5	8.643	8.723	8.791	8.849	8.901	8.947	8.989	9.027	9.063	9.096	9.126	85
4	722	789	848	899	946	988	9.026	061	094	125	153	86
3	789	847	898	944	936	9.025	060	093	123	152	179	87
2	846	897	943	985	9.023	059	092	122	150	177	202	88
1	897	943	984	9.022	058	090	121	149	176	201	225	89
0	8.942	8.984	9.022	9.057	9.089	9.119	9.148	9.175	9.200	9.224	9.246	90
− 1	983	9.021	056	088	119	147	173	199	222	245	267	91
− 2	9.020	055	088	118	146	173	197	221	244	265	286	92
− 3	055	087	117	145	172	197	220	243	264	285	305	93
− 4	087	117	145	171	196	220	242	263	284	303	322	94
− 5	9.116	9.144	9.171	9.195	9.219	9.241	9.263	9.283	9.303	9.321	9.339	95
− 6	144	170	195	218	241	262	282	302	320	338	355	96
− 7	170	195	218	240	261	282	301	320	337	354	371	97
− 8	194	218	240	261	281	301	319	337	354	370	386	98
− 9	218	240	261	281	300	319	336	353	370	385	401	99
−10	9.240	9.261	9.281	9.300	9.318	9.336	9.353	9.369	9.385	9.400	9.415	100
−11	261	281	300	318	335	352	369	384	400	414	428	101
−12	281	300	318	335	352	368	384	399	414	428	441	102
−13	300	318	335	352	368	384	399	413	428	441	454	103
−14	318	335	352	368	384	399	413	427	441	454	466	104
−15	9.336	9.352	9.368	9.384	9.399	9.413	9.427	9.440	9.454	9.466	9.478	105
−16	353	369	384	399	413	427	440	453	466	478	490	106
−17	369	384	399	413	427	440	453	466	478	490	502	107
−18	385	399	414	427	441	453	466	478	490	502	513	108
−19	400	414	428	441	454	466	478	490	502	513	524	109
−20	9.415	9.428	9.442	9.454	9.466	9.479	9.490	9.502	9.513	9.524	9.534	110
−21	429	442	455	467	479	491	502	513	524	534	544	111
−22	443	455	468	479	491	502	513	524	535	544	554	112
−23	456	468	480	492	503	514	524	535	545	554	564	113
−24	469	481	492	504	514	525	535	545	555	564	574	114
Dec.	80°	79°	78°	77°	76°	75°	74°	73°	72°	71°	70°	Polar Dist.
	Co-Latitude.											

Time-Azimuths: Log B.

Dec.	Latitude.											Polar Dist.
	10°	11°	12°	13°	14°	15°	16°	17°	18°	19°	20°	
35°	0.407	0.398	0.390	0.383	0.375	0.367	0.360	0.353	0.346	0.339	0.332	55°
34	417	408	400	392	384	376	369	361	354	347	340	56
33	427	418	410	401	393	385	378	370	362	355	348	57
32	437	429	420	411	403	394	387	379	371	363	356	58
31	448	439	430	421	412	404	396	388	379	372	364	59
30	0.459	0.450	0.440	0.431	0.422	0.413	0.405	0.397	0.388	0.380	0.372	60
29	470	461	451	442	432	423	414	406	397	389	381	61
28	482	472	462	452	442	433	424	415	406	398	390	62
27	494	483	473	463	453	443	434	425	416	407	399	63
26	506	495	484	474	463	454	444	435	425	416	408	64
25	0.518	0.507	0.496	0.485	0.474	0.464	0.454	0.445	0.435	0.426	0.417	65
24	531	519	508	496	486	475	465	455	445	436	426	66
23	544	532	520	508	497	486	476	465	455	446	436	67
22	557	545	532	520	509	498	487	476	466	456	446	68
21	571	558	545	533	521	510	498	487	476	466	456	69
20	0.585	0.572	0.559	0.546	0.533	0.522	0.510	0.498	0.487	0.476	0.466	70
19	600	586	572	559	546	534	522	510	498	487	476	71
18	615	601	586	573	559	547	534	522	510	498	487	72
17	631	616	601	587	573	560	547	534	522	510	498	73
16	647	631	616	601	587	573	560	547	534	522	510	74
15	0.664	0.648	0.632	0.616	0.601	0.587	0.573	0.560	0.546	0.534	0.522	75
14	682	665	648	632	616	601	587	573	559	546	534	76
13	700	682	665	648	632	616	601	587	573	559	546	77
12	719	700	682	665	648	632	616	601	587	572	559	78
11	739	719	700	682	665	648	631	616	601	586	572	79
10	0.760	0.739	0.719	0.700	0.682	0.664	0.647	0.631	0.615	0.600	0.585	80
9	782	760	739	719	700	681	664	647	630	615	599	81
8	806	782	760	739	719	699	681	663	646	630	614	82
7	830	805	782	760	739	718	699	680	663	646	629	83
6	856	830	805	782	759	738	718	698	680	662	645	84
5	0.884	0.856	0.829	0.805	0.781	0.759	0.737	0.717	0.698	0.679	0.661	85
4	913	883	855	829	804	780	758	737	716	697	678	86
3	945	913	883	855	828	803	780	757	736	715	695	87
2	980	945	912	882	854	827	803	779	756	735	714	88
1	1.017	979	944	912	882	853	827	802	778	755	733	89
0	1.058	1.016	0.978	0.943	0.911	0.881	0.852	0.826	0.800	0.776	0.754	90
− 1	103	057	1.016	978	942	910	879	851	824	799	775	91
− 2	154	103	056	1.015	977	941	909	878	850	823	798	92
− 3	211	153	102	056	1.014	975	940	907	877	848	821	93
− 4	278	211	152	101	054	1.012	974	939	906	875	847	94
− 5	1.357	1.277	1.209	1.151	1.099	1.053	1.011	0.973	0.937	0.904	0.874	95
− 6	453	355	276	208	150	098	052	1.010	971	936	903	96
− 7	577	452	354	275	207	148	097	050	1.008	970	934	97
− 8	753	576	451	353	273	205	147	095	048	1.006	968	98
− 9	2.053	751	575	449	351	272	204	145	093	047	1.004	99
−10	+ ∞	2.052	1.750	1.573	1.448	1.350	1.270	1.202	1.143	1.091	1.045	100
−11	2.052	+ ∞	2.050	748	572	446	348	268	200	141	089	101
−12	1.750	2.050	+ ∞	2.049	747	570	444	346	266	198	139	102
−13	573	1.748	2.049	+ ∞	2.047	745	568	442	344	264	196	103
−14	448	572	1.747	2.047	+ ∞	2.045	743	566	440	342	262	104
−15	1.350	1.446	1.570	1.745	2.045	+ ∞	2.043	1.741	1.564	1.438	1.340	105
−16	270	348	444	568	1.743	2.043	+ ∞	2.041	739	561	435	106
−17	202	268	346	442	566	1.741	2.041	+ ∞	2.039	736	559	107
−18	143	200	266	344	440	564	1.739	2.039	+ ∞	2.036	734	108
−19	091	141	198	264	342	438	561	1.736	2.036	+ ∞	2.033	109
−20	1.045	1.089	1.139	1.196	1.262	1.340	1.435	1.559	1.734	2.033	+ ∞	110
−21	002	043	087	137	194	259	337	433	556	1.731	2.031	111
−22	0.964	000	040	085	135	191	257	335	430	554	1.728	112
−23	928	0.961	0.998	038	082	132	189	254	332	427	551	113
−24	895	925	959	0.995	035	080	129	186	251	329	424	114
Dec.	80°	79°	78°	77°	76°	75°	74°	73°	72°	71°	70°	Polar Dist.
	Co-Latitude.											

Time-Azimuths: Log A.

Dec.	Latitude.											Polar Dist.
	20°	21°	22°	23°	24°	25°	26°	27°	28°	29°	30°	
35	9.168	9.140	9.110	9.077	9.042	9.003	8.959	8.911	8.855	8.790	8.714	55°
34	136	106	073	038	8.998	8.955	906	850	786	709	614	56
33	102	069	034	8.994	951	902	846	781	704	610	487	57
32	065	030	8.990	947	898	842	777	700	605	483	309	58
31	026	8.987	943	894	838	773	696	601	478	304	006	59
30	8.983	8.939	8.890	8.834	8.769	8.692	8.597	8.474	8.300	8.001	— ∞	60
29	936	886	830	765	688	593	470	296	7.997	— ∞	8.001	61
28	883	827	762	684	589	466	292	7.993	— ∞	7.997	300	62
27	823	758	681	586	462	288	7.989	— ∞	7.993	8.296	474	63
26	755	677	582	459	285	7.985	— ∞	7.989	8.292	470	597	64
25	8.674	8.579	8.456	8.281	7.982	— ∞	7.985	8.288	8.466	8.593	8.692	65
24	576	452	278	7.978	— ∞	7.982	8.285	462	589	688	769	66
23	449	275	7.975	— ∞	7.978	8.281	459	586	684	765	834	67
22	272	7.972	— ∞	7.975	8.278	456	582	681	762	830	890	68
21	7.969	— ∞	7.972	8.275	452	579	677	758	827	886	939	69
20	— ∞	7.969	8.272	8.449	8.576	8.674	8.755	8.823	8.883	8.936	8.983	70
19	7.966	8.269	446	573	671	752	820	880	932	980	9.023	71
18	8.266	444	570	668	749	817	876	929	976	9.019	059	72
17	441	567	665	746	814	873	926	973	9.016	055	092	73
16	565	663	743	811	871	923	970	9.013	052	088	122	74
15	8.660	8.741	9.809	8.868	8.920	8.967	9.010	9.049	9.085	9.119	9.150	75
14	738	806	865	918	965	9.007	046	082	116	147	176	76
13	804	863	915	962	9.005	044	080	113	144	173	201	77
12	861	913	960	9.002	041	077	110	141	171	198	224	78
11	911	957	9.000	039	075	108	139	168	195	221	246	79
10	8.955	8.998	9.036	9.072	9.105	9.136	9.165	9.193	9.219	9.243	9.267	80
9	996	9.034	070	103	134	163	190	216	241	264	286	81
8	9.032	068	101	132	161	188	214	238	262	284	305	82
7	066	099	130	159	186	212	236	259	281	302	323	83
6	097	128	157	184	209	234	257	279	300	320	340	84
5	9.126	9.155	9.182	9.207	9.232	9.255	9.277	9.298	9.318	9.337	9.356	85
4	153	180	206	230	253	275	296	316	335	354	372	86
3	179	204	228	251	273	294	314	333	351	369	387	87
2	202	226	249	271	292	312	331	349	367	384	401	88
1	225	248	269	290	310	329	348	365	382	399	415	89
0	9.246	9.268	9.289	9.309	9.328	9.346	9.363	9.380	9.397	9.413	9.428	90
— 1	267	287	307	326	344	362	379	395	411	426	441	91
— 2	286	306	325	343	360	377	393	409	424	439	453	92
— 3	305	323	341	359	376	392	407	423	437	452	466	93
— 4	322	340	357	374	391	406	421	436	450	464	477	94
— 5	9.339	9.356	9.373	9.389	9.405	9.420	9.434	9.448	9.462	9.476	9.489	95
— 6	355	372	388	403	418	433	447	461	474	487	500	96
— 7	371	387	402	417	432	446	459	473	485	498	510	97
— 8	386	401	416	431	445	458	471	484	497	509	521	98
— 9	401	415	430	444	457	470	483	495	508	519	531	99
—10	9.415	9.429	9.443	9.456	9.469	9.482	9.494	9.506	9.518	9.530	9.541	100
—11	428	442	455	468	481	493	505	517	528	540	550	101
—12	441	455	467	480	492	504	516	527	538	549	560	102
—13	454	467	479	492	503	515	526	537	548	559	569	103
—14	466	479	491	503	514	526	537	547	558	568	578	104
—15	9.478	9.491	9.502	9.514	9.525	9.536	9.546	9.557	9.567	9.577	9.587	105
—16	490	502	513	524	535	546	556	566	576	586	595	106
—17	502	513	524	535	545	555	565	575	585	594	604	107
—18	513	524	534	545	555	565	575	584	594	603	612	108
—19	524	534	544	555	564	574	584	593	602	611	620	109
—20	9.534	9.544	9.554	9.564	9.574	9.583	9.593	9.602	9.610	9.619	9.628	110
—21	544	554	564	574	583	592	601	610	619	627	635	111
—22	554	564	574	583	592	601	610	618	627	635	643	112
—23	564	574	583	592	601	609	618	626	634	642	650	113
—24	574	583	592	601	609	618	626	634	642	650	658	114
Dec.	70°	69°	68°	67°	66°	65°	64°	63°	62°	61°	60°	Polar Dist.
	Co-Latitude.											

Time-Azimuths: Log B.

Dec	Latitude.											Polar Dist.
	20°	21°	22°	23°	24°	25°	26°	27°	28°	29°	30°	
35°	0.332	0.325	0.319	0.312	0.306	0.299	0.293	0.287	0.281	0.275	0.269	55°
34	340	333	326	319	313	306	300	294	288	282	276	56
33	348	341	333	326	320	313	307	300	294	288	282	57
32	356	349	341	334	327	320	314	307	301	294	288	58
31	364	357	349	342	335	328	321	314	308	301	295	59
30	0.372	0.365	0.357	0.350	0.342	0.335	0.328	0.321	0.314	0.308	0.301	60
29	381	373	365	358	350	343	335	328	321	314	308	61
28	390	381	373	366	358	350	343	336	328	321	314	62
27	399	390	382	374	366	358	350	343	336	328	321	63
26	408	399	390	382	374	366	358	350	343	335	328	64
25	0.417	0.408	0.399	0.391	0.382	0.374	0.366	0.358	0.350	0.342	0.335	65
24	426	417	408	399	391	382	374	366	358	350	342	66
23	436	426	417	408	399	391	382	374	366	358	350	67
22	446	436	426	417	408	399	390	382	374	365	357	68
21	456	446	436	426	417	408	399	390	382	373	365	69
20	0.466	0.456	0.446	0.436	0.426	0.417	0.407	0.399	0.390	0.381	0.372	70
19	476	466	456	445	435	426	416	407	398	389	380	71
18	487	476	466	455	445	435	425	416	406	397	388	72
17	498	487	476	465	455	445	435	425	415	406	396	73
16	510	498	487	476	465	454	444	434	424	414	405	74
15	0.522	0.509	0.498	0.486	0.475	0.464	0.454	0.443	0.433	0.423	0.413	75
14	534	521	509	497	486	474	464	453	442	432	422	76
13	546	533	520	508	497	485	474	463	452	441	431	77
12	559	545	532	520	508	496	484	473	462	451	440	78
11	572	558	544	532	519	507	495	483	472	461	450	79
10	0.585	0.571	0.557	0.544	0.531	0.518	0.506	0.494	0.482	0.471	0.459	80
9	599	585	570	556	543	530	517	505	492	481	469	81
8	614	599	584	569	555	542	529	516	503	491	479	82
7	629	613	598	583	568	554	541	527	515	502	490	83
6	645	628	612	597	581	567	553	539	526	513	500	84
5	0.661	0.644	0.627	0.611	0.595	0.580	0.566	0.552	0.538	0.524	0.511	85
4	678	660	643	626	609	594	579	564	550	536	523	86
3	695	677	659	641	624	608	593	577	563	548	535	87
2	714	694	675	657	640	623	607	591	576	561	547	88
1	733	712	693	674	656	638	621	605	589	574	559	89
0	0.754	0.732	0.711	0.691	0.672	0.654	0.637	0.620	0.603	0.587	0.572	90
− 1	775	752	731	710	690	671	653	635	618	601	585	91
− 2	798	774	751	729	708	688	669	651	633	616	599	92
− 3	821	796	772	749	727	706	686	667	649	631	614	93
− 4	847	820	794	770	747	725	704	684	665	646	629	94
− 5	0.874	0.845	0.818	0.793	0.768	0.745	0.723	0.702	0.682	0.663	0.644	95
− 6	903	872	843	816	791	766	743	721	700	680	660	96
− 7	934	901	870	841	814	789	764	741	719	698	677	97
− 8	968	932	899	868	839	812	786	762	738	716	695	98
− 9	1.004	966	930	897	866	837	810	784	759	736	714	99
−10	1.045	1.002	0.964	0.928	0.895	0.864	0.835	0.807	0.781	0.757	0.733	100
−11	089	043	1.000	961	925	892	861	832	805	779	754	101
−12	139	087	040	998	959	923	890	859	829	802	776	102
−13	196	137	085	1.038	995	957	920	887	856	827	799	103
−14	262	194	135	082	1.035	993	954	918	884	853	824	104
−15	1.340	1.259	1.191	1.132	1.080	1.033	0.990	0.951	0.915	0.881	0.850	105
−16	435	337	257	189	129	077	1.030	987	948	912	878	106
−17	559	433	335	254	186	126	074	1.027	984	945	908	107
−18	734	556	430	332	251	183	123	071	1.024	981	942	108
−19	2.033	731	554	427	329	248	180	120	068	1.020	977	109
−20	+ ∞	2.031	1.728	1.551	1.424	1.326	1.245	1.177	1.117	1.064	1.017	110
−21	2.031	+ ∞	2.028	725	548	421	323	242	173	114	061	111
−22	1.728	2.028	+ ∞	2.025	722	544	418	319	238	170	110	112
−23	551	1.725	2.025	+ ∞	2.022	719	541	414	316	235	166	113
−24	424	548	1.722	2.022	+ ∞	2.018	715	538	411	312	231	114
Dec.	70°	69°	68°	67°	66°	65°	64°	63°	62°	61°	60°	Polar Dist.
	Co-Latitude.											

Time-Azimuths: Log A.

Dec.	Latitude. 30°	31°	32°	33°	34°	35°	36°	37°	38°	39°	40°	Polar Dist.
35°	8.714	8.619	8.497	8.323	8.025	— ∞	8.030	8.334	8.513	8.641	8.740	55°
34	614	492	318	8.020	— ∞	8.025	329	507	635	735	817	56
33	487	314	8.015	— ∞	8.020	323	502	629	729	811	881	57
32	309	8.010	— ∞	8.015	318	497	624	724	805	875	936	58
31	8.006	— ∞	8.010	313	492	619	719	800	870	930	984	59
30	— ∞	8.006	8.308	8.487	8.614	8.714	8.795	8.865	8.925	8.979	9.027	60
29	8.001	304	483	610	709	790	860	920	974	9.022	066	61
28	300	478	605	704	786	855	915	969	9.017	061	101	62
27	474	601	700	781	850	911	964	9.012	056	096	133	63
26	597	696	777	846	906	959	9.007	051	091	128	162	64
25	8.692	8.773	8.842	8.902	8.955	9.003	9.046	9.086	9.123	9.158	9.190	65
24	769	838	898	951	999	042	082	119	153	185	215	66
23	834	894	947	994	9.038	077	114	148	180	211	239	67
22	890	943	990	9.034	073	110	144	176	206	234	261	68
21	939	987	9.030	069	105	140	172	202	230	257	282	69
20	8.983	9.026	9.066	9.102	9.136	9.168	9.198	9.226	9.253	9.278	9.302	70
19	9.023	062	098	132	164	194	222	248	274	298	321	71
18	059	095	129	160	190	218	244	270	294	317	339	72
17	092	125	157	186	214	241	265	290	313	335	356	73
16	122	153	183	211	237	262	286	309	331	352	372	74
15	9.150	9.180	9.207	9.234	9.259	9.282	9.305	9.327	9.348	9.368	9.387	75
14	176	204	230	255	279	302	323	344	364	384	402	76
13	201	227	252	276	298	320	341	361	380	399	416	77
12	224	249	273	295	317	337	357	376	395	413	430	78
11	246	270	292	313	334	354	373	391	409	427	443	79
10	9.267	9.289	9.310	9.331	9.351	9.370	9.388	9.406	9.423	9.440	9.456	80
9	286	308	328	348	367	385	403	420	436	452	468	81
8	305	325	345	364	382	400	417	433	449	465	480	82
7	323	342	361	379	397	414	430	446	461	476	491	83
6	340	358	376	394	411	427	443	458	473	483	502	84
5	9.356	9.374	9.391	9.408	9.424	9.440	9.455	9.470	9.485	9.499	9.513	85
4	372	389	406	422	437	453	467	482	496	510	523	86
3	387	403	419	435	450	465	479	493	507	520	533	87
2	401	417	432	448	462	476	490	504	517	530	542	88
1	415	430	445	460	474	488	501	514	527	540	552	89
0	9.428	9.443	9.457	9.472	9.485	9.499	9.512	9.524	9.537	9.549	9.561	90
— 1	441	455	469	483	496	509	522	534	547	558	570	91
— 2	453	467	481	494	507	520	532	544	556	567	579	92
— 3	465	479	492	505	518	530	542	554	565	576	587	93
— 4	477	490	503	516	528	540	551	563	574	585	595	94
— 5	9.488	9.501	9.514	9.526	9.538	9.549	9.560	9.572	9.582	9.593	9.603	95
— 6	499	512	524	536	547	558	569	580	591	601	611	96
— 7	510	522	534	545	557	567	578	589	599	609	619	97
— 8	521	532	544	555	566	576	587	597	607	617	627	98
— 9	531	542	553	564	575	585	595	605	615	625	634	99
—10	9.541	9.552	9.562	9.573	9.583	9.593	9.603	9.613	9.623	9.632	9.641	100
—11	551	561	571	582	592	602	611	621	630	639	648	101
—12	560	570	580	590	600	610	619	628	637	646	655	102
—13	569	579	589	599	608	617	627	636	644	653	662	103
—14	578	588	597	607	616	625	634	643	651	660	668	104
—15	9.587	9.596	9.606	9.615	9.624	9.633	9.641	9.650	9.658	9.667	9.675	105
—16	595	605	614	623	631	640	648	657	665	673	681	106
—17	604	613	622	630	639	647	655	664	671	680	688	107
—18	612	621	629	638	646	654	662	670	678	686	694	108
—19	620	628	637	645	653	661	669	677	685	692	700	109
—20	9.628	9.636	9.644	9.652	9.660	9.668	9.676	9.684	9.691	9.698	9.706	110
—21	635	644	652	659	667	675	683	690	697	704	712	111
—22	643	651	659	666	674	682	689	696	703	710	717	112
—23	650	658	666	673	681	688	695	702	709	716	723	113
—24	658	665	673	680	687	694	701	708	715	722	728	114
Dec.	60°	59°	58°	57°	56°	55°	54°	53°	52°	51°	50° Co-Latitude.	Polar Dist.

Time-Azimuths: Log B.

Dec.	Latitude. 30°	31°	32°	33°	34°	35°	36°	37°	38°	39°	40°	Polar Dist.
35°	0.269	0.264	0.258	0.252	0.247	0.241	0.236	0.231	0.226	0.220	0.215	55°
34	276	270	264	258	252	247	241	236	231	225	220	56
33	282	276	270	264	258	252	247	241	236	230	225	57
32	288	282	276	270	264	258	252	247	241	235	230	58
31	295	288	282	276	270	264	258	252	246	240	235	59
30	0.301	0.295	0.288	0.282	0.276	0.269	0.263	0.257	0.251	0.246	0.240	60
29	308	301	294	288	282	275	269	263	257	251	245	61
28	314	308	301	294	288	281	275	269	262	256	250	62
27	321	314	307	300	294	287	281	274	268	261	255	63
26	328	321	314	307	300	293	287	280	273	267	261	64
25	0.335	0.328	0.320	0.313	0.306	0.299	0.293	0.286	0.279	0.273	0.266	65
24	342	335	327	320	313	306	299	292	285	278	272	66
23	350	342	334	327	319	312	305	298	291	284	277	67
22	357	349	341	334	326	318	311	304	297	290	283	68
21	365	356	348	341	333	325	318	310	303	296	289	69
20	0.372	0.364	0.356	0.348	0.340	0.332	0.324	0.316	0.309	0.302	0.294	70
19	380	372	363	355	347	339	331	323	315	308	300	71
18	388	380	371	362	354	346	338	330	322	314	306	72
17	396	388	379	370	361	353	345	336	328	320	312	73
16	405	396	387	377	369	360	352	343	335	327	319	74
15	0.413	0.404	0.394	0.385	0.376	0.367	0.359	0.350	0.342	0.333	0.325	75
14	422	412	403	393	384	375	366	357	349	340	332	76
13	431	421	411	401	392	383	373	364	356	347	338	77
12	440	430	420	410	400	391	381	372	363	354	345	78
11	450	439	429	418	408	399	389	379	370	361	352	79
10	0.459	0.448	0.438	0.427	0.417	0.407	0.397	0.387	0.378	0.368	0.359	80
9	469	458	447	436	426	415	405	395	385	376	366	81
8	479	468	456	445	435	424	413	403	393	383	374	82
7	490	478	466	455	444	433	422	411	401	391	381	83
6	500	488	476	464	453	442	431	420	409	399	389	84
5	0.511	0.499	0.485	0.474	0.462	0.451	0.440	0.428	0.418	0.407	0.397	85
4	523	510	497	484	472	460	449	437	426	415	405	86
3	535	521	508	495	482	470	458	447	435	424	413	87
2	547	533	519	506	493	480	468	456	444	433	421	88
1	559	545	531	517	504	491	478	466	453	442	430	89
0	0.572	0.557	0.543	0.528	0.515	0.501	0.488	0.476	0.463	0.451	0.439	90
− 1	585	570	555	540	526	512	499	486	473	460	448	91
− 2	599	583	568	552	538	524	510	496	483	470	458	92
− 3	614	597	581	565	550	535	521	507	493	480	467	93
− 4	629	611	594	578	563	547	533	518	504	491	477	94
− 5	0.644	0.626	0.609	0.592	0.576	0.560	0.545	0.530	0.515	0.501	0.488	95
− 6	660	642	624	606	589	573	557	542	527	512	498	96
− 7	677	658	639	621	603	587	570	554	539	524	509	97
− 8	695	675	655	636	618	601	584	567	551	536	520	98
− 9	714	692	672	652	633	615	598	580	564	548	532	99
−10	0.733	0.711	0.690	0.669	0.649	0.630	0.612	0.594	0.577	0.560	0.544	100
−11	754	730	708	687	666	646	627	609	591	573	557	101
−12	776	751	727	705	683	663	643	624	605	587	570	102
−13	799	773	748	724	702	680	659	639	620	602	584	103
−14	824	796	770	745	721	698	677	656	636	617	598	104
−15	0.850	0.820	0.793	0.765	0.741	0.718	0.695	0.673	0.652	0.632	0.613	105
−16	878	847	817	789	763	738	714	691	669	648	628	106
−17	908	875	843	814	786	759	734	710	687	665	644	107
−18	942	905	871	840	810	782	756	730	706	683	661	108
−19	977	938	902	868	836	806	778	752	726	702	679	109
−20	1.017	0.974	0.935	0.898	0.864	0.832	0.802	0.774	0.748	0.722	0.698	110
−21	061	1.013	970	931	894	860	828	798	770	744	718	111
−22	110	057	1.010	966	927	890	856	824	794	766	739	112
−23	166	106	053	1.006	962	923	886	852	820	789	761	113
−24	231	162	102	049	1.002	958	918	881	847	815	785	114
Dec.	60°	59°	58°	57°	56°	55°	54°	53°	52°	51°	50°	Polar Dist.
	Co-Latitude.											

Time-Azimuths: Log A.

Dec.	Latitude.											Polar Dist.
	40°	41°	42°	43°	44°	45°	46°	47°	48°	49°	50°	
35°	8.740	8.822	8.892	8.953	9.007	9.056	9.101	9.141	9.179	9.215	9.248	55°
34	817	886	947	9.001	050	094	135	173	208	241	273	56
33	881	941	995	044	088	129	167	202	235	266	295	57
32	936	989	9.038	082	123	160	195	228	259	289	317	58
31	984	9.032	076	117	154	189	222	253	282	310	337	59
30	9.027	9.071	9.111	9.149	9.184	9.216	9.247	9.276	9.304	9.330	9.355	60
29	066	106	143	178	211	241	270	298	324	349	373	61
28	101	138	173	205	236	264	292	318	343	367	390	62
27	133	167	200	230	259	286	312	337	361	384	406	63
26	162	195	225	254	281	307	332	355	378	400	421	64
25	9.190	9.220	9.249	9.276	9.302	9.326	9.350	9.373	9.395	9.416	9.436	65
24	215	244	271	297	321	345	367	389	410	430	450	66
23	239	266	292	316	340	362	384	405	425	444	463	67
22	261	287	311	335	357	379	399	419	439	457	476	68
21	282	307	330	352	374	394	414	434	452	470	488	69
20	9.302	9.325	9.348	9.369	9.390	9.409	9.429	9.447	9.465	9.483	9.500	70
19	321	343	364	385	405	424	442	460	478	495	511	71
18	339	360	380	400	419	437	455	473	490	506	522	72
17	356	376	396	415	433	450	468	485	501	517	532	73
16	372	391	410	429	446	463	480	496	512	527	542	74
15	9.387	9.406	9.424	9.442	9.459	9.476	9.492	9.507	9.523	9.538	9.552	75
14	402	420	438	455	471	487	503	518	533	547	562	76
13	416	434	451	467	483	498	514	528	543	557	571	77
12	430	447	463	479	494	509	524	538	553	566	580	78
11	443	459	475	490	505	520	534	548	562	575	588	79
10	9.456	9.471	9.487	9.502	9.516	9.530	9.544	9.558	9.571	9.584	9.597	80
9	468	483	498	512	526	540	554	567	580	592	605	81
8	480	494	509	523	536	550	563	576	588	600	613	82
7	491	505	519	533	546	559	572	584	596	608	620	83
6	502	516	529	543	555	568	580	593	604	616	628	84
5	9.513	9.526	9.539	9.552	9.565	9.577	9.589	9.601	9.612	9.624	9.635	85
4	523	536	549	561	573	585	597	609	620	631	642	86
3	533	545	558	570	582	594	605	616	627	638	649	87
2	542	555	567	579	590	602	613	624	635	645	656	88
1	552	564	576	587	598	610	620	631	642	652	662	89
0	9.561	9.573	9.584	9.595	9.606	9.617	9.628	9.638	9.649	9.659	9.669	90
− 1	570	581	593	603	614	625	635	645	655	665	675	91
− 2	579	590	601	611	622	632	642	652	662	672	681	92
− 3	587	598	609	619	629	639	649	659	668	678	687	93
− 4	595	606	616	626	636	646	656	665	675	684	693	94
− 5	9.603	9.614	9.624	9.634	9.643	9.653	9.662	9.672	9.681	9.690	9.699	95
− 6	611	621	631	641	650	660	669	678	687	696	704	96
− 7	619	629	638	648	657	666	675	684	693	701	710	97
− 8	627	636	645	655	664	673	681	690	699	707	715	98
− 9	634	643	652	661	670	679	687	696	704	713	721	99
−10	9.641	9.650	9.659	9.668	9.676	9.685	9.693	9.702	9.710	9.718	9.726	100
−11	648	657	666	674	683	691	699	707	715	723	731	101
−12	655	664	672	681	689	697	705	713	721	729	736	102
−13	662	670	679	687	695	703	711	718	726	734	741	103
−14	668	677	685	693	701	708	716	724	731	739	746	104
−15	9.675	9.683	9.691	9.699	9.706	9.714	9.722	9.729	9.736	9.744	9.751	105
−16	681	689	697	705	712	720	727	734	741	749	756	106
−17	688	695	703	710	718	725	732	739	746	753	760	107
−18	694	701	709	716	723	730	737	744	751	758	765	108
−19	700	707	714	721	729	736	742	749	756	763	769	109
−20	9.706	9.713	9.720	9.727	9.734	9.741	9.747	9.754	9.761	9.767	9.774	110
−21	712	718	725	732	739	746	752	759	765	772	778	111
−22	717	724	731	738	744	751	757	764	770	776	782	112
−23	723	730	736	743	749	756	762	768	774	780	787	113
−24	728	735	741	748	754	760	767	773	779	785	791	114
Dec.	50°	49°	48°	47°	46°	45°	44°	43°	42°	41°	40°	Polar Dist.
	Co-Latitude.											

Time-Azimuths: Log B.

Dec.	Latitude.											Polar Dist.
	40°	41°	42°	43°	44°	45°	46°	47°	48°	49°	50°	
35°	0.215	0.210	0.205	0.200	0.195	0.190	0.186	0.181	0.176	0.171	0.167	55°
34	220	215	210	205	199	194	190	185	180	175	170	56
33	225	219	214	209	204	199	194	189	184	179	174	57
32	230	224	219	214	208	203	198	193	188	183	178	58
31	235	229	224	218	213	208	202	197	192	187	181	59
30	0.240	0.234	0.228	0.223	0.217	0.212	0.207	0.201	0.196	0.191	0.185	60
29	245	239	233	228	222	216	211	205	200	195	189	61
28	250	244	238	232	227	221	215	210	204	199	193	62
27	255	249	243	237	231	225	220	214	208	203	197	63
26	261	254	248	242	236	230	224	218	212	207	201	64
25	0.266	0.260	0.253	0.247	0.241	0.235	0.229	0.223	0.217	0.211	0.205	65
24	272	265	259	252	246	240	233	227	221	215	209	66
23	277	270	264	257	251	244	238	232	226	220	213	67
22	283	276	269	263	256	249	243	236	230	224	218	68
21	289	282	275	268	261	254	248	241	235	228	222	69
20	0.294	0.287	0.280	0.273	0.266	0.259	0.253	0.246	0.239	0.233	0.226	70
19	300	293	286	279	271	264	258	251	244	237	231	71
18	306	299	291	284	277	270	263	256	249	242	235	72
17	312	305	297	290	282	275	268	261	254	247	240	73
16	319	311	303	296	288	280	273	266	259	251	245	74
15	0.325	0.317	0.309	0.301	0.294	0.286	0.278	0.271	0.264	0.256	0.249	75
14	332	323	315	307	299	292	284	276	269	261	254	76
13	338	330	322	313	305	297	289	282	274	266	259	77
12	345	336	328	319	311	303	295	287	279	271	264	78
11	352	343	334	326	317	309	301	293	285	277	269	79
10	0.359	0.350	0.341	0.332	0.324	0.315	0.307	0.298	0.290	0.282	0.274	80
9	366	357	348	339	330	321	313	304	296	287	279	81
8	374	364	355	345	336	327	319	310	301	293	285	82
7	381	371	362	352	343	334	325	316	307	299	290	83
6	389	379	369	359	350	340	331	322	313	304	296	84
5	0.397	0.386	0.376	0.366	0.357	0.347	0.338	0.328	0.319	0.310	0.301	85
4	405	394	384	374	364	354	344	335	325	316	307	86
3	413	402	392	381	371	361	351	341	332	322	313	87
2	421	410	399	389	378	368	358	348	338	328	319	88
1	430	419	407	397	386	375	365	355	345	335	325	89
0	0.439	0.427	0.416	0.405	0.394	0.383	0.372	0.362	0.351	0.341	0.331	90
— 1	448	436	424	413	402	390	380	369	358	348	338	91
— 2	458	445	433	421	410	398	387	376	365	355	344	92
— 3	467	455	442	430	418	406	395	384	373	362	351	93
— 4	477	464	451	439	427	415	403	391	380	369	358	94
— 5	0.488	0.474	0.461	0.448	0.436	0.423	0.411	0.399	0.388	0.376	0.365	95
— 6	498	484	471	457	445	432	420	408	396	384	372	96
— 7	509	495	481	467	454	441	428	416	404	392	380	97
— 8	520	506	491	477	464	450	437	424	412	400	387	98
— 9	532	517	502	488	474	460	446	433	420	408	395	99
—10	0.544	0.529	0.513	0.499	0.484	0.470	0.456	0.442	0.429	0.416	0.403	100
—11	557	541	525	510	495	480	466	452	438	425	412	101
—12	570	553	537	521	506	491	476	462	447	434	421	102
—13	584	566	549	533	517	502	486	472	457	443	429	103
—14	598	580	562	545	629	513	497	482	467	453	438	104
—15	0.613	0.594	0.576	0.558	0.541	0.525	0.508	0.493	0.477	0.463	0.448	105
—16	628	609	590	571	554	537	520	504	488	473	458	106
—17	644	624	604	585	567	549	532	515	499	483	468	107
—18	661	640	620	600	581	563	545	527	510	494	478	108
—19	679	657	636	615	596	577	558	540	522	505	489	109
—20	0.698	0.675	0.653	0.631	0.611	0.591	0.572	0.553	0.535	0.517	0.500	110
—21	718	693	670	648	626	606	586	567	548	530	512	111
—22	739	713	689	665	643	621	601	581	561	543	524	112
—23	761	734	708	684	660	638	616	595	575	556	537	113
—24	785	756	729	703	679	655	633	611	590	570	550	114
Dec.	50°	49°	48°	47°	46°	45°	44°	43°	42°	41°	40°	Polar Dist.
	Co-Latitude.											

Time-Azimuths: Log A.

Dec.	Latitude. 50°	51°	52°	53°	54°	55°	56°	57°	58°	59°	60°	Polar Dist.
35°	9.248	9.280	9.309	9.337	9.364	9.390	9.415	9.439	9.462	9.484	9.506	55°
34	273	302	330	357	383	407	431	454	476	498	518	56
33	295	323	350	376	400	424	447	468	490	510	530	57
32	317	343	369	393	417	439	461	482	503	523	542	58
31	337	362	386	410	432	454	475	495	515	534	553	59
30	9.355	9.380	9.403	9.425	9.447	9.468	9.488	9.508	9.527	9.545	9.564	60
29	373	396	419	440	461	481	501	520	538	556	574	61
28	390	412	434	454	474	494	513	531	549	566	583	62
27	406	427	448	468	487	506	524	542	559	576	593	63
26	421	442	462	481	499	518	535	552	569	586	602	64
25	9.436	9.456	9.475	9.493	9.511	9.529	9.546	9.562	9.579	9.595	9.611	65
24	450	469	487	505	523	540	556	572	588	604	619	66
23	463	481	499	517	533	550	566	582	597	612	627	67
22	476	493	511	527	544	560	575	591	606	620	635	68
21	488	505	522	538	554	569	585	600	614	628	643	69
20	9.500	9.516	9.532	9.548	9.564	9.579	9.594	9.608	9.622	9.636	9.650	70
19	511	527	543	558	573	588	602	616	630	644	657	71
18	522	537	553	567	582	596	610	624	638	651	664	72
17	532	547	562	577	591	605	618	632	645	658	671	73
16	542	557	571	586	599	613	626	639	652	665	677	74
15	9.552	9.566	9.580	9.594	9.608	9.621	9.634	9.646	9.659	9.671	9.683	75
14	562	575	589	603	616	628	641	653	666	678	689	76
13	571	584	598	611	623	636	648	660	672	684	695	77
12	580	593	606	618	631	643	655	667	679	690	701	78
11	588	601	614	626	638	650	662	673	685	696	707	79
10	9.597	9.609	9.621	9.633	9.645	9.657	9.668	9.680	9.691	9.702	9.713	80
9	605	617	629	641	652	664	675	686	697	707	718	81
8	613	624	636	648	659	670	681	692	702	713	723	82
7	620	632	643	654	665	676	687	698	708	718	728	83
6	628	639	650	661	672	682	693	703	713	724	733	84
5	9.635	9.646	9.657	9.668	9.678	9.688	9.699	9.709	9.719	9.729	9.738	85
4	642	653	663	674	684	694	704	714	724	734	743	86
3	649	659	670	680	690	700	710	720	729	739	748	87
2	656	666	676	686	696	706	715	725	734	743	753	88
1	662	672	682	692	702	711	721	730	739	748	757	89
0	9.669	9.679	9.688	9.698	9.707	9.717	9.726	9.735	9.744	9.753	9.762	90
− 1	675	685	694	703	713	722	731	740	748	757	766	91
− 2	681	691	700	709	718	727	736	744	753	762	770	92
− 3	687	696	705	714	723	732	741	749	758	766	774	93
− 4	693	702	711	720	728	737	745	754	762	770	778	94
− 5	9.699	9.708	9.716	9.725	9.733	9.742	9.750	9.758	9.766	9.774	9.782	95
− 6	704	713	722	730	738	747	755	763	771	778	786	96
− 7	710	718	727	735	743	751	759	767	775	782	790	97
− 8	715	724	732	740	748	756	764	771	779	786	794	98
− 9	721	729	737	745	753	760	768	775	783	790	798	99
−10	9.726	9.734	9.742	9.750	9.757	9.765	9.772	9.780	9.787	9.794	9.801	100
−11	731	739	747	754	762	769	776	784	791	798	805	101
−12	736	744	751	759	766	773	780	787	795	802	809	102
−13	741	749	756	763	770	777	784	791	798	805	812	103
−14	746	753	760	768	775	782	788	795	802	809	816	104
−15	9.751	9.758	9.765	9.772	9.779	9.786	9.792	9.799	9.806	9.812	9.819	105
−16	756	763	769	776	783	790	796	803	809	816	822	106
−17	760	767	774	780	787	794	800	807	813	819	825	107
−18	765	771	778	785	791	797	804	810	816	823	829	108
−19	769	776	782	789	795	801	807	814	820	826	832	109
−20	9.774	9.780	9.786	9.793	9.799	9.805	9.811	9.817	9.823	9.829	9.835	110
−21	778	784	791	797	803	809	815	821	827	832	838	111
−22	782	789	795	801	807	812	818	824	830	836	841	112
−23	787	793	799	804	810	816	822	828	833	839	844	113
−24	791	797	802	808	814	820	825	831	836	842	847	114
Dec.	40°	39°	38°	37°	36°	35°	34°	33°	32°	31°	30° Co-Latitude.	Polar Dist.

Time-Azimuths: Log B.

Dec.	50°	51°	52°	53°	54°	55°	56°	57°	58°	59°	60°	Polar Dist.
	Latitude.											
35°	0.167	0.162	0.157	0.153	0.148	0.144	0.139	0.135	0.131	0.126	0.122	55°
34	170	166	161	156	152	147	142	138	133	129	125	56
33	174	169	164	160	155	150	145	141	136	132	127	57
32	178	173	168	163	158	153	149	144	139	135	130	58
31	181	176	171	166	161	157	152	147	142	137	133	59
30	0.185	0.180	0.175	0.170	0.165	0.160	0.155	0.150	0.145	0.140	0.135	60
29	199	184	179	173	168	163	158	153	148	143	138	61
28	193	188	182	177	172	167	161	156	151	146	141	62
27	197	191	186	181	175	170	165	159	154	149	144	63
26	201	195	190	184	179	173	168	163	157	152	147	64
25	0.205	0.199	0.194	0.188	0.182	0.177	0.171	0.166	0.160	0.155	0.150	65
24	209	203	198	192	186	180	175	169	164	158	153	66
23	213	207	201	196	190	184	178	173	167	161	156	67
22	218	212	205	200	194	187	182	176	170	164	159	68
21	222	216	210	203	197	191	185	179	173	168	162	69
20	0.226	0.220	0.214	0.207	0.201	0.195	0.189	0.183	0.177	0.171	0.165	70
19	231	224	218	211	205	199	193	186	180	174	168	71
18	235	229	222	215	209	203	196	190	184	177	171	72
17	240	233	226	220	213	207	200	194	187	181	175	73
16	245	238	231	224	217	210	204	197	191	184	178	74
15	0.249	0.242	0.235	0.228	0.221	0.214	0.208	0.201	0.194	0.188	0.181	75
14	254	247	240	232	225	218	212	205	198	191	185	76
13	259	252	244	237	230	223	216	209	202	195	188	77
12	264	256	249	241	234	227	220	213	205	198	192	78
11	269	261	253	246	239	231	224	216	209	202	195	79
10	0.274	0.266	0.258	0.251	0.243	0.235	0.228	0.220	0.213	0.206	0.199	80
9	279	271	263	255	248	240	232	225	217	210	202	81
8	285	276	268	260	252	244	237	229	221	214	206	82
7	290	282	273	265	257	249	241	233	225	218	210	83
6	296	287	278	270	262	253	245	237	230	222	214	84
5	0.301	0.292	0.284	0.275	0.267	0.258	0.250	0.242	0.234	0.226	0.218	85
4	307	298	289	280	272	263	255	246	238	230	222	86
3	313	304	295	286	277	268	260	251	242	234	226	87
2	319	309	300	291	282	273	264	256	247	238	230	88
1	325	315	306	297	287	278	269	260	252	243	234	89
0	0.331	0.321	0.312	0.302	0.293	0.283	0.274	0.265	0.256	0.247	0.239	90
− 1	338	328	318	308	298	289	279	270	261	252	243	91
− 2	344	334	324	314	304	294	285	275	266	257	247	92
− 3	351	341	330	320	310	300	290	281	271	261	252	93
− 4	358	347	337	326	316	306	296	286	276	266	257	94
− 5	0.365	0.354	0.343	0.332	0.322	0.312	0.301	0.291	0.281	0.271	0.262	95
− 6	372	361	350	339	328	318	307	297	287	276	267	96
− 7	380	368	357	346	335	324	313	302	292	282	272	97
− 8	387	376	364	353	341	330	319	308	298	287	277	98
− 9	395	383	371	360	348	336	325	314	303	293	282	99
−10	0.403	0.391	0.379	0.367	0.355	0.343	0.332	0.320	0.309	0.298	0.287	100
−11	412	399	386	374	362	350	338	327	315	304	293	101
−12	421	407	394	382	369	357	345	333	321	310	299	102
−13	429	416	402	390	377	364	352	340	328	316	305	103
−14	438	425	411	398	384	372	359	347	334	322	310	104
−15	0.448	0.434	0.420	0.406	0.392	0.379	0.366	0.354	0.341	0.329	0.317	105
−16	458	443	429	414	401	387	374	361	348	335	323	106
−17	468	453	438	423	409	395	382	368	355	342	329	107
−18	478	463	447	433	418	404	390	376	362	349	336	108
−19	489	473	457	442	427	412	398	384	370	356	343	109
−20	0.500	0.484	0.468	0.452	0.436	0.421	0.406	0.392	0.378	0.364	0.350	110
−21	512	495	478	462	446	431	415	400	386	372	357	111
−22	524	507	489	473	456	440	425	409	394	380	365	112
−23	537	519	501	484	467	450	434	418	403	388	373	113
−24	550	531	513	495	478	461	444	428	412	396	381	114
Dec.	40°	39°	38°	37°	36°	35°	34°	33°	32°	31°	30°	Polar Dist.
	Co-Latitude.											

Time-Azimuths: Log A.

Dec.	Latitude.											Polar Dist.
	60°	61°	62°	63°	64°	65°	66°	67°	68°	69°	70°	
35°	9.506	9.527	9.547	9.567	9.586	9.605	9.623	9.641	9.659	9.677	9.694	55°
34	518	538	558	577	596	614	632	650	667	684	701	56
33	530	550	569	587	606	623	641	658	675	691	707	57
32	542	561	579	597	615	632	649	666	682	698	714	58
31	553	571	589	606	624	640	657	673	689	705	720	59
30	9.564	9.581	9.598	9.615	9.632	9.648	9.665	9.680	9.696	9.711	9.726	60
29	574	591	607	624	640	656	672	687	702	717	732	61
28	583	600	616	632	648	664	679	694	709	723	737	62
27	593	609	625	640	656	671	686	700	715	729	743	63
26	602	618	633	648	663	678	692	706	721	734	748	64
25	9.611	9.626	9.641	9.656	9.670	9.685	9.699	9.712	9.726	9.740	9.753	65
24	619	634	649	663	677	691	705	718	732	745	758	66
23	627	642	656	670	684	697	711	724	737	750	763	67
22	635	649	663	677	690	703	717	730	742	755	768	68
21	643	656	670	683	696	709	722	735	747	760	772	69
20	9.650	9.663	9.677	9.690	9.702	9.715	9.728	9.740	9.752	9.765	9.776	70
19	657	670	683	696	708	721	733	745	757	769	781	71
18	664	677	689	702	714	726	738	750	762	773	785	72
17	671	683	695	708	720	731	743	755	766	778	789	73
16	677	689	701	713	725	737	748	760	771	782	793	74
15	9.683	9.695	9.707	9.719	9.730	9.742	9.753	9.764	9.775	9.786	9.797	75
14	689	701	713	724	735	747	758	769	779	790	801	76
13	695	707	718	729	740	751	762	773	783	794	804	77
12	701	713	724	734	745	756	767	777	787	798	808	78
11	707	718	729	739	750	760	771	781	791	801	811	79
10	9.713	9.723	9.734	9.744	9.755	9.765	9.775	9.785	9.795	9.805	9.815	80
9	718	728	739	749	759	769	779	789	799	809	818	81
8	723	733	744	754	764	774	783	793	803	812	821	82
7	728	738	748	758	768	778	787	797	806	815	825	83
6	733	743	753	763	772	782	791	800	810	819	828	84
5	9.738	9.748	9.758	9.767	9.776	9.786	9.795	9.804	9.813	9.822	9.831	85
4	743	753	762	771	780	789	798	807	816	825	834	86
3	748	757	766	775	784	793	802	811	819	828	837	87
2	753	761	771	779	788	797	806	814	823	831	840	88
1	757	766	775	783	792	801	809	818	826	834	842	89
0	9.762	9.770	9.779	9.787	9.796	9.804	9.813	9.821	9.829	9.837	9.845	90
— 1	766	774	783	791	799	808	816	824	832	840	848	91
— 2	770	778	787	795	803	811	819	827	835	843	851	92
— 3	774	782	790	799	807	815	822	830	838	846	853	93
— 4	778	786	794	802	810	818	826	833	841	848	856	94
— 5	9.782	9.790	9.798	9.806	9.813	9.821	9.829	9.836	9.844	9.851	9.858	95
— 6	786	794	802	809	817	824	832	839	846	854	861	96
— 7	790	798	805	813	820	827	835	842	849	856	863	97
— 8	794	801	809	816	823	830	838	845	852	859	866	98
— 9	798	805	812	819	826	833	841	848	854	861	868	99
—10	9.801	9.809	9.815	9.823	9.830	9.836	9.843	9.850	9.857	9.864	9.871	100
—11	805	812	819	826	833	839	846	853	860	866	873	101
—12	809	815	822	829	836	842	849	856	862	869	875	102
—13	812	819	825	832	839	845	852	858	865	871	877	103
—14	816	822	829	835	842	848	854	861	867	873	880	104
—15	9.819	9.825	9.832	9.838	9.845	9.851	9.857	9.863	9.869	9.876	9.882	105
—16	822	828	835	841	847	854	860	866	872	878	884	106
—17	825	832	838	844	850	856	862	868	874	880	886	107
—18	829	835	841	847	853	859	865	871	877	882	888	108
—19	832	838	844	850	856	862	867	873	879	885	890	109
—20	9.835	9.841	9.847	9.853	9.858	9.864	9.870	9.875	9.881	9.887	9.892	110
—21	838	844	850	855	861	867	872	878	883	889	894	111
—22	841	847	852	858	864	869	875	880	886	891	896	112
—23	844	850	855	861	866	872	877	882	888	893	898	113
—24	847	853	858	864	869	874	879	885	890	895	900	114
Dec.	30°	29°	28°	27°	26°	25°	24°	23°	22°	21°	20°	Polar Dist.
	Co-Latitude.											

Time-Azimuths: Log B.

Dec.	Latitude. 60°	61°	62°	63°	64°	65°	66°	67°	68°	69°	70°	Polar Dist.
° 35	0.122	0.118	0.113	0.109	0.105	0.101	0.097	0.092	0.088	0.084	0.080	° 55
34	125	120	116	111	107	103	099	094	090	086	082	56
33	127	123	118	114	109	105	101	096	092	088	083	57
32	130	125	121	116	112	107	103	098	094	090	085	58
31	133	128	123	119	114	110	105	100	096	091	087	59
30	0.135	0.131	0.126	0.121	0.117	0.112	0.107	0.103	0.098	0.093	0.089	60
29	138	133	129	124	119	114	109	105	100	095	091	61
28	141	136	131	126	121	116	112	107	102	097	092	62
27	144	139	134	129	124	119	114	109	104	099	094	63
26	147	142	136	131	126	121	116	111	106	101	096	64
25	0.150	0.144	0.139	0.134	0.129	0.124	0.118	0.113	0.108	0.103	0.098	65
24	153	147	142	136	131	126	121	115	110	105	100	66
23	156	150	145	139	134	128	123	118	112	107	102	67
22	159	153	147	142	136	131	125	120	114	109	104	68
21	162	156	150	145	139	133	128	122	117	111	106	69
20	0.165	0.159	0.153	0.147	0.142	0.136	0.130	0.125	0.119	0.113	0.108	70
19	168	162	156	150	144	138	133	127	121	115	110	71
18	171	165	159	153	147	141	135	129	123	118	112	72
17	175	168	162	156	150	144	138	132	126	120	114	73
16	178	171	165	159	153	146	140	134	128	122	116	74
15	0.181	0.175	0.168	0.162	0.155	0.149	0.143	0.137	0.131	0.124	0.118	75
14	185	178	171	165	158	152	146	139	133	127	120	76
13	188	181	175	168	161	155	148	142	135	129	123	77
12	192	185	178	171	164	158	151	144	138	131	125	78
11	195	188	181	174	167	161	154	147	140	134	127	79
10	0.199	0.191	0.185	0.177	0.170	0.163	0.157	0.150	0.143	0.136	0.129	80
9	202	195	188	181	174	166	159	153	146	139	132	81
8	206	199	191	184	177	170	162	155	148	141	134	82
7	210	202	195	187	180	173	165	158	151	144	137	83
6	214	206	198	191	183	176	168	161	154	146	139	84
5	0.218	0.210	0.202	0.194	0.187	0.179	0.171	0.164	0.156	0.149	0.142	85
4	222	214	206	198	190	182	174	167	159	152	144	86
3	226	218	210	201	193	185	178	170	162	154	147	87
2	230	222	213	205	197	189	181	173	165	157	149	88
1	234	226	217	209	201	192	184	176	168	160	152	89
0	0.239	0.230	0.221	0.213	0.204	0.196	0.188	0.179	0.171	0.163	0.155	90
− 1	243	234	225	217	208	199	191	183	174	166	158	91
− 2	247	239	229	221	212	203	194	186	177	169	160	92
− 3	252	243	234	225	216	207	198	189	181	172	163	93
− 4	257	247	238	229	220	211	202	193	184	175	166	94
− 5	0.262	0.252	0.242	0.233	0.224	0.214	0.205	0.196	0.187	0.178	0.169	95
− 6	267	257	247	237	228	218	209	200	190	181	172	96
− 7	272	262	252	242	232	222	213	203	194	185	175	97
− 8	277	267	256	246	236	226	217	207	197	188	179	98
− 9	282	272	261	251	241	231	221	211	201	191	182	99
−10	0.287	0.277	0.266	0.256	0.245	0.235	0.225	0.215	0.205	0.195	0.185	100
−11	293	282	271	261	250	239	229	219	209	199	189	101
−12	299	287	276	266	255	244	233	223	213	202	192	102
−13	305	293	282	271	260	249	238	227	217	206	196	103
−14	310	299	287	276	265	253	242	231	221	210	199	104
−15	0.317	0.305	0.293	0.281	0.270	0.258	0.247	0.236	0.225	0.214	0.203	105
−16	323	311	299	287	275	263	252	240	229	218	207	106
−17	329	317	305	292	280	269	257	245	234	222	211	107
−18	336	323	311	298	286	274	262	250	238	227	215	108
−19	343	330	317	304	292	279	267	255	243	231	219	109
−20	0.350	0.337	0.324	0.310	0.298	0.285	0.272	0.260	0.248	0.235	0.224	110
−21	357	344	330	317	304	291	278	265	253	240	228	111
−22	365	351	337	323	310	297	283	270	258	245	232	112
−23	373	358	344	330	316	303	289	276	263	250	237	113
−24	381	366	351	337	323	309	295	282	268	255	242	114
Dec.	30°	29°	28°	27°	26°	25°	24°	23°	22°	21°	20°	Polar Dist.
	Co-Latitude.											

Time-Azimuths: Log A.

Dec.	Latitude. 70°	71°	72°	73°	74°	75°	76°	77°	78°	79°	80°	Polar Dist.
35°	9.694	9.711	9.727	9.743	9.760	9.775	9.791	9.807	9.822	9.838	9.853	55°
34	701	717	733	749	765	780	796	811	826	841	856	56
33	707	723	739	755	770	785	800	815	830	844	859	57
32	714	729	745	760	775	790	804	819	833	848	862	58
31	720	735	750	765	780	794	808	823	837	851	865	59
30	9.726	9.741	9.755	9.770	9.784	9.798	9.812	9.826	9.840	9.854	9.867	60
29	732	746	761	775	789	802	816	830	843	857	870	61
28	737	752	766	779	793	806	820	833	846	860	873	62
27	743	757	770	784	797	810	824	837	849	862	875	63
26	748	762	775	788	801	814	827	840	852	865	878	64
25	9.753	9.766	9.779	9.792	9.805	9.818	9.830	9.843	9.855	9.868	9.880	65
24	758	771	784	796	809	821	834	846	858	870	882	66
23	763	775	788	800	813	825	837	849	861	873	885	67
22	768	780	792	804	816	828	840	852	863	875	887	68
21	772	784	796	808	820	831	843	855	866	878	889	69
20	9.776	9.788	9.800	9.812	9.823	9.835	9.846	9.857	9.869	9.880	9.891	70
19	781	792	804	815	827	838	849	860	872	882	893	71
18	785	796	807	819	830	841	852	863	874	884	895	72
17	789	800	811	822	833	844	854	865	876	886	897	73
16	793	804	815	826	836	847	857	868	878	888	899	74
15	9.797	9.808	9.818	9.829	9.839	9.850	9.860	9.870	9.880	9.890	9.900	75
14	801	811	822	832	842	852	862	872	882	892	902	76
13	804	815	825	835	845	855	865	875	884	894	904	77
12	808	818	828	838	848	857	867	877	887	896	906	78
11	811	821	831	841	850	860	870	879	889	898	907	79
10	9.815	9.825	9.834	9.844	9.853	9.863	9.872	9.881	9.891	9.900	9.909	80
9	818	828	837	846	856	865	874	883	893	902	911	81
8	821	831	840	849	858	867	877	885	895	903	912	82
7	825	834	843	852	861	870	879	887	896	905	914	83
6	828	837	846	855	863	872	881	889	898	907	915	84
5	9.831	9.840	9.848	9.857	9.866	9.874	9.883	9.891	9.900	9.908	9.917	85
4	834	842	851	860	868	877	885	893	902	910	918	86
3	837	845	854	862	871	879	887	895	903	911	920	87
2	840	848	856	865	873	881	889	897	905	913	921	88
1	842	851	859	867	875	883	891	899	907	915	923	89
0	9.845	9.853	9.861	9.869	9.877	9.885	9.893	9.901	9.908	9.916	9.924	90
−1	848	856	864	872	879	887	895	902	910	918	925	91
−2	851	858	866	874	881	889	897	904	912	919	926	92
−3	853	861	868	876	883	891	898	906	913	920	928	93
−4	856	863	871	878	885	893	900	907	915	922	929	94
−5	9.858	9.866	9.873	9.880	9.887	9.895	9.902	9.909	9.916	9.923	9.930	95
−6	861	868	875	882	889	897	904	911	918	925	932	96
−7	863	871	878	884	891	898	905	912	919	926	933	97
−8	866	873	880	886	893	900	907	914	920	927	934	98
−9	868	875	882	888	895	902	909	915	922	928	935	99
−10	9.871	9.877	9.884	9.890	9.897	9.904	9.910	9.917	9.923	9.930	9.936	100
−11	873	879	886	892	899	905	912	918	925	931	937	101
−12	875	882	888	894	901	907	913	920	926	932	938	102
−13	877	884	890	896	903	909	915	921	927	933	939	103
−14	880	886	892	898	904	910	916	922	929	935	940	104
−15	9.882	9.888	9.894	9.900	9.906	9.912	9.918	9.924	9.930	9.936	9.942	105
−16	884	890	896	902	908	914	919	925	931	937	943	106
−17	886	892	898	904	909	915	921	927	932	938	944	107
−18	888	894	900	905	911	917	922	928	934	939	945	108
−19	890	896	901	907	913	918	924	929	935	940	946	109
−20	9.892	9.898	9.903	9.909	9.914	9.920	9.925	9.931	9.936	9.941	9.947	110
−21	894	900	905	910	916	921	927	932	937	942	948	111
−22	896	902	907	912	917	923	928	933	938	943	949	112
−23	898	903	909	914	919	924	929	934	939	945	950	113
−24	900	905	910	915	921	926	931	936	941	946	951	114
Dec.	20°	19°	18°	17°	16°	15°	14°	13°	12°	11°	10° Co-Latitude.	Polar Dist.

Time-Azimuths: Log B.

Dec.	Latitude. 70°	71°	72°	73°	74°	75°	76°	77°	78°	79°	80°	Polar Dist.
35°	0.080	0.076	0.072	0.068	0.064	0.060	0.056	0.052	0.048	0.044	0.040	55°
34	082	078	073	069	065	061	057	053	049	044	040	56
33	083	079	075	071	066	062	058	054	050	045	041	57
32	085	081	076	072	068	064	059	055	051	046	042	58
31	087	082	078	074	069	065	060	056	052	047	043	59
30	0.089	0.084	0.079	0.075	0.071	0.066	0.062	0.057	0.053	0.048	0.044	60
29	091	086	081	076	072	067	063	058	054	049	045	61
28	092	088	083	078	073	069	064	060	055	050	046	62
27	094	089	085	080	075	070	065	061	056	051	047	63
26	096	091	086	081	076	072	067	062	057	052	048	64
25	0.098	0.093	0.088	0.083	0.078	0.073	0.068	0.063	0.058	0.053	0.048	65
24	100	095	090	085	079	074	069	064	059	054	049	66
23	102	097	091	086	081	076	071	066	060	055	050	67
22	104	098	093	088	083	077	072	067	062	056	051	68
21	106	100	095	090	084	079	073	068	063	057	052	69
20	0.108	0.102	0.097	0.091	0.086	0.080	0.075	0.069	0.064	0.059	0.053	70
19	110	104	099	093	087	082	076	071	065	060	054	71
18	112	106	100	095	089	083	078	072	066	061	055	72
17	114	108	102	096	091	085	079	073	068	062	056	73
16	116	110	104	098	092	087	081	075	069	063	057	74
15	0.118	0.112	0.106	0.100	0.094	0.088	0.082	0.076	0.070	0.064	0.058	75
14	120	114	108	102	096	090	084	078	071	065	059	76
13	123	116	110	104	097	091	085	079	073	067	060	77
12	125	118	112	106	099	093	087	080	074	068	062	78
11	127	121	114	108	101	095	088	082	075	069	063	79
10	0.129	0.123	0.116	0.110	0.103	0.096	0.090	0.083	0.077	0.070	0.064	80
9	132	125	118	112	105	098	091	085	078	072	065	81
8	134	127	120	114	107	100	093	086	080	073	066	82
7	137	129	122	116	109	102	095	088	081	074	067	83
6	139	132	125	118	111	103	096	089	082	075	068	84
5	0.142	0.134	0.127	0.120	0.113	0.105	0.098	0.091	0.084	0.077	0.070	85
4	144	137	129	122	115	107	100	093	085	078	071	86
3	147	139	132	124	117	109	102	094	087	080	072	87
2	149	142	134	126	119	111	103	096	088	081	074	88
1	152	144	136	128	121	113	105	098	090	082	075	89
0	0.155	0.147	0.139	0.131	0.123	0.115	0.107	0.099	0.092	0.084	0.076	90
− 1	158	149	141	133	125	117	109	101	093	085	077	91
− 2	160	152	144	135	127	119	111	103	095	087	079	92
− 3	163	155	146	138	130	121	113	105	097	089	080	93
− 4	166	158	149	140	132	123	115	107	098	090	082	94
− 5	0.169	0.160	0.152	0.143	0.134	0.126	0.117	0.109	0.100	0.092	0.083	95
− 6	172	163	154	145	137	128	119	111	102	093	085	96
− 7	175	166	157	148	139	130	121	113	104	095	086	97
− 8	179	169	160	151	142	133	123	115	106	097	088	98
− 9	182	172	163	154	144	135	126	117	108	098	089	99
−10	0.185	0.176	0.166	0.156	0.147	0.137	0.128	0.119	0.109	0.100	0.091	100
−11	189	179	169	159	150	140	130	121	111	102	093	101
−12	192	182	172	162	152	143	133	123	113	104	094	102
−13	196	185	175	165	155	145	135	125	116	106	096	103
−14	199	189	178	168	158	148	138	128	118	108	098	104
−15	0.203	0.192	0.182	0.171	0.161	0.150	0.140	0.130	0.120	0.110	0.100	105
−16	207	196	185	174	164	153	143	132	122	112	101	106
−17	211	200	189	178	167	156	146	135	124	114	103	107
−18	215	204	192	181	170	159	148	137	127	116	105	108
−19	219	208	196	185	173	162	151	140	129	118	107	109
−20	0.224	0.212	0.200	0.188	0.177	0.165	0.154	0.143	0.131	0.120	0.109	110
−21	228	216	204	192	180	169	157	145	134	122	111	111
−22	232	220	208	196	184	172	160	148	136	125	113	112
−23	237	224	212	200	187	175	163	151	139	127	115	113
−24	242	229	216	203	191	179	166	154	142	130	118	114
Dec.	20°	19°	18°	17°	16°	15°	14°	13°	12°	11°	10°	Polar Dist.
	Co-Latitude.											

Time-Azimuths: Log A.

Lat.	Declination.											Co-Lat.
	−24°	−25°	−26°	−27°	−28°	−29°	−30°	−31°	−32°	−33°	−34°	
0°	9.328	9.346	9.363	9.380	9.397	9.413	9.428	9.443	9.457	9.471	9.485	90°
1	344	362	379	395	411	426	441	455	469	483	496	89
2	360	377	393	409	424	439	453	467	481	494	507	88
3	375	392	407	423	437	452	465	479	492	505	518	87
4	390	406	421	436	450	464	477	490	503	516	528	86
5	9.404	9.420	9.434	9.448	9.462	9.476	9.489	9.501	9.514	9.526	9.538	85
6	418	433	447	461	474	487	500	512	524	536	547	84
7	431	446	459	472	485	498	510	522	534	545	556	83
8	444	458	471	484	497	509	521	532	544	555	566	82
9	457	470	483	495	508	519	531	542	553	564	575	81
10	9.469	9.482	9.494	9.506	9.518	9.529	9.541	9.552	9.562	9.573	9.584	80
11	481	493	505	517	528	539	550	561	571	582	592	79
12	492	504	516	527	538	549	560	570	580	590	600	78
13	503	515	526	537	548	558	569	579	589	599	608	77
14	514	525	536	547	557	568	578	588	597	607	616	76
15	9.525	9.536	9.546	9.557	9.567	9.577	9.586	9.596	9.605	9.615	9.624	75
16	535	546	556	565	576	586	595	604	613	623	631	74
17	545	555	565	575	585	594	603	612	621	630	639	73
18	555	565	575	584	594	603	612	620	629	638	646	72
19	564	574	584	593	602	611	620	628	637	645	653	71
20	9.574	9.583	9.593	9.601	9.610	9.619	9.628	9.636	9.644	9.652	9.660	70
21	583	592	602	610	618	627	635	643	652	659	667	69
22	592	601	610	618	626	635	643	651	659	666	674	68
23	601	609	618	626	634	642	650	658	666	673	681	67
24	609	618	626	634	642	650	658	665	673	680	687	66
25	9.618	9.626	9.634	9.642	9.650	9.657	9.665	9.672	9.680	9.687	9.694	65
26	626	634	642	649	657	664	672	679	686	693	700	64
27	634	642	649	657	664	672	679	686	693	700	706	63
28	642	650	657	664	672	679	686	692	699	706	712	62
29	650	657	664	672	679	686	692	699	706	712	718	61
30	9.658	9.665	9.672	9.679	9.685	9.692	9.699	9.706	9.712	9.718	9.724	60
31	665	672	679	686	692	699	705	712	718	724	730	59
32	673	679	686	693	699	705	712	718	724	730	736	58
33	680	687	693	700	706	712	718	724	730	736	742	57
34	687	694	700	706	712	718	724	730	736	742	748	56
35	9.694	9.701	9.707	9.713	9.719	9.725	9.731	9.736	9.742	9.748	9.753	55
36	701	708	713	719	725	731	737	742	748	753	759	54
37	708	714	720	726	731	737	743	748	753	759	764	53
38	715	721	727	732	738	743	749	754	759	764	769	52
39	722	727	733	738	744	749	754	760	765	770	775	51
40	9.728	9.734	9.739	9.745	9.750	9.755	9.760	9.765	9.771	9.775	9.780	50
41	735	740	746	751	756	761	766	771	776	781	785	49
42	741	747	752	757	762	767	772	776	781	786	790	48
43	748	753	758	763	768	772	777	782	786	791	795	47
44	754	759	764	769	773	778	783	787	792	796	800	46
45	9.760	9.765	9.770	9.775	9.779	9.784	9.788	9.792	9.797	9.801	9.805	45
46	767	771	776	780	785	789	793	798	802	806	810	44
47	773	777	782	785	790	795	799	803	807	811	815	43
48	779	783	788	792	796	800	804	808	812	816	820	42
49	785	789	793	797	801	805	809	813	817	821	825	41
50	9.791	9.795	9.799	9.803	9.807	9.811	9.815	9.818	9.822	9.826	9.830	40
51	797	801	804	808	812	816	820	823	827	831	834	39
52	802	806	810	814	818	821	825	829	832	836	839	38
53	808	812	816	819	823	826	830	834	837	840	844	37
54	814	818	821	825	828	832	835	838	842	845	848	36
55	9.820	9.823	9.827	9.830	9.833	9.837	9.840	9.843	9.847	9.850	9.853	35
56	825	829	832	835	839	842	845	848	851	854	858	34
57	831	834	837	841	844	847	850	853	856	859	862	33
58	836	840	843	846	849	852	855	858	861	864	866	32
59	842	845	848	851	854	857	860	863	865	868	871	31
Lat.	114°	115°	116°	117°	118°	119°	120°	121°	122°	123°	124°	Co-Lat.
	Polar Distance.											

Time-Azimuths: Log B.

Lat.	Declination.											Co-Lat.
	−24°	−25°	−26°	−27°	−28°	−29°	−30°	−31°	−32°	−33°	−34°	
0°	0.672	0.654	0.637	0.620	0.603	0.587	0.572	0.557	0.542	0.528	0.515	90°
1	690	671	653	635	618	601	585	570	555	540	526	89
2	708	688	669	651	633	616	599	583	568	552	538	88
3	727	706	686	667	649	631	613	597	581	565	550	87
4	747	725	704	684	665	646	628	611	594	578	563	86
5	0.768	0.745	0.723	0.702	0.682	0.663	0.644	0.626	0.609	0.592	0.576	85
5	791	765	743	721	700	680	660	642	624	606	589	84
7	814	788	764	741	719	698	677	658	639	621	603	83
8	839	812	786	762	738	716	695	675	655	636	618	82
9	866	837	810	784	759	736	714	692	672	652	633	81
10	0.895	0.864	0.835	0.807	0.781	0.757	0.733	0.711	0.690	0.669	0.649	80
11	925	892	861	832	805	779	754	730	708	687	666	79
12	959	923	890	859	829	802	776	751	727	705	683	78
13	995	956	920	887	856	827	799	773	748	724	702	77
14	1.035	993	954	918	884	853	824	796	770	745	721	76
15	1.080	1.033	0.990	0.951	0.915	0.881	0.850	0.820	0.793	0.766	0.741	75
16	129	077	1.030	987	948	912	878	847	817	789	763	74
17	186	127	074	1.027	984	945	909	875	843	814	786	73
18	251	183	124	071	1.024	981	941	905	871	840	810	72
19	329	248	180	120	068	1.020	977	938	902	868	836	71
20	1.424	1.326	1.245	1.177	1.117	1.064	1.017	0.974	0.934	0.898	0.864	70
21	548	421	323	242	173	114	061	1.013	970	931	894	69
22	722	544	418	319	238	170	110	057	1.010	966	927	68
23	2.022	719	541	414	316	235	166	106	053	1.006	962	67
24	+ ∞	2.018	715	538	411	312	231	162	102	049	1.001	66
25	2.018	+ ∞	2.015	1.712	1.534	1.407	1.308	1.227	1.158	1.098	1.045	65
26	1.715	2.015	+ ∞	2.011	708	530	403	304	223	154	094	64
27	538	1.712	2.011	+ ∞	2.007	704	526	399	300	219	150	63
28	411	534	1.708	2.007	+ ∞	2.003	700	522	395	296	214	62
29	312	407	530	1.704	2.003	+ ∞	999	696	517	390	291	61
30	1.231	1.308	1.403	1.526	1.700	1.999	+ ∞	1.994	1.691	1.513	1.386	60
31	162	227	304	399	522	696	1.995	+ ∞	990	686	508	59
32	102	158	223	300	395	517	691	1.990	+ ∞	985	682	58
33	049	098	154	219	296	390	513	686	1.985	+ ∞	980	57
34	002	045	094	150	214	291	386	508	682	1.980	+ ∞	56
35	0.958	0.997	1.041	1.089	1.145	1.210	1.286	1.381	1.503	1.677	1.975	55
36	918	954	0.993	036	085	140	205	281	376	498	671	54
37	881	914	949	0.988	031	080	135	200	276	371	493	53
38	847	877	909	944	0.983	026	075	130	195	271	365	52
39	815	842	872	904	939	0.978	021	070	125	189	265	51
40	0.785	0.810	0.838	0.867	0.899	0.934	0.973	1.016	1.064	1.119	1.183	50
41	756	780	805	833	862	894	929	0.968	011	059	114	49
42	729	751	775	800	828	857	889	924	0.962	005	053	48
43	703	724	746	770	795	822	851	883	918	0.956	0.999	47
44	679	698	719	741	764	789	816	846	877	912	950	46
45	0.655	0.674	0.693	0.714	0.735	0.759	0.784	0.811	0.840	0.871	0.906	45
46	633	650	668	688	708	730	753	778	805	833	865	44
47	611	627	645	663	682	702	724	747	772	798	827	43
48	590	605	622	639	657	676	696	718	741	765	792	42
49	570	584	600	616	633	651	670	690	711	734	759	41
50	0.550	0.564	0.579	0.594	0.610	0.627	0.645	0.663	0.683	0.705	0.727	40
51	531	544	558	573	588	604	620	638	657	877	698	39
52	513	525	538	552	566	581	597	614	631	650	670	38
53	495	507	519	532	546	560	575	590	607	624	643	37
54	477	489	501	513	526	539	553	568	583	600	617	36
55	0.460	0.471	0.482	0.494	0.506	0.519	0.532	0.546	0.561	0.576	0.593	35
56	444	454	465	476	487	499	512	525	539	553	569	34
57	428	437	448	458	469	480	492	505	518	532	546	33
58	412	421	431	441	451	462	473	485	497	510	524	32
59	396	405	414	424	434	444	455	466	477	490	502	31
Lat.	114°	115°	116°	117°	118°	119°	120°	121°	122°	123°	124°	Co-Lat.
	Polar Distance.											

0^h]					Time-Azimuths: Log C.							
m	$0^m.0$	$0^m.1$	$0^m.2$	$0^m.3$	$0^m.4$	$0^m.5$	$0^m.6$	$0^m.7$	$0^m.8$	$0^m.9$	$1^m.0$	m
0	+ ∞	3.661	3.360	3.184	3.059	2.962	2.883	2.816	2.758	2.707	2.661	59
1	2.661	2.620	2.582	2.547	2.515	485	457	431	406	382	360	58
2	360	339	319	299	281	263	246	230	214	199	184	57
3	184	170	156	143	130	117	105	093	081	070	059	56
4	059	048	038	028	018	008	1.998	1.989	1.980	1.971	1.962	55
5	1.962	1.954	1.945	1.937	1.929	1.921	1.913	1.905	1.898	1.890	1.883	54
6	883	876	869	862	855	848	842	835	829	822	816	53
7	816	810	804	798	792	786	780	775	769	764	758	52
8	758	753	747	742	737	732	727	722	717	712	707	51
9	707	702	697	693	688	683	679	674	670	666	661	50
10	1.661	1.657	1.653	1.648	1.644	1.640	1.636	1.632	1.628	1.624	1.620	49
11	620	616	612	608	604	600	597	593	589	586	582	48
12	582	578	575	571	568	564	561	557	554	551	547	47
13	547	544	541	537	534	531	528	524	521	518	515	46
14	515	512	509	506	503	500	497	494	491	488	485	45
15	1.485	1.482	1.479	1.476	1.474	1.471	1.468	1.465	1.462	1.460	1.457	44
16	457	454	452	449	446	444	441	438	436	433	431	43
17	431	428	425	423	420	418	415	413	411	408	406	42
18	406	403	401	399	396	394	391	389	387	384	382	41
19	382	380	378	375	373	371	369	366	364	362	360	40
20	1.360	1.358	1.356	1.353	1.351	1.349	1.347	1.345	1.343	1.341	1.339	39
21	339	337	335	333	330	328	326	324	322	320	318	38
22	318	316	315	313	311	309	307	305	303	301	299	37
23	299	297	295	293	292	290	288	286	284	282	281	36
24	281	279	277	275	273	272	270	268	266	265	263	35
25	1.263	1.261	1.259	1.258	1.256	1.254	1.253	1.251	1.249	1.247	1.246	34
26	246	244	242	241	239	237	236	234	233	231	229	33
27	229	228	226	225	223	221	220	218	217	215	214	32
28	214	212	210	209	207	206	204	203	201	200	198	31
29	198	197	195	194	192	191	189	188	186	185	183	30
30	1.183	1.182	1.181	1.179	1.178	1.176	1.175	1.173	1.172	1.171	1.169	29
31	169	168	166	165	164	162	161	159	158	157	155	28
32	155	154	153	151	150	149	147	146	145	143	142	27
33	142	141	139	138	137	135	134	133	132	130	129	26
34	129	128	126	125	124	123	121	120	119	118	116	25
35	1.116	1.115	1.114	1.113	1.111	1.110	1.109	1.108	1.106	1.105	1.104	24
36	104	103	102	100	099	098	097	096	094	093	092	23
37	092	091	090	089	087	086	085	084	083	082	080	22
38	080	079	078	077	076	075	074	072	071	070	069	21
39	069	068	067	066	065	064	062	061	060	059	058	20
40	1.058	1.057	1.056	1.055	1.054	1.053	1.052	1.050	1.049	1.048	1.047	19
41	047	046	045	044	043	042	041	040	039	038	037	18
42	037	036	035	034	033	032	031	030	029	027	026	17
43	026	025	024	023	022	021	020	019	018	017	016	16
44	016	015	014	013	012	011	011	010	009	008	007	15
45	1.007	1.006	1.005	1.004	1.003	1.002	1.001	1.000	0.999	0.998	0.997	14
46	0.997	0.996	0.995	0.994	0.993	0.992	0.991	0.990	989	989	988	13
47	988	987	986	985	984	983	982	981	980	979	978	12
48	978	977	977	976	975	974	973	972	971	970	969	11
49	969	968	968	967	966	965	964	963	962	961	961	10
50	0.961	0.960	0.959	0.958	0.957	0.956	0.955	0.954	0.954	0.953	0.952	9
51	952	951	950	949	948	948	947	946	945	944	943	8
52	943	942	942	941	940	939	938	937	937	936	935	7
53	935	934	933	933	932	931	930	929	928	928	927	6
54	927	926	925	924	924	923	922	921	920	920	919	5
55	0.919	0.918	0.917	0.916	0.916	0.915	0.914	0.913	0.912	0.912	0.911	4
56	911	910	909	909	908	907	906	905	905	904	903	3
57	903	902	902	901	900	899	899	898	897	896	895	2
58	895	895	894	893	892	892	891	890	889	888	888	1
59	888	887	886	886	885	884	884	883	882	881	881	0
m	$1^m.0$	$0^m.9$	$0^m.8$	$0^m.7$	$0^m.6$	$0^m.5$	$0^m.4$	$0^m.3$	$0^m.2$	$0^m.1$	$0^m.0$	m

With Hour-Angles greater than 6^h read from bottom, and subtract tabular Log from 10.000. [11^h

1h]

Time-Azimuths: Log C.

m	0m.0	0m.1	0m.2	0m.3	0m.4	0m.5	0m.6	0m.7	0m.8	0m.9	1m.0	m
0	0.881	0.880	0.879	0.878	0.878	0.877	0.876	0.875	0.875	0.874	0.873	59
1	873	873	872	871	870	870	869	868	868	867	866	58
2	866	865	865	864	863	863	862	861	861	860	859	57
3	859	858	858	857	856	856	855	854	854	853	852	56
4	852	852	851	850	849	849	848	847	847	846	845	55
5	0.845	0.845	0.844	0.843	0.843	0.842	0.841	0.841	0.840	0.839	0.839	54
6	839	838	837	837	836	835	835	834	833	833	832	53
7	832	831	831	830	829	829	828	827	827	826	826	52
8	826	825	824	824	823	822	822	821	820	820	819	51
9	819	818	818	817	817	816	815	815	814	813	813	50
10	0.813	0.812	0.811	0.811	0.810	0.810	0.809	0.808	0.808	0.807	0.806	49
11	806	806	805	805	804	803	803	802	802	801	800	48
12	800	800	799	798	798	797	797	796	795	795	794	47
13	794	794	793	792	792	791	791	790	789	789	788	46
14	788	788	787	786	786	785	785	784	783	783	782	45
15	0.782	0.782	0.781	0.780	0.780	0.779	0.779	0.778	0.778	0.777	0.776	44
16	776	776	775	775	774	773	773	772	772	771	771	43
17	771	770	769	769	768	768	767	767	766	765	765	42
18	765	764	764	763	763	762	762	761	760	760	759	41
19	759	759	758	758	757	756	756	755	755	754	754	40
20	0.754	0.753	0.753	0.752	0.751	0.751	0.750	0.750	0.749	0.749	0.748	39
21	748	748	747	747	746	745	745	744	744	743	743	38
22	743	742	742	741	741	740	739	739	738	738	737	37
23	737	737	736	736	735	735	734	734	733	733	732	36
24	732	732	731	730	730	729	729	728	728	727	727	35
25	0.727	0.726	0.726	0.725	0.725	0.724	0.724	0.723	0.723	0.722	0.722	34
26	722	721	721	720	720	719	718	718	717	717	716	33
27	716	716	715	715	714	714	713	713	712	712	711	32
28	711	711	710	710	709	709	708	708	707	707	706	31
29	706	706	705	705	704	704	703	703	702	702	701	30
30	0.701	0.701	0.700	0.700	0.699	0.699	0.698	0.698	0.697	0.697	0.696	29
31	696	696	695	695	694	694	693	693	693	692	692	28
32	692	691	691	690	690	689	689	688	688	687	687	27
33	687	686	686	685	685	684	684	683	683	682	682	26
34	682	681	681	681	680	680	679	679	678	678	677	25
35	0.677	0.677	0.676	0.676	0.675	0.675	0.674	0.674	0.673	0.673	0.673	24
36	673	672	672	671	671	670	670	669	669	668	668	23
37	668	667	667	667	666	666	665	665	664	664	663	22
38	663	663	662	662	661	661	661	660	660	659	659	21
39	659	658	658	657	657	656	656	656	655	655	654	20
40	0.654	0.654	0.653	0.653	0.652	0.652	0.652	0.651	0.651	0.650	0.650	19
41	650	649	649	648	648	648	647	647	646	646	645	18
42	645	645	644	644	644	643	643	642	642	641	641	17
43	641	641	640	640	639	639	638	638	638	637	637	16
44	637	636	636	635	635	634	634	634	633	633	632	15
45	0.632	0.632	0.631	0.631	0.631	0.630	0.630	0.629	0.629	0.628	0.628	14
46	628	628	627	627	626	626	626	625	625	624	624	13
47	624	623	623	623	622	622	621	621	620	620	620	12
48	620	619	619	618	618	618	617	617	616	616	615	11
49	615	615	615	614	614	613	613	613	612	612	611	10
50	0.611	0.611	0.611	0.610	0.610	0.609	0.609	0.609	0.608	0.608	0.607	9
51	607	607	606	606	606	605	605	604	604	604	603	8
52	603	603	602	602	602	601	601	600	600	600	599	7
53	599	599	598	598	598	597	597	596	596	596	595	6
54	595	595	594	594	594	593	593	592	592	592	591	5
55	0.591	0.591	0.590	0.590	0.590	0.589	0.589	0.589	0.588	0.587	0.587	4
56	587	587	587	586	586	585	585	585	584	584	583	3
57	583	583	583	582	582	582	581	581	580	580	580	2
58	580	579	579	578	578	578	577	577	577	576	576	1
59	576	575	575	575	574	574	573	573	573	572	572	0
m	1m.0	0m.9	0m.8	0m.7	0m.6	0m.5	0m.4	0m.3	0m.2	0m.1	0m.0	m

With Hour-Angles greater than 6h read from bottom, and subtract tabular Log from 10.000. [10h

2h]	Time-Azimuths: Log C.										
m	0m.0	0m.1	0m.2	0m.3	0m.4	0m.5	0m.6	0m.7	0m.8	0m.9	1m.0	m
0	0.572	0.572	0.571	0.571	0.570	0.570	0.570	0.569	0.569	0.569	0.568	59
1	568	568	567	567	567	566	565	566	565	565	564	58
2	564	564	564	563	563	563	562	562	561	561	561	57
3	561	560	560	560	559	559	558	558	558	557	557	56
4	557	557	556	556	556	555	555	554	554	554	553	55
5	0.553	0.553	0.553	0.552	0.552	0.552	0.551	0.551	0.550	0.550	0.550	54
6	550	549	549	549	548	548	548	547	547	546	546	53
7	545	545	545	545	545	544	544	544	543	543	543	52
8	543	542	542	542	541	541	540	540	540	539	539	51
9	539	539	538	538	538	537	537	536	536	536	535	50
10	0.535	0.535	0.535	0.534	0.534	0.534	0.533	0.533	0.533	0.532	0.532	49
11	532	532	531	531	530	530	530	529	529	529	528	48
12	528	528	528	527	527	527	526	526	525	525	525	47
13	525	525	524	524	524	523	523	523	522	522	521	46
14	521	521	521	520	520	520	519	519	519	518	518	45
15	0.518	0.518	0.517	0.517	0.517	0.516	0.516	0.516	0.515	0.515	0.515	44
16	515	514	514	514	513	513	513	512	512	512	511	43
17	511	511	511	510	510	510	509	509	509	508	508	42
18	508	508	507	507	507	506	506	506	505	505	505	41
19	505	504	504	504	503	503	503	502	502	502	501	40
20	0.501	0.501	0.501	0.500	0.500	0.500	0.499	0.499	0.499	0.498	0.498	39
21	498	498	497	497	497	496	496	496	495	495	495	38
22	495	494	494	494	493	493	493	492	492	492	491	37
23	491	491	491	490	490	490	490	489	489	489	488	36
24	488	488	488	487	487	487	486	485	485	485	485	35
25	0.485	0.485	0.484	0.484	0.484	0.483	0.483	0.483	0.482	0.482	0.482	34
26	482	481	481	481	481	480	480	480	479	479	479	33
27	479	478	478	478	477	477	477	476	476	476	475	32
28	475	475	475	475	474	474	474	473	473	473	472	31
29	472	472	472	471	471	471	470	470	470	470	469	30
30	0.469	0.469	0.469	0.468	0.468	0.468	0.467	0.467	0.467	0.466	0.466	29
31	466	466	465	465	465	465	464	464	464	463	463	28
32	463	463	462	462	462	461	461	461	461	460	460	27
33	460	460	459	459	459	458	458	458	458	457	457	26
34	457	457	456	456	456	455	455	455	454	454	454	25
35	0.454	0.454	0.453	0.453	0.453	0.452	0.452	0.452	0.451	0.451	0.451	24
36	451	451	450	450	450	449	449	449	448	448	448	23
37	448	448	447	447	447	446	446	446	445	445	445	22
38	445	445	444	444	444	443	443	443	442	442	442	21
39	442	442	441	441	441	440	440	440	440	439	439	20
40	0.439	0.439	0.438	0.438	0.438	0.437	0.437	0.437	0.437	0.436	0.436	19
41	436	436	435	435	435	435	434	434	434	433	433	18
42	433	433	432	432	432	432	431	431	431	430	430	17
43	430	430	430	429	429	429	428	428	428	428	427	16
44	427	427	427	426	426	426	426	425	425	425	424	15
45	0.424	0.424	0.424	0.424	0.423	0.423	0.423	0.422	0.422	0.422	0.422	14
46	422	421	421	421	420	420	420	420	419	419	419	13
47	419	418	418	418	418	417	417	417	416	416	416	12
48	416	416	415	415	415	414	414	414	414	413	413	11
49	413	413	412	412	412	412	411	411	411	410	410	10
50	0.410	0.410	0.410	0.409	0.409	0.409	0.409	0.408	0.408	0.408	0.407	9
51	407	407	407	407	406	406	406	405	405	405	405	8
52	405	404	404	404	403	403	403	403	402	402	402	7
53	402	402	401	401	401	400	400	400	400	399	399	6
54	399	399	399	398	398	398	397	397	397	397	396	5
55	0.396	0.396	0.396	0.396	0.395	0.395	0.395	0.394	0.394	0.394	0.394	4
56	394	393	393	393	393	392	392	392	391	391	391	3
57	391	391	390	390	390	390	389	389	389	388	388	2
58	388	388	388	387	387	387	387	386	386	386	385	1
59	385	385	385	385	384	384	384	384	383	383	383	0
m	1m.0	0m.9	0m.8	0m.7	0m.6	0m.5	0m.4	0m.3	0m.2	0m.1	0m.0	m

With Hour-Angles greater than 6h read from bottom, and subtract tabular Log from 10.000. [9h

Time-Azimuths: Log C.

3h]

m	0m.0	0m.1	0m.2	0m.3	0m.4	0m.5	0m.6	0m.7	0m.8	0m.9	1m.0	m
0	0.383	0.383	0.382	0.382	0.382	0.381	0.381	0.381	0.381	0.380	0.380	59
1	380	380	380	379	379	379	379	378	378	378	377	58
2	377	377	377	377	376	376	376	376	375	375	375	57
3	375	375	374	374	374	373	373	373	373	372	372	56
4	372	372	372	371	371	371	371	370	370	370	370	55
5	0.370	0.369	0.369	0.369	0.368	0.368	0.368	0.368	0.367	0.367	0.367	54
6	367	367	366	366	366	366	365	365	365	365	364	53
7	364	364	364	364	363	363	363	362	362	362	362	52
8	362	361	361	361	361	360	360	360	360	359	359	51
9	359	359	359	358	358	358	358	357	357	357	357	50
10	0.357	0.356	0.356	0.356	0.356	0.355	0.355	0.355	0.354	0.354	0.354	49
11	354	354	353	353	353	353	352	352	352	352	351	48
12	351	351	351	351	350	350	350	350	349	349	349	47
13	349	349	348	348	348	348	347	347	347	347	346	46
14	346	346	346	346	345	345	345	345	344	344	344	45
15	0.344	0.344	0.343	0.343	0.343	0.343	0.342	0.342	0.342	0.342	0.341	44
16	341	341	341	341	340	340	340	340	339	339	339	43
17	339	339	338	338	338	338	337	337	337	337	336	42
18	336	336	336	336	335	335	335	335	334	334	334	41
19	334	334	333	333	333	333	332	332	332	332	331	40
20	0.331	0.331	0.331	0.331	0.330	0.330	0.330	0.330	0.329	0.329	0.329	39
21	329	329	328	328	328	328	327	327	327	327	326	38
22	326	326	326	326	325	325	325	325	324	324	324	37
23	324	324	323	323	323	323	322	322	322	322	322	36
24	322	321	321	321	321	320	320	320	320	319	319	35
25	0.319	0.319	0.319	0.318	0.318	0.318	0.318	0.317	0.317	0.317	0.317	34
26	317	316	316	316	316	315	315	315	315	314	314	33
27	314	314	314	314	313	313	313	313	312	312	312	32
28	312	312	311	311	311	311	310	310	310	310	309	31
29	309	309	309	309	308	308	308	308	308	307	307	30
30	0.307	0.307	0.307	0.306	0.306	0.306	0.306	0.305	0.305	0.305	0.305	29
31	305	304	304	304	304	303	303	303	303	303	302	28
32	302	302	302	302	301	301	301	301	300	300	300	27
33	300	300	299	299	299	299	298	298	298	298	298	26
34	298	297	297	297	297	296	296	296	296	295	295	25
35	0.295	0.295	0.295	0.294	0.294	0.294	0.294	0.294	0.293	0.293	0.293	24
36	293	293	292	292	292	292	291	291	291	291	290	23
37	290	290	290	290	290	289	289	289	289	288	288	22
38	288	288	288	287	287	287	287	287	286	286	286	21
39	286	286	285	285	285	285	284	284	284	284	284	20
40	0.284	0.283	0.283	0.283	0.283	0.282	0.282	0.282	0.282	0.281	0.281	19
41	281	281	281	281	280	280	280	280	279	279	279	18
42	279	279	278	278	278	278	278	277	277	277	277	17
43	277	276	276	276	276	275	275	275	275	275	274	16
44	274	274	274	274	273	273	273	273	272	272	272	15
45	0.272	0.272	0.272	0.271	0.271	0.271	0.271	0.270	0.270	0.270	0.270	14
46	270	270	269	269	269	269	268	268	268	268	267	13
47	267	267	267	267	267	266	266	266	266	265	265	12
48	265	265	265	265	264	264	264	264	263	263	263	11
49	263	263	263	262	262	262	262	261	261	261	261	10
50	0.261	0.261	0.260	0.260	0.260	0.260	0.259	0.259	0.259	0.259	0.258	9
51	258	258	258	258	258	257	257	257	257	256	256	8
52	256	256	256	256	255	255	255	255	254	254	254	7
53	254	254	254	253	253	253	253	252	252	252	252	6
54	252	252	251	251	251	251	250	250	250	250	250	5
55	0.250	0.249	0.249	0.249	0.249	0.248	0.248	0.248	0.248	0.248	0.247	4
56	247	247	247	247	246	246	246	246	246	245	245	3
57	245	245	245	244	244	244	244	244	243	243	243	2
58	243	243	243	242	242	242	242	241	241	241	241	1
59	241	241	240	240	240	240	239	239	239	239	239	0
m	1m.0	0m.9	0m.8	0m.7	0m.6	0m.5	0m.4	0m.3	0m.2	0m.1	0m.0	m

With Hour-Angles greater than 6h read from bottom, and subtract tabular Log from 10.000. [8h

4h] **Time-Azimuths: Log C.**

m	0m.0	0m.1	0m.2	0m.3	0m.4	0m.5	0m.6	0m.7	0m.8	0m.9	1m.0	m
0	0.239	0.238	0.238	0.238	0.238	0.237	0.237	0.237	0.237	0.237	0.236	59
1	236	236	236	236	236	235	235	235	235	234	234	58
2	234	234	234	234	233	233	233	233	232	232	232	57
3	232	232	232	231	231	231	231	231	230	230	230	56
4	230	230	229	229	229	229	229	228	228	228	228	55
5	0.228	0.227	0.227	0.227	0.227	0.227	0.226	0.226	0.226	0.226	0.226	54
6	226	225	225	225	225	224	224	224	224	224	223	53
7	223	223	223	223	223	222	222	222	222	222	222	52
8	222	221	221	221	220	220	220	220	220	219	219	51
9	219	219	219	218	218	218	218	218	217	217	217	50
10	0.217	0.217	0.217	0.216	0.216	0.216	0.216	0.215	0.215	0.215	0.215	49
11	215	215	214	214	214	214	214	213	213	213	213	48
12	213	212	212	212	212	212	211	211	211	211	211	47
13	211	210	210	210	210	209	209	209	209	209	208	46
14	208	208	208	208	208	207	207	207	207	207	206	45
15	0.206	0.205	0.206	0.206	0.205	0.205	0.205	0.205	0.205	0.204	0.204	44
16	204	204	204	204	203	203	203	203	203	202	202	43
17	202	202	202	201	201	201	201	201	200	200	200	42
18	200	200	200	199	199	199	199	199	198	198	198	41
19	198	198	197	197	197	197	197	196	196	196	196	40
20	0.195	0.195	0.195	0.195	0.195	0.195	0.195	0.194	0.194	0.194	0.194	39
21	194	194	193	193	193	193	192	192	192	192	192	38
22	192	191	191	191	191	191	190	190	190	190	190	37
23	190	189	189	189	189	189	188	188	183	188	187	36
24	187	187	187	187	187	186	186	186	186	186	185	35
25	0.185	0.185	0.185	0.185	0.185	0.184	0.184	0.184	0.184	0.184	0.183	34
26	183	183	183	183	183	182	182	182	182	181	181	33
27	181	181	181	181	180	180	180	180	180	179	179	32
28	179	179	179	179	178	178	178	178	178	177	177	31
29	177	177	177	177	176	176	176	176	176	175	175	30
30.	0.175	0.175	0.175	0.174	0.174	0.174	0.174	0.174	0.173	0.173	0.173	29
31	173	173	173	172	172	172	172	172	171	171	171	28
32	171	171	171	170	170	170	170	170	169	169	169	27
33	169	169	169	168	168	168	168	168	167	167	167	26
34	167	167	167	166	166	166	166	166	165	165	165	25
35	0.165	0.165	0.164	0.164	0.164	0.164	0.164	0.163	0.163	0.163	0.163	24
36	163	163	162	162	162	162	162	161	161	161	161	23
37	161	161	160	160	160	160	160	159	159	159	159	22
38	159	159	158	158	158	158	158	157	157	157	157	21
39	157	157	156	156	156	156	156	155	155	155	155	20
40	0.155	0.155	0.154	0.154	0.154	0.154	0.154	0.153	0.153	0.153	0.153	19
41	153	153	152	152	152	152	152	151	151	151	151	18
42	151	151	150	150	150	150	150	149	149	149	149	17
43	149	149	148	148	148	148	148	147	147	147	147	16
44	147	147	146	146	146	146	146	145	145	145	145	15
45	0.145	0.145	0.144	0.144	0.144	0.144	0.144	0.143	0.143	0.143	0.143	14
46	143	143	142	142	142	142	142	141	141	141	141	13
47	141	141	140	140	140	140	140	139	139	139	139	12
48	139	139	138	138	138	138	138	137	137	137	137	11
49	137	137	136	136	136	136	136	135	135	135	135	10
50	0.135	0.135	0.134	0.134	0.134	0.134	0.134	0.133	0.133	0.133	0.133	9
51	133	133	132	132	132	132	132	131	131	131	131	8
52	131	131	130	130	130	130	130	129	129	129	129	7
53	129	129	128	128	128	128	128	127	127	127	127	6
54	127	127	126	126	126	126	126	125	125	125	125	5
55	0.125	0.125	0.124	0.124	0.124	0.124	0.124	0.123	0.123	0.123	0.123	4
56	123	123	122	122	122	122	122	122	121	121	121	3
57	121	121	121	120	120	120	120	120	119	119	119	2
58	119	119	119	118	118	118	118	118	117	117	117	1
59	117	117	117	116	116	116	116	116	115	115	115	0
m	1m.0	0m.9	0m.8	0m.7	0m.6	0m.5	0m.4	0m.3	0m.2	0m.1	0m.0	m

With Hour-Angles greater than 6h read from bottom, and subtract tabular Log from 10.000. **[7h**

Time-Azimuths: Log C.

5ʰ]

m	0ᵐ.0	0ᵐ.1	0ᵐ.2	0ᵐ.3	0ᵐ.4	0ᵐ.5	0ᵐ.6	0ᵐ.7	0ᵐ.8	0ᵐ.9	1ᵐ.0	m
0	0.115	0.115	0.115	0.114	0.114	0.114	0.114	0.114	0.113	0.113	0.113	59
1	113	113	113	112	112	112	112	112	111	111	111	58
2	111	111	111	111	110	110	110	110	110	109	109	57
3	109	109	109	109	108	108	108	108	108	107	107	56
4	107	107	107	107	106	106	106	106	106	105	105	55
5	0.105	0.105	0.105	0.105	0.104	0.104	0.104	0.104	0.104	0.103	0.103	54
6	103	103	103	103	103	102	102	102	102	102	101	53
7	101	101	101	101	101	100	100	100	100	100	099	52
8	099	099	099	099	099	098	098	098	098	098	097	51
9	097	097	097	097	097	096	096	096	096	096	096	50
10	0.096	0.095	0.095	0.095	0.095	0.095	0.094	0.094	0.094	0.094	0.094	49
11	094	093	093	093	093	093	092	092	092	092	092	48
12	092	091	091	091	091	091	090	090	090	090	090	47
13	090	090	089	089	089	089	089	088	088	088	088	46
14	088	088	087	087	087	087	087	086	086	086	086	45
15	0.086	0.086	0.085	0.085	0.085	0.085	0.085	0.084	0.084	0.084	0.084	44
16	084	084	084	083	083	083	083	083	082	082	082	43
17	082	082	082	081	081	081	081	081	080	080	080	42
18	080	080	080	079	079	079	079	079	078	078	078	41
19	078	078	078	078	077	077	077	077	077	076	076	40
20	0.076	0.076	0.076	0.076	0.075	0.075	0.075	0.075	0.075	0.074	0.074	39
21	074	074	074	074	073	073	073	073	073	073	072	38
22	072	072	072	072	072	071	071	071	071	071	070	37
23	070	070	070	070	070	069	069	069	069	069	069	36
24	069	068	068	068	068	068	067	067	067	067	067	35
25	0.067	0.066	0.066	0.066	0.066	0.066	0.065	0.065	0.065	0.065	0.065	34
26	065	064	064	064	064	064	064	063	063	063	063	33
27	063	063	062	062	062	062	062	061	061	061	061	32
28	061	061	060	060	060	060	060	059	059	059	059	31
29	059	059	059	058	058	058	058	058	057	057	057	30
30	0.057	0.057	0.057	0.056	0.056	0.056	0.056	0.056	0.055	0.055	0.055	29
31	055	055	055	055	054	054	054	054	054	053	053	28
32	053	053	053	053	052	052	052	052	052	051	051	27
33	051	051	051	051	051	050	050	050	050	050	049	26
34	049	049	049	049	049	048	048	048	048	048	047	25
35	0.047	0.047	0.047	0.047	0.047	0.047	0.046	0.046	0.046	0.046	0.046	24
36	046	045	045	045	045	045	044	044	044	044	044	23
37	044	043	043	043	043	043	043	042	042	042	042	22
38	042	042	041	041	041	041	041	040	040	040	040	21
39	040	040	039	039	039	039	039	039	038	038	038	20
40	0.038	0.038	0.038	0.037	0.037	0.037	0.037	0.037	0.036	0.036	0.036	19
41	036	036	036	035	035	035	035	035	035	034	034	18
42	034	034	034	034	033	033	033	033	033	032	032	17
43	032	032	032	032	031	031	031	031	031	031	030	16
44	030	030	030	030	030	029	029	029	029	029	028	15
45	0.028	0.028	0.028	0.028	0.028	0.027	0.027	0.027	0.027	0.027	0.027	14
46	027	026	026	026	026	026	025	025	025	025	025	13
47	025	024	024	024	024	024	024	023	023	023	023	12
48	023	023	022	022	022	022	022	021	021	021	021	11
49	021	021	020	020	020	020	020	020	019	019	019	10
50	0.019	0.019	0.019	0.018	0.018	0.018	0.018	0.018	0.017	0.017	0.017	9
51	017	017	017	016	016	016	016	016	016	015	015	8
52	015	015	015	015	014	014	014	014	014	013	013	7
53	013	013	013	013	013	012	012	012	012	012	011	6
54	011	011	011	011	011	010	010	010	010	010	009	5
55	0.009	0.009	0.009	0.009	0.009	0.009	0.008	0.008	0.008	0.008	0.008	4
56	008	007	007	007	007	007	006	006	006	006	006	3
57	006	005	005	005	005	005	005	004	004	004	004	2
58	004	004	003	003	003	003	003	002	002	002	002	1
59	002	002	002	001	001	001	001	001	000	000	000	0
m	1ᵐ.0	0ᵐ.9	0ᵐ.8	0ᵐ.7	0ᵐ.6	0ᵐ.5	0ᵐ.4	0ᵐ.3	0ᵐ.2	0ᵐ.1	0ᵐ.0	m

[6ʰ

With Hour-Angles greater than 6ʰ read from bottom, and subtract tabular Log from 10.000.

Time-Azimuths: Log Tangents X and Y.

Angles X and Y.	0°.0	0°.1	0°.2	0°.3	0°.4	0°.5	0°.6	0°.7	0°.8	0°.9	Angles X and Y.
0°	— ∞	7.242	7.543	7.719	7.844	7.941	8.020	8.087	8.145	8.196	0°
1	8.242	8.283	8.321	8.356	8.388	8.418	446	472	497	521	1
2	543	564	585	604	622	640	657	674	689	705	2
3	719	734	747	761	774	786	799	811	822	834	3
4	845	855	866	876	886	896	906	915	924	933	4
5	8.942	8.951	8.959	8.967	8.976	8.984	8.991	8.999	9.007	9.014	5
6	9.022	9.029	9.036	9.043	9.050	9.057	9.063	9.070	076	083	6
7	089	095	102	108	114	119	125	131	137	142	7
8	148	153	159	164	169	174	180	185	190	195	8
9	200	205	209	214	219	224	228	233	237	242	9
10	9.246	9.251	9.255	9.259	9.264	9.268	9.272	9.276	9.280	9.285	10
11	289	293	297	301	305	308	312	316	320	324	11
12	327	331	335	339	342	346	349	353	356	360	12
13	363	367	370	374	377	380	384	387	390	394	13
14	397	400	403	406	410	413	416	419	422	425	14
15	9.428	9.431	9.434	9.437	9.440	9.443	9.446	9.449	9.452	9.455	15
16	457	460	463	466	469	472	474	477	480	483	16
17	485	488	491	493	496	499	501	504	507	509	17
18	512	514	517	519	522	525	527	530	532	535	18
19	537	539	542	544	547	549	552	554	556	559	19
20	9.561	9.563	9.566	9.568	9.570	9.573	9.575	9.577	9.580	9.582	20
21	584	586	589	591	593	595	598	600	602	604	21
22	606	609	611	613	615	617	619	621	624	626	22
23	628	630	632	634	636	638	640	642	644	647	23
24	649	651	653	655	657	659	661	663	665	667	24
25	9.669	9.671	9.673	9.675	9.677	9.678	9.680	9.682	9.684	9.686	25
26	688	690	692	694	696	698	700	702	703	705	26
27	707	709	711	713	715	716	718	720	722	724	27
28	726	728	729	731	733	735	737	738	740	742	28
29	744	746	747	749	751	753	754	756	758	760	29
30	9.761	9.763	9.765	9.767	9.768	9.770	9.772	9.774	9.775	9.777	30
31	779	780	782	784	786	787	789	791	792	794	31
32	796	797	799	801	803	804	806	808	809	811	32
33	813	814	816	817	819	821	822	824	826	827	33
34	829	831	832	834	836	837	839	840	842	844	34
35	9.845	9.847	9.848	9.850	9.852	9.853	9.855	9.856	9.858	9.860	35
36	861	863	864	866	868	869	871	872	874	876	36
37	877	879	880	882	883	885	887	888	890	891	37
38	893	894	896	897	899	901	902	904	905	907	38
39	908	910	911	913	915	916	918	919	921	922	39
40	9.924	9.925	9.927	9.928	9.930	9.931	9.933	9.935	9.936	9.938	40
41	939	941	942	944	945	947	948	950	951	953	41
42	954	956	957	959	961	962	964	965	967	968	42
43	970	971	973	974	976	977	979	980	982	983	43
44	985	986	988	989	991	992	994	995	997	998	44
45	0.000	0.002	0.003	0.005	0.006	0.008	0.009	0.011	0.012	0.014	45

FIRST CASE: Half sum of Polar Distance and Co-latitude less than 90°.—The sum or difference of the Angles X and Y, according as the Polar Distance is greater or less than the Co-latitude, is the Azimuth.

SECOND CASE: Half sum of Polar Distance and Co-latitude greater than 90°.—The difference of the Angles X and Y subtracted from 180° is always the Azimuth.

Time-Azimuths: Log Tangents X and Y.

Angles X and Y.	0°.0	0°.1	0°.2	0°.3	0°.4	0°.5	0°.6	0°.7	0°.8	0°.9	Angles X and Y.
45°	0.000	0.002	0.003	0.005	0.006	0.008	0.009	0.011	0.012	0.014	45°
46	015	017	018	020	021	023	024	026	027	029	46
47	030	032	033	035	036	038	039	041	043	044	47
48	046	047	049	050	052	053	055	056	058	059	48
49	061	062	064	065	067	069	070	072	073	075	49
50	0.076	0.078	0.079	0.081	0.082	0.084	0.085	0.087	0.089	0.090	50
51	092	093	095	096	098	099	101	103	104	106	51
52	107	109	110	112	113	115	117	118	120	121	52
53	123	124	126	128	129	131	132	134	136	137	53
54	139	140	142	144	145	147	148	150	152	153	54
55	0.155	0.156	0.158	0.160	0.161	0.163	0.164	0.166	0.168	0.169	55
56	171	173	174	176	178	179	181	183	184	186	56
57	187	189	191	192	194	196	197	199	201	203	57
58	204	206	208	209	211	213	214	216	218	220	58
59	221	223	225	226	228	230	232	233	235	237	59
60	0.239	0.240	0.242	0.244	0.246	0.247	0.249	0.251	0.253	0.254	60
61	256	258	260	262	263	265	267	269	271	272	61
62	274	276	278	280	282	284	285	287	289	291	62
63	293	295	297	298	300	302	304	306	308	310	63
64	312	314	316	318	320	322	323	325	327	329	64
65	0.331	0.333	0.335	0.337	0.339	0.341	0.343	0.345	0.347	0.349	65
66	351	353	356	358	360	362	364	366	368	370	66
67	372	374	376	379	381	383	385	387	389	391	67
68	394	396	398	400	402	405	407	409	411	414	68
69	416	418	420	423	425	427	430	432	434	437	69
70	0.439	0.441	0.444	0.446	0.448	0.451	0.453	0.456	0.458	0.461	70
71	463	465	468	470	473	475	478	481	483	486	71
72	488	491	493	496	499	501	504	507	509	512	72
73	515	517	520	523	526	528	531	534	537	540	73
74	543	545	548	551	554	557	560	563	566	569	74
75	0.572	0.575	0.578	0.581	0.584	0.587	0.590	0.594	0.597	0.600	75
76	603	606	610	613	616	620	623	626	630	633	76
77	637	640	644	647	651	654	658	661	665	669	77
78	673	676	680	684	688	692	695	699	703	707	78
79	711	715	720	724	728	732	736	741	745	749	79
80	0.754	0.758	0.763	0.767	0.772	0.776	0.781	0.786	0.791	0.795	80
81	800	805	810	815	820	826	831	836	841	847	81
82	852	858	863	869	875	881	886	892	898	905	82
83	911	917	924	930	937	943	950	957	964	971	83
84	978	986	993	1.001	1.009	1.016	1.024	1.033	1.041	1.049	84
85	1.058	1.067	1.076	1.085	1.094	1.104	1.114	1.124	1.134	1.145	85
86	155	166	178	189	201	214	226	239	253	266	86
87	281	295	311	326	343	360	378	396	415	436	87
88	457	479	503	528	554	582	612	644	679	717	88
89	758	804	855	913	980	2.059	2.156	2.281	2.457	2.758	89
90	+ ∞										90

The Azimuth is marked N or S according to the Latitude, and E or W according to the Hour-Angle.

The Position-Angle is found by reversing the process of the preceding Rule; that is to say, by operating with the difference instead of the sum, and the sum instead of the difference, in the two Cases.

Time-Azimuths: Direct and Limiting Values.

Lat.	Hour-Angle West or East of the Meridian.													On Horizon.	
	0h	1h	2h	3h	4h	5h	6h	7h	8h	9h	10h	11h	12h	Az.	H.A.
	Polar Distance 30°, or Declination 60° of same name as the Latitude.														
°	°	°	°	°	°	°	°	°	°	°	°	°	°	°	h m
0	0.0	8.5	16.1	22.2	26.6	29.1	30.0	29.1						30.0	6 0
10	0.0	9.6	17.8	24.1	28.2	30.2	30.4	28.9	25.8					28.4	7 11
20	0.0	11.3	20.6	27.0	30.7	32.1	31.6	29.4	25.7	20.7	14.6	7.5	0.0	22.8	8 36
30	0.0	14.3	25.1	31.7	34.7	35.2	33.7	30.7	26.3	20.9	14.5	7.4	0.0	0.0	12 0
40	0.0	20.1	33.0	39.0	40.7	39.8	37.0	32.9	27.7	21.7	14.9	7.6	0.0		
50	0.0	34.7	48.0	51.0	49.9	46.6	41.9	36.4	30.1	23.1	15.7	7.9	0.0		
60	Indet.	83.5	76.9	70.3	63.4	56.4	49.1	41.6	33.7	25.6	17.2	8.6	0.0		
70	180.0	140.6	113.9	95.8	82.0	70.1	59.4	49.2	39.2	29.4	19.6	9.8	0.0		
80	180.0	158.3	137.8	119.2	102.5	87.3	73.3	60.1	47.5	35.3	23.4	11.7	0.0		
	Polar Distance 40°, or Declination 50° of same name.														
°	°	°	°	°	°	°	°	°	°	°	°	°	°	°	h m
0	0.0	12.2	22.8	30.7	36.0	39.0	40.0	39.0						40.0	6 0
10	0.0	14.4	26.0	33.9	38.5	40.6	40.4	38.4						38.9	6 49
20	0.0	18.1	31.3	38.8	42.4	43.1	41.7	38.6	33.8					35.4	7 43
30	0.0	25.2	39.8	46.2	47.9	47.0	44.1	39.7	34.0	27.0	18.8	9.7	0.0	27.8	8 50
40	0.0	41.6	54.5	57.1	55.7	52.3	47.6	41.8	35.1	27.3	18.8	9.6	0.0	0.0	12 0
50	Indet.	84.2	78.4	72.4	66.1	59.6	52.6	45.0	37.0	28.4	19.3	9.8	0.0		
60	180.0	132.9	107.1	91.3	79.4	69.0	59.2	49.7	40.1	30.3	20.4	10.2	0.0		
70	180.0	152.6	129.1	110.0	94.1	80.4	67.8	56.0	44.6	33.4	22.3	11.1	0.0		
80	180.0	160.8	142.3	124.7	108.3	92.8	78.3	64.4	51.1	38.0	25.3	12.6	0.0		
	Polar Distance 50°, or Declination 40° of same name.														
°	°	°	°	°	°	°	°	°	°	°	°	°	°	°	h m
0	0.0	17.1	30.8	40.1	45.9	49.0	50.0	49.0						50.0	6 0
10	0.0	21.4	36.5	45.2	49.5	51.0	50.4	48.0						49.2	6 34
20	0.0	29.5	45.4	52.3	54.5	54.1	51.7	47.8	42.1					46.8	7 11
30	0.0	46.7	59.6	62.2	61.2	58.3	54.0	48.4	41.6					42.1	7 56
40	Indet.	85.2	80.2	75.1	69.6	63.8	57.3	50.0	41.9	32.8	22.6	11.6	0.0	32.9	8 59
50	180.0	127.8	103.9	90.2	79.8	70.5	61.7	52.6	43.2	33.2	22.6	11.4	0.0	0.0	12 0
60	180.0	148.2	123.5	105.3	90.9	78.6	67.2	56.3	45.4	34.4	23.2	11.6	0.0		
70	180.0	157.4	136.5	118.1	101.9	87.4	74.0	61.2	48.8	36.6	24.4	12.2	0.0		
80	180.0	162.2	144.8	127.9	111.8	96.4	81.7	67.5	53.6	40.0	26.6	13.3	0.0		
	Polar Distance 60°, or Declination 30° of same name.														
°	°	°	°	°	°	°	°	°	°	°	°	°	°	°	h m
0	0.0	24.1	40.9	50.8	56.3	59.1	60.0	59.1						60.0	6 0
10	0.0	32.8	50.1	57.8	60.9	61.5	60.4	57.6						59.5	6 23
20	0.0	50.6	63.8	67.0	66.8	64.8	61.5	56.8						57.9	6 49
30	Ind.t.	86.2	82.4	78.3	73.9	69.0	63.4	56.9	49.1					54.7	7 18
40	180.0	124.6	102.9	91.0	82.1	74.1	66.1	57.8	48.6					49.3	7 56
50	180.0	144.9	120.3	103.6	90.8	79.8	69.6	59.5	49.0	37.8	25.8	13.1	0.0	38.9	8 54
60	180.0	154.7	132.7	114.6	99.5	86.2	73.9	62.0	50.2	38.1	25.7	12.9	0.0	0.0	12 0
70	180.0	160.0	140.9	123.4	107.5	92.7	78.8	65.5	52.4	39.4	26.3	13.2	0.0		
80	180.0	163.1	146.4	130.1	114.4	99.1	84.3	69.8	55.6	41.6	27.7	13.8	0.0		
	Polar Distance 70°, or Declination 20° of same name.														
°	°	°	°	°	°	°	°	°	°	°	°	°	°	°	h m
0	0.0	35.4	53.9	62.7	67.2	69.4	70.0	69.4						70.0	6 0
10	0.0	53.6	67.4	71.6	72.6	72.0	70.3	67.3						69.7	6 15
20	Indet.	87.4	84.8	81.9	78.8	75.3	71.1	66.0						68.6	6 30
30	180.0	123.0	103.3	93.1	85.7	79.1	72.5	65.3						66.7	6 49
40	180.0	142.9	119.1	104.0	92.8	83.4	74.4	65.3	55.3					63.5	7 11
50	180.0	152.9	130.7	113.5	99.8	87.9	76.8	65.9	54.5					57.9	7 43
60	180.0	158.4	138.6	121.3	106.2	92.5	79.7	67.2	54.6	41.7	28.2	14.3	0.0	46.8	8 36
70	180.0	161.7	144.0	127.4	111.7	97.0	82.9	69.2	55.5	41.9	28.1	14.1	0.0	0.0	12 0
80	180.0	163.8	147.6	131.8	116.4	101.2	86.4	71.8	57.3	43.0	28.6	14.3	0.0		

The Azimuths in smaller figures answer to actual depressions of the object below the True Horizon, and are used for differences with the adjacent Azimuths.

Time-Azimuths: Direct and Limiting Values.

Lat.	Hour-Angle West or East of the Meridian.													On Horizon.	
	0h	1h	2h	3h	4h	5h	6h	7h	8h	9h	10h	11h	12h	Az.	H.A.
	Pol. Dist. 80°, or Declination 10° of same name as the Latitude.														
°	°	°	°	°	°	°	°	°						°	h m
0	0.0	55.8	70.6	76.0	78.5	79.7	80.0	79.7						80.0	6 0
10	Indet.	88.7	87.3	85.9	84.3	82.4	80.2	77.2						79.8	6 7
20	180.0	122.5	104.6	96.2	90.4	85.4	80.6	75.3						79.3	6 15
30	180.0	141.9	119.3	105.9	96.4	88.6	81.3	73.7						78.4	6 23
40	180.0	152.0	130.1	114.3	102.2	91.9	82.3	72.7						76.9	6 34
50	180.0	157.6	137.7	121.2	107.3	95.0	83.5	72.1						74.3	6 49
60	180.0	160.9	142.9	126.6	111.7	98.0	85.0	72.1	58.9					69.7	7 11
70	180.0	163.0	146.4	130.5	115.3	100.7	86.6	72.6	58.5	49.3	29.8	15.0	0.0	59.5	7 56
80	180.0	164.3	148.7	133.3	118.1	103.1	88.3	73.5	58.9	44.2	29.5	14.8	0.0	0.0	12 0
	Pol. Dist. 90°, or Declination 0°.														
°	°	°	°	°	°	°	°	°						°	h m
0	Indet.	90.0	90.0	90.0	90.0	90.0	90.0	90.0						90.0	6 0
10	180.0	123.0	106.7	99.9	95.7	92.7	90.0	87.3						90.0	6 0
20	180.0	141.9	120.6	108.9	101.2	95.2	90.0	84.8						90.0	6 0
30	180.0	151.8	130.9	116.6	106.1	97.6	90.0	82.4						90.0	6 0
40	180.0	157.4	138.0	122.7	110.4	99.8	90.0	80.2						90.0	6 0
50	180.0	160.7	143.0	127.5	113.9	101.6	90.0	78.4						90.0	6 0
60	180.0	162.8	146.3	130.9	116.6	103.1	90.0	76.9						90.0	6 0
70	180.0	164.1	148.4	133.2	118.5	104.1	90.0	75.9						90.0	6 0
80	180.0	164.8	149.6	134.6	119.6	104.8	90.0	75.2						90.0	6 0
	Pol. Dist. 100°, or Declination 10° of contrary name.														
°	°	°	°	°	°	°	°	°						°	h m
0	180.0	124.3	109.4	104.0	101.5	100.3	100.0	100.3						100.0	6 0
10	180.0	142.8	123.0	112.7	106.7	102.8	99.8							100.2	5 53
20	180.0	152.5	132.7	120.0	111.3	104.8	99.4							100.7	5 45
30	180.0	157.8	139.5	125.6	114.9	106.3	98.7							101.6	5 37
40	180.0	161.1	144.1	129.8	117.8	107.3	97.7							103.1	5 26
50	180.0	163.1	147.2	132.8	119.8	107.8	96.5							105.7	5 11
60	180.0	164.4	149.2	134.7	121.1	107.9								110.3	4 49
70	180.0	165.0	150.2	135.7	121.5	107.5								120.5	4 4
80	180.0	165.2	150.5	135.8	121.1									180.0	0 0
	Pol. Dist. 110°, or Declination 20° of contrary name.														
°	°	°	°	°	°	°	°	°						°	h m
0	180.0	144.6	126.0	117.3	112.8	110.6	110.0	110.6						110.0	6 0
10	180.0	153.8	135.5	124.2	117.2	112.7	109.7							110.3	5 45
20	180.0	159.0	141.9	129.5	120.6	114.0	108.9							111.4	5 30
30	180.0	162.0	146.2	133.4	123.1	114.7	107.5							113.3	5 11
40	180.0	164.0	149.1	136.1	124.7	114.7								116.5	4 49
50	180.0	165.1	150.9	137.6	125.5	114.1								122.1	4 17
60	180.0	165.7	151.8	138.3	125.4									133.2	3 24
70	180.0	165.9	151.9	138.1										180.0	0 0
	Pol. Dist. 120°, or Declination 30° of contrary name.														
°	°	°	°	°	°	°	°	°						°	h m
0	180.0	155.8	139.1	129.2	123.7	120.9	120.0	120.9						120.0	6 0
10	180.0	160.6	145.2	134.4	127.1	122.4	119.6							120.5	5 37
20	180.0	163.5	149.2	138.0	129.5	123.2	118.5							122.1	5 11
30	180.0	165.2	151.8	140.4	130.9	123.1								125.3	4 42
40	180.0	166.3	153.4	141.7	131.4	122.3								130.7	4 4
50	180.0	166.9	154.2	142.2	131.1									141.1	3 6
60	180.0	167.0	154.3	141.9										180.0	0 0
	Pol. Dist. 130°, or Declination 40° of contrary name.														
°	°	°	°	°	°	°	°	°						°	h m
0	180.0	162.9	149.2	139.9	134.1	131.0	130.0	131.0						130.0	6 0
10	180.0	165.4	152.9	143.3	136.5	132.0	129.6							130.8	5 26
20	180.0	167.0	155.3	145.6	137.9	132.2								133.2	4 49
30	180.0	167.9	156.7	146.8	138.4	131.6								137.9	4 4
40	180.0	168.4	157.4	147.2	138.1									147.9	3 1
50	180.0	168.6	157.4	146.8										180.0	0 0

Position-Angles for Direct and Limiting Time-Azimuths.

Lat.	0h	1h	2h	3h	4h	5h	6h	7h	8h	9h	10h	11h	12h	Lat.
	Hour-Angle West or East of the Meridian.													
	Pol. Dist. 30°, or Declination 60° of same name as the Latitude.													
0	180.0	162.8	146.3	130.9	116.6	103.1	90.0	76.9						0
10	180.0	160.9	142.9	126.6	111.7	98.0	85.0	71.1	59.0					10
20	180.0	158.4	138.7	121.2	106.2	92.5	79.7	67.2	54.6	41.7	28.2	14.3	0.0	20
30	180.0	154.7	132.7	114.6	99.5	86.2	73.9	62.0	50.2	38.1	25.7	12.9	0.0	30
40	180.0	148.2	123.5	105.3	80.9	78.6	67.2	56.3	45.4	34.4	23.2	11.6	0.0	40
50	180.0	132.9	107.1	91.3	79.4	69.0	59.2	49.7	40.1	30.3	20.4	10.2	0.0	50
60	Indet.	83.5	76.9	70.3	63.4	56.4	49.1	41.6	33.7	25.6	17.2	8.6	0.0	60
70	0.0	25.7	38.7	42.9	42.6	40.0	36.1	31.2	25.6	19.6	13.3	6.7	0.0	70
80	0.0	7.4	13.5	17.6	19.8	20.3	19.4	17.5	14.8	11.6	7.9	4.0	0.0	80
	Pol. Dist. 40°, or Declination 50° of same name.													
0	180.0	160.7	143.0	127.4	113.9	101.6	90.0	78.4						0
10	180.0	157.6	137.7	121.2	107.3	95.0	83.5	72.1						10
20	180.0	152.9	130.7	113.5	99.8	87.9	76.9	65.9	54.5					20
30	180.0	144.9	120.3	103.6	90.8	79.9	69.6	59.5	48.9	37.8	25.8	13.1	0.0	30
40	180.0	127.8	103.9	90.2	79.8	70.5	61.7	52.6	43.2	33.2	22.6	11.4	0.0	40
50	Indet.	84.2	78.4	72.4	66.1	59.6	52.6	45.0	37.0	28.4	19.3	9.8	0.0	50
60	0.0	34.7	48.0	51.0	49.9	46.6	41.9	36.4	30.1	22.1	15.7	8.0	0.0	60
70	0.0	14.2	24.4	30.0	32.1	31.7	29.5	26.2	22.0	17.0	11.6	5.9	0.0	70
80	0.0	5.1	9.5	12.8	14.9	15.6	15.3	14.1	12.1	9.6	6.6	3.4	0.0	80
	Pol. Dist. 50°, or Declination 40° of same name.													
0	180.0	157.4	138.0	122.8	110.4	99.8	90.0	80.2						0
10	180.0	152.0	130.1	114.3	102.2	91.9	82.3	72.7						10
20	180.0	142.9	119.1	104.0	92.8	83.4	74.4	65.3	55.3					20
30	180.0	124.6	102.9	91.0	82.1	74.1	66.1	57.8	48.6					30
40	Indet	85.2	80.2	75.1	69.6	63.8	57.3	50.0	41.9	32.8	22.6	11.6	0.0	40
50	0.0	41.6	54.6	57.1	55.7	52.3	47.6	41.8	35.0	27.3	18.8	9.6	0.0	50
60	0.0	20.1	33.0	39.0	40.7	39.8	37.0	32.9	27.7	21.6	14.9	7.6	0.0	60
70	0.0	9.9	17.9	23.2	25.9	26.5	25.4	23.0	19.6	15.4	10.6	5.4	0.0	70
80	0.0	4.0	7.5	10.3	12.1	13.0	13.0	12.1	10.5	8.4	5.8	3.0	0.0	80
	Pol. Dist. 60°, or Declination 30° of same name.													
0	180.0	151.8	130.9	116.6	106.1	97.6	90.0	82.4						0
10	180.0	141.9	119.3	105.9	96.4	88.6	81.3	73.7						10
20	180.0	123.0	103.3	93.1	85.7	79.1	72.5	65.3						20
30	Indet.	86.2	82.4	78.3	73.9	69.0	63.4	56.9	49.1					30
40	0.0	46.7	59.6	62.2	61.2	58.3	54.0	48.4	41.5					40
50	0.0	25.2	39.8	46.2	48.0	46.9	44.1	39.7	34.0	27.0	18.8	9.7	0.0	50
60	0.0	14.3	25.1	31.7	34.7	35.2	33.7	30.7	26.3	20.7	14.5	7.4	0.0	60
70	0.0	7.8	14.4	19.2	22.1	23.2	22.8	21.1	18.2	14.5	10.1	5.2	0.0	70
80	0.0	3.3	6.4	8.8	10.5	11.4	11.5	10.8	9.5	7.6	5.4	2.7	0.0	80
	Pol. Dist. 70°, or Declination 20° of same name.													
0	180.0	141.9	120.7	108.9	101.2	95.2	90.0	84.8						0
10	180.0	122.5	104.6	96.1	90.4	85.4	80.6	75.3						10
20	Indet.	87.4	84.8	81.9	78.8	75.3	71.1	66.0						20
30	0.0	50.6	63.8	67.0	66.8	64.8	61.5	56.8						30
40	0.0	29.5	45.4	52.3	54.5	54.1	51.7	47.7	42.1					40
50	0.0	18.1	31.3	38.8	42.4	43.1	41.8	38.6	33.8					50
60	0.0	11.3	20.6	27.0	30.7	32.1	31.6	29.4	25.7	20.7	14.6	7.5	0.0	60
70	0.0	6.5	12.3	16.8	19.8	21.2	21.2	19.9	17.5	14.1	9.8	5.1	0.0	70
80	0.0	3.0	5.7	7.9	9.5	10.5	10.6	10.1	8.9	7.2	5.1	2.6	0.0	80

Position-Angles in smaller figures correspond to depressions of the object below the True Horizon.

Position-Angles for Direct and Limiting Time-Azimuths.

Lat.	0h	1h	2h	3h	4h	5h	6h	7h	8h	9h	10h	11h	12h	Lat.
	Hour-Angle West or East of the Meridian.													
	Pol. Dist. 80°, or Declination 10° of same name as the Latitude.													
0°	180.0	123.0	106.7	99.8	95.7	92.7	90.0	87.3						0°
10	Indet.	88.7	87.3	85.9	84.3	82.4	80.2	77.2						10
20	0.0	53.6	67.4	71.6	72.6	72.0	70.3	67.3						20
30	0.0	32.9	50.1	57.8	60.9	61.5	60.4	57.6						30
40	0.0	21.5	36.5	45.2	49.5	51.0	50.4	48.0						40
50	0.0	14.4	26.0	33.9	38.5	40.6	40.4	38.4						50
60	0.0	9.5	17.8	24.1	28.2	30.2	30.4	28.9	25.8					60
70	0.0	5.8	11.1	15.3	18.3	19.9	20.3	19.4	17.1	14.0	9.9	6.1	0.0	70
80	0.0	2.7	5.3	7.4	8.9	9.9	10.2	9.7	8.7	7.1	5.0	2.6	0.0	80
	Pol. Dist. 90°, or Declination 0°.													
0°	Indet.	90.0	90.0	90.0	90.0	90.0	90.0	90.0						0°
10	0.0	55.7	70.6	76.0	78.5	79.7	80.0	79.7						10
20	0.0	35.4	54.0	62.8	67.2	69.4	70.0	69.4						20
30	0.0	24.1	40.9	50.8	56.3	59.1	60.0	59.1						30
40	0.0	17.1	30.8	40.1	45.9	49.0	50.0	49.0						40
50	0.0	12.2	22.7	30.6	36.0	39.0	40.0	39.0						50
60	0.0	8.5	16.1	22.2	26.5	29.1	30.0	29.1						60
70	0.0	5.4	10.3	14.4	17.5	19.4	20.0	19.4						70
80	0.0	2.6	5.0	7.1	8.7	9.7	10.0	9.7						80
	Pol. Dist. 100°, or Declination 10° of contrary name.													
0°	0.0	57.0	73.3	80.1	84.3	87.3	90.0	92.7						0°
10	0.0	37.1	57.0	67.2	73.3	77.2	80.1							10
20	0.0	26.1	44.5	55.7	62.8	67.3	70.3							20
30	0.0	19.3	34.8	45.6	52.8	57.6	60.4							30
40	0.0	14.6	27.1	36.7	43.4	47.9	50.4							40
50	0.0	10.9	20.7	28.6	34.5	38.5	40.4							50
60	0.0	7.8	15.1	21.1	25.8	28.9								60
70	0.0	5.1	9.9	14.0	17.2	19.3								70
80	0.0	2.6	5.0	7.1	8.7									80
	Pol. Dist. 110°, or Declination 20° of contrary name.													
0°	0.0	38.1	59.4	71.1	78.8	84.8	90.0	95.2						0°
10	0.0	27.5	47.2	60.0	68.8	75.3	80.6							10
20	0.0	21.0	38.1	50.4	59.4	66.0	71.1							20
30	0.0	16.5	30.8	42.0	50.5	56.8	61.5							30
40	0.0	13.0	24.7	34.4	42.0	47.8								40
50	0.0	10.1	19.4	27.4	33.8	38.6								50
60	0.0	7.5	14.6	20.7	25.7									60
70	0.0	5.1	9.9	14.1										70
	Pol. Dist. 120°, or Declination 30° of contrary name.													
0°	0.0	28.2	49.1	63.4	73.9	82.4	90.0	97.6						0°
10	0.0	22.1	40.5	54.4	65.1	73.5	81.3							10
20	0.0	17.9	33.7	46.6	56.9	65.3	72.5							20
30	0.0	14.7	28.2	39.6	49.1	56.9								30
40	0.0	12.1	23.3	33.2	41.6	48.4								40
50	0.0	9.7	18.8	27.0	34.0									50
60	0.0	7.4	14.5	20.9										60
	Pol. Dist. 130°, or Declination 40° of contrary name.													
0°	0.0	22.6	41.9	57.2	69.6	80.2	90.0	99.8						0°
10	0.0	18.9	35.9	50.2	62.2	72.7	82.3							10
20	0.0	16.0	30.9	43.9	55.3	65.3								20
30	0.0	13.7	26.6	38.2	48.6	57.8								30
40	0.0	11.6	22.6	32.8	41.9									40
50	0.0	9.6	18.8	27.4										50

Altitudes for Direct and Limiting Time-Azimuths.

Lat.	Hour-Angle West or East of the Meridian.													Lat.
	0h	1h	2h	3h	4h	5h	6h	7h	8h	9h	10h	11h	12h	
	Pol. Dist. 30°, or Declination 60° of same name as the Latitude.													
0°	30°.0	28°.9	25°.5	20°.7	14°.4	7°.3	0°.0	7°.3						0°
10	40.0	38.7	35.0	30.0	23.4	16.1	8.7	1.2	5°.5					10
20	50.0	48.6	44.6	38.9	32.1	24.7	17.3	10.0	3.3	1°.7	6°.6	8°.9	10°.0	20
30	60.0	58.4	53.9	47.5	40.5	33.0	25.6	18.7	12.4	7.3	3.2	0.9	0.0	30
40	70.0	67.9	62.7	55.8	48.4	40.9	33.8	27.2	21.4	16.6	13.1	10.8	10.0	40
50	80.0	76.9	70.4	62.9	55.5	48.3	41.6	35.5	30.2	25.8	22.7	20.7	20.0	50
60	90.0	82.3	75.1	68.0	61.0	54.6	48.6	43.3	38.7	34.9	32.3	30.6	30.0	60
70	80.0	78.2	74.3	69.1	64.1	59.1	54.5	50.3	46.7	43.8	41.8	40.4	40.0	70
80	70.0	69.5	68.2	66.0	63.7	61.1	58.5	56.1	54.0	52.3	51.1	50.2	50.0	80
	Pol. Dist. 40°, or Declination 50° of same name.													
0°	40°.0	38°.2	33°.8	27°.1	18°.8	9°.7	0°.0	9°.7						0°
10	50.0	48.1	42.9	35.5	26.7	17.2	7.7	1.8						10
20	60.0	57.7	51.8	43.6	34.3	24.6	15.2	6.0	2°.2					20
30	70.0	67.0	59.9	50.9	41.4	31.8	22.5	13.8	5.9	0°.7	5°.8	8°.6	10°.0	30
40	80.0	75.5	66.8	57.2	47.6	38.3	29.5	21.4	14.3	8.1	3.9	0.9	0.0	40
50	90.0	80.3	70.8	61.5	52.5	43.9	35.9	28.7	22.2	17.1	13.4	10.8	10.0	50
60	80.0	76.8	70.4	62.9	55.5	48.3	41.5	35.5	30.2	25.8	22.7	20.7	20.0	60
70	70.0	68.7	65.5	61.1	56.1	51.0	46.1	41.5	37.6	34.3	32.0	30.5	30.0	70
80	60.0	59.6	58.3	56.4	54.1	51.6	49.0	46.5	44.3	42.6	41.2	40.3	40.0	80
	Pol. Dist. 50°, or Declination 40° of same name.													
0°	50°.0	47°.7	41°.5	32°.8	22°.5	11°.4	0°.0	11°.4						0°
10	60.0	57.2	49.9	40.2	29.3	17.9	6.4	4.8						10
20	70.0	66.2	57.5	46.8	35.4	24.0	12.7	2.1	8°.0					20
30	80.0	74.2	63.6	52.2	40.8	29.5	18.7	8.8	0.7					30
40	90.0	78.5	67.1	55.9	45.0	34.4	24.4	15.2	6.9	0°.1	5°.8	8°.8	10°.0	40
50	80.0	75.6	66.7	57.2	47.6	38.3	29.5	21.4	14.3	8.2	3.7	0.6	0.0	50
60	70.0	67.9	62.7	55.8	48.4	41.0	33.8	27.3	21.4	16.6	13.1	10.6	10.0	60
70	60.0	59.0	56.2	52.1	47.3	42.2	37.1	32.4	28.2	24.8	22.2	20.5	20.0	70
80	50.0	49.6	48.4	46.6	44.4	41.9	39.3	36.8	34.5	32.6	31.2	30.4	30.0	80
	Pol. Dist. 60°, or Declination 30° of same name.													
0°	60°.0	56°.8	48°.6	37°.8	25°.6	12°.9	0°.0	12°.9						0°
10	70.0	65.6	55.6	43.6	30.9	17.9	5.0	7.8						10
20	80.0	73.2	61.1	48.3	35.3	22.4	9.9	2.5						20
30	90.0	77.0	64.1	51.3	38.7	26.3	14.5	3.0	7°.0					30
40	80.0	74.2	63.6	52.2	40.8	29.5	18.8	8.6	0.6					40
50	70.0	67.0	59.9	50.9	41.4	31.8	22.5	13.8	5.9	0°.8	6°.0	9°.0	10°.0	50
60	60.0	58.3	53.9	47.7	40.5	33.0	25.7	18.7	12.4	7.2	3.0	0.5	0.0	60
70	50.0	49.1	46.6	42.8	38.2	33.1	28.0	23.2	18.8	15.1	12.4	10.3	10.0	70
80	40.0	39.6	38.5	36.8	34.6	32.1	29.5	26.9	24.6	22.5	21.4	20.2	20.0	80
	Pol. Dist. 70°, or Declination 20° of same name.													
0°	70°.0	65°.2	54°.5	41°.6	28°.0	14°.1	0°.0	14°.1						0°
10	80.0	72.4	59.4	45.6	31.5	17.4	3.3	10.4						10
20	90.0	75.9	61.8	47.8	33.9	20.2	6.7	6.4						20
30	80.0	73.2	61.1	48.3	35.3	22.4	9.9	2.2						30
40	70.0	66.2	57.5	46.8	35.4	24.0	12.7	2.0	8°.1					40
50	60.0	57.7	51.7	43.6	34.3	24.7	15.2	6.1	2.4					50
60	50.0	48.6	44.7	38.9	32.2	24.7	17.2	10.1	3.5	1°.8	6°.2	9°.2	10°.0	60
70	40.0	39.2	36.8	33.3	28.8	23.9	18.7	13.8	9.2	5.4	2.5	0.4	0.0	70
80	30.0	29.6	28.6	26.9	24.7	22.3	19.7	17.1	14.8	12.8	11.3	10.3	10.0	80

The Altitudes in smaller figures are depressions below the True Horizon; that is, negative Altitudes.

Altitudes for Direct and Limiting Time-Azimuths.

Lat.	Hour-Angle West or East of the Meridian.													Lat.
	0h	1h	2h	3h	4h	5h	6h	7h	8h	9h	10h	11h	12h	
	Pol. Dist. 80°, or Declination 10° of same name as the Latitude.													
°	°	°	°	°	°	°	°	°						°
0	80.0	72.1	58.5	44.1	29.5	14.8	0.0	14.8						0
10	90.0	75.2	60.5	45.7	31.0	16.3	1.8	12.8						10
20	80.0	72.4	59.4	45.6	31.5	17.4	3.3	10.4						20
30	70.0	65.6	55.6	43.6	30.9	17.9	4.9	7.7						30
40	60.0	57.2	49.9	40.2	29.3	17.9	6.4	4.9						40
50	50.0	48.1	42.9	35.5	26.7	17.3	7.6	1.8	°					50
60	40.0	38.8	35.2	29.9	23.4	16.1	8.6	0.3	5.5	°	°	°	°	60
70	30.0	29.2	27.1	23.7	19.4	14.5	9.9	4.2	0.0	5.8	7.1	9.4	10.0	70
80	20.0	19.6	18.6	17.0	14.8	12.4	9.8	7.3	4.9	3.0	2.0	0.2	0.0	80
	Pol. Dist. 90°, or Declination 0°.													
°	°	°	°	°	°	°	°	°						°
0	90.0	75.0	60.0	45.0	30.0	15.0	0.0	15.0						0
10	80.0	72.0	58.5	44.1	29.5	14.8	0.0	14.8						10
20	70.0	65.2	54.5	41.6	28.0	14.1	0.0	14.1						20
30	60.0	56.8	48.6	37.7	25.7	12.9	0.0	12.9						30
40	50.0	47.7	41.6	32.8	22.5	11.5	0.0	11.5						40
50	40.0	38.4	33.8	27.0	18.7	9.6	0.0	9.6						50
60	30.0	28.9	25.7	20.7	14.5	7.5	0.0	7.5						60
70	20.0	19.3	17.2	14.0	9.9	5.2	0.0	5.2						70
80	10.0	9.7	8.7	7.0	5.1	2.7	0.0	2.7						80
	Pol. Dist. 100°, or Declination 10° of contrary name.													
°	°	°	°	°	°	°	°	°						°
0	80.0	72.0	58.5	44.1	29.5	14.8	0.0	14.8						0
10	70.0	65.0	54.1	41.0	27.0	12.8	1.7							10
20	60.0	56.5	47.9	36.5	23.7	10.4	3.4							20
30	50.0	47.5	40.7	31.1	19.8	7.7	5.0							30
40	40.0	38.1	32.8	24.9	15.4	4.8	6.4							40
50	30.0	28.6	24.5	18.3	10.5	2.3	7.6							50
60	20.0	18.9	16.0	11.4	5.4	1.1								60
70	10.0	9.3	7.4	4.3	0.3	4.4								70
80	0.0	0.1	1.2	2.9	4.9									80
	Pol. Dist. 110°, or Declination 20° of contrary name.													
°	°	°	°	°	°	°	°	°						°
0	70.0	65.2	54.5	41.6	28.0	14.1	0.0	14.1						0
10	60.0	56.5	47.9	36.5	23.7	10.4	3.9							10
20	50.0	47.4	40.4	30.5	18.9	6.5	6.7							20
30	40.0	38.0	32.2	23.9	13.6	2.4								30
40	30.0	28.4	23.8	16.8	8.1	1.9								40
50	20.0	18.8	15.1	9.4	2.4	6.1								50
60	10.0	9.1	6.4	2.0	3.4									60
70	0.0	0.2	2.4	5.4										70
	Pol. Dist. 120°, or Declination 30° of contrary name.													
°	°	°	°	°	°	°	°	°						°
0	60.0	56.8	48.6	37.8	25.6	12.9	0.0	12.9						0
10	50.0	47.4	40.7	31.1	19.8	7.7	5.1							10
20	40.0	38.0	32.2	23.9	13.6	2.3	9.9							20
30	30.0	28.3	23.5	16.2	7.1	3.2								30
40	20.0	18.6	14.6	8.5	0.4	8.3								40
50	10.0	8.8	5.8	0.9	6.0									50
60	0.0	0.5	3.2	7.3										60
	Pol. Dist. 130°, or Declination 40° of contrary name.													
°	°	°	°	°	°	°	°	°						°
0	50.0	47.7	41.5	32.8	22.5	11.4	0.0	11.4						0
10	40.0	38.1	32.8	25.0	15.4	4.8	6.4							10
20	30.0	28.3	23.8	16.8	8.0	1.9								20
30	20.0	18.7	14.6	8.6	0.4	8.2								30
40	10.0	8.8	5.5	0.5	6.9									40
50	0.0	0.6	3.6	8.3										50

Error of the Time-Azimuth for an Error of 1m in the Hour-Angle.

Hour-Angle 1h or 11h.

Az.	90°	85°	80°	75°	70°	65°	60°	55°	50°	45°	40°	30°	20°	10°	0°	Az.
0°	0′	0′	0′	0′	0′	0′	0′	0′	0′	0′	0′	0′	0′	0′	0′	180°
5	0	0	1	1	2	2	3	3	3	4	4	4	5	5	5	175
10	0	1	2	3	3	4	5	6	6	7	8	9	9	10	10	170
15	0	1	3	4	5	6	7	9	10	11	12	13	14	15	15	165
20	0	2	3	5	7	8	10	11	13	14	15	17	19	20	20	160
25	0	2	4	6	8	10	12	14	16	17	19	21	23	24	25	155
30	0	3	5	7	10	12	14	17	19	20	22	25	27	28	29	150
35	0	3	6	9	11	14	17	19	21	23	26	29	31	33	33	145
40	0	3	6	10	13	16	19	21	24	26	28	32	35	37	37	140
45	0	4	7	11	14	17	20	23	26	29	31	35	38	40	41	135
50	0	4	8	12	15	19	22	26	28	31	34	39	42	44	44	130
60	0	4	9	13	17	21	25	29	32	35	39	43	47	49	50	120
70	0	5	9	14	19	23	27	31	35	38	42	47	51	54	55	110
80	0	5	10	15	20	24	28	33	37	40	44	49	54	56	57	100
90	0	5	10	15	20	25	29	33	37	41	44	50	55	57	58	90
Az.	90°	95°	100°	105°	110°	115°	120°	125°	130°	135°	140°	150°	160°	170°	180°	Az.

Position-Angle.

Hour-Angle 2h or 10h.

Az.	90°	85°	80°	75°	70°	65°	60°	55°	50°	45°	40°	30°	20°	10°	0°	Az.
0°	0′	0′	0′	0′	0′	0′	0′	0′	0′	0′	0′	0′	0′	0′	0′	180°
5	0	0	0	1	1	1	1	1	2	2	2	2	3	3	3	175
10	0	0	1	1	2	2	3	3	3	4	4	5	5	5	5	170
15	0	1	1	2	3	3	4	4	5	6	6	7	7	8	8	165
20	0	1	2	3	3	4	5	6	7	7	8	9	10	10	10	160
25	0	1	2	3	4	5	6	7	8	9	10	11	12	12	13	155
30	0	1	3	4	5	6	7	9	10	11	12	13	14	15	15	150
35	0	1	3	4	6	7	9	10	11	12	13	15	16	17	17	145
40	0	2	3	5	7	8	10	11	12	14	15	17	18	19	19	140
45	0	2	4	6	7	9	11	12	14	15	16	18	20	21	21	135
50	0	2	4	6	8	10	12	13	15	16	18	20	22	23	23	130
60	0	2	5	7	9	11	13	15	17	18	20	22	24	26	26	120
70	0	3	5	7	10	12	14	16	18	20	22	24	26	28	28	110
80	0	3	5	8	10	12	15	17	19	21	23	26	28	29	29	100
90	0	3	5	8	10	13	15	17	19	21	23	26	28	29	30	90
Az.	90°	95°	100°	105°	110°	115°	120°	125°	130°	135°	140°	150°	160°	170°	180°	Az.

Position-Angle.

Hour-Angle 3h or 9h.

Az.	90°	85°	80°	75°	70°	65°	60°	55°	50°	45°	40°	30°	20°	10°	0°	Az.
0°	0′	0′	0′	0′	0′	0′	0′	0′	0′	0	0′	0′	0′	0′	0′	180°
5	0	0	0	1	1	1	1	1	1	1	1	2	2	2	2	175
10	0	0	1	1	1	2	2	2	2	3	3	3	4	4	4	170
15	0	1	1	1	2	2	3	3	3	4	4	5	5	5	6	165
20	0	1	1	2	2	3	4	4	5	5	6	6	7	7	7	160
25	0	1	2	2	3	4	4	5	6	6	7	8	8	9	9	155
30	0	1	2	3	4	4	5	6	7	7	8	9	10	10	11	150
35	0	1	2	3	4	5	6	7	8	9	9	10	11	12	12	140
40	0	1	2	3	5	6	7	8	9	10	10	12	13	13	14	145
45	0	1	3	4	5	6	7	9	10	11	12	13	14	15	15	135
50	0	1	3	4	6	7	8	9	10	12	13	14	15	16	16	130
60	0	2	3	5	6	8	9	10	12	13	14	16	17	18	18	120
70	0	2	4	5	7	8	10	11	13	14	15	17	19	20	20	110
80	0	2	4	5	7	9	10	12	13	15	16	18	20	21	21	100
90	0	2	4	6	7	9	11	12	14	15	16	18	20	21	21	90
Az.	90°	95°	100°	105°	110°	115°	120°	125°	130°	135°	140°	150°	160°	170°	180°	Az.

Position-Angle.

Error of the Time-Azimuth for an Error of 1^m in the Hour-Angle.

Hour-Angle 4^h or 8^h.

Az.	Position-Angle.															Az.
	90°	85°	80°	75°	70°	65°	60°	55°	50°	45°	40°	30°	20°	10°	0°	
0°	0′	0′	0′	0′	0′	0′	0′	0′	0′	0′	0′	0′	0′	0′	0′	180°
5	0	0	0	0	1	1	1	1	1	1	1	1	1	1	2	175
10	0	0	0	1	1	1	1	2	2	2	2	3	3	3	3	170
15	0	0	1	1	1	2	2	3	3	3	3	4	4	4	5	165
20	0	1	1	1	2	2	3	3	4	4	4	5	6	6	6	160
25	0	1	1	2	2	3	4	4	5	5	6	6	7	7	7	155
30	0	1	1	2	3	4	4	5	6	6	7	7	8	8	9	150
35	0	1	2	3	3	4	5	6	6	7	8	9	9	10	10	145
40	0	1	2	3	4	5	6	6	7	8	9	10	10	11	11	140
45	0	1	2	3	4	5	6	7	8	9	9	11	11	12	12	135
50	0	1	2	3	4	6	7	8	9	9	10	11	12	13	13	130
60	0	1	3	4	5	6	7	9	10	11	11	13	14	15	15	120
70	0	1	3	4	6	7	8	9	10	11	12	14	15	16	16	110
80	0	1	3	4	6	7	8	10	11	12	13	15	16	17	17	100
90	0	2	3	5	6	7	9	10	11	12	13	15	16	17	17	90
Az.	90°	95°	100°	105°	110°	115°	120°	125°	130°	135°	140°	150°	160°	170°	180°	Az.
	Position-Angle.															

Hour-Angle 5^h or 7^h.

Az.	Position-Angle.															Az.
	90°	85°	80°	75°	70°	65°	60°	55°	50°	45°	40°	30°	20°	10°	0°	
0°	0′	0′	0′	0′	0′	0′	0′	0′	0′	0′	0′	0′	0′	0′	0′	180°
5	0	0	0	0	0	1	1	1	1	1	1	1	1	1	1	175
10	0	0	0	1	1	1	1	1	2	2	2	2	2	3	3	170
15	0	0	1	1	1	2	2	2	3	3	3	3	4	4	4	165
20	0	0	1	1	2	2	3	3	3	4	4	5	5	5	5	160
25	0	1	1	2	2	3	3	4	4	5	5	6	6	6	7	155
30	0	1	1	2	3	3	4	4	5	5	6	7	7	8	8	150
35	0	1	1	2	3	4	4	5	6	6	7	8	8	9	9	145
40	0	1	2	3	3	4	5	6	6	7	8	9	9	10	10	140
45	0	1	2	3	4	5	5	6	7	8	8	9	10	11	11	135
50	0	1	2	3	4	5	6	7	8	8	9	10	11	12	12	130
60	0	1	2	3	5	6	7	8	9	9	10	11	13	13	13	120
70	0	1	2	4	5	6	7	8	9	10	11	13	14	14	15	110
80	0	1	3	4	5	6	8	9	10	11	12	13	14	15	15	100
90	0	1	3	4	5	7	8	9	10	11	12	13	15	15	16	90
Az.	90°	95°	100°	105°	110°	115°	120°	125°	130°	135°	140°	150°	160°	170°	180°	Az.
	Position-Angle.															

Hour-Angle 6^h.

Az.	Position-Angle.															Az.
	90°	85°	80°	75°	70°	65°	60°	55°	50°	45°	40°	30°	20°	10°	0°	
0°	0′	0′	0′	0′	0′	0′	0′	0′	0′	0′	0′	0′	0′	0′	0′	180°
5	0	0	0	0	0	1	1	1	1	1	1	1	1	1	1	175
10	0	0	0	1	1	1	1	1	2	2	2	2	2	3	3	170
15	0	0	1	1	1	2	2	2	2	3	3	3	4	4	4	165
20	0	0	1	1	2	2	3	3	3	4	4	4	5	5	5	160
25	0	1	1	2	2	3	3	4	4	4	5	5	6	6	6	155
30	0	1	1	2	3	3	4	4	5	5	6	6	7	7	7	150
35	0	1	1	2	3	4	4	5	5	6	7	7	8	8	9	145
40	0	1	2	2	3	4	5	5	6	7	7	8	9	9	10	140
45	0	1	2	3	4	4	5	6	7	7	8	9	10	10	11	135
50	0	1	2	3	4	5	6	7	7	8	9	10	11	11	12	130
60	0	1	2	3	4	5	6	7	8	9	10	11	12	13	13	120
70	0	1	2	4	5	6	7	8	9	10	11	12	13	14	14	110
80	0	1	3	4	5	6	7	8	9	10	11	13	14	15	15	100
90	0	1	3	4	5	6	7	9	10	11	12	13	14	15	15	90
Az.	90°	95°	100°	105°	110°	115°	120°	125°	130°	135°	140°	150°	160°	170°	180°	Az.
	Position-Angle.															

Error of the Time-Azimuth for an Error of 1^m in the Hour-Angle.

Hour-Angle $0^h\ 10^m$ or $11^h\ 50^m$.

Az.	Position-Angle.															Az.
	90°	85°	80°	75°	70°	65°	60°	55°	50°	45°	40°	30°	20°	10°	0°	
0°	0.0°	0.0°	0.0°	0.0°	0.0°	0.0°	0.0°	0.0°	0.0°	0.0°	0.0°	0.0°	0.0°	0.0°	0.0°	180°
5	0	0	1	1	2	2	2	3	3	4	4	4	5	5	5	175
10	0	1	2	3	3	4	5	6	6	7	8	9	9	1.0	1.0	170
15	0	1	3	4	5	6	7	9	1.0	1.0	1.1	1.3	1.4	5	5	165
20	0	2	3	5	7	8	1.0	1.1	3	4	5	7	8	9	2.0	160
25	0.0	0.2	0.4	0.6	0.8	1.0	1.2	1.4	1.6	1.7	1.9	2.1	2.3	2.4	2.4	155
30	0	2	5	7	1.0	2	4	6	8	2.0	2.2	5	7	8	9	150
35	0	3	6	9	1	4	6	9	2.1	3	5	8	3.1	3.2	3.3	145
40	0	3	6	1.0	3	6	8	2.1	4	6	8	3.2	5	6	7	140
45	0	4	7	0	4	7	2.0	3	6	9	3.1	5	8	4.0	4.1	135
50	0.0	0.4	0.8	1.1	1.5	1.9	2.2	2.5	2.8	3.1	3.4	3.8	4.1	4.3	4.4	130
60	0	4	9	3	7	2.1	5	8	3.2	5	8	4.3	7	9	5.0	120
70	0	5	9	4	8	3	7	3.1	5	8	4.1	7	5.1	5.3	4	110
80	0	5	1.0	5	9	4	8	2	6	4.0	3	9	3	6	6	100
90	0	5	0	5	2.0	4	9	3	7	1	4	5.0	4	6	7	90
Az.	90°	95°	100°	105°	110°	115°	120°	125°	130°	135°	140°	150°	160°	170°	180°	Az.
	Position-Angle.															

Hour-Angle $0^h\ 20^m$ or $11^h\ 40^m$.

Az.	Position-Angle.															Az.
	90°	85°	80°	75°	70°	65°	60°	55°	50°	45°	40°	30°	20°	10°	0°	
0°	0.0°	0.0°	0.0°	0.0°	0.0°	0.0°	0.0°	0.0°	0.0°	0.0°	0.0°	0.0°	0.0°	0.0°	0.0°	180°
5	0	0	0	1	1	1	1	1	2	2	2	2	2	2	3	175
10	0	0	1	1	2	2	2	3	3	4	4	4	5	5	5	170
15	0	1	1	2	3	3	4	4	5	5	6	6	7	7	7	165
20	0	1	2	3	3	4	5	6	6	7	8	9	9	1.0	1.0	160
25	0.0	0.1	0.2	0.3	0.4	0.5	0.6	0.7	0.8	0.9	0.9	1.1	1.1	1.2	1.2	155
30	0	1	2	4	5	6	7	8	9	1.0	1.1	2	3	4	4	150
35	0	1	3	4	6	7	8	9	1.1	2	3	4	5	6	6	145
40	0	2	3	5	6	8	9	1.1	2	3	4	6	7	8	8	140
45	0	2	4	5	7	9	1.0	2	3	4	6	8	9	2.0	2.0	135
50	0.0	0.2	0.4	0.6	0.8	0.9	1.1	1.3	1.4	1.6	1.7	1.9	2.1	2.2	2.2	130
60	0	2	4	6	9	1.1	2	4	6	8	9	2.2	3	4	5	120
70	0	2	5	7	9	1	3	5	7	9	2.1	3	5	7	7	110
80	0	2	5	7	1.0	2	4	6	8	2.0	2	4	7	8	8	100
90	0	3	5	7	0	2	4	6	8	0	2	5	7	8	9	90
Az.	90°	95°	100°	105°	110°	115°	120°	125°	130°	135°	140°	150°	160°	170°	180°	Az.
	Position-Angle.															

Hour-Angle $0^h\ 30^m$ or $11^h\ 30^m$.

Az.	Position-Angle.															Az.
	90°	85°	80°	75°	70°	65°	60°	55°	50°	45°	40°	30°	20°	10°	0°	
0°	0.0°	0.0°	0.0°	0.0°	0.0°	0.0°	0.0°	0.0°	0.0°	0.0°	0.0°	0.0°	0.0°	0.0°	0.0°	180°
5	0	0	0	0	1	1	1	1	1	1	1	1	2	2	2	175
10	0	0	1	1	1	1	2	2	2	2	3	3	3	3	3	170
15	0	0	1	1	2	2	2	3	3	3	4	4	5	5	5	165
20	0	1	1	2	2	3	3	4	4	5	5	6	6	6	7	160
25	0.0	0.1	0.1	0.2	0.3	0.3	0.4	0.5	0.5	0.6	0.6	0.7	0.8	0.8	0.8	155
30	0	1	2	2	3	4	5	5	6	7	7	8	9	9	1.0	150
35	0	1	2	3	4	5	5	6	7	8	8	9	1.0	1.1	1	145
40	0	1	2	3	4	5	6	7	8	9	9	1.0	2	2	2	140
45	0	1	2	3	5	6	7	8	9	1.0	1.0	2	3	3	4	135
50	0.0	0.1	0.3	0.4	0.5	0.6	0.7	0.8	0.9	1.0	1.1	1.3	1.4	1.4	1.5	130
60	0	1	3	4	6	7	8	9	1.0	2	3	4	6	6	7	120
70	0	2	3	5	6	8	9	1.0	2	3	4	6	7	8	8	110
80	0	2	3	5	6	8	9	1	2	3	4	6	8	9	9	100
90	0	2	3	5	7	8	1.0	1	2	4	5	7	8	9	9	90
Az.	90°	95°	100°	105°	110°	115°	120°	125°	130°	135°	140°	150°	160°	170°	180°	Az.
	Position-Angle.															

Error of Time-Azimuth for an Error of 12′, or 0°.2, in Latitude.

Az.	Altitude. 0°	10°	20°	30°	40°	50°	60°	70°	75°	80°	82°	84°	86°	88°	90°	Az.
0°	0′	0′	0′	0′	0′	0′	0′	0′	0.0	0.0	0.0	0.0	0.0	0.0	Indet.	180°
2	0	0	0	0	0	1	1	1	0	0	1	1	1	2	∞	178
4	0	0	0	1	1	1	1	2	1	1	1	1	2	4	∞	176
6	0	0	1	1	1	2	2	3	1	1	2	2	3	6	∞	174
8	0	0	1	1	1	2	3	5	1	2	2	3	4	8	∞	172
10	0	0	1	1	2	3	4	6	0.1	0.2	0.3	0.3	0.5	1.0	∞	170
12	0	0	1	1	2	3	4	7	2	2	3	4	6	2	∞	168
14	0	1	1	2	2	4	5	8	2	3	3	5	7	4	∞	166
16	0	1	1	2	3	4	6	9	2	3	4	5	8	6	∞	164
18	0	1	1	2	3	4	6	10	2	3	4	6	9	8	∞	162
20	0	1	2	2	3	5	7	11	0.3	0.4	0.5	0.7	1.0	2.0	∞	160
25	0	1	2	3	4	6	8	14	3	5	6	8	2	4	∞	155
30	0	1	2	3	5	7	10	16	4	6	7	1.0	4	9	∞	150
35	0	1	3	4	6	8	12	19	4	6	8	1	6	3.3	∞	145
40	0	1	3	5	7	9	13	21	5	7	9	2	8	7	∞	140
45	0	2	3	5	7	10	15	23	0.5	0.8	1.0	1.4	2.0	4.1	∞	135
50	0	2	3	5	8	11	16	25	6	9	1	5	2	4	∞	130
55	0	2	4	6	8	12	17	27	6	9	2	6	3	7	∞	125
60	0	2	4	6	9	12	18	29	6	1.0	2	7	5	5.0	∞	120
65	0	2	4	6	9	13	19	30	7	0	3	7	6	2	∞	115
70	0	2	4	7	10	13	19	31	0.7	1.1	1.3	1.8	2.7	5.4	∞	110
75	0	2	4	7	10	14	20	32	7	1	4	8	8	5	∞	105
80	0	2	4	7	10	14	20	32	7	1	4	9	8	6	∞	100
85	0	2	4	7	10	14	21	33	7	1	4	9	8	7	∞	95
90	0	2	4	7	10	14	21	33	7	1	4	9	9	7	∞	90

TABLE XXXVI.

Error of Time-Azimuth for an Error of 6′, or 0°.1, in Declination.

Pos. Ang.	Altitude. 0°	10°	20°	30°	40°	50°	60°	70°	75°	80°	82°	84°	86°	88°	90°	Pos. Ang.
0°	0′	0′	0′	0′	0′	0′	0′	0′	0.0	0.0	0.0	0.0	0.0	0.0	Indet.	180°
2	0	0	0	0	0	0	0	1	0	0	0	0	1	1	∞	178
4	0	0	0	1	1	1	1	1	0	0	1	1	1	2	∞	176
6	1	1	1	1	1	1	1	2	0	1	1	1	2	3	∞	174
8	1	1	1	1	1	1	2	2	1	1	1	1	2	4	∞	172
10	1	1	1	1	1	2	2	3	0.1	0.1	0.1	0.2	0.3	0.5	∞	170
12	1	1	1	1	2	2	3	4	1	1	2	2	3	6	∞	168
14	1	2	2	2	2	2	3	4	1	1	2	2	3	7	∞	166
16	2	2	2	2	2	3	3	5	1	2	2	3	4	8	∞	164
18	2	2	2	2	2	3	4	5	1	2	2	3	4	9	∞	162
20	2	2	2	2	3	3	4	6	0.1	0.2	0.2	0.3	0.5	1.0	∞	160
25	2	3	3	3	3	4	5	7	2	2	3	4	6	2	∞	155
30	3	3	3	4	4	5	6	9	2	3	4	5	7	4	∞	150
35	3	4	4	4	5	5	7	10	2	3	4	5	8	6	∞	145
40	4	4	4	5	5	6	8	11	2	4	5	6	9	8	∞	140
45	4	4	5	5	6	7	9	12	0.3	0.4	0.5	0.7	1.0	2.0	∞	135
50	5	5	5	5	6	7	9	13	3	4	5	7	1	2	∞	130
55	5	5	5	6	6	8	10	14	3	5	6	8	2	4	∞	125
60	5	5	6	6	7	8	10	15	3	5	6	8	2	5	∞	120
65	5	6	6	6	7	9	11	16	3	5	7	9	3	6	∞	115
70	6	6	6	7	7	9	11	17	0.4	0.5	0.7	0.9	1.3	2.7	∞	110
75	6	6	6	7	8	9	12	17	4	6	7	9	4	8	∞	105
80	6	6	6	7	8	9	12	17	4	6	7	9	4	8	∞	100
85	6	6	6	7	8	9	12	18	4	6	7	1.0	4	9	∞	95
90	6	6	6	7	8	9	12	18	4	6	7	0	4	9	∞	90

Limiting Errors of Time-Azimuths.

Hour-Angle.	First Supposition.				Second Supposition.				Third Supposition.			
	Partial Az. Error.			Prob. Total Az. Error.	Partial Az. Error.			Prob. Total Az. Error.	Partial Az. Error.			Prob. Total Az. Error.
	H. A. Error ± 1m.	Lat. Error ± 12′.	Dec. Error ± 3′.		H. A. Error ± 2m.	Lat. Error ± 18′.	Dec. Error ± 3′.		H. A. Error ± 3m.	Lat. Error ± 30′.	Dec. Error ± 3′.	
h m	°	°	°	°	°	°	°	°	°	°	°	°
1 0	±0.6	±0.8	±0.2	±1.0	±0.9	±1.1	±0.2	±1.4	±1.9	±1.9	±0.2	±1.9
2 0	0.4	0.5	0.2	0.7	0.7	0.8	0.2	1.1	1.1	1.3	0.2	1.7
3 0	0.3	0.4	0.1	0.6	0.5	0.5	0.1	0.8	0.9	0.9	0.1	1.3
4 0	0.3	0.3	0.1	0.5	0.5	0.4	0.1	0.7	0.8	0.6	0.1	1.0
5 0	0.3	0.2	0.1	0.4	0.5	0.3	0.1	0.6	0.7	0.4	0.1	0.8
6 0	0.3	0.1	0.1	0.4	0.5	0.2	0.1	0.6	0.7	0.3	0.1	0.8
7 0	0.3	0.1	0.0	0.4	0.5	0.1	0.0	0.6	0.7	0.2	0.0	0.8
8 0	0.3	0.1	0.0	0.3	0.5	0.1	0.0	0.6	0.7	0.2	0.0	0.8
9 0	0.3	0.0	0.0	0.3	0.5	0.1	0.0	0.5	0.7	0.1	0.0	0.7
10 0	0.3	0.0	0.0	0.3	0.5	0.0	0.0	0.5	0.7	0.1	0.0	0.7
11 0	0.3	0.0	0.0	0.3	0.5	0.0	0.0	0.5	0.7	0.0	0.0	0.7
12 0	0.3	0.0	0.0	0.3	0.5	0.0	0.0	0.5	0.7	0.0	0.0	0.7

TABLE XXXVIII.

Limiting Errors of Time-Azimuths in High Latitudes.

Hour-Angle.	First Supposition.				Second Supposition.				Third Supposition.			
	Partial Az. Error.			Prob. Total Az. Error.	Partial Az. Error.			Prob. Total Az. Error.	Partial Az. Error.			Prob. Total Az. Error.
	± 1m.	± 12′.	± 3′.		± 2m.	± 18′.	± 3′.		± 3m.	± 30′.	± 6′.	
h m	°	°	°	°	°	°	°	°	°	°	°	°
0 0	±0.4	0.0	0.0	±0.4	±0.7	0.0	0.0	±0.7	±1.1	0.0	0.0	±1.1
0 10	0.4	0.0	0.0	0.4	0.7	0.0	0.0	0.7	1.1	±0.1	0.0	1.1
0 30	0.4	0.0	0.0	0.4	0.7	±0.1	0.0	0.7	1.1	0.2	0.0	1.1
1 0	0.4	±0.1	0.0	0.4	0.7	0.2	0.0	0.8	1.1	0.3	±0.1	1.2
2 0	0.3	0.2	0.0	0.4	0.6	0.2	0.0	0.7	0.9	0.4	0.1	1.0
3 0	0.3	0.2	0.0	0.4	0.5	0.2	0.0	0.6	0.8	0.4	0.1	0.9
4 0	0.3	0.2	0.0	0.4	0.5	0.2	0.0	0.6	0.8	0.4	0.1	0.9
5 0	0.3	0.1	0.0	0.4	0.5	0.2	0.0	0.6	0.8	0.3	0.1	0.9
6 0	0.3	0.1	0.0	0.4	0.5	0.2	0.0	0.6	0.8	0.3	0.1	0.8
7 0	0.3	0.1	0.0	0.3	0.5	0.1	0.0	0.5	0.7	0.2	0.1	0.8
8 0	0.3	0.1	0.0	0.3	0.5	0.1	0.0	0.5	0.7	0.2	0.1	0.8
9 0	0.3	0.0	0.0	0.3	0.5	0.1	0.0	0.5	0.7	0.1	0.1	0.7
10 0	0.3	0.0	0.0	0.3	0.5	0.0	0.0	0.5	0.7	0.0	0.0	0.7
11 0	0.3	0.0	0.0	0.3	0.5	0.0	0.0	0.5	0.7	0.0	0.0	0.7
12 0	0.3	0.0	0.0	0.3	0.5	0.0	0.0	0.5	0.7	0.0	0.0	0.7

TABLE XXXIX.

Limiting Errors of Serial Time-Azimuths.

Hour-Angle.	Observations in Port.				At Sea: In all Latitudes.				At Sea: In all Latitudes.			
	Partial Az. Error.			Prob. Total Az. Error.	Partial Az. Error.			Prob. Total Az. Error.	Partial Az. Error.			Prob. Total Az. Error.
	H. A. Error ± 4s.	Lat. Error ± 1′.	Dec. Error ± 0′.5.		H. A. Error ± 10s.	Lat. Error ± 3′.	Dec. Error ± 1′.		H. A. Error ± 30s.	Lat. Error ± 6′.	Dec. Error ± 1′.	
h m	′	′	′	′	′	′	′	′	′	′	′	′
6 0	±0.9	±0.4	±0.5	±1.1	±2.2	±1.2	±1.1	±2.7	±6.5	±2.5	±1.1	±7.1
5 0	0.9	0.6	0.5	1.2	2.2	1.7	1.1	2.8	6.7	3.4	1.1	7.6
4 0	1.0	0.8	0.6	1.4	2.6	2.3	1.2	3.7	7.8	4.6	1.2	9.1
3 0	1.3	1.2	0.8	1.9	3.3	3.6	1.6	5.1	10.0	7.2	1.6	12.4
2 30	1.6	1.6	1.0	2.4	4.0	4.9	1.9	6.6	12.1	9.7	1.9	15.6

Circumpolar Azimuths: Polaris, or the Pole-Star.

Lat.	Western Elongations. Greatest Elongation West. Sid. T.	Az.	Star moving from Meridian. Sid. Time of Azimuths. 6 13	5 13	4 13	3 13	2 13	Sid. T. on Mer'n above the Pole. 1 13	Eastern Elongations. Star moving towards Meridian. Sid. Time of Azimuths. 0 13	23 13	22 13	21 13	20 13	Greatest Elongation East. Az.	Sid. T.	Lat.
°	h m	°	h m	h m	h m	h m	h m	h m	h m	h m	h m	h m	h m	°	h m	°
0	7 13.0	1.4	1.3	1.2	1.0	0.7	0.3	0.0	0.3	0.7	1.0	1.2	1.3	1.4	19 13.0	0
2	12.8	4	3	2	0	7	3	0	3	7	0	2	3	4	13.2	2
4	12.6	4	3	2	0	7	3	0	3	7	0	2	3	4	13.4	4
6	12.4	4	3	2	0	7	4	0	4	7	0	2	3	4	13.6	6
8	12.2	4	3	2	0	7	4	0	4	7	0	2	3	4	13.8	8
10	7 12.0	1.4	1.3	1.2	1.0	0.7	0.4	0.0	0.4	0.7	1.0	1.2	1.3	1.4	19 14.0	10
12	11.8	4	3	2	0	7	4	0	4	7	0	2	3	4	14.2	12
14	11.6	4	4	2	0	7	4	0	4	7	0	2	4	4	14.4	14
16	11.4	4	4	3	0	7	4	0	4	7	0	3	4	4	14.6	16
18	11.2	4	4	3	0	7	4	0	4	7	0	3	4	4	14.8	18
20	7 11.0	1.5	1.4	1.3	1.0	0.7	0.4	0.0	0.4	0.7	1.0	1.3	1.4	1.5	19 15.0	20
21	10.9	5	4	3	0	7	4	0	4	7	0	3	4	5	15.1	21
22	10.8	5	4	3	0	7	4	0	4	7	0	3	4	5	15.2	22
23	10.7	5	4	3	0	7	4	0	4	7	0	3	4	5	15.3	23
24	10.6	5	4	3	1	7	4	0	4	7	1	3	4	5	15.4	24
25	7 10.5	1.5	1.4	1.3	1.1	0.8	0.4	0.0	0.4	0.8	1.1	1.3	1.4	1.5	19 15.5	25
26	10.4	5	5	3	1	8	4	0	4	8	1	3	5	5	15.6	26
27	10.2	5	5	3	1	8	4	0	4	8	1	3	5	5	15.8	27
28	10.1	5	5	3	1	8	4	0	4	8	1	3	5	5	15.9	28
29	10.0	6	5	4	1	8	4	0	4	8	1	4	5	6	16.0	29
30	7 9.9	1.6	1.5	1.4	1.1	0.8	0.4	0.0	0.4	0.8	1.1	1.4	1.5	1.6	19 16.1	30
31	9.7	6	5	4	1	8	4	0	4	8	1	4	5	6	16.3	31
32	9.6	6	6	4	1	8	4	0	4	8	1	4	6	6	16.4	32
33	9.5	6	6	4	2	8	4	0	4	8	2	4	6	6	16.5	33
34	9.3	6	6	4	2	8	4	0	4	8	2	4	6	6	16.7	34
35	7 9.2	1.7	1.6	1.4	1.2	0.8	0.4	0.0	0.4	0.8	1.2	1.4	1.6	1.7	19 16.8	35
36	9.1	7	6	5	2	8	4	0	4	8	2	5	6	7	16.9	36
37	8.9	7	6	5	2	8	4	0	4	8	2	5	6	7	17.1	37
38	8.8	7	7	5	2	9	4	0	4	9	2	5	7	7	17.2	38
39	8.6	8	7	5	2	9	5	0	5	9	2	5	7	8	17.4	39
40	7 8.4	1.8	1.7	1.5	1.3	0.9	0.5	0.0	0.5	0.9	1.3	1.5	1.7	1.8	19 17.6	40
41	8.3	8	7	6	3	9	5	0	5	9	3	6	7	8	17.7	41
42	8.1	8	8	6	3	9	5	0	5	9	3	6	8	8	17.9	42
43	7.9	9	8	6	3	9	5	0	5	9	3	6	8	9	18.1	43
44	7.8	9	8	6	3	1.0	5	0	5	1.0	3	6	8	9	18.2	44
45	7 7.6	1.9	1.9	1.7	1.4	1.0	0.5	0.0	0.5	1.0	1.4	1.7	1.9	1.9	19 18.4	45
46	7.4	9	9	7	4	0	5	0	5	0	4	7	9	9	18.6	46
47	7.2	2.0	9	7	4	0	5	0	5	0	4	7	9	2.0	18.8	47
48	7.0	0	2.0	8	4	0	5	0	5	0	4	8	2.0	0	19.0	48
49	6.8	1	0	8	5	0	5	0	5	0	5	8	0	1	19.2	49
50	7 6.5	2.1	2.0	1.8	1.5	1.1	0.5	0.0	0.5	1.1	1.5	1.8	2.0	2.1	19 19.5	50
51	6.3	2	1	9	5	1	6	0	6	1	5	9	1	2	19.7	51
52	6.0	2	1	9	6	1	6	0	6	1	6	9	1	2	20.0	52
53	5.8	3	2	2.0	6	1	6	0	6	1	6	2.0	2	3	20.2	53
54	5.5	3	2	0	6	2	6	0	6	2	6	0	2	3	20.5	54
55	7 5.2	2.4	2.3	2.1	1.7	1.2	0.6	0.0	0.6	1.2	1.7	2.1	2.3	2.4	19 20.8	55
56	4.9	4	4	1	7	2	6	0	6	2	7	1	4	4	21.1	56
57	4.6	5	4	2	8	3	6	0	6	3	8	2	4	5	21.4	57
58	4.3	6	5	2	8	3	7	0	7	3	8	2	5	6	21.7	58
59	4.0	6	6	3	9	3	7	0	7	3	9	3	6	6	22.0	59
60	7 3.6	2.7	2.6	2.4	2.0	1.4	0.7	0.0	0.7	1.4	2.0	2.4	2.6	2.7	19 22.4	60
	Sid. T.	Az.	h m 8 13	h m 9 13	h m 10 13	h m 11 13	h m 12 13	h m 13 13	h m 14 13	h m 15 13	h m 16 13	h m 17 13	h m 18 13	Az.	Sid. T.	
Lat.	Greatest Elongation West.		Sid. Time of Azimuths. Star moving towards Meridian.					Sid. T. on Mer'n below the Pole.	Sid. Time of Azimuths. Star moving from Meridian.					Greatest Elongation East.		Lat.

Subtract R. A. True Sun (Tab. LIX) from Sid. T. to get Ship A. T., or subtract R. A. Mean Sun (by applying E. T. to R. A. True Sun) to get Ship M. T.

Altitude-Azimuths: Part I.

Alt.	Latitude. 0°	2°	4°	6°	8°	10°	12°	14°	16°	18°	20°	22°	24°	26°	28°	30°	Alt.
0°	0	0	0	1	2	3	5	6	8	11	13	16	20	23	27	31	0°
2	0	0	0	1	2	3	5	6	8	11	13	16	20	23	27	31	2
4	0	0	1	2	3	4	5	7	9	11	14	17	20	24	28	32	4
6	1	1	2	2	3	4	6	8	10	12	15	18	21	24	28	32	6
8	2	2	3	3	4	5	7	9	11	13	16	19	22	25	29	33	8
10	3	3	4	4	5	6	8	10	12	14	17	20	23	26	30	34	10
12	5	5	5	6	7	8	10	11	13	16	18	21	24	28	32	36	12
14	6	6	7	8	9	10	11	13	15	17	20	23	26	30	34	38	14
16	8	8	9	10	11	12	13	15	17	19	22	25	28	32	36	40	16
18	11	11	11	12	13	14	16	17	19	22	24	27	30	34	38	42	18
20	13	13	14	15	16	17	18	20	22	24	27	30	33	37	41	45	20
22	16	16	17	18	19	20	21	23	25	27	30	33	36	39	43	48	22
24	20	20	20	21	22	23	24	26	28	30	33	36	39	43	47	51	24
26	23	23	23	24	25	26	28	30	32	34	37	40	43	46	50	54	26
28	27	27	27	28	29	30	32	33	35	38	41	44	47	50	54	58	28
30	31	31	31	32	33	34	36	38	40	42	45	48	51	54	58	62	30
32	36	36	36	37	38	39	41	42	44	47	49	52	55	59	63	67	32
34	41	41	41	42	43	44	46	47	49	52	54	57	60	64	68	72	34
36	46	46	46	47	48	49	51	52	54	57	59	62	66	69	73	77	36
38	52	52	52	53	54	55	57	58	60	63	65	68	71	75	79	83	38
40	58	58	58	59	60	61	63	64	66	69	71	74	77	81	85	89	40
42	64	64	65	66	67	68	69	71	73	75	78	81	84	88	92	96	42
44	71	71	72	73	74	75	76	78	80	82	85	88	91	95	99	103	44
46	79	79	80	80	81	82	84	86	88	90	93	96	99	102	106	110	46
48	87	87	88	88	89	90	92	94	96	98	101	104	106	110	114	118	48
50	96	96	96	97	98	99	101	102	104	107	109	112	115	119	123	127	50
52	105	105	106	106	107	109	110	112	114	116	119	122	125	128	132	136	52
54	115	115	116	116	117	119	120	122	124	126	129	132	135	138	142	146	54
56	126	126	127	127	128	129	131	133	135	137	140	143	146	149	153	157	56
58	138	138	138	139	140	141	143	144	146	149	151	154	157	161	165	169	58
60	150	150	151	152	153	154	155	157	159	161	164	167	170	174	178	182	60
62	164	164	164	165	166	167	169	171	173	175	178	181	184	187	191	195	62
64	179	179	179	180	181	182	184	185	187	190	192	195	199	202	206	210	64
66	195	195	196	196	197	199	200	202	204	206	209	212	215	218	222	226	66
68	213	213	214	214	215	217	218	220	222	224	227	230	233	236	240	244	68
70	233	233	233	234	235	236	238	239	241	244	246	249	253	256	260	264	70
72	255	255	255	256	257	258	260	261	263	266	268	271	275	278	282	286	72
74	280	280	280	281	282	283	285	286	288	291	293	296	299	303	307	311	74
76	308	308	309	309	310	311	313	315	317	319	322	324	328	331	335	339	76
78	341	341	341	342	343	344	346	347	349	352	354	357	361	364	368	372	78
80	380	380	381	382	383	384	385	387	389	391	394	397	400	404	408	411	80
82	428	428	429	429	430	431	433	435	437	439	442	445	448	451	455	459	82
84	490	491	491	491	492	494	495	497	499	501	504	507	510	513	517	521	84
86	578	578	579	579	580	581	583	585	587	589	592	595	598	601	605	609	86
88	729	729	729	730	731	732	733	735	737	739	742	745	748	752	756	759	88

Entering Part I with the Lat. and Alt., and Part II with the Dec. and Diff. of the Lat. and Alt., take out the corresponding numbers. Then, with the Sum of these two numbers, the corresponding Azimuth is found in Part III.

Altitude-Azimuths: Part I.

Alt.	Latitude. 30°	32°	34°	36°	38°	40°	42°	44°	46°	48°	50°	52°	54°	56°	58°	60°	Alt.
0°	31	36	41	46	52	58	64	71	79	87	96	105	115	126	138	150	0°
2	31	36	41	46	52	58	64	71	79	87	96	105	115	126	138	151	2
4	32	36	41	46	52	58	65	72	80	88	96	106	116	127	139	151	4
6	32	37	42	47	53	59	66	73	80	88	97	106	116	127	139	152	6
8	33	38	43	48	54	60	67	74	81	89	98	107	117	128	140	153	8
10	34	39	44	49	55	61	68	75	82	90	99	109	119	129	141	154	10
12	36	41	46	51	57	63	69	76	84	92	101	110	120	131	143	155	12
14	38	42	47	52	58	64	71	78	86	94	102	112	122	133	144	157	14
16	40	44	49	54	60	66	73	80	88	96	104	114	124	135	146	159	16
18	42	47	52	57	63	69	75	82	90	98	107	116	126	137	149	161	18
20	45	49	54	59	65	71	78	85	93	101	109	119	129	140	151	164	20
22	48	52	57	62	68	74	81	88	96	104	112	122	132	143	154	167	22
24	51	55	60	66	71	77	84	91	99	107	115	125	135	146	158	170	24
26	54	59	64	69	75	81	88	95	102	110	119	128	138	149	161	174	26
28	58	63	68	73	79	85	92	99	106	114	123	132	142	153	165	178	28
30	62	67	72	77	83	89	96	103	110	118	127	136	147	157	169	182	30
32	67	72	77	82	88	94	100	107	115	123	132	141	151	162	174	186	32
34	72	76	81	87	92	98	105	112	120	128	137	146	156	167	179	191	34
36	77	82	87	92	98	104	110	117	125	133	142	151	161	172	184	196	36
38	83	88	93	98	104	110	116	123	131	139	148	157	167	178	190	202	38
40	89	94	99	104	110	116	122	129	137	145	154	163	173	184	196	208	40
42	96	100	105	110	116	122	129	136	144	152	161	170	180	191	202	215	42
44	103	107	112	117	123	129	136	143	151	159	168	177	187	198	209	222	44
46	110	115	120	125	131	137	143	151	158	166	176	184	194	205	217	230	46
48	118	123	128	133	139	145	152	159	166	174	184	192	202	213	225	238	48
50	127	132	137	142	148	154	161	168	175	183	192	201	211	222	234	246	50
52	136	141	146	151	157	163	170	177	184	192	201	211	221	231	243	255	52
54	146	151	156	161	167	173	180	187	194	202	211	221	231	241	253	266	54
56	157	162	167	172	178	184	191	198	205	213	222	231	242	252	264	277	56
58	169	174	179	184	190	196	202	209	217	225	233	243	253	264	275	288	58
60	182	186	191	196	202	208	215	222	230	238	246	256	266	277	288	301	60
62	195	200	205	210	216	222	229	236	243	251	260	269	280	291	302	315	62
64	210	215	220	225	231	237	244	251	258	266	275	284	295	306	317	330	64
66	226	231	236	241	247	253	260	267	274	283	291	301	311	323	334	—	66
68	244	249	254	259	265	271	277	285	292	300	309	319	329	341			68
70	264	269	274	279	285	291	297	305	312	320	329	338	349				70
72	286	291	296	301	307	313	319	327	334	342	351	360					72
74	311	316	321	326	332	338	344	352	359	367	376						74
76	339	344	349	354	360	366	372	380	387	395							76
78	372	377	382	387	393	399	405	413	420								78
80	411	416	421	426	432	438	445	452									80
82	459	464	469	474	480	486	493										82
84	521	526	531	536	542	548											84
86	609	614	619	624	630												86
88	759	764	769	774													88

Mark the Azimuth N or S according to the Latitude, and E or W according as the object observed is East or West of the Meridian.

When the Lat. exceeds 60° use Alt. for Lat. and Lat. for Alt.

Altitude-Azimuths: Part II.

Diff. Alt. and Lat.	Declination of same name as the Latitude.																Diff. Alt. and Lat.
	0°	2°	4°	6°	8°	10°	12°	14°	16°	18°	20°	22°	24°	26°	28°	30°	
0°	849	842	834	825	817	808	799	789	779	769	759	748	736	724	712	699	0°
2	849	842	834	825	817	808	799	789	779	769	758	748	736	724	712	699	2
4	849	841	833	825	816	807	798	789	779	768	758	747	735	723	711	698	4
6	848	840	832	824	815	806	797	788	778	767	757	746	734	722	710	697	6
8	847	839	831	823	814	805	796	786	776	766	755	744	732	720	708	695	8
10	846	838	830	822	813	804	796	785	775	764	753	742	730	718	705	692	10
12	845	837	829	820	811	802	793	783	773	762	751	740	728	715	702	689	12
14	843	835	827	818	809	800	791	781	770	760	748	737	725	712	699	685	14
16	841	833	824	816	807	798	788	778	767	757	745	734	721	708	695	681	16
18	838	830	822	813	804	795	785	775	764	753	742	730	717	704	691	677	18
20	836	828	819	810	801	792	782	771	760	749	738	726	713	699	686	672	20
22	833	825	816	807	798	788	778	767	756	745	733	721	708	694	680	665	22
24	830	821	812	803	794	784	774	763	752	740	728	715	702	688	673	658	24
26	826	818	808	799	790	780	769	758	747	735	722	709	695	681	666	650	26
28	822	814	804	795	785	775	764	753	741	729	716	702	688	673	658	641	28
30	818	809	800	790	780	769	758	747	735	723	709	695	680	665	649	631	30
32	814	804	795	785	775	764	752	741	729	716	702	687	672	656	639	620	32
34	809	799	790	779	769	758	746	734	721	708	693	678	662	645	627	608	34
36	803	794	784	773	762	751	739	726	713	699	684	668	651	634	615	595	36
38	797	788	778	767	755	744	731	718	704	689	674	657	640	621	601	579	38
40	791	781	771	760	748	736	723	709	695	679	663	646	627	607	585	562	40
42	785	774	764	753	740	727	714	699	684	668	651	633	613	591	568	542	42
44	778	767	756	744	731	718	704	689	673	656	638	618	597	574	548	520	44
46	770	759	747	735	722	708	693	677	660	642	623	602	579	554	526	494	46
48	762	750	738	725	711	697	681	665	646	628	607	584	558	532	500	464	48
50	753	741	729	715	700	685	669	651	632	611	588	563	535	505	469	427	50
52	744	732	718	704	688	672	655	636	615	593	568	540	509	474	432	381	52
54	734	721	707	691	675	658	639	619	597	572	545	514	478	437	386	321	54
56	723	709	694	678	661	642	622	600	576	548	518	482	441	390	326	236	56
58	711	696	681	664	645	625	603	579	552	521	486	445	395	330	240	87	58
60	698	683	666	648	628	606	582	555	525	489	449	399	334	244	92		60
62	685	668	650	631	609	585	558	528	493	452	402	338	248	96			62
64	670	652	633	611	587	561	531	496	455	405	341	252	99				64
66	654	635	613	589	563	533	499	458	408	344	255	103					66
68	636	615	591	565	535	501	460	411	347	258	106						68
70	616	593	567	537	503	462	413	350	260	109							70
72	594	568	539	505	464	415	352	263	111								72
74	569	540	506	466	417	354	265	113									74
76	541	507	467	418	355	267	115										76
78	508	468	419	357	268	117											78
80	469	420	358	269	118												80
82	421	358	270	119													82
84	359	271	120														84
86	271	121															86
88	121																88

Altitude-Azimuths: Part III.

Sum.	Az.	Sum.	Az.	Sum.	Az.	Sum.	Az.	Sum.	Az.	Sum.	Az.	Sum.	Az.	Sum.	Az.	Sum.	Az.
		240	20°	413	30°	534	40°	626	50°	699	60°	759	70°	808	80°	850	90°
		261	21	427	31	544	41	634	51	705	61	764	71	813	81	851	91
19	12°	281	22	440	32	554	42	642	52	712	62	769	72	817	82	857	92
54	13	300	23	453	33	564	43	650	53	718	63	774	73	821	83	861	93
86	14	318	24	466	34	574	44	657	54	724	64	779	74	826	84	864	94
116	15	335	25	478	35	583	45	664	55	730	65	784	75	830	85	868	95
141	16	352	26	490	36	592	46	672	56	736	66	789	76	834	86	871	96
170	17	368	27	501	37	601	47	679	57	742	67	794	77	838	87	874	97
194	18	384	28	512	38	609	48	686	58	748	68	799	78	842	88	878	98
218	19	399	29	523	39	618	49	692	59	753	69	804	79	846	89	881	99

Altitude-Azimuths: Part II.

Diff. Alt. and Lat.	Declination of contrary name to the Latitude.																Diff. Alt. and Lat.
	0°	2°	4°	6°	8°	10°	12°	14°	16°	18°	20°	22°	24°	26°	28°	30°	
0°	849	857	864	871	878	884	890	896	902	908	913	918	923	928	933	937	0°
2	849	857	864	871	878	884	890	896	902	908	913	918	923	928	933	937	2
4	849	856	864	871	877	884	890	896	902	907	913	918	923	928	933	937	4
6	848	856	863	870	877	883	889	895	901	907	912	918	923	928	933	937	6
8	847	855	862	869	876	882	888	895	901	906	912	917	922	927	932	936	8
10	846	854	861	868	875	881	887	894	900	905	911	916	921	926	931	935	10
12	845	852	859	867	874	880	886	893	899	904	910	915	920	925	930	934	12
14	843	850	858	865	872	879	885	891	897	903	909	914	919	924	929	933	14
16	841	848	856	863	870	877	883	890	896	901	907	912	917	922	927	932	16
18	838	846	854	861	868	875	881	888	894	900	905	911	916	921	926	930	18
20	836	844	851	859	866	873	879	886	892	898	903	909	914	919	924	929	20
22	833	841	849	856	863	870	877	883	889	895	901	907	912	917	922	927	22
24	830	838	846	853	860	867	874	881	887	893	899	904	910	915	920	925	24
26	826	834	842	850	857	864	871	878	884	890	896	901	907	913	917	922	26
28	822	831	839	847	854	861	868	875	881	887	893	899	905	910	915	920	28
30	818	827	835	843	851	858	865	872	878	884	890	896	902	907	912	917	30
32	814	823	831	839	847	854	861	868	875	881	887	893	898	904	909	914	32
34	809	818	826	834	842	850	857	864	871	877	884	890	895	901	906	911	34
36	804	813	821	830	838	846	853	860	867	874	880	886	892	897	903	908	36
38	798	807	816	825	833	841	849	856	863	870	876	882	888	894	899	904	38
40	792	801	810	819	828	836	844	851	858	865	872	878	884	890	895	901	40
42	785	795	804	813	821	830	839	846	853	860	867	874	880	886	891	897	42
44	778	788	798	807	816	825	833	841	848	855	862	869	875	881	887	892	44
46	770	781	791	801	810	819	827	835	843	850	857	864	870	877	882	888	46
48	762	773	784	794	803	812	821	829	837	845	852	859	865	872	878	883	48
50	753	765	776	786	796	805	814	823	831	839	846	853	860	866	873	878	50
52	744	756	767	778	788	797	807	816	824	832	840	847	854	861	867	873	52
54	734	747	758	769	780	790	800	809	818	826	834	841	848	855	862	868	54
56	723	736	749	760	771	782	792	801	810	819	827	835	842	849	856	862	56
58	711	725	738	751	762	773	783	793	802	811	820	828	835	842	850	856	58
60	698	713	727	740	752	764	774	784	794	803	812	820	828	836	843		60
62	685	700	715	729	742	754	765	775	785	795	804	812	821	828			62
64	670	687	702	717	730	743	755	766	776	786	796	804	813				64
66	654	672	688	704	718	731	744	755	766	777	787	796					66
68	636	656	673	690	705	719	732	744	756	767	777						68
70	616	638	657	674	691	705	719	732	745	756							70
72	594	618	639	658	675	691	706	720	733								72
74	569	595	619	639	658	676	692	706									74
76	541	570	596	619	640	659	676										76
78	508	542	571	596	620	640											78
80	469	509	543	571	599												80
82	421	470	509	543													82
84	359	422	470														84
86	271	359															86
88	121																88

Altitude-Azimuths: Part III.

Sum.	Az.	Sum.	Az.	Sum.	Az.	Sum.	Az.	Sum.	Az.	Sum.	Az.	Sum.	Az.	Sum.	Az.
884	100°	913	110°	938	120°	957	130°	973	140°	985	150°	993	160°	998	170°
887	101	916	111	940	121	959	131	974	141	986	151	994	161	999	171
890	102	919	112	942	122	961	132	976	142	987	152	995	162	999	172
894	103	921	113	944	123	962	133	977	143	988	153	995	163	999	173
897	104	924	114	946	124	964	134	978	144	989	154	996	164	999	174
899	105	926	115	948	125	966	135	979	145	990	155	996	165	1000	175
902	106	928	116	950	126	967	136	981	146	990	156	997	166	1000	176
905	107	931	117	952	127	969	137	982	147	991	157	997	167	1000	177
908	108	933	118	954	128	970	138	983	148	992	158	998	168	1000	178
911	109	935	119	955	129	972	139	984	149	993	159	998	169	1000	180

Altitude-Azimuths: Direct and Limiting Values.

Lat.	Altitude. 0°	10°	20°	30°	40°	50°	60°	70°	80°	90°	Lat.
Pol. Dist. 60°, or Declination 30° of same name as the Latitude.											
°	°	°	°	°	°	°	°	°	°		°
0	60.0	59.5	57.9	54.7	49.3	38.9	0.0				0
10	59.5	61.0	61.5	61.0	59.0	54.6	44.8	0.0			10
20	57.9	61.5	64.3	66.2	67.1	66.8	64.3	56.2	0.0		20
30	54.7	61.0	66.2	70.5	74.4	77.9	81.1	84.1	87.1	Indet.	30
40	49.3	59.0	67.1	74.4	81.5	89.1	98.5	113.4	180.0		40
50	38.9	54.6	66.8	77.9	89.1	102.1	120.6	180.0			50
60	0.0	44.8	64.3	81.1	98.5	120.6	180.0				60
70		0.0	56.2	84.1	113.4	180.0					70
80			0.0	87.1	180.0						80
Pol. Dist. 70°, or Declination 20° of same name.											
°	°	°	°	°	°	°	°	°	°		°
0	70.0	69.7	68.6	66.7	63.5	57.9	46.8	0.0			0
10	69.7	71.2	72.2	72.6	72.2	70.7	67.1	57.9	0.0		10
20	68.6	72.2	75.2	77.9	80.2	82.4	84.4	86.3	88.2	Indet.	20
30	66.7	72.6	77.9	82.9	88.2	94.2	102.1	115.6	180.0		30
40	63.5	72.2	80.2	88.2	96.9	107.8	124.1	180.0			40
50	57.9	70.7	82.4	94.2	107.8	126.3	180.0				50
60	46.8	67.1	84.4	102.1	124.1	180.0					60
70	0.0	57.9	86.3	115.6	180.0						70
80		0.0	88.2	180.0							80
Pol. Dist. 80°, or Declination 10° of same name.											
°	°	°	°	°	°	°	°	°	°		°
0	80.0	79.8	79.3	78.4	76.9	74.3	69.7	59.5	0.0		0
10	79.8	81.5	82.9	84.1	85.3	86.3	87.3	88.2	89.1	Indet.	10
20	79.3	82.9	86.3	89.8	93.7	98.4	105.1	117.4	180.0		20
30	78.4	84.1	89.8	95.8	102.9	112.1	126.8	180.0			30
40	76.9	85.3	93.7	102.9	114.1	130.3	180.0				40
50	74.3	86.3	98.4	112.1	130.3	180.0					50
60	69.7	87.3	105.1	126.8	180.0						60
70	59.5	88.2	117.4	180.0							70
80	0.0	89.1	180.0								80
Pol. Dist. 90°, or Declination 0°.											
°	°	°	°	°	°	°	°	°	°		°
0	90.0	90.0	90.0	90.0	90.0	90.0	90.0	90.0	90.0	Indet.	0
10	90.0	90.8	93.7	95.8	98.5	102.1	107.8	119.0	180.0		10
20	90.0	93.7	97.6	102.1	107.8	115.7	129.1	180.0			20
30	90.0	95.8	102.1	109.5	119.0	133.5	180.0				30
40	90.0	98.5	107.8	119.0	134.8	180.0					40
50	90.0	102.1	115.7	133.5	180.0						50
60	90.0	107.8	129.1	180.0							60
70	90.0	119.0	180.0								70
80	90.0	180.0									80
Pol. Dist. 100°, or Declination 10° of contrary name.											
°	°	°	°	°	°	°	°	°	°		°
0	100.0	100.2	100.7	101.6	103.1	105.7	110.3	120.5	180.0		0
10	100.2	102.1	104.6	107.8	112.2	119.0	131.1	180.0			10
20	100.7	104.6	109.2	115.1	123.1	136.2	180.0				20
30	101.6	107.8	115.1	124.4	138.3	180.0					30
40	103.1	112.2	123.1	138.3	180.0						40
50	105.7	119.0	136.2	180.0							50
60	110.3	131.1	180.0								60
70	120.5	180.0									70
80	180.0										80

Position-Angles for Direct and Limiting Altitude-Azimuths.

Lat.	Altitude. 0°	10°	20°	30°	40°	50°	60°	70°	80°	90°	Lat.
Pol. Dist. 60°, or Declination 30° of same name as the Latitude.											
°	°	°	°	°	°	°	°	°	°		°
0	90.0	95.8	102.2	109.5	119.0	133.5	180.0				0
10	78.4	84.6	88.2	96.0	102.9	112.1	126.8	180.0			10
20	66.7	72.5	77.3	83.1	88.2	94.1	102.1	115.6	180.0		20
30	54.7	61.0	66.2	70.5	74.3	77.9	81.1	84.1	87.0	Indet.	30
40	42.1	49.3	54.5	58.4	61.0	62.2	61.0	54.3	0.0		40
50	27.8	37.2	43.0	46.5	47.9	46.5	39.7	0.0			50
60	0.0	24.0	31.3	34.8	34.8	29.8	0.0				60
70		0.0	19.2	23.1	21.2	0.0					70
80			0.0	11.6	0.0						80
Pol. Dist. 70°, or Declination 20° of same name.											
°	°	°	°	°	°	°	°	°	°		°
0	90.0	93.7	97.6	102.1	107.8	115.7	129.1	180.0			0
10	79.4	82.7	86.1	88.8	93.9	98.5	105.2	117.4	180.0		10
20	68.7	72.2	75.2	77.9	80.2	82.4	84.4	86.3	88.3	Indet.	20
30	57.8	61.5	64.3	66.1	67.1	66.8	64.3	56.2	0.0		30
40	46.8	50.9	53.4	54.6	54.0	50.9	42.4	0.0			40
50	35.4	40.2	42.7	43.0	40.6	33.4	0.0				50
60	22.9	29.3	32.0	31.3	26.1	0.0					60
70	0.0	18.0	21.3	19.2	0.0						70
80		0.0	10.6	0.0							80
Pol. Dist. 80°, or Declination 10° of same name.											
°	°	°	°	°	°	°	°	°	°		°
0	90.0	91.7	93.7	95.8	98.5	102.1	107.8	119.0	180.0		0
10	79.9	81.5	82.9	84.1	85.2	86.3	87.3	88.3	89.1	Indet.	10
20	69.7	71.3	72.2	72.6	72.2	70.7	67.1	57.9	0.0		20
30	59.5	61.0	61.6	61.0	59.0	54.6	44.8	0.0			30
40	49.3	50.5	50.9	48.1	45.3	36.3	0.0				40
50	38.9	40.6	40.2	37.2	29.8	0.0					50
60	28.4	30.5	29.3	24.0	0.0						60
70	17.4	20.3	18.0	0.0							70
80	0.0	10.2	0.0								80
Pol. Dist. 90°, or Declination 0°.											
°	°	°	°	°	°	°	°	°	°		°
0	90.0	90.0	90.0	90.0	90.0	90.0	90.0	90.0	90.0	Indet.	0
10	80.0	80.0	79.3	78.4	76.9	74.3	69.7	59.5	0.0		10
20	70.0	69.3	68.7	66.7	63.5	57.9	46.8	0.0			20
30	60.0	59.5	57.8	54.7	49.3	38.9	0.0				30
40	50.0	49.3	46.8	42.1	32.9	0.0					40
50	40.0	38.9	35.4	27.8	0.0						50
60	30.0	28.4	22.8	0.0							60
70	20.0	17.4	0.0								70
80	10.0	0.0									80
Pol. Dist. 100°, or Declination 10° of contrary name.											
°	°	°	°	°	°	°	°	°	°		°
0	90.0	88.3	86.3	84.2	81.5	77.9	72.2	61.0	0.0		0
10	79.9	77.9	75.4	72.3	67.8	61.0	48.9	0.0			10
20	69.7	67.5	64.3	59.8	53.0	41.4	0.0				20
30	59.5	56.9	52.8	46.5	35.8	0.0					30
40	49.3	46.1	40.6	31.2	0.0						40
50	38.9	34.8	26.9	0.0							50
60	28.4	22.5	0.0								60
70	17.4	0.0									70
80	0.0										80

Altitude-Azimuths: Direct and Limiting Values.

Lat.	Altitude. 0°	10°	20°	30°	40°	50°	60°	70°	80°	90°	Lat.
	Pol. Dist. 100°, or Declination 10° of contrary name to Latitude.										
0°	100.0°	100.2°	100.7°	101.6°	103.1°	105.7°	110.3°	120.5°	180.0°		0°
10	100.2	102.1	104.6	107.8	112.2	119.0	131.1	180.0			10
20	100.7	104.6	109.2	115.1	123.1	136.2	180.0				20
30	101.6	107.8	115.1	124.4	138.3	180.0					30
40	103.1	112.2	123.1	138.3	180.0						40
50	105.7	119.0	136.2	180.0							50
60	110.3	131.1	180.0								60
70	120.5	180.0									70
80	180.0										80
	Pol. Dist. 110°, or Declination 20° of contrary name.										
0°	110.0°	110.3°	111.4°	113.3°	116.5°	122.1°	133.2°	180.0°			0°
10	110.3	112.6	115.7	120.2	126.9	138.6	180.0				10
20	111.4	115.7	121.3	129.1	141.3	180.0					20
30	113.3	120.2	129.1	142.1	180.0						30
40	116.5	126.9	141.3	180.0							40
50	122.1	138.6	180.0								50
60	133.2	180.0									60
70	180.0										70
	Pol. Dist. 120°, or Declination 30° of contrary name.										
0°	120.0°	120.5°	122.1°	125.3°	130.7°	141.1°	180.0°				0°
10	120.5	123.1	127.2	133.5	144.2	180.0					10
20	122.1	127.2	134.3	145.5	180.0						20
30	125.3	133.5	145.5	180.0							30
40	130.7	144.2	180.0								40
50	141.1	180.0									50
60	180.0										60

TABLE XLIV.

Error of the Altitude-Azimuth for an Error of 6′, or 0°.1, in the Altitude.

Pos. Ang.	Altitude. 0°	10°	20°	30°	40°	50°	60°	70°	75°	80°	82°	84°	86°	88°	90°	Pos. Ang.
90°	0′	0′	0′	0′	0′	0′	0′	0′	0°.0	0°.0	0°.0	0°.0	0°.0	0°.0	Indet.	90°
85	1	1	1	1	1	1	1	2	0	1	1	1	1	3	∞	95
80	1	1	1	1	1	2	2	3	1	1	1	2	3	5	∞	100
75	2	2	2	2	2	3	3	5	1	2	2	3	4	8	∞	105
70	2	2	2	3	3	3	4	6	1	2	3	3	5	1.0	∞	110
65	3	3	3	3	4	4	6	9	0.2	0.3	0.3	0.5	0.7	1.3	∞	115
60	4	4	4	4	5	5	7	10	2	3	4	6	8	7	∞	120
55	4	4	5	5	6	7	8	12	3	4	5	7	1.0	2.0	∞	125
50	5	5	5	6	7	8	10	15	3	5	6	8	2	4	∞	130
45	6	6	6	7	8	9	12	18	4	6	7	1.0	4	9	∞	135
40	7	7	8	8	9	12	14	21	0.5	0.7	0.9	1.1	1.7	3.4	∞	140
35	9	9	9	10	11	13	17	25	6	8	1.0	4	2.1	4.1	∞	145
30	10	11	11	12	14	16	21	30	7	1.0	2	7	5	5.0	∞	150
25	13	13	14	15	17	20	26	38	8	2	5	2.0	3.1	6.2	∞	155
20	17	17	18	19	22	26	33	48	1.1	6	2.0	6	9	7.9	∞	160
18	19	19	20	21	24	29	37	54	1.2	1.8	2.2	3.0	4.4	8.8		162
16	21	21	22	24	27	33	42	61	3	2.0	5	3	5.0			164
14	24	24	26	28	31	37	48	70	5	3	9	8				166
12	28	29	30	33	37	44	57	83	8	7	3.4					168
10	34	35	36	39	44	53	68	100	2.2	3.3						170
8	43	43	45	49	56	66	85	125	2.7							172
6	57	58	61	66	75	89	114									174
4	86	87	91	99	112	133										176
2	172	175	183	198	225											178
0	∞	∞	∞	∞												180

Position-Angles for Direct and Limiting Altitude-Azimuths.

Lat.	Altitude. 0°	10°	20°	30°	40°	50°	60°	70°	80°	90°	Lat.
	Pol. Dist. 100°, or Declination 10° of contrary name.										
°	°	°	°	°	°	°	°	°	°		°
0	90.0	88.8	86.3	84.2	81.5	77.9	72.3	61.0	0.0		0
10	79.9	77.9	75.4	72.3	67.8	61.0	48.9	0.0			10
20	69.7	67.5	64.3	59.8	53.0	41.4	0.0				20
30	59.5	56.9	52.8	46.5	35.8	0.0					30
40	49.3	46.1	40.6	31.2	0.0						40
50	38.9	34.8	26.9	0.0							50
60	28.4	22.5	0.0								60
70	17.4	0.0									70
80	0.0										80
	Pol. Dist. 110°, or Declination 20° of contrary name.										
°	°	°	°	°	°	°	°	°			°
0	90.0	86.3	82.4	77.9	72.2	64.3	50.9	0.0			0
10	79.4	72.8	70.8	64.9	56.9	43.8	0.0				10
20	68.7	64.3	58.7	50.9	38.7	0.0					20
30	57.8	52.8	45.7	34.5	0.0						30
40	46.8	40.6	30.6	0.0							40
50	35.4	26.9	0.0								50
60	22.9	0.0									60
70	0.0										70
	Pol. Dist. 120°, or Declination 30° of contrary name.										
°	°	°	°	°	°	°	°				°
0	90.0	84.2	77.8	70.5	61.0	46.5	0.0				0
10	78.4	72.2	64.9	55.6	41.7	0.0					10
20	66.7	59.8	50.9	37.9	0.0						20
30	54.7	46.5	34.5	0.0							30
40	42.1	31.2	0.0								40
50	27.8	0.0									50
60	0.0										60

TABLE XLV.

Error of the Altitude-Azimuth for an Error of 12′, or 0°.2, in Latitude.

Hour-Angle.	Latitude. 0°	10°	20°	30°	40°	50°	60°	65°	70°	72°	74°	76°	78°	80°	Hour-Angle.
h m	°	°	°	°	°	°	°	°	°	°	°	°	°	°	h m
6 0	0.0	0.0	0.0	0.0	0.0	0.0	0.0	0.0	0.0	0.0	0.0	0.0	0.0	0.0	6 0
5 40	0	0	0	0	0	0	0	0	0	1	1	1	1	1	20
20	0	0	0	0	1	1	1	1	1	1	1	1	2	2	40
0	1	1	1	1	1	1	1	1	2	2	2	2	3	3	7 0
4 40	1	1	1	1	1	1	1	2	2	2	3	3	3	4	20
4 20	0.1	0.1	0.1	0.1	0.1	0.1	0.2	0.2	0.3	0.3	0.3	0.4	0.5	0.5	7 40
0	1	1	1	1	2	2	2	3	3	4	4	5	6	7	8 0
3 40	1	1	2	2	2	2	3	3	4	5	5	6	7	8	20
20	2	2	2	2	2	3	3	4	5	5	6	7	8	1.0	40
0	2	2	2	2	3	3	4	5	6	6	7	8	1.0	2	9 0
2 40	0.2	0.2	0.3	0.3	0.3	0.4	0.5	0.6	0.7	0.8	0.9	1.0	1.1	1.4	9 20
20	3	3	3	3	4	4	6	7	8	9	1.0	2	4	6	40
0	3	4	4	4	5	5	7	8	1.0	1.1	3	4	7	2.0	10 0
1 40	4	4	4	5	5	7	9	1.0	3	4	6	8	2.1	5	20
20	5	6	6	6	7	9	1.1	3	6	8	2.0	2.3	6	3.2	40
1 12	0.6	0.6	0.7	0.7	0.8	1.0	1.2	1.5	1.8	2.0	2.2	2.5	3.0	3.5	10 48
4	7	7	7	8	9	1	4	7	2.0	3	5	9	4		56
0 56	8	8	9	9	1.0	2	6	2.0	3	6	9	3.3			11 4
48	9	1.0	1.0	1.1	2	4	9	2	7	3.0	3.4				12
40	1.1	2	2	3	5	8	2.3	7	3.3	7					20
0 32	1.4	1.4	1.5	1.6	1.9	2.2	2.8	3.4							11 28
24	1.9	1.9	2.0	2.2	2.5										36
16	2.9	2.9	3.0	3.3											44
8	5.7	5.8													52
0	∞														12 0

Error of Altitude-Azimuth for an Error of 6′, or 0°.1, in Declination.

Hour-Angle.	Latitude. 0°	10°	20°	30°	40°	50°	60°	65°	70°	72°	74°	76°	78°	80°	Hour-Angle.
h m	°	°	°	°	°	°	°	°	°	°	°	°	°	°	h m
6 0	0.1	0.1	0.1	0.1	0.1	0.2	0.2	0.2	0.3	0.3	0.4	0.4	0.5	0.6	6 0
5 40	1	1	1	1	1	2	2	2	3	3	4	4	5	6	20
20	1	1	1	1	1	2	2	2	3	3	4	4	5	6	40
0	1	1	1	1	1	2	2	2	3	3	4	4	5	6	7 0
4 40	1	1	1	1	1	2	2	3	3	3	4	4	5	6	20
4 20	0.1	0.1	0.1	0.1	0.1	0.2	0.2	0.3	0.3	0.4	0.4	0.5	0.5	0.6	7 40
0	1	1	1	1	2	2	2	3	3	4	4	5	6	7	8 0
3 40	1	1	1	1	2	2	2	3	4	4	4	5	6	7	20
20	1	1	1	2	2	2	3	3	4	4	5	5	6	8	40
0	1	1	2	2	2	2	3	3	4	5	5	6	7	8	9 0
2 40	0.2	0.2	0.2	0.2	0.2	0.2	0.3	0.4	0.5	0.5	0.6	0.6	0.7	0.9	9 20
20	2	2	2	2	2	3	3	4	5	6	6	7	8	1.0	40
0	2	2	2	2	3	3	4	5	6	6	7	8	1.0	2	10 0
1 40	2	2	3	3	3	4	5	6	7	8	9	1.0	1	4	20
20	3	3	3	3	4	5	6	7	9	9	1.1	2	4	7	40
1 12	0.3	0.3	0.3	0.4	0.4	0.5	0.6	0.8	1.0	1.0	1.2	1.3	1.6	1.9	10 48
4	4	4	4	4	5	6	7	9	1	2	3	5	7	2.1	56
0 56	4	4	4	5	5	6	8	1.0	2	4	5	7	2.0		11 4
48	5	5	5	6	6	7	1.0	1	4	6	7	2.0			12
40	6	6	6	7	8	9	2	4	7	8	2.1				20
0 32	0.7	0.7	0.8	0.8	0.9	1.1	1.4	1.7	2.1	2.3					11 28
24	1.0	1.0	1.0	1.1	1.2	5	9	2.3	2.8						36
16	4	5	5	6	9	2.2	2.9	3.4							44
8	2.9	2.9	3.0	3.3	3.7	4.4	5.7								52
0	∞	∞	∞												12 0

TABLE XLVII.

Limiting Errors of Altitude-Azimuths.

Lat.	Least Hour-Angle 1ʰ. Partial Az. Error. Alt. Error ± 6′.	Lat. Error ± 12′.	Dec. Error ± 3′.	Prob. Total Az. Error.	Least Hour-Angle 2ʰ. Partial Az. Error. Alt. Error ± 6′.	Lat. Error ± 12′.	Dec. Error ± 3′.	Prob. Total Az. Error.	Least Hour-Angle 3ʰ. Partial Az. Error. Alt. Error ± 6′.	Lat. Error ± 12′.	Dec. Error ± 3′.	Prob. Total Az. Error.
°	°	°	°	°	°	°	°	°	°	°	°	°
0	±0.4	±0.8	±0.2	±0.9	±0.2	±0.4	±0.1	±0.5	±0.1	±0.2	±0.1	±0.3
10	0.4	0.8	0.2	0.9	0.2	0.4	0.1	0.5	0.1	0.2	0.1	0.3
20	0.4	0.8	0.2	1.0	0.2	0.4	0.1	0.5	0.1	0.2	0.1	0.3
30	0.5	0.9	0.3	1.1	0.3	0.4	0.2	0.6	0.1	0.3	0.1	0.4
40	0.5	1.0	0.3	1.2	0.3	0.5	0.2	0.6	0.2	0.3	0.1	0.4
50	0.6	1.2	0.3	1.7	0.4	0.6	0.2	0.8	0.2	0.3	0.2	0.5
60	0.8	1.6	0.4	1.9	0.4	0.7	0.2	0.8	0.3	0.4	0.2	0.6
70	1.1	2.3	0.6	2.6	0.6	1.0	0.3	1.2	0.4	0.6	0.2	0.8
80	2.8	4.5	1.2	5.5	1.3	2.0	0.6	2.5	1.0	1.2	0.4	1.7

Time-Alt. Azimuths: Log. A.

Az.	Declination. 0°	5°	10°	15°	20°	25°	30°	35°	40°	45°	50°	Diff. for 0°.1.	Az.
0°	+∞	+∞	+∞	+∞	+∞	+∞	+∞	+∞	+∞	+∞	+∞		180°
1	1.758	1.756	1.751	1.743	1.731	1.715	1.695	1.671	1.642	1.607	1.566		179
2	457	455	450	442	430	414	394	370	341	306	265	30.1	178
3	281	279	274	266	254	238	218	194	165	130	089	17.6	177
4	156	154	149	141	129	113	093	069	040	005	0.964	12.5	176
												9.6	
5	1.060	1.058	1.053	1.045	1.033	1.017	0.997	0.973	0.944	0.909	0.868		175
6	0.981	0.979	0.974	0.966	0.954	0.938	918	894	865	830	789	7.9	174
7	914	912	907	899	887	871	851	827	798	763	722	6.7	173
8	856	854	849	841	829	813	793	769	740	705	664	5.8	172
9	806	804	799	791	779	763	743	719	690	655	614	5.0	171
												4.6	
10	0.760	0.759	0.753	0.745	0.733	0.717	0.697	0.673	0.644	0.609	0.568		170
11	719	717	712	704	692	676	656	632	603	568	527	4.1	169
12	682	680	675	667	655	639	619	595	566	531	490	3.7	168
13	648	646	641	633	621	605	585	561	532	497	456	3.4	167
14	616	614	609	601	589	573	553	529	500	465	424	3.2	166
												2.9	
15	0.587	0.585	0.580	0.572	0.560	0.544	0.524	0.500	0.471	0.436	0.395		165
16	560	558	553	545	533	517	497	473	444	409	368	2.7	164
17	534	532	527	519	507	491	471	447	418	383	342	2.6	163
18	510	508	503	495	483	467	447	423	394	359	318	2.4	162
19	488	486	481	473	461	445	425	401	372	337	296	2.2	161
												2.2	
20	0.466	0.464	0.459	0.451	0.439	0.423	0.403	0.379	0.350	0.315	0.274		160
21	446	444	439	431	419	403	383	359	330	295	254	2.0	159
22	427	425	420	412	400	384	364	340	311	276	235	1.9	158
23	408	406	401	393	381	365	345	321	292	257	216	1.9	157
24	391	389	384	376	364	348	328	304	275	240	199	1.7	156
												1.7	
25	0.374	0.372	0.367	0.359	0.347	0.331	0.311	0.287	0.258	0.223	0.182		155
26	358	356	351	343	331	315	295	271	242	207	166	1.6	154
27	343	341	336	328	316	300	280	256	227	192	151	1.5	153
28	328	326	321	313	301	285	265	241	212	177	136	1.5	152
29	314	312	307	299	287	271	251	227	198	163	122	1.4	151
												1.3	
30	0.301	0.299	0.294	0.286	0.274	0.258	0.238	0.214	0.185	0.150	0.109		150
31	288	286	281	273	261	245	225	201	172	137	096	1.3	149
32	276	274	269	261	249	233	213	189	160	125	084	1.2	148
33	264	262	257	249	237	221	201	177	148	113	072	1.2	147
34	253	251	246	238	226	210	190	166	137	102	061	1.1	146
												1.1	
35	0.242	0.240	0.235	0.227	0.215	0.199	0.179	0.155	0.126	0.091	0.050		145
36	231	229	224	216	204	188	168	144	115	080	039	1.1	144
37	221	219	214	206	194	178	158	134	105	070	029	1.0	143
38	211	209	204	196	184	168	148	124	095	060	019	1.0	142
39	201	199	194	186	174	158	138	114	085	050	009	1.0	141
												0.9	
40	0.192	0.190	0.185	0.177	0.165	0.149	0.129	0.105	0.076	0.041	0.000		140
42	175	173	168	160	148	132	112	088	059	024	9.983	0.85	138
44	158	156	151	143	131	115	095	071	042	007	966	0.85	136
46	143	141	136	128	116	100	080	056	027	9.992	951	0.75	134
48	129	127	122	114	102	086	066	042	013	978	937	0.70	132
												0.65	
50	0.116	0.114	0.109	0.101	0.089	0.073	0.053	0.029	0.000	9.965	9.924		130
52	104	102	097	089	077	061	041	017	9.988	953	912	0.60	128
54	092	090	085	077	065	049	029	005	976	941	900	0.60	126
56	082	080	075	067	055	039	019	9.995	966	931	890	0.50	124
58	072	070	065	057	045	029	009	985	956	921	880	0.50	122
												0.45	
60	0.063	0.061	0.056	0.048	0.036	0.020	0.000	9.976	9.947	9.912	9.871		120
65	043	041	036	028	016	000	9.980	956	927	892	851	0.40	115
70	027	025	020	012	000	9.984	964	940	911	876	835	0.32	110
75	015	013	008	000	9.988	972	952	928	899	864	823	0.24	105
80	007	005	000	9.992	980	964	944	920	891	856	815	0.16	100
												0.07	
90	0.000	9.998	9.993	9.985	9.973	9.957	9.937	9.913	9.884	9.849	9.808		90
Az.	Difference for 0°.1 of Declination: 0.04	0.10	0.16	0.24	0.32	0.40	0.48	0.58	0.70	0.82		For Az.	Az.

Time-Alt. Azimuths; Log B.

Hour-Angle or Position-Angle. Arc.	Time.	Altitude or Latitude. 0°	10°	15°	20°	25°	30°	32°	34°	36°	38°	40°	Hour-Angle or Position-Angle. Time.	Arc.
°	h m												h m	°
0	0 0	+ ∞	+ ∞	+ ∞	+ ∞	+ ∞	+ ∞	+ ∞	+ ∞	+ ∞	+ ∞	+ ∞	12 0	180
1	0 4	1.758	1.751	1.743	1.731	1.715	1.695	1.686	1.676	1.666	1.654	1.642	11 56	179
2	0 8	457	450	442	430	414	394	385	375	365	353	341	11 52	178
3	0 12	281	274	266	254	238	218	209	199	189	177	165	11 48	177
4	0 16	156	149	141	129	113	093	084	074	064	052	040	11 44	176
5	0 20	1.060	1.053	1.045	1.033	1.017	0.997	0.988	0.978	0.968	0.956	0.944	11 40	175
6	0 24	0.981	0.974	0.966	0.954	0.938	918	909	899	889	877	865	11 36	174
7	0 28	914	907	899	887	871	851	842	832	822	810	798	11 32	173
8	0 32	856	849	841	829	813	793	784	774	764	752	740	11 28	172
9	0 36	806	799	791	779	763	743	734	724	714	702	690	11 24	171
10	0 40	0.760	0.753	0.745	0.733	0.717	0.697	0.688	0.678	0.668	0.656	0.644	11 20	170
11	0 44	719	712	704	692	676	656	647	637	627	615	603	11 16	169
12	0 48	682	675	667	655	639	619	610	600	590	578	566	11 12	168
13	0 52	648	641	633	621	605	585	576	566	556	544	532	11 8	167
14	0 56	616	609	601	589	573	553	544	534	524	512	500	11 4	166
15	1 0	0.587	0.580	0.572	0.560	0.544	0.524	0.515	0.505	0.495	0.483	0.471	11 0	165
16	1 4	560	553	545	533	517	497	488	478	468	456	444	10 56	164
17	1 8	534	527	519	507	491	471	462	452	442	430	418	10 52	163
18	1 12	510	503	495	483	467	447	438	428	418	406	394	10 48	162
19	1 16	488	481	473	461	445	425	416	406	396	384	372	10 44	161
20	1 20	0.466	0.459	0.451	0.439	0.423	0.403	0.394	0.384	0.374	0.362	0.350	10 40	160
21	1 24	446	439	431	419	403	383	374	364	354	342	330	10 36	159
22	1 28	427	420	412	400	384	364	355	345	335	323	311	10 32	158
23	1 32	408	401	393	381	365	345	336	326	316	304	292	10 28	157
24	1 36	391	384	376	364	348	328	319	309	299	287	275	10 24	156
25	1 40	0.374	0.367	0.359	0.347	0.331	0.311	0.302	0.292	0.282	0.270	0.258	10 20	155
26	1 44	358	351	343	331	315	295	286	276	266	254	242	10 16	154
27	1 48	343	336	328	316	300	280	271	261	251	239	227	10 12	153
28	1 52	328	321	313	301	285	265	256	246	236	224	212	10 8	152
29	1 56	314	307	299	287	271	251	242	232	222	210	198	10 4	151
30	2 0	0.301	0.294	0.286	0.274	0.258	0.238	0.229	0.219	0.209	0.197	0.185	10 0	150
31	2 4	288	281	273	261	245	225	216	206	196	184	172	9 56	149
32	2 8	276	269	261	249	233	213	204	194	184	172	160	9 52	148
33	2 12	264	257	249	237	221	201	192	182	172	160	148	9 48	147
34	2 16	253	246	238	226	210	190	181	171	161	149	137	9 44	146
35	2 20	0.242	0.235	0.227	0.215	0.199	0.179	0.170	0.160	0.150	0.138	0.126	9 40	145
36	2 24	231	224	216	204	188	168	159	149	139	127	115	9 36	144
37	2 28	221	214	206	194	178	158	149	139	129	117	105	9 32	143
38	2 32	211	204	196	184	168	148	139	129	119	107	095	9 28	142
39	2 36	201	194	186	174	158	138	129	119	109	097	085	9 24	141
40	2 40	0.192	0.185	0.177	0.165	0.149	0.129	0.120	0.110	0.100	0.088	0.076	9 20	140
42	2 48	175	168	160	148	132	112	103	093	083	071	059	9 12	138
44	2 56	158	151	143	131	115	095	086	076	066	054	042	9 4	136
46	3 4	143	136	128	116	100	080	071	061	051	039	027	8 56	134
48	3 12	129	122	114	102	086	066	057	047	037	025	013	8 48	132
50	3 20	0.116	0.109	0.101	0.089	0.073	0.053	0.044	0.034	0.024	0.012	0.000	8 40	130
52	3 28	104	097	089	077	061	041	032	022	012	000	9.988	8 32	128
54	3 36	092	085	077	065	049	029	020	010	000	9.988	976	8 24	126
56	3 44	082	075	067	055	039	019	010	000	9.990	978	966	8 16	124
58	3 52	072	065	057	045	029	009	000	9.990	980	968	956	8 8	122
60	4 0	0.063	0.056	0.048	0.036	0.020	0.000	9.991	9.981	9.971	9.959	9.947	8 0	120
65	4 20	043	036	028	016	000	9.980	971	961	951	939	927	7 40	115
70	4 40	027	020	012	000	9.984	964	955	945	935	923	911	7 20	110
75	5 0	015	008	000	9.988	972	952	943	933	923	911	899	7 0	105
80	5 20	007	000	9.992	980	964	944	935	925	915	903	891	6 40	100
90	6 0	0.000	9.993	9.985	9.973	9.957	9.937	9.928	9.918	9.908	9.896	9.884	6 0	90
		0.07	0.16	0.24	0.32	0.40	0.45	0.50	0.50	0.60	0.60			

Differences for 0°.1 of Altitude or Latitude.

Differences for Side-Arguments are the same as for Azimuths under Log A.

Time-Alt. Azimuths: Log B.

Hour-Angle or Position-Angle. Arc.	Time.	Altitude or Latitude. 40°	42°	44°	46°	48°	50°	51°	52°	53°	54°	55°	Hour-Angle or Position-Angle. Time.	Arc.
°	h m												h m	°
0	0 0	+ ∞	+ ∞	+ ∞	+ ∞	+ ∞	+ ∞	+ ∞	+ ∞	+ ∞	+ ∞	+ ∞	12 0	180
1	0 4	1.642	1.629	1.615	1.600	1.583	1.566	1.557	1.547	1.537	1.527	1.517	11 56	179
2	0 8	341	328	314	299	282	265	256	246	236	226	216	11 52	178
3	0 12	165	152	138	123	106	089	080	070	060	050	040	11 48	177
4	0 16	040	027	013	0.998	0.981	0.964	0.955	0.945	0.935	0.925	0.915	11 44	176
5	0 20	0.944	0.931	0.917	0.902	0.885	0.868	0.859	0.849	0.839	0.829	0.819	11 40	175
6	0 24	865	852	838	823	806	789	780	770	760	750	740	11 36	174
7	0 28	798	785	771	756	739	722	713	703	693	683	673	11 32	173
8	0 32	740	727	713	698	681	664	655	645	635	625	615	11 28	172
9	0 36	690	677	663	648	631	614	605	595	585	575	565	11 24	171
10	0 40	0.644	0.631	0.617	0.602	0.585	0.568	0.559	0.549	0.539	0.529	0.519	11 20	170
11	0 44	603	590	576	561	544	527	518	508	498	488	478	11 16	169
12	0 48	566	553	539	524	507	490	481	471	461	451	441	11 12	168
13	0 52	532	519	505	490	473	456	447	437	427	417	407	11 8	167
14	0 56	500	487	473	458	441	424	415	405	395	385	375	11 4	166
15	1 0	0.471	0.458	0.444	0.429	0.412	0.395	0.386	0.376	0.366	0.356	0.346	11 0	165
16	1 4	444	431	417	402	385	368	359	349	339	329	319	10 56	164
17	1 8	418	405	391	376	369	342	333	323	313	303	293	10 52	163
18	1 12	394	381	367	352	335	318	309	299	289	279	269	10 48	162
19	1 16	372	359	345	330	313	296	287	277	267	257	247	10 44	161
20	1 20	0.350	0.337	0.323	0.308	0.291	0.274	0.265	0.255	0.245	0.235	0.225	10 40	160
21	1 24	330	317	303	288	271	254	245	235	225	215	205	10 36	159
22	1 28	311	298	284	269	252	235	226	216	206	196	186	10 32	158
23	1 32	292	279	265	250	233	216	207	197	187	177	167	10 28	157
24	1 36	275	262	248	233	216	199	190	180	170	160	150	10 24	156
25	1 40	0.258	0.245	0.231	0.216	0.199	0.182	0.173	0.163	0.153	0.143	0.133	10 20	155
26	1 44	242	229	215	200	183	166	157	147	137	127	117	10 16	154
27	1 48	227	214	200	185	168	151	142	132	122	112	102	10 12	153
28	1 52	212	199	185	170	153	136	127	117	107	097	087	10 8	152
29	1 56	198	185	171	156	149	122	113	103	093	083	073	10 4	151
30	2 0	0.185	0.172	0.158	0.143	0.126	0.109	0.100	0.090	0.080	0.070	0.060	10 0	150
31	2 4	172	159	145	130	113	096	087	077	067	057	047	9 56	149
32	2 8	160	147	133	118	101	084	075	065	055	045	035	9 52	148
33	2 12	148	135	121	106	089	072	063	053	043	033	023	9 48	147
34	2 16	137	124	110	095	078	061	052	042	032	022	012	9 44	146
35	2 20	0.126	0.113	0.099	0.084	0.067	0.050	0.041	0.031	0.021	0.011	0.000	9 40	145
36	2 24	115	102	088	073	056	039	030	020	010	000	9.990	9 36	144
37	2 28	105	092	078	063	046	029	020	010	000	9.990	980	9 32	143
38	2 32	095	082	068	053	036	019	010	000	9.990	980	970	9 28	142
39	2 36	085	072	058	043	026	009	000	9.990	980	970	960	9 24	141
40	2 40	0.076	0.063	0.049	0.034	0.017	0.000	9.991	9.981	9.971	9.961	9.951	9 20	140
42	2 48	059	046	032	017	000	9.983	974	964	954	944	934	9 12	138
44	2 56	042	029	015	000	9.983	966	957	947	937	927	917	9 4	136
46	3 4	027	014	000	9.985	968	951	942	932	922	912	902	8 56	134
48	3 12	013	000	9.986	971	954	937	928	918	908	898	888	8 48	132
50	3 20	0.000	9.987	9.973	9.958	9.941	9.924	9.915	9.905	9.895	9.885	9.875	8 40	130
52	3 28	9.988	975	961	946	939	912	903	893	883	873	863	8 32	128
54	3 36	976	963	949	934	917	900	891	881	871	861	851	8 24	126
56	3 44	966	953	939	924	907	890	881	871	861	851	841	8 16	124
58	3 52	956	943	929	914	897	880	871	861	851	841	831	8 8	122
60	4 0	9.947	9.934	9.920	9.905	9.888	9.871	9.862	9.852	9.842	9.832	9.822	8 0	120
65	4 20	927	914	900	885	868	851	842	832	822	812	802	7 40	115
70	4 40	911	898	884	869	852	835	826	816	806	796	786	7 20	110
75	5 0	899	886	872	857	840	823	814	804	794	784	774	7 0	105
80	5 20	891	878	864	849	832	815	806	796	786	776	766	6 40	100
90	6 0	9.884	9.871	9.857	9.842	9.825	9.808	9.799	9.789	9.779	9.769	9.759	6 0	90
		0.65	0.70	0.75	0.85	0.85	0.9	1.0	1.0	1.0	1.0			
		Differences for 0°·1 of Altitude or Latitude.												

Differences for Side-Arguments are the same as for Azimuths under Log A.

Time-Alt. Azimuths: Log B.

Hour-Angle or Position-Angle. Arc.	Time.	Altitude or Latitude. 55°	56°	57°	58°	59°	60°	61°	62°	63°	64°	65°	Hour-Angle or Position-Angle. Time.	Arc.
°	h m												h m	°
0	0 0	+∞	+∞	+∞	+∞	+∞	+∞	+∞	+∞	+∞	+∞	+∞	12 0	180
1	0 4	1.517	1.506	1.494	1.482	1.470	1.457	1.444	1.430	1.415	1.400	1.384	11 56	179
2	0 8	216	205	193	181	169	156	143	129	114	099	083	11 52	178
3	0 12	040	029	017	005	0.993	0.980	0.967	0.953	0.938	0.923	0.907	11 48	177
4	0 16	0.915	0.904	0.892	0.880	868	855	842	828	813	798	782	11 44	176
5	0 20	0.819	0.808	0.796	0.784	0.772	0.759	0.746	0.732	0.717	0.702	0.686	11 40	175
6	0 24	740	729	717	705	693	680	667	653	638	623	607	11 36	174
7	0 28	673	662	650	638	626	613	600	586	571	556	540	11 32	173
8	0 32	615	604	592	580	568	555	542	528	513	498	482	11 28	172
9	0 36	565	554	542	530	518	505	492	478	463	448	432	11 24	171
10	0 40	0.519	0.508	0.496	0.484	0.472	0.459	0.446	0.432	0.417	0.402	0.386	11 20	170
11	0 44	478	467	455	443	431	418	405	391	376	361	345	11 16	169
12	0 48	441	430	418	406	394	381	368	354	339	324	308	11 12	168
13	0 52	407	396	384	372	360	347	334	320	305	290	274	11 8	167
14	0 56	375	364	352	340	328	315	302	288	273	258	242	11 4	166
15	1 0	0.346	0.335	0.323	0.311	0.299	0.286	0.273	0.259	0.244	0.229	0.213	11 0	165
16	1 4	319	308	296	284	272	259	246	232	217	202	186	10 56	164
17	1 8	293	282	270	258	246	233	220	206	191	176	160	10 52	163
18	1 12	269	258	246	234	222	209	196	182	167	152	136	10 48	162
19	1 16	247	236	224	212	200	187	174	160	145	130	114	10 44	161
20	1 20	0.225	0.214	0.202	0.190	0.178	0.165	0.152	0.138	0.123	0.108	0.092	10 40	160
21	1 24	205	194	182	170	158	145	132	118	103	088	072	10 36	159
22	1 28	186	175	163	151	139	126	113	099	084	069	053	10 32	158
23	1 32	167	156	144	132	120	107	094	080	065	050	034	10 28	157
24	1 36	150	139	127	115	103	090	077	063	048	033	017	10 24	156
25	1 40	0.133	0.122	0.110	0.098	0.086	0.073	0.060	0.046	0.031	0.016	0.000	10 20	155
26	1 44	117	106	094	082	070	057	044	030	015	000	9.984	10 16	154
27	1 48	102	091	079	067	055	042	029	015	000	985	969	10 12	153
28	1 52	087	076	064	052	040	027	014	000	9.985	9.970	954	10 8	152
29	1 56	073	062	050	038	026	013	000	9.986	971	956	940	10 4	151
30	2 0	0.060	0.049	0.037	0.025	0.013	0.000	9.987	9.973	9.958	9.943	9.927	10 0	150
31	2 4	047	036	024	012	000	9.987	974	960	945	930	914	9 56	149
32	2 8	035	024	012	000	9.988	975	962	948	933	918	902	9 52	148
33	2 12	023	012	000	9.988	976	963	950	936	921	906	890	9 48	147
34	2 16	012	000	9.989	977	965	952	939	925	909	895	879	9 44	146
35	2 20	0.000	9.990	9.978	9.966	9.954	9.941	9.928	9.914	9.899	9.884	9.868	9 40	145
36	2 24	9.990	979	967	955	943	930	917	903	888	873	857	9 36	144
37	2 28	980	969	957	945	933	920	907	893	878	863	847	9 32	143
38	2 32	970	959	947	935	923	910	897	883	868	853	837	9 28	142
39	2 36	960	949	937	925	913	900	887	873	858	843	827	9 24	141
40	2 40	9.951	9.940	9.928	9.916	9.904	9.891	9.878	9.864	9.849	9.834	9.818	9 20	140
42	2 48	934	923	911	899	887	874	861	847	832	817	801	9 12	138
44	2 56	917	906	894	882	870	857	844	830	815	800	784	9 4	136
46	3 4	902	891	879	867	855	842	829	815	800	785		8 56	134
48	3 12	888	877	865	853	841	828	815	801	786			8 48	132
50	3 20	9.875	9.864	9.852	9.840	9.828	9.815	9.802	9.788				8 40	130
52	3 28	863	852	840	828	816	803	790					8 32	128
54	3 36	851	840	828	816	804	791						8 24	126
56	3 44	841	830	818	806	794							8 16	124
58	3 52	831	820	808	796								8 8	122
60	4 0	9.822	9.811	9.799									8 0	120
65	4 20	802	791										7 40	115
70	4 40												7 20	110
75	5 0												7 0	105
80	5 20												6 40	100
90	6 0												6 0	90

1.1	1.2	1.2	1.2	1.3	1.3	1.4	1.5	1.5	1.6

Differences for 0°.1 of Altitude or Latitude.

Differences for Side-Arguments are the same as those for Azimuths under Log A.

Time-Alt. Azimuths: Log B.

Hour-Angle or Position-Angle.		Altitude or Latitude.											Hour-Angle or Position-Angle.	
Arc.	Time.	65°	66°	67°	68°	69°	70°	71°	72°	73°	74°	75°	Time.	Arc.
°	h m												h m	°
0	0 0	+ ∞	+ ∞	+ ∞	+ ∞	+ ∞	+ ∞	+ ∞	+ ∞	+ ∞	+ ∞	+ ∞	12 0	180
1	0 4	1.384	1.367	1.350	1.331	1.312	1.292	1.270	1.248	1.224	1.198	1.171	11 56	179
2	0 8	083	066	049	030	011	0.991	0.979	0.947	0.923	0.897	0.870	11 52	178
3	0 12	0.907	0.890	0.873	0.854	0.835	815	793	771	747	721	694	11 48	177
4	0 16	782	765	748	729	710	690	668	636	622	596	569	11 44	176
5	0 20	0.686	0.669	0.652	0.633	0.614	0.594	0.572	0.550	0.526	0.500	0.473	11 40	175
6	0 24	607	590	573	554	535	515	493	471	447	421	394	11 36	174
7	0 28	540	523	506	487	468	448	426	404	380	354	327	11 32	173
8	0 32	482	465	448	429	410	390	368	346	322	296	269	11 28	172
9	0 36	432	415	398	379	360	340	318	296	272	246	219	11 24	171
10	0 40	0.386	0.369	0.352	0.333	0.314	0.294	0.272	0.250	0.226	0.200	0.173	11 20	170
11	0 44	345	328	311	292	273	253	231	209	185	159	132	11 16	169
12	0 48	308	291	274	255	236	216	194	172	148	122	095	11 12	168
13	0 52	274	257	240	221	202	182	160	138	114	088	061	11 8	167
14	0 56	242	225	208	189	170	150	128	106	082	056	029	11 4	166
15	1 0	0.213	0.196	0.179	0.160	0.141	0.121	0.099	0.077	0.053	0.027	0.000	11 0	165
16	1 4	186	169	152	133	114	094	072	050	026	000	9.973	10 56	164
17	1 8	160	143	126	107	088	068	046	024	000	9.974	947	10 52	163
18	1 12	136	119	102	083	064	044	022	000	9.976	950	923	10 48	162
19	1 16	114	097	080	061	042	022	000	9.978	954	928	901	10 44	161
20	1 20	0.092	0.075	0.058	0.039	0.020	0.000	9.978	9.956	9.932	9.906	9.879	10 40	160
21	1 24	072	055	038	019	000	9.980	958	936	912	886	859	10 36	159
22	1 28	053	036	019	000	9.981	961	949	917	893	867	840	10 32	158
23	1 32	034	017	000	9.981	962	942	920	898	874	848	821	10 28	157
24	1 36	017	000	9.983	964	945	925	903	881	857	831	804	10 24	156
25	1 40	0.000	9.983	9.966	9.947	9.928	9.908	9.886	9.864	9.840	9.814	9.787	10 20	155
26	1 44	984	967	950	931	912	892	870	848	824	798		10 16	154
27	1 48	969	952	935	916	897	877	855	833	809	783		10 12	153
28	1 52	954	937	920	901	882	862	840	818	794			10 8	152
29	1 56	940	923	906	887	868	848	826	804				10 4	151
30	2 0	9.927	9.910	9.893	9.874	9.855	9.835	9.813	9.791				10 0	150
31	2 4	914	897	880	861	842	822	800					9 56	149
32	2 8	902	885	868	849	830	810	788					9 52	148
33	2 12	890	873	856	837	818	798						9 48	147
34	2 16	879	862	845	826	807	787						9 44	146
35	2 20	9.868	9.851	9.834	9.815	9.796							9 40	145
36	2 24	857	840	823	804								9 36	144
37	2 28	847	830	813	794								9 32	143
38	2 32	837	820	803									9 28	142
39	2 36	827	810	793									9 24	141
40	2 40	9.818	9.801										9 20	140
42	2 48	801											9 12	138
44	2 56												9 4	136
46	3 4												8 56	134
48	3 12												8 48	132
50	3 20												8 40	130
52	3 28												8 32	128
54	3 36												8 24	126
56	3 44												8 16	124
58	3 52												8 8	122
60	4 0												8 0	120
65	4 20												7 40	115
70	4 40												7 20	110
75	5 0												7 0	105
80	5 20												6 40	100
90	6 0												6 0	90
		1.7	1.7	1.9	1.9	2.0	2.2	2.2	2.4	2.6	2.7			
		Differences for 0°.1 of Altitude or Latitude.												

Differences for Side-Arguments are the same as those for Azimuths under Log A.

Error of Time-Alt. Azimuth for an Error of $0^m.2$, or 12^s, in Hour-Angle.

Az.	Hour-Angle.													Az.
	6h 0m	5h 20m	4h 40m	4h 0m	3h 20m	2h 40m	2h 0m	1h 40m	1h 20m	1h 0m	0h 40m	0h 20m	0h 0m	
0°	0°.0	0′	0′	0′	0′	0′	0′	0°.0	0°.0	0°.0	0°.0	0°.0	Indet.	180°
10	0	0	0	1	1	1	1	0	0	0	1	1	∞	170
20	0	0	1	1	1	1	2	0	1	1	1	2	∞	160
30	0	1	1	1	2	2	3	1	1	1	2	3	∞	150
40	0	1	1	2	2	3	4	1	1	2	2	5	∞	140
50	0.0	1	1	2	3	4	6	0.1	0.2	0.2	0.3	0.7	∞	130
60	0	1	2	3	4	6	9	2	2	3	5	1.0	∞	120
65	0	1	2	4	5	8	11	2	3	4	6	2	∞	115
70	0	1	3	5	7	10	14	3	4	5	8	6	∞	110
75	0	2	4	7	9	13	19	4	5	7	1.1	2.1	∞	105
80	0.0	3	6	10	15	20	29	0.6	0.8	1.1	1.6	3.2	∞	100
81	0	3	7	11	16	23	33	7	9	2	8	6	∞	99
82	0	4	8	12	18	25	37	8	1.0	3	2.0	4.1	∞	98
83	0	4	9	14	21	29	42	9	1	5	3	6	∞	97
84	0	5	10	17	24	34	49	1.0	3	8	7	5.4	∞	96
85	0.0	6	13	20	29	41	60	1.2	1.6	2.1	3.2	6.5		95
86	0	8	16	25	36	51	75	5	2.0	7	4.0			94
87	0	10	21	33	48	69	99	2.0	6	3.6				93
88	0	15	32	50	72	103	149	3	3.9					92
89	0	30	63	99	144	205	297	6.1						91
90	Indet.	∞	∞	∞	∞	∞	∞	∞						90
Az.	6h 0m	6h 40m	7h 20m	8h 0m	8h 40m	9h 20m	10h 0m	10h 20m	10h 40m	11h 0m	11h 20m	11h 40m	12h 0m	Az.
	Hour-Angle.													

TABLE L.

Error of Time-Alt. Azimuth for an Error of 3′ in Altitude or Declination.

Az.	Altitude or Declination.													Az.
	0°	10°	20°	30°	40°	50°	60°	65°	70°	75°	80°	85°	90°	
0°	0′	0′	0′	0′	0′	0′	0′	0°.0	0°.0	0°.0	0.0	0°.0	Indet.	180°
10	0	0	0	1	1	1	1	0	0	0	1	1	∞	170
20	0	0	1	1	1	1	2	0	1	1	1	2	∞	160
30	0	1	1	1	2	2	3	1	1	1	2	3	∞	150
40	0	1	1	2	2	3	4	1	1	2	2	5	∞	140
50	0	1	1	2	3	4	6	0.1	0.2	0.2	0.3	0.7	∞	130
60	0	1	2	3	4	6	9	2	2	3	5	1.0	∞	120
65	0	1	2	4	5	8	11	2	3	4	6	2	∞	115
70	0	1	3	5	7	10	14	3	4	5	8	6	∞	110
75	0	2	4	7	9	13	19	4	5	7	1.1	2.1	∞	105
80	0	3	6	10	15	20	29	0.6	0.8	1.1	1.6	3.2	∞	100
81	0	3	7	11	16	23	33	7	9	2	8	6	∞	99
82	0	4	8	12	18	25	37	8	1.0	3	2.0	4.1	∞	98
83	0	4	9	14	21	29	42	9	1	5	3	6	∞	97
84	0	5	10	17	24	34	49	1.0	3	8	7	5.4	∞	96
85	0	6	13	20	29	41	60	1.2	1.6	2.1	3.2	6.5		95
86	0	8	16	25	36	51	75	5	2.0	7	4.0			94
87	0	10	21	33	48	69	99	2.0	6	3.6				93
88	0	15	32	50	72	103	149	3	3.9					92
89	0	30	63	99	144	205	297	6.1						91
90	Indet.	∞	∞	∞	∞	∞	∞							90

Transition-Azimuths.

Change of Altitude in One Minute of Time.

Lat.	0′	1′	2′	3′	4′	5′	6′	7′	8′	9′	10′	11′	12′	13′	14′	15′
°	°	°	°	°	°	°	°	°	°	°	°	°	°	°	°	°
0	0.0	3.8	7.7	11.5	15.5	19.5	23.6	27.8	32.2	36.9	41.8	47.2	53.1	60.1	69.0	90.0
4	0	3.8	7.7	11.6	15.5	19.5	23.6	27.9	32.3	37.0	41.9	47.3	53.3	60.3	69.3	
8	0	3.9	7.7	11.7	15.6	19.7	23.8	28.1	32.6	37.3	42.3	47.8	53.9	61.1	70.5	
12	0	3.9	7.8	11.8	15.8	19.9	24.1	28.5	33.0	37.8	43.0	48.6	54.9	62.4	72.6	
16	0	4.0	8.0	12.0	16.1	20.3	24.6	29.0	33.7	38.6	43.9	49.7	56.3	64.4	76.1	
20	0.0	4.1	8.2	12.3	16.5	20.8	25.2	29.8	34.6	39.7	45.2	51.3	58.3	67.3	83.3	
22	0	4.1	8.3	12.4	16.7	21.1	25.5	30.2	35.1	40.3	46.0	52.3	59.6	69.2		
24	0	4.2	8.4	12.6	17.0	21.4	26.0	30.7	35.7	41.0	46.9	53.4	61.1	71.6		
26	0	4.2	8.5	12.8	17.3	21.8	26.4	31.3	36.4	41.9	47.9	54.7	62.9	74.6		
28	0	4.3	8.7	13.1	17.6	22.2	26.9	31.9	37.2	42.8	49.0	56.1	65.0	79.0		
30	0.0	4.4	8.8	13.3	17.9	22.6	27.5	32.6	38.0	43.8	50.3	57.9	67.5			
31	0	4.5	8.9	13.5	18.1	22.9	27.8	33.0	38.5	44.4	51.0	58.8	68.9			
32	0	4.5	9.0	13.6	18.3	23.1	28.1	33.4	39.0	45.0	51.8	59.8	70.6			
33	0	4.6	9.1	13.8	18.5	23.4	28.5	33.8	39.5	45.7	52.6	61.0	72.5			
34	0	4.6	9.2	14.0	18.8	23.7	28.8	34.3	40.0	46.4	53.5	62.2	74.8			
35	0.0	4.7	9.4	14.1	19.0	24.0	29.2	34.7	40.6	47.1	54.5	63.5	77.6			
36	0	4.7	9.5	14.3	19.2	24.3	29.6	35.2	41.2	47.9	55.5	65.0	81.4			
37	0	4.8	9.6	14.5	19.5	24.7	30.0	35.7	41.9	48.7	56.6	66.7				
38	0	4.8	9.7	14.7	19.8	25.0	30.5	36.3	42.6	49.6	57.8	68.5				
39	0	4.9	9.9	14.9	20.1	25.4	31.0	36.9	43.3	50.5	59.1	70.7				
40	0.0	5.0	10.0	15.1	20.4	25.8	31.5	37.5	44.1	51.6	60.5	73.2				
41	0	5.1	10.2	15.4	20.7	26.2	32.0	38.2	45.0	52.6	62.0	76.3				
42	0	5.2	10.3	15.6	21.2	26.6	32.6	38.9	45.9	53.8	63.8	80.7				
43	0	5.2	10.5	15.9	21.4	27.1	33.1	39.6	46.8	55.1	65.7					
44	0	5.3	10.7	16.1	21.8	27.6	33.8	40.4	47.8	56.5	67.9					
45	0.0	5.4	10.9	16.4	22.1	28.1	34.4	41.3	49.0	58.0	70.5					
46	0	5.5	11.1	16.7	22.6	28.7	35.1	42.2	50.2	59.7	73.7					
47	0	5.6	11.3	17.0	23.0	29.3	35.9	43.2	51.4	61.6	77.8					
48	0	5.7	11.5	17.4	23.5	29.9	36.7	44.2	52.9	63.7	85.1					
49	0	5.8	11.7	17.7	24.0	30.5	37.6	45.3	54.4	66.1						
50	0.0	6.0	12.0	18.1	24.5	31.2	38.5	46.5	56.1	69.0						
51	0	6.1	12.2	18.5	25.1	32.0	39.5	47.9	57.9	72.4						
52	0	6.2	12.5	18.9	25.7	32.8	40.5	49.3	60.0	77.0						
53	0	6.4	12.8	19.4	26.3	33.6	41.6	50.8	62.4	85.6						
54	0	6.5	13.1	19.9	27.0	34.5	42.9	52.5	65.1							
55	0.0	6.7	13.4	20.4	27.7	35.5	44.2	54.4	68.4							
56	0	6.8	13.8	20.9	28.5	36.6	45.7	56.6	72.5							
57	0	7.0	14.2	21.5	29.3	37.7	47.3	59.0	78.3							
58	0	7.2	14.6	22.2	30.2	39.0	49.0	61.7								
59	0	7.4	15.0	22.8	31.2	40.3	50.9	65.0								
60	0.0	7.7	15.5	23.6	32.2	41.8	53.1	69.0								
61	0	7.9	16.0	24.4	33.4	43.4	55.6	74.3								
62	0	8.2	16.5	25.2	34.6	45.2	58.4	83.7								
63	0	8.4	17.1	26.1	36.0	47.2	61.8									
64	0	8.7	17.7	27.1	37.5	49.5	65.8									
65	0.0	9.1	18.4	28.2	39.1	52.1	71.2									
66	0	9.4	19.1	29.4	41.0	55.0	79.5									
67	0	9.8	19.9	30.8	43.0	58.6										
68	0	10.3	20.8	32.3	45.4	62.8										
69	0	10.7	21.8	33.9	48.1	68.5										
70	0.0	11.2	22.9	35.8	51.2	77.1										
71	0	11.8	24.2	37.9	55.0											
72	0	12.5	25.6	40.3	59.6											
73	0	13.2	27.1	43.2	65.8											
74	0	14.0	28.9	46.5												

The Azimuths of this Table correspond to the stated changes in the Altitude of a Heavenly Body in One Minute of Time.

Direct Bearings of a Fixed Object: Limiting Distance of the Object.

Radius of Swing.	Distance-Ratio, or Distance of the Object divided by the Radius of Swing.																	Radius of Swing.
	30	40	50	75	100	150	200	250	300	350	400	500	600	700	800	900	1000	
Feet.	N. M.	N. M.	N. M.	N. M.	N. M.	N. M.	N. M.	N. M.	N. M.	N. M.	N. M.	N. M.	N. M.	N. M.	N. M.	N. M.	N. M.	Feet.
50	0.2	0.3	0.4	0.6	0.8	1.2	1.6	2.1	2.5	2.9	3.3	4	5	6	7	7	8	**50**
75	0.4	0.5	0.6	0.9	1.2	1.8	2.5	3.1	3.7	4.3	4.9	6	7	9	10	11	12	**75**
100	0.5	0.7	0.8	1.2	1.6	2.5	3.3	4.1	4.9	5.7	6.6	8	10	11	13	15	16	**100**
125	0.6	0.8	1.0	1.5	2.0	3.1	4.1	5.1	6.1	7.2	8.2	10	12	14	16	18	20	**125**
150	0.7	1.0	1.2	1.8	2.5	3.7	4.9	6.2	7.4	8.6	9.9	12	15	17	20	22	25	**150**
175	0.9	1.2	1.4	2.2	2.9	4.3	5.7	7.2	8.6	10.1	11.5	14	17	20	23	26	29	**175**
200	1.0	1.3	1.6	2.4	3.3	4.9	6.6	8.2	9.9	11.5	13.1	16	20	23	26	30	33	**200**
225	1.1	1.5	1.8	2.8	3.7	5.5	7.4	9.2	11.1	12.9	14.7	18	22	26	30	33	37	**225**
250	1.2	1.6	2.0	3.1	4.1	6.2	8.2	10.3	12.3	14.4	16.4	21	25	29	33	38	42	**250**
275	1.4	1.8	2.3	3.4	4.5	6.8	9.0	11.3	13.5	15.8	18.0	23	27	32	36	41	45	**275**
300	1.5	2.0	2.5	3.7	4.9	7.4	9.9	12.3	14.8	17.2	19.7	25	30	34	39	44	49	**300**
325	1.6	2.1	2.7	4.0	5.3	8.0	10.7	13.3	16.0	18.7	21.4	27	32	37	43	48	53	**325**
350	1.7	2.3	2.9	4.3	5.8	8.6	11.5	14.4	17.2	20.1	23.0	29	34	40	40	52	57	**350**
375	1.8	2.5	3.1	4.6	6.2	9.2	12.3	15.4	18.5	21.6	24.6	31	37	43	49	55	62	**375**
400	2.0	2.6	3.3	4.9	6.6	9.9	13.1	16.4	19.7	23.0	26.3	33	40	47	53	60	67	**400**

The Distances are expressed in Nautical Miles of 6,086 feet.

TABLE LIII.

Direct Bearings of a Fixed Object: Parallactic Errors of the Bearings.

Angle of Swing.	Distance-Ratio, or Distance of the Object divided by the Radius of Swing.																	Angle of Swing.
	30	40	50	75	100	150	200	250	300	350	400	500	600	700	800	900	1000	
°	°	°	°	°	°	°	°	°	°	°	°	°	°	°	°	°	°	°
0	0.0	0.0	0.0	0.0	0.0	0.0	0.0	0.0	0.0	0.0	0.0	0.0	0.0	0.0	0.0	0.0	0.0	**0**
10	3	2	2	1	1	1	1	0	0	0	0	0	0	0	0	0	0	**10**
20	7	5	4	3	2	1	1	1	1	0	0	0	0	0	0	0	0	**20**
30	1.0	7	6	4	3	2	1	1	1	1	1	1	0	0	0	0	0	**30**
40	2	9	7	5	4	2	2	1	1	1	1	1	1	1	0	0	0	**40**
50	1.5	1.1	0.9	0.6	0.4	0.3	0.2	0.2	0.1	0.1	0.1	0.1	0.1	0.1	0.1	0.1	0.0	**50**
60	7	2	1.0	7	5	3	2	2	2	1	1	1	1	1	1	1	0	**60**
70	8	3	1	7	5	4	3	2	2	2	1	1	1	1	1	1	1	**70**
80	9	4	2	8	6	4	3	2	2	2	1	1	1	1	1	1	1	**80**
90	1.9	1.4	1.2	0.8	0.6	0.4	0.3	0.2	0.2	0.2	0.2	0.1	0.1	0.1	0.1	0.1	0.1	**90**
100	1.9	1.4	1.2	0.8	0.6	0.4	0.3	0.2	0.2	0.2	0.1	0.1	0.1	0.1	0.1	0.1	0.1	**100**
110	8	3	1	7	5	4	3	2	2	2	1	1	1	1	1	1	1	**110**
120	7	2	0	7	5	3	2	2	2	1	1	1	1	1	1	1	0	**120**
130	5	1	0.9	6	4	3	2	2	1	1	1	1	1	1	1	1	0	**130**
140	1.2	0.9	0.7	0.5	0.4	0.2	0.2	0.1	0.1	0.1	0.1	0.1	0.1	0.1	0.0	0.0	0.0	**140**
150	0	7	6	4	3	2	1	1	1	1	1	1	0	0	0	0	0	**150**
160	0.7	5	4	3	2	1	1	1	1	0	0	0	0	0	0	0	0	**160**
170	3	2	2	1	1	1	1	0	0	0	0	0	0	0	0	0	0	**170**
180	0	0	0	0	0	0	0	0	0	0	0	0	0	0	0	0	0	**180**

The Parallactic Error is applied to the Right or Left of the Compass-Error (Total or Deviation) according as the Angle of Swing falls to the Left or Right of the Bearing of the Object; that is, contrariwise to the Angle of Swing.

Products of Arcs multiplied by the Sines of the Rhumbs.

Arcs.	Sines of the Rhumbs.									Arcs.
	$S_0 =$ 0.000	$S_1 =$ 0.195	$S_2 =$ 0.383	$S_3 =$ 0.556	$S_4 =$ 0.707	$S_5 =$ 0.831	$S_6 =$ 0.924	$S_7 =$ 0.981	$S_8 =$ 1.000	
0°.0	0°.0	0°.00	0°.00	0°.00	0°.00	0°.00	0°.00	0°.00	0°.00	0°.0
1	0	02	04	06	07	08	09	10	10	1
2	0	04	08	11	14	17	18	20	20	2
3	0	06	11	17	21	25	28	29	30	3
4	0	08	15	22	28	33	37	39	40	4
0.5	0.0	0.10	0.19	0.28	0.35	0.42	0.46	0.49	0.50	0.5
6	0	12	23	33	42	50	55	59	60	6
7	0	14	27	39	49	58	65	69	70	7
8	0	16	31	44	57	66	74	78	80	8
9	0	18	34	50	64	75	83	88	90	9
1.0	0.0	0.20	0.38	0.56	0.71	0.83	0.92	0.98	1.00	1.0
1	0	21	42	61	78	91	1.02	1.08	10	1
2	0	23	46	67	85	1.00	11	18	20	2
3	0	25	50	72	92	08	20	28	30	3
4	0	27	54	78	99	16	29	37	40	4
1.5	0.0	0.29	0.57	0.83	1.06	1.25	1.39	1.47	1.50	1.5
6	0	31	61	89	13	33	48	57	60	6
7	0	33	65	94	20	41	57	67	70	7
8	0	35	69	1.00	27	50	66	77	80	8
9	0	37	73	06	34	58	75	86	90	9
2.0	0.0	0.39	0.77	1.11	1.41	1.66	1.85	1.96	2.00	2.0
1	0	41	80	17	48	75	94	2.06	10	1
2	0	43	84	22	56	83	2.03	16	20	2
3	0	45	88	28	63	91	12	26	30	3
4	0	47	92	33	70	99	22	35	40	4
2.5	0.0	0.49	0.96	1.39	1.77	2.07	2.31	2.45	2.50	2.5
6	0	51	1.00	44	84	16	40	55	60	6
7	0	53	03	50	91	24	49	65	70	7
8	0	55	07	56	98	33	59	75	80	8
9	0	57	11	61	2.05	41	68	84	90	9
3.0	0.0	0.59	1.15	1.67	2.12	2.49	2.77	2.94	3.00	3.0
1	0	60	19	72	19	58	86	3.04	10	1
2	0	62	22	78	26	66	95	14	20	2
3	0	64	26	83	33	74	3.05	24	30	3
4	0	66	30	89	40	83	14	33	40	4
3.5	0.0	0.68	1.34	1.95	2.47	2.91	3.23	3.43	3.50	3.5
6	0	70	38	2.00	55	99	33	53	60	6
7	0	72	42	06	62	3.08	42	63	70	7
8	0	74	45	11	69	16	51	73	80	8
9	0	76	49	17	76	24	60	83	90	9
4.0	0.0	0.78	1.53	2.22	2.83	3.33	3.69	3.92	4.00	4.0
1	0	80	57	28	90	41	78	4.02	10	1
2	0	82	61	33	97	49	88	12	20	2
3	0	84	65	39	3.04	57	97	22	30	3
4	0	86	68	44	11	66	4.06	32	40	4
4.5	0.0	0.88	1.72	2.50	3.18	3.74	4.16	4.41	4.50	4.5
6	0	90	76	56	25	82	25	51	60	6
7	0	92	79	61	32	91	34	61	70	7
8	0	94	83	67	39	99	43	71	80	8
9	0	96	87	72	46	4.07	53	81	90	9
5.0	0.0	0.98	1.91	2.78	3.54	4.16	4.62	4.90	5.00	5.0
1	0	1.00	95	83	61	24	71	5.00	10	1
2	0	01	99	89	68	32	80	10	20	2
3	0	03	2.03	95	75	40	90	20	30	3
4	0	05	07	3.00	82	49	99	30	40	4
5.5	0.0	1.07	2.10	3.06	3.89	4.57	5.08	5.39	5.50	5.5
6	0	09	14	11	96	66	17	49	60	6
7	0	11	18	17	4.03	74	27	59	70	7
8	0	13	22	22	10	82	36	69	80	8
9	0	15	26	28	17	91	45	79	90	9
6.0	0.0	1.17	2.30	3.33	4.24	4.99	5.54	5.89	6.00	6.0

Products of Arcs multiplied by the Sines of the Rhumbs.

Arcs.	Sines of the Rhumbs.									Arcs.
	S_0 = 0.000	S_1 = 0.195	S_2 = 0.383	S_3 = 0.556	S_4 = 0.707	S_5 = 0.831	S_6 = 0.924	S_7 = 0.981	S_8 = 1.000	
°	°	°	°	°	°	°	°	°	°	°
6.0	0.0	1.17	2.30	3.33	4.24	4.99	5.54	5.89	6.00	**6.0**
1	0	19	33	39	31	5.07	63	98	10	**1**
2	0	21	37	44	38	15	73	6.08	20	**2**
3	0	23	41	50	46	24	82	18	30	**3**
4	0	25	45	55	53	32	91	28	40	**4**
6.5	0.0	1.27	2.49	3.61	4.60	5.40	6.00	6.37	6.50	**6.5**
6	0	29	52	67	67	48	09	47	60	**6**
7	0	31	56	72	74	57	19	57	70	**7**
8	0	33	60	78	81	65	28	67	80	**8**
9	0	34	64	83	88	74	37	77	90	**9**
7.0	0.0	1.36	2.68	3.89	4.95	5.82	6.47	6.87	7.00	**7.0**
1	0	38	72	94	5.02	90	56	96	10	**1**
2	0	40	75	4.00	09	99	65	7.06	20	**2**
3	0	42	79	05	16	6.07	74	16	30	**3**
4	0	44	83	11	23	15	84	26	40	**4**
7.5	0.0	1.46	2.87	4.17	5.30	6.24	6.93	7.36	7.50	**7.5**
6	0	48	91	22	37	32	7.02	45	60	**6**
7	0	50	95	28	44	40	11	55	70	**7**
8	0	52	98	33	51	48	21	65	80	**8**
9	0	54	3.02	39	58	57	30	75	90	**9**
8.0	0.0	1.56	3.06	4.44	5.65	6.65	7.39	7.85	8.00	**8.0**
1	0	58	10	50	73	73	48	94	10	**1**
2	0	60	14	55	80	82	58	8.04	20	**2**
3	0	62	18	61	87	90	67	14	30	**3**
4	0	64	21	67	94	98	76	24	40	**4**
8.5	0.0	1.66	3.25	4.72	6.01	7.07	7.85	8.34	8.50	**8.5**
6	0	68	29	78	08	15	94	43	60	**6**
7	0	70	33	83	15	23	8.04	53	70	**7**
8	0	72	37	89	22	32	13	63	80	**8**
9	0	74	41	95	29	40	22	73	90	**9**
9.0	0.0	1.75	3.44	5.00	6.36	7.48	8.31	8.83	9.00	**9.0**
1	0	77	48	05	43	56	41	92	10	**1**
2	0	79	52	11	51	65	50	9.02	20	**2**
3	0	81	56	17	58	73	59	12	30	**3**
4	0	83	60	22	65	81	68	22	40	**4**
9.5	0.0	1.85	3.63	5.28	6.72	7.90	8.78	9.32	9.50	**9.5**
6	0	87	67	33	79	98	87	42	60	**6**
7	0	89	71	39	86	8.06	96	51	70	**7**
8	0	91	75	44	93	15	9.05	61	80	**8**
9	0	93	79	50	7.00	23	15	71	90	**9**
10.0	0.0	1.95	3.83	5.56	7.07	8.31	9.24	9.81	10.00	**10.0**
1	0	97	86	61	14	40	33	91	10	**1**
2	0	99	90	67	21	48	42	10.00	20	**2**
3	0	2.01	94	72	28	56	51	10	30	**3**
4	0	03	98	78	35	65	61	20	40	**4**
10.5	0.0	2.05	4.01	5.83	7.42	8.73	9.70	10.30	10.50	**10.5**
6	0	07	05	89	50	81	79	40	60	**6**
7	0	09	09	94	57	90	88	49	70	**7**
8	0	11	13	6.00	64	98	98	59	80	**8**
9	0	13	17	05	71	9.06	10.07	69	90	**9**
11.0	0.0	2.15	4.21	6.11	7.78	9.15	10.16	10.79	11.00	**11.0**
1	0	16	25	17	85	23	25	89	10	**1**
2	0	18	29	22	92	31	35	98	20	**2**
3	0	20	32	27	99	39	44	11.08	30	**3**
4	0	22	36	33	8.06	48	53	18	40	**4**
11.5	0.0	2.24	4.40	6.39	8.13	9.56	10.62	11.28	11.50	**11.5**
6	0	26	44	44	20	64	72	38	60	**6**
7	0	28	48	50	27	73	81	47	70	**7**
8	0	30	51	56	34	81	90	57	80	**8**
9	0	32	55	61	41	89	99	67	90	**9**
12.0	0.0	2.34	4.59	6.67	8.49	9.98	11.09	11.77	12.00	**12.0**

Products of Arcs multiplied by the Sines of the Rhumbs.

Arcs.	Sines of the Rhumbs. S_0 = 0.000	S_1 = 0.195	S_2 = 0.383	S_3 = 0.556	S_4 = 0.707	S_5 = 0.831	S_6 = 0.924	S_7 = 0.981	S_8 = 1.000	Arcs.
12°.0	0°.0	2°.34	4°.59	6°.67	8°.49	9°.98	11°.09	11°.77	12°.00	12°.0
1	0	36	63	72	56	10.06	18	87	10	1
2	0	38	67	78	63	14	27	97	20	2
3	0	40	71	83	70	23	36	12.06	30	3
4	0	42	74	89	77	31	46	16	40	4
12.5	0.0	2.44	4.78	6.94	8.84	10.39	11.55	12.26	12.50	12.5
6	0	46	82	7.00	91	48	64	36	60	6
7	0	48	86	05	98	56	73	46	70	7
8	0	50	90	11	9.05	64	82	56	80	8
9	0	52	94	16	12	72	92	65	90	9
13.0	0.0	2.54	4.98	7.22	9.19	10.81	12.01	12.75	13.00	13.0
1	0	56	5.01	28	26	89	10	85	10	1
2	0	57	05	33	33	97	19	95	20	2
3	0	59	09	39	40	11.06	29	13.05	30	3
4	0	61	12	44	47	14	38	15	40	4
13.5	0.0	2.63	5.16	7.50	9.54	11.23	12.47	13.24	13.50	13.5
6	0	65	20	55	61	31	56	34	60	6
7	0	67	24	61	69	39	66	44	70	7
8	0	69	28	67	76	47	75	54	80	8
9	0	71	32	72	83	56	84	63	90	9
14.0	0.0	2.73	5.36	7.78	9.90	11.64	12.93	13.73	14.00	14.0
1	0	75	39	83	97	72	13.03	83	10	1
2	0	77	43	89	10.04	91	12	93	20	2
3	0	79	47	94	11	89	21	14.03	30	3
4	0	81	51	8.00	18	97	30	13	40	4
14.5	0.0	2.83	5.55	8.06	10.25	12.06	13.40	14.22	14.50	14.5
6	0	85	59	11	32	14	49	32	60	6
7	0	87	63	17	39	22	58	42	70	7
8	0	89	67	22	46	31	67	52	80	8
9	0	91	70	28	54	39	77	62	90	9
15.0	0.0	2.93	5.74	8.33	10.61	12.47	13.86	14.71	15.00	15.0
1	0	95	78	39	68	56	95	81	10	1
2	0	96	82	44	75	64	14.04	91	20	2
3	0	98	85	50	82	72	13	15.01	30	3
4	0	3.00	89	55	89	80	23	10	40	4
15.5	0.0	3.02	5.93	8.61	10.96	12.89	14.32	15.20	15.50	15.5
6	0	04	97	67	11.03	97	41	30	60	6
7	0	06	6.01	72	10	13.05	50	40	70	7
8	0	08	05	78	17	14	60	50	80	8
9	0	10	09	83	24	22	69	60	90	9
16.0	0.0	3.12	6.12	8.89	11.31	13.30	14.78	15.69	16.00	16.0
1	0	14	16	94	38	38	87	79	10	1
2	0	16	20	9.00	45	47	97	89	20	2
3	0	18	24	06	53	55	15.06	99	30	3
4	0	20	27	11	60	63	15	16.08	40	4
16.5	0.0	3.22	6.31	9.17	11.67	13.72	15.24	16.18	16.50	16.5
6	0	24	35	22	74	80	34	28	60	6
7	0	26	39	28	81	88	43	38	70	7
8	0	28	43	33	88	97	52	48	80	8
9	0	30	47	39	95	14.05	61	58	90	9
17.0	0.0	3.32	6.51	9.44	12.02	14.14	15.71	16.68	17.00	17.0
1	0	34	54	50	09	22	80	77	10	1
2	0	35	58	55	16	30	89	87	20	2
3	0	37	62	61	23	38	98	97	30	3
4	0	39	66	67	30	47	16.08	17.07	40	4
17.5	0.0	3.41	6.70	9.72	12.37	14.55	16.17	17.16	17.50	17.5
6	0	43	73	78	45	63	26	26	60	6
7	0	45	77	83	52	72	35	36	70	7
8	0	47	81	89	59	80	44	46	80	8
9	0	49	85	94	66	88	54	56	90	9
18.0	0.0	3.51	6.89	10.00	12.73	14.97	16.63	17.65	18.00	18.0

Products of Arcs multiplied by the Sines of the Rhumbs.

Arcs.	Sines of the Rhumbs.									Arcs.
	$S_0 =$ 0.000	$S_1 =$ 0.195	$S_2 =$ 0.383	$S_3 =$ 0.556	$S_4 =$ 0.707	$S_5 =$ 0.831	$S_6 =$ 0.924	$S_7 =$ 0.981	$S_8 =$ 1.000	
°	°	°	°	°	°	°	°	°	°	°
18.0	0.0	3.51	6.89	10.00	12.73	14.97	16.63	17.65	18.00	**18.0**
1	0	53	93	06	80	15.05	72	75	10	**1**
2	0	55	96	11	87	13	82	85	20	**2**
3	0	57	7.00	17	94	22	91	95	30	**3**
4	0	59	04	22	13.01	30	17.00	18.05	40	**4**
18.5	0.0	3.61	7.08	10.28	13.08	15.38	17.09	18.14	18.50	**18.5**
6	0	63	12	33	15	46	18	24	60	**6**
7	0	65	15	39	22	55	27	34	70	**7**
8	0	67	19	44	29	63	37	44	80	**8**
9	0	69	23	50	36	71	46	54	90	**9**
19.0	0.0	3.71	7.27	10.56	13.43	15.80	17.55	18.64	19.00	**19.0**
1	0	73	31	61	50	88	64	73	10	**1**
2	0	74	35	67	58	96	74	83	20	**2**
3	0	76	39	72	65	16.05	83	93	30	**3**
4	0	78	42	78	72	13	92	19.03	40	**4**
19.5	0.0	3.80	7.46	10.83	13.79	16.21	18.01	19.13	19.50	**19.5**
6	0	82	50	89	86	30	11	22	60	**6**
7	0	84	54	94	93	38	20	32	70	**7**
8	0	86	58	11.00	14.00	46	29	42	80	**8**
9	0	88	62	06	07	55	39	52	90	**9**
20.0	0.0	3.90	7.66	11.11	14.14	16.63	18.48	19.62	20.00	**20.0**
1	0	92	69	17	21	71	57	72	10	**1**
2	0	94	73	22	29	80	66	81	20	**2**
3	0	96	77	28	36	88	75	91	30	**3**
4	0	98	81	33	43	96	84	20.01	40	**4**
20.5	0.0	4.00	7.84	11.39	14.50	17.05	18.94	20.11	20.50	**20.5**
6	0	02	88	45	57	13	19.03	21	60	**6**
7	0	04	92	50	64	21	12	30	70	**7**
8	0	06	96	56	71	29	22	40	80	**8**
9	0	08	8.00	61	78	38	31	50	90	**9**
21.0	0.0	4.10	8.04	11.66	14.85	17.46	19.40	20.59	21.00	**21.0**
1	0	12	08	72	92	54	49	69	10	**1**
2	0	13	11	78	99	62	58	79	20	**2**
3	0	15	15	83	15.06	71	68	89	30	**3**
4	0	17	19	89	13	79	77	99	40	**4**
21.5	0.0	4.19	8.23	11.94	15.20	17.87	19.86	21.09	21.50	**21.5**
6	0	21	27	12.00	28	96	96	19	60	**6**
7	0	23	30	06	35	18.04	20.05	29	70	**7**
8	0	25	34	11	42	13	14	38	80	**8**
9	0	27	38	17	49	21	23	48	90	**9**
22.0	0.0	4.29	8.42	12.22	15.56	18.29	20.33	21.58	22.00	**22.0**
1	0	31	46	28	63	37	42	68	10	**1**
2	0	33	50	33	70	46	51	78	20	**2**
3	0	35	53	39	77	54	60	87	30	**3**
4	0	37	57	45	84	62	69	97	40	**4**
22.5	0.0	4.39	8.61	12.50	15.91	18.71	20.79	22.07	22.50	**22.5**
6	0	41	65	56	98	79	88	17	60	**6**
7	0	43	69	61	16.05	87	97	26	70	**7**
8	0	45	72	67	12	96	21.06	36	80	**8**
9	0	47	76	72	19	19.04	15	46	90	**9**
23.0	0.0	4.49	8.80	12.78	16.26	19.12	21.25	22.56	23.00	**23.0**
1	0	51	84	83	34	21	34	66	10	**1**
2	0	53	88	89	41	29	43	76	20	**2**
3	0	55	92	95	48	38	53	86	30	**3**
4	0	56	95	13.00	55	46	62	95	40	**4**
23.5	0.0	4.58	8.99	13.06	16.62	19.54	21.71	23.05	23.50	**23.5**
6	0	60	9.03	11	69	62	80	15	60	**6**
7	0	62	07	17	76	71	90	25	70	**7**
8	0	64	11	22	83	79	99	35	80	**8**
9	0	66	15	28	90	87	22.08	45	90	**9**
24.0	0.0	4.68	9.18	13.33	16.97	19.95	22.17	23.54	24.00	**24.0**

Products of Arcs multiplied by the Sines of the Rhumbs.

Arcs.	Sines of the Rhumbs.									Arcs.
	S_0 = 0.000	S_1 = 0.195	S_2 = 0.383	S_3 = 0.556	S_4 = 0.707	S_5 = 0.831	S_6 = 0.924	S_7 = 0.981	S_8 = 1.000	
24°.0	0°.0	4°.68	9°.18	13°.33	16°.97	19°.95	22°.17	23°.54	24°.00	**24°.0**
1	0	70	22	39	17.04	20.03	26	64	10	**1**
2	0	72	26	44	11	12	36	74	20	**2**
3	0	74	30	50	18	20	45	83	30	**3**
4	0	76	34	56	25	29	54	93	40	**4**
24.5	0.0	4.78	9.38	13.61	17.32	20.37	22.63	24.03	24.50	**24.5**
6	0	80	41	66	39	45	72	13	60	**6**
7	0	82	45	72	46	53	82	23	70	**7**
8	0	84	49	78	54	62	91	33	80	**8**
9	0	86	53	83	61	70	23.00	42	90	**9**
25.0	0.0	4.88	9.57	13.89	17.68	20.78	23.09	24.52	25.00	**25.0**
1	0	90	60	94	75	87	19	62	10	**1**
2	0	92	64	14.00	82	95	28	72	20	**2**
3	0	93	68	05	89	21.03	37	81	30	**3**
4	0	95	72	11	96	11	46	91	40	**4**
25.5	0.0	4.97	9.76	14.16	18.03	21.20	23.56	25.01	25.50	**25.5**
6	0	99	79	22	10	28	65	11	60	**6**
7	0	5.01	83	28	17	37	74	21	70	**7**
8	0	03	87	33	25	45	83	30	80	**8**
9	0	05	91	39	32	53	93	40	90	**9**
26.0	0.0	5.07	9.95	14.44	18.39	21.62	24.02	25.50	26.00	**26.0**
1	0	09	99	50	46	70	11	60	10	**1**
2	0	11	10.03	55	53	78	20	70	20	**2**
3	0	13	06	61	60	87	30	80	30	**3**
4	0	15	10	67	67	95	39	89	40	**4**
26.5	0.0	5.17	10.14	14.72	18.74	22.03	24.48	25.99	26.50	**26.5**
6	0	19	18	78	81	12	57	26.09	60	**6**
7	0	21	22	83	88	20	67	19	70	**7**
8	0	23	25	89	95	28	76	29	80	**8**
9	0	25	29	94	19.02	36	85	38	90	**9**
27.0	0.0	5.27	10.33	15.00	19.09	22.45	24.95	26.48	27.00	**27.0**
1	0	29	37	06	16	53	25.04	58	10	**1**
2	0	31	41	11	23	62	13	68	20	**2**
3	0	33	45	17	31	70	22	78	30	**3**
4	0	35	48	22	38	78	31	88	40	**4**
27.5	0.0	5.36	10.52	15.28	19.45	22.86	25.40	26.97	27.50	**27.5**
6	0	38	56	33	52	95	50	27.07	60	**6**
7	0	40	60	39	59	23.03	59	17	70	**7**
8	0	42	64	44	66	11	68	27	80	**8**
9	0	44	68	50	73	20	77	37	90	**9**
28.0	0.0	5.46	10.72	15.55	19.80	23.28	25.87	27.47	28.00	**28.0**
1	0	48	75	61	87	36	96	56	10	**1**
2	0	50	79	67	94	45	26.05	66	20	**2**
3	0	52	83	72	20.01	53	15	76	30	**3**
4	0	54	87	78	08	61	24	86	40	**4**
28.5	0.0	5.56	10.91	15.83	20.15	23.69	26.33	27.95	28.50	**28.5**
6	0	58	94	89	22	78	42	28.05	60	**6**
7	0	60	98	94	29	86	52	15	70	**7**
8	0	62	11.02	16.00	37	94	61	25	80	**8**
9	0	64	06	05	44	24.03	70	35	90	**9**
29.0	0.0	5.66	11.10	16.11	20.51	24.11	26.79	28.44	29.00	**29.0**
1	0	68	13	17	58	19	88	54	10	**1**
2	0	70	17	22	65	28	98	64	20	**2**
3	0	72	21	28	72	36	27.07	74	30	**3**
4	0	74	25	33	79	44	16	84	40	**4**
29.5	0.0	5.75	11.29	16.39	20.86	24.52	27.25	28.93	29.50	**29.5**
6	0	77	33	44	93	61	35	29.03	60	**6**
7	0	79	36	50	21.00	69	44	13	70	**7**
8	0	81	40	55	07	77	53	23	80	**8**
9	0	83	44	61	14	86	62	33	90	**9**
30.0	0.0	5.85	11.48	16.66	21.22	24.94	27.72	29.43	30.00	**30.0**

Products of Arcs multiplied by the Sines of the Rhumbs.

Arcs.	Sines of the Rhumbs.									Arcs.
	S_0 = 0.000	S_1 = 0.195	S_2 = 0.383	S_3 = 0.556	S_4 = 0.707	S_5 = 0.831	S_6 = 0.924	S_7 = 0.981	S_8 = 1.000	
°	°	°	°	°	°	°	°	°	°	°
30.0	0.0	5.85	11.48	16.66	21.22	24.94	27.72	29.43	30.00	**30.0**
1	0	87	52	72	29	25.03	81	53	10	**1**
2	0	89	56	78	36	11	90	62	20	**2**
3	0	91	59	83	43	19	99	72	30	**3**
4	0	93	63	89	50	28	28.09	82	40	**4**
30.5	0.0	5.95	11.67	26.94	21.57	25.36	28.18	29.92	30.50	**30.5**
6	0	97	71	17.00	64	44	27	30.01	60	**6**
7	0	99	75	05	71	52	36	11	70	**7**
8	0	6.01	79	11	78	61	46	21	80	**8**
9	0	03	83	17	85	69	55	31	90	**9**
31.0	0.0	6.05	11.86	17.22	21.92	25.78	28.64	30.41	31.00	**31.0**
1	0	07	90	28	99	86	73	51	10	**1**
2	0	09	94	33	22.06	94	82	61	20	**2**
3	0	10	98	39	13	26.02	91	70	30	**3**
4	0	12	12.02	44	20	10	29.01	80	40	**4**
31.5	0.0	6.14	12.05	17.50	22.27	26.19	29.10	30.90	31.50	**31.5**
6	0	16	09	55	35	27	19	31.00	60	**6**
7	0	18	13	61	42	35	29	10	70	**7**
8	0	20	17	66	49	44	38	19	80	**8**
9	0	22	21	72	56	52	47	29	90	**9**
32.0	0.0	6.24	12.24	17.78	22.63	26.61	29.57	31.39	32.00	**32.0**
1	0	26	28	83	70	69	66	49	10	**1**
2	0	28	32	89	77	77	75	59	20	**2**
3	0	30	36	94	84	85	84	68	30	**3**
4	0	32	40	18.00	91	94	94	78	40	**4**
32.5	0.0	6.34	12.44	18.05	22.98	27.02	30.03	31.88	32.50	**32.5**
6	0	36	47	11	23.05	10	12	98	60	**6**
7	0	38	51	17	13	19	22	32.08	70	**7**
8	0	40	55	22	20	27	31	17	80	**8**
9	0	42	59	28	27	35	40	27	90	**9**
33.0	0.0	6.44	12.63	18.33	23.34	27.44	30.49	32.37	33.00	**33.0**
1	0	46	67	39	41	52	58	47	10	**1**
2	0	48	70	44	48	60	67	56	20	**2**
3	0	50	74	50	55	68	76	66	30	**3**
4	0	52	78	56	62	77	86	76	40	**4**
33.5	0.0	6.53	12.82	18.61	23.69	27.85	30.95	32.86	33.50	**33.5**
6	0	55	86	66	76	93	31.04	95	60	**6**
7	0	57	90	72	83	28.02	13	33.05	70	**7**
8	0	59	93	78	90	10	23	15	80	**8**
9	0	61	97	83	97	19	32	25	90	**9**
34.0	0.0	6.63	13.01	18.89	24.04	28.27	31.41	33.35	34.00	**34.0**
1	0	65	05	94	12	35	51	45	10	**1**
2	0	67	09	19.00	19	43	60	54	20	**2**
3	0	69	13	05	26	52	69	64	30	**3**
4	0	71	16	11	33	60	78	74	40	**4**
34.5	0.0	6.73	13.20	19.16	24.40	28.68	31.87	33.84	34.50	**34.5**
6	0	75	24	22	47	77	97	94	60	**6**
7	0	77	28	27	54	85	32.06	34.03	70	**7**
8	0	79	32	33	61	93	15	13	80	**8**
9	0	81	35	39	68	29.01	24	23	90	**9**
35.0	0.0	6.83	13.39	19.44	24.75	29.10	32.34	34.33	35.00	**35.0**
1	0	85	43	50	82	18	43	43	10	**1**
2	0	87	47	55	89	26	52	52	20	**2**
3	0	89	51	61	96	35	61	62	30	**3**
4	0	91	54	67	25.03	43	70	72	40	**4**
35.5	0.0	6.92	13.58	19.72	25.10	29.51	32.80	34.82	35.50	**35.5**
6	0	94	62	78	18	60	89	92	60	**6**
7	0	96	66	83	25	68	98	35.02	70	**7**
8	0	98	70	89	32	77	33.08	12	80	**8**
9	0	7.00	74	94	39	85	17	21	90	**9**
36.0	0.0	7.02	13.78	20.00	25.46	29.93	33.26	35.31	36.00	**36.0**

Products of Arcs multiplied by the Sines of the Rhumbs.

Arcs.	Sines of the Rhumbs.									Arcs.
	$S_0 =$ 0.000	$S_1 =$ 0.195	$S_2 =$ 0.383	$S_3 =$ 0.556	$S_4 =$ 0.707	$S_5 =$ 0.831	$S_6 =$ 0.924	$S_7 =$ 0.981	$S_8 =$ 1.000	
°	°	°	°	°	°	°	°	°	°	°
36.0	0.0	7.02	13.78	20.00	25.46	29.93	33.26	35.31	36.00	**36.0**
1	0	04	81	05	53	30.01	35	41	10	**1**
2	0	06	85	11	60	10	44	51	20	**2**
3	0	08	89	16	67	18	54	61	30	**3**
4	0	10	93	22	74	26	63	70	40	**4**
36.5	0.0	7.12	13.97	20.28	25.81	30.35	33.72	35.80	36.50	**36.5**
6	0	14	14.00	33	88	43	81	90	60	**6**
7	0	16	04	39	95	52	91	36.00	70	**7**
8	0	18	08	44	26.02	60	34.00	10	80	**8**
9	0	20	12	50	09	68	09	19	90	**9**
37.0	0.0	7.22	14.16	20.55	26.16	30.76	34.18	36.29	37.00	**37.0**
1	0	24	20	61	23	85	28	39	10	**1**
2	0	26	23	66	30	93	37	49	20	**2**
3	0	28	27	72	38	31.01	46	59	30	**3**
4	0	30	31	78	45	10	55	69	40	**4**
37.5	0.0	7.31	14.35	20.83	26.52	31.18	34.64	36.78	37.50	**37.5**
6	0	33	39	89	59	26	74	88	60	**6**
7	0	35	42	94	66	34	83	98	70	**7**
8	0	37	46	21.00	73	43	92	37.08	80	**8**
9	0	39	50	05	80	51	35.01	17	90	**9**
38.0	0.0	7.41	14.54	21.11	26.87	31.59	35.11	37.27	38.00	**38.0**
1	0	43	58	16	94	67	20	37	10	**1**
2	0	45	62	22	27.01	76	29	47	20	**2**
3	0	47	66	28	08	84	38	57	30	**3**
4	0	49	70	33	15	92	47	66	40	**4**
38.5	0.0	7.51	14.73	21.39	27.22	32.01	35.57	37.76	38.50	**38.5**
6	0	53	77	44	30	09	66	86	60	**6**
7	0	55	81	50	37	17	75	96	70	**7**
8	6	57	85	55	44	26	84	38.06	80	**8**
9	0	59	89	61	51	34	94	16	90	**9**
39.0	0.0	7.61	14.92	21.67	27.58	32.42	36.03	38.26	39.00	**39.0**
1	0	63	96	72	65	51	13	35	10	**1**
2	0	65	15.00	78	72	59	22	45	20	**2**
3	0	67	04	83	79	68	31	55	30	**3**
4	0	69	08	89	86	76	40	65	40	**4**
39.5	0.0	7.71	15.11	21.94	27.93	32.84	36.49	38.74	39.50	**39.5**
6	0	73	15	22.00	28.00	92	59	84	60	**6**
7	0	75	19	05	07	33.01	68	94	70	**7**
8	0	77	23	11	15	09	77	39.04	80	**8**
9	0	79	27	17	22	17	86	14	90	**9**
40.0	0.0	7.80	15.31	22.22	28.29	33.26	36.95	39.24	40.00	**40.0**
1	0	82	34	27	36	34	37.04	33	10	**1**
2	0	84	38	33	43	42	14	43	20	**2**
3	0	86	42	39	50	51	23	53	30	**3**
4	0	88	46	44	57	59	33	63	40	**4**
40.5	0.0	7.90	15.50	22.50	28.64	33.68	37.42	39.73	40.50	**40.5**
6	0	92	54	55	71	76	51	82	60	**6**
7	0	94	57	61	78	84	60	92	70	**7**
8	0	96	61	67	85	93	69	40.02	80	**8**
9	0	98	65	72	92	34.01	78	12	90	**9**
41.0	0.0	8.00	15.69	22.78	28.99	34.09	37.88	40.22	41.00	**41.0**
1	0	02	72	83	29.07	17	97	31	10	**1**
2	0	04	76	89	14	25	38.06	41	20	**2**
3	0	06	80	95	21	34	16	51	30	**3**
4	0	08	84	23.00	28	42	25	61	40	**4**
41.5	0.0	8.10	15.88	23.06	29.35	34.51	38.34	40.71	41.50	**41.5**
6	0	12	92	11	42	59	43	80	60	**6**
7	0	13	95	16	49	67	52	90	70	**7**
8	0	15	99	22	56	75	62	41.00	80	**8**
9	0	17	16.03	28	63	83	71	10	90	**9**
42.0	0.0	8.19	16.07	23.33	29.70	34.92	38.81	41.19	42.00	**42.0**

Products of Arcs multiplied by the Sines of the Rhumbs.

Arcs.	Sines of the Rhumbs.									Arcs.
	S_0 = 0.000	S_1 = 0.195	S_2 = 0.383	S_3 = 0.556	S_4 = 0.707	S_5 = 0.831	S_6 = 0.924	S_7 = 0.981	S_8 = 1.000	
°	°	°	°	°	°	°	°	°	°	°
42.0	0.0	8.19	16.07	23.33	29.70	34.92	38.81	41.19	42.00	42.0
1	0	21	11	39	77	35.00	90	29	10	1
2	0	23	15	44	84	08	99	39	20	2
3	0	25	19	50	91	16	39.08	49	30	3
4	0	27	23	56	98	25	17	59	40	4
42.5	0.0	8.29	16.26	23.61	30.05	35.34	39.26	41.69	42.50	42.5
6	0	31	30	66	12	42	36	78	60	6
7	0	33	34	72	19	50	45	88	70	7
8	0	35	38	77	26	58	54	98	80	8
9	0	37	42	83	24	67	64	42.08	90	9
43.0	0.0	8.39	16.46	23.89	30.41	35.75	39.73	42.18	43.00	43.0
1	0	41	49	94	48	83	82	28	10	1
2	0	43	53	24.00	55	92	91	37	20	2
3	0	45	57	05	62	36.00	40.00	47	30	3
4	0	47	61	11	69	08	10	57	40	4
43.5	0.0	8.49	16.65	24.17	30.76	36.17	40.19	42.67	43.50	43.5
6	0	51	68	22	83	25	28	77	60	6
7	0	53	72	28	90	33	37	86	70	7
8	0	55	76	33	97	42	47	96	80	8
9	0	57	80	39	31.04	50	56	43.06	90	9
44.0	0.0	8.58	16.84	24.45	31.11	36.58	40.65	43.16	44.00	44.0
1	0	60	87	50	18	66	74	25	10	1
2	0	62	91	55	26	75	83	35	20	2
3	0	64	95	61	33	83	93	45	30	3
4	0	66	99	67	40	92	41.02	55	40	4
44.5	0.0	8.68	17.03	24.72	31.47	37.00	41.11	43.65	44.50	44.5
6	0	70	07	77	54	08	20	74	60	6
7	0	72	10	83	61	16	30	84	70	7
8	0	74	14	89	68	25	39	94	80	8
9	0	76	18	95	75	33	48	44.04	90	9
45.0	0.0	8.78	17.22	25.00	31.82	37.41	41.57	44.14	45.00	45.0
1	0	80	26	06	89	50	67	24	10	1
2	0	82	29	11	96	58	76	33	20	2
3	0	84	33	17	32.03	66	85	43	30	3
4	0	86	37	22	11	75	95	53	40	4
45.5	0.0	8.88	17.41	25.28	32.18	37.83	42.04	44.63	45.50	45.5
6	0	90	45	33	25	91	13	73	60	6
7	0	92	49	39	32	99	22	83	70	7
8	0	94	53	45	39	38.08	32	93	80	8
9	0	95	56	50	46	16	41	45.02	90	9
46.0	0.0	8.97	17.60	25.56	32.53	38.25	42.50	45.12	46.00	46.0
1	0	99	64	61	60	33	59	22	10	1
2	0	9.01	68	66	67	41	68	31	20	2
3	0	03	72	72	74	49	78	41	30	3
4	0	05	75	78	81	57	87	51	40	4
46.5	0.0	9.07	17.79	25.84	32.88	38.66	42.96	45.61	46.50	46.5
6	0	09	83	89	95	74	43.05	71	60	6
7	0	11	87	94	33.02	82	14	81	70	7
8	0	13	91	26.00	10	91	24	91	80	8
9	0	15	95	06	17	99	33	46.01	90	9
47.0	0.0	9.17	17.99	26.11	33.24	39.08	43.42	46.10	47.00	47.0
1	0	19	18.02	16	31	16	51	20	10	1
2	0	21	06	22	38	24	60	29	20	2
3	0	23	10	28	45	33	70	39	30	3
4	0	25	14	33	52	41	79	49	40	4
47.5	0.0	9.27	18.18	26.39	33.59	39.49	43.88	46.59	47.50	47.5
6	0	29	22	44	66	57	97	69	60	6
7	0	31	25	50	73	66	44.07	78	70	7
8	0	32	29	55	80	74	16	88	80	8
9	0	34	33	61	87	82	25	98	90	9
48.0	0.0	9.36	18.37	26.66	33.94	39.90	44.34	47.08	48.00	48.0

Magnetic Elements of the Earth: The Magnetic Variation.

IN ARCTIC LATITUDES.

Longitude West of Greenwich.

Lat.	0°	5°	10°	15°	20°	25°	30°	35°	40°	45°	Lat.
60° N.	22° W.	25° W.	30° W.	35° W.	39° W.	43° W.	46° W.	49° W.	51° W.	52° W.	60° N.
65	24	28	33	38	43	46	50	54	58	61	65
70	26	30	35	39	44	48	53	58	62	67	70
75	27	31	36	40	45	49	54	59	64	69	75
80	28	32	37	41	45	50	55	60	65	70	80
	45°	50°	55°	60°	65°	70°	75°	80°	85°	90°	
60° N.	52° W.	54° W.	54° W.	53° W.	52° W.	49° W.	43° W.	32° W.	20° W.	4° W.	60° N.
65	61	64	66	67	67	66	64	60	50	25	65
70	67	72	75	78	81	82	83	84	85	85	70
75	69	75	80	86	90	96	103	112	124	135	75
80	70	77	84	91	98	105	114	123	132	141	80
	90°	95°	100°	105°	110°	115°	120°	125°	130°	135°	
60° N.	4° W.	10° E.	19° E.	24° E.	27° E.	29° E.	31° E.	33° E.	33° E.	33° E.	60° N.
65	25	10 E.	23	31	38	43	45	45	44	42	65
70	85	80 W.	70 E.	68	66	65	63	60	58	54	70
75	135	150	172 W.	156 E.	130	110	95	88	81	71	75
80	141	150	160	175 W.	172 E.	160	140	128	110	98	80
	135°	140°	145°	150°	155°	160°	165°	170°	175°	180°	
60° N.	33° E.	32° E.	31° E.	29° E.	27° E.	25° E.	23° E.	21° E.	18° E.	16° E.	60° N.
65	42	40	37	35	33	30	27	24	21	19	65
70	54	50	46	42	39	35	32	29	26	23	70
75	71	62	56	50	45	40	37	35	32	30	75
80	98	84	70	59	54	49	45	42	40	38	80

Longitude East of Greenwich.

Lat.	0°	5°	10°	15°	20°	25°	30°	35°	40°	45°	Lat.
60° N.	22° W.	19° W.	15° W.	12° W.	9° W.	6° W.	2° W.	1° E.	4° E.	6° E.	60° N.
65	24	20	16	14	8	5	2	2	5	8	65
70	26	22	18	13	9	5	1	2	6	9	70
75	27	22	18	13	10	6	2	2	6	9	75
80	28	23	19	13	10	6	2	2	7	10	80
	45°	50°	55°	60°	65°	70°	75°	80°	85°	90°	
60° N.	6° E.	8° E.	10° E.	11° E.	12° E.	12° E.	13° E.	12° E.	11° E.	10° E.	60° N.
65	8	10	12	14	16	16	16	16	14	13	65
70	9	12	14	16	18	18	18	18	17	15	70
75	9	13	15	18	21	24	25	25	24	22	75
80	10	13	15	18	22	25	28	31	33	32	80
	90°	95°	100°	105°	110°	115°	120°	125°	130°	135°	
60° N.	10° E.	7° E.	5° E.	2° E.	0°	2° W.	3° W.	5° W.	6° W.	5° W.	60° N.
65	13	9	7	5	3 E.	0	1	2	3	3	65
70	15	13	11	9	7	6 E.	5 E.	4 E.	3 E.	3 E.	70
75	22	20	18	16	15	14	13	13	12	12	75
80	32	31	30	29	28	27	27	27	27	27	80
	135°	140°	145°	150°	155°	160°	165°	170°	175°	180°	
60° N.	5° W.	4° W.	2° W.	0°	3° E.	5° E.	8° E.	10° E.	13° E.	16° E.	60° N.
65	3	1	1 E.	2 E.	5	7	10	13	16	19	65
70	3 E.	4 E.	6	8	10	12	15	17	20	23	70
75	12	13	14	16	18	20	22	24	27	30	75
80	27	27	28	29	30	31	32	34	36	38	80

Magnetic Elements of the Earth: The Magnetic Variation.

IN LATITUDES FROM 70° N. TO 60° S.

Lat.	Longitude West of Greenwich.										Lat.
	0°	5°	10°	15°	20°	25°	30°	35°	40°	45°	
70° N.	25°.7 W.	30°.2 W.	35°.0 W.	39°.5 W.	44°.2 W.	48°.6 W.	52°.7 W.	57°.5 W.	62°.5 W.	67°.5 W.	70° N.
65	23.7	28.0	32.8	38.0	42.6	46.6	50.5	54.5	58.5	61.0	65
60	22.0	25.4	30.0	34.8	39.4	43.3	46.5	49.0	50.3	52.6	60
55	20.6	23.4	27.0	31.3	35.0	38.5	41.3	43.2	44.3	44.8	55
50	19.3	21.8	24.4	27.5	30.8	33.5	35.5	37.0	37.8	37.6	50
45 N.	18.2 W.	20.3 W.	22.6 W.	24.9 W.	27.4 W.	29.8 W.	31.3 W.	32.0 W.	31.9 W.	31.0 W.	45 N.
40	17.3	19.1	21.0	23.0	24.7	26.4	27.3	27.5	27.0	25.5	40
35	16.6	18.2	19.8	21.4	23.8	24.0	24.2	23.8	23.0	21.4	35
30	16.4	17.6	18.9	20.2	21.2	21.7	21.5	20.8	19.5	17.0	30
25	16.4	17.4	18.4	19.4	20.2	20.3	19.9	18.8	16.5	13.8	25
20 N.	16.6 W.	17.5 W.	18.2 W.	19.0 W.	19.5 W.	19.5 W.	18.7 W.	16.5 W.	14.0 W.	10.7 W.	20 N.
15	17.1	17.7	18.3	19.0	19.4	19.2	17.3	15.0	11.6	8.2	15
10	17.6	18.2	18.6	19.2	19.5	18.7	16.4	13.3	9.8	6.0	10
5	18.4	18.8	19.3	19.5	19.4	18.2	15.8	12.5	8.8	5.0	5
0	19.8	20.5	20.7	20.3	19.5	18.9	15.3	12.0	8.3	4.4	0
5 S.	21.8 W.	22.4 W.	22.5 W.	21.6 W.	19.9 W.	17.5 W.	15.0 W.	11.7 W.	8.0 W.	4.0 W.	5 S.
10	24.0	24.2	23.8	22.0	19.6	17.0	14.3	11.0	7.4	3.6	10
15	25.8	25.6	24.2	21.6	18.8	16.2	13.5	10.4	6.6	3.0	15
20	27.0	25.8	23.4	20.7	18.0	15.3	12.5	9.2	5.4	2.2	20
25	26.9	25.0	22.3	19.6	16.8	14.1	11.2	7.7	4.3	1.2	25
30 S.	26.0 W.	23.7 W.	21.1 W.	18.4 W.	15.6 W.	12.7 W.	9.6 W.	6.4 W.	3.0 W.	0.0	30 S.
35	24.8	22.4	19.8	17.0	14.3	11.2	8.2	5.0	1.6	1.9 E.	35
40	23.4	21.0	18.4	15.7	12.8	9.8	6.6	3.4	0.0	3.5	40
45	21.9	19.5	16.8	14.2	11.2	8.0	5.0	1.5	2.0 E.	5.3	45
50	20.3	17.7	15.2	12.4	9.5	6.3	3.0	0.3 E.	3.7	7.0	50
55 S.	18.5 W.	15.9 W.	13.3 W.	10.5 W.	7.4 W.	4.2 W.	0.8 W.	2.4 E.	5.6 E.	8.6 E.	55 S.
60	16.8	14.0	11.4	8.3	5.2	2.8	1.2 E.	4.4	7.3	10.3	60

Lat.	Longitude West of Greenwich.										Lat.
	45°	50°	55°	60°	65°	70°	75°	80°	85°	90°	
70° N.	67°.5 W.	71°.5 W.	75°.0 W.	78°.0 W.	81°.0 W.	82°.0 W.	83°.0 W.	84°.0 W.	85°.0 W.	84°.0 W.	70° N.
65	61.0	64.5	66.5	67.0	67.5	66.5	64.5	60.0	50.0	22.5	65
60	52.6	53.8	54.0	53.3	51.7	44.0	42.5	32.0	20.0	3.5	60
55	44.8	44.8	43.8	42.0	38.0	33.0	27.0	18.0	8.0	3.0 E.	55
50	37.6	36.3	34.2	31.0	27.0	22.4	16.5	10.0	2.2	6.0	50
45 N.	31.0 W.	29.3 W.	26.8 W.	23.7 W.	20.3 W.	15.0 W.	10.0 W.	4.5 W.	1.0 E.	7.0 E.	45 N.
40	25.5	23.5	20.9	17.5	13.4	9.4	5.3	1.0	3.3	7.3	40
35	21.4	19.0	15.7	12.3	9.0	5.8	2.3	1.1 E.	4.4	7.4	35
30	17.0	14.0	11.1	8.5	5.7	2.7	0.0	2.6	5.0	7.3	30
25	13.8	10.9	8.4	5.8	3.0	0.5	1.6 E.	3.5	5.4	7.2	25
20 N.	10.7 W.	7.0 W.	5.2 W.	2.7 W.	0.1 W.	1.4 E.	2.8 E.	4.4 E.	5.9 E.	7.3 E.	20 N.
15	8.2	5.2	2.4	0.2 E.	1.4 E.	2.5	3.8	5.2	6.5	7.4	15
10	6.0	3.0	0.1 E.	1.4	2.5	3.7	4.9	6.3	7.2	7.7	10
5	5.0	1.8	0.8	2.1	3.3	4.6	6.0	7.1	7.8	8.3	5
0	4.4	1.0	1.3	2.7	4.0	5.6	7.0	8.0	8.6	8.7	0
5 S.	4.0 W.	0.6 W.	1.7 E.	3.3 E.	5.0 E.	6.5 E.	8.0 E.	9.0 E.	9.4 E.	9.5 E.	5 S.
10	3.6	0.2	2.1	4.2	5.8	7.7	9.0	10.1	10.5	10.5	10
15	3.0	0.2 E.	2.6	5.0	7.0	9.0	10.2	11.2	11.5	11.5	15
20	2.2	1.0	3.7	6.3	8.5	10.3	11.6	12.5	12.8	12.6	20
25	1.2	2.3	5.0	7.8	10.0	11.8	12.2	14.2	14.3	13.8	25
30 S.	0.0	3.5 E.	6.5 E.	9.4 E.	11.6 E.	13.8 E.	15.2 E.	15.8 E.	15.8 E.	15.1 E.	30 S.
35	1.9 E.	5.2	8.3	11.0	13.5	15.5	16.8	17.4	17.2	16.4	35
40	3.5	6.8	10.0	12.8	15.4	17.3	18.5	19.1	19.0	18.2	40
45	5.3	8.4	11.6	14.7	16.8	19.0	20.4	21.2	21.1	20.4	45
50	7.0	10.0	13.3	16.1	18.3	20.5	22.1	23.2	23.2	22.7	50
55 S.	8.6 E.	11.8 E.	15.0 E.	17.5 E.	20.0 E.	21.8 E.	24.0 E.	25.0 E.	25.5 E.	25.3 E.	55 S.
60	10.3	13.5	16.5	19.2	21.6	24.3	26.0	27.1	27.7	27.8	60

Magnetic Elements of the Earth: The Magnetic Variation.

IN LATITUDES FROM 70° N. TO 60° S.

Lat.	Longitude West of Greenwich.										Lat.
	90°	95°	100°	105°	110°	115°	120°	125°	130°	135°	
70 N.	84.0 W.	80.0 W.	70.0 E.	68.0 E.	67.0 E.	65.0 E.	63.0 E.	60.0 E.	58.0 E.	54.0 E.	70 N.
65	22.5	7.5 E.	23.0	31.5	38.0	42.6	45.0	45.0	44.0	42.0	65
60	3.5	10.0	19.0	24.0	27.2	29.5	31.0	33.0	33.0	32.6	60
55	3.0 E.	11.0	17.0	21.0	23.1	25.0	26.3	27.2	27.5	27.4	55
50	6.0	10.8	15.3	18.4	21.6	22.0	22.8	23.4	23.7	23.6	50
45 N.	7.0 E.	10.4 E.	13.4 E.	16.0 E.	17.8 E.	19.3 E.	20.0 E.	20.4 E.	20.5 E.	20.4 E.	45 N.
40	7.3	10.0	12.0	14.0	15.4	16.4	17.0	17.5	17.7	17.7	40
35	7.4	9.3	11.0	12.5	13.5	14.3	14.9	15.2	15.4	15.4	35
30	7.3	8.9	10.0	11.0	11.7	12.2	12.5	12.7	12.8	12.9	30
25	7.2	8.4	9.1	9.8	10.3	10.6	10.7	10.8	10.8	10.8	25
20 N.	7.3 E	8.1 E.	8.5 E.	8.8 E.	9.0 E.	9.0 E.	9.0 E.	9.0 E.	8.9 E.	8.9 E.	20 N.
15	7.4	8.0	8.3	8.1	7.9	7.6	7.3	7.1	7.0	7.0	15
10	7.7	8.1	7.9	7.3	6.9	6.5	6.2	6.0	5.8	5.8	10
5	8.3	8.3	7.7	7.0	6.4	6.0	5.5	5.0	4.8	4.8	5
0	8.7	8.6	8.0	7.0	6.3	5.7	5.1	4.5	4.0	4.0	0
5 S.	9.5 E.	9.2 E.	8.4 E.	7.5 E.	6.6 E.	6.0 E.	5.4 E.	5.0 E.	4.5 E.	4.4 E.	5 S.
10	10.5	10.0	9.1	8.1	7.2	6.6	6.0	5.7	5.5	5.5	10
15	11.5	10.9	9.9	9.0	8.0	7.4	7.0	6.6	6.4	6.3	15
20	12.6	11.8	10.8	9.9	8.9	8.2	7.8	7.5	7.3	7.2	20
25	13.8	12.9	11.7	10.7	9.8	9.0	8.6	8.3	8.2	8.1	25
30 S.	15.1 E.	14.0 E.	13.0 E.	11.8 E.	10.7 E.	9.8 E.	9.3 E.	9.0 E.	8.7 E.	8.7 E.	30 S.
35	16.4	15.4	14.1	13.0	11.9	10.9	10.1	9.7	9.5	9.4	35
40	18.2	17.0	15.6	14.4	13.2	12.2	11.3	10.6	10.3	10.1	40
45	20.4	19.3	17.8	16.2	14.6	13.6	12.7	12.0	11.5	11.2	45
50	22.7	21.6	20.2	18.6	17.0	15.3	14.2	13.5	13.0	12.6	50
55 S.	25.3 E.	24.5 E.	23.0 E.	21.4 E.	19.8 E.	18.2 E.	16.6 E.	15.5 E.	14.8 E.	14.4 E.	55 S.
60	27.8	27.5	26.7	25.2	23.6	22.0	20.4	19.1	18.1	17.5	60

Lat.	Longitude West of Greenwich.										Lat.
	135°	140°	145°	150°	155°	160°	165°	170°	175°	180°	
70 N.	54.0 E.	50.0 E.	46.5 E.	42.0 E.	39.0 E.	35.0 E.	32.5 E.	29.3 E.	25.8 E.	23.0 E.	70 N.
65	42.0	40.0	37.0	34.5	32.5	30.0	26.6	23.9	21.0	18.5	65
60	32.6	32.0	30.7	28.7	26.7	24.8	22.9	20.7	18.3	16.0	60
55	27.4	26.8	26.0	24.8	23.5	22.0	20.6	18.7	16.8	14.7	55
50	23.6	23.2	22.6	21.9	21.0	19.9	18.5	17.0	15.6	14.0	50
45 N.	20.4 E.	20.0 E.	19.8 E.	19.3 E.	18.7 E.	18.0 E.	16.0 E.	15.8 E.	14.7 E.	13.5 E.	45 N.
40	17.7	17.6	17.3	17.0	16.6	16.0	15.4	14.7	14.0	13.0	40
35	15.4	15.3	15.0	14.9	14.7	14.4	14.3	13.9	13.3	12.4	35
30	12.9	12.9	13.0	13.0	13.0	13.0	13.0	12.9	12.6	12.0	30
25	10.8	10.9	11.0	11.1	11.3	11.5	11.7	11.8	11.9	11.6	25
20 N.	8.9 E.	8.9 E.	8.9 E.	9.0 E.	9.3 E.	9.7 E.	10.1 E.	10.6 E.	10.8 E.	10.8 E.	20 N.
15	7.0	7.1	7.3	7.5	8.0	8.4	9.0	9.5	9.8	10.0	15
10	5.8	5.9	6.1	6.4	6.8	7.3	8.0	8.7	9.1	9.5	10
5	4.8	4.8	5.0	5.6	6.2	6.7	7.4	8.1	8.6	9.0	5
0	4.0	4.0	4.2	5.2	5.9	6.5	7.2	7.9	8.3	8.7	0
5 S.	4.4 E.	4.5 E.	4.8 E.	5.4 E.	6.0 E.	6.6 E.	7.3 E.	8.0 E.	8.4 E.	8.8 E.	5 S.
10	5.5	5.5	5.7	6.0	6.5	7.1	7.6	8.3	8.8	9.2	10
15	6.3	6.3	6.4	6.7	7.2	7.6	8.2	8.7	9.3	9.6	15
20	7.2	7.2	7.3	7.6	7.8	8.4	8.9	9.4	9.8	10.2	20
25	8.1	8.1	8.2	8.4	8.7	9.2	9.6	10.0	10.7	11.1	25
30 S.	8.7 E.	8.7 E.	8.8 E.	9.2 E.	9.5 E.	9.8 E.	10.3 E.	10.9 E.	11.6 E.	12.3 E.	30 S.
35	9.4	9.4	9.6	9.8	10.2	10.7	11.3	12.0	12.7	13.4	35
40	10.1	10.2	10.4	10.7	11.2	11.7	12.4	13.0	13.8	14.6	40
45	11.2	11.2	11.5	11.8	12.3	12.9	13.5	14.3	15.2	16.0	45
50	12.6	12.7	12.8	13.2	13.6	14.2	15.0	15.8	16.7	17.5	50
55 S.	14.4 E.	14.4 E.	14.5 E.	15.0 E.	15.4 E.	16.2 E.	17.0 E.	17.8 E.	18.4 E.	19.0 E.	55 S.
60	17.5	17.3	17.4	17.7	18.2	18.7	19.2	19.7	20.3	21.2	60

Magnetic Elements of the Earth: The Magnetic Variation.

IN LATITUDES FROM 70° N. TO 60° S.

Lat.	Longitude East of Greenwich.										Lat.
	0°	5°	10°	15°	20°	25°	30°	35°	40°	45°	
70° N.	25°.7 W.	21°.8 W.	17°.6 W.	13°.5 W.	9°.5 W.	5°.0 W.	1°.2 W.	2°.4 E.	5°.6 E.	9°.0 E.	70° N.
65	23.7	20.0	16.4	12.6	8.9	5.3	1.6	2.0	4.9	7.7	65
60	22.0	18.8	15.4	12.0	8.6	5.7	2.4	1.0	3.7	6.1	60
55	20.6	17.7	14.5	11.5	8.5	6.0	3.2	0.4 W.	2.0	4.3	55
50	19.3	16.7	13.8	11.3	8.6	6.3	4.0	1.7	0.3	2.3	50
45 N.	18.2 W.	16.0 W.	13.5 W.	11.3 W.	8.8 W.	6.7 W.	4.6 W.	2.5 W.	1.0 W.	0.8 E.	45 N.
40	17.3	15.3	13.3	11.4	9.2	7.2	5.0	3.4	1.8	0.5 W.	40
35	16.6	15.0	13.2	11.5	9.6	7.6	5.6	3.9	2.5	1.3	35
30	16.4	15.0	13.3	11.7	10.0	8.1	6.2	4.4	3.1	1.9	30
25	16.4	15.2	13.7	12.0	10.3	8.6	6.7	5.0	3.7	2.4	25
20 N.	16.6 W.	15.6 W.	14.2 W.	12.7 W.	11.0 W.	9.2 W.	7.3 W.	5.6 W.	4.2 W.	3.0 W.	20 N.
15	17.1	16.2	15.0	13.4	11.7	10.0	8.2	6.4	4.8	3.6	15
10	17.6	16.9	15.9	14.5	12.8	11.0	9.2	7.4	6.0	4.4	10
5	18.4	17.6	16.7	15.5	14.0	12.3	10.4	8.6	6.8	5.3	5
0	19.8	18.9	17.9	16.8	15.5	13.9	12.0	10.0	8.2	6.5	0
5 S.	21.8 W.	20.8 W.	19.5 W.	18.2 W.	17.0 W.	15.6 W.	14.0 W.	12.0 W.	9.8 W.	8.0 W.	5 S.
10	24.0	23.2	22.0	20.3	19.0	17.4	15.8	14.0	11.8	9.8	10
15	25.8	25.4	24.6	23.5	21.7	20.0	18.2	16.2	14.4	12.2	15
20	27.0	27.1	26.8	26.0	24.6	23.0	21.0	19.3	17.3	15.0	20
25	26.9	28.1	28.2	27.9	27.0	25.7	24.2	22.5	20.7	18.8	25
30 S.	26.0 W.	27.8 W.	28.8 W.	29.1 W.	28.9 W.	28.3 W.	27.0 W.	25.4 W.	23.7 W.	22.0 W.	30 S.
35	24.8	26.8	28.6	29.6	30.2	30.2	29.8	28.9	27.5	26.0	35
40	23.4	25.7	27.7	29.5	30.9	31.6	31.7	31.3	30.6	29.6	40
45	21.9	24.4	26.6	28.8	30.8	32.2	33.2	33.4	33.0	32.4	45
50	20.3	23.0	25.3	27.8	30.2	32.3	33.8	34.9	35.2	35.2	50
55 S.	18.5 W.	21.2 W.	23.8 W.	26.4 W.	29.2 W.	32.0 W.	34.2 W.	35.8 W.	36.8 W.	37.4 W.	55 S.
60	16.8	19.7	22.3	25.0	28.1	31.3	34.0	36.0	37.3	38.4	60

Lat.	Longitude East of Greenwich.										Lat.
	45°	50°	55°	60°	65°	70°	75°	80°	85°	90°	
70° N.	9°.0 E.	12°.0 E.	14°.0 E.	16°.0 E.	18°.0 E.	18°.0 E.	18°.0 E.	18°.0 E.	17°.0 E.	15°.0 E.	70° N.
65	7.7	10.1	12.5	14.0	16.0	16.5	16.5	16.0	14.0	13.0	65
60	6.1	8.2	10.0	11.3	12.0	12.5	12.6	12.5	11.3	9.7	60
55	4.3	6.2	7.9	9.1	9.7	10.0	10.0	9.9	9.4	8.0	55
50	2.3	4.0	5.7	5.9	7.8	8.3	8.6	8.5	8.2	7.1	50
45 N.	0.8 E.	2.4 E.	3.9 E.	5.0 E.	6.2 E.	6.8 E.	7.2 E.	7.4 E.	7.4 E.	6.7 E.	45 N.
40	0.5 W.	0.9	2.2	3.2	4.2	5.2	6.0	6.3	6.4	6.3	40
35	1.3	0.2 W.	0.9	1.8	2.7	3.5	4.2	4.7	5.1	5.2	35
30	1.9	1.1	0.2 W.	0.6	1.4	2.0	2.6	3.1	3.5	3.6	30
25	2.4	1.6	0.8	0.0	0.7	1.1	1.7	2.2	2.7	2.8	25
20 N.	3.0 W.	2.0 W.	1.3 W.	0.5 W.	0.2 E.	0.7 E.	1.2 E.	1.6 E.	2.1 E.	2.3 E.	20 N
15	3.6	2.5	1.6	0.9	0.0	0.4	0.8	1.3	1.6	2.0	15
10	4.4	3.2	2.1	1.3	0.5 W.	0.2	0.6	1.0	1.3	1.6	10
5	5.3	4.0	2.8	1.8	1.0	0.2 W.	0.4	0.7	1.1	1.4	5
0	6.5	5.0	3.8	2.7	1.7	0.8	0.0	0.4	0.7	1.1	0
5 S.	8.0 W.	6.5 W.	4.9 W.	3.7 W.	2.7 W.	1.8 W.	0.9 W.	0.0	0.3 E.	0.5 E.	5 S.
10	9.8	8.1	6.5	5.0	4.0	3.0	2.1	1.4 W.	0.7 W.	0.2 W.	10
15	12.2	10.0	8.5	7.1	5.8	4.7	3.9	3.2	2.6	2.1	15
20	15.0	13.0	11.0	9.5	8.2	7.1	6.2	5.5	4.9	4.5	20
25	18.8	15.6	14.7	13.0	11.5	10.3	9.6	9.0	8.4	7.7	25
30 S.	22.0 W.	20.2 W.	18.5 W.	16.8 W.	15.3 W.	14.2 W.	13.0 W.	12.4 W.	12.0 W.	11.5 W.	30 S.
35	26.0	24.3	22.8	21.5	20.2	19.1	18.1	17.5	17.0	16.0	35
40	29.6	28.2	27.0	25.8	24.7	23.7	23.0	22.4	21.6	20.5	40
45	32.4	31.7	30.8	30.0	29.2	28.4	27.7	27.2	26.7	25.7	45
50	35.2	34.7	34.2	33.7	33.3	32.8	32.5	32.2	32.0	31.2	50
55 S.	37.4 W.	37.7 W.	38.0 W.	38.2 W.	38.5 W.	39.0 W.	39.3 W.	39.5 W.	39.2 W.	38.3 W.	55 S.
60	38.4	39.3	40.0	41.7	43.5	45.0	46.5	47.0	46.2	45.0	60

Magnetic Elements of the Earth: The Magnetic Variation.

FROM LATITUDES 70° N. TO 60° S.

Lat.	Longitude East of Greenwich.										Lat.
	90°	95°	100°	105°	110°	115°	120°	125°	130°	135°	
70° N.	15°.0 E.	13°.0 E.	11°.0 E.	9°.0 E.	7°.0 E.	5°.5 E.	4°.5 E.	3°.5 E.	2°.7 E.	3°.5 E.	70° N.
65	13.0	9.4	7.0	5.0	2.5	0.0	1.2 W.	2.5 W.	3.0 W.	2.7 W.	65
60	9.7	7.3	5.0	2.5	0.0	1.6 W.	3.4	5.2	6.0	5.2	60
55	8.0	6.0	3.8	1.4	0.7 W.	2.4	4.1	5.7	6.5	6.0	55
50	7.1	5.4	3.3	1.0	0.8	2.5	4.2	5.8	6.5	6.1	50
45 N.	6.7 E.	5.0 E.	3.0 E.	1.0 E.	0.7 W.	2.2 W.	3.9 W.	5.6 W.	6.4 W.	6.0 W.	45 N.
40	6.3	4.8	3.0	1.2	0.3	1.7	3.3	4.8	5.7	5.5	40
35	5.2	4.3	3.1	1.4	0.2	1.2	2.5	3.9	4.5	4.4	35
30	3.6	3.4	2.7	1.7	0.6 E.	0.6	1.7	2.6	3.0	2.9	30
25	2.8	2.9	2.5	2.0	1.0	0.1 E.	0.8	1.6	1.8	1.6	25
20 N.	2.3 E.	2.5 E.	2.3 E.	2.2 E.	1.5 E.	0.6 E.	0.0	0.7 W.	0.9 W.	0.5 W.	20 N.
15	2.0	2.2	2.4	2.2	1.7	1.2	0.6 E.	0.0	0.0	0.5 E.	15
10	1.6	1.9	2.1	2.0	1.6	1.4	1.3	1.1 E.	1.1 E.	1.4	10
5	1.4	1.6	1.7	1.7	1.7	1.6	1.4	1.4	1.5	1.9	5
0	1.1	1.3	1.4	1.4	1.4	1.4	1.5	1.7	1.8	2.3	0
5 S.	0.5 E.	0.8 E.	1.0 E.	1.1 E.	1.1 E.	1.2 E.	1.3 E.	1.6 E.	1.8 E.	2.7 E.	5 S.
10	0.2 W.	0.1	0.2	0.3	0.4	0.5	1.0	1.4	1.9	3.0	10
15	2.1	1.7 W.	1.4 W.	1.1 W.	0.8 W.	0.5 W.	0.0	0.8	1.7	3.1	15
20	4.5	4.0	3.4	2.8	2.2	1.5	0.8 W.	0.0	1.4	3.2	20
25	7.7	7.0	6.0	4.9	3.8	2.6	1.7	0.6 W.	0.9	3.3	25
30 S.	11.5 W.	10.6 W.	9.3 W.	7.7 W.	6.0 W.	4.3 W.	2.5 W.	1.1 W.	0.5 E.	3.3 E.	30 S.
35	16.0	14.6	13.0	11.0	9.0	6.5	4.3	1.8	0.0	3.2	35
40	20.5	19.0	16.8	14.4	11.6	9.0	6.0	3.0	0.3 W.	3.0	40
45	25.7	24.0	21.4	18.4	15.5	11.9	8.3	4.8	1.0	2.8	45
50	31.2	29.5	27.0	23.0	19.0	15.0	10.7	6.5	2.0	2.5	50
55 S.	38.3 W.	35.8 W.	33.0 W.	29.0 W.	24.3 W.	19.8 W.	14.7 W.	9.2 W.	3.8 W.	1.8 E.	55 S.
60	45.0	43.2	41.0	36.0	31.0	25.0	20.0	13.8	7.0	0.0	60

Lat.	Longitude East of Greenwich.										Lat.
	135°	140°	145°	150°	155°	160°	165°	170°	175°	180°	
70° N.	3°.5 E.	4°.5 E.	6°.0 E.	8°.0 E.	10°.0 E.	12°.5 E.	15°.0 E.	17°.5 E.	20°.0 E.	23°.0 E.	70° N.
65	2.7 W.	1.4 W.	0.5	2.5	4.6	7.3	9.8	12.6	15.8	18.5	65
60	5.2	3.6	1.8 W.	0.2	2.8	5.3	7.8	10.3	13.2	16.0	60
55	6.0	4.6	2.5	0.4 W.	2.0	4.4	7.0	9.7	12.3	14.7	55
50	6.1	4.8	2.8	0.7	1.9	4.3	7.0	9.6	12.0	14.0	50
45 N.	6.0 W.	4.7 W.	2.8 W.	0.5 W.	2.0 E.	4.7 E.	7.3 E.	9.8 E.	11.8 E.	13.5 E.	45 N.
40	5.5	4.4	2.2	0.0	2.5	5.0	7.6	10.0	11.6	13.0	40
35	4.4	3.4	1.5	0.5 E.	3.1	5.5	7.8	10.0	11.4	12.4	35
30	2.9	2.0	0.4	1.4	3.8	6.0	8.1	10.0	11.1	12.0	30
25	1.6	0.8	0.5 E.	2.2	4.3	6.4	8.2	10.0	11.0	11.6	25
20 N.	0.5 W.	0.5 E.	1.5 E.	3.1 E.	5.0 E.	6.8 E.	8.4 E.	9.7 E.	10.5 E.	10.8 E.	20 N.
15	0.5 E.	1.2	2.5	3.9	5.6	7.1	8.4	9.4	9.9	10.0	15
10	1.4	2.2	3.2	4.7	6.0	7.4	8.4	9.2	9.5	9.5	10
5	1.9	2.9	4.0	5.2	6.4	7.7	8.4	9.0	9.3	9.0	5
0	2.3	3.4	4.6	5.7	6.8	8.0	8.4	8.7	9.0	8.7	0
5 S.	2.7 E.	3.8 E.	5.0 E.	6.1 E.	7.2 E.	8.2 E.	8.6 E.	9.0 E.	9.1 E.	8.8 E.	5 S.
10	3.0	4.2	5.4	6.6	7.6	8.4	9.0	9.3	9.3	9.2	10
15	3.1	4.5	5.8	7.1	8.2	9.0	9.5	9.7	9.7	9.6	15
20	3.2	4.8	6.3	7.7	8.8	9.5	10.0	10.3	10.4	10.2	20
25	3.3	5.2	7.0	8.3	9.5	10.3	11.0	11.3	11.4	11.1	25
30 S.	3.3 E.	5.6 E.	7.5 E.	9.1 E.	10.3 E.	11.3 E.	12.0 E.	12.5 E.	12.6 E.	12.3 E.	30 S.
35	3.2	6.0	8.1	10.0	11.3	12.4	13.2	13.7	13.7	13.4	35
40	3.0	6.3	8.8	10.7	12.3	13.6	14.4	14.9	15.0	14.6	40
45	2.8	6.6	9.7	11.7	13.5	14.8	15.7	16.2	16.3	16.0	45
50	2.5	7.0	10.3	12.7	14.7	16.2	17.2	17.7	17.8	17.5	50
55 S.	1.8 E.	6.8 E.	11.0 E.	14.0 E.	16.3 E.	18.1 E.	14.1 E.	19.6 E.	18.4 E.	19.0 E.	55 S.
60	0.0	6.0	11.4	15.6	18.5	20.7	22.0	22.4	22.0	21.2	60

Magnetic Elements of the Earth: The Magnetic Dip.

Lat.	Longitude West of Greenwich.																			Lat.
	0°	10°	20°	30°	40°	50°	60°	70°	80°	90°	100°	110°	120°	130°	140°	150°	160°	170°	180°	
75° N.	+81°	+82°	+83°	+83°	+85°	+86°	+86°	+87°	+89°	+89°	+89°	+87°	+87°	+86°	+85°	+83°	+82°	+82°	+82°	75° N.
70	79	81	81	82	84	85	85	86	88	89	89	87	86	84	83	81	80	80	79	70
65	75	76	77	78	79	81	83	85	87	87	86	85	85	83	81	79	77	76	75	65
60	72	73	74	76	78	80	82	84	86	86	85	83	82	79	77	75	73	72	71	60
55	70	72	73	74	76	78	80	82	83	83	82	80	78	76	74	72	70	68	66	55
50 N.	+57	+69	+71	+73	+75	+77	+78	+79	+80	+79	+78	+76	+74	+72	+69	+57	+65	+63	+61	50 N.
45	64	66	68	71	73	75	76	77	77	76	74	72	70	68	65	63	60	58	56	45
40	60	62	65	68	70	72	72	72	72	71	69	67	65	62	60	57	55	52	51	40
35	56	58	61	65	67	68	63	68	67	65	64	62	59	57	55	52	50	48	47	35
30	51	54	57	61	63	64	64	63	62	60	58	56	54	52	50	48	47	45	43	30
25 N.	+46	+50	+54	+57	+58	+59	+58	+57	+56	+53	+51	+49	+48	+47	+46	+44	+43	+42	+39	25 N.
20	38	43	48	52	54	55	53	52	49	45	43	42	42	42	41	40	38	35	30	20
15	30	37	42	47	49	49	47	44	40	38	36	34	33	33	32	32	30	27	22	15
10	20	29	36	40	42	41	40	37	33	31	28	26	24	24	23	23	21	19	14	10
5	10	20	29	33	35	34	33	30	27	22	17	14	13	13	13	13	11	+ 9	+ 5	5
0	0	+10	+20	+26	+28	+27	+25	+20	+16	+10	+ 5	+ 3	+ 2	+ 2	+ 2	+ 2	+ 1	- 1	- 4	0
5 S.	- 8	+ 2	12	19	21	20	18	12	+ 8	+ 2	- 3	- 5	- 7	- 7	- 7	- 7	- 7	10	14	5 S.
10	18	- 6	+ 4	11	14	13	9	+ 2	- 3	- 9	12	14	16	16	16	16	17	20	23	10
15	28	16	- 5	+ 2	+ 5	+ 4	0	- 7	12	17	20	22	24	24	24	26	27	30	32	15
20	34	26	15	- 8	- 4	- 5	-10	15	20	25	28	30	32	33	33	34	35	37	39	20
25 S.	-38	32	-24	-18	-14	-14	-18	-23	-28	-32	-35	-38	-40	-41	-41	-41	-42	-44	-46	25 S.
30	42	37	31	27	23	23	26	30	34	38	41	44	46	47	48	49	50	51	53	30
35	46	41	36	33	30	30	33	36	40	44	47	50	51	52	53	54	55	56	58	35
40	50	45	40	38	36	36	39	42	46	50	53	55	56	57	58	59	60	61	62	40
45	53	50	45	43	42	42	45	48	51	55	58	60	61	62	63	63	64	65	66	45
50 S.	-55	-52	-49	-47	-47	-48	-50	-52	-55	-59	-62	-54	-65	-66	-67	-67	-68	-69	-70	50 S.
55	57	55	53	52	52	53	55	57	60	64	67	68	69	70	71	71	72	73	73	55
60	59	57	56	55	56	57	59	62	65	68	70	72	73	74	75	75	76	76	76	60

Lat.	Longitude East of Greenwich.																			Lat.
	0°	10°	20°	30°	40°	50°	60°	70°	80°	90°	100°	110°	120°	130°	140°	150°	160°	170°	180°	
75° N.	+81°	+81°	+81°	+80°	+80°	+80°	+81°	+81°	+81°	+81°	+81°	+81°	+81°	+81°	+81°	+81°	+81°	+82°	+82°	75° N.
70	79	79	78	77	77	77	78	79	79	80	80	80	80	80	80	79	79	79	79	70
65	75	75	74	74	74	75	76	76	76	77	77	77	77	77	76	76	75	74	75	65
60	72	72	71	71	71	71	72	72	72	73	73	73	73	73	72	72	70	70	71	60
55	70	69	68	68	68	68	69	70	70	71	71	71	71	70	69	68	66	65	66	55
50 N.	+67	+66	+65	+64	+64	+64	+64	+65	+65	+65	+66	+66	+66	+65	+64	+63	+61	+60	+51	50 N.
45	64	62	61	60	60	60	60	60	60	60	60	61	61	60	59	57	55	55	56	45
40	60	57	55	54	53	53	53	53	54	55	55	56	56	55	53	50	49	49	51	40
35	56	53	50	48	47	47	47	48	49	50	50	50	50	49	48	46	44	45	47	35
30	51	47	43	41	40	39	39	40	40	41	42	43	43	42	42	40	40	41	43	30
25 N.	+46	+40	+35	+31	+30	+29	+29	+30	+31	+33	+34	+35	+35	+35	+35	+33	+33	+35	+39	25 N.
20	38	30	23	20	19	19	20	20	21	22	23	25	27	28	28	24	24	25	30	20
15	30	20	14	10	10	10	10	10	10	11	12	15	17	18	19	15	15	17	22	15
10	20	10	+ 4	0	0	0	0	0	0	0	+ 1	+ 3	+ 5	+ 8	9	9	8	9	14	10
5	10	0	- 6	-10	-10	-10	-10	-10	-10	- 9	- 7	- 5	- 3	- 1	0	0	0	0	+ 5	5
0	0	- 9	-16	-20	-22	-22	-21	-20	-20	-18	-16	-14	-12	-11	-10	-10	-10	- 9	- 4	0
5 S.	- 8	19	25	30	30	30	30	30	29	27	24	22	20	20	20	21	21	19	14	5 S.
10	18	28	33	37	39	40	40	39	38	36	33	32	31	30	31	32	31	28	23	10
15	27	34	40	44	47	48	48	47	46	44	43	42	41	40	40	40	38	35	32	15
20	34	40	46	50	53	54	53	52	52	51	51	51	50	49	47	46	44	42	39	20
25 S.	-38	-44	-50	-54	-57	-58	-57	-56	-56	-55	-55	-55	-55	-54	-53	-53	-52	-50	-46	25 S.
30	42	49	53	57	59	60	61	60	60	60	59	59	59	58	57	57	56	55	53	30
35	46	52	56	59	61	63	64	64	65	65	65	65	65	64	63	63	62	60	58	35
40	50	54	58	61	63	65	66	67	67	68	69	70	70	69	68	67	66	64	62	40
45	53	56	60	62	65	67	68	69	70	71	72	74	75	74	73	72	70	68	66	45
50 S.	-55	-58	-61	-63	-66	-68	-69	-71	-72	-73	-75	-76	-77	-77	-76	-75	-74	-72	-70	50 S.
55	57	60	62	65	67	69	71	72	74	76	78	79	80	80	79	78	77	75	73	55
60	59	62	64	66	68	70	72	73	75	77	80	82	83	83	82	81	80	77	76	60

Magnetic Elements of the Earth: The Horizontal Force.

Longitude West of Greenwich.

Lat.	0°	10°	20°	30°	40°	50°	60°	70°	80°	90°	100°	110°	120°	130°	140°	150°	160°	170°	180°	Lat.
75° N.	0.6	0.5	0.5	0.4	0.4	0.3	0.1	0.0	0.0	0.0	0.0	0.0	0.1	0.2	0.3	0.3	0.4	0.4	0.4	75° N.
70	7	6	6	5	4	3	2	0	0	0	0	0	3	4	5	5	6	6	7	70
65	8	7	7	6	5	4	3	1	0	0	1	3	4	6	6	7	8	8	9	65
60	9	8	7	6	6	5	4	3	3	3	4	5	6	7	8	9	1.0	1.0	1.0	60
55	9	9	8	8	7	6	6	5	4	5	6	7	8	9	1.0	1.0	1	2	2	55
50 N.	1.0	1.0	0.9	0.9	0.8	0.7	0.7	0.6	0.6	0.7	0.8	0.9	1.0	1.1	1.1	1.2	1.3	1.3	1.4	50 N.
45	2	1	1.0	9	9	8	8	8	9	1.0	1.1	1.1	2	2	3	4	4	4	4	45
40	3	2	1	1.0	1.0	1.0	1.0	1.0	1.1	2	3	3	4	4	5	5	5	5	5	40
35	4	3	2	2	1	1	2	2	3	4	5	5	6	6	6	6	6	6	6	35
30	5	4	4	3	3	3	4	5	5	6	7	7	7	7	7	6	6	6	6	30
25 N.	1.6	1.5	1.5	1.4	1.4	1.5	1.5	1.6	1.7	1.8	1.9	1.9	1.9	1.8	1.8	1.7	1.7	1.7	1.7	25 N.
20	7	6	6	5	5	6	7	8	9	2.0	2.0	2.0	9	9	8	7	7	7	7	20
15	8	7	7	6	6	7	8	9	2.0	1	1	1	2.0	9	8	8	8	8	8	15
10	9	8	8	7	7	8	9	2.0	1	2	2	1	1	2.0	9	8	8	9	9	10
5	9	8	8	8	8	9	2.0	0	1	2	2	1	1	0	5	9	9	9	9	5
0	1.9	1.9	1.9	1.9	1.9	1.9	2.0	2.0	2.1	2.2	2.1	2.1	2.1	2.0	2.0	1.9	1.9	2.0	2.0	0
5 S.	8	8	8	9	9	9	0	0	1	1	1	1	0	0	0	2.0	2.0	0	0	5 S.
10	7	7	7	8	8	9	1.9	0	0	1	1	0	0	0	0	0	0	0	0	10
15	6	6	6	7	7	8	8	1.9	0	0	0	0	0	0	0	0	0	0	0	15
20	4	5	6	6	6	7	8	9	1.9	0	0	0	0	0	0	0	0	0	0	20
25 S.	1.4	1.4	1.5	1.5	1.6	1.6	1.7	1.8	1.9	2.0	2.0	2.0	1.9	1.9	1.9	1.9	1.9	1.9	1.9	25 S.
30	3	4	4	5	5	6	7	8	9	1.9	1.9	1.9	9	9	9	8	8	8	7	30
35	3	3	4	5	5	6	7	8	9	8	8	9	8	8	8	7	7	7	6	35
40	3	3	4	5	5	6	7	7	8	8	8	8	7	7	6	6	6	5	5	40
45	3	3	4	5	5	6	6	7	7	7	7	6	6	5	5	5	4	4	3	45
50 S.	1.3	1.3	1.4	1.5	1.5	1.6	1.6	1.6	1.6	1.6	1.5	1.5	1.4	1.4	1.4	1.3	1.3	1.3	1.2	50 S.
55	3	4	4	5	5	6	6	5	5	5	4	3	3	2	2	2	1	1	0	55
60	3	4	4	5	5	5	5	5	4	3	2	1	1	0	0	0.9	0.9	0.8	0.8	60

Longitude East of Greenwich.

Lat.	0°	10°	20°	30°	40°	50°	60°	70°	80°	90°	100°	110°	120°	130°	140°	150°	160°	170°	180°	Lat.
75° N.	0.6	0.6	0.6	0.6	0.6	0.6	0.6	0.6	0.6	0.6	0.6	0.5	0.5	0.5	0.5	0.5	0.5	0.5	0.4	75° N.
70	7	7	7	8	8	8	8	8	7	7	6	6	6	6	6	6	8	8	7	70
65	8	8	8	8	8	8	8	9	9	8	8	8	8	8	8	9	9	9	9	65
60	9	9	9	9	9	9	1.0	1.0	1.0	1.0	1.0	1.0	1.0	1.0	1.0	1.0	1.0	1.0	1.0	60
55	9	1.0	1.0	1.1	1.1	1.1	2	2	1	1	1	1	1	1	1	2	2	2	2	55
50 N.	1.0	1.1	1.1	1.2	1.2	1.2	1.3	1.3	1.3	1.3	1.3	1.3	1.3	1.2	1.3	1.3	1.4	1.4	1.4	50 N.
45	2	2	3	3	4	4	4	4	4	4	4	4	4	4	4	4	4	4	4	45
40	3	3	4	4	5	5	5	6	6	6	6	6	6	6	6	6	5	5	5	40
35	4	4	5	6	6	6	7	7	7	7	7	7	7	7	7	6	6	6	6	35
30	5	5	6	7	8	8	9	9	2.0	2.0	9	9	8	8	7	7	6	6	6	30
25 N.	1.6	1.7	1.7	1.8	1.9	1.9	2.0	2.1	2.2	2.1	2.0	2.0	1.9	1.9	1.8	1.8	1.7	1.7	1.7	25 N.
20	7	8	9	9	9	2.0	0	1	3	2	1	1	2.0	2.0	9	8	8	7	7	20
15	8	9	9	9	9	1.9	0	1	2	3	2	1	1	0	2.0	9	9	8	8	15
10	9	9	9	8	8	9	1.9	0	1	2	2	2	1	1	0	2.0	9	9	9	10
5	9	9	8	7	7	8	9	0	1	1	2	2	2	1	1	0	2.0	2.0	9	5
0	1.9	1.8	1.7	1.6	1.6	1.7	1.8	1.9	2.0	2.1	2.1	2.1	2.2	2.2	2.1	2.1	2.0	2.0	2.0	0
5 S.	8	7	6	5	5	6	7	8	1.9	0	1	1	2	2	1	1	1	0	0	5 S.
10	7	6	5	5	5	5	6	7	8	1.9	0	1	0	1	1	1	1	1	0	10
15	6	5	4	4	4	4	5	6	7	8	1.9	0	0	1	1	1	0	0	0	15
20	4	4	3	3	3	3	4	5	6	7	8	1.8	1.9	1.9	0	0	0	0	0	20
25 S.	1.4	1.3	1.3	1.3	1.3	1.3	1.3	1.4	1.5	1.5	1.6	1.7	1.8	1.8	1.8	1.8	1.8	1.8	1.9	25 S.
30	3	3	3	2	2	2	2	3	4	4	5	6	6	7	7	7	7	7	7	30
35	3	2	2	1	1	1	1	2	2	3	3	4	4	4	4	5	5	6	6	35
40	3	2	2	1	1	1	1	1	1	2	2	3	3	3	3	3	4	4	5	40
45	3	2	1	1	1	0	0	0	1	1	1	1	1	2	2	2	2	3	3	45
50 S.	1.3	1.2	1.1	1.1	1.0	1.0	1.0	1.0	1.0	1.0	1.0	1.0	1.0	1.0	1.0	1.0	1.1	1.1	1.2	50 S.
55	3	2	2	1	0	0	0	0.9	0.9	0.9	0.8	0.8	0.7	0.7	0.8	0.8	0.9	0.9	0	55
60	3	3	2	1	1	0	0	9	8	8	7	6	5	5	5	5	7	8	8	60

Right Ascension of the True Sun and Equation of Time.

1875: At Greenwich Mean Noon.

Day.	January. ☉'s R. A.	January. E. T.	February. ☉'s R. A.	February. E. T.	March. ☉'s R. A.	March. E. T.	April. ☉'s R. A.	April. E. T.	May. ☉'s R. A.	May. E. T.	June. ☉'s R. A.	June. E. T.
	h m	m	h m	m	h m	m	h m	m	h m	m	h m	m
1	18 46.7	− 3.8	20 59.0	−13.8	22 48.1	−12.6	0 41.8	− 4.0	2 33.0	+ 3.0	4 35.7	+ 2.5
2	51.1	4.2	21 3.0	14.0	51.9	12.4	45.4	3.7	36.9	3.1	39.8	2.4
3	55.5	4.7	7.1	14.1	55.6	12.2	49.0	3.4	40.7	3.2	43.9	2.2
4	59.9	5.1	11.1	14.2	59.3	12.0	52.7	3.1	44.5	3.3	48.0	2.0
5	19 4.3	5.6	15.2	14.3	23 3.0	11.7	56.3	2.8	48.4	3.4	52.2	1.9
6	8.7	6.0	19.2	14.3	6.8	11.5	1 0.0	2.5	52.2	3.5	56.3	1.7
7	13.1	6.5	23.2	14.4	10.5	11.3	3.6	2.2	56.1	3.6	5 0.4	1.5
8	19 17.4	− 6.9	21 27.2	−14.4	23 14.2	−11.0	1 7.3	− 2.9	3 0.0	+ 3.6	5 4.5	+ 1.3
9	21.8	7.3	31.2	14.5	17.9	10.8	11.0	1.7	3.9	3.7	8.7	1.1
10	26.2	7.7	35.1	14.5	21.5	10.5	14.6	1.4	7.7	3.8	12.8	0.9
11	30.5	8.2	39.1	14.5	25.2	10.3	18.3	1.1	11.7	3.8	16.9	0.7
12	34.8	8.5	43.0	14.5	28.9	10.0	22.0	0.9	15.6	3.8	21.1	0.5
13	39.2	8.9	46.9	14.5	32.6	9.7	25.7	0.6	19.5	3.8	25.2	0.3
14	43.5	9.3	50.8	14.4	36.2	9.4	29.3	0.3	23.4	3.9	29.4	0.1
15	19 47.8	− 9.7	21 54.7	−14.4	23 39.9	− 9.2	1 33.0	− 0.1	3 27.4	+ 3.9	5 33.5	− 0.1
16	52.1	10.0	58.6	14.3	43.5	8.9	36.7	+ 0.2	31.3	3.8	37.7	0.3
17	56.3	10.3	22 2.5	14.3	47.2	8.6	40.4	0.4	35.3	3.8	41.8	0.5
18	20 0.6	10.7	6.4	14.2	50.8	8.3	44.1	0.6	39.2	3.8	46.0	0.7
19	4.9	11.0	10.2	14.1	54.5	8.0	47.9	0.9	43.2	3.8	50.1	0.9
20	9.1	11.3	14.0	14.0	58.1	7.7	51.6	1.1	47.2	3.7	54.3	1.2
21	13.3	11.5	17.9	13.9	0 1.8	7.4	55.3	1.3	51.2	3.7	58.5	1.4
22	20 17.5	−11.8	22 21.7	−13.8	0 5.4	− 7.1	1 59.0	+ 1.5	3 55.2	+ 3.6	6 2.6	− 1.6
23	21.7	12.1	25.5	13.6	9.0	6.8	2 2.8	1.7	59.2	3.5	6.8	1.8
24	25.9	12.3	29.3	13.5	12.7	6.5	6.5	1.9	4 3.2	3.5	10.9	2.0
25	30.1	12.6	33.1	13.3	16.3	6.2	10.3	2.1	7.3	3.4	15.1	2.2
26	34.3	12.8	36.8	13.1	19.9	5.8	14.1	2.2	11.3	3.3	19.2	2.4
27	38.4	13.0	40.6	13.0	23.6	5.5	17.8	2.4	15.4	3.2	23.4	2.7
28	42.6	13.2	44.4	12.8	27.2	5.2	21.6	2.6	19.4	3.0	27.6	2.9
29	20 46.7	−13.4			0 30.8	− 4.9	2 25.4	+ 2.7	4 23.5	+ 2.9	6 31.7	− 3.1
30	50.8	13.5			34.5	4.6	29.2	2.9	27.6	2.8	35.9	3.3
31	54.9	13.7			38.1	4.3			31.6	2.7		

Day.	July. ☉'s R. A.	July. E. T.	August. ☉'s R. A.	August. E. T.	September. ☉'s R. A.	September. E. T.	October. ☉'s R. A.	October. E. T.	November. ☉'s R. A.	November. E. T.	December. ☉'s R. A.	December. E. T.
	h m	m	h m	m	h m	m	h m	m	h m	m	h m	m
1	6 40.0	− 3.5	8 44.8	− 6.1	10 40.9	+ 0.0	12 29.0	+10.3	14 25.2	+16.3	16 28.9	+10.9
2	44.1	3.6	48.7	6.0	44.5	0.4	32.6	10.6	29.1	16.3	33.2	10.5
3	48.2	3.8	52.6	6.0	48.2	0.7	36.2	10.9	33.0	16.3	37.5	10.1
4	52.4	4.0	56.5	5.9	51.8	1.0	39.9	11.2	37.0	16.3	41.9	9.7
5	56.5	4.2	9 0.3	5.8	55.4	1.3	43.5	11.5	40.9	16.3	46.2	9.3
6	7 0.6	4.4	4.2	5.7	59.0	1.7	47.2	11.8	44.9	16.3	50.6	8.9
7	4.7	4.5	8.0	5.6	11 2.6	2.0	50.8	12.1	48.9	16.2	55.0	8.4
8	7 8.8	− 4.7	9 11.8	− 5.4	11 6.2	+ 2.4	12 54.4	+12.4	14 52.9	+16.1	16 59.3	+ 8.0
9	12.9	4.8	15.6	5.3	9.8	2.7	58.2	12.6	56.9	16.1	17 3.7	7.6
10	17.0	5.0	19.4	5.2	13.4	3.0	13 1.8	12.9	15 1.0	16.0	8.1	7.1
11	21.1	5.2	23.2	5.0	17.0	3.4	5.5	13.2	5.0	15.9	12.5	6.6
12	25.2	5.3	27.0	4.9	20.6	3.7	9.2	13.4	9.1	15.7	16.9	6.2
13	29.2	5.4	30.8	4.7	24.2	4.1	12.9	13.7	13.2	15.6	21.4	5.7
14	33.3	5.5	34.5	4.5	27.8	4.4	16.6	13.9	17.2	15.5	25.8	5.2
15	7 37.3	− 5.6	9 38.3	− 4.3	11 31.4	+ 4.8	13 20.3	+14.1	15 21.4	+15.3	17 30.2	+ 4.7
16	41.4	5.7	42.0	4.1	35.0	5.1	24.0	14.4	25.5	15.1	34.6	4.3
17	45.4	5.8	45.7	3.9	38.6	5.5	27.8	14.5	29.6	14.9	39.0	3.8
18	49.5	5.9	49.5	3.7	42.2	5.8	31.5	14.8	33.8	14.7	43.5	3.3
19	53.5	6.0	53.2	3.5	45.7	6.2	35.3	14.9	37.9	14.5	47.9	2.8
20	57.5	6.0	56.9	3.3	49.3	6.5	39.0	15.1	42.1	14.3	52.4	2.3
21	8 0.5	6.1	10 0.6	3.0	52.9	6.9	42.8	15.3	46.3	14.0	56.8	1.8
22	8 5.5	− 6.2	10 4.3	− 2.8	11 56.5	+ 7.2	13 46.6	+15.4	15 50.5	+13.8	18 1.2	+ 1.3
23	9.5	6.2	8.0	2.5	12 0.1	7.6	50.4	15.6	54.7	13.5	5.7	0.8
24	13.4	6.2	11.7	2.3	3.7	7.9	54.2	15.7	58.9	13.2	10.1	0.3
25	17.4	6.2	15.4	2.0	7.3	8.3	58.1	15.8	16 3.2	12.9	14.6	− 0.2
26	21.3	6.2	19.0	1.7	10.9	8.6	14 1.9	15.9	7.4	12.6	19.0	0.7
27	25.3	6.2	22.7	1.4	14.5	9.0	5.7	16.0	11.7	12.3	23.5	1.2
28	29.2	6.2	26.4	1.2	18.1	9.3	9.6	16.1	16.0	11.9	27.9	1.7
29	8 33.1	− 6.2	10 30.0	− 0.9	12 21.7	+ 9.6	14 13.4	+16.2	16 20.3	+11.6	18 32.3	− 2.2
30	37.1	6.2	33.6	0.5	25.4	9.9	17.4	16.2	24.6	11.2	36.8	2.7
31	40.9	6.1	37.3	0.3			21.2	16.3			41.2	3.2

Right Ascension of the True Sun and Equation of Time.

1876: At Greenwich Mean Noon.

Day.	January.		February.		March.		April.		May.		June.	
	☉'s R. A.	E. T.	☉'s R. A.	E. T.	☉'s R. A.	E. T.	☉'s R. A.	E. T.	☉'s R. A.	E. T.	☉'s R. A.	E. T.
	h m	m	h m	m	h m	m	h m	m	h m	m	h m	m
1	18 45.6	− 3.6	20 58.0	−13.8	22 51.0	−12.5	0 44.5	− 3.8	2 35.9	+ 3.1	4 38.8	+ 2.4
2	50.0	4.1	21 2.1	13.9	54.7	12.2	48.2	3.5	39.8	3.2	43.0	2.2
3	54.4	4.6	6.1	14.0	58.4	12.0	51.8	3.2	43.6	3.3	47.1	2.1
4	58.8	5.0	10.2	14.2	23 2.2	11.8	55.5	2.9	47.4	3.4	51.2	1.9
5	19 3.2	5.5	14.2	14.2	5.9	11.6	59.1	2.6	51.3	3.5	55.3	1.7
6	7.6	5.9	18.2	14.3	9.6	11.3	1 2.8	2.3	55.1	3.6	59.4	1.5
7	12.0	6.4	22.2	14.4	13.3	11.1	6.4	2.0	59.0	3.6	5 3.5	1.4
8	19 16.4	− 6.8	21 26.2	−14.4	23 17.0	−10.8	1 10.1	− 1.7	3 2.9	+ 3.7	5 7.7	+ 1.2
9	20.7	7.2	30.2	14.5	20.7	10.6	13.7	1.4	6.8	3.8	11.8	1.0
10	25.1	7.6	34.2	14.5	24.3	10.3	17.4	1.2	10.7	3.8	15.9	0.8
11	29.4	8.0	38.1	14.5	28.0	10.1	21.1	0.9	14.6	3.8	20.1	0.6
12	33.8	8.4	42.0	14.5	31.7	9.8	24.8	0.7	18.5	3.9	24.2	0.4
13	38.1	8.8	46.0	14.5	35.3	9.5	28.5	0.4	22.5	3.9	28.4	0.2
14	42.4	9.2	49.9	14.4	39.0	9.2	32.1	0.1	26.4	3.9	32.5	0.0
15	19 46.7	− 9.5	21 53.8	−14.4	23 42.6	− 8.9	1 35.8	+ 0.1	3 30.4	+ 3.9	5 36.7	− 0.2
16	51.0	9.9	57.7	14.3	46.3	8.6	39.5	0.3	34.3	3.8	40.8	0.4
17	55.3	10.2	22 1.5	14.3	49.9	8.3	43.2	0.6	38.3	3.8	45.0	0.7
18	59.6	10.6	5.4	14.2	53.6	8.1	47.0	0.8	42.3	3.8	49.2	0.9
19	20 3.8	10.9	9.3	14.1	57.2	7.7	50.7	1.0	46.2	3.8	53.3	1.1
20	8.1	11.2	13.1	14.0	0 0.9	7.5	54.4	1.2	50.2	3.7	57.5	1.3
21	12.3	11.5	16.9	13.9	4.5	7.1	58.1	1.5	54.3	3.6	6 1.6	1.5
22	20 16.5	−11.7	22 20.8	−13.8	0 8.1	− 6.8	2 1.9	+ 1.6	3 58.3	+ 3.5	6 5.8	− 1.8
23	20.7	12.0	24.6	13.7	11.8	6.5	5.6	1.8	4 2.3	3.5	10.0	2.0
24	24.9	12.3	28.4	13.5	15.4	6.2	9.4	2.0	6.3	3.4	14.1	2.2
25	29.1	12.5	32.2	13.4	19.1	5.9	13.2	2.2	10.3	3.3	18.3	2.4
26	33.3	12.7	35.9	13.2	22.7	5.6	16.9	2.4	14.4	3.2	22.4	2.6
27	37.4	12.9	39.7	13.0	26.3	5.3	20.7	2.5	18.5	3.0	26.6	2.8
28	41.6	13.2	43.5	12.8	30.0	5.0	24.5	2.7	22.5	2.9	30.7	3.0
29	20 45.7	−13.3	22 47.2	−12.6	0 33.6	− 4.7	2 28.3	+ 2.8	4 26.6	+ 2.8	6 34.9	− 3.2
30	49.8	13.5			37.3	4.4	32.1	3.0	30.7	2.7	39.0	3.4
31	53.9	13.7			40.9	4.1			34.8	2.5		

Day.	July.		August.		September.		October.		November.		December.	
	☉'s R. A.	E. T.	☉'s R. A.	E. T.	☉'s R. A.	E. T.	☉'s R. A.	E. T.	☉'s R. A.	E. T.	☉'s R. A.	E. T.
	h m	m	h m	m	h m	m	h m	m	h m	m	h m	m
1	6 43.1	− 3.6	8 47.8	− 6.0	10 43.7	+ 0.3	12 31.7	+10.5	14 28.1	+16.3	16 32.2	+10.6
2	47.3	3.8	51.7	6.0	47.3	0.6	35.4	10.8	32.1	16.3	36.5	10.2
3	51.4	4.0	55.5	5.9	50.9	0.9	39.0	11.1	36.0	16.3	40.8	9.8
4	55.5	4.2	59.4	5.8	54.5	1.3	42.6	11.4	40.0	16.3	45.2	9.4
5	59.6	4.3	9 3.2	5.7	58.1	1.6	46.3	11.7	43.9	16.3	49.5	9.0
6	7 3.7	4.5	7.0	5.6	11 1.7	1.9	49.9	12.0	47.9	16.2	53.9	8.5
7	7.8	4.6	10.9	5.5	5.3	2.3	53.6	12.3	51.9	16.2	58.3	8.1
8	7 11.9	− 4.8	9 14.7	− 5.3	11 9.0	+ 2.6	12 57.2	+12.6	14 56.0	+16.1	17 2.7	+ 7.7
9	16.0	5.0	18.5	5.2	12.5	3.0	13 0.9	12.9	15 0.0	16.0	7.1	7.2
10	20.1	5.1	22.3	5.1	16.1	3.3	4.6	13.1	4.0	15.9	11.5	6.7
11	24.2	5.2	26.1	4.9	19.7	3.7	8.3	13.4	8.1	15.8	15.9	6.3
12	28.3	5.4	29.8	4.7	23.3	4.0	12.0	13.6	12.2	15.6	20.3	5.8
13	32.3	5.5	33.6	4.5	26.9	4.4	15.7	13.9	16.3	15.5	24.7	5.3
14	36.4	5.6	37.4	4.4	30.5	4.7	19.4	14.1	20.4	15.3	29.1	4.9
15	7 40.4	− 5.7	9 41.1	− 4.2	11 34.1	+ 5.1	13 23.1	+14.3	15 24.5	+15.2	17 33.6	+ 4.4
16	44.5	5.8	44.8	3.9	37.7	5.4	26.9	14.5	28.6	15.0	38.0	3.9
17	48.5	5.9	48.6	3.8	41.3	5.8	30.6	14.7	32.8	14.8	42.4	3.4
18	52.5	6.0	52.3	3.5	44.9	6.1	34.4	14.9	36.9	14.6	46.9	2.9
19	56.5	6.0	56.0	3.3	48.5	6.4	38.1	15.1	41.1	14.3	51.3	2.4
20	8 0.5	6.1	59.7	3.1	52.1	6.8	41.9	15.2	45.3	14.1	55.8	1.9
21	4.5	6.1	10 3.4	2.8	55.7	7.1	45.7	15.4	49.5	13.8	18 0.2	1.4
22	8 8.5	− 6.2	10 7.1	− 2.6	11 59.3	+ 7.5	13 49.5	+15.5	15 53.7	+13.6	18 4.6	+ 0.9
23	12.5	6.2	10.8	2.3	12 2.9	7.8	53.3	15.7	57.9	13.3	9.1	0.4
24	16.4	6.2	14.5	2.1	6.4	8.2	57.1	15.8	16 2.2	13.0	13.5	− 0.1
25	20.4	6.2	18.2	1.8	10.1	8.5	14 1.0	15.9	6.4	12.7	18.0	0.6
26	24.3	6.2	21.8	1.5	13.6	8.9	4.8	16.0	10.7	12.3	22.4	1.1
27	28.2	6.2	25.5	1.2	17.3	9.2	8.7	16.1	15.0	12.0	26.8	1.6
28	32.2	6.2	29.1	0.9	20.9	9.5	12.5	16.2	19.2	11.7	31.3	2.1
29	8 36.1	− 6.2	10 32.8	− 0.6	12 24.5	+ 9.9	14 16.4	+16.2	16 23.5	+11.3	18 35.7	− 2.6
30	40.0	6.1	36.4	0.3	28.1	10.2	20.3	16.3	27.8	11.0	40.1	3.1
31	43.9	6.1	40.0	0.0			24.2	16.3			44.5	3.5

Right Ascension of the True Sun and Equation of Time.

1877: At Greenwich Mean Noon.

Day.	January.		February.		March.		April.		May.		June.	
	☉'s R. A.	E. T.	☉'s R. A.	E. T.	☉'s R. A.	E. T.	☉'s R. A.	E. T.	☉'s R. A.	E. T.	☉'s R. A.	E. T.
	h m	m	h m	m	h m	m	h m	m	h m	m	h m	m
1	18 49.0	− 4.0	21 1.1	−13.9	22 50.1	−12.5	0 43.7	− 3.9	2 35.0	+ 3.1	4 37.9	+ 2.4
2	53.4	4.5	5.1	14.0	53.8	12.3	47.3	3.6	38.8	3.2	41.9	2.3
3	57.8	4.9	9.2	14.1	57.5	12.1	50.9	3.2	42.7	3.3	46.1	2.1
4	19 2.2	5.4	13.2	14.2	23 1.3	11.9	54.6	3.0	46.5	3.4	50.2	1.9
5	6.5	5.8	17.3	14.3	5.0	11.6	58.2	2.7	50.4	3.5	54.3	1.8
6	10.9	6.3	21.3	14.4	8.7	11.4	1 1.9	2.4	54.2	3.6	58.4	1.6
7	15.3	6.7	25.3	14.4	12.4	11.2	5.5	2.1	58.1	3.6	5 2.5	1.4
8	19 19.7	− 7.1	21 29.3	−14.5	23 16.1	−10.9	1 9.2	− 1.8	3 2.0	+ 3.7	5 6.7	+ 1.2
9	24.0	7.5	33.2	14.5	19.8	10.7	12.9	1.5	5.9	3.7	10.8	1.0
10	28.4	7.9	37.2	14.5	23.5	10.4	16.5	1.2	9.8	3.8	14.9	0.8
11	32.7	8.3	41.1	14.5	27.1	10.1	20.2	1.0	13.7	3.8	19.1	0.6
12	37.1	8.7	45.0	14.5	30.8	9.9	23.9	0.7	17.6	3.8	23.2	0.4
13	41.4	9.1	49.0	14.5	34.5	9.6	27.6	0.5	21.5	3.9	27.4	0.2
14	45.7	9.5	52.9	14.4	38.1	9.3	31.3	0.2	25.4	3.9	31.5	0.0
15	19 50.0	− 9.8	21 56.8	−14.4	23 41.8	− 9.0	1 35.0	+ 0.0	3 29.4	+ 3.9	5 35.7	− 0.2
16	54.3	10.2	22 0.6	14.3	45.4	8.7	38.6	0.3	33.4	3.8	39.8	0.4
17	58.6	10.5	4.5	14.2	49.1	8.4	42.4	0.5	37.3	3.8	44.0	0.6
18	20 2.8	10.8	8.4	14.2	52.7	8.1	46.1	0.7	41.3	3.8	48.1	0.8
19	7.0	11.1	12.2	14.1	56.4	7.8	49.8	1.0	45.3	3.7	52.3	1.0
20	11.3	11.4	16.1	14.0	0 0.0	7.5	53.5	1.2	49.3	3.7	56.5	1.3
21	15.5	11.7	19.9	13.8	3.7	7.3	57.3	1.4	53.3	3.6	6 0.6	1.5
22	20 19.7	−12.0	22 23.7	−13.7	0 7.3	− 6.9	2 1.0	+ 1.6	3 57.3	+ 3.6	6 4.8	− 1.7
23	23.9	12.2	27.5	13.6	10.9	6.6	4.7	1.8	4 1.3	3.5	8.9	1.9
24	28.1	12.5	31.3	13.4	14.6	6.3	8.5	2.0	5.4	3.4	13.1	2.1
25	32.3	12.7	35.0	13.2	18.2	6.0	12.3	2.1	9.4	3.3	17.2	2.3
26	36.4	12.9	38.8	13.1	21.8	5.7	16.0	2.3	13.4	3.2	21.4	2.6
27	40.6	13.1	42.6	12.9	25.5	5.4	19.8	2.5	17.5	3.1	25.6	2.8
28	44.7	13.3	46.3	12.7	29.1	5.1	23.6	2.6	21.5	3.0	29.7	3.0
29	20 48.8	−13.5			0 32.7	− 4.8	2 27.4	+ 2.8	4 25.6	+ 2.9	6 33.9	− 3.2
30	52.9	13.6			36.4	4.5	31.2	2.9	29.7	2.7	38.0	3.4
31	57.0	13.8			40.0	4.2			33.8	2.6		

Day.	July.		August.		September.		October.		November.		December.	
	☉'s R. A.	E. T.	☉'s R. A.	E. T.	☉'s R. A.	E. T.	☉'s R. A.	E. T.	☉'s R. A.	E. T.	☉'s R. A.	E. T.
	h m	m	h m	m	h m	m	h m	m	h m	m	h m	m
1	6 42.1	− 3.5	8 46.8	− 6.0	10 42.8	+ 0.2	12 30.8	+10.5	14 27.2	+16.3	16 31.1	+10.7
2	46.2	3.7	50.7	6.0	46.4	0.5	34.5	10.7	31.1	16.3	35.4	10.3
3	50.4	3.9	54.6	5.9	50.0	0.9	38.1	11.1	35.1	16.3	39.8	9.9
4	54.5	4.1	58.4	5.8	53.7	1.2	41.7	11.4	39.0	16.3	44.1	9.5
5	58.6	4.3	9 2.3	5.7	57.3	1.5	45.4	11.7	43.0	16.3	48.5	9.1
6	7 2.7	4.4	6.1	5.6	11 0.9	1.8	49.0	12.0	47.0	16.2	52.9	8.6
7	6.8	4.6	9.9	5.5	4.5	2.2	52.7	12.2	51.0	16.2	57.2	8.2
8	7 10.9	− 4.8	9 13.8	− 5.4	11 8.1	+ 2.5	12 56.4	+12.5	14 55.0	+16.1	17 1.6	+ 7.8
9	15.0	4.9	17.6	5.2	11.7	2.9	13 0.0	12.8	59.0	16.0	6.0	7.3
10	19.1	5.1	21.4	5.1	15.3	3.2	3.7	13.0	15 3.1	15.9	10.4	6.9
11	23.2	5.2	25.1	4.9	18.9	3.6	7.4	13.3	7.1	15.8	14.8	6.4
12	27.3	5.3	28.9	4.8	22.5	3.9	11.1	13.5	11.2	15.7	19.2	5.9
13	31.3	5.4	32.7	4.6	26.1	4.2	14.8	13.8	15.3	15.5	23.6	5.5
14	35.4	5.6	36.5	4.4	29.7	4.6	18.5	14.0	19.4	15.4	28.1	5.0
15	7 39.5	− 5.7	9 40.2	− 4.2	11 33.2	+ 5.0	13 22.3	+14.2	15 23.5	+15.2	17 32.5	+ 4.5
16	43.5	5.8	43.9	4.0	36.8	5.3	26.0	14.4	27.6	15.0	36.9	4.0
17	47.5	5.9	47.7	3.8	40.4	5.7	29.7	14.7	31.8	14.8	41.4	3.5
18	51.5	5.9	51.4	3.6	44.0	6.0	33.5	14.8	35.9	14.6	45.8	3.0
19	55.6	6.0	55.1	3.4	47.6	6.4	37.2	15.0	40.1	14.4	50.2	2.5
20	59.6	6.1	58.8	3.1	51.2	6.7	41.0	15.2	44.3	14.1	54.7	2.0
21	8 3.5	6.1	10 2.5	2.9	54.8	7.1	44.8	15.3	48.5	13.9	59.1	1.5
22	8 7.5	− 6.2	10 6.2	− 2.6	11 58.4	+ 7.4	13 48.6	+15.5	15 52.7	+13.6	18 3.5	+ 1.1
23	11.5	6.2	9.9	2.4	12 2.0	7.8	52.4	15.6	56.9	13.4	8.0	0.5
24	15.5	6.2	13.6	2.1	5.6	8.1	56.2	15.8	16 1.1	13.1	12.4	0.1
25	19.4	6.2	17.2	1.8	9.2	8.5	14 0.0	15.9	5.4	12.8	16.9	− 0.5
26	23.4	6.2	20.9	1.6	12.8	8.8	3.9	16.0	9.6	12.5	21.3	1.0
27	27.3	6.2	24.6	1.3	16.4	9.1	7.7	16.1	13.9	12.1	25.7	1.4
28	31.2	6.2	28.2	1.0	20.0	9.5	11.6	16.1	18.2	11.8	30.2	1.9
29	8 35.1	− 6.2	10 31.9	− 0.7	12 23.6	+ 9.8	14 15.5	+16.2	16 22.5	+11.4	18 34.6	− 2.4
30	39.0	6.1	35.5	0.4	27.2	10.1	19.4	16.2	26.8	11.1	39.0	2.9
31	42.9	6.1	39.2	0.1			23.3	16.3			43.5	3.4

Right Ascension of the True Sun and Equation of Time.

1878: At Greenwich Mean Noon.

Day.	January.		February.		March.		April.		May.		June.	
	☉'s R. A.	E. T.	☉'s R. A.	E. T.	☉'s R. A.	E. T.	☉'s R. A.	E. T.	☉'s R. A.	E. T.	☉'s R. A.	E. T.
	h m	m	h m	m	h m	m	h m	m	h m	m	h m	m
1	18 47.9	— 3.9	21 0.1	—13.9	22 49.2	—12.5	0 42.8	— 3.9	2 34.1	+ 3.0	4 36.9	+ 2.4
2	52.3	4.3	4.2	14.0	52.9	12.3	46.4	3.6	37.9	3.1	41.0	2.3
3	56.7	4.8	8.2	14.1	56.6	12.1	50.0	3.3	41.8	3.2	45.1	2.1
4	19 1.1	5.3	12.3	14.2	23 0.4	11.9	53.7	3.0	45.6	3.3	49.2	2.0
5	5.5	5.7	16.3	14.3	4.1	11.7	57.3	2.7	49.4	3.4	53.3	1.8
6	9.9	6.2	20.3	14.4	7.8	11.5	1 1.0	2.5	53.3	3.5	57.4	1.6
7	14.3	6.6	24.3	14.4	11.5	11.2	4.7	2.2	57.2	3.6	5 1.6	1.4
8	19 18.6	— 7.0	21 28.3	—14.5	23 15.2	—11.0	1 8.3	— 1.9	3 1.0	+ 3.7	5 5.7	+ 1.2
9	23.0	7.4	32.3	14.5	18.9	10.7	12.0	1.6	4.9	3.7	9.8	1.1
10	27.3	7.8	36.2	14.5	22.6	10.5	15.6	1.3	8.8	3.8	14.0	0.8
11	31.7	8.2	40.2	14.5	26.2	10.2	19.3	1.0	12.7	3.8	18.1	0.7
12	36.0	8.6	44.1	14.5	29.9	9.9	23.0	0.8	16.7	3.8	22.2	0.5
13	40.3	9.0	48.0	14.5	33.6	9.7	26.7	0.5	20.6	3.8	26.4	0.3
14	44.6	9.4	51.9	14.4	37.2	9.3	30.4	0.3	24.5	3.9	30.5	0.1
15	19 48.9	— 9.7	21 55.8	—14.4	23 40.9	— 9.1	1 34.1	0.0	3 28.5	+ 3.8	5 34.7	— 0.2
16	53.2	10.1	59.7	14.3	44.6	8.8	37.8	+ 0.2	32.4	3.8	38.9	0.4
17	57.5	10.4	22 3.5	14.2	48.2	8.5	41.4	0.5	36.4	3.8	43.0	0.6
18	20 1.8	10.7	7.4	14.2	51.8	8.2	45.2	0.7	40.4	3.8	47.2	0.8
19	6.0	11.0	11.3	14.1	55.5	7.9	48.9	0.9	44.3	3.8	51.3	1.0
20	10.2	11.3	15.1	14.0	59.1	7.6	52.6	1.1	48.3	3.7	55.5	1.2
21	14.5	11.6	18.9	13.8	0 2.8	7.3	56.3	1.4	52.3	3.6	59.6	1.4
22	20 18.7	—11.9	22 22.7	—13.7	0 6.4	— 7.0	2 0.1	+ 1.6	3 56.3	+ 3.6	6 3.8	— 1.7
23	22.9	12.1	26.5	13.6	10.0	6.7	3.8	1.8	4 0.4	3.5	8.0	1.9
24	27.1	12.4	30.3	13.4	13.7	6.4	7.6	1.9	4.4	3.4	12.1	2.1
25	31.2	12.6	34.1	13.3	17.3	6.1	11.3	2.1	8.4	3.3	16.3	2.3
26	35.4	12.8	37.9	13.1	21.0	5.8	15.1	2.3	12.5	3.2	20.4	2.5
27	39.5	13.0	41.7	12.9	24.6	5.5	18.9	2.5	16.5	3.1	24.6	2.7
28	43.7	13.2	45.4	12.7	28.2	5.1	22.7	2.6	20.6	3.0	28.7	2.9
29	20 47.8	—13.4			0 31.8	— 4.8	2 26.5	+ 2.8	4 24.6	+ 2.9	6 32.9	— 3.1
30	51.9	13.6			35.5	4.5	30.3	2.9	28.7	2.7	37.0	3.3
31	56.0	13.7			39.1	4.2			32.8	2.6		

Day.	July.		August.		September.		October.		November.		December.	
	☉'s R. A.	E. T.	☉'s R. A.	E. T.	☉'s R. A.	E. T.	☉'s R. A.	E. T.	☉'s R. A.	E. T.	☉'s R. A.	E. T.
	h m	m	h m	m	h m	m	h m	m	h m	m	h m	m
1	6 41.1	— 3.5	8 45.9	— 6.1	10 42.0	+ 0.1	12 30.0	+10.3	14 26.3	+16.3	16 30.1	+10.7
2	45.3	3.7	49.8	6.0	45.6	0.4	33.6	10.7	30.2	16.3	34.4	10.4
3	49.4	3.9	53.7	6.0	49.2	0.7	37.3	10.9	34.1	16.3	38.7	10.0
4	53.6	4.1	57.5	5.9	52.8	1.1	40.9	11.3	38.1	16.3	43.1	9.6
5	57.7	4.3	9 1.4	5.8	56.4	1.4	44.5	11.6	42.0	16.3	47.4	9.2
6	7 1.8	4.4	5.2	5.7	11 0.1	1.7	48.2	11.9	46.1	16.2	51.8	8.8
7	5.9	4.6	9.1	5.6	3.6	2.1	51.8	12.2	50.0	16.2	56.2	8.3
8	7 10.0	— 4.8	9 12.9	— 5.4	11 7.3	+ 2.4	12 55.5	+12.4	14 54.0	+16.1	17 0.6	+ 7.9
9	14.1	4.9	16.7	5.3	10.8	2.8	59.2	12.7	58.1	16.0	4.9	7.4
10	18.2	5.1	20.5	5.2	14.4	3.1	13 2.8	13.0	15 2.1	15.9	9.3	7.0
11	22.3	5.2	24.3	5.0	18.1	3.4	6.5	13.2	6.2	15.8	13.7	6.5
12	26.3	5.3	28.0	4.8	21.6	3.8	10.2	13.5	10.2	15.7	18.1	6.1
13	30.4	5.5	31.8	4.7	25.2	4.2	13.9	13.7	14.3	15.6	22.6	5.6
14	34.4	5.6	35.6	4.5	28.8	4.5	17.6	14.0	18.4	15.4	27.0	5.1
15	7 38.5	— 5.7	9 39.3	— 4.3	11 32.4	+ 4.9	13 21.4	+14.2	15 22.5	+15.3	17 31.4	+ 4.6
16	42.5	5.8	43.1	4.1	36.0	5.2	25.1	14.4	26.6	15.1	35.8	4.2
17	46.6	5.9	46.8	3.9	39.6	5.6	28.8	14.6	30.8	14.9	40.3	3.6
18	50.6	5.9	50.5	3.7	43.2	5.9	32.6	14.8	34.9	14.7	44.7	3.2
19	54.6	6.0	54.2	3.4	46.7	6.3	36.3	15.0	39.1	14.4	49.1	2.7
20	58.6	6.1	58.0	3.2	50.4	6.6	40.1	15.1	43.3	14.2	53.6	2.2
21	8 2.6	6.1	10 1.7	3.0	53.9	7.0	43.9	15.3	47.4	14.0	58.0	1.7
22	8 6.6	— 6.2	10 5.3	— 2.7	11 57.5	+ 7.3	13 47.7	+15.4	15 51.7	+13.7	18 2.4	+ 1.2
23	10.6	6.2	9.1	2.5	12 1.1	7.7	51.5	15.6	55.9	13.4	6.9	0.7
24	14.5	6.2	12.7	2.2	4.7	8.0	55.3	15.7	16 0.1	13.1	11.3	0.2
25	18.5	6.3	16.4	1.9	8.3	8.4	59.1	15.8	4.4	12.8	15.8	— 0.3
26	22.4	6.2	20.1	1.7	11.9	8.7	14 3.0	15.9	8.6	12.5	20.2	0.8
27	26.4	6.3	23.7	1.4	15.6	9.0	6.8	16.0	12.9	12.2	24.7	1.3
28	30.3	6.2	27.4	1.1	19.4	9.4	10.7	16.1	17.2	11.8	29.1	1.8
29	8 34.2	— 6.2	10 31.0	— 0.8	11 22.8	+ 9.7	14 14.5	+16.2	16 21.5	+11.5	18 33.5	— 2.3
30	38.1	6.2	34.7	0.5	26.4	10.0	18.4	16.2	25.8	11.1	38.0	2.8
31	42.0	6.1	38.3	0.2			22.3	16.3			42.4	3.3

Declination of the Sun.

1875: At Greenwich Mean Noon.

Day.	Jan.	Feb.	Mar.	Apr.	May.	June.	July.	Aug.	Sept.	Oct.	Nov.	Dec.
	°	°	°	°	°	°	°	°	°	°	°	°
1	23.0 S.	17.1 S.	7.6 S.	4.5 N.	15.0 N.	22.0 N.	23.1 N.	18.1 N.	8.4 N.	3.1 S.	14.4 S.	21.8 S.
2	22.9	16.8	7.2	4.9	15.3	22.2	23.1	17.8	8.0	3.5	14.7	22.0
3	22.8	16.6	6.9	5.3	15.6	22.3	23.0	17.6	7.6	3.9	15.0	22.1
4	22.7	16.3	6.5	5.6	15.9	22.4	22.9	17.3	7.3	4.3	15.4	22.2
5	22.6	16.0	6.1	6.0	16.2	22.5	22.8	17.0	6.9	4.7	15.7	22.4
6	22.5	15.6	5.7	6.4	16.5	22.6	22.7	16.8	6.5	5.1	16.0	22.5
7	22.4	15.3	5.3	6.8	16.8	22.7	22.6	16.5	6.1	5.5	16.3	22.6
8	22.3 S.	15.0 S.	4.9 S.	7.2 N.	17.1 N.	22.8 N.	22.5 N.	16.2 N.	5.8 N.	5.8 S.	16.6 S.	22.7 S.
9	22.1	14.7	4.5	7.5	17.3	22.9	22.4	15.9	5.4	6.2	16.8	22.8
10	22.0	14.4	4.1	7.9	17.6	23.0	22.3	15.6	5.0	6.6	17.1	22.9
11	21.8	14.1	3.8	8.3	17.9	23.1	22.1	15.3	4.6	7.0	17.4	23.0
12	21.7	13.7	3.4	8.6	18.1	23.2	22.0	15.0	4.2	7.4	17.7	23.1
13	21.5	13.4	3.0	9.0	18.4	23.2	21.9	14.7	3.9	7.7	17.9	23.2
14	21.3	13.1	2.6	9.4	18.6	23.3	21.7	14.4	3.5	8.1	18.2	23.2
15	21.1 S.	12.7 S.	2.2 S.	9.7 N.	18.8 N.	23.3 N.	21.6 N.	14.1 N.	3.1 N.	8.5 S.	18.5 S.	23.3 S.
16	21.0	12.4	1.8	10.1	19.1	23.4	21.4	13.8	2.7	8.8	18.7	23.3
17	20.8	12.0	1.4	10.4	19.3	23.4	21.2	13.5	2.3	9.2	19.0	23.4
18	20.6	11.7	1.0	10.8	19.5	23.4	21.1	13.2	1.9	9.6	19.2	23.4
19	20.4	11.3	0.6	11.1	19.7	23.4	20.9	12.8	1.5	9.9	19.5	23.4
20	20.1	11.0	0.2 S.	11.5	20.0	23.5	20.7	12.5	1.2	10.3	19.7	23.4
21	19.9	10.6	0.2 N.	11.8	20.2	23.5	20.5	12.2	0.8	10.7	19.9	23.5
22	19.7 S.	10.2 S.	0.6 N.	12.2 N.	20.4 N.	23.5 N.	20.3 N.	11.9 N.	0.4 N.	11.0 S.	20.1 S.	23.5 S.
23	19.5	9.9	1.0	12.5	20.6	23.4	20.1	11.5	0.0 S.	11.4	20.3	23.5
24	19.2	9.5	1.4	12.8	20.7	23.4	19.9	11.2	0.4	11.7	20.5	23.4
25	19.0	9.1	1.8	13.1	20.9	23.4	19.7	10.8	0.8	12.1	20.7	23.4
26	18.7	8.8	2.2	13.5	21.1	23.4	19.5	10.5	1.2	12.4	20.9	23.4
27	18.5	8.4	2.6	13.8	21.3	23.3	19.3	10.1	1.6	12.8	21.1	23.3
28	18.2	8.0	2.9	14.1	21.4	23.3	19.0	9.8	2.0	13.1	21.3	23.3
29	18.0 S.		3.3 N.	14.4 N.	21.6 N.	23.3 N.	18.8 N.	9.4 N.	2.4 S.	13.4 S.	21.5 S.	23.2 S.
30	17.7		3.7	14.7	21.8	23.2	18.6	9.1	2.7	13.8	21.6	23.2
31	17.4		4.1		21.9		18.3	8.7		14.1		23.1

1876: At Greenwich Mean Noon.

Day.	Jan.	Feb.	Mar.	Apr.	May.	June.	July.	Aug.	Sept.	Oct.	Nov.	Dec.
	°	°	°	°	°	°	°	°	°	°	°	°
1	23.0 S.	17.2 S.	7.3 S.	4.8 N.	15.3 N.	22.1 N.	23.1 N.	17.9 N.	8.1 N.	3.4 S.	14.6 S.	21.9 S.
2	23.0	16.9	7.0	5.2	15.6	22.3	23.0	17.6	7.7	3.8	15.0	22.1
3	22.9	16.6	6.6	5.6	15.9	22.4	22.9	17.4	7.3	4.2	15.3	22.2
4	22.8	16.3	6.2	5.9	16.2	22.5	22.8	17.1	7.0	4.6	15.6	22.3
5	22.7	16.0	5.8	6.3	16.4	22.6	22.7	16.8	6.6	5.0	15.9	22.5
6	22.5	15.7	5.4	6.7	16.7	22.7	22.6	16.6	6.2	5.4	16.2	22.6
7	22.4	15.4	5.0	7.1	17.0	22.8	22.5	16.3	5.9	5.7	16.5	22.7
8	22.3 S.	15.1 S.	4.6 S.	7.4 N.	17.3 N.	22.9 N.	22.4 N.	16.0 N.	5.5 N.	6.1 S.	16.8 S.	22.8 S.
9	22.2	14.8	4.2	7.8	17.5	23.0	22.3	15.7	5.1	6.5	17.1	22.9
10	22.0	14.5	3.8	8.2	17.8	23.1	22.2	15.4	4.7	6.9	17.3	23.0
11	21.9	14.1	3.5	8.6	18.0	23.1	22.0	15.1	4.3	7.3	17.6	23.1
12	21.7	13.8	3.1	8.9	18.3	23.2	21.9	14.8	4.0	7.6	17.9	23.1
13	21.5	13.5	2.7	9.3	18.5	23.3	21.8	14.5	3.6	8.0	18.2	23.2
14	21.4	13.1	2.3	9.6	18.8	23.3	21.6	14.2	3.2	8.4	18.4	23.3
15	21.2 S.	12.8 S.	1.9 S.	10.0 N.	19.0 N.	23.3 N.	21.5 N.	13.9 N.	2.8 N.	8.8 S.	18.7 S.	23.3 S.
16	21.0	12.4	1.5	10.3	19.2	23.4	21.3	13.6	2.4	9.1	18.9	23.4
17	20.8	12.1	1.1	10.7	19.5	23.4	21.1	13.2	2.0	9.5	19.2	23.4
18	20.6	11.8	0.7	11.0	19.7	23.4	20.9	12.9	1.6	9.9	19.4	23.4
19	20.4	11.4	0.3 S.	11.4	19.9	23.4	20.8	12.6	1.2	10.2	19.6	23.4
20	20.2	11.0	0.1 N.	11.7	20.1	23.5	20.6	12.3	0.9	10.6	19.9	23.5
21	20.0	10.7	0.5	12.1	20.3	23.5	20.4	11.9	0.5	10.9	20.1	23.5
22	19.8 S.	10.3 S.	0.9 N.	12.4 N.	20.5 N.	23.5 N.	20.2 N.	11.6 N.	0.1 N.	11.3 S.	20.3 S.	23.5 S.
23	19.5	10.0	1.3	12.7	20.7	23.4	20.0	11.3	0.3 S.	11.6	20.5	23.4
24	19.3	9.6	1.7	13.1	20.9	23.4	19.8	10.9	0.7	12.0	20.7	23.4
25	19.0	9.2	2.1	13.4	21.1	23.4	19.5	10.6	1.1	12.3	20.9	23.4
26	18.8	8.8	2.5	13.7	21.2	23.4	19.3	10.2	1.5	12.7	21.1	23.4
27	18.5	8.5	2.8	14.0	21.4	23.3	19.1	9.9	1.9	13.0	21.3	23.3
28	18.3	8.1	3.2	14.4	21.6	23.3	18.9	9.5	2.3	13.3	21.4	23.3
29	18.0 S.	7.7 S.	3.6 N.	14.7 N.	21.7 N.	23.2 N.	18.6 N.	9.2 N.	2.6 S.	13.7 S.	21.6 S.	23.2 S.
30	17.8		4.0	15.0	21.9	23.2	18.4	8.8	3.0	14.0	21.8	23.1
31	17.5		4.4		22.0		18.1	8.4		14.3		23.1

Declination of the Sun.

1877: At Greenwich Mean Noon.

Day.	Jan.	Feb.	Mar.	Apr.	May.	June.	July.	Aug.	Sept.	Oct.	Nov.	Dec.
1	23°.0 S.	17°.0 S.	7°.4 S.	4°.7 N.	15°.2 N.	22°.1 N.	23°.1 N.	17°.9 N.	8°.2 N.	3°.3 S.	14°.6 S.	21°.9 S.
2	22.9	16.7	7.0	5.1	15.5	22.2	23.0	17.7	7.8	3.7	14.9	22.0
3	22.8	16.4	6.7	5.5	15.8	22.4	23.0	17.4	7.4	4.1	15.2	22.2
4	22.7	16.1	6.3	5.8	16.1	22.5	22.9	17.2	7.1	4.5	15.5	22.3
5	22.6	15.8	5.9	6.2	16.4	22.6	22.8	16.9	6.7	4.9	15.8	22.4
6	22.5	15.5	5.5	6.6	16.6	22.7	22.7	16.6	6.3	5.3	16.1	22.6
7	22.3	15.2	5.1	7.0	16.9	22.8	22.6	16.3	5.9	5.6	16.4	22.7
8	22.2 S.	14.9 S.	4.7 S.	7.4 N.	17.2 N.	22.9 N.	22.5 N.	16.1 N.	5.6 N.	6.0 S.	16.7 S.	22.8 S.
9	22.1	14.5	4.3	7.7	17.5	23.0	22.3	15.8	5.2	6.4	17.0	22.9
10	21.9	14.2	3.9	8.1	17.7	23.1	22.2	15.5	4.8	6.8	17.3	23.0
11	21.7	13.9	3.5	8.5	18.0	23.1	22.1	15.2	4.4	7.2	17.5	23.1
12	21.6	13.6	3.2	8.8	18.2	23.2	21.9	14.9	4.0	7.5	17.8	23.1
13	21.4	13.2	2.8	9.2	18.5	23.2	21.8	14.6	3.7	7.9	18.1	23.2
14	21.2	12.9	2.4	9.6	18.7	23.3	21.6	14.3	3.3	8.3	18.3	23.3
15	21.1 S.	12.5 S.	2.0 S.	9.9 N.	19.0 N.	23.3 N.	21.5 N.	14.0 N.	2.9 N.	8.7 S.	18.6 S.	23.3 S.
16	20.9	12.2	1.6	10.3	19.2	23.4	21.3	13.6	2.5	9.0	18.9	23.4
17	20.7	11.8	1.2	10.6	19.4	23.4	21.2	13.3	2.1	9.4	19.1	23.4
18	20.5	11.5	0.8	11.0	19.6	23.4	21.0	13.0	1.7	9.8	19.3	23.4
19	20.3	11.1	0.4 S.	11.3	19.9	23.4	20.8	12.7	1.3	10.1	19.6	23.4
20	20.0	10.8	0.0	11.7	20.1	23.5	20.6	12.3	1.0	10.5	19.8	23.5
21	19.8	10.4	0.4 N.	12.0	20.3	23.5	20.4	12.0	0.6	10.8	20.0	23.5
22	19.6 S.	10.0 S.	0.8 N.	12.3 N.	20.5 N.	23.5 N.	20.2 N.	11.7 N.	0.2 N.	11.2 S.	20.2 S.	23.5 S.
23	19.3	9.7	1.2	12.7	20.7	23.4	20.0	11.3	0.2 S.	11.5	20.4	23.4
24	19.1	9.3	1.6	13.0	20.8	23.4	19.8	11.0	0.6	11.9	20.6	23.4
25	18.9	8.9	2.0	13.3	21.0	23.4	19.6	10.7	1.0	12.2	20.8	23.4
26	18.6	8.6	2.4	13.6	21.2	23.4	19.4	10.3	1.4	12.6	21.0	23.4
27	18.4	8.2	2.8	14.0	21.4	23.3	19.2	10.0	1.8	12.9	21.2	23.3
28	18.1	7.8	3.1	14.3	21.5	23.3	18.9	9.6	2.2	13.3	21.4	23.3
29	17.8 S.		3.5 N.	14.6 N.	21.7 N.	23.2 N.	18.7 N.	9.2 N.	2.6 S.	13.6 S.	21.6 S.	23.2 S.
30	17.5		3.9	14.9	21.8	23.2	18.6	8.9	2.9	13.9	21.7	23.2
31	17.3		4.3		22.0		18.2	8.5		14.2		23.1

1878: At Greenwich Mean Noon.

Day.	Jan.	Feb.	Mar.	Apr.	May.	June.	July.	Aug.	Sept.	Oct.	Nov.	Dec.
1	23°.0 S.	17°.1 S.	7°.5 S.	4°.6 N.	15°.1 N.	22°.1 N.	23°.1 N.	18°.0 N.	8°.2 N.	3°.2 S.	14°.5 S.	21°.8 S.
2	22.9	16.8	7.1	5.0	15.4	22.2	23.0	17.8	7.9	3.6	14.8	22.0
3	22.8	16.5	6.8	5.4	15.7	22.3	23.0	17.5	7.5	4.0	15.1	22.1
4	22.7	16.2	6.4	5.8	16.0	22.5	22.9	17.2	7.1	4.4	15.4	22.3
5	22.6	15.9	6.0	6.1	16.3	22.6	22.8	17.0	6.8	4.8	15.7	22.4
6	22.5	15.6	5.6	6.5	16.6	22.7	22.7	16.7	6.4	5.2	16.0	22.5
7	22.4	15.3	5.2	6.9	16.9	22.8	22.6	16.4	6.0	5.6	16.3	22.6
8	22.2 S.	14.9 S.	4.8 S.	7.3 N.	17.1 N.	22.9 N.	22.5 N.	16.1 N.	5.7 N.	5.9 S.	16.6 S.	22.8 S.
9	22.1	14.6	4.4	7.6	17.4	23.0	22.4	15.8	5.3	6.3	16.9	22.9
10	21.9	14.3	4.0	8.0	17.7	23.0	22.2	15.5	4.9	6.7	17.2	22.9
11	21.8	14.0	3.6	8.4	17.9	23.1	22.1	15.3	4.5	7.1	17.5	23.0
12	21.6	13.6	3.3	8.7	18.2	23.2	22.0	15.0	4.1	7.5	17.8	23.1
13	21.5	13.3	2.9	9.1	18.4	23.2	21.8	14.6	3.8	7.8	18.0	23.2
14	21.3	13.0	2.5	9.5	18.7	23.3	21.7	14.3	3.4	8.2	18.3	23.2
15	21.1 S.	12.6 S.	2.1 S.	9.8 N.	18.9 N.	23.3 N.	21.5 N.	14.1 N.	3.0 N.	8.6 S.	18.5 S.	23.3 S.
16	20.9	12.3	1.7	10.2	19.1	23.4	21.4	13.7	2.6	8.9	18.8	23.3
17	20.7	11.9	1.3	10.5	19.4	23.4	21.2	13.4	2.2	9.3	19.0	23.4
18	20.5	11.6	0.9	10.9	19.6	23.4	21.0	13.1	1.8	9.7	19.3	23.4
19	20.3	11.2	0.5	11.2	19.8	23.4	20.8	12.8	1.4	10.0	19.5	23.4
20	20.1	10.9	0.1 S.	11.6	20.0	23.5	20.7	12.4	1.0	10.4	19.7	23.4
21	19.9	10.5	0.3 N.	11.9	20.2	23.5	20.5	12.1	0.7	10.8	20.0	23.5
22	19.6 S.	10.1 S.	0.7 N.	12.2 N.	20.4 N.	23.5 N.	20.3 N.	11.8 N.	0.3 N.	11.1 S.	20.2 S.	23.5 S.
23	19.4	9.8	1.1	12.6	20.6	23.4	20.1	11.4	0.1 S.	11.5	20.4	23.4
24	19.2	9.4	1.5	12.9	20.8	23.4	19.9	11.1	0.5	11.8	20.6	23.4
25	18.9	9.0	1.9	13.2	21.0	23.4	19.7	10.7	0.9	12.2	20.8	23.4
26	18.7	8.7	2.3	13.6	21.2	23.4	19.4	10.4	1.3	12.5	21.0	23.4
27	18.4	8.3	2.7	13.9	21.3	23.3	19.2	10.0	1.7	12.8	21.2	23.3
28	18.2	7.9	3.1	14.2	21.5	23.3	19.0	9.7	2.1	13.2	21.4	23.3
29	17.9 S.		3.4 N.	14.5 N.	21.6 N.	23.2 N.	18.7 N.	9.3 N.	2.5 S.	13.5 S.	21.5 S.	23.2 S.
30	17.6		3.8	14.8	21.8	23.2	18.5	9.0	2.9	13.8	21.7	23.2
31	17.3		4.2		21.9		18.3	8.6		14.2		23.1

Mean Places of Twenty-five Fixed Stars. 1875: January 1, Greenwich.

Common Name.	Mag.	Right Ascension.	Annual Diff.	Declination.	Annual Diff.	Name of Constellation.	Systematic Name of Star.
		h m	m	°	°		
Alpheratz,	2	0 1.93	0.05	28.40 N.	+0.005	Androm'eda,	α Andromedæ.
Polaris (P. Star),	2	1 13.00	35	88.64 N.	+ 005	The Little Bear,	α Ursæ Minoris.
Acher'nar,	1	1 33.05	04	57.87 S.	— 005	Erid'anus,	α Eridani,
Hamel,	2	2 0.13	06	22.87 N.	+ 005	The Ram,	α Arietis.
Aldebar'an,	1	4 28.75	06	16.26 N.	+ 002	The Bull,	α Tauri.
Capella,	1	5 7.46	0.07	45.87 N.	+0.001	The Charioteer,	α Aurigæ.
Rigel,	1	5 8.53	05	8.35 S.	— 001	Ori'on,	β Orionis.
Betelguese,	Var.	5 48.41	05	7.38 N.	+ 000	Ori'on,	α Orionis,
Cano'pus,	1	6 21.18	02	52.63 S.	+ 000	The Ship Argo,	α Argûs.
Sir'ius,	1	6 39.64	04	16.55 S.	+ 001	The Great Dog,	α Canis Majoris.
Castor,	2	7.26.62	0.06	32.16 N.	—0.002	The Twins,	α Geminorum.
Pro'cyon,	1	7 32.76	05	5.54 N.	— 002	The Little Dog,	σ Canis Minoris.
Pollux,	1	7 37.66	06	28.33 N.	— 002	The Twins,	β Geminorum.
Alphard,	2	9 21.45	05	8.12 S.	+ 004	The Hydra,	α Hydræ.
Reg'ulus,	1	10 1.71	05	12.58 N.	— 005	The Lion,	α Leonis.
α^1 Crucis,	1	12 19.65	0.05	62.43 S.	+0.005	The Cross,	α^1 Crucis.
Spica,	1	13 18.61	05	10.51 S.	+ 005	The Virgin,	α Virginis.
β Centauri,	1	13 55.02	07	59.77 S.	+ 005	The Centaur,	β Centauri.
Arctu'rus,	1	14 9.96	05	19.83 N.	— 005	The Bear-Watcher,	α Boötis.
α^2 Centauri,	1	14 31.14	07	60.31 S.	+ 004	The Centaur,	α^2 Centauri.
Anta'res,	1	16 21.75	0.06	26.15 S.	+0.002	The Scorpion,	α Scorpii.
Vega,	1	18 32.71	03	38.67 N.	+ 001	The Harp,	α Lyræ.
Altair,	1	19 44.68	05	8.54 N.	+ 003	The Eagle,	α Aquilæ.
Fo'malhaut,	1	22 50.74	05	30.28 S.	— 005	The Southern Fish,	α Piscis Australis.
Mar'kab,	2	22 58.53	05	14.53 N.	+ 005	Peg'asus,	α Pegasi.

The Diff. in R. A. is always additive. The Diff. in Dec. is additive or subtractive according as the sign is + or —.

TABLE LXII.

Meridian-Passages of Twenty-five Fixed Stars.
1875: At Greenwich Mean Noon on the First Day of the Month.

Name of Star.	Jan.	Feb.	Mar.	Apr.	May.	June.	July.	Aug.	Sept.	Oct.	Nov.	Dec.
	h m	h m	h m	h m	h m	h m	h m	h m	h m	h m	h m	h m
Alpheratz,	5 15	3 3	1 14	23 20	21 29	19 26	17 22	15 17	13 21	11 33	9 37	7 33
Polaris,	6 26	4 14	2 25	0 31	22 40	20 37	18 33	16 28	14 32	12 44	10 48	8 44
Achernar,	6 46	4 34	2 45	0 51	23 0	20 57	18 53	16 48	14 52	13 4	11 8	9 4
Hamel,	7 13	5 1	3 12	1 18	23 27	21 24	19 20	17 15	15 19	13 31	11 35	9 31
Aldebaran,	9 42	7 30	5 41	3 47	1 56	23 53	21 49	19 44	17 48	16 0	14 4	12 0
Capella,	10 21	8 9	6 20	4 26	2 35	0 32	22 28	20 23	18 27	16 39	14 43	12 39
Rigel,	10 22	8 10	6 21	4 27	2 36	0 33	22 29	20 24	18 28	16 40	14 44	12 40
Betelguese,	11 2	8 50	7 1	5 7	3 16	1 13	23 9	21 4	19 8	16 20	15 24	13 20
Canopus,	11 34	9 22	7 33	5 39	3 48	1 45	23 41	21 36	19 40	17 52	15 56	13 52
Sirius,	11 53	9 41	7 52	5 58	4 7	2 4	24 0	21 55	19 59	18 11	16 15	14 11
Castor,	12 40	10 28	8 39	6 45	4 54	2 51	0 47	22 42	20 46	18 58	17 2	14 58
Procyon,	12 46	10 34	8 45	6 51	5 0	2 57	0 53	22 48	20 52	19 4	17 8	15 4
Pollux,	12 51	10 39	8 50	6 56	5 5	3 2	0 58	22 53	20 57	19 9	17 13	15 9
Alphard,	14 35	12 23	10 34	8 40	6 49	4 46	2 42	0 37	22 41	20 53	18 57	16 53
Regulus,	15 15	13 3	11 14	9 20	7 29	5 26	3 22	1 17	23 21	21 33	19 37	17 33
α^1 Crucis,	17 33	15 21	13 32	11 38	9 47	7 44	5 40	3 35	1 39	23 51	21 55	19 51
Spica,	18 32	16 20	14 31	12 37	10 46	8 43	6 39	4 34	2 38	0 50	22 54	20 50
β Centauri,	19 8	16 56	15 7	13 13	11 22	9 19	7 15	5 10	3 14	1 26	23 30	21 26
Arcturus,	19 23	17 11	15 22	13 28	11 37	9 34	7 30	5 25	3 29	1 41	23 45	21 41
α^2 Centauri,	19 44	17 32	15 43	13 49	11 58	9 55	7 51	5 46	3 50	2 2	0 6	22 2
Antares,	21 35	19 23	17 34	15 40	13 49	11 46	9 42	7 37	5 41	3 53	1 57	23 53
Vega,	23 46	21 34	19 45	17 51	16 0	13 57	11 53	9 48	7 52	6 4	4 8	2 4
Altair,	0 58	22 46	20 57	19 3	17 12	15 9	13 5	11 0	9 4	7 16	5 20	3 16
Fomalhaut,	4 4	1 52	0 3	22 9	20 18	18 15	16 11	14 6	12 10	10 22	8 26	6 22
Markab,	4 12	2 0	0 11	22 17	20 26	18 23	16 19	14 14	12 18	10 30	8 34	6 30

Reductions of Meridian Passages of the Fixed Stars.

1875: At Greenwich Mean Noon on each day of the month.

Day.	Jan.	Feb.	Mar.	Apr.	May.	June.	July.	Aug.	Sept.	Oct.	Nov.	Dec.
1	$0^h\ 0^m$	$0^h\ 0^m$	$0^h\ 0^m$	$0^h\ 0^m$	$0^h\ 0^m$	$0^h\ 0^m$	$0^h\ 0^m$	$0^h\ 0^m$	$0^h\ 0^m$	$0^h\ 0^m$	$0^h\ 0^m$	$0^h\ 0^m$
2	4	4	4	4	4	4	4	4	4	4	4	4
3	9	8	7	7	8	8	8	8	7	7	8	9
4	13	12	11	11	11	12	12	12	11	11	12	13
5	18	16	15	14	15	16	16	15	14	14	16	17
6	22	20	19	18	19	21	21	19	18	18	20	22
7	26	24	22	22	23	25	25	23	22	22	24	26
8	0 31	0 28	0 26	0 25	0 27	0 29	0 29	0 27	0 25	0 25	0 28	0 30
9	35	32	30	29	31	33	33	31	29	29	32	35
10	39	36	33	33	35	37	37	35	32	33	36	39
11	44	40	37	36	39	41	41	38	36	36	40	44
12	48	44	41	40	43	45	45	42	40	40	44	48
13	52	48	44	44	46	49	49	46	43	44	48	52
14	57	52	48	47	50	54	53	50	47	48	52	57
15	1 1	0 56	0 52	0 51	0 54	0 58	0 57	0 53	0 50	0 51	0 56	1 1
16	5	1 0	55	55	58	1 2	1 1	57	54	55	1 0	6
17	10	3	59	59	1 2	6	5	1 1	58	59	4	10
18	14	7	1 3	1 2	6	10	9	5	1 1	1 2	9	15
19	18	11	6	6	10	15	13	8	5	6	13	19
20	22	15	10	10	14	19	17	12	8	10	17	23
21	27	19	14	13	18	23	21	16	12	14	21	28
22	1 31	1 23	1 17	1 17	1 22	1 27	1 25	1 19	1 16	1 18	1 25	1 32
23	35	26	21	21	26	31	29	23	19	21	29	37
24	39	30	25	25	30	35	33	27	23	25	34	41
25	43	34	28	28	34	39	37	31	26	29	38	46
26	48	38	32	32	38	43	41	34	30	33	42	50
27	52	42	35	36	42	48	45	38	34	37	46	55
28	56	45	39	40	46	52	49	42	37	41	51	59
29	2 0	1 49	1 43	1 44	1 50	1 56	1 53	1 45	1 41	1 44	1 55	2 3
30	4		46	47	55	2 0	57	48	44	48	59	8
31	8		50		59		2 1	52		52		12

The Reduction is to be subtracted from the Time in Table LXII. The result will be Apparent Time; and this, although adapted to 1875, will be within 2^m for many years.

Reduction of Daily or Hourly changes in Right Ascension.

Daily Change.	Decimal Parts of the Hour.											Hourly Change.
	0h.0	0h.1	0h.2	0h.3	0h.4	0h.5	0h.6	0h.7	0h.8	0h.9	1h.0	
m	m	m	m	m	m	m	m	m	m	m	m	s
0.0	0.0	0.00	0.00	0.00	0.00	0.00	0.00	0.00	0.00	0.00	0.00	0.00
1	0	00	00	00	00	00	00	00	00	00	00	25
2	0	00	00	00	00	00	00	01	01	01	01	50
3	0	00	00	00	00	01	01	01	01	01	01	75
4	0	00	00	00	01	01	01	01	01	01	02	1.00
0.5	0.0	0.00	0.00	0.01	0.01	0.01	0.01	0.01	0.02	0.02	0.02	1.25
6	0	00	00	01	01	01	01	02	02	02	02	50
7	0	00	01	01	01	02	02	02	02	03	03	75
8	0	00	01	01	01	02	02	02	03	03	03	2.00
9	0	00	01	01	01	02	02	03	03	03	04	25
1.0	0.0	0.00	0.01	0.01	0.02	0.02	0.02	0.03	0.03	0.04	0.04	2.50
1	0	00	01	01	02	02	03	03	04	04	05	75
2	0	00	01	01	02	02	03	03	04	04	05	3.00
3	0	01	01	02	02	03	03	04	04	05	05	25
4	0	01	01	02	02	03	03	04	05	05	06	50
1.5	0.0	0.01	0.01	0.02	0.02	0.03	0.04	0.04	0.05	0.06	0.06	3.75
6	0	01	01	02	03	03	04	05	05	06	07	4.00
7	0	01	01	02	03	03	04	05	06	06	07	25
8	0	01	01	02	03	04	04	05	06	07	07	50
9	0	01	02	02	03	04	05	06	06	07	08	75
2.0	0.0	0.01	0.02	0.02	0.03	0.04	0.05	0.06	0.07	0.07	0.08	5.00
1	0	01	02	03	03	04	05	06	07	08	09	25
2	0	01	02	03	04	05	05	06	07	08	09	50
3	0	01	02	03	04	05	06	07	08	09	10	75
4	0	01	02	03	04	05	06	07	08	09	10	6.00
2.5	0.0	0.01	0.02	0.03	0.04	0.05	0.06	0.07	0.08	0.09	0.10	6.25
6	0	01	02	03	04	05	06	08	09	10	11	50
7	0	01	02	03	04	06	07	08	09	10	11	75
8	0	01	02	03	05	06	07	08	09	10	12	7.00
9	0	01	02	04	05	06	07	09	10	11	12	25
3.0	0.0	0.01	0.02	0.04	0.05	0.06	0.07	0.09	0.10	0.11	0.12	7.50
1	0	01	03	04	05	06	08	09	10	12	13	75
2	0	01	03	04	05	07	08	09	11	12	13	8.00
3	0	01	03	04	05	07	08	10	11	12	14	25
4	0	01	03	04	06	07	08	10	11	13	14	50
3.5	0.0	0.01	0.03	0.04	0.06	0.07	0.09	0.10	0.12	0.13	0.15	8.75
6	0	01	03	04	06	07	09	10	12	13	15	9.00
7	0	02	03	05	06	08	09	11	12	14	15	25
8	0	02	03	05	06	08	09	11	13	14	16	50
9	0	02	03	05	06	08	10	11	13	15	16	75
4.0	0.0	0.02	0.03	0.05	0.07	0.08	0.10	0.12	0.13	0.15	0.17	10.00
1	0	02	03	05	07	09	10	12	14	15	17	25
2	0	02	03	05	07	09	10	12	14	16	17	50
3	0	02	04	05	07	09	11	13	14	16	18	75
4	0	02	04	05	07	09	11	13	15	16	18	11.00
4.5	0.0	0.02	0.04	0.06	0.08	0.09	0.11	0.13	0.15	0.17	0.19	11.25
6	0	02	04	06	08	09	11	13	15	17	19	50
7	0	02	04	06	08	10	12	14	16	18	20	75
8	0	02	04	06	08	10	12	14	16	18	20	12.00
9	0	02	04	06	08	10	12	14	16	18	20	25
5.0	0.0	0.02	0.04	0.06	0.08	0.10	0.12	0.15	0.17	0.19	0.21	12.50
1	0	02	04	06	08	11	13	15	17	19	21	75
2	0	02	04	06	09	11	13	15	17	19	22	13.00
3	0	02	04	07	09	11	13	15	18	20	22	25
4	0	02	04	07	09	11	13	16	18	20	22	50
5.5	0.0	0.02	0.05	0.07	0.09	0.11	0.14	0.16	0.18	0.21	0.23	13.75
6	0	02	05	07	09	12	14	16	19	21	23	14.00
7	0	02	05	07	09	12	14	17	19	21	24	25
8	0	02	05	07	10	12	14	17	19	22	24	50
9	0	02	05	07	10	12	14	17	20	22	25	75
6.0	0.0	0.02	0.05	0.07	0.10	0.13	0.15	0.17	0.20	0.22	0.25	15.00

TABLE LXIV.

Reduction of Daily or Hourly Changes in Right Ascension.

Daily Change.	Hours of the Day. 2h.0	4h.0	6h.0	8h.0	10h.0	12h.0	14h.0	16h.0	18h.0	20h.0	22h.0	Hourly Change.
m	m	m	m	m	m	m	m	m	m	m	m	s
0.0	0.00	0.00	0.00	0.00	0.00	0.00	0.00	0.00	0.00	0.00	0.00	**0.00**
1	01	01	02	03	04	05	06	06	07	08	09	**25**
2	02	03	05	07	08	10	12	13	15	16	18	**50**
3	02	05	07	10	12	15	17	20	22	25	27	**75**
4	03	07	10	13	17	20	23	27	30	33	37	**1.00**
0.5	0.04	0.08	0.12	0.17	0.21	0.25	0.29	0.33	0.38	0.42	0.46	**1.25**
6	05	10	15	20	25	30	35	40	45	50	55	**50**
7	06	12	17	23	29	35	41	46	52	58	64	**75**
8	07	13	20	27	33	40	46	53	60	67	73	**2.00**
9	07	15	22	30	37	45	52	60	67	75	82	**25**
1.0	0.08	0.17	0.25	0.33	0.42	0.50	0.58	0.67	0.75	0.83	0.92	**2.50**
1	09	18	27	37	46	55	64	73	82	92	1.01	**75**
2	10	20	30	40	50	60	70	80	90	1.00	10	**3.00**
3	11	22	32	43	54	65	76	86	97	08	19	**25**
4	12	23	35	47	58	70	81	93	1.05	17	28	**50**
1.5	0.12	0.25	0.37	0.50	0.62	0.75	0.87	1.00	1.12	1.25	1.37	**3.75**
6	13	27	40	53	67	80	93	07	20	33	47	**4.00**
7	14	28	42	57	71	85	99	13	27	42	56	**25**
8	15	30	45	60	75	90	1.05	20	35	50	65	**50**
9	16	32	47	63	79	95	11	26	42	58	74	**75**
2.0	0.17	0.33	0.50	0.67	0.83	1.00	1.17	1.33	1.50	1.67	1.83	**5.00**
1	17	35	52	70	87	05	22	40	57	75	92	**25**
2	18	37	55	73	92	10	28	47	65	83	2.02	**50**
3	19	38	58	77	96	15	34	54	72	92	11	**75**
4	20	40	60	80	1.00	20	40	60	80	2.00	20	**6.00**
2.5	0.21	0.42	0.62	0.83	1.04	1.25	1.46	1.66	1.87	2.08	2.29	**6.25**
6	22	43	65	87	08	30	51	73	95	17	38	**50**
7	22	45	67	90	12	35	57	80	2.02	25	47	**75**
8	23	47	70	93	17	40	63	87	10	33	57	**7.00**
9	24	48	72	97	21	45	69	94	17	42	66	**25**
3.0	0.25	0.50	0.75	1.00	1.25	1.50	1.75	2.00	2.25	2.50	2.75	**7.50**
1	26	52	77	03	29	55	81	06	32	58	84	**75**
2	27	53	80	07	33	60	86	13	40	67	93	**8.00**
3	27	55	82	10	37	65	92	20	47	75	3.02	**25**
4	28	57	85	13	42	70	98	27	55	83	12	**50**
3.5	0.29	0.58	0.87	1.17	1.46	1.75	2.04	2.33	2.62	2.92	3.21	**8.75**
6	30	60	90	20	50	80	10	40	70	3.00	30	**9.00**
7	31	62	92	23	54	85	16	46	77	08	39	**25**
8	32	63	95	27	58	90	21	53	85	17	48	**50**
9	32	65	97	30	62	95	27	60	92	25	57	**75**
4.0	0.33	0.67	1.00	1.33	1.67	2.00	2.33	2.67	3.00	3.33	3.67	**10.00**
1	34	68	02	37	71	05	39	73	07	42	76	**25**
2	35	70	05	40	75	10	45	80	15	50	85	**50**
3	36	72	07	43	79	15	51	86	22	58	94	**75**
4	37	73	10	47	83	20	56	93	30	67	4.03	**11.00**
4.5	0.37	0.75	1.12	1.50	1.87	2.25	2.62	3.00	3.37	3.75	4.12	**11.25**
6	38	77	15	53	92	30	68	07	45	83	22	**50**
7	39	78	17	57	96	35	74	13	52	92	31	**75**
8	40	80	20	60	2.00	40	80	20	60	4.00	40	**12.00**
9	41	82	22	63	04	45	86	26	67	08	49	**25**
5.0	0.42	0.83	1.25	1.67	2.08	2.50	2.91	3.33	3.75	4.17	4.58	**12.50**
1	42	85	27	70	12	55	97	40	82	25	67	**75**
2	43	87	30	73	17	60	3.03	47	90	33	77	**13.00**
3	44	88	32	77	21	65	09	53	97	42	86	**25**
4	45	90	35	80	25	70	15	60	4.05	50	95	**50**
5.5	0.46	0.92	1.37	1.83	2.29	2.75	3.21	3.66	4.12	4.58	5.04	**13.75**
6	47	93	40	87	33	80	26	73	20	67	13	**14.00**
7	47	95	42	90	37	85	32	80	27	75	22	**25**
8	48	97	45	93	42	90	38	87	35	83	32	**50**
9	49	98	47	97	46	95	44	93	42	92	41	**75**
6.0	0.50	1.00	1.50	2.00	2.50	3.00	3.50	4.00	4.50	5.00	5.50	**15.00**

Reduction of Hourly Changes in the Moon's Right Ascension.

Parts of the Hour.	$1^m.0$	$1^m.1$	$1^m.2$	$1^m.3$	$1^m.4$	$1^m.5$	$1^m.6$	$1^m.7$	$1^m.8$	$1^m.9$	$2^m.0$	Parts of the Hour.
	Change in One Hour.											
m	m	m	m	m	m	m	m	m	m	m	m	m
0	0.00	0.00	0.00	0.00	0.00	0.00	0.00	0.00	0.00	0.00	0.00	0
1	02	02	02	02	02	02	03	03	03	03	03	1
2	03	04	04	04	05	05	05	06	06	06	07	2
3	05	05	06	06	07	07	08	08	09	09	10	3
4	07	07	08	09	09	10	11	11	12	13	13	4
5	0.08	0.09	0.10	0.11	0.12	0.12	0.13	0.14	0.15	0.16	0.17	5
6	10	11	12	13	14	15	16	17	18	19	20	6
7	12	13	14	15	16	17	19	20	21	22	23	7
8	13	15	16	17	19	20	21	23	24	25	27	8
9	15	16	18	19	21	22	24	25	27	28	30	9
10	0.17	0.18	0.20	0.22	0.23	0.25	0.27	0.28	0.30	0.32	0.33	10
11	18	20	22	24	26	27	29	31	33	35	37	11
12	20	22	24	26	28	30	32	34	36	38	40	12
13	22	24	26	28	30	32	35	37	39	41	43	13
14	23	26	28	30	33	35	37	40	42	44	47	14
15	0.25	0.27	0.30	0.32	0.35	0.37	0.40	0.42	0.45	0.47	0.50	15
16	27	29	32	35	37	40	43	45	48	51	53	16
17	28	31	34	37	40	42	45	48	51	54	57	17
18	30	33	36	39	42	45	48	51	54	57	60	18
19	32	35	38	41	44	47	51	54	57	60	63	19
20	0.33	0.37	0.40	0.43	0.47	0.50	0.53	0.57	0.60	0.63	0.67	20
21	35	38	42	45	49	52	56	59	63	66	70	21
22	37	40	44	48	51	55	59	62	66	70	73	22
23	38	42	46	50	54	57	61	65	69	73	77	23
24	40	44	48	52	56	60	64	68	72	76	80	24
25	0.42	0.46	0.50	0.54	0.58	0.62	0.67	0.71	0.75	0.79	0.83	25
26	43	48	52	56	61	65	69	74	78	82	87	26
27	45	49	54	58	63	67	72	76	81	85	90	27
28	47	51	56	61	66	70	75	79	84	89	93	28
29	48	53	58	63	68	72	77	82	87	92	97	29
30	0.50	0.55	0.60	0.65	0.70	0.75	0.80	0.85	0.90	0.95	1.00	30
31	52	57	62	67	72	77	83	88	93	98	03	31
32	53	59	64	69	75	80	85	91	96	1.01	07	32
33	55	60	66	71	77	82	88	93	99	04	10	33
34	57	62	68	74	79	85	91	96	1.02	08	13	34
35	0.58	0.64	0.70	0.76	0.82	0.87	0.93	0.99	1.05	1.11	1.17	35
36	60	66	72	78	84	90	96	1.02	08	14	20	36
37	62	68	74	80	86	92	99	05	11	17	23	37
38	63	70	76	82	89	95	1.01	08	14	20	27	38
39	65	71	78	84	91	97	04	10	17	23	30	39
40	0.67	0.73	0.80	0.87	0.93	1.00	1.07	1.13	1.20	1.27	1.33	40
41	68	75	82	89	96	02	09	16	23	30	37	41
42	70	77	84	91	98	05	12	19	26	33	40	42
43	72	79	86	93	1.00	07	15	22	29	36	43	43
44	73	81	88	95	03	10	17	25	32	39	47	44
45	0.75	0.82	0.90	0.97	1.05	1.12	1.20	1.27	1.35	1.42	1.50	45
46	77	84	92	1.00	07	15	23	30	38	46	53	46
47	78	86	94	02	10	17	25	33	41	49	57	47
48	80	88	96	04	12	20	28	36	44	52	60	48
49	82	90	98	06	14	22	31	39	47	55	63	49
50	0.83	0.92	1.00	1.08	1.17	1.25	1.33	1.42	1.50	1.58	1.67	50
51	85	93	02	10	19	27	36	44	53	61	70	51
52	87	95	04	13	21	30	39	47	56	65	73	52
53	88	97	06	15	24	32	41	50	59	68	77	53
54	90	99	1.08	17	26	35	44	53	62	71	80	54
55	0.92	1.01	1.10	1.19	1.28	1.37	1.47	1.56	1.65	1.74	1.83	55
56	93	03	12	21	31	40	49	59	68	77	87	56
57	95	04	14	23	33	42	52	61	71	80	90	57
58	97	06	16	26	35	45	55	64	74	84	93	58
59	98	08	18	28	38	47	57	67	77	87	97	59
60	1.00	1.10	1.20	1.30	1.40	1.50	1.60	1.70	1.80	1.90	2.00	60
	$1^s.00$	$1^s.10$	$1^s.20$	$1^s.30$	$1^s.40$	$1^s.50$	$1^s.60$	$1^s.70$	$1^s.80$	$1^s.90$	$2^s.00$	
	Change in One Minute.											

TABLE LXV.

Reduction of Hourly Changes in the Moon's Right Ascension.

Parts of the Hour.	Change in One Hour.											Parts of the Hour.
	2m.0	2m.1	2m.2	2m.3	2m.4	2m.5	2m.6	2m.7	2m.8	2m.9	3m.0	
m	m	m	m	m	m	m	m	m	m	m	m	m
0	0.00	0.00	0.00	0.00	0.00	0.00	0.00	0.00	0.00	0.00	0.00	**0**
1	03	03	.04	04	04	04	04	04	05	05	05	**1**
2	07	07	07	08	08	08	09	09	09	10	10	**2**
3	10	10	11	11	12	12	13	13	14	14	15	**3**
4	13	14	15	15	16	17	17	18	19	19	20	**4**
5	0.17	0.17	0.18	0.19	0.20	0.21	0.22	0.22	0.23	0.24	0.25	**5**
6	20	21	22	23	24	25	26	27	28	29	30	**6**
7	23	24	26	27	28	29	30	31	33	34	35	**7**
8	27	28	29	31	32	33	35	36	37	39	40	**8**
9	30	31	33	34	36	37	39	40	42	43	45	**9**
10	0.33	0.35	0.37	0.38	0.40	0.42	0.43	0.45	0.47	0.48	0.50	**10**
11	37	38	40	42	44	46	48	49	51	53	55	**11**
12	40	42	44	46	48	50	52	54	56	58	60	**12**
13	43	45	48	50	52	54	56	58	61	63	65	**13**
14	47	49	51	54	56	58	61	63	65	68	70	**14**
15	0.50	0.52	0.55	0.57	0.60	0.62	0.65	0.67	0.70	0.72	0.75	**15**
16	53	56	59	61	64	67	69	72	75	77	80	**16**
17	57	59	62	65	68	71	74	76	79	82	85	**17**
18	60	63	66	69	72	75	78	81	84	87	90	**18**
19	63	66	70	73	76	79	82	85	89	92	95	**19**
20	0.67	0.70	0.73	0.77	0.80	0.83	0.87	0.90	0.93	0.97	1.00	**20**
21	70	73	77	80	84	87	91	94	98	1.01	05	**21**
22	73	77	81	84	88	92	95	99	1.03	06	10	**22**
23	77	80	84	88	92	96	1.00	1.03	07	11	15	**23**
24	80	84	88	92	96	1.00	04	08	12	16	20	**24**
25	0.83	0.87	0.92	0.96	1.00	1.04	1.08	1.12	1.17	1.21	1.25	**25**
26	87	91	95	1.00	04	08	13	17	21	26	30	**26**
27	90	94	99	03	08	12	17	21	26	30	35	**27**
28	93	98	1.03	07	12	17	21	26	31	35	40	**28**
29	97	1.01	06	11	16	21	26	30	35	40	45	**29**
30	1.00	1.05	1.10	1.15	1.20	1.25	1.30	1.35	1.40	1.45	1.50	**30**
31	03	08	14	19	24	29	34	39	45	50	55	**31**
32	07	12	17	23	28	33	39	44	49	55	60	**32**
33	10	15	21	26	32	37	43	48	54	59	65	**33**
34	13	19	25	30	36	42	47	53	59	64	70	**34**
35	1.17	1.22	1.28	1.34	1.40	1.46	1.52	1.57	1.63	1.69	1.75	**35**
36	20	26	32	38	44	50	56	62	68	74	80	**36**
37	23	29	36	42	48	54	60	66	73	79	85	**37**
38	27	33	39	46	52	58	65	71	77	84	90	**38**
39	30	36	43	49	56	62	69	75	82	88	95	**39**
40	1.33	1.40	1.47	1.53	1.60	1.67	1.73	1.80	1.87	1.93	2.00	**40**
41	37	43	50	57	64	71	78	84	91	98	05	**41**
42	40	47	54	61	68	75	82	89	96	2.03	10	**42**
43	43	50	58	65	72	79	86	93	2.01	08	15	**43**
44	47	54	61	69	76	83	91	98	05	13	20	**44**
45	1.50	1.57	1.65	1.72	1.80	1.87	1.95	2.02	2.10	2.17	2.25	**45**
46	53	61	69	76	84	92	99	07	15	22	30	**46**
47	57	64	72	80	88	96	2.04	11	19	27	35	**47**
48	60	68	76	84	92	2.00	08	16	24	32	40	**48**
49	63	71	80	88	96	04	12	20	29	37	45	**49**
50	1.67	1.75	1.83	1.92	2.00	2.08	2.17	2.25	2.33	2.42	2.50	**50**
51	70	78	87	95	04	12	21	29	38	46	55	**51**
52	73	82	91	99	08	17	25	34	43	51	60	**52**
53	77	85	94	2.03	12	21	30	38	47	56	65	**53**
54	80	89	98	07	16	25	34	43	52	61	70	**54**
55	1.83	1.92	2.02	2.11	2.20	2.29	2.38	2.47	2.57	2.66	2.75	**55**
56	87	96	05	15	24	33	43	52	61	71	80	**56**
57	90	99	09	18	28	37	47	56	66	75	85	**57**
58	93	2.03	13	22	32	42	51	61	71	80	90	**58**
59	97	06	16	26	36	46	56	65	75	85	95	**59**
60	2.00	2.10	2.20	2.30	2.40	2.50	2.60	2.70	2.80	2.90	3.00	**60**
	2s.00	**2s.10**	**2s.20**	**2s.30**	**2s.40**	**2s.50**	**2s.60**	**2s.70**	**2s.80**	**2s.90**	**3s.00**	
	Change in One Minute.											

Reduction of the Mean Sun's Right Ascension.

Time.	Tenths of the Hour.										Arc.
	0h.0	0h.1	0h.2	0h.3	0h.4	0h.5	0h.6	0h.7	0h.8	0h.9	
h	m	m	m	m	m	m	m	m	m	m	°
0	0.00	0.02	0.03	0.05	0.07	0.08	0.10	0.11	0.13	0.15	**0**
1	16	18	20	21	23	25	26	28	29	31	**15**
2	33	34	36	38	39	41	43	44	46	47	**30**
3	49	51	53	54	56	57	59	61	62	64	**45**
4	66	67	69	71	72	74	75	77	79	80	**60**
5	0.82	0.84	0.85	0.87	0.89	0.90	0.92	0.94	0.95	0.97	**75**
6	99	1.00	1.02	1.03	1.05	1.07	1.08	1.10	1.12	1.13	**90**
7	1.15	17	18	20	22	23	25	26	28	30	**105**
8	31	33	35	36	38	40	41	43	44	46	**120**
9	48	49	51	53	54	56	58	59	61	63	**135**
10	1.64	1.66	1.68	1.69	1.71	1.72	1.74	1.76	1.77	1.79	**150**
11	81	82	84	86	87	89	90	92	94	95	**165**
12	97	99	2.00	2.02	2.04	2.05	2.07	2.09	2.10	2.12	**180**
13	2.13	2.15	17	18	20	22	23	25	27	28	**195**
14	30	32	33	35	37	38	39	41	43	45	**210**
15	2.46	2.48	2.50	2.51	2.53	2.55	2.56	2.58	2.59	2.61	**225**
16	63	64	66	68	69	71	73	74	76	88	**240**
17	79	81	83	84	86	87	89	91	92	94	**255**
18	96	97	99	3.01	3.02	3.04	3.05	3.07	3.09	3.10	**270**
19	3.12	3.14	3.15	17	19	20	22	24	25	27	**285**
20	3.28	3.30	3.32	3.33	3.35	3.37	3.38	3.40	3.42	3.43	**300**
21	45	47	48	50	52	53	55	56	58	60	**315**
22	61	63	65	66	68	70	71	73	74	76	**330**
23	78	79	81	83	84	86	88	89	91	93	**345**
	0°.0	**1°.5**	**3°.0**	**4°.5**	**6°.0**	**7°.5**	**9°.0**	**10°.5**	**12°.0**	**13°.5**	
	Tenths of the Hour in Arc.										

www.ingramcontent.com/pod-product-compliance
Lightning Source LLC
Chambersburg PA
CBHW020857020726
47497CB00005B/1447

* 9 7 8 3 3 3 7 4 1 8 5 1 9 *